£1·40

Martina Cole is the No. ... ...en
hugely successful novels. ... ...ily,
went straight to No. 1 ... ...ack
bestseller list and was the No. 1 bestselling ... ...dult
fiction title of 2010. *The Take*, which won the British Book
Award for Crime Thriller of the Year in 2006, was adapted for
Sky One. *The Runaway* has also followed. Two of her novels
have been adapted for stage, *Two Women* and *The Graft*,
which were both highly acclaimed when performed at the
Theatre Royal Stratford East.

Martina Cole is a phenomenon. Her hard-hitting, uncom-
promising and haunting writing makes for an incredible read,
and sales of her books now stand at over ten million copies.
She is the person who dares to tell it like it really is.

Praise for Martina Cole's bestsellers:

'Cole has the amazing talent of making characters larger than
life. Another fabulous effort' *Sun*

'Right from the start, she has enjoyed unqualified approval
for her distinctive and powerfully written fiction' *The Times*

'A masterpiece of plotting, characterisation and drama . . .
Terrific stuff from a terrific lady' *Mirror*

'Cole at her finest . . . gritty dialogue, shocking violence and
a gripping storyline' *Daily Express*

'A rough, tough tale . . . Cole is one of the most popular
novelists of our time' *Literary Review*

By Martina Cole and available from Headline

Dangerous Lady
The Ladykiller
Goodnight Lady
The Jump
The Runaway
Two Women
Broken
Faceless
Maura's Game
The Know
The Graft
The Take
Close
Faces
The Business
Hard Girls
The Family

MARTINA COLE

THE RUNAWAY

headline

Copyright © 1997 Martina Cole

The right of Martina Cole to be identified as the Author
of the Work has been asserted by her in accordance with the
Copyright, Designs and Patents Act 1988.

First published in 1997
by HEADLINE BOOK PUBLISHING

First published in paperback in 1998
by HEADLINE BOOK PUBLISHING

This edition published in paperback in 2011
by HEADLINE PUBLISHING GROUP

1

Cataloguing in Publication Data is available from the British Library

ISBN 978 0 7553 7810 4

Typeset in Galliard by Avon DataSet Ltd,
Bidford-on-Avon, Warwickshire

Printed and bound in Great Britain by Clays Ltd, St Ives plc

Headline's policy is to use papers that are natural, renewable and
recyclable products and made from wood grown in sustainable forests.
The logging and manufacturing processes are expected to conform
to the environmental regulations of the country of origin.

HEADLINE PUBLISHING GROUP
An Hachette UK Company
338 Euston Road
London NW1 3BH

www.headline.co.uk
www.hachette.co.uk

For D
Love always
M

In loving memory of Michael James Williams
Always remembered

Non omnis moriar
I shall not altogether die
– Horace

Always in your hearts, always in your minds.
He can never therefore be far from you.

For Zena and Maurice with sorrow and love.

Prologue

London 1995

'Do you think she'll pull through?'

The policeman's face wore a dark frown, all deep creases and premature age. His bald head shone faintly with a sheen of perspiration.

The young doctor shrugged. 'I'm not sure she'd want to. We put over two hundred stitches in her face alone. Her nose was completely obliterated and we had to operate to relieve a deep depression of the skull. In reality she should be dead – no one should survive a beating like that. Yet she's breathing, she's stabilised, her vital signs are good, the bones are beginning to mend. Until she comes out of the coma – that's assuming she does, of course – we can't really ascertain whether or not she's brain-damaged. Whoever cut her up . . .

'Well, let's get this straight, she was cut to ribbons – one breast practically severed. Must have been a lunatic who did it. I have never in my life seen anything like it.'

He stared down at the patient, the lines of stitches criss-crossing her swollen, battered face, stark against the white hospital bedding. She was unrecognisable as a woman, looking more like something from a horror film.

The whirring of the machines by her bed broke the silence, and the young doctor sighed gently, a barely audible sound.

'Do you know who did it?'

The policeman nodded. 'Let's say I have a pretty good idea why she was beaten, and that's a start, isn't it? It'll be proving the bastard's motive that'll be the hard one. Placing him in the frame.'

He tore his glance away from the woman and looked the doctor in the eye. 'She was a very beautiful woman, was my Cathy. Not in an obvious way, but she had class. Had a way about her. Know what I mean?' His thick cockney accent was harsh in the quiet of the ICU.

The doctor smiled faintly. 'You knew her, then?'

Now the policeman smiled, a sad wistful expression. His face softened, giving the doctor a glimpse of the ruggedly attractive man he had once been.

'Oh, I knew her all right. Everyone in the West End knew Cathy one way or another. I came across her over twenty years ago, just before she came to Soho. She's travelled a long way in that time, a very long way.'

He paused as if forgetting the doctor was there. 'Yes, a bloody long way, God help her.'

He stroked her thin arm gently, a caressing motion. 'She's the owner of Dukes – you know, the big revue bar in Soho. Where the great and the good mingle with the not-so-great and not-so-good. But it's a respectable place for all that. Tourists love it, the Germans especially. Men dressed as women are a big attraction. It's *La Cage* of Soho, and this little lady was the brains behind it.

'Cathy's trouble was, she never managed to leave the

past behind her. It always seemed to follow her, and this is the upshot.'

The doctor heard the man swallow loudly, knew he was battling to keep tears from falling, and kept his glance on the woman in the bed.

'She wasn't bad, you know, my Cathy. Not really. She was just a survivor, who did what she had to, to win through. It was all about survival, never anything worse.'

The doctor squeezed the policeman's shoulder and said gently, 'Well, let's hope she survives this, eh?' But his voice didn't hold out much hope. Deep inside he doubted whether this patient would open her eyes or indeed ever recognise anyone again. Part of him hoped this for her sake, because the beating she had taken had left its mark all right. Apart from the colour of her hair there was nothing left of her to say what she had once looked like.

'She never had a chance really,' the policeman said softly. 'Women in Soho normally die of drink or drugs. Often it's like this, battered and bruised in a hospital room, all alone.' He paused for a second, gathering his composure once more before looking the doctor in the eye. 'I loved her in my own way from the first day I saw her, alone and afraid, just a kid. I loved her.'

Then he walked from the room like an old man, slowly, as if in pain.

A young policewoman took up a vigil beside the bed. In the unlikely event that the patient regained consciousness, she was to write down any words spoken. Armed guards stood outside the room twenty-four hours of the day.

'Was that your boss?' The doctor's voice was still low, as if in the presence of death.

The young redhead grinned impishly, thrilled to be noticed by the handsome young dark-eyed medic.

'He's my boss, all right. That was Chief Inspector Richard Gates, Head of the Vice Squad.'

New York

The man looked out of his office window, and for once in his life didn't thrill at the sight of the skyline before him. Normally it brought a tightening in his guts, a feeling of euphoria, that he, Eamonn Docherty, London bootboy, was now a respected businessman with an office the size of a tennis court and a desk that looked as if it should be in the Victoria and Albert Museum, not on the eighty-second floor of Plaza Tower, one of his many property holdings.

He picked up the phone for the tenth time that morning and tapped in a number. The dialling tone shrilled loudly in his ear, as if he were phoning the deli round the corner, not London, England. He replaced the phone as a recording of a woman's voice came on the answerphone.

'Where the fuck is she?'

He spoke to no one, voice loud in the quiet of the room. Getting to his feet, he walked to the glass wall and stared unseeing at the view before him. Closing his eyes, he envisaged his first glimpse of America as a young man.

His father, Eamonn Docherty Senior, was drunk and snoring beside him on the boat as they entered the Hudson, the Statue of Liberty before them in all her glory. Unlike their forebears there was no Ellis Island for them. They had been brought in illegally on an English container boat. A friend of a friend had arranged it – that was his father's favourite expression.

Eamonn Junior had been the perpetrator of a violent murder that had haunted him all his life. He had had to disappear from the East End, and his father had arranged it so that they both went together.

It was the only time the old man had ever come up trumps for him in his whole life.

He had lost his father within the year, and had been left at just eighteen to make the best he could of his life in the States. And as eventful, dirty and violent as it had been, it had eventually brought him here to Plaza Tower.

He'd worked for it, using anyone and anything to get here. Even Cathy, his Cathy as he always thought of her. Always his.

The phone rang and the sudden noise made him jump. His heartbeat hammered in his ears. It was his private line.

Now the phone was ringing he was frightened to pick it up, frightened of what he was going to hear.

Knowing in his heart exactly what he was going to hear.

The voice on the other end was unmistakable, a husky, female voice only ever mastered by transvestites: more feminine than Elizabeth Taylor, more masculine than his own.

'Oh my God, Eamonn, she's dying! Cathy's dying! Oh, please come. Please. I don't know what to do . . . They've cut her to ribbons. You can barely see her face for the stitches! Oh God, oh dear God, help her someone . . .'

Then, after the babbling broken sentences, the heartfelt crying, the gut-wrenching sobs.

'I'll be there. Don't worry.' He replaced the receiver gently, the sobbing still audible in the quiet of the room.

Putting his head in his well-manicured hands, Eamonn wept. He'd thought he was prepared for the news, but he wasn't. He wasn't prepared at all.

He had started something, and didn't know how to stop it.

Book One

Chapter One

January 1960

'I ain't going in there, he'll start on us.'

Cathy sighed deeply and pushed a stray hair from the boy's forehead. 'So where are we going to go then, smart arse?'

'Can't we go next door, Cath?' Eamonn's voice was a soft whine and she shook her head slowly.

Mrs Sullivan had the flat next door to theirs on the second-floor landing. A kindly soul, she would give the children shelter when a fight between their parents was raging – a very frequent occurrence. They could hear Eamonn Docherty Senior's voice raised in anger through the front door as they stood outside, interspersed with Madge's shrieks in reply.

'We can't take the piss, or when we really need her she'll tell us to take a hike. Tell you what . . .'

The front door was opened abruptly and Madge Connor stood before them in all her glory. Her fifteen-stone frame was wrapped in a pink quilted housecoat and make-up was smeared around her moon face. Only the cigarette dangling from her swollen lips moved, bobbing up and down as she stared at them, eyes narrowed. Finally she shrilled at them in a voice that could cut glass: 'You got home then, you lazy pair of bastards! Get in here, Eamonn, and sort your old man out, will you? He's going up the wall.'

Cathy could hear Eamonn Senior shouting about Ireland, and after Eamonn Junior had walked through the door she closed her eyes tightly.

She had always wondered what it must be like to have a father, but after two years of living with Eamonn Senior she was glad inside that all she had to contend with was her mother. Though, between the two adults, both Cathy's and Eamonn's lives were a constant nightmare. The adults were always either kissing or kicking one another. There was never, ever a happy medium. Walking into the flat, she was engulfed in the usual smells: cooking fat and cat's urine, mixed with an underlying beer-bottle smell that she just couldn't get to terms with. It burned her nose and throat until once more she became accustomed to it. It always made her stomach revolt, always depressed her. The stench of poverty.

As she entered the tiny front room, her mother's lover was removing his belt. His large frame, without an ounce of spare fat, was imposing. Eamonn Senior was huge, from his size twelve feet to his bulbous blue eyes, and exuded an animal strength and cunning that made lesser men wary before even speaking a word to him.

'I'll cut the fecking legs from under you, you dirty swine. I'll put your names in me book with a line through them. Now how would you like that?'

Cathy sighed with delight and relief. The blue eyes were twinkling now, his temper apparently over, the violent rage soothed by drink and giving way to an all-encompassing

10

happiness with the world. This was his favourite joke, old IRA talk from the days of the freedom fighters. They put your name in a book, apparently, and if a line was crossed through it, you were shot at dawn the next day.

Cathy grinned as she heard the big man bellow: 'Shot at dawn, the pair of you. How'd you like that, eh?'

He lowered his huge face down to their level, his heart apparently bursting with love for the two children. Especially for his son, his namesake, his only child.

'Is it chips you're wanting?' He smiled, a huge toothy grin that creased his face in all the right places and made people understand what women saw in him, because women loved Eamonn Docherty – they always had.

A certain kind of woman anyway.

Madge Connor, face full of disbelief, shook her head in wonderment. 'You never know what the fucker's going to do. Never.' It was said in a thick cockney accent, with just a hint of rough pride. Her big, fighting, drinking, whoring common-law husband was a mystery to her. Which, she admitted in soberer moments, was his chief attraction.

'I better get ready for work. Cathy, do me a favour, mate. Iron me red dress.'

Cathy went into the small kitchenette and began to plug in the iron and place the cleanest towel she could find on the table. It was all done automatically. You never refused an order in this house, even when it sounded like a request. If you wanted to get through the night, you jumped when they told you to jump, simple as that.

Twenty minutes later, with a cat's lick for a wash and heavy make-up piled on to yesterday's, her red dress straining at the seams, Madge was ready for work. As she gave her hair one final backcomb she looked at her daughter and said gently: 'Do I look all right, love?'

Cathy smiled, the gap-toothed smile of a seven-year-old

ancient, and said honestly, 'You look lovely, Mum. 'Andsome.'

It was the required answer.

'Get me bag from the bedroom.'

Cathy skipped off, grinning at Eamonn Junior who was now ensconced on his dad's lap, searching through a big handful of change for the chip money.

They looked each other in the eye, relief and childish joy flooding through them both at this unexpected outcome. It was a Wednesday, normally a fraught day for the children. Middle of the week, skint and argumentative, both parents generally had tempers on them when the kids arrived back from school. Today, for some unknown reason, they were happy. And if the grown-ups were happy, the children were ecstatic.

Who'd ever heard of chips on a Wednesday?

Cathy skipped back to the kitchen with her mother's beaded bag. 'Thanks, love. You'll have a clear-up for me tonight, eh?'

Cathy nodded solemnly.

Madge pressed her cheek to her daughter's and laughed gently, her sour breath, a mixture of cheap Scotch and onions, hitting Cathy's nostrils like a week-dead dog.

'I'll bring you back some crisps, what do you say to that?'

Cathy nodded, loath to open her mouth and let the stale smell enter her body.

There was a knock on the front door and she used it as an excuse to escape. It would be her mum's friend Betty. They worked together in a small drinking club in Custom House where they served foreign sailors drinks and anything else they wanted, though this was never discussed openly in front of Eamonn Senior unless he brought up the subject himself. Even though he'd drink the money and eat the food it provided, and go so far as to give the two women a lift to work some days, he pretended to know nothing about it – until once a fortnight or so he decided to batter Madge's brains out to prove a point. That point being that he, as a man, didn't like the set-up.

Betty wafted into the small hallway, all Max Factor and beaver lamb coat.

'Hello, Daffy Cathy!' Her booming voice seemed too big for her slim frame. Betty Jones was slender to the point of emaciation, though she had the constitution of a horse, as she'd tell anyone who'd listen. She shoved a threepenny bit into Cathy's hand and winked.

Cathy adored Betty. Eamonn Junior adored Betty. Eamonn Senior hated her and the feeling was mutual.

Madge hurried into the hallway, pulling on her coney fur coat. It was going bald in places but with snow on the ground it was a warmer bet than her usual cotton jacket.

'That coat's being held together by spit and hope, girl! Get him to provide you with a new one. He don't do fuck all else. The least he could do is clothe yer.'

Eamonn Junior closed his eyes in distress. He felt his father's body stiffen at Betty's words. Her voice was like a red rag to a bull where his father was concerned and as the man stood up and unceremoniously dropped him to the floor, Eamonn rolled away.

Betty and Madge were on their way out of the front door when a booming voice stayed them.

'What have I told you about coming into my house?'

Betty pulled her coat around her like a shield. 'You talking to me?' This was said with a rough edge to her voice, a fighting edge.

'And what other piece of shite would I be referring to?' Eamonn Senior's voice was deadly quiet. He was standing in the doorway of the front room now.

'You don't scare me, mate, you never have. If you was any kind of a man you'd provide for these kids, and your old woman wouldn't be flogging her arse in three feet of fucking snow! You don't impress me, *Mister* Docherty. There's only one piece of shite in here and I'm looking at it!'

The man's face was purple with rage now, and as he stepped forward Madge pushed vainly at his chest.

'Leave it out, Eamonn. You know what Betty's like, all wind and water. She's had a drink and—'

'Get outta me way before I knock your head off!'

He slammed Madge against the wall, causing her to lose balance. Cathy stood in front of Betty as the big man approached her. Betty, with a maddening smile, egged him on.

'Come on then, hit me! You're good at hitting women, ain't ya? But not men though, eh? As big as you are, you don't hit men, do you?'

Cathy pushed Betty towards the open front door. The cold air was rushing inside now and the small hallway was freezing.

'Get out, Betty! Stop causing trouble.'

Turning, she threw herself at the big man's legs. Picking her up in one arm, he pointed at Betty with a trembling finger.

'One of these days, lady, I'll break your fucking neck.'

Betty laughed raucously. She knew exactly how to wind up Eamonn Docherty. 'Get stuffed, you Irish ponce!'

Roughly, Madge pushed her friend out of the front door. 'Leave it out, Betty. I've got to live here, you know.'

'I'll see *you* when you get home, lady.'

Madge looked into the big man's face and nodded.

Young Eamonn pulled his father back into the front room, and the air of menace left the narrow hallway.

Madge pulled the front door to behind her. 'Thanks a

fucking bundle, Betty. He'll trounce me now. Happy, are you? You just got me a hammering.'

Betty shook her head in distress, her dyed yellow hair stiff as a board under the sugar and water setting it. 'I'm sorry, Madge, but you know how I feel about him – he's a ponce.'

Madge smiled faintly. 'I'm well aware of that, Betty, but he's *my* ponce.'

Both women grinned as they click-clacked across the tiled floor to the stairwell in the stiletto-heeled shoes unsuitable for the weather but mandatory for their jobs. Giggling like schoolgirls they walked down the stairs, a pair of ageing tarts who still thought they had it.

Cathy and Eamonn lay together in the darkness, arms entwined. At ten he was much bigger than she, but she had the edge because even at seven Cathy was a born diplomat.

After tidying up the flat, they had all eaten chips and saveloys, washed down with mugs of hot sweet tea. Then Cathy had made connie-onnie sandwiches from condensed milk for them both before they went to bed.

Eamonn Senior had gone to the pub at eight-thirty, and the two children were able to relax. The ever-present sense of danger had disappeared out of the front door with him. Now they had been woken by his return and in the dim light of the streetlamp outside they waited with bated breath for him to fall asleep. They could never relax of a night unless they could hear his tell-tale snores. Until then, anything could happen and frequently did.

They heard a cup smash and, sighing heavily, Cathy slipped from the bed.

'Don't go, Cathy, leave him to it.'

She pulled on a dirty dressing gown. The room was freezing and her breath made little clouds as she spoke.

'You stay here and keep warm, all right? I'll make him his Bovril and get him to bed, otherwise none of us will get any sleep.'

The big man was standing in the small kitchen scratching his belly, wearing only vest and underpants. He tried hard to focus on the broken china at his feet, his drink-filled body impervious to the cold.

Cathy picked up the broken cup. Quickly and expertly, she put it in the bin then led him into the front room by the hand. He dropped on to the battered settee with a thump.

'You're a good girl. Where's me boy?' His soured question needed no answer and Cathy didn't offer any. Instead she slipped into the kitchen and put on the water for his nightly Bovril. No matter how drunk he was, Eamonn Docherty had to have his Bovril or he wouldn't sleep. Cathy knew from experience that it was easier to make it for him, watch him drink it and put him to bed, even though her tired eyes were straining to stay open and felt as if they'd been sprayed with hot sand.

When she brought him in his drink, he took it gratefully. 'You're a good girlie, aren't you? Me own little pickaheen! Come and sit on me lap, child.'

Cathy shook her head warily. 'You can't hold me and the mug. Drink your Bovril, Mr Docherty.'

Eamonn surveyed her through heavy-lidded eyes. She was so tiny, sitting there on the stool, her skinny little legs poking out of her dressing gown like sticks of chalk. But the child had the face of a grown woman, so knowing was it.

'I wouldn't hurt you, child, you must believe that.' It was said soberly and Cathy felt a moment's regret for the way she'd answered him. For all his faults, she felt safe with him in that way.

'We've been through all this before, Mr Docherty. I don't like sitting on people's laps. I never have.'

'I'm not like the other men your mother took up with, I know how to treat a child. You're like me own.'

Part of his brain was wondering why he always felt the need to justify himself with this girl, but then, her demeanour was that of a woman, a knowing experienced woman. He half guessed what she'd endured before he came on the scene.

He closed his eyes at the implication. He would never want a child like that, yet he knew it was what Cathy Connor thought he wanted and that hurt his pride. Worse than that, the realisation that she knew as much already, at just seven, grieved him.

It was his only saving grace. For all he was, for all he'd done, *that* would never be on the agenda. Never. He wanted Cathy to know that and to trust him. It was a conversation they had regularly.

'You should get to bed, Mr Docherty. You've got to go to work in the morning.'

He nodded, then running his hand through his thick dark hair, laughed. 'You'll never end up like your mother, you're too fecking sure of yourself. Get away to bed, child. I'm fine now. I'll have a quick draw and be away in meself.'

Cathy nodded, saying a quiet goodnight and slipping back into the bedroom. The large overcoat that covered the bed was falling on to the floor and she pulled it back on top, tucking a sleeve under the mattress to secure it.

Eamonn was already asleep and as she slipped in beside him, the warmth of his body was like balm.

Madge was frozen. As she felt the man's hands grope inside the bodice of her dress she cursed softly under her breath. He was a small Chinese with bad teeth and the haunting smell of Chow Mein on his hair. Freeing her pendulous breasts, he squeezed them painfully, causing her to shove him away from her.

'Don't get flash, mate, I ain't in the mood. And as I've got about six stone on you, I wouldn't advise you to try nothing too rough.'

The man smiled in the dimness and once more pushed her against the wall, but more gently this time. She felt his lips on her nipple and smiled in the darkness. They were like three-inch rivets with the cold. As she hitched her dress up over her hips the icy wind made her shiver all over. The Chinese man thought he was doing something right for once and sucked furiously on her breast. Madge felt an urge to crush his skull in her bare hands. Instead she placed her leg up on a wooden crate and encouraged him to enter her.

'Come on, mate, it's fucking freezing.'

He was strong for his size and as he began a steady rhythmic thrusting she set about her real business of the night. Murmuring encouragement, she pulled him into the warmth of her coat. She ran her hands over his body, gently and expertly relieving him of his wallet. He had already given her a brand new ten-shilling note; now she went for the big one. Expertly, in the guise of caresses, she checked him for a knife. Though most sailors carried them in their boots, it was as well to be prepared. Her own knife was safely tucked into the back of her dress, in a thin belt, in case she needed it. She felt the shuddering of his body and the slimy wetness between her legs, and then as always she held him for a few seconds until he regained the use of his legs. His hot heavy breath coming in short gasps, he spoke to her in Cantonese and she smiled at him gaily.

'All right, love?'

He seemed to understand her tone and smiled again.

Madge realised he was only young, no more than nineteen. Why was it she never looked at them properly till after the event?

She shrugged. Pulling her coat around her, she made her way through the back of the building and into the warmth of the bar.

'Give us a hot toddy, Pete,' she shouted to the barman as she made her way to the ladies' toilet. Inside she put her leg on the dirty seat and wiped herself clean. Then, rinsing her hands under the icy cold tap, she shook them dry. Wiping away the last of the water on her dress, she took the wallet from her pocket. It was a cheap plastic affair with 'Buenos Aires' written boldly across it. A souvenir of her john's travels. Madge smiled because it had 'Made in China' on the back.

'Long way to go for a wallet made in your own country!' Her voice was loud in the small cubicle.

Inside the wallet there were three five-pound notes and a photograph of an elderly-looking woman, probably his grandmother. Grinning now, Madge tossed the wallet into her bag and made her way out to the warmth of the bar once more.

Pushing through the throng, she picked up her hot toddy. When she saw Betty sitting at a table with two sailors, she joined them.

Pete's Bar was an old container depot, rented from a local bullyboy called Jimmy Capper who saw to it that the place was never raided and that it was 'protected'. He was twenty-five, shrewd and violent. Perfect credentials for Custom House, and the perfect foil for Peter Lawson, the bar's owner. Peter encouraged his girls to work, and looked after them in his rough way. He would loan them money and sort out disputes. All his girls respected him, few of them liked him. They paid 'scrum' money to work the bar and resented this, arguing that they kept his trade coming in. Pete argued back that their whole livelihoods revolved around robbing the sailors, so if they wanted his protection it would cost them. It was a chicken and egg situation, and no one would ever win.

Tonight Pete's clientele was the usual mixture of Chinese, Russian and European seamen. Gambling was the major attraction, and Pete watered down their drinks, over-charged them, and smiled at their jokes. He kept a sawn-off shotgun under his counter to scare them when they fought, and a baseball bat in the ladies' toilets for when the whores argued among themselves. In fact, he preferred fighting the men; breaking up two women, kicking, screaming and scratching, was far more dangerous as far as he was concerned. Especially waterfront women. They were the hardest, meanest bitches he had ever come across. But, he conceded, they had to be.

Part of him admired them for their toughness. They spent their lives in the pox clinic, his bar or up against walls. Anyone who could sustain that lifestyle for years deserved a certain respect. He watched the bar constantly, and kept up eye contact with his two bouncers. In Pete's Bar, anything could happen but he averaged £700 a week and that was what kept him here, and his wife and children in a detached house in Maida Vale.

Madge was on her second rum toddy when the Chinese sailor walked back into the bar. She didn't see him until he stepped in front of her. For a second she didn't realise who he was.

'Money, lady. Want money.'

He stood there in dignified silence as everyone turned to stare at him. His white suit, crumpled and stained, was bright under the harsh lights.

'Money, lady. Want money.'

20

Madge grinned. 'Fuck off! I don't know what you're talking about.'

She resumed drinking her toddy. Betty watched the little man warily as he stood before her friend. People, women especially, had been knifed for much less than a wallet on the waterfront at Custom House.

A record came on the jukebox and as the strains of Del Shannon belted out, the little Chinese man once more asked politely for his money. The two sailors Betty had found were Russians – great bears of men who spoke perfect English.

'Do you have his money?' The Russian sailor's thick guttural voice was hard. Sailors were the same the world over. If the woman had stolen the Chinese man's wallet, the chances were she could already have his. Instinctively he put his hand to his pocket and was relieved to find the reassuring bulge still there.

Madge lit a cigarette and shook her head dismissively. 'I ain't got his fucking money. He's a nutter.' She leant forward in her seat and said: 'Look, you had a nice time, didn't you? You probably lost your money or something.' She smiled at the Russian nearer her and hunched her shoulders in a 'They all try this' kind of way. She didn't want to lose this one; if she could score again tonight, she could have tomorrow off.

Two women made their way to the table and stood nearby, sipping their drinks. Like sailors, whores stuck together. One of the women, a large-boned African called Dobie, smiled slightly at the little Chinese man. A gold tooth glinted in the light and her tribal markings made her face look like a death mask.

'Go on, piss off, you little runt!' Betty's voice had a finality about it that even the Chinese man understood.

Before anyone realised what had happened he had

stabbed Madge in the upper arm. The three-inch blade hung unsteadily against the bone for a few seconds before dropping to the table. Madge looked at the wound in wonderment. A deep tear was oozing blood and the open flap of skin seemed to hover in the air for a second before closing over the wound once more.

The Chinese was instantly knocked flying by Dobie's handbag. He was launched unceremoniously into the lap of a Swedish sailor who was playing cards and hadn't bothered to look up during the argument.

Within seconds the whole bar was in uproar as sailors began fighting among themselves. All the Chinese patrons were determined to look after their countryman.

Pete Lawson was hauling out his sawn-off shotgun as all the women made a hasty retreat. Outside they hurried towards Commercial Road; an all-night cafe would be their final destination. As they hurried along, the African woman opened her bag and removed a housebrick, flinging it away with animal strength.

In the brightly lit Commercial Road their footsteps slowed. A few snowflakes shone in the light of the street-lamps and they all pulled their coats tighter around them.

'Brass monkey weather this, eh, girls?' Betty's voice was loud but no one answered her. They burst into Lenny's all-night cafe, bringing with them the cold and the smell of cheap perfume. Sitting at a large table at the back, they looked at one another and burst into loud nervous laughter.

'Breakfast's on you, Madge Connor, seeing's how you started all the hag in the first place.'

Madge grinned and slipped out of her coat. They all surveyed her wound.

'You'll live. A couple of stitches and you'll be right as ninepence. We'll nip up the Old London before we go home.'

Madge lit a cigarette and coughed heavily. 'Fucking rinky dink dinks! No wonder they dropped a fucking bomb on them.'

'That was the Japs, you prat. Here, did you see in the paper today about Hedy Lamarr? Got caught shoplifting in Hollywood! With all that money, she's out skanking!'

Lenny automatically began pouring them out tea laced with whisky. He didn't mind the whores, they were a good earner. The women chatted on about nothing very much, all aware that they had got off lightly, all unwilling to admit that fact. It was common for women to be found dead in the docks; they all knew they were prime targets. Used and abused by sailors who came and went within days, hours in some cases, the police didn't bother looking too hard into the case when one of them was murdered. The attitude seemed to be: one fewer to harass, one fewer to police. Their age, lifestyle and looks condemned them to such a livelihood in Custom House. Even the dingiest bars in Soho would shun them. They were the lowest of their kind and all too well aware of that fact.

Yet, united, they possessed a certain rough dignity of their own.

Young Eamonn opened his eyes and yawned heavily. At ten he knew he was getting too old to sleep with his stepsister but her warm presence reassured him. He lay listening to her soft snores. Then, remembering she'd been up in the night, he felt a pang of guilt. He knew he should have got up with her; instead he had gone straight back to sleep. He looked at the curtains and saw the weak winter sunshine coming through them and snuggled down under the covers once more. Cathy didn't mind getting up and she would soon have the kitchen nice and warm for them. Under the pretence of turning over, he pushed against her roughly, knowing she would waken. Then, pretending still to be asleep, he burrowed down deeper into the bed. As he felt her get up, he smiled to himself.

Cathy was good, she knew what had to be done and she did it. In twenty minutes she would have tea and toast ready for him and he could get up and scamper through to the heat of the kitchen.

Cathy shivered as she lit the small stove, turning on two burners to try and heat the place up. She cut the bread expertly and put it under the grill, then pulling down the door to the wooden larder, she checked over the provisions. There was margarine and a small amount of jam. Humming now, she began to prepare breakfast. Just as she had made a large pot of tea Madge let herself in the front door.

'A nice cup of tea! Just the thing, it's freezing out there.' Opening a newspaper parcel, she revealed some cold sausages. 'I got these from the cafe for you, love.'

'I'll put them into sandwiches. I love sausages.'

Cathy smiled at her mother, grateful for the small kindness. Good money was earned with regularity in this house, but the amount that went on food was paltry. Drink was the mainstay of the household, as were new clothes for Madge when she was flush, and elaborate furniture, which was always repossessed.

Somehow, doing a weekly shop was beyond her. They got tick, like everyone else, at Tamlin's, and lived from day to day, paying a bit off the back only when refused more food or cigarettes.

Madge took off her old coat and grinned. 'Bleeding thing! I'll have to get a new one. I look like fucking Yogi Bear walking about!'

Cathy laughed delightedly. 'That means Betty must be Boo Boo!'

They laughed together at the joke.

Madge, full up with bacon, eggs, tomatoes and sausages, turned her nose up at the sandwiches. As she watched her daughter deftly work in the small kitchen, she felt a momentary pang of regret. Looking at the tangled blond hair hanging down the child's back, and her large blue eyes, she realised that she loved Cathy dearly. She was a good kid, you could rely on her to do what needed to be done. In a few years she'd be a real little asset . . .

'Give us a kiss, baby.'

Cathy went dutifully to her mother. Putting her thin arms around Madge's ample waist, she kissed the cheek which her mother bent to offer her.

'I love you, Mum.'

Madge nodded sadly. 'I know you do, darlin'.'

Madge hugged her little girl against her, savouring the sweetness of her smell and her wiry thinness. Cathy would be all right, she was a survivor. Madge told herself this every day of her life.

Eamonn Senior watched them from the doorway and shook his head in wonderment. How had God in His wisdom ever seen fit to give them both children?

He surveyed Madge's smeared make-up and fat belly, her varicose veins and swollen feet in tight silver stilettos. In her big moon face there was still a trace of the beauty she had possessed once. Madge was just thirty-five years old.

Pulling his braces up over his shoulders, he walked into the little kitchen. 'Sausages, is it? Have we no eggs?'

Cathy shook her head, happy at the jovial tone of his voice. Madge took a pound note from her bag as Eamonn Junior came into the kitchen, face still creased with sleep.

'Go down the shop and get a dozen eggs and a paper. Pay this nicker off the bill, and get yourselves some sweets too.'

The boy took the money and ran from the room.

'Leave the sandwiches there, child. I'll cook us a couple of eggs to go with them, eh?'

Cathy nodded happily.

As the big Irishman poured himself out a cup of tea he spoke to Madge. 'How was the night then?'

'Fifteen quid. Rolled a Chink, and he only came back, didn't he? Talk about run! We poodled up the Commercial Road like greyhounds! He stabbed me, look.' She showed them the dressing on her arm. 'Nothing too serious though, just three stitches. They put 'em in up the London, that's why I'm late home. He was only little and all. Four foot and a fag paper!'

Eamonn laughed. 'It's a fine woman you are, Madge.' He wiped a hand across his stubbly chin. 'Any chance of a loan, like? A fiver would do it.'

Cathy watched her mother give him the five-pound note and sighed inwardly with relief. Madge had had a tickle, as she called it. That meant they would all get a good breakfast and the house would be ringing with laughter instead of oaths. All in all, not a bad start to a Thursday.

She was looking forward to school. Cathy liked it there. It was orderly, it was warm and her teacher, Mrs Platting, called her 'darling'.

Grinning now, she watched her mother and the big man chatting and smiling, and after she'd poured them both out another cup of tea, she had a sneaky puff on her mother's cigarette.

Madge saw her and laughed once more. 'Did you see that, Eamonn! She's smoking.'

They both looked at her delightedly and Cathy basked in their affection.

Moments like this were rare and she had learned long ago to enjoy good things, because you never knew just how long they would last.

Chapter Two

1965

Madge poured herself a large measure of Black and White whisky and settled once more into her chair. Belching loudly, she glanced at the clock. Eleven o'clock in the morning and still no sign of her man.

Lighting a cigarette, she turned the radio beside her down low, letting the smooth strains of the choral music wash over her. She could hear Cathy's voice in the kitchen as she prepared the chicken for their Christmas dinner. Young Eamonn's laughter mingled with her daughter's and for a few seconds Madge smiled in contentment. Then, remembering that the boy's father had not come home last night, the smile faded.

He was staying out more and more of late, and Madge Connor, who prided herself on the fact that she could smell a rat long before it was stinking, was forced to accept that there was a bird in the offing. Now her Eamonn having a roll on the side wasn't anything unusual, but this bird had been a regular thing for weeks and that meant it was serious.

After five years, he was going on the trot. She knew it in her heart as surely as she knew her own name. Stinging tears of drunkenness filled her faded blue eyes, and her chin trembled dangerously. Swallowing more Scotch, she forced herself to be calm.

Cathy walked into the room with a bacon sandwich and a cup of coffee for her. 'Here you are, Mum, a bit of breakfast.' She eyed the empty glass in her mother's hand and rolled her eyes. 'Oh, come on, Mum, you promised. No drinking until dinner. Mrs Cartwright at school says that drinking during the day means you've got a problem with—'

Madge cut off her daughter's voice with a bellow. 'Bollocks to Mrs know-it-all fucking Cartwright! If I want a drink on Christmas Day, I'll have one. All right?'

Cathy's face paled at the vitriolic attack and Madge felt a second's shame. It was her old man she was angry with, not her daughter. As Cathy walked back into the kitchen, the suppressed tears spilled over on to Madge's cheeks.

Where was her Irish boy, the bastard? Christmas Day and he was nowhere to be seen.

In the kitchen Cathy sipped her coffee and pulled on her cigarette. At twelve she looked fifteen and knew it. Acting as if she were older was something she had done ever since she could remember. Now she got herself wolf whistles with her walk, and the nickname of 'Jailbait' roundabouts.

'Do you know where your old man is, Eamonn?'

The boy, who at fifteen already topped six feet, shrugged nonchalantly. 'If I did, I wouldn't tell her anyway. What would be the point? You know what me dad's like – he'll be home eventually and they'll have a fight and that'll be it until the next time.'

Cathy nodded. Putting out her cigarette, she checked on the small chicken in the oven.

'That smells handsome, girl.'

Cathy smiled. 'I know! Eamonn, can I ask you something without you laughing at me?'

The boy nodded, a smile already curving his wide mouth. Like his father, he had the black-haired good looks of the Irish.

'Would you ever get married?'

He shook his head vigorously. 'Not in a million years, Cath. Have this all me life? I don't think so! I'm off, mate, as soon as I can earn me own dosh.'

She lit another cigarette. 'I want to get married, and I want a nice house and a couple of kids. I want to have a garden with nice flowers in, and a husband who adores me and goes to work regularly. And I'll cook him lovely dinners and he'll kiss me all the time . . .'

Her voice was wistful, and instead of laughing Eamonn put his arm around her shoulders and cuddled her. 'And that's exactly what you'll get, love.'

Cathy pulled on her cigarette and shook her head. 'No, I won't. Any decent bloke would run a mile from her in there, and I don't blame them. Do you know what Desmond Blackburn's dad said to me the other day? "You'll soon be pulling your skirts up like your mother, girl, and I'll be first in line." The dirty old git! I told him to fuck off, I was so annoyed, and he laughed and said: "You've already learned the language. What else has Eamonn Docherty taught you?" I didn't know if he meant you or your father.'

'Oh, he did, did he?'

Cathy pushed her heavy blond hair away from her forehead. 'Don't get all het up, they ain't worth it. Anyway, you can't blame the neighbours, the way our two go on.

31

Look at last Friday – me mum and Betty fighting in the bloody street! I'm sick of the lot of it. She could get a proper job, Christ knows there are enough of them about, but no, not her. We could move away where no one knows our business. When I suggested it to her, she went barmy. I hate her sometimes. I know it's wicked, but I can't help it.'

Eamonn nodded sympathetically. 'At least you're not the namesake of a fucking lunatic Irishman. I hope he don't come back. I hope he's dead somewhere. It's the only way I'll ever be shot of him. Anyway, Merry Christmas.'

He smiled at her then and they both began to laugh for no reason.

'Do you know the funniest thing of all?' Cathy said, looking up into his merry blue eyes. 'I love me mum really and I don't know why. She sits on her arse all day, and then flogs it all night. She won't do a hand's turn in the house and yet she expects clean clothes miraculously to appear from nowhere. She'll eat herself unconscious and yet she wouldn't cook a boiled egg! But, despite all that, I look at her sometimes and I get a tight feeling in me guts. It's as if she's the kid and I'm the grown-up.'

She shook her head in wonderment and laughed again. 'It's mad, ain't it? Then, in the next breath, I see her waddle down the street and I hate her with all my heart. Yet if someone says anything about her, I want to kill them. Even though I know what they're saying is true.'

Eamonn watched her as she began to peel the potatoes, cigarette dangling from her lip, her eyes screwed up against the smoke.

'I can leave school next year – I can't wait to earn me own money,' he told her. 'I'm going in the docks. I've got the size and the savvy, as me old man would say.'

'You'll do all right there, they earn a good wedge. I wish I could get a proper job.' Cathy pointed the potato knife at his chest. 'One day, right, I'll have everything that everyone else has – and more. Loads more. Because this ain't gonna be my life, Eamonn, and I intend to make that statement a fact.'

Before he could answer, the front door opened and Betty's voice was heard throughout the flat.

'Merry Christmas!' The fight with Madge already forgotten, she bowled in with an armful of presents. 'Something smells handsome! I wish you'd come and live with me, Cath. I'd pay you to do all this, straight up.'

Cathy smiled, showing small white teeth. 'I know you would, Auntie Bet, but me mum's put a block on it.'

Betty followed her back into the kitchen. 'Here, Eamonn, you big git, take these presents. How is she?'

Cathy shrugged as she put the potatoes into a dish for roasting. 'Pissed, as usual. He ain't come home again. You know the scenario, Auntie Bet. Why should Christmas be any different? As me mum will say later, it's only a day like any other.'

Betty took off her beaver lamb coat and folded it carefully over the back of a kitchen chair. 'It's serious this time, love.'

Both Eamonn and Cathy looked at her.

'Who is it then?' Cathy asked.

'It's Junie Blacklock, her that was widowed. No disrespect, Eamonn, but you know your father as well as any of us. Junie's insurance was a tidy sum, plus she's an Irish like him. She ain't got chick nor child and she's a looker, I'll give her that. Kept herself nice always, even during the war. She'll never see forty again, but that's neither here nor there, is it? I got the SP from old Mother Wacker, and you know her – if it's not true she won't

33

mouth a word of it. According to her, Eamonn's moving in with Junie, so that means you'll be moving in and all, boy, because where he goes, you go.'

Cathy closed her eyes and shook her head in consternation. 'The rotten bastard! The least he could do was wait until after the holidays. This'll finish Mum now. Apart from me, he's all she's ever had.'

Eamonn put the kettle on and said, 'Still, look on the bright side. At least I won't be far from you. That's something, I suppose.'

Betty bit on her thumbnail nervously. 'I'll have to tell Madge. I mean, at the end of the day she is me best mate. She'd rather hear it from me than someone else, and if Mother Wacker knows about it, then the whole world and his dog will know by the morning. Mouthy old bat she is.'

Cathy turned off the oven.

'What you doing? I'm starving,' Eamonn protested.

Cathy looked into his eyes and said sadly, 'There'll be no dinner here today. She'll go garrity when she finds out. There'll be ambulances arriving and no prizes for guessing who the occupant will be, eh? Go on, Auntie Bet, tell her. Before someone else does, and not as kindly.'

Five minutes later Cathy heard the high keening coming from the front room and an answering cry rose inside her. For all Madge Connor's faults, she was Cathy's mother and the girl loved her.

More, perhaps, than she deserved.

Junie Blacklock was a small woman, with a handspan waist and good teeth. She prided herself on her neat home, her neat figure and even neater bank balance. A woman whose husband had joked she could put elastic on a shilling and stretch it through to the next week, she had saved a tidy sum over the years and now added to this was his life assurance money, which meant she had a good sum and was comfortably off. Meeting Eamonn Docherty, her heart had been stolen from her breast by his smooth Irish tongue and impressive appearance. For the first time in her life, Junie was in love and it showed.

Lying in the woman's sweet-smelling bed, Eamonn savoured the aroma of the turkey cooking below and the full feeling in his belly from the eggs and bacon she had fried him earlier. The house smelled of furniture polish and Eamonn loved it. He and the boy would be well set on here. Junie was Irish by birth and understood a man's need for a drink. As long as he worked at the docks and provided that at least for himself, he'd live the life of fecking Riley here. He was fifty-six, and the thought of going into his twilight years with Madge frightened him. He'd turn over a new leaf now, marry the little pickaheen in the kitchen below and look forward to an old age full of the finer things in life. Food, drink and a bit of the other now and again. What more could a man ask?

Getting out of bed, he pulled on his trousers. He glanced idly towards the window and froze. Through the clean nets he saw Madge weaving unsteadily up the street, with Betty and Cathy in tow. Sinking down on to the edge of the bed, he put his hands to his head and said: 'Feck!' over and over to himself.

Junie opened the front door with a wide smile on her face. She had been expecting these visitors for some time and was both frightened and exhilarated that the moment had finally come.

'Can I help you, dearie?' Her soft Cork voice was polite-sounding, with an undertone of pure steel.

'I want my old man, and I want him now!' Madge's voice was loud, slurred and agitated.

Junie smiled then. 'Is it your husband you're looking for? Only I wasn't aware you had one.' She put a finger to her lip as if thinking then said, 'Would it be your lodger you're after? Mr Docherty?'

Cathy felt a moment's pleasure as her mother went for the stuck-up piece. She and Betty watched the fight in stone cold silence, until Madge had gained the advantage and was straddling the other woman, banging her head on the pathway.

'Where is he, the dirty Irish git? I'll fucking kill him first, before I let him come to you!'

At that moment the man himself arrived on the doorstep and lifted Madge off the little Irishwoman with easy grace.

'Calm down, woman. Sure you're making a show of yourself to the whole street. Have you no shame?'

Cathy pulled her mother from his arms. 'After her years in the docks, shame is the last thing she'd possess, don't you think? Well, let me tell you something, Eamonn Docherty – you're a rotten bastard for doing this to her! And as for *her* . . .' She poked Junie in the chest. 'If that's what you really want, I wish you well, but she put her old man in the grave and hopefully she'll do the same thing to you and all. My mother's worth better than you, you drunken Irish ponce.'

'I couldn't have put it better meself,' Betty chimed in loudly, enjoying the scene they were creating before Junie Blacklock's neighbours. 'And if I was you, lady, I'd get yourself to a pox doctor. Docherty's normally dosed up to the fucking eyebrows!'

Madge was still crying uncontrollably. Pulling herself from her daughter's arms, she beseeched Eamonn: 'Please come home, love. We'll sort everything out, I promise you. Just come home, Eamonn, please come home.'

The big man looked at her in disgust and said through his teeth, 'Go home, woman. Would you look at yourself for once? What man would want you? Even one like me. You're an old whore – look like one and smell like one. You're a disgusting article. Get away out of here now before I put me boot in your arse.'

As he walked back into the house with Junie, his arm around the sobbing woman's shoulders, Cathy followed him inside. In the neat and tidy front room she stared around her for a moment in wonder. Through a doorway she could see a polished wooden table set for two people with a holly centrepiece and a proper cloth napkin beside each plate. Everywhere was polished or scrubbed, and the warmth was somehow clean, not the stuffy cloying warmth to be found in her own home. It was a room to aspire to, a room of which Cathy admitted deep inside herself she would love to be mistress. The anger left her abruptly. Who could blame Eamonn for wanting this, laid out on a plate for him, without even having to pay towards the rent? He was a man who used women, lived off them. Junie could offer more than her mother. It was an easy choice to make.

'Eamonn will bring your clothes round, OK?'

The big man held Junie in his arms and shook his head in distress. 'I'm sorry for what I said, but you're a sensible child. You can see how it is.'

Cathy smiled nastily. 'I can see how it is, all right. You fell on your feet here. I wouldn't advise knocking her from pillar to post like you did me mother, though. Do you know what I can't understand in all this?' She looked into the little woman's face. 'I don't get what it is exactly that you see in him. Because my mum might not be Woman of the Year, I accept that, but I always thought even *she* was too good for him. He's Irish scum, lady. But then again, so are you, I suppose.'

She walked out into the hallway. Then: 'Oh, by the way, you'd better set another place, his son will be here soon. My mum wouldn't give him house room after this.'

Outside she looked at her mother crumpled in Betty's arms and felt the first stirrings of a headache. As they walked down the neat pathway to the gate, Cathy glanced at the neighbours standing curiously on their doorsteps. Brazenly she bent down and picked up a stone, hurling it through the front window of the neat and tidy little house.

'Had a look, have you? Want a bleeding photograph!' she called to the onlookers.

Betty, despite herself, started to laugh. 'You're a girl, Cathy Connor, and no mistake.'

She shrugged. 'Well, that's Christmas fucked. Another fun day in the Connor household. Here, give me an arm and I'll help you carry her home.'

The three women walked along with as much dignity as they could muster, which as they all secretly acknowledged wasn't much.

Eamonn Junior had left and Madge was in bed sleeping off the bottle of Scotch she had put away soon after getting home. Cathy tidied round and then, finding she was hungry, opened the oven door.

All that was left of the chicken was the bones: Eamonn had picked the bird clean. Putting her head in her hands, she cried.

Looking around the tiny cramped kitchen, with the damp on the walls and the faded lino on the floor, Cathy Connor saw the rest of her life.

In her mind's eye, she saw once again the tidy house with its clean curtains, polished furniture and newly papered walls. Eamonn would be in his element there after years sleeping in a bed piled high with coats, her own haphazard cleaning and her mother's cloying scent pervading the house. The boy would think he had died and gone to heaven.

Much as she hated to admit it, Cathy envied him.

Junie was over the worst of her shock, and a few sherries later was dishing up the dinner and chatting twenty to the dozen about how everything would be grand. Madge would understand now, and they could start life together in peace.

Young Eamonn's eyes nearly popped from his head as a plate was piled high for him with turkey, stuffing, carrots, cabbage and roast potatoes. He saw his father smile and smiled back happily. After wolfing down the turkey dinner, he was further amazed to see a huge sherry trifle brought wobbling to the table in Junie's capable hands. Thanking God that he had finally landed on his feet, he'd polished off two bowls before his father admitted defeat and retired upstairs with Junie 'for a rest'.

Turning on the brand new television set, the boy sat and laughed at Tony Hancock. He was cracking nuts and drinking a beer when Junie came down in her dressing gown.

Taking the cut-glass bowl from his lap, she replaced it on the sideboard. Grim-faced she slid a doily under the glass he used for his beer and peered at him closely.

'Let's get this straight first off, young man. You are here on sufferance because your father's here. I'll feed you and water you, and we'll be civil. But you don't touch anything in this house without my express permission. Do you understand me?'

Eamonn Junior looked into her cold grey eyes and nodded.

'Now get yourself up and have a bath, you smell of the

slums, boy. In future you'll bathe twice a week and you'll leave your boots outside the front door. And if you don't like it . . . well, you know what you can do, don't you? Your father burned his boats today. If I give you both your marching orders, what else is there for you? Think on that.'

In the shiny bathroom, Eamonn thought of sausage sandwiches and Madge's haphazard attentions and realised that he had been better off where he was. His dad was doing all right, but what was there in all this for him, he wondered. The old biddy didn't like him, and he certainly didn't like her.

Downstairs he could hear his father's booming laughter. Eamonn shuddered. He was missing the old place already. For all the niceness of this house, he knew he'd never be welcome. Hadn't June gone out of her way to tell him he was only here on sufferance?

When he arrived downstairs, she was all sweetness and light, making them turkey sandwiches and cups of sweet tea. When she finally went out to the kitchen to wash up, Eamonn Senior looked at his son and said with pride: 'I'm for marrying her, son.'

The boy laughed softly. 'You're joking, Dad!'

His father frowned. 'What's to joke about? Are you blind or something? Look around you, for Christ Himself's sake. We're well set on here, you fecking eejit!'

The boy shook his head and sighed. 'And you called poor old Madge a whore! You're no better. You lived off her and now you'll live off this one.'

His father's expression changed then, a subtle change that told Eamonn he had better watch his step. His father was still on his best behaviour but he'd hammer the boy if the need arose.

'And you're no better than me. You've always looked out for number one, and no doubt you always will. I'd exchange you in the morning for young Cathy, because she's got more heart than you'll ever have. Madge will be all right all the time she has Cathy to look out for her. I only wish I'd been blessed with such a child, because you'd see me dying and look for the angle before offering me help!'

Eamonn Junior stared at his father. 'Well, I had a good teacher, didn't I?'

The big man was not offended. He nodded solemnly. 'Aye, son, you did that. If I gave you nothing else, I gave you a shrewd brain.'

Junie bustled into the room once more, pleased as punch to have the big Irish navvy sitting in her late husband's chair. Smiling at him, she settled into her own and began to sew, humming softly under her breath.

Eamonn watched his father put away beer after beer and sandwich after sandwich. Looking round the room, he costed up everything in his head. One day, when he was older, he'd clear this place out and leave the pair of them with nothing.

The thought cheered him, more so when he saw his father making sheep's eyes at the little dark-haired widow with her soft Irish accent and heart of steel.

Later, lying between the crisp white sheets of a proper bed, he decided to go round to Madge's the next day. He'd eat and sleep here, but he wouldn't forego Madge's and Cathy's attention. In this house he'd be starved of it. That old bitch would launch him out like a rocket given half a chance.

But he'd play the pair of them at their own game, and bide his time. He wasn't the son of Eamonn Docherty for nothing. As he had said to his father earlier, he'd had a very good teacher.

*

Betty, in a bid to cheer up her friend, had rustled up two men of indeterminate age and occupation. Both wore suspenders on their socks and both had brightly coloured braces, National Health false teeth and thinning hair. Their names were Charlie and Bill. Charlie was obviously a regular customer of Betty's, and as such felt he was in charge. As he topped up her mother's glass, he winked jovially at Cathy.

'What did you get for Christmas, love?'

Cathy looked into his cold eyes and said quietly, 'What I get every year. Sweet fuck-all.'

Charlie grinned and gave his exaggerated wink once more. Grabbing the front of his trousers, he said loudly: 'I've got something here for you, if you think you can handle it.'

Cathy rolled her eyes at the ceiling. 'Leave it where it is, little boy. I want nourishment not punishment!'

Madge and Betty roared with laughter.

Bill, realising what the girl had said, put in, 'She's a bit knowing, ain't she?'

'Oh, leave her alone, you two. She's only twelve.'

'Big girl for twelve, if you ask me.'

Betty turned on the man beside her and cried, 'Well, no one is asking you, are they? Cut her a bit of slack, for Christ's sake.'

But there was an underlying note of jealousy in the woman's voice and Cathy got up and walked out. Pulling a dresser against her bedroom door, she began to tidy up her room. Hearing the radio and the laughter in the background, she sighed heavily. Another man and her mother was the old Madge once more. Tomorrow she'd be crying and threatening suicide again, but for the moment all was well with her.

Looking out of the window Cathy saw all the

neighbours' Christmas trees and the warm glow from the fairy lights around them and wondered what it must be like to live in a normal household, with a normal mother and father and a normal life.

Closing her eyes, she bit back tears. She was missing Eamonn badly. For the last seven Christmases they had been together, the two of them against the world – or against their parents anyway. She could put up with anything if he was there beside her. Now they were parted and she wasn't sure she could cope. He was her ally, her brother, her friend. Eamonn was everything to her.

In the front room she heard a glass break, and a man swearing, then loud laughter once more. This would be her life from now on – she had to accept that or go mad.

It would be back to the bad old days of errant men, haphazard money, and the phantom pregnancies her mother suffered every few months. Back to prying money from Madge to provide food and warmth. Back to listening to the groans and snores of men she would never see again, if God were good. Listening to bedsprings and fights or bedsprings and laughter.

She glanced around the room which was about to become her nightly prison, and sighed heavily. Living with her mother, a lunatic alcoholic, was one thing – she could cope with that – but living without Eamonn was a different kettle of fish altogether.

From now on she'd be living without love.

The love he'd given her was what had kept her going this long. Madge's love didn't count in the equation, because her mother's love was transient, only really apparent when there was no man on the scene. Betty's petty jealousy had struck a warning note in Cathy's mind and she knew, deep inside, that she had to sort herself out now. In a year or two it would be all too easy to go the way of her mother and Betty, and that was something she was determined wasn't going to happen to her. Not in a million years. Her life would be different. She had decided that much.

Finally she slept with images of Eamonn before her eyes, a tiny terraced house full of shining furniture, and herself, her belly full of arms and legs, waiting for her conquering hero to come home.

She had a smile on her face as she slept, and her eyelids fluttered as she dreamed of the good life, her other life. The life she knew was waiting for her.

One day it would all come true, she had to believe that. Because without her dreams Cathy Connor had nothing, and no one was more painfully aware of that than she was herself.

Chapter Three

1966

Madge Connor was having trouble breathing. Clearing her throat loudly, she sat up straighter in her chair and downed the rum in front of her in one swallow. The coughing abated and she smiled lazily before hawking in her throat once more, bringing the spittle and phlegm into her mouth.

A voice protested loudly: 'Leave it out, Madge, you're making me feel sick!'

She spat into the spittoon by the bar and shrugged. 'Better out than in.' Holding up her glass, she signalled for another large drink and lit another cigarette.

Betty shook her head and sighed. 'One of these days, Madge Connor, them fags is going to kill you.'

'Blow it out your arse, Bet, and let's get to work.'

The barman brought the drink and Madge downed it at a gulp, wiping her mouth with the back of her hand, smearing lipstick and spit across her face.

'You're pissed.'

Madge put on a surprised expression and said

sarcastically, 'No? Thank Gawd you told me, Betty, I'd never have sussed that one by meself!'

Betty sighed again. 'You're always pissed lately, ever since that Irish ponce got married.' Her voice became softer then. 'Come on, Madge, let's get to work before all the blokes are taken.'

Madge shook her head. 'I can't be bothered any more. We're pissing against the wind there. Can't you see, we're too old for this lark?'

Her faded eyes were alight with honesty and Betty couldn't stand looking into them any longer. The trouble with Madge was, when she got drunk, she told the truth. And the truth hurt.

Betty patted her hair, dyed black these days, looking in the bar mirror. 'Suit your fucking self! I've got to earn a few quid even if you ain't.' Slipping off the stool, she made her way out of The Blind Beggar pub and towards Victoria Park. She'd pick up the bus and be in Custom House within half an hour.

As she approached the bus stop she heard Madge's tell-tale high heels behind her.

'Hold on, girl, I'll break me neck in a minute!'

Taking out a crumpled tissue, Betty wiped her friend's face clean and helped her apply more lipstick. As the bus came into sight two young boys on the opposite side of the street started shouting.

'Oi, you old slappers, how much for a quick flash?'

Ignoring them, Betty helped her friend on to the bus, oblivious to the hostile stares of the women already seated. Madge and Betty's cheap fur coats and plastered-on make-up were a dead giveaway. They were ridiculed wherever they went and both stared stoically ahead, as they'd learned to years ago.

*

'Come on, Cathy, let me.'

She shook her head as she pulled his hands from under her jumper.

'Stop it. You know I won't do that.'

Eamonn leaned back against the settee, gritting his teeth. 'I don't believe you, Cathy. We've done everything else but, and at the last minute you knock me back!' Jumping up, he arranged himself and pulled up his flies.

Cathy watched him, full of fear that he'd walk away from her, this time for ever.

'You're a tease, Cathy, you know that, don't you?' he complained bitterly.

She closed her eyes. The cider he had given her had made her drunk and she wished she was in bed asleep, instead of lying on a settee, half naked and upset.

'I'm frightened, Eamonn.'

Picking up his coat from the floor, he smiled unpleasantly. 'Thanks a lot, Cath. That says it all, don't it? After all these years, you're frightened of me. Well, don't worry, I won't be coming back, love.'

As he made for the door, she ran to him, her unbuttoned tartan skirt hanging loose around her waist and threatening to slip to the floor.

'I'm sorry, Eamonn, really I am. Don't go.'

He turned and looked at her hard. 'Does that mean you're going to let me then?'

She dropped her gaze and concentrated on the old scarred dresser in the corner of the room. She heard his sharp intake of breath.

'I can't, Eamonn.' Her low voice was barely audible.

'Not can't, Cathy. Won't. See you sometime.'

He turned from her and left the room. At the front door he waited a few seconds, sure that she'd beg him to come back. But she didn't, and feeling the temper rise within him, he slammed out of the door.

Cathy heard his footsteps clattering downstairs as she was pulling on her panties, and swallowed down the urge to cry. Sex was a major part of her mother's life and Cathy had always accepted that. But sex for herself was something else altogether. She wanted to be a virgin when she got married, and even at thirteen she understood exactly what Eamonn was offering her: the chance to get pregnant, the chance to be used, the chance to become what her mother was. She adored Eamonn but years of living with him had left her with no illusions as far as he was concerned. That, coupled with the fact that she still adored him, was the root of all her problems.

The worst of it was, she wanted to do what he asked, but was too frightened.

After tidying herself, she began washing the glasses and straightening the furniture. Then she went to her room, lay down on the bed and took deep breaths.

She was lulled to sleep by images of Eamonn and herself, in a nice house, with a wedding ring on her finger and a baby in her arms. Respectability was all-important to Cathy because it was something to aspire to. Most people wouldn't understand that. But then, most people weren't the child of a dock dolly like Madge.

Since her Irishman had married, she had even started to bring her work home.

It was the shrill laughter of drunkenness that woke Cathy. Rubbing her eyes, she realised she was still fully dressed. She sat up on the bed and glanced at the small bedside clock. It was three-thirty in the morning. Her head ached from the cider and her mouth felt as dry as the Gobi Desert. Yawning heavily, she walked from the bedroom into the narrow hallway. As she made her way to the kitchen she heard a man's voice.

'Pour out more drinks, Alan.'

'Yeah, large ones!' Betty's voice was slurred and Cathy closed her eyes in distress.

If it was a foursome, the noise level was likely to increase and she wasn't in the mood. Hearing the clink of glasses, she poured herself some milk and tiptoed back to her room with it. Inside she drank the milk and undressed hurriedly, hanging up her skirt and smoothing out her jumper. Pulling on a large flannelette nightie, she pulled back the covers and climbed into bed. But she was wide awake now.

By the light of the streetlamp she could make out the furniture in her room, even the damp patches on the wallpaper. She replayed the scene of earlier in her mind and sighed heavily. In her young life only two people had remained a constant fixture: her mother and Eamonn.

Now he wanted something from her, and she knew she would eventually let him have it. Putting her hands behind her head, she comforted herself with wild imaginings: Eamonn waiting for her at the altar, the moment he slid the ring on to her finger, Madge all respectable in a navy-blue two-piece wiping away tears of pride.

She was smiling slightly when the bedroom door was thrust open and the harsh light from the hallway dazzled her.

'Well, well! What have we here?'

The man was tall and thin, with a beaked nose and thick lips. He smiled at her but there was a gloating quality in his voice and eyes.

'Get out! Go on, mate, get yourself out of here.' Cathy could hear the sounds of the radio and raucous laughter coming from the lounge.

The man approached the bed. 'Come on, love, I ain't stupid. Got the painters in, is that it?'

Cathy closed her eyes at this disgusting reference to periods. Leaping from the bed, she screamed out: 'Mum! Mum! Get in here!'

The loudness of that voice, coming from such a fragile slip of a girl, took him by surprise. Sidestepping him, Cathy ran into the front room, causing the three of them to fall quiet. The second man sat staring at her in shock.

'Who's this then?'

Cathy put her hands on her hips and said nastily, 'Come on, Mum, do the honours. I have to get up for school in the morning, and there's a man in my room trying to get his leg over.'

Madge winked at her and said, 'He's all right, girl. Tell him the score and send him back in here. You're safe as houses, love.'

Cathy shook her head in consternation. 'You go and get him, please – he's your punter, not mine. I'd appreciate it if you'd tell him that and all. He seems to think I work with you two.'

The man walked back into the room as she said that. He was pulling up his flies and belched loudly before saying: 'Leave it out, girl, you're ripe for it. Next you'll be telling us you're a virgin and your mother's Lady Docker!'

The men laughed together.

Cathy screwed up her eyes in exasperation and Betty stood up. Taking the girl's arm she said in a soothing voice: 'Don't get in a state, Cathy. Come on, I'll take you back to bed.'

'I'll come with you.' The second man's voice was full of innuendo. 'See you tucked in, like.'

Betty looked at him and said laughingly, 'Stop it, Alan. The girl's only thirteen. Leave her alone.'

Alan, a heavy-set man with steel-grey Brylcreemed hair and a red nose, said seriously, 'Thirteen, my arse! She looks old enough to me. Old enough for what I want anyway.'

Cathy pulled herself from Betty's grasp. Her voice hard and reminiscent of her mother's, she said loudly and forcefully: 'That's it! I want both of you out – now.' She picked up the two overcoats from the back of the settee and threw them on the floor.

'I beg your pardon?' The tall thin man sounded amazed.

'You heard. What are you, deaf as well as stupid? I said out.'

'You'll get a slap around the face, young la—'

But Ron's voice was cut off by Madge who butted in: 'If there's any fucking slapping to be done, mate, I'll do it! Now then, Cathy, get yourself back to bed and I'll sort these two out myself.'

The girl gritted her teeth. 'I want them out, Mum.'

Madge stood up. Pushing out her considerable chest, she said heavily, 'What you want and what you'll get is two different things. Now, get back to bed and I'll see you in the morning. OK?'

Her eyes spoke volumes and Cathy turned abruptly and walked from the room. The tall man stood in the doorway. She had to squeeze past him to get out.

He smiled down at her, his breath rank in her face as she made her escape. 'I'll see you again, love.'

She shouted over her shoulder, 'Not if I see you first, mate!' Then slammed the bedroom door and made a big production of wedging a chair underneath the handle.

This was becoming a nightly occurrence and she hated it. Twice in the last few weeks she had been disturbed by men trying to touch her, or had woken to find them leering at her. It was getting beyond a joke. Cathy had long ago come to terms with her mother's way of life. The taunts of the other kids were like water off a duck's back now. But as she herself approached womanhood, things were changing, becoming frightening. Because Cathy knew, in her heart of hearts, that if offered enough money Madge would try and talk even her daughter into the 'life', something Cathy emphatically did not want. Madge Connor patently could not understand her reluctance. To Madge, men were there to rip off, to take from, and if they wanted something in return, well, what was wrong with that?

Memories of her young life assailed Cathy. Visiting men would sit her on their lap and all Madge would do was laugh shrilly and pour herself another drink. Cathy could almost see herself trying to squirm free from their harsh beards and loose-lipped kisses. It made her shudder even now.

As bad as Eamonn Senior was, he had never tried that with her, only ever wanting to be her friend. In a strange way, she missed him. At least with him there, she'd been safe, and Eamonn, her Eamonn had been there too. Now it seemed the only way to get him back was to give in to him; let him have what he wanted. Feeling tears sting her eyes, she wondered what the end of all this would be.

Cathy sat at the kitchen table with a plastic-backed mirror propped up against the teapot. She made up her face carefully, sipping from the cup of sweet tea beside her and munching a piece of toast. As she applied lipstick her mother walked into the kitchen and began to pour out two teas, letting the mirror fall to the table.

'Is he still here?' Cathy's voice was low.

Madge stared at her. 'What if he is? This is my flat, love, not yours. Remember?'

'How could I forget? By the way, Mrs Carter from next door is complaining to the landlord again. She told me when I was bringing in the milk.'

Madge yawned, tongue like a yellow snake inside her mouth. 'Fuck her, silly old cow!' Walking to the door she called: 'Tea up! Breakfast's extra!'

The tall thin man walked into the kitchen in nothing but his trousers. His braces hung by his legs and his eyes still had white beads of sleep round them. Cathy felt the toast rise inside her as she looked at him.

'Drink your tea and fuck off.' Her voice was matter-of-fact.

Madge laughed. 'She likes you, Ron. Normally she don't speak to anyone!'

The man grinned and Cathy grinned back. A fake grin that held so much hatred he was taken aback for a few moments.

'You're such a stroppy mare, Cathy. You always shoot yourself in the foot, you,' Madge ran on. 'If you could give people a kind word, you'd get rewarded. Look at that man a while ago – he gave you half a crown!' She looked at Ron and said in exasperation, 'She told him to shove it. Straight up!' Madge's voice held pride and annoyance at the same time. 'She's a nice girl, this one. No one will ever own her, mate.'

Cathy lit a cigarette and took a deep draw on it. Then, making her voice sweet, she said, 'So, Ron, have you a wife and kids, and where do you work? Is this how you want me, Mum? The talkative teenager?'

Madge laughed heartily. 'You should go on the bleeding stage, Cath. You're a card and no mistake.'

'She wants a slap round the earhole, Madge, and if I was her father she'd get one.'

Madge turned on him viciously. 'You and whose fucking army, mate? Because if you so much as raised your hand, I'd stick a knife through your heart without a second's thought.'

The man looked at her for long moments. 'I'll bear that in mind, lady.'

Madge lit a cigarette and said, 'Get your coat and piss off, I'll see you later.' Her voice had lost its fierceness now and was almost cajoling.

When Ron had left she poured out two fresh teas and said sadly, 'Another day, another dollar.'

'How much did you get?' Cathy asked with genuine interest.

'A couple of quid. Nothing to write home about. How's young Eamonn?'

Cathy shrugged. 'Same as usual, Mum. He said his dad's well, before you ask.'

As Madge nodded, cigarette ash fell on to the slip which was all she wore and she wiped at it haphazardly. 'I loved him, you know, Cathy.' Her voice was small, crushed-sounding.

Cathy looked sadly at her. The streaked mascara and faded lipstick gave her mother's face a clown-like appearance. Holding her hand tightly, Cathy said, 'I know you did, Mum. I know you did.'

Madge sniffed. 'I got a new job last night. I'm going to work in a clip joint near Soho.'

Cathy smiled even though her heart wasn't in it. 'Why the long face then, Mum? After all, you've been promoted.'

Madge laughed harshly. 'You're a sarcastic little mare, ain't ya?'

Cathy pulled a brush through her thick blond hair and said, 'Why don't you get a proper job, Mum? Like everyone else.'

Madge shook her head and said hotly: 'I should bleeding well cocoa! Let's not start all that old fanny again. Fine mess we'd be in with about three quid a week to live on. Have you thought of that, eh?'

'Well, other people manage.'

'I ain't other people. Anyway, I like me job.'

Putting on her school coat, Cathy kissed her mother and said, 'That's the trouble, you like it too much. See you tonight.'

Madge swung round in her chair and said, 'Before you rush off, what do you think of Ron?'

Cathy shrugged. 'Why?'

'He wants to move in, I think. It's him what got me the new job.'

Cathy's face was a picture of terror as she said, 'Oh, Mum! You're not moving him in, are you? He's horrible.'

'No, he ain't. He's a man, that's all. Surely you're not going to hold that against him? Anyway, nothing's final. I might change me mind.'

'You'd better, Mum. I'm sick of people in and out of my bedroom, and you know that'll be the upshot. It always is.'

Her mother grinned slyly. 'You could make us a fortune, Cathy. You're ripe for it.'

The girl's face blanched. 'You're not serious, surely?'

' 'Course not, you silly mare. I'm just winding you up.'

Cathy slammed out of the flat, her heart beating a tattoo in her chest.

More and more often lately her mother made jokes that Cathy didn't think were funny. In her heart she knew they were real threats; in the night she admitted this to herself because, as much as her mother loved her, Cathy knew Madge was a brass through and through. Like a piece of Southend rock, if you cut Madge Connor in half it would be written there in big pink letters.

As she walked to school Cathy's mind was on what her mother had told her, and for the first time in ages, Eamonn was not in the forefront of her thoughts.

*

'Hello, me little pickaheen!' Eamonn Senior's welcome was loud and Junie's face pinched as they saw Cathy sitting in their neat little kitchen.

'Hello, Junie. Eamonn.' Cathy's voice was civil, and against her better judgement the older woman smiled kindly at her.

'You've just mashed the tea then? Good girl, we'll both have a cup. Bring them through to the parlour, there's a dear.'

'I'll have a bottle of beer meself. Now then, child, where's the eejit?' the big man asked her.

'He's popped over the road to Mr Burrows's. He said there's a chance of a job in the docks.'

Eamonn Senior's eyes widened. 'Good for him!'

Cathy nodded solemnly.

'How's your mother?' Cathy knew he only asked out of politeness. She pushed her blond hair back from her face and stared at him with an adult expression.

'She's fine, thanks. Got a new job in a clip joint and seems pleased enough about it. It's a step up as far as she's concerned.'

The man's face was a picture as he listened to the news. 'A clip joint, is it? Well, I hope it keeps fine for her.' This was said in a derogatory way but Cathy was saved from answering by Eamonn Junior's return.

'All right, Cath? I thought *you* was going to work today,' he said, looking at his father with a sneer on his face. 'Many more days off and you'll be out, mate.'

His father blew out his lips in derision. 'They can't get rid of me, I've told you that. They can't get rid of any of the Irish at the moment. You'd do well to remember that.'

Young Eamonn pulled himself up to his full height and said quietly, 'I told you over and over again, Dad – I ain't fucking Irish, I'm English!' Before his father could retort he had pulled Cathy from her seat and they were out the back door and up the path to the lane.

'I hate that bastard at times.'

Cathy grinned. 'What with him and me mother, it's a wonder either of us is even remotely normal.'

Eamonn pulled her against him, and pushed his hand up her skirt. 'Give us a kiss, Cathy.'

She kissed him then, smelling Coal Tar soap and Park Drive cigarettes.

'Me mate has a bedsit. He says we can use it tonight.'

Eamonn's eyes were a deep sea blue. Looking into them, she felt herself drowning. He was half smiling, his face already showing signs of five o'clock shadow. He was as dark as the gypsies he was said to descend from.

Seeing her expression he said softly, 'Come on, Cathy. What you got to lose? I want you.'

Shaking her head, she sighed heavily. 'No, Eamonn. I'm sorry, but I'm not ready yet. I told you – I'm frightened.'

She was pleading with her eyes. Eamonn stared hungrily into her pretty heart-shaped face and felt the pull of her then. Closing his own eyes, he said through gritted teeth: 'For fuck's sake, Cathy, you're thirteen going on thirty! You're not a kid, none of us is. Never bleeding well had the chance! I promise you, I'll be really nice to you. You'll love it.'

Cathy felt something inside her give way. Burning her boats, she said: 'All right then, Eamonn.'

He crushed her to him tightly, feeling the strong steady beat of her heart against his ribs. She was so tiny, yet so female. He loved the smell of her, the feel of her. They were interrupted by the sound of heavy footfalls coming down the alley.

'Eamonn! You'd better come, mate.'

Titchy O'Mara was a small stocky boy of sixteen. He

had the roundness of his mother and the harsh features of his father. Out of breath, he put his hands on his knees and steadied himself.

He smiled briefly at Cathy before gasping: 'There's a big fight tonight, Bethnal Green against Bermondsey Boys. There's been fucking murders today! Harry Clark got a hammering in Bermondsey market – he's in the Old London being stitched and all sorts. They've really pushed it this time. We're going over the water at ten tonight, but we're tooling up beforehand. You coming or what?'

Eamonn's face was stiff with anger. 'Harry Clark? But he's only a kid, no more than fifteen. The dirty bastards! Have you told the rest of the firm?'

Titchy nodded. ' 'Course I have. We need to get everyone for this. I'm telling you now, this is the big one, mate. We've got to sort the fuckers once and for all.'

Eamonn nodded, all thoughts of Cathy forgotten. 'I'm coming. Wait here while I get me gear.'

She rolled her eyes heavenwards as he disappeared through the back gate into his house. Titchy smiled at her shyly. He liked Cathy Connor, they had a lot in common. His mother was a dock dolly as well.

Five minutes later Eamonn was dressed in his battle clothes: black trousers, black shirt and black leather jacket. His fashionable elephant's trunk hairstyle was freshly Brylcreemed and he carried a bicycle chain and an iron cosh in a tool bag.

Kissing his cheek, Cathy watched him disappear with Titchy and sighed with relief that the inevitable had been put off for a few days by the actions of the Bermondsey Boys.

Eamonn was easily the tallest of his cronies and they looked to him for guidance. Even the older boys looked to him, because Eamonn had the edge. Unlike his pals, who just liked to act it, Eamonn was really hard. He didn't just fight, he set out to maim. His name was synonymous with real fear in the East End. It wasn't just his size, impressive though that was. He had a coldness about him that the others picked up on.

At fifteen, he had beaten unconscious a North Londoner called Teddy Spinelli, a loan shark of Italian descent. Once, Teddy had been respected – feared even. Since the hammering he had received at Eamonn's hands, he had not been seen or heard of anywhere in the Smoke. Even the older villains gave Eamonn his due, impressed with this young boy, this fighter. Seeing themselves in him when young.

This was duly noted and gave him a mystique which Eamonn used shamelessly for his own ends.

There was one drawback to all this, however: every firm with dreams of the big time wanted to be the one to hammer Eamonn Docherty, therefore acquiring his reputation by default. Eamonn knew this and it was why he was so adamant about getting this South London firm put away once and for all. All in the name of poor Harry, of course.

If he pulled this one off, his entry into the real London gangs was assured. He was just sixteen years old.

He began passing out the weapons they had stashed away for such occasions. Putting his bicycle chain around his neck and his cosh down the back of his trousers, he pulled from his jacket a small handgun, ostentatiously checking it for ammunition.

The other boys all stared at him in awe.

'Where the fuck did you get that?'

Eamonn grinned. 'It was me old man's. Let's just say I borrowed it.'

Titchy's eyes were round and staring. 'Surely you're not

going to use it?' His voice was high, scared-sounding, and Eamonn loved it.

Looking around him at the fourteen-strong gang he had been leading for the past few years, he shook his head.

'Anyone who can't handle it had better fuck off now, I ain't playing kids' games tonight. Harry Clark is lying in the Old London battered to fuck. Tonight we avenge him, and we go down in London history.'

He smiled at them all, a chilling sight.

'South London get their comeuppance, and we become the number ones. Within a week we'll all be on a wage with the big boys. Who needs the docks, eh, when we can pull in big money for doing what we like best? Kicking people's heads in.'

Titchy laughed nervously. 'You're a fucking nutter!'

Eamonn Junior grinned. 'I'll take that as a compliment, coming from you!'

Everyone laughed, but the sound was tinged with hysteria. Tonight wasn't just a rumble. Tonight they were going to be blooded – whether they liked it or not.

Eamonn had always had the edge, and each and every one of them knew it. There was no turning back now.

Chapter Four

'Hello, Cathy love. I see your woman going out done up to the nines. In on your own again the night?'

Mrs Fowler's voice was kind, and Cathy stood in the lobby to the flats and smiled at the old woman.

'Yes, I'm on me own tonight, Mrs Fowler. And believe me, with my mother that's a Godsend at times!'

'She's a bleeding case, her,' the old lady said comfortably. 'Still, as I always say, each to their own, girl. If you fancy a cuppa later, give me a knock, all right?'

Cathy nodded and took the stairs two at a time, her kitten-heeled shoes clattering all the way up to the second floor. Some people were nice, really nice.

Pulling the key through the letter box on its piece of string, she opened the front door. The worn paint and scarred surface were unchanged from the day they'd first walked in here.

Cathy stepped into the seedy flat. Slipping out of her coat, she looked around her in dismay. Madge had once more completely trashed the tiny kitchen and living room in her hurry to get out to work.

The worn horsehair sofa was covered with sequinned

dresses and discarded stockings, most with ladders or badly repaired holes. The floor was littered with shoes and handbags, strewn everywhere, left for her to tidy up.

Walking into the kitchen, she groaned. Make-up in various stages of decay covered all the surfaces. Spit-covered mascara brushes were scattered over the table next to dirty dishes. Exotic blushers were everywhere and gaudy cream eyeshadows were left, minus their lids, by the overflowing ashtray.

Putting on the kettle, Cathy began clearing away. As she carried things into her mother's bedroom she wrinkled her nose at the stale smell. She threw open the window and looked down into the street, at children playing and women gossiping, and took in a good deep lungful of London air. Leaving the window wide open, she picked up her mother's large make-up bag and went back into the kitchen. She gathered up the make-up and unzipped the bag. Inside were several packs of French letters. Closing her eyes, she took a deep breath. Then, taking one of the packets, she slipped it into her own clutchbag.

If she was going to lose her cherry, at least she'd do it with proper precautions.

She made herself a cup of tea then began cleaning the lounge, putting all her mother's dresses on hangers and arraying her shoes in neat lines around Madge's bedroom walls. The handbags she stacked in the wardrobe, checking them first for change as she always did. Finally she pulled her mother's bedclothes over the bed and, using the carpet sweeper, cleaned the floor.

Afterwards she made herself a coffee, lit a cigarette and listened to the Beatles on the radio, wondering if she'd ever have the chance to be part of the wild sixties – though, she admitted to herself ruefully, her mother had practised if not exactly free love, then certainly promiscuous love for years.

In a funny way she envied her mother. Everything was cut and dried with Madge. You either did something, or you didn't. There was no middle ground.

Cathy sighed. She rinsed out her cup and then began sorting through the washing basket. As she worked she dreamed of washing clothes in a nice kitchen, like the one on the Tide advert, and cooking elaborate meals for her husband Eamonn. In her dream her mother and Eamonn Senior were miraculously dead and buried, leaving their two children to live the good life with no painful reminders of the past.

Thinking of Eamonn she imagined him taking her sexually and the thought made her breath come in quick jolting gasps. He was right, she admitted. She was ripe for it. What she wasn't ripe for was a child, a flat like this one and the hard life of the women around her: old before their time and knocking out children like Ford assembly lines.

Smiling, she decided that she, Cathy Connor, would have her cake and eat it too.

As she scrubbed, she sang along happily with the Crystals.

'What on earth is *that* sitting at the end of my bar!'

Jessie Houston's voice was scandalised and Madge's face hardened as the words intended for her rang out over the small bar.

'Are you off your fucking head, Ron? I've seen better-looking things in bombed-out houses!'

He wiped a hand across his sweating face and tried to placate his sister-in-law. 'Leave it out, Jess.'

Jessie, eight stone of pure malevolence, looked into his face and shrieked: 'Leave *her* out, more like! Outside with the bleeding rubbish. I know some of our girls are a bit long in the tooth, but at least they're not dock dollies. And she's a dock dolly from head to foot. I smelt the fucker before her beak came round the door.' She looked along the bar to Madge and said in a quieter voice: 'No disrespect, love, but I can't have you here, sorry. The other girls will be here soon and they'll go spare.'

Madge swallowed down her humiliation and stared challengingly at Ron.

'She stays and that's my final word,' he put in.

Jessie thumped the bar. Turning on Ron, she screamed, 'Then you run this place yourself! I ain't being made a laughing stock. Even if we employed her, who'd have her? Look at her, Ron, for Christ's sakes.'

Ron, used to letting the fierce little woman in front of him have her own way, said through gritted teeth, 'She stays, Jessie – all right? I own half this club and you'd better remember that.'

Jessie's face was white with fury. Since the death of her husband, she had come into the whoring business, and both she and Ron had been relieved to find that she had a natural aptitude for it. With no children and no real scruples, Jessie had found her vocation in life. The only bugbear was the fact that she had ruled her husband, and now she ruled Ron and the little empire they had created.

Even the bigger boys were wary of Jessie. Just looking at her you could see she was capable of literally anything. She could evict a fifteen-stone man with the minimum of fuss, pour the drinks and head count the girls without thinking. Ron's brother Danny had once been the brains of the business. Jessie had effortlessly taken over where he had left off.

This was the first time Ron had tried to assert himself, and in all honesty it wasn't so much Madge herself as the fact that he was trying to take a decision on his own that bothered Jessie. She had to be in charge. It was just her way.

'Come on, Jess, do the honours, love.' Ron's voice was cajoling now, tinged with desperation.

Jessie took a deep breath. Pulling herself up to her full five foot two, she said, 'On your own head be it, Ron. It's half yours as you point out, but if you done a bit of collar here now and then I'd be more inclined to take your point of view like . . .'

She droned on and he smiled at Madge, raising his eyebrows in triumph.

Madge looked from him to Jessie and stored the insults away for future reference. Jessie should have known better than to pull down a dock dolly because dock girls never forgot nothing.

Jessie went into the back room where the gambling would take place and Ron poured Madge a stiff drink of rum.

'She's all right, Madge. Don't take any notice of her. She's always the same, don't mean anything by it. Once the other girls arrive, you'll see I'm right. The main job here is getting the punters to bet. It's more a gambling club than a clippie really. Remember always to keep your paper with you when you score a lump. Because Jessie will head count you all and she don't miss a trick, but if you don't know your score, she won't tell you. Understand me?'

Madge nodded. 'I thought you said it was your club?'

Ron stared down into her face and sighed heavily. 'It is. Half mine anyway. Look, Madge, if you don't like the set-up, fuck off, love. There's plenty more where you came from.'

Madge licked her bright orange lips and attempted a smile. 'Don't be like that, Ron. I thought me and you was mates.'

He relented and smiled thinly at her. 'We are, providing you do as I say.'

Before she had a chance to answer the door burst open and two of the other hostesses arrived. Looking at them, Madge saw that they weren't really very different from her.

Her dreams of the big time were shattered in seconds. Instead of ripping off sailors, she'd be ripping off local men. Who, unlike the sailors, could easily track her down. Knocking back her drink, she looked at the hubbub around her and sighed.

Well, it was a step up in its own way, and if nothing else she had Ron. Because a man in her bed was worth two in her hand, any day of the week.

It was just after eleven when the boys made their way along Upper Thames Street. They looked like trouble, which was exactly the impression they wished to create. Some were walking, others were on Vespas, the engines humming in the darkness. All were alert and ready for the trouble they were to cause.

'Show us your gun again, Eamonn. Go on.' Doughal Feenan was fascinated by the weapon and Eamonn handed it to him, laughing at the boy's incredulity.

Doughal, all red hair and freckles, looked at his friend and said seriously: 'You wouldn't really shoot someone dead, would you?'

Eamonn could hear fear tinged with awe in the boy's voice and shrugged nonchalantly. 'Watch me. Those bastards need to be taught a lesson and a bullet up their arses should achieve that much at least!'

He laughed and the others laughed with him, all thinking this was just a frightener for the South London boys. At the end of the day, with the eldest there just sixteen, they weren't like the big timers, though all of them wanted to be seen that way. By their peer group at least.

Eamonn took the gun and put it back in his jacket pocket. He loved the attention it created. Loved the feeling of being in charge of them all, being the main man. Eamonn Docherty craved the limelight. Craved the feeling of being someone important, and the gun guaranteed him that.

No one would dare disrespect him with a gun aimed at their heads. No one.

Looking at his gang he felt a moment's intense happiness. He loved to lead people, loved to be the one telling them all what they were to do, where they were to go. They all looked up to him as if he were something special. He had made up his mind that one day soon everyone would know him, would understand he was a dangerous man, a force to be reckoned with.

The gun, and his natural leadership abilities, would guarantee him that. After tonight his name would be known everywhere in London while simultaneously his East End cronies would retreat behind a wall of silence and he would, in effect, get away with murder.

He had been living for this night for too long. All he wanted now was to get it and his dirty work over with. Then he could start his career, his real life.

The Krays would give him a job; they liked a face with bottle and he had plenty of it. No more listening to his father's old crap, no more living in a two up, two down with an Irish drunk and a houseproud bitch. No more scraping along, doing a little bit here and a little bit there.

If everything went to plan, he'd finally hit the big one. Payola. He would be a real villain now, and that meant the fast track to money, cars and prestige.

Tonight was to be his watershed, his blooding. He couldn't wait to get started.

He didn't have to wait long. The South London firm was waiting for them at the top of the Embankment.

James Carter was a Bermondsey boy through and through. Of Irish descent, he had a lot in common with Eamonn Docherty though neither of them would admit that.

He watched the other gang's arrival with cold green eyes. Taking out his steel comb, he pulled it through his hair, fastidiously pushing his quiff into place and replacing the comb in his pocket. His full-lipped mouth was set in a cruel smile and inside his jacket was a cut-throat razor. Eamonn Docherty was to get the biggest shock of his life tonight and James Carter was going to be the man to give it to him.

Behind him his gang stood stock still. Every face was hard. Every hand was shaking. Not with fear, but with excitement.

As the East Enders drew close, they stopped and the two gangs stared each other out. Then, as if all of one mind, they pulled out their weapons.

A car driving past speeded up, rattling towards Westminster. Gang fights were common, but it was unusual to see one on a common thoroughfare.

The Embankment was quiet at eleven-thirty at night; most revellers had gone on to other places or were already home. The only sound now was of the Thames lapping gently against the green-slimed wall.

Eamonn touched the bicycle chain around his neck, his cosh down the back of his trousers. They waited patiently for everyone to arm themselves. This was the unwritten rule. When the streetlamp glinted on the gun pulled from Eamonn's pocket there was a collective exhalation of shock from the South Londoners.

James Carter's voice was deep, resonant with an Irish

inflection. 'Fuck off, Docherty. No one uses guns.' Even though his voice was heavy with menace, everyone sensed the underlying fear there.

They were all experiencing it too.

Eamonn smiled lazily, his voice matter-of-fact and terrifyingly normal. 'You should have thought of that when you beat up poor Harry. Eight to one, I heard. So I thought I'd even the odds up like – for him.'

The flash that came from the gun was a surprise to all there. The East London boys closed their eyes in fright and the South Londoners opened theirs to see if the bullet was aimed at them.

James Carter seemed to fall to the pavement in slow motion. Half his face flew into the air, bits of skin and eyeball spraying his friends and causing them to step back involuntarily.

Eamonn's low laughter was clearly heard by them all. A stunned silence reigned, the sense of shock almost tangible.

Looking at the boy on the ground, Eamonn felt as if the bullet had hit him. There was a tight feeling in his chest, he was fighting for breath. Shock at what he'd done ballooned up inside him.

One of the South London boys knelt by his friend. Seeing the single staring eye and the position of the boy's body, he looked at Eamonn. With tears in his voice, he said hysterically: 'You're fucking mad, Docherty! He's an Irish like you. You don't shoot people, don't kill people . . .' His voice trailed off as they heard the sound of police cars in the distance.

Everyone began running away, fear lending wings to their feet.

Titchy pulled on Eamonn's jacket. 'Come on, Eamonn, the Old Bill will be here any second. Come on, man, for fuck's sake.'

Eamonn heard the anguish in the other boy's voice. After one last look at James Carter, he turned away and began running. His heart was hammering in his chest and his blood ran cold.

He'd done it.

Jesus help me, he thought. *I've actually done it. I've killed someone.*

Madge was in her element. A drunken gambler had won a game and given her ten pounds. After telling her she was his lucky mascot, he had then offered her another ten to 'do the business' for him. So in less than an hour she had earned herself twenty pounds and had actually enjoyed herself.

She loved the heady atmosphere of the gambling room, and also the unaccustomed comfort of the 'business' room. To ply her trade with a mattress under her back seemed the height of sophistication so far as she was concerned.

After deciding she would live with Jessie's taunts in order to keep this job, she sipped a large rum and Coke, staring around the gambling room.

It was relatively small and windowless. Police raids made that inevitable. You got into the club through the one narrow door and if ever there were a fire, the chances were you'd burn to death in the stampede to get back out the same way. Anyway, gamblers didn't need natural light. Electric was fine, they needed no reminder of the time of day. People had been known to come in on a Thursday and leave on a Saturday morning, wondering where Friday had gone. From Thursday to Sunday the club was open literally all day and all night.

It was a good earner, and Jessie made sure that it reached its full potential. Most of the police force was paid off, except for the die-hards, the punters were happy and the drink was never watered – three good reasons to use the place.

The girls were all of a certain age, guaranteeing no trouble with the men. Young girls wrought havoc in gambling clubs, their youth distracting the men from the serious business of gambling. Jessie knew that the punters who frequented her club would sleep with the Pope if the lighting was right. It was gambling that brought on their sexual rush, not a pretty face or a shapely leg. Sex was just another high, another bit of fun.

As Madge listened to the noise and breathed in the foetid air of the place, she felt a moment's exhilaration. After a bad start the night was turning out better than she'd expected. One of the other girls smiled at her and she nodded in a friendly fashion. At the end of the day, whatever Jessie had said, whores all looked out for one another.

They had to.

As a man sidled up to her and offered to buy her a drink, she grinned at him coquettishly and stifled a yawn. The drink, the sex, the excitement and the heat had all made her tired. Grinning, she accepted the drink, and told herself to liven up. This could be a lucrative little earner and she needed to keep her wits about her.

Cathy was sitting on the settee, listening to the radio, when she heard a low call through the letter box.

'Is that you, Eamonn?' As she walked into the hallway she heard his voice again.

'Open the door, you silly cow! Don't let anyone know I'm here, Cathy. Keep your voice down.'

Unchaining the door, she let him in. One look at his white face told her he was in trouble. Big trouble.

'What's happened?' Her voice, too, was low.

Eamonn looked down at Cathy then, realising just how

small she was. Without her usual heels on she stood barely five foot two. Her tiny elfin face was all eyes, big blue eyes, and rosebud mouth. Seeing the fear there, he smiled, knowing the reaction his words would get from her.

'I done it, Cath. I finally done it. I'm there, girl, right up there!' He pointed to the ceiling and laughed softly.

She stared at him blankly. 'What have you done, Eamonn?'

Pushing his face down level with hers, he whispered hoarsely: 'I fucking shot James Carter! Shot the bastard dead.' He watched as her eyes widened into twin pools of blue.

'You're joking! Dear Christ, tell me you're joking!'

Walking into the front room, he flopped down on the settee, stretching out his legs, all bravado.

'It's no joke, Cathy love. He wanted it and he fucking got it, mate, right in the boatrace.' Putting out his fingers like a gun, he pointed them at her and went: 'Bang, bang. That easy, girl. Like combing me hair, it was that easy.'

Cathy just looked at him, sure she must be dreaming. 'You're bloody mad. Are you having me on? Only if you are, I don't think it's very funny, Eamonn. It's sick. Shooting someone . . . Whatever next!' She attempted to laugh, all the time knowing he was telling her the truth, yet unable to believe he would really do it.

Eamonn laughed then, really laughed. 'I'm there now, Cath – can't you see that? I'm blooded, girl. I'm on the borrow, I'm the main man. Me life's settled.' Sitting up quickly, he looked into her eyes and said: 'I'm on me way, Cath.'

Cathy shook her head so hard her hair whipped around her face. 'You're nowhere, you silly bastard, except on your way to getting a fucking rope around your neck. James

Carter was fifteen years old! Fifteen, for crying out loud. We're still kids, Eamonn – *kids*. No matter how much we think we know, we're ignorant of real life. You're telling me you stole his life away, and then laughing like it's a joke or something?' Her voice broke as she fought back the tears.

'James Carter was even worse off than us – the eldest of nine kids, his mother depended on him for money. You think you know it all and you know fucking nothing! It's always *you*, Eamonn, what *you* want. Only what you want. And this is the upshot. You've shot poor James Carter, and he's dead, and now you want me to alibi you. That's why you're here, ain't it?'

Eamonn stared at the little girl before him. In all his wildest fantasies he'd never expected this. Oh, he'd expected she might be a bit upset, but surely she should understand why he'd done what he had?

Desperation in his voice, he said harshly, 'I don't know nothing, eh? I know enough. I know that what I want won't come from unloading ships in the docks. I want what the real world's got. The real people. I want cars and clothes and a nice drum. I want to walk down the street and be recognised as a man to respect, not the son of a drunken Irish docker. I want to be able to hold me bleeding head up. I want people to look up to me, Cathy. I want what every other fucker's given at birth – I want to *be* someone. Someone important.

'Fuck James Carter! Another time and it could have been me on the receiving end of that bullet, not him. He wanted what I wanted, love, and like me he'd have done anything to get it.'

Cathy stared down into the face she adored. Saw the lighter flecks in his eyes and the beginnings of the dark shadow around his cheeks. Saw the strength of his brow and chin, and the harsh set of them. She shook her head sadly, swallowing back the words she wanted to say to him. To yell at him.

Eamonn slouched back on the settee, picking nervously at a small slit in the arm, pulling out wads of horsehair, the tremor in his hand noticeable to both of them now.

'What do you want, Cathy? Do you want to end up like your mum, lying down with every Tom, Dick and Harry for a couple of quid? Because that will be your life if you're not careful. How many women round here moonlight, eh? So-called respectable women with kids and husbands. They look down on Madge but they're no fucking better. None of them. What you see here is what we will end up with unless we do something about it. People like us are the shit on the shoes of everyone else. We're the grafters, the lifters, the scrubbers. We're supposed to be grateful for having a roof over our heads, having enough to eat. I've heard it all me life, first at school and then from the Labour Exchange. Well, I want to have too much of everything, not just enough. I want things, Cathy.

'When me mum died, I was left with him, the fucking old ponce! I've been dragged all over the bleeding show. Have to live with the knowledge of him and his escapades. Have to watch me step in case his new wife slings me out the door. Have to listen to them, night after night, at it in their bed. Then I have to listen to his drunken ramblings.'

He pushed his hands through his hair and sighed, before continuing.

'The only way out is up, Cath. And going up in the world for the likes of us means either villainy or the forces – and I'm fucked if I'll join the army! If Madge has her way, you'll be flogging your fanny before the year's out. You know it, and I know it. I'm offering you a way out with me. Me and you, girl, together. I came here tonight because you're the closest person to me. You're the only person I really care about. Not just to alibi me. I could get a dozen people to do that.'

He was near to tears, and sitting beside him Cathy put her arm around his shoulders. Burying his face in her neck he let her hold him until the shameful sobs had ceased. The sixteen-year-old hard man was now a frightened boy. Wiping his nose with the back of his hand, he whispered, 'It could just as easily have been me shot tonight, Cathy, and you know that.'

Holding him close to her, she closed her eyes tightly. Eamonn had done what he felt he had to do, and nothing would convince him otherwise.

When his hands went to her breasts, she didn't attempt to stop him.

Eamonn needed her, and no matter what he had done, what she really thought, loyalty to him overrode everything else.

He was the most stable element in her life. She worshipped him. Without him she had nothing.

Kissing the top of his head, she felt his probing fingers, all thoughts of James Carter, guns and policemen forced from her mind.

Eamonn needed her.

That was enough to be going on with.

Chapter Five

Eamonn looked at his father and smirked.

'You did it, didn't you?' The older man's voice was low, tense.

Eamonn nodded slowly. Maddeningly.

'So what if I did?' His voice was a curious mixture of childish bravado and manly insolence.

Eamonn Docherty looked down at his son and felt the pull of him. In all his life he had loved only one thing: his child, his boy. As bad as he had ever been, whoring and fighting were his worst sins. The child of his body, however, was a different kettle of fish.

'Don't you realise what you've done, son?'

The boy shrugged nonchalantly.

The large hand that swung out and knocked him from his seat came as a total surprise. As the beating began the boy curled himself into a tight ball, taking the blows, moving around on the floor to minimise the damage.

Finally spent, Eamonn Docherty leant against the wall of the dining room and wiped one hand across his sweating face. 'They'll hang you out to dry, boy. What are you?

Stupid? Are you that fecking eggity you think you can get away with murder?'

The boy slowly pulled himself to his feet, using the mahogany table for support, his fingerprints standing out like beacons on the highly polished surface.

They looked at one another then, both men, each wary of the other.

'That's the last time you raise your hand to me, Dad. Next time I'll fight you back.'

They stared each other out, both battling with the rage inside them. Eamonn was pleased to see his father drop his eyes first.

'You're a fecking fool, boy, if you think you can walk away from this one.'

Eamonn laughed then. 'But I have, Dad. It's been a week and not a sniff from the Old Bill. They don't care about the likes of Carter, no more than they do the likes of us. It made the *Evening Standard*, and not a fucking dicky bird since. Except for locally, that is. In fact, I've been offered a job.'

The derogatory snort from his father made Eamonn's whole body tense up.

'A job, is it? What kind of job would that be? Bashing old ladies over the head for their bit of pension? Armed robbery? Or how about a nice clean minding job, a sixteen-year-old hard man? Jasus save us, I've heard everything now.'

Eamonn watched as his father dropped into a chair, an old man suddenly, the usual surly cockiness gone from him. He looked defeated, and instead of being pleased at this change in his antagonist, it hurt the boy. His father, for all his faults, real or imagined, had always seemed the epitome of the hard man. Now he found this hard man had feet of clay, and that inability to understand his son's actions hurt deeply.

'I've been offered a job by Dixon. It's only picking up rents, but it's a start. I can go great guns from there, I know I can.'

Eamonn Docherty looked at his son, noted his size, his dark good looks, and patent lack of intelligence.

'Picking up rents, eh? Lucrative job that. If you don't get caught, of course, or fall foul of anyone.'

The big man leant forward in his chair then, a desperate note in his voice as he pleaded with his son. 'Is that what you really want? I wanted you to be someone, a normal person, son. I didn't want you to end up like me. I thought you despised what I was, what I became? I thought you wanted better?'

'I do, Dad. That's why I'm taking the job. I won't end my days like you, mate, poncing off some little widow, trying to con her last few quid out of her. Living for the pub opening and a decent bit of dinner on the table. You did what you set out to do, Dad. You made me want more, and this is the only way I'm going to get it.'

'Have you no remorse at all, son? For stealing that young lad's life away?'

Eamonn shrugged once more. 'Not really, no. Why should I? He wouldn't have if the boot had been on the other foot. I'm nearly seventeen, Dad, a man in my own right. What you think is nothing to me. The funny thing is, it never was. You're nothing to me, mate. Nothing to anyone except yourself. You have a high opinion of yourself, always did. But I could see you for what you were – a big Irish ponce. You lived off Madge. Her earnings kept you in the pub. She slept with men and you slept with her, knowing that. I think more of her than I do of you, Dad. Because Madge, for all her faults, never pretended to be something she wasn't. If you died in the morning, I wouldn't shed a tear. So now you know.'

The older man hung his head and stared at the lino below his feet. Tears stung his eyes and he blinked them away before looking once more into his son's face.

'I tried my best, Eamonn son. We can only do our best.'

'That's exactly the point I'm trying to make. One man's meat is another man's gravy, eh? I'll be moved out by the weekend.'

As the man watched his son leave the room he felt an overwhelming loneliness and defeat. He'd wanted life to be different for his son and now it looked as if it would be. For all the father had been a drunkard, a wastrel and a womaniser, he'd never actually resorted to criminal actions – well, no more than the odd bit of petty pilfering in the docks. Now, at sixteen, his son had launched into a criminal career by murdering a fellow teenager. And the killing wouldn't stop there, he knew. From now on, Eamonn Junior would live like a villain and die a villain's death. That was to be his destiny and nothing on God's earth could save him from it.

Madge was happy, which meant that her daughter should have been ecstatic. Instead Cathy was withdrawn and nervous. Watching the girl as she made them both tea and toast, Madge noticed the deep shadows under her eyes and the sunken cheeks.

'Are you sure everything's all right, love?'

Cathy smiled gently. 'For the millionth time, Mum, I'm all right. Stop questioning me. I'm just tired, that's all.'

'It's Eamonn, ain't it? This is something to do with him. He's never been off the doorstep all week. Anyone would think you two were joined at the hip.'

Cathy made an effort not to look in her mother's direction, knowing that the shrewd blue eyes would immediately read the thoughts inside her head. Say what you liked about Madge Connor: she ignored her daughter shamelessly at times, but when she wanted to know something, she had a way of finding it out.

'I don't know what you mean, Mum. I've always seen a lot of him.'

'Well, girl, you're seeing too much of him for my liking. I know the score there so don't try and give me any old fanny. If he topped Carter then he's for the chop himself. Don't get involved, love.'

Cathy's eyes flashed a steely blue as she turned on her mother. 'What do you know about anything? He was with me, and if the filth come knocking on this door, I'll tell them the same thing. Bloody hell, Mum, I expected it off everyone else but not you! He was the closest thing to a son you ever had. If it was his father in trouble you'd be moving heaven and earth to help him.'

Madge sipped her tea and smiled, further irritating her already strung-out daughter. 'His father, for all his bleeding faults, wouldn't be in this kind of trouble, as you so nicely put it. That boy's a natural villain. The sooner you accept that, the easier your life will be. Believe me, I know exactly what I'm talking about. He ain't just a ducker and diver no more, love, he's a face, and faces have a habit of getting kicked in round these parts. Just you bear that in mind. Everyone is for him at the moment but that could change overnight. You know what the East End's like. That Carter boy was an Irish, and the Irish stick together. They ain't like Londoners.'

Cathy cracked her knuckles, a sure sign of agitation. 'He's an Irish and all, Mum, remember? You should do, you was trumping his father for long enough.'

Madge grinned, her usual good humour coming to the fore. 'We are getting on our high horse today, aren't we, dearie? Who gives a fuck anyway? If the Filth come snooping I'll back the boy up and all, you know that. I just don't want you getting too involved, love. I know I ain't Mother of the Year, but I do care about you in me own way.'

Cathy picked up her cup of tea and took a swig. 'You're a funny woman, Mum. I should hate you really. I do sometimes, but it never lasts. You always end up making me laugh. At times I feel like I'm the mum and you're the kid.'

Madge stared into her daughter's lovely face and smiled, a real smile that softened her rough features and made her cheeks look round and rosy, her only Irish feature.

'You've not had the greatest childhood, I understand that, love. But I am as I am. As me old mum used to say: "I'll never change all the time I've got a hole in me arse." But I just want you to know that life is a complicated thing. It's not all cut and dried.'

Now Cathy did laugh, a loud raucous sound born of nerves and genuine amusement. 'You're right there, Mum. How could it be, living with you?'

They laughed together and peace was restored, but for the first time ever Madge was frightened for her daughter and the feeling was strange. She realised that never before in her life had she had to look after her own child. Cathy Connor, now coming up to fourteen years of age, had always looked after her.

It was a sobering thought.

Eamonn Junior was watching the man before him warily. The heavy smell of camphor was hanging in the air and he felt his insides heave at the unaccustomed taint permeating his nose and even his mouth. As the man hawked deep in his throat, he pulled his head from beneath the towel and spat into a small jug by his side.

'I feel like shit on a stick! That's what smoking does for

you, boy, and don't ever forget it. I've been bringing up fucking soot and all sorts the last few months.'

Eamonn nodded, holding on to his breakfast with all his might. The steaming bowl of water slopped everywhere as the man pushed it away from him impatiently.

'Word on the street is you topped James Carter. Is this true?'

Eamonn looked into the heavy face before him and weighed up exactly what he was going to say before nodding gently.

'Yes, Mr Dixon.'

The man laughed. Wiping his sweating face with a handkerchief of brilliant whiteness, he said, 'You little fucker! Bold as brass, ain't you? Well, the offer's still on for the job if you want it. I was amazed to hear you're not seventeen yet, but I'll swallow that because you've got size on your side, see. I like to keep a lookout for new faces, new people. It keeps everything sweet. The firm gets stronger and I get more manpower. One thing though . . .'

He leant ominously close over the table.

'Don't get ambitious for anything that's mine, right? If I tell you to run, you run. If I tell you to drop your kecks and shit on a table, you do it, right? What I say goes. If you have trouble with discipline then let me know now. I do not suffer fools gladly.'

Eamonn nodded, pleased to be inside the world of real villainy, over the moon at the prospect of being a face, one of Dixon's gang. A known man.

'One last thing, boy. The Filth will be on to you in the next few days. You bluff it out. The famous wall of silence is on your side now because you are under my protection. Don't fuck me up. Be polite to the Old Bill, be amenable. Tell all the old pony and trap you like. But whatever they say, deny it.'

Dixon lit a cigarette and coughed until his heavy-jowled face was like a red ball.

'I'm starting you off on debts, right. Do you understand the logic behind buying debts?'

Eamonn shook his head. 'No, Mr Dixon.'

The man smiled, cigarette smoke curling around his yellow teeth and up towards his badly fitting toupee. 'Mr Dixon, eh? I like respect. Respect is earned, boy, always remember that. You earn it with this.'

He tensed one huge arm and shook his fist. 'No fucker in their right mind disrespects people stronger than them, physically or mentally. Be wary of some of the little bastards because sometimes they have the edge. The nutter element.' He tapped his head to illustrate his point before carrying on in his amiable, sing-song voice, as if he was discussing the weather or a mundane daily happening.

'Anyway, as I was saying, the debts. Say you owed someone five grand, and you didn't pay them, and no matter how much they asked for it back you told them to fuck off out of it. They get right fed up, and they come to see me. Now I buy the debt off them for, say, two grand. They're happy because two grand in the bin is better than nothing, see. I have now laid out two grand on your behalf. Already, you've caused me hag. I have it in for you, see.

'I then come after you for seven grand – the five you owed muggins and the two I've been so kind as to lay out on your behalf. So I send someone round to have a word. If I get the seven grand in fourteen days, you're laughing. If I don't it goes up a hundred a week for interest, see. So it's to your advantage to pay me, because after a couple of weeks – and this is where you come in, son – I begin to get really upset, see. And I send a friend round to negotiate like. You may be required to break an arm or a leg. In extreme cases I might want to have the fucker shot. I say extreme but it's getting quite common, actually. I don't like doing it, but I have to set an example, don't I? After all, they have cost me money and that upsets me dearly.

'Money is God. Remember that, son. It's also the root of all evil, thank fuck, otherwise we'd be paupers!' He laughed at his joke, causing another spasm of coughing. 'Now, do you think you've grasped the fundamentals?'

Eamonn nodded. 'Yes, Mr Dixon.'

The man smiled. 'Well, we all know you can shoot a gun anyway, so at least I ain't got that added worry. I'm teaming you up with Marcus Devlin. He's an Irish nutter who'll show you the ropes. You start work in fourteen days. Give the Old Bill a chance to get sorted out. I can't say no fairer than that, can I?'

Eamonn nodded once more, bowled over by the complete assurance and friendliness of Danny Dixon, procurer, brothel-keeper and debt collector, to name but a few of his lucrative businesses.

Taking out his wallet, Dixon removed three twenty-pound notes and placed them before the boy, saying shrewdly, 'This money means I own you, son. Before you pick it up, bear that in mind. I own ya, lock, stock and fucking barrel.'

Taking the money in trembling hands, Eamonn looked straight at the man before him. 'Thank you, Mr Dixon.'

Dixon grinned. 'Respect and manners, a good combination.' He pointed at the money. 'That's called a retainer. It means you work for me and no one else, right? Go out, get laid, do what you like. But make sure you're on call when I need you.'

'How will I know you need me, Mr Dixon?'

The man laughed again. 'You'll know. Now fuck off out of it and wait for me call. With sixty sobs of my poke, you'll hear from me soon enough.'

Eamonn stood up and held out his hand. 'It's been nice doing business with you, sir.'

Danny Dixon shook his head. 'We ain't done no business yet, boy. All that's happened is I've given you some of my hard-earned cash.' He poked a finger at Eamonn's chest. 'You're the one who'll be doing the business, son. My business. Now on the trot and I'll be in touch.'

Eamonn walked from the room dazed with pride. He was finally someone, he was finally a face.

Grinning like a Cheshire cat he walked out of the small house in Bethnal Green and held on to the feeling inside him. Thanks to James Carter he was now in the big league and he intended to stay there for as long as possible. Carter had been his stepping stone to the good life. He now felt no remorse whatsoever over the murder. As far as Eamonn was concerned it couldn't have happened at a better time.

Madge was at work and Cathy having a well-earned rest when the door was hammered on violently. The noise was shocking in the quiet flat and Cathy jumped from her seat in terror.

'Open the door, Cathy! Let me in, love!'

She sighed with relief on hearing Eamonn's voice. Running to the door, she opened it, smiling widely. 'I thought you was the Old Bill, banging the bleeding door down like that!'

Picking her up in his arms, he kicked the front door shut and crushed her to him, drinking in her familiar odour of rosewater and Max Factor. He carried her through to the front room and placed her on the couch, simultaneously forcing her mouth open and exploring it with his tongue. Cathy could taste whisky and smell beer as she responded to his kisses. Pulling her face away, she protested, 'You're half cut, Eamonn!'

Pushing her legs open with his knee, he positioned himself between them before crushing her to him once more and kissing her urgently. Sucking on her lips and face, covering her with his mouth and his hands.

'Oh, Cathy love . . . Cathy.' His words were low, brought from the depths of him. They were a plea and a demand all at once.

Dragging up her lacy top, he pawed at her breasts, fondling them roughly, while Cathy tried to squirm away from him.

'Eamonn, for God's sake! You're hurting me.'

Embarrassed to open to him under the harsh lights, she tried once more to push him away.

'Oh no you don't, Cathy, not tonight.' His voice was heavy with drink and sexual energy. 'You do not push me away tonight.' Putting a hand between her legs, he ripped her knickers away and slipped a finger inside her, the dryness and tensing of her muscles affecting him not at all.

'Relax, Cathy, enjoy it. Just relax, girl.'

Stepping back, he knelt between her legs and forced his head down between them, his tongue probing her clitoris, wetting it. As Cathy tried to pull him away by grabbing at his hair, he pinned her arms to her sides, holding her down with a strength born of determination. As he sucked at her she felt the tears come. Bucking her hips, she tried to force him away from her once more.

'Stop it, Eamonn, you're frightening me. You're hurting me.'

Raising his head, he smiled at her. 'You love it as much as I do. I love you, Cathy, you know I do. Now relax and let's get on with it.'

Opening his trousers, he pulled them down to his knees. Cathy stared at him as if she had never seen him before. This was a new Eamonn. A frightening Eamonn.

'Please . . .'

The plea was cut off as roughly he pushed himself inside her. Riding her hard now, he was oblivious to her fighting beneath him; the pain inside her unbelievable. His thrusting increased and as he began to groan aloud, Cathy scratched at his face, drawing her nails down his cheek with all her strength.

Holding her down once more, he stared into her white face as he pushed himself into her as hard as he could, focusing on her eyes as she beseeched him to stop what he was doing. To please let her go. As he reached orgasm, she felt his body begin to stiffen and the pain in her wrists was made unbearable as he gripped her tighter and tighter. He was moving inside her more slowly now. She felt the hot wetness as it dribbled down between her legs, and when he collapsed on top of her, his whole body limp, she let out one sob before pushing him from her.

Nearly hysterical with pain and fear, she cried. The burning between her legs was almost unbearable, and her wrists were numb.

Kneeling up, Eamonn looked at her for a few seconds as if unable to believe what he'd done. Cathy was curled up on the sofa. He saw how small she was, how fragile. The blood smeared on her white thighs stood out in stark contrast. Putting his hand on her shoulder, he said: 'Cathy . . . I'm sorry. I am so sorry.'

Looking over her shoulder at him, she hissed, 'Get out, Eamonn. Get away from me.'

He put up a hand to stroke her face and she flinched away from him, covering her head with her arms. The enormity of what he'd done hit him then. The sheer terror in every line of her body sobered him up instantly. Picking her up like a baby, he tried to caress her, tried to make it better, and she fought him then. All nails and teeth, kicking out with her feet and punching him with her fists.

'You bastard! You dirty, stinking bastard! Get away from me.' She fought her way free and ran towards her bedroom. When he grabbed at her arm, she screamed.

The banging on the wall made them both stand stock still.

'Keep the bleeding noise down, you two. I'm trying to fucking sleep!'

Pulling her into his arms, Eamonn held her tightly to him, all the while murmuring endearments into her hair, stroking her face, trying to calm her down. Trying to make sense of what had happened to her and to himself.

As she cried he realised he had taken from her something that was hers alone. He knew that instantly, even in his drink-fuddled mind. And that she would never really forgive him for it.

Finally he picked her up and took her into her bedroom where he placed her gently on her bed.

'Cathy, please stop crying, darlin'. I'm sorry, love, all right? I'm really sorry. I don't know what happened, I've had such a great day . . .' He was gabbling and he knew it. 'I got the job today, Cathy, look.'

Pulling the remainder of the money Dixon had given him from his pockets, he laid it on the bed. 'You have it. Look, there's over fifty quid there. You have it, Cathy, get yourself something nice . . .'

Body heaving with sobs, she pushed the money from the bed. 'Get out, Eamonn. Just get out, please. Leave me alone.'

Her eyes were red and swollen now, her face blotchy, even her hair looked lifeless. Her lips, swollen and bruised from his kisses, looked deformed. She looked ugly for once, and he knew that he was responsible. He had made his little Cathy ugly inside and outside.

'I just want to be alone. Please leave me alone.'

He belted his trousers and began picking up the money from the floor. Wiping a hand across his face, he saw blood on the back of it and felt a moment's irritation. When he looked in the mirror he saw the four long red welts on his skin and cursed under his breath.

'For fuck's sake, Cathy, it ain't like we don't know one another, is it? I said I was sorry, girl. What more do you want?' He knew it was just bravado, knew he was trying to justify his actions to himself as much as to her, and still he heard his voice carrying on. 'It'll be better next time, love, you'll know what to expect. It's always hard on the bird the first time, but you'll get used to it . . .'

His voice trailed off. 'Please, Cathy. Please . . .'

He could no longer pretend. He had done something unforgivable, had hurt Cathy. But she must forgive him, she *had* to, or all his triumph counted for nothing. Without her, he was a beaten and neglected child all over again.

'I don't know what to do, Cathy. Please, darlin', tell me what to do?' Kneeling by the side of the bed, he began to cry. He pressed his face into the covers as tears bubbled out of his eyes and into the musty bedding.

Finally, after what seemed an age, she put one hand on his head. Looking up into her white face he was amazed to hear her say, 'Don't cry, Eamonn. Just go home.'

She had touched him. He was halfway to getting her back, they both knew that. As his arm went around her waist and he lay beside her, holding her to him tightly, he cried with her. When both her arms eventually went around him and she held on to him as tightly he knew a moment's intense relief.

They lay entwined, tears eventually ceasing, and only the beating of their hearts and the soft sounds of their breathing broke the silence of the room. As the shadows deepened on the walls, still they lay together.

They had crossed a bridge that night, and a further bond had been formed between them. Two broken children, they were both well aware that all they had ever really had was each other.

Cathy would forgive him anything, Eamonn knew that now. As he held her to him, he felt the excitement of a man who owned another person wholly.

Like Dixon owned him, he owned Cathy. Lock, stock and barrel.

Chapter Six

'Are you sure you're all right, love?'

Madge's voice was low and husky-sounding from too many cigarettes and too much booze when she came into her daughter's room later that night.

Cathy nodded, closing her eyes against the harsh light and the sound of the radio playing loudly in the front room. She could hear men's voices too, and sighed. 'Mum, go back to your punter. I'm fine. Really.'

Madge stared down into her daughter's white pinched face and said gently. 'Is it your time of the month, love?'

Cathy shook her head. 'I've got a bellyache, Mum, that's all. I'm fine.'

Madge stared down at her for a few seconds more then, screwing up her eyes, said, 'You ain't been up to nothing with that Eamonn, have you?'

Sitting up in bed, Cathy cried out: 'No, I bleeding well ain't! And if I had been, who are you to criticise anyway? I mean, be fair, Mum. It's a wonder I ain't out on the bash with you. That's what a lot of people think I do anyway.'

Her temper faded as quickly as it had erupted, and lying down again, she said wearily, 'Please leave me alone, Mum.

I feel so bloody rough. I'm probably coming down with something.'

Madge stood up and said snidely, 'As long as it ain't a bellyful of arms and legs.'

'Oh, piss off, Mother. You get on my wick at times.'

Cathy's voice was so virulent, Madge was shocked for a few moments.

'Don't you talk to me like that, lady! Whatever you think of me, I'm still your mother . . .'

Cathy interrupted her by saying nastily, 'Pity you don't think of that when you go out on the gatter and bringing home half the docks.'

The sharp slap on Cathy's cheek shocked both mother and daughter. When the girl started to cry it was as if she would never stop. Tears drenched her face and rolled on the sheet unchecked. Looking down at her daughter once more, Madge found herself in the grip of unaccustomed emotions. Unable to understand Cathy as a child, the emerging woman was becoming like a sister to her, a friend, and it grieved her that they were at loggerheads.

'I'm sorry, baby. I could cut me bleeding hand off.'

She pulled her daughter roughly into her arms. The two of them held each other and cried. Madge, motherly for once, caressed her child's narrow back and whispered endearments into her hair. 'I'm sorry, Cathy. I'm so sorry, love.'

Enjoying the feel of her mother's arms around her, she tightened her grip on Madge's waist. 'I love you too, Mum. I'm sorry I was such a crosspatch.'

Madge smiled through her tears. 'Crosspatch' was Cathy's word from when she was a small child, a tiny little bundle, all stick-thin legs and huge blue eyes.

'You're not a crosspatch, darlin'. You were right in what you said. I'm an old trout. It's the way God made me, but I love you, Cathy. In me own way, I love you very much.'

At that point the door was pushed open and Ron came into the room. 'What's going on here then, eh? A fucking mother's meeting? Get your fat arse back into the front room, girl. I'm getting lonely all on me Jack Jones.'

Madge tutted loudly. 'Piss off, Ron. Can't you see the girl's upset?'

'What's the matter with her then?' Pushing his face towards Cathy's, he bellowed, 'What's up with you, you silly little mare?'

She closed her eyes and sighed. 'Get him out of here, Mum.'

Ron, drunk and on his dignity, bellowed, ' "Get him out of here"? Are you talking about me, young lady? Only if you are, I'll have you know that I put the fucking roof over your head these days, and it would do you no harm to remember that.'

Stepping towards the bed, he poked Cathy in the chest as he ranted: 'I took your mother off the streets and turned her into a real professional. No one talks to me like that, especially not a jumped-up little girl who should keep her big trap shut and her snotty nose to herself!'

Standing up, Madge bolstered her chest with one meaty forearm and said, 'Are you quite finished?' Her voice was quiet, dignified and calm. A sure sign to Cathy that her mother was ready to explode at any moment.

Ron, on the other hand, unaware of Madge's little ways, carried on regardless. 'No, I ain't fucking finished. When I am you'll be the first to know, all right? Now get your arse in that front room and pour me a drink.'

Cathy watched wide-eyed as her mother figured out whether she was going to kill him or kiss him.

To Cathy's horror, kissing won.

Taking Ron's arm, she pulled him from the room, cajoling him with a merry voice as she cried: 'Come on then, let's get a nice drink down our gregorys, and then we can all have a laugh, eh?'

Ron, stretching himself to his full height, smiled benignly at her and allowed himself to be removed from Cathy's room. Over her shoulder Madge winked at her daughter before rolling heavily painted eyes at the ceiling.

Lying down again, Cathy wrapped her arms around herself and sighed. If this was how her life was always going to be, maybe it wasn't worth the effort.

Ron, full of drink and bravado, began baiting Madge in the lounge next door.

'You treat her like a fucking china doll. She should be out grafting, bringing in a few bob. With her hair and eyes, she'd earn a fortune. A bleeding fortune.' His voice was low now as he contemplated the vast sums of money to be earned off that little girl with her huge blue eyes and thick blond hair. He wouldn't be averse to breaking her in himself; unless that toerag Docherty had got there first, of course. The thought annoyed him.

Pouring Ron a large Scotch, Madge closed her eyes tightly. Ron's eyes had strayed a few times towards her daughter's burgeoning charms and she had ignored it. Now, though, he was putting it into words, saying it out loud, and Madge was not happy about it.

'Don't talk like that, Ron.' The steely tone was back in Madge's voice. There was a coldness, a hardness, she could project in her voice, and anyone who knew her well always dropped the subject that had upset her. Madge with a drink taken could be a lunatic. Like most whores, she harboured grudges and gave vent to them every now and again. When she did, her outbursts were of Olympian standards.

'Leave it out, Ron,' she warned him now. 'The girl was upset. At the end of the day, she's still my kid.'

He snorted derisively through his long beaked nose. 'Pity you don't think of that when she's walking around like a replica whore. All that make-up on, those little tits pressing against her clothes . . . She's her mother's fucking daughter all right.'

Madge looked at the man beside her, seeing the thinning hair, the moist mouth and slack lips, those grimy fingernails. Without a second's thought she threw her drink in his face.

'How dare you? How dare you talk about my child like that? I might not be an ideal mother, I know that, but she's still my baby. My flesh and blood. No one speaks about my kid like that. No one, do you hear me?'

She pressed her face to his and screamed into it: 'You jumped-up pox doctor's clerk! Look at you – take a fucking good butcher's hook, mate. You're a piece of shit. You and all your cronies, you're scared of your own shadow. You're a coward, mate, a twenty-two-carat coward. Now you want my girl, do you? You want my baby. Putting me on the game ain't enough. You want the two of us whoring for you, do you? Well, let me tell you, even if I did want her on the bash, I wouldn't let you touch her with a barge pole. My girl is worth fifty . . . no, a hundred of you and all your ilk, mate. She'll *be* somebody.'

Laughing scornfully, she said to him then: 'Who the fucking hell do you think *you* are, with your tin pot club and your one-inch cock? What use are you to any woman, eh? Even an old whore like me. At least Eamonn could get me going, mate, get me all loved up. You couldn't turn on a fucking light switch!'

Somewhere in Madge's drink-fuddled brain she was aware that she was going too far. But the drink seemed to have triggered something inside her. All her anger and frustration came bubbling to the surface and Ron was the recipient of her hatred of herself, her life, and all the ugliness she'd had to endure.

'A step up, your club?' Her voice was a screech by now. 'That's a fucking laugh! I've had better punters down the docks, mate. And as for you – I've been fucked by four-foot sailors with more going for them than what you've got. That dinky little cock, and all your moaning and groaning and sweating . . . It makes me sick to my stomach to think of you. So now you fucking know.'

Ron was staring at her as if he'd never seen her before. He had never been spoken to like that by a whore. Especially not one of his own whores. He was enraged and his back slap to Madge's face shocked them both. Then the real fight began.

With her extra bulk, Madge was a formidable opponent. Grabbing at Ron's hair, she dragged him unceremoniously off the settee, her heavy breasts straining with the exertion. She had fought men all her life, it was a part of her job, survival to her. This time, though, it was personal. It was an act of vengeance. Madge had been abused all her life; now this man wanted to abuse her child. She felt the white heat of anger and jealousy as it rose inside her. Felt the strength of her hatred of him, and of all men, overwhelm her. She dug her nails into his neck and spat into his eye.

Looking blearily up into her face, Ron saw that the woman was completely out of control. The watery eyes, caked with mascara and blue eyeshadow, were positively manic. Madge had lost it. After years of being abused she was fighting back.

Ron was every man who had roughed her up, every decent woman who had made a joke at her expense, every punter, good, bad or indifferent, who had contemptuously dropped money into her hand.

Using the last of his strength, the man pushed her away

with all his might, sending her careering across the room. She landed with a heavy thump against the far wall. As Ron got to his feet, she watched him warily, her heaving bulk trembling now from head to foot.

'I'll break your fucking neck, woman.' As he advanced on her, both were unaware of Cathy standing in the door-way watching everything. She flew across the room and pulled frantically at Ron's hair.

'Leave me mum alone! Let her be. Go home, Ron, for Christ's sake!'

He shrugged her off without a thought.

'Go home, man. My mum's drunk and so are you. Come back in the morning.' Cathy's voice was high-pitched, terrified.

The long-suffering Sullivans next door were once more banging on the walls for quiet. Used to noise and shouting, they didn't take the situation seriously enough actually to do anything. Like battered wives, whores were to be ignored or at best tolerated. Such people were always left to their own devices. It was the way of the world.

Ron began to beat Madge in a calm methodical way. Shock had given way to rage by then. As he began systematically to punish her, Madge crumpled to the floor. Curling up, she covered her head with her arms and let herself relax as all people used to violence learn to do. Blows are easily absorbed by a slack body; only the tensing of the muscles causes real pain. Madge was used to pain, she lived with it every day, took her life in her hands at work. A beating wasn't such a big deal to her.

Not so for Cathy, though. Picking up the breadknife from the table, she stood beside Ron, beseeching him to stop hurting her mother. She could see Madge's body taking the blows and as Ron's anger was almost spent, he drew back his leg for a final kick.

It was when he did this that Cathy plunged the knife into his neck. It was a reflex action. She just wanted him to stop hurting her mother.

The girl watched in horror as his skin opened, inch by inch. It was like a slow-motion picture. She looked dumbly at the knife in her hand, realising for the first time what she had done. Ron, bewildered now, looked at the girl in front of him and registered her huge terrified eyes and trembling hand as he fell heavily to his knees, his hand to his neck.

After what seemed the longest time blood began to pulse from the jagged wound. His carotid artery sent dark red jets two feet into the air. His hands were covered within seconds. With every beat of his rapidly failing heart more blood was pumped out of his body. It was only when Cathy was sprayed with its warm rankness that she began to scream.

The sound seemed to be coming from someone else and the volume was overwhelming in the small room.

Madge watched her lover die and finally, after what seemed an age, she started screaming too.

DI Richard Gates pushed roughly through the small crowd in the hallway and bellowed: 'All right, all right, had your look? Now move outside, and please be quiet. We'll take statements later from all of you.'

He was hustling them out of the doorway as DC Fuller walked into the Connors' flat. Two bobbies were stationed outside the door to keep onlookers at bay as Gates, smoothing down his thinning hair, walked into the small lounge.

The carnage that met his eyes was unbelievable.

'Fucking hell! What happened here?' The words were out of his mouth as soon as they entered his mind.

The blood-splattered walls ran crimson, and the slender

girl before him seemed to be soaked through with blood. The deep red stain on her white nightdress looked obscene somehow. She held a knife. Taking a handkerchief from his pocket, he walked towards her and took it from her gently.

A pair of terrified blue eyes looked into his beseechingly. Against his better judgement, the policeman wanted to take the suspect into his arms and comfort her. Instead, placing the knife on the table, he looked around him once more.

'All right, Madge. What's happened here then?'

'Please, Mum.' The girl's voice was thread-like, the note of pleading in it audible to everyone. Gates sighed heavily. He had known Madge for years, from his beat days. Now, at twenty-nine, he was the youngest DI in the East End, and had cut his teeth running in the likes of Madge and her cronies. They had a sort of hostile friendship, one that was mutually beneficial at times. Whores were natural born grasses, and always ready to cover their own arse. Gates smiled grimly at her.

'What's he then?' He poked Ron's corpse with his foot. 'Not a punter, surely? Pimp? I know Ronnie was a worker.'

DC Fuller said snidely, 'He won't be working any more, will he?'

The smirk on his face set the tone for the night. It was an old whore's problem. The dead man was a piece of scum. They would wrap it up quickly and go home. It was already cut and dried. No one respectable, so no one to worry about, and apart from all that blood, no different from most other East End murders. Knives were the order of the day, unless you had poke and could afford a gun.

Cathy stood as still as a statue, the shaking of her legs visible to everyone in the room.

'Why don't you sit down, love?'

Gates's voice was unexpectedly gentle. Taking her arm,

he led her to the sofa and lowered her on to it. He went into a bedroom and brought back a heavy coat from the bed, draping it around her.

'She's in shock, and I ain't fucking surprised. Poor little mare.'

Cathy was sobbing now. The unexpected display of kindness had opened up the floodgates of emotion once more.

'She stabbed him.' Madge pointed at her daughter with a trembling hand.

Gates looked at her in disgust.

'It's true, Mr Gates. We was fighting and she came out and somehow he ended up dead. She's always had a temper, little mare! You couldn't control her half the time . . . She picked up the knife and the next thing I knew he was stabbed. I don't think she did it deliberately, she was trying to help me, like.'

'Sling them in the motor, Bernie. Forensics are here. We'll sort this out down the station.' As Madge walked from the room, Gates whispered to her: 'You're a real bitch, Madge, do you know that? Your sort never change. You bring scum into your home with a teenage girl there . . .' His voice trailed off in contempt.

Madge dropped her head in shame.

'Get in the car, whore, and think on what you just said.' His voice was low, tired-sounding, disgusted.

He picked Cathy up effortlessly and carried her down the stairs, placing her in the front seat of the car as the neighbours stared at them with ghoulish interest. The blood soaking Cathy was very noticeable and Mrs Sullivan, a kind woman at heart, pushed her eldest son in the chest and said quietly: 'Away round to the Irishman's house. Tell him what's happened and say Cathy needs him.'

Then, gathering her own brood around her, she herded

them once more up the stairs and out of the coldness of the night.

Inside the police station, Cathy was given hot sweet tea and wrapped in a blanket. Her hair was sticky with blood and fingers stained brown with it. Gates came into the cell they had placed her in carrying a bowl of warm water and washed her gently.

She stared at the man all the while, saying nothing. To her he looked frightening, with his large round face and piercing blue eyes. Usually he had a friendly expression that onlookers found engaging; only now, with his anger carefully suppressed, did he look formidable and frightening. Cathy mistakenly thought the anger was directed at her, his gentle ministrations notwithstanding.

A large man, with thinning blond hair and huge biceps, he was an unknown quantity to her. His large belly jutted before him and Cathy could feel the warmth of it through the blanket. When his heavy hand came out to wipe her face, she flinched involuntarily.

Gates stared down at the frail teenager and sighed heavily. This girl had struck a chord in him somewhere. He knew Madge, knew the problems of whores and their children, and though he would never have admitted it out loud in a million years, sympathised with Cathy Connor. Madge was going to leave her high and dry, and he knew what lay in store for the young girl then. At nearly fourteen she would be detained indefinitely at Her Majesty's Pleasure, a thought that made him rage inside himself.

People like Madge had nothing in their minds but themselves. Unlike most whores, who sold themselves for their children, Madge was the one in a million who actually liked what she did; revelled in it even. Now she would let her child take the consequences of her own lifestyle without a second's thought.

'Cathy?' Gates's voice was quiet, low, his most distinctive feature. 'Come on, love. Tell me what happened and we'll see if we can sort it all out, eh?' Putting one heavy arm around her thin shoulders, he pulled her roughly against him, her head cradled on his barrel chest.

'Cry – that's right,' he said, seeing the big fat tears rolling down her face. 'Let it all out, and then we'll have a chat and see what can be made out of this mess.'

He held Cathy until she fell asleep, and then carefully laid her on the bed, putting a pillow under her head and covering her with a blanket. Fuller, watching through the spyhole, was struck dumb with amazement.

Madge looked demented: her hair was wild, her make-up streaked all over her fat face. Her cheeks were swollen and blotched red from crying – over her own situation though, not Ron's death. Sitting on the narrow cot in her cell, she stared at the pale yellow walls covered in graffiti and felt the tears flow once more.

What was she going to do?

The question had been hammering in her brain for the last few hours. Other than being given a cup of tea and a few cigarettes, she had had no contact with anyone at all. Restlessly, she sat herself up and tried to tidy her hair. All the time she was scheming. Inside herself she knew she should be protecting her daughter, but the fact was she had looked out for number one all her life and couldn't stop now.

Madge could not do time. Adult time. The few occasions she had been banged up in Holloway as a teenage delinquent had been an education, and Madge, knowing what lay in store, couldn't bear to face more time inside.

A long time inside at that.

Life.

She convinced herself once more that Cathy was young, would be out in no time and would cope quite adequately. Whereas she herself, the wrong side of forty and used to being outside, couldn't.

Anyway, Cathy had wielded the knife.

Cathy had stabbed Ron.

Cathy was quite old enough to take the consequences of her own actions.

But a glimmer of shame deep within her could not be ignored. Getting up, she paced the cell. Her heart was beating a tattoo inside her chest and her breath was coming in heavy gasps. Fear had taken hold of her and she knew it. She could taste it inside her mouth and it was bitter.

Gates watched his superior officer, DCI Bannister, with a resigned expression on his face. Bannister was of the old school. Find a suspect and nail them, was his philosophy.

The airless room was making both men testy, and Bannister, watching his DI in turn, smothered a small impulse of dislike.

Since Gates had come into his life he had for the first time found himself at a loss. This man looked more like a criminal than a policeman with his hair cropped close to his large balding head, his bull neck and hard blue eyes. Gates also had a strange philosophy of life, made apparent by his obvious kinship with many of the criminals he dealt with.

Being born in the East End, he had taken a circuitous route to respectability. His father had been a pub landlord who had, in his day, entertained some of the leading criminals of his era. DI Richard Gates was an anomaly to everyone who met him, and knowing this, he played on it relentlessly. His soft voice struck terror into the hearts of his men and criminals alike. With his brawny arms and big belly, he could look amiable one day and menacing the next.

Now, staring into his superior's eyes, he knew the effect he was creating and enjoyed it immensely. Inside himself he had no respect for anyone or anything. It was this that set him apart from other policemen and he used it shamelessly.

'I think it was the mother's doing, meself. The girl had nothing to do with it.'

Bannister nodded then said, 'I understand Madge Connor was screaming blue murder that it was her daughter who was the culprit?'

Gates shrugged. 'Madge is a whore and whores will say anything to cover their own arses. Surely you know that much?'

The insult was taken on board and filed away for future reference. One day Bannister intended to get rid of Gates, and get rid of him for good.

'So what are you going to do?'

Gates smiled then. He knew he'd won the battle; all that was left was the war.

'I'm going to have a little chat with Madge, and see if I can talk a bit of sense into her. Show her the error of her ways, so to speak.'

Bannister nodded. 'Good man. I'll leave it to you, then?'

Gates nodded and strode out, leaving his superior to reflect that the DI's transfer to another station couldn't come too fast for him.

Chapter Seven

Richard Gates ran one hand across his forehead and sighed. Madge watched him as he lit a cigarette and took a deep drag on it.

'So what you're saying, Madge, is that the girl, your daughter, stabbed Ron while the two of you were fighting?'

She nodded vigorously, all innocence and smeared mascara. 'She didn't mean it, Mr Gates, but her temper's terrible. He was hammering the life out of me and she came in the room and just lost it. I've never seen anything like it in me life.' Madge closed her eyes in mock horror.

Gates laughed softly. 'You missed your vocation, Madge. You should have been a fucking actress. Now let's stop fannying around and you can sign a nice statement telling me how you topped Ron and then we can all go home and get a bit of kip, eh? Except you, of course.' His voice was low and menacing now.

Madge lit a cigarette and sighed heavily. 'I'm sorry, Mr Gates, but I can't lie to you. I know what happened, see. I was there, you wasn't.'

Walking round the table, Richard Gates looked hard

into the face of the old harridan before him. 'Do you remember a few years ago, Madge, when that sailor was stabbed to death in the docks?'

She nodded vaguely. 'That rings a bell, yes. But what's it got to do with me?'

Gates stubbed out his cigarette and smiled. 'I interviewed you, Madge, together with that skinny bitch of a mate of yours and the big black bird.'

'Sod off, Gates. If you think I had anything to do with that, you must be a nutter. I didn't know the bloke, none of us did. You can't try and pin anything on me. It's not fair!'

Gates rubbed a hand once more across his balding head, feeling the thin hair and smiling.

'If it's left to me, Madge, you'll go down at some point. I am known as the villain's friend. I'm quite aware of me nickname and made a point of earning it. I put away anyone I want, see. Because I can. I can get people banged up; I can even make them disappear. If I were to tell people that you'd begun grassing, I could make your life a misery.

'Now, there's a young girl banged up not ten feet from here. She's your daughter and I want to see her get a bit of a chance in life. Get her out of here and away from you. Maybe then she'll have that chance.'

Madge watched the man before her in amazement. 'Why should you care about her, or about anyone? I know your reputation, mate – the whore's friend as well as the villain's. Not above getting yourself a quick blow job now and then. Frightening the tarts into doing what you want. Why, all of a sudden, are you worried about my girl?'

She pulled herself up by leaning on the wooden table. Smiling lop-sidedly, she shook her head. 'I ain't doing it. Not for her, and especially not for you. I can't be banged up, I just can't. I'm too old for all that. She'll be out before she knows it and things will soon get back to normal. It ain't that I don't want to do it, I can't do it. I just can't.' Her voice broke and she hung her head in shame as she listened to the man before her.

'I know whores who'd kill for their kids, but not you,' he hissed. 'You're the scum of the fucking earth. They'll eat her alive in the poke and you know it. She's not fourteen. Too young to be charged with the murder itself, but old enough to be shut away for fucking years, in and out of lock-ups. Is that what you want for your child? Detained at Her Majesty's Pleasure? Locked up and forgotten about? Because that is what will happen to her. She'll be at the mercy of everyone and anyone. Ron won't be in it. I know about these things, Madge. She won't get an easy ride. You will. In the nick you'll be a murderess which guarantees you kudos, don't it. You're over the hill and on your way out. You'll be free in five to seven. Why are you making this so difficult for everyone, yourself included? Because if I want you away, Madge, away you'll go, girl.'

She shook her head once more. 'I'm sorry, I just can't do it.'

Gates closed his eyes and tried to control his temper. 'Think on what I said and make the right decision.'

As he walked from the room he lit another cigarette and inhaled deeply. The night was wearing on and his temper was wearing thin.

Opening the spyhole on Cathy's cell, he looked at her, huddled in a blanket, and wondered why the hell he cared what happened to her.

'There's an Irishman to see you, Mr Gates – Docherty, the big mouth from the docks. Says he's here for the girl's sake.'

Gates nodded and said, 'Send him in, and bring in a couple of teas. Not that stewed shit, either.'

The PC grinned. No one above his own rank cared for Gates, but the officers below him liked and respected him in their own way.

He had a natural sense of fair play that appealed to them, plus an uncanny knack of remembering their details: wives' names, mothers' illnesses, children's ailments and achievements were always remarked on. As everyone knew, Richard Gates made a point of knowing everything about everyone. It was this fact above all that frightened his superiors, and frequently gave him the upper hand in his dealings with them.

Gates finished writing his report as the door opened and Eamonn Docherty walked into the office accompanied by the PC carrying two mugs of tea.

The two men stared at each other warily. Eventually, smiling slightly, Gates sipped his tea and said: 'It's been a long time, you Irish ponce. How are you?'

Eamonn Senior laughed then, a hollow laugh that sounded forced even to his own ears. 'I'm all right with me little wife. And yourself?'

Gates shrugged, an elaborate movement that accentuated the size of him. 'All right.' His low voice was no longer menacing but fairly friendly.

Eamonn sipped his own tea and waited for the bigger man to talk. It was unusual for him to be smaller than another man, and this gave him an unaccustomed feeling of inadequacy. Gates played on this by taking his time lighting a cigarette.

'You've heard then?'

Eamonn nodded. 'Mrs Sullivan sent round one of her lads – she's a neighbour, like. Knew them for years. How's the girl taking it? She loves Madge in her own way, you know. As bad as Madge can be, the child was a priority for her most of the time. I love the little pickaheen meself. I'll take her home with me and the wife can go and fuck herself. Cathy's like me own.'

Gates chewed on his lip before saying, 'Well, your own boy was nearly up on a murder charge a while ago, wasn't he?'

Eamonn frowned, wishing he had not drunk so much earlier in the night. He tried to understand the reasoning behind the man's words. As his face took on an expression of disbelief, Gates tapped the desk.

'Penny dropped, has it? Madge is letting the kid take the blame.'

'You're joking?'

'I wish I was. In fact, there's no doubt the girl did do it. Helping the mother, from what I can gather. You know Madge, you lived with her long enough. She's a whore through and through. She's quite happy to let the girl take the heat and to walk away from it herself. I've put the fuck on her, told her I'll get her anyway, and she still won't budge. So what can I use against her?'

Eamonn began to roll himself a cigarette, making the process long and laborious to give himself time to think. As he licked the paper, he said: 'Will all this be secret like, between us?'

'Of course. What do you think I'm going to do – take out an ad in the fucking local paper?'

Eamonn listened to the man with a heavy heart. Gates was renowned in the criminal fraternity, not as a bent copper but as one with a sense of fair play and a penchant for being swayed by a logical argument. That he had his seniors in his great big hands went without saying; Eamonn only hoped he could get the girl out of trouble. The thought of her, frightened and alone in a prison cell, made him feel physically sick.

'All I'll say without putting anyone else's face in the

frame is: remind Madge of how she worked with Susan P a while back. That should terrify her enough to make her do anything.'

Gates raised his eyebrows in surprise. 'Susan P? She's a bit out of Madge's league. Now what could Susan want from her, eh? I'll have to dig into this meself, I think – find out what I've been missing.'

Eamonn closed his eyes and sighed heavily. 'Believe me when I say you don't want to dig too deep into it. I don't know the score, but from what I've guessed, there's some heavy people involved.'

'Curiouser and curiouser, as the cat said.' Gates's voice was low and menacing once more.

'Well, curiosity killed the fecking cat, Gates, remember that.'

He grinned, showing white teeth. 'I'll remember, don't you worry. Now, Mr Docherty, finish your tea and start at the beginning. I need to know everything. And I think you're just the man to tell me.'

'Before I say anything – if Madge won't budge, I'll take the can for the child. Say I came in and saw him there, some such shite. Either way, I'll get her out of here.'

Richard Gates stared at the man before him with steely blue eyes then shook his head in reluctant admiration. 'You've just gone right up in my estimation, Docherty. I'd have thought you'd have fucked off out of it and kept as far away from old Madge as possible.'

'I would if it was just her. I lived off her for years, everyone knows that, and yet I cared for her too in a strange way. She can be a laugh, old Madge. Still, I wouldn't put me head in a noose for her. But Cathy, she's different. I wouldn't want to see her young life ruined. She's had it hard enough, yet the little mare's a fighter all right.'

Eamonn smiled as he said it, and Gates answered it with a smile of his own.

'We'll sort something out between us, I'm sure.'

Eamonn relit his roll-up and enquired, 'Why are you doing this? What's in it for you?'

Gates shrugged. 'That's the funny thing – there is no angle. I just feel sorry for the kid, I suppose. She's too young and vulnerable to be thrown on the scrap heap, and that's exactly what'll happen to her if we don't step in, believe me. Now, are you going to tell me what the story is?'

Eamonn shook his head slowly. 'I don't want to get involved unless I have to. Press Madge, she'll open her big trap, I can guarantee it.'

'I'll go one better than that,' Gates said. 'I'll ask young Susan P. We go back a long way – we're old friends.'

Eamonn wasn't surprised. Gates was a policeman with a difference: he actually liked most of the criminals he dealt with, though you had to be practically psychic to realise that. There were exceptions.

A story had gone the rounds for years, concerning Gates and a suspected rapist. The man had supposedly fallen down a flight of stairs, and subsequently died in hospital.

Such stories enhanced his reputation, both in the service and outside it. Judges were wary of him yet they respected him because, love him or loathe him, Gates had never tried to frame an innocent man. All his collars were real, even if the charges were sometimes fabricated. If he couldn't hang them for a sheep, Gates would hang them for a lamb. He always got them in the end.

'Cathy seems like a nice kid,' he said now.

Eamonn Senior nodded vigorously. 'She's a diamond, as you cockneys say. Bright, intelligent, too fecking good for

Madge, although the girl would walk over red-hot coals for her, Mr Gates, and that's a fact.'

'Yeah, I can see that, and I intend to do right by her. Let's face it,' he paused to light himself a cigarette, 'someone has to. Let's just say it's something to do to make a boring night a bit more interesting.'

Both of them knew he was lying but neither man mentioned the fact.

Susan P was watching her best girl at work. The whirring of the small camera was audible in the room, and as the Right Honourable Dennis Crumb, Labour MP and pillar of the Welsh mining community, began to perform oral sex on the supine young lady before him, Susan P actually began to laugh out loud.

'Go on, girl, give him the works.'

The two-way mirror was Susan's main entertainment. Watching people having paid sex interested her. She liked to see the different ways men thought they turned women on, and the different ways the girls reacted to the situation.

It always amazed her the way most men were so bloody amateurish. They really believed a woman they had never met, had bought and paid for, and who had nothing even remotely in common with them, actually enjoyed the clandestine sex they offered. Did they honestly believe that twiddling a girl's nipples as if they were tuning in the radio and performing oral sex like a wet-brushed Hoover guaranteed the recipient of their attentions even a modicum of enjoyment? She watched Naomi squirming and moaning. That girl sure could act! Just then the whore looked straight into her madam's eyes and winked heavily. Then she began the moaning and groaning once more, this time louder and more staged. The Right Honourable sucked harder, no end pleased with himself. Susan P grinned. He had probably been getting a similar performance for years from his wife.

She heard the door open but carried on observing the scene before her avidly. A few minutes elapsed while she watched the man bring himself to orgasm all over the girl's breasts before turning off the mirror light and saying: 'Richard Gates, you always turn up at the most interesting moment in my little films.'

She turned to him then, opening her arms in welcome as she walked up to him and hugged him to her as close as his belly would allow.

'Not an ounce of fat. Just scar tissue, as usual.'

Gates grinned. 'And it's all yours, any time you want it.'

Susan pushed her chestnut hair from her eyes and said, 'Thanks for the offer but I prefer being in the audience.' Then with a whisky poured for each of them and cigarettes lit they settled on the small sofa in her office and Susan said expansively: 'So, what do you want?'

Richard studied her for a moment. Her eyes were a deep sea green and her bone structure was perfect. Tall and slim, she was the mother of two grown children, though no one would believe that. She lived on coffee, cocaine and cigarettes, had a wonderful dress sense and an even more wonderful sense of humour. Her eyes were deep-set and gave the impression of a privately sensual nature; her movements were neat and contained, with an animal grace.

She had never slept with a man for money or prestige, she just had the knack of finding women who would do this, and do it well. She was the most successful madam in London, and looked after her girls with a protective zeal that guaranteed them not only respect, but a safe passage into their thirties – something few other whores could take for granted.

'I want some help, Sue, and I think you're the only person who can give it to me.'

'Why is it that the nicer you are, Richard, the less I trust you?'

'That's because you know me so well, and when I want something important I'm nicer than usual.'

'You're a lot of things, Richard, and I've heard you called a lot of things too – but nice isn't one of them.' He feigned distress and they both laughed.

'Oh my God!' Susan P stood up and switched on the mirrored light once more. 'Look at this prat! Honestly, men are children really. Spoilt, babyish and utterly stupid. Present company excepted, of course.'

'Of course. Well, I wouldn't vote for the fucker meself, but the housewives like him, I'm told.'

The Right Honourable was now regaling a bored Naomi with tales of his sexual prowess and she was listening with every appearance of rapt interest.

'The girl's good. What's her name?'

Susan P grinned, showing expensive white teeth. 'You wouldn't get within smelling distance. Her old man's doing an eighteen. Loves him to death, bless her little cotton socks. Won't shackle an Old Bill for love nor money, dear. Even turned down a Chief Constable at a Masonic do.'

Gates shook his head in mock despair. 'I wanted to fuck it, not marry it.'

Susan grinned again.

'No chance of doing either, I'm afraid. She just won't swallow it, if you'll excuse the pun?'

Gates laughed with her. Then: 'Turn the light off, Susan. Hairy arses never did much for me, I'm afraid. Now, down to business. I want to nail Madge Connor and I heard through the grapevine you can give me the necessary info to do just that.'

Susan P's expression changed noticeably and her eyelids dropped, giving her a sleepy expression. 'I don't grass, Gates, you should know that better than anyone.' Her voice was cold now, clipped and hard.

He finished his Scotch. 'You will when I tell you the reason. Her daughter stabbed a punter to death last night, and Madge is willing to let her carry the can. I don't want that to happen. The girl's only a kid, and what she's done is bad enough without her having to take the consequences. I need a handle on Madge to ensure she takes the appropriate steps and saves the girl's skin. Anything you tell me will not be used in any other way, I give you my word on that.'

'Why the interest in this kid? So what if she did it? Why should I give a flying fuck?'

Gates shook his head.

'Imagine it was your girl, Susan, and she was liable to be banged up. What would you, her mother, do, eh? I'll tell you what you'd do – you'd move heaven and earth to save her. Well, rightly or wrongly, I want Madge Connor to do the same. If I have to, I'll play the heavy. So let's get on with what I came here for. Talk to me, woman.'

Susan dropped her guard and sat back in her seat once more. 'I remember the kid. I saw her when I went to the flat. To be honest, I thought she'd end up the same way as the mother. I even thought I might take her on meself. Good-looking little thing, all big eyes and blonde hair. If I didn't know you better, I'd be inclined to think that's why you're so concerned.'

Gates looked annoyed and Susan hastened to reassure him. 'I just mean, if it was anyone else . . . Christ, man, there's plenty of them about. You should know that better than anyone.'

She stared into her empty glass, debating with herself

how much it was safe to tell. After an age she said quietly, 'I used her to do a put up. You know, when you take one whore and use another for the actual bagging? Madge, dressed up and scrubbed, delivered a parcel for me. She was the decoy, though she didn't know that at the time. She delivered the parcel to the house of a High Court judge. It was the start of a blackmail scam against him. Madge delivered a few stills. I used a younger whore to deliver the actual film to his chambers. You know how it works. His wife wants to know what an old brass is doing leaving him letters, and his arsehole goes when he realises that at the same time a film of him shagging a young filly has arrived at his place of work. I use the two in case the Filth are following anyone. If one don't shut the fuckers up, then two will. You know the scenario, Gates. I used Madge once.'

He listened carefully then said: 'So who was the judge?'

Susan P shook her head. 'I can't tell even you that. Not unless I have your word you'll get my Molly out of Holloway?'

Gates rolled his eyes and nodded. 'Always a rider with you, ain't there?'

'Molly's a good worker, but a bastard with a drink in her,' Susan explained. 'She's been done for affray. Her case comes up on Tuesday.'

'It's as good as done,' Gates told her. 'Now what's the fucker's name?'

Susan, happier now, said jokingly: 'You won't believe me.'

'Try me?'

'It's the Lord Chief Justice himself. Has a penchant for young girls in school uniforms – hardly original but there you go. Enough for the *News of the World* to have a fit of the vapours if the pictures ever hit their desks.'

Gates shook his head and laughed gently. 'The dirty old fucker!'

Susan P grinned. 'My sentiments entirely. Now, would you like another drink?'

Gates held out his empty glass but declined. 'Not for me, girl. I have to see a woman about a dog.'

Chapter Eight

Cathy was being examined by the doctor and Richard Gates was watching the procedure impassively. The police doctor felt nervous as usual while in Gates's company and his hands shook slightly as he rebuttoned Cathy's night-dress. Wrapping her once more in the rough blanket, he turned to the female PC and said, 'She's in extreme shock.'

Gates swiftly interrupted him. 'She can't make a statement then?'

Dr Angus Miller looked closely into the bigger man's eyes. 'Not if you think that's inadvisable . . .' His voice trailed off.

Gates smiled. 'I do. Thanks, Dr Miller, you have been a diamond geezer.' The mockery in his voice was evident and the other man tidied his things away in his black bag and hastily departed.

'Something will have to be done soon, sir,' said the WPC.

Gates nodded slightly. 'All right, Doreen. Give the poor little mare a wash and brush up and I'll sort out her mother.'

*

Madge was bewildered and annoyed. It was now ten-fifteen in the morning and she had been given neither tea, coffee nor breakfast since her last encounter with that bastard Gates. She knew he had ordered this, and now, thirsty, hungry and scared, she was wondering what his next step would be. One thing she was sure of: he wouldn't give in without a fight, and Madge was no longer sure she was a match for him and his iron will.

Gates covertly watched her pacing her cell and smiled to himself. He was well aware of the psychological advantage he had gained by cutting her off from everything. Even the offer of a simple cup of tea would be seen as contact with the outside world and could help bolster her resolve. If he had had the time he would have left her a couple of days without toilet facilities, food or drink. That was always good for a result. Stripping them naked helped also, especially with the women. But time, unfortunately, was not on his side. Someone had to be charged or he had to let them go. And charge Madge he would.

When she heard the door being unlocked she didn't know whether to feel fear or relief. Seeing Gates, she decided on the former.

'Hello, Madge. You're looking distinctly worried. Now why would that be?' His voice had a sing-song quality to it that frightened her more than if he'd shouted at her. But Gates rarely shouted. His soft voice was his trademark and he had a saying: *You can do more with a soft voice than a big stick.*

Looking at his set face, the tight line in his lips and terrifying coldness in his eyes, Madge started to waver. 'Look, Mr Gates . . .'

He interrupted her. 'You're beginning to get right on my nerves, Madge. In all my years I've never had to do so much running around for an old brass. I feel like you're taking the piss out of me, see.' He held up his hands expressively. 'I feel like you're having a laugh at my expense.'

Madge was shaking her head and mumbling, 'No, no, Mr Gates.'

Pushing her roughly down on the narrow bed, he said, 'I found out about your scam with Susan P. Now she's all upset. Wants to know who grassed her up, don't she? Out on the street you wouldn't last five minutes if I told her that you'd opened your big mouth about her blackmailing the Lord Chief Justice. I mean, that's a lucrative business she has there. Imagine if it was stopped or she was arrested. Susan P is not a woman to fall out with. She has a phenomenal temper. She also likes kids. But then, you know that.'

Madge looked horrified. Stifling a smile, Gates carried on with the psychological pressure.

'Asked after your little girl she did, when I spoke to her. Wanted to know if the girl would be taken care of while you were banged up like. Offered to see the kid all right. What a touch, eh, Madge? Susan P championing your little Cathy. Now doesn't that make you feel better? I mean, think about it. Both me and Susan P looking out for her. She'll have more protection than the fucking Queen and that Greek ponce she married!'

Madge, knowing she was defeated, stared up at the big man before her and accepted the inevitable. If he'd told Susan P she had opened her mouth, she was already as good as dead. Susan P was famously fair – and famously violent when the fancy took her.

Just like Richard Gates.

Both had their own way of looking at and doing things, and such was their strength of mind, they achieved whatever it was they decided on.

A wave of hatred washed over Madge as she thought of her daughter. Cathy had youth, good looks and friends. A winning combination by anyone's standards.

A big fat tear squeezed itself from the corner of her eye and she wiped it away with one tobacco-stained finger.

'Want a cup of tea, Madge, and a bit of nosebag?'

Gates's voice was softer, friendlier. He had what he wanted, there was no need to keep the pressure on.

She nodded sadly and he smiled at her, a real smile that changed his whole demeanour. 'Cheer up, girl. Worse things happen in the nick – or so I'm told anyway!'

He had done what he'd set out to do. As usual, once he had achieved his aim, he was bored and wanted to get on with the next item on his agenda. Outside the cell he said to his DC, 'Get her a cooked brekker and a statement form. Once she's signed, charge her. Then get Social Services in for the kid. I'm going home for a shit, a shave and a shampoo.'

With that he left the building. DC Fuller watched his boss's retreating back with a shocked expression on his face. It had seemed as though the big brass was never going to hold her hand up, but a bit of the Gates treatment and suddenly it was *I Confess*. Yes, another interesting night at Bethnal Green police station.

You could shove *Dixon of Dock Green* and *Z Cars*!

Cathy was washed and dressed. Sitting in the interview room she stared around her in bewilderment. The dingy walls and scarred table were testament to the many hours people had spent confined in here. Dark stains on walls and floor also showed that many had been taken there against their will, to be prompted into statements by physical force. Even at her young age, Cathy knew that. Stories of police brutality were common where she lived, and were related with a strange sort of pride. It was as if the day you got your first police hammering you had finally made it as a criminal. It was a red-letter day for the younger men, like their first fumbling attempt at sex or their first ever burglary.

Looking at those stains now, Cathy shivered as she imagined the punishment meted out in this room. Instinctively, she knew the nice man, Gates, would be one of the chief offenders. He wouldn't treat everybody the way he did her. Closing her eyes, she imagined where she would be going next. All she knew was that her mother had been charged and she herself was to be taken by a social worker, to be put into care eventually. The very words were frightening.

Care. Knowing what she did already from friends at school, the word 'care' was used by the Social Services in its loosest sense. The door opened. Wide-eyed she looked at the tall woman before her, wearing a green cloche hat and orange lipstick.

'Is this the child?'

The policewoman nodded silently. She felt for the kid. This hatchet-faced bitch looked about as friendly as the Wicked Witch of the West. She was all angles, from her high cheekbones to her bony wrists and ankles. As she sat herself down, the policewoman thought that the woman had knees like a bag of hammers.

'Name, child?'

Cathy looked at the woman mutely.

The young WPC's heart went out to the girl and she said gently, 'She's still in shock.'

The woman turned cold eyes on her and said scathingly, 'When I want your opinion, I will ask for it.'

Cathy stared straight ahead. Sighing, the woman said curtly, 'It's no good being surly, young lady. My advice to you is to cooperate with me. I can make life as easy or as hard as I decide. It would serve you well to remember that.' Glancing at the WPC she said, 'Bring some tea.'

The WPC left the room reluctantly.

Mrs Mary Barton, social worker, studied the girl before her. The cupid's bow mouth and naturally arched eyebrows irritated her. Really, the child looked more like an adult. The breasts already jutting through the thin material of the borrowed dress annoyed her. In fact, everything about the child set her on edge. Working-class girls were born women. They developed much earlier, they looked at men much earlier, and as she herself could attest, produced children much earlier.

This one here with her brassy blond hair and big blue eyes needed taking in hand, and Mary Barton knew just the person to do it. But not now. She had thought of fostering the girl with the Henderson family in Totteridge.

Cathy pushed her hair from her eyes and settled it over one shoulder. It was a graceful, completely unconscious gesture and it made Mrs Barton's false teeth grind.

Definitely a whore in the making here. Well, a few months at the Benton School for Girls would sort this little hussy out! No need to waste any time on tea and sympathy.

'Come along, child, we have a long journey ahead of us.'

'Can I see me mum before we go?'

Mrs Barton shook her head vehemently. 'No, you cannot. This is a police station, not a holiday camp. Your mother is on a murder charge and will be on her way to Holloway by now. Good riddance to bad rubbish, say I. You'll see her eventually. If you're good.'

The words were a threat and Cathy knew that, even though her mind was in turmoil. Watching Mrs Barton fussily gather together her papers and files, she tried again. 'Can't I even say goodbye?'

Mrs Barton acted as if she had not heard the outrageous demand, but her body language said it all. Bowing her head, Cathy swallowed down the tears.

The nice WPC had told her earlier that Madge had taken the blame for the stabbing, and that Cathy was to keep quiet and not say a word about it to anyone. She had hugged Cathy then, smelling nicely of lavender and toothpaste. Cathy had felt like hugging her back, but hadn't dared.

All she knew was that her mother had finally come through for her and the knowledge was like balm. She had thought her mother didn't care but she did.

Cathy's eyes filled with tears again and she hastily wiped them away. A little voice was prompting her to tell the truth. But she couldn't. The nice WPC had said that the big man with the balding head and quiet voice would be very cross with Cathy if she opened her mouth. That her mother owed her this and it was the right thing for her to do.

Still, even though she'd wanted her mother to do it, now that she had Cathy was frightened for her. She loved her mum very much, and understood her.

Following Mrs Barton out to her small car, she looked back one final time at the police station. Then, straightening her back, she got into the car. Wherever they took her, Eamonn would come and get her. Everything would be all right then.

She hung on to that thought as they set out on the journey to Kent and finally, exhausted and afraid, sought refuge in sleep.

*

On remand, Madge was allowed a visit from Eamonn Docherty Senior and smiled wanly to see him.

'It took this to get you to visit me without a fight, eh?' Her voice was hard, but her face was drawn and tired.

'Social Services have taken Cathy. I tried to see you earlier, came as soon as I could.'

Madge nodded, placated.

'You took it for her then? That was a very fine thing to do,' he said.

She lit a cigarette and snorted derisively. 'Under duress, Eamonn. Don't go thinking I've any noble sentiments because I ain't. If I had that little mare here now, I'd break her fucking neck! She stabbed him, and at nearly fourteen she should have carried the can, mate. She'd have been in and out in no time. As it is, I'm away for the duration, ain't I? As for that bastard Gates, I'll see me day with him. With the pair of them.'

Eamonn Senior shook his head in distress. 'Madge, I really thought you'd finally become a worthwhile person. After all, if you hadn't brought that Filth into your home, none of this would have happened. *You* caused it all. Everything. That girl was a rock to you but you could never see it. You gave her a bit of affection, as and when the fancy took you. As she grew up, you let her take on more and more of the responsibility that should have been yours. You used and abused her.

'Well, let me tell you something, lady. I'm glad Gates put a stop to your gallop. I'm glad you're going to do a long time, Madge, because that's all you're fit for. Any decent mother would have looked out for the girl, but not you. Oh, no. You'd have had her on the streets with you. That was your man's intention, whatever you chose to believe. Well, I'll leave you to stew in your own juice. By

Christ, I hope it burns a hole through your heart, I do that. I don't know why I even came here.'

'Why did you, Eamonn?' Madge's voice was low now, a pleading note in it to which he responded despite his temper.

'I came, Madge, because we were together for years and the girl was like me own child. I came hoping I'd find a different Madge Connor. A contrite woman, who had finally done something worthwhile with her shite of a life. That's why I came.' He looked into her watery eyes and hoped against hope he would find some sign of humanity there.

'Well, you had a wasted journey then, didn't you?' Laughing contemptuously, Madge got up and dismissed him by turning her back on him and calling for the PO to take her back to her cell.

Watching her, he was amazed at the hardness that had come over her in the space of twenty-four hours. She was afraid of prison. Well, who wasn't? But surely she must realise it was better that she be incarcerated than that young girl?

Shaking his head at the vagaries of women, Eamonn Senior walked out of Holloway and made his way to the nearest public house where he drank himself unconscious.

Cathy woke up as they reached Deal seafront. The lights and the sea were so different from anything she had ever seen before that she stared at them in fascination before she remembered where she was going and why.

Holidaymakers walked along the rainy prom carrying paper-wrapped fish and chips. Small children tagged along behind them. Kiss-me-quick hats and huge sticks of pink rock were evident everywhere, and the women looked wonderful with their brightly coloured clothes and backcombed hairstyles.

Cathy saw a man pick up his tiny daughter and hold her above his head. She could see his wife looking on, face alight with happiness. Cathy envied them their sheer exuberance, the contentment and the stability of their lives.

As they left the seafront they began to drive up a long winding road. Every now and then there were lovely houses to be seen, with neatly kept gardens and expensive cars in the drives. The houses were lit up like beacons and looked warm and inviting.

It was as they turned into a small lane that Cathy felt the first stirrings of apprehension.

'Nearly there.' Mrs Barton's voice was clipped.

As they approached a pair of huge wrought-iron gates she stopped the car. Getting out, she pulled on a long old-fashioned bell rope. The cold had made its way into the car and Cathy shivered. It was a damp cold, which chilled her to the bone. Unlike the other houses they had passed, this one looked far from jolly and inviting. It had a cold and hostile air. There were no snow-white nets at the windows, only ornamental metalwork. No decorative brick walls, only a heavy chain-link fence and barbed wire. It looked more like a fortress.

An elderly man opened the gates. As they drove past him, he peered into the car with rheumy eyes. Standing still, he watched until they had rounded a bend in the drive.

Seeing the full extent of the house, Cathy was shocked. It was huge. An old Victorian building, built for prestige not comfort. As they got out of the car, a biting wind swirled around her and permeated her thin borrowed clothes.

The impressive front door opened and they were ushered inside. The entrance hall was high-ceilinged and incredibly cold. The woman who came to greet them had a heavy bosom and a hawklike face. Her nose was like a beak and she wiped a dewdrop from it with a dirty handkerchief.

'Who's this then?'

Mrs Barton gave a contemptuous gesture for reply, pushing the woman from her forcibly. 'Where's Miss Henley? Tell her I'm here. Then take the girl and give her something to eat, and bring me a scalding hot cup of tea. Do you think you can remember all that, Deirdre?'

'Yes, Mrs Barton, ma'am.' The woman nodded, her hawk nose quivering with suppressed indignation.

Grabbing Cathy by the arm, she pulled her across the hallway and into a small office. As she opened the door, warmth seeped out and engulfed them.

'Mrs Barton's here to see you, brought this little madam with her.' Deirdre's voice was all affronted dignity and the small plump woman behind the desk looked at Cathy in amazement.

'She wants tea and she wants you,' Deirdre continued.

'Take the girl to the kitchens and bring the tea through. I'll see Mrs Barton.'

Cathy heard the steely tone in her voice and smiled to herself. Here was one person with no fear of the social worker.

'What are you looking at, girl?' The voice was hard, brooking no argument.

Cathy shook her head in distress.

'In this establishment, you speak when you're spoken to. Answer me, girl.'

She shook her head and tried to explain herself, but no words would come out.

'Take her away, Deirdre. She's obviously retarded or something.' The contemptuous tone was too much for Cathy and she felt her eyes filling with tears.

'I'm not a bloody retard!' The words were out before she knew what she'd done. They were loud and shrill in the overheated room, and the plump woman's face was a picture of shock and disbelief.

'Take her away, Deirdre. Take her to the quiet room. No food, no nothing, until I say otherwise.'

Deirdre took Cathy roughly by the arm and dragged her down a long flight of stairs. She tried to struggle and was given a sharp pinch for her trouble.

'You're for it, madam. Miss Henley won't have misbehaviour here. She'll slap your face till your earholes rattle. And it's no good crying and carrying on, that don't cut no ice with her.' She dragged Cathy bodily through the kitchen and, opening a heavy metal door, pushed her into darkness.

Cold darkness.

Realising what had happened, Cathy tried to get out by the closing door. A hefty shove sent her sprawling across the damp floor. The door banged to with terrifying finality and Cathy lay there, her heart beating a tattoo in her chest and her brain working overtime.

Her sobs of fear and rage were hysterical but nothing could be heard through the thick metal door, and no one would have been interested if they had heard her.

It was that kind of place.

Leona Henley listened avidly to Mrs Barton's tale of woe, refilling her cup and offering her biscuits, small dainty sandwiches and slices of rich moist fruit cake.

'I knew the girl was trouble from the moment I set eyes on her. Now you understand why I brought her here,' the social worker finished.

Miss Henley listened with interest and then said, 'I really shouldn't take her. This is, after all, a criminal establishment. The girls here are too young for prison and so I get them. Thieves and bullies mainly, as you well know. I'd need a court order to take her.'

She was interrupted by Mrs Barton.

'I can get the necessary documents. The girl practically attacked me. I'll lodge a complaint, and you must too. I really can't be expected to inflict her on foster parents, can I? She witnessed her whore of a mother murdering a man, and between me and you, Miss Henley, I think she was of the same occupation as the mother. On the doctor's report it said sexual relations had recently taken place.'

Miss Henley, suitably scandalised, raised her eyebrows.

'It's my guess the mother caught her at it so to speak and that's how the tragedy happened. She's a little tart, I tell you. Needs a firm hand. And that was why I thought of you. If I can't place her legitimately then you're the last resort anyway, and I always speak so highly of you to everyone.'

Miss Henley knew she was caught between a rock and a very hard place. The hatchet-faced bitch in front of her wanted the girl away, and so away she would go. It was inevitable. She had seen this woman beat a recalcitrant child unconscious before now, with a ferocity that had astonished even her who had herself been guilty of the same thing, God knows. Mrs Barton was a doubly danger- ous woman because she had an in with everyone. Everyone important that was. She could close a place down overnight if she wanted to; her power was great and she wielded it shamelessly.

Her husband was Mr Justice Barton and her brother the regional head of Social Services for London and the Home Counties.

'I'm sure we can fit her in here. And you'll provide the necessary paperwork?' Miss Henley asked.

Mrs Barton smiled happily. 'Of course, dear. Now how

about another slice of that delicious cake? Who made it – one of the gels?'

Contented now she had achieved her aim, she relaxed and began actually to enjoy herself. It was so nice when one managed to deal with a difficult problem, as she was to remark to her husband later on.

'A job well done, dear. I mean, how could you inflict a child like that on a nice family like the Hendersons?'

Cathy woke up on the freezing cold floor. It was pitch dark, and a musty smell of dampness hung in the air. Remembering where she was, she opened her eyes wide, hoping she would see something, anything, to dispel the total blackness. It was deathly quiet, only a faint scuffling noise, which Cathy knew instinctively was mice, breaking the silence. The mice didn't frighten her; she had lived with worse all her life.

The floor was damp under her hands and Cathy pulled herself into a sitting position, dragging herself across the floor to sit against the wall, knees tucked up before her, arms wrapped around herself to try and keep warm.

In her mind she saw Ron's body once more, and Eamonn's face as he stole her virginity. Both events were mixed together in her mind and she tried desperately to try and fix on something else. Her heart was beating too fast and she fought down the hysteria welling inside her. Crying was pointless, she knew. She had to try and focus on something else, and so she thought of her mother, pleased inside that Madge had finally done something for her after all these years.

Silently Cathy thanked her. In that dark void she believed that maybe Madge would hear her and know how grateful she really was.

It was the only thing that kept her sane.

*

Miss Henley finally remembered to let Cathy out fifteen hours later. After Mrs Barton had left, they had gone to bed, thinking the girl would be more malleable after a night in the quiet room. But in the morning two of the inmates had had a fight, and it was early-afternoon before they remembered Cathy.

Opening the heavy door, Miss Henley was surprised to find the girl sitting against the wall quite calmly. Her huge blue eyes were vacant, but as Miss Henley remarked to herself, that wasn't anything unusual after a first taste of the quiet room.

'Up you get.'

Cathy pulled herself to her feet and awaited further instructions. The girl's thin coat was covered in a layer of green mould from the damp walls and her legs were blue with the cold. Still she did not say one word. Just followed her jailer from the store room, clumsy from the cold and her own lack of movement. The kitchen was warm, and Cathy noticed twin girls watching her warily.

'Give her some tea, bread and jam. Then bring her to see me in my office.'

The girls nodded in sequence and watched the woman's retreating back.

The twins had thick black hair and big brown eyes; each had a small blue spot on their face above the right cheekbone. They were borstal spots, Cathy recognised that much straight off and knew immediately what kind of place she was in.

'I'm Maureen and this is Doreen. We're in for arson. Burned our mum's house down.' They smiled at one another as if they had told a great joke. 'What you here for?'

Cathy shook her head. 'I don't know.'

The two girls stared at each other and shrugged. 'Keep your own counsel if you like, but we'll find out.'

They busied themselves getting bread and margarine from the store and pouring out a mug of thick black tea from a boiling urn.

'Get that down you, and tell us your name.'

Cathy ate the food ravenously, and sipped at the scalding black tea as she felt her arms and legs begin to defrost.

'I'm Cathy Connor. I'm from the East End.'

'What you doing here? 'Tis for young offenders. You must have did something.'

Cathy shook her head. 'I ain't. I ain't done nothing.' She remembered what the nice man and the WPC had told her.

Maureen looked into her face and smiled. 'All right then, keep your trap shut. But I warn you now, girl. Denise will want to know and she'll find out.'

Just then Deirdre came back into the kitchen, and Cathy and the twins had to stop their discussion.

Cathy wasn't to find out any more about Denise until much later.

Miss Henley looked at the girl before her and felt an unaccustomed twinge of guilt. The thick blond hair was knotted, her eyes had dark circles beneath them and her legs were mottled blue from the freezing floor. This in itself didn't bother her so much as the fact that, technically, the girl should not be here. She hadn't actually done anything wrong.

'Well, girl? What have you to say for yourself?'

Cathy shook her head slightly. 'Nothing, miss. I have nothing to say.'

Miss Henley could see the confusion on her face.

'While you're in my establishment, I will have no back-chat, no fighting and no bad language. Do you understand what I'm telling you? If you do not, I will repeat myself. If you do understand me and you break my rules, I will hang you out to dry.' Miss Henley smiled as she said this and Cathy felt her heart sink inside her.

'Now I will hand you over to Deirdre who will provide you with your uniform and sleeping quarters. One word of advice: be careful of the girls here. They do not suffer fools gladly. They are, for the most part, vicious young women with a tendency towards violent behaviour. I do not tolerate it but I know that it can be, shall we say, difficult for some of the girls to control themselves. This is not a warning, it's a statement of fact. Be careful, and abide by my rules, and you will survive here. Now, is there anything you want to ask me?'

'Why am I here? I understand this place is for offenders.' Cathy's voice was carefully polite. She watched the woman's eyes cloud over, and held her breath.

'That will all be explained to you in due course. Deirdre, take her to her sleeping quarters.'

Cathy knew she had just made an enemy, but didn't see any way she could have avoided the situation. If what the twins said was true, she shouldn't even be here in the first place.

Deirdre furnished her with a blue pinafore dress, which was miles too long, and three pairs of thick black stockings. Also three hankies and two pairs of knickers. (One on, one washed, as Deirdre explained.) They were large navy blue ones with grey piping. Lastly there were two vests. Her house slippers and outside shoes would be given to her in the evening when Miss Henley opened the shoe stores.

Cathy was then led through a warren of green-painted

hallways until they reached the top of the house and what were once the maids' quarters. Deirdre pushed her gently into a small room with a high dormer window and two beds.

'You're in with a girl called Sally Wilden. She's a little mare too. I reckon you'll get on like a house on fire. Sally's trouble, and I have a feeling on me you'll be trouble as well. I've looked after girls all me life. Been here ten years and know a bad 'un when I see her. A word in your shell-like: don't push Miss Henley. She can be a bastard and you've already made an enemy of Barton. Watch your step, girl. Just watch your step. Take good care of yourself here because I can tell you now, no one else will.'

Cathy looked straight into the hawklike face. 'I shouldn't be here, this place is for offenders. I'm not an offender.'

Deirdre smiled. 'If Barton wants you here, here is where you'll stay. Keep your head down and your trap shut and you'll be all right. Once you're here, no one from outside will get near you. Believe me, I know.'

Troubled now, Cathy left her things in the room and followed Deirdre downstairs. The smell of carbolic was overpowering, underlaid with the taint of overcooked cabbage. It was a nauseating combination.

All Cathy wanted was a bath and something proper to eat. She held on to these thoughts as they walked into the classroom. About thirty pairs of eyes turned to stare at her in open curiosity and Cathy felt herself reddening with embarrassment. Deirdre left her there without a word and Cathy stood before the class and waited to be introduced.

It was a long wait. The teacher, a tall heavy-set woman, ignored her and carried on teaching the class about personal hygiene. Cathy stood watching, taking everything in, but her face betrayed nothing.

Staring around her, she studied the girls and the teacher and decided that she'd be out of this place at the first opportunity.

Cathy Connor knew she must concentrate her mind on escape, and escape alone.

At least one of these people seemed friendly and that was something to be going on with.

Keeping her face carefully impassive, she listened and watched for the next hour and a half.

Chapter Nine

No one spoke to Cathy after the lesson ended, not even the teacher, Mrs Daggers – a name that had brought a smile to all the girls' faces when they had first heard it. Those smiles didn't last long, however. Mrs Daggers was known as the hardest teacher there and could give as good as she got; even the legendary Denise didn't give Mrs Daggers any trouble.

Following the girls from the room, Cathy walked slowly towards the dining room. One girl dropped behind and whispered, 'It's teatime. Eat as much as you can get hold of. We get a cup of cocoa after this and that's it till the morning.'

Cathy smiled her thanks, and they entered the dining room, where she stood behind the girl in the long crocodile waiting to be served. It was then that she met Denise.

The girl was fat, unusually so, with a pretty Oriental face. Her hands and feet seemed too small for her swollen body and her eyes were a greeny-blue instead of the brown that might have been expected. She had an air of joviality about her and Cathy smiled as the other girl spoke to her for the first time.

'Who are you then?' The voice was pure South London and Cathy answered confidently.

'Cathy Connor. I'm from Bethnal Green.'

Denise smiled. 'You're not a Northerner then?'

Cathy said in a hard voice: 'I hope not. Ain't I got enough troubles?'

The Southern girls laughed and Denise grinned. 'You'll do, I suppose. What you in for?'

Cathy was shrewd. She'd had to be to live with Madge all these years, so she dropped her voice and said, 'I'll tell you later, when we ain't got an audience.'

Denise stared her down for a moment. She was in a quandary now. The girl was here for a good one or she wouldn't be so cocky. That meant Denise would want her on her team. Most girls shouted their case from the second they got through the door. This one was asking for privacy, something the others had surrendered years ago. Against her better judgement, Denise decided to be lenient this once.

'Fair enough. Come and sit with me and we'll discuss it.' This way she would find out and not lose any face. The new girl intrigued her and she wanted to know what was what before she made up her mind about her.

Cathy nodded, and as they served themselves with Spam, bread and mustard pickle, all the girls watched.

Sitting opposite Denise at a long table, Cathy waited patiently for the other girl to talk.

'I'm Denise Wong,' she said finally. 'You probably guessed I'm a half chat by me face. I run this place in me own way. Miss Henley relies on me, see. Without me there would be anarchy. She accepts this and we have a good working relationship. She's a stupid old bitch and I know that. I do a lot of her dirty work for her, so she treats me with respect. Everyone does. I'm in for demanding money with menaces and prostitution. Now you know my life story, tell me yours.'

Cathy took a bite of her food and pondered how much to tell Denise. She decided on the truth.

'I murdered a bloke, me mum's pimp. I stabbed him. Me mum's put her hand up for me like, to save my arse. Some old bitch called Barton took me out of the nick and here I am. But I ain't been charged with nothing.'

Denise grinned. 'You will be. Barton's a slag. Same story with Sally. Barton had her here and all she did was mouth off a bit. Barton's usual is to say you attacked someone and that you can't appear in court because you're off your trolley. They deal with it in your absence and you get sentenced. We have a joke here, that this school is so good you have to be sent here by a judge. The thing is, you'll need to find out what your sentence is and when you're liable for a release date. I can do that for you. For a price, of course.'

That seemed fair enough. 'What's the price?' Cathy asked.

'I want you on my team. I run this shithole and I need all the help I can get. This place was once a home for unmarried mothers. Now it's a secure unit for girls – or gels, as the social workers call us. I'm the strong arm of the place. What I say goes. Can you cope with that? If not, say so now and I won't waste me fucking time. I'll batter you straight away and get it over with.'

Cathy knew the girl was not talking for effect.

'Suits me all right,' she said calmly. 'I just need to see how the land lies. I have to know what's happening with me mum and others. Me bloke is probably wondering where I am too. We had a bit of a disagreement – I need to see him to sort it out.'

Denise nodded sympathetically. 'You'll be all right. Now go and get some more food. Tell Ugly on the counter I said to load you up properly. Other than a hot drink later, this is it for the night. Food is a bastard here – you never seem to get enough. The cold's bad enough, but hungry *and* cold are the pits. I hear you've already had a touch of the quiet room. That's nothing. Tie down is the bastard. That's Mr Hodges's department, and I'm warning you now, girl, watch that old fucker! He's a dirty old git. Straying hands and tongue. Keep away from him.'

'What's tie down?' Cathy was frightened despite herself.

Denise shrugged. 'You'll find out. It's pointless me explaining it, it's different for everyone. That's his favourite pastime. Hodges is the official head of this place, but he lets old Mother Henley run it for him. Fuck knows what he does with himself most of the time because we don't see him for weeks on end, then he turns up and there's murders. You'll soon get used to it all. You'll have to. I can honestly say I'm sorry for you, though, girl. It's bad enough when you've been sent here official like. Did you stab the bloke because he was after you?'

Cathy shook her head. 'He was beating me mum up.'

'And your mum's took the fuck for you?'

Cathy nodded.

'What a touch! I don't even know who my mum is.' This was said with complete honesty and no trace of self-pity.

'Well, mine's no angel but she's me mum, you know?' Cathy smiled gently.

'You done the business yet?' Cathy looked puzzled and Denise laughed loudly. 'You had a bit of the other?'

Cathy went bright red and nodded.

Denise laughed once more, bringing all eyes to them. 'Go and get your grub. You're funny, Connor. I think me and you will get along nicely.'

When the girl serving the food got the nod from

Denise, she furnished Cathy with a large slice of fruit cake and a cup of tea with milk and sugar. She also told Cathy that she could have as much bread and Spam as she wanted.

Taking her stacked plate back to the table, Cathy tried to work out in her own head what she was going to do, and more importantly, how she was going to get away from this place. That was the most important thing.

Getting out and getting back to Eamonn.

At that moment Eamonn was with two heavies in a cafe on the Commercial Road. They were waiting for a man to deliver some money and they were early. Drinking coffee and eating bacon sandwiches, they chatted idly.

'That was a blow for you, though, Eamonn, the girl getting taken off like that, eh?' This from Big Joe McCarthy. Joe was second-generation Irish, and like Eamonn wanted better than his father had had.

Eamonn stared at him levelly, and kept his voice carefully casual. 'Yeah, that's right.'

'I heard the girl did it and the mother's carrying the can. Got that one from one of Susan P's girls. They say the little 'un was nearly sent down over it and Gates forced the mother to take the blame. Nice little thing and all, that Cathy. Pretty as a picture and twice as lifelike, as my old mum used to say.'

Eamonn looked at the older heavy. Paddy Clark was in his forties and the picture of a thug for hire, but he was a nice bloke with daughters of his own and a little wife whom he loved dearly.

'Cathy's all right.'

Eamonn's voice was harsh now and the men knew he wanted the subject dropped. Going up to the counter, he ordered more coffee, and Big Joe McCarthy said snidely,

'She was his girl. You'd think he'd be moving heaven and earth to help her, wouldn't you?'

The older man nodded. 'He's a cold one all right.'

Eamonn knew exactly what they were saying and it suited him. Far better they believe he was a selfish, heartless bastard than realise the truth: that without Cathy he felt confused, powerless as a child against the misery of this loss. There was only one way to drown out the pain: become the toughest, most ruthless enforcer the East End had ever seen.

The door opened, letting in chilly air, and the man they were waiting for breezed over to their table.

'He's tucked us up. I phoned in and we're to go after him.' He looked at Eamonn. 'The boss said you knew what to do?'

Eamonn nodded. 'Get yourself a coffee and we'll away and look for the bastard. He's had his last warning. He won't see the sun come up the morrow.' The men were all quiet as they digested this bit of information and Eamonn Junior enjoyed the atmosphere he had created.

Life was good, except for the fact that he missed his girl. But once she was back, everything would return to normal. Whatever normal was.

He smiled to himself, thinking of Cathy beneath him, of himself riding her. She was sweet, in all ways she was sweet, and he was looking forward to seeing her again.

The institution that housed the girls had been built in the 1890s and had once been the home of an affluent local businessman. It had subsequently been named Blake's Folly, because after he'd built it for her, Blake's wife had died in childbirth and the impossibly large house had been no good to him. He had succumbed to illness some years later and his family had closed down the house. It had been left unoccupied for many years. Eventually it had become a home for young women in difficult situations, as unmarried mothers were then described, until it had been made into a secure unit-cum-school for children unable to serve the appropriate legal penalty for their crimes because of their age or mental capacity.

Edward Blake had designed a house on a grand scale that furnished space without light. The windows, now barred, fought off the sun on a daily basis and the rooms were always dark and chilly, even at the height of summer. In winter, the house was so cold the inside of the windows iced up frequently and pipes burst on a regular basis.

Cathy came there in early October when it was just getting cold. Sometimes the girls were given a fire in the dining room, but only at Christmas or other holidays. For the most part they were left cold, hungry and tired.

Their day started at six a.m. and they were then kept occupied for the rest of the time until bed at seven-thirty. In winter the girls were glad of the regime; in summer they were heartbroken.

The sound of the gulls and the noise of the holiday-makers beyond the fence tormented them, and the inmates would listen and dream that they too were part of the outside world once more and free to enjoy Deal.

Cathy was not to know that a few of the girls in Denise's circle had found a way to stop the boredom from growing too intense. In fact they had a system, and soon Cathy would be offered the use of it. It was just a question of whether she would have the guts actually to implement their daring plan of action, as other girls frequently had.

Only time would tell.

Denise wanted to make sure that Cathy was definitely kosher before she offered her the out.

Cathy was already classed as an 'A' girl by the fact that

she was at the top of the house and not in one of the dormitories on the middle floor. These were the original bedrooms, made into bigger rooms with only butler's sinks for sanitation. The girls were expected to defecate into buckets and empty them in the morning. Urine was put straight down the sink and washed away. They also washed themselves in the sink, under supervision of course. Girls with periods were treated no differently. They washed their 'monthly rags' out after each use and dried them as best they could on the towel rail.

In the 1960s and early 1970s girls' institutions were not commonly discussed. Most people didn't even know they existed. Many of the girls were sentenced for trivial offences, often caused by appalling home circumstances, and then promptly forgotten about, even by their own families. Problem children were taken away and that was that.

Cathy was to a certain extent at home in this environment. After living all these years with a prostitute, the girls' talk of violence, theft and their own premature sexual activity was not shocking to her. In fact she was swiftly made aware that what had happened to her at Eamonn's hands had not been nearly so shocking as she'd thought at the time. He did after all love her in his own way, and was free to do so. Some of the girls had received treatment far worse from their brothers, fathers or uncles. Often all were using them at the same time. Denise had been offering fellatio for money since the age of seven and as she had been in care for a great deal of her life, the beneficiaries of her money-earning talents were the people who were supposed to be guiding and looking after her.

She had bragged over cocoa that she could bring a man to full orgasm in under two minutes, using only her tongue. After listening to Madge and Betty's talk, this sounded pretty tame to Cathy, which was noted and respected by Denise who was really trying to psych her out.

The tough little angelic blonde intrigued Denise. She realised that there was a lot to the girl she hadn't yet fathomed. Denise believed her when she said she had knifed the man. There was an underlying current of ferocity in Cathy Connor and she wanted to make full use of it if she could. As small as she was, she had an air about her of a girl who knew what was going on, who knew the score, and in institutions such as Benton School for Girls, this was a rare occurrence.

Most of the girls were dumb animals. A few were cunning, really cunning, and they ruled the roost.

Denise had a feeling that Cathy, once she was initiated into the school properly, would be an asset and wanted to use her as soon as she could.

The strict regime, instead of cowing the girls, made them more violent with each other. Constant humiliation, both physical and mental, made them crafty. They were meek in the face of their superiors, and gave vent to their feelings of suppressed rage by fighting each other.

It was the survival of the fittest, as in any institution, and the brains used the brawn all the time.

All were broken, all were hurting inside, all wanted to hurt others. It was a brutal and frightening environment and each girl had adapted as children do and worked out her own way of coping. Some were weaker and so became gofers, even offering sexual favours to older girls as well as their possessions. The stronger ones just took what they wanted and didn't think twice about it. It was, after all, their right as top dogs.

In fact, many of them blossomed in the Home. They felt they had a place there, a niche, they were someone. They were important in their own little world. For many of them, Denise especially, that was enough.

Cathy unconsciously took all this in on her first day, and after the events of the previous forty-eight hours it was almost a relief to have something else to think about.

She had already relegated Ron to a distant unpleasant memory, just as she had rewritten history and turned the bruising encounter with Eamonn into a romantic interlude. She was already learning, as all the other girls had, that you must adapt. If you didn't, you were as good as dead.

Cathy was escorted to her room on the second night by Sally Wilden; Denise had called her over to the table and introduced them. Cathy recognised the girl who had winked at her in the dining-room queue. Sally was a lot like Cathy and they hit it off at once.

So at seven-thirty the two girls were locked into their room and finally made each other's acquaintance properly.

Sally was tall and slim, with a lean boyish figure. She had thick honey-coloured hair – her best feature – and greeny-brown eyes. She had a cheerful, easygoing manner and her voice was low and musical. She and Cathy were the perfect foil for one another. Sally, for her part, was pleased as punch to share with the new girl, as she was pretty and intelligent and had a nice way about her. Which was a welcome change after some of the girls she had roomed with over the last few years.

'So what you here for?' Sally's friendly voice was reassuring in the dimness and Cathy quickly explained the situation.

Sally shook her head sadly. 'You're finished, girl. I'm sorry to put the kibosh on you, but I was in the same boat. Old Mother Barton hated me on sight. She knew it wasn't me who'd caused the trouble . . .' She paused then and explained exactly what had happened.

'I was a witness to a fight between me brother and me

stepfather. Me stepfather's a bastard. All right when he's sober but a fucker with a drink in him. Me brother battered the shite out of him and I helped, so to speak. Anyway, the upshot was Mrs Barton was sent round our house and I gave her some lip. This was made into a statement to the police and I was then arrested for threatening to kill her. I know that sounds crazy but it's true. In court I was made out to be the cause of the fighting in my home, the cause of everything that had gone wrong with the world including the Second fucking World War! Mrs Barton put on her act so well even *I* felt fucking sorry for her! She blew my mind.

'Anyway I got three years because the judge said I was a menace to society and that a woman of Mrs Barton's stature should not be threatened and terrified when carrying out her legitimate tasks. So I was sent here and for the first week I was in the quiet room. It was a psychological thing, I realise that now. That place can really break some of the girls, you know. The dark and cold are terrifying things. Often the most terrifying to the people who come here. I was finally forced to lick condensation off the fucking walls to quench me thirst.'

She laughed again as she said this, but it was a bitter sound.

'Still, I survived and I'm still here to tell the tale. One girl was found dead in there, and didn't that cause a fucking furore? Officially she died of pneumonia. But really she died of fright. We all knew that, and Henley and Hodges gave us an easy time for a few months because of it. The last thing they wanted was all of us up in arms. We used poor old Mary's death as they used her. So in a way we're as bad as them. But you have to survive, girl.

'I'm seventeen soon and then I'll be out of here and back in the real world. I'll be honest and tell you there have been times over the last few years when I thought I would

151

never walk out of here. Now I use the system. It's all you can do.'

Cathy was quiet after hearing this and both of them thought about the girl who had died. Then Sally continued with her advice.

'I've heard the SP on why you're here and all I can say is: use it. Let them know you were the murderer. It will give you kudos, even with Hodges and Henley. They won't trust you, and that's what you want. Be nice to their face, but a bit insolent like. You know what I'm saying, don't you? Never give them cause for actual complaint, nothing they can accuse you of. Just have it in your face, in your eyes, and they'll give you an easier time of it. Denise is all right, a bit of a nutter but fair. Cultivate her friendship. You might need it. Don't stick up for the weaker ones. I made that mistake. They either learn to take it or to fight back; either way they survive without you getting involved. Now I'm going to ask you to do something, and I swear there's no weird motive to it. Take the blankets off your bed and put them on mine.'

She grinned at Cathy's expression and said jovially: 'Then get in with me. Believe me, this isn't a sex thing, though it would be if Denise or Harriet said the same thing. This is purely for practical reasons. Two bodies are warmer than one and, believe me, after a night in this room you'll see exactly what I mean. Like, you're pretty but you're not manly enough for me!'

The two girls both giggled then and soon were ensconced in one bed.

By morning Cathy understood her new friend perfectly. Even cuddled up together, the room was like an icebox.

Breakfast was cold porridge, and bread and marge. Cathy was given sugar and honey with her porridge, and sugar and milk in her tea. Her new garments were huge and she laughed when Denise called out: 'Fuck me, it's the orphan in the storm!'

After breakfast they were all assigned jobs and Cathy was informed that she was to scrub the hallway by the front door with Denise. The work was hard, but at least the movement warmed them up and the scalding water gave their freezing hands some relief.

They chatted amicably as they worked and though the scrubbing was tough, Cathy soon had the swing of things. Denise was good company and regaled Cathy with stories and anecdotes about the school which shocked but intrigued her.

Suddenly, though, Denise went very quiet. Cathy looked at her and realised that something was very wrong.

A shadow passed over them and Cathy stared up into the most terrifying face she had ever seen.

The man was tall, and thin to the point of emaciation. He was in his late fifties or early sixties, it was difficult to tell because of the enormous beard that covered practically three-quarters of his face. It was a gingery colour with a lot of silver in it. Even in the dim light Cathy could see that his eyes were a flat grey and his eyebrows met in the middle, giving him a threatening look.

The worst thing of all was his slack red lips. She could see spittle at the corners of his mouth and he licked at it in an unconscious, habitual way.

'Who are you?'

His voice was thick, as if he had a phlegmy cold, but she somehow knew this was how he always sounded. It was sick-making and Cathy swallowed down a mouthful of bile before she answered him. Something told her to beware of this man, that he was dangerous to her. Nevertheless, she stood up. Wiping her hands on her rough apron, she looked into the man's face and said, gently but firmly, 'I'm

Cathy Connor and I shouldn't be here.'

Denise closed her eyes in shock and waited for the explosion she was sure was going to come.

Instead, to her surprise, she heard Mr Hodges laugh gently.

'From what I understand, Mrs Barton will soon remedy that situation. I'll see you in my office at seven this evening.' He walked deliberately across their clean floor and Denise let out a sigh of relief at his departure.

Cathy looked down at her and said pleasantly: 'Mr Hodges?'

'Mr Arsehole Hodges himself,' the other girl confirmed. 'Tonight, tell him you think you've got a dose. Because he likes to break the new ones in. Funny, he don't touch the likes of me. It's the little ones like you he's after. Skinny mares with blue eyes and a bit of tit.'

She grinned and tried to lighten the situation. 'Still, gives you something to look forward to, don't it? Almost a date, if you think about it.' She roared with laughter at her own joke and they carried on washing the floor in silence.

Cathy felt sick with apprehension as the real force of her predicament hit her then. She had been chucked out of the frying pan and into the fire. Her eyes filled with tears and for the first time in years she wanted her mother. The thought of what Madge had done for her made her even more upset and she wished she could have her mother beside her once more.

She hoped Madge was faring better than she herself, wherever they had sent her.

Mr Hodges walked past them a while later and Cathy stared at his thin retreating back and stuck out her tongue. It was a childish gesture and she knew it would not do any good, but for those few seconds it made her feel much better.

Chapter Ten

Harold Peter Hodges was a secretive man. It was a conscious trait and had served him in good stead all his life. He had risen to be head of Benton School for Girls after taking over a young offenders' institute in Dartmouth and terrorising the boys there so completely he was rewarded near retirement age with the cushier job of running a girls' institution.

For him it was a dream come true.

Girls and boys of a certain age and build interested him. He kidded himself that he was a sort of father figure to them, taking a philanthropic interest only, but a few times over the years he had sailed pretty close to the wind. One young lad had committed suicide after an encounter with Hodges and that had caused a bit of an uproar. His mother, a meddling woman, had caused trouble before Hodges had finally managed to pull the wool over the investigating civil servant's eyes.

After all, he excused his actions to himself, just because he got a little lonely sometimes and maybe *played* with the children, it did not make him a bad person at heart. These were children who knew a lot from an early age. Nothing he did to them could ever be as bad as what they had experienced in their own sordid, deprived homes.

He made himself believe this and after an attack, or as he termed it one of his 'games', he often went away for a while to a Catholic retreat, there to come to terms with his sin and properly repent of it.

Not that it had ever stopped his lust from recurring. Now the new girl had intrigued him. It was her small build that had caught his eye. She was nearly fourteen, he understood, but looked like a much younger child.

Her direct stare had been a challenge to his authority, though it had amused and excited him too. She obviously needed taking down a peg and he was the man to do it. According to Miss Henley, she was another of Barton's fuck ups. He would have to wait to do anything really effective until the girl was legally in their custody. But he could live with that.

In fact, the waiting would be an added stimulus. And tonight he would start the game . . . His breathing quickened in anticipation.

She would taste so sweet – the girls always did – though he preferred boys in many ways. They were easier to cow. The act of buggery broke the most strong-minded lad. It was that fear and the vulnerability of the children that gave him the desired feeling of absolute power. Made him feel strong and capable of fulfilling his sexual fantasies.

He had never been able to perform a sexual act with an adult, no matter how he tried. It was this that had brought him to working with children. Outwardly he came over as a caring and kind teacher, having taught in legitimate private schools at first, though that had been dangerous to an extent because his colleagues had realised eventually that there was something not quite right with him. That there was something missing.

It had taken a chat with a likeminded fellow to lead him in the direction of the correctional institutions. Here the children were captive and pliant. For the most part anyway.

The evening meal over, the girls were allowed an hour's recreation. This consisted of playing cards or chatting. Denise used this time to sort out any problems she had encountered during the day with the various girls she minded.

The smaller or younger girls would give part of their allowance to her in exchange for protection. Some of the girls had families who would send in money or leave it on visits; this was used to help make their stay at Benton easier and happier.

One of these girls was a tiny mouselike child called Cynthia. She was very, very upper-class and they called her Lady C. She had burned her sisters to death quite deliberately. Taking the two younger girls out for a walk, she had doused them with petrol and set them alight, watching as they both went up in flames. Everyone was wary of her; Denise watched her closely, remarking to the others that even the biggest nutter must give way when they met a complete lunatic. Lady C was a lunatic.

Small and waiflike, she had terrible temper tantrums that amazed the other girls with their violence. Then, for months, she would be docile and pliant as could be. Now she was after a box of matches, a regular request from Lady C though no one was daft enough to let her have them. The last thing they wanted was to be burned to death in a locked room, and with her that would most definitely be the upshot.

Lady C made her way over to Cathy and smiled. Cathy, already warned about her, smiled back in friendly fashion. In Lady C's face was a childlike happiness, and for a few seconds Cathy saw her the way she could have been, before madness struck and she murdered her own flesh and blood.

'I hear you're to see Hodges?'

Cathy nodded and the girl's face clouded over. Her fine features became pinched and drawn, eyes just a little unfocused, her mouth too tight for a girl's. She looked like a very old woman in a child's body. She picked constantly at her pinafore with excessively long nails which had apparently been used more than once as weapons, especially when a temper was on her.

'I like your hair,' she said.

Cathy unconsciously put her hand to her head. 'Thank you.'

Lady C nodded happily. 'I like you.'

Cathy smiled, and thanked her once again. Denise was watching the performance with interest. It was unusual for Lady C to instigate a conversation that wasn't to do with matches. She waited for this to come up, ready to put her off.

'Mr Hodges isn't a nice man. You must be very careful,' the girl warned Cathy solemnly. Opening her hand, Lady C placed a small blade on the table. 'Take that with you. It might help you when he begins his games.'

All eyes were on the small sharp blade before them. Denise's were like saucers. 'Where the hell did you get that?'

Lady C grinned. 'I stole it from the workman who was mending the doors.'

Denise frowned. 'But that was ages ago. You've had it all this time?'

Lady C grinned once more. 'I want it back, though. *I* need it myself.' Her refined voice was hard, not like a child's at all. 'I want it for Mrs Barton. I owe her.'

All the girls were amazed. It was the first time she had

ever voluntarily joined in a conversation. The blade was such a shock most of them stood staring at it as if they expected it to disappear.

Denise picked up the blade and whistled softly. 'Fuck me, you're a dark horse!'

Lady C's face was sad as she answered, 'Your language is terrible, Denise.'

The big one laughed. 'I know. And you're frightening, lady. You've had this blade for months.'

'I've another as well. The man was changing them all the time and as he threw them away, I would just retrieve them from the bin in the kitchen. It was easy. No one watches me, really. Not unless there's matches around anyway.' She was pleased as punch. Happy to have put one over on everyone.

'Mark him with it, but not where it will show,' she instructed Cathy. 'Not the face. Maybe the stomach or his hands. Let him know you're not putting up with him.' Lady C kept her voice low. 'Don't let him get to you.'

Cathy took the blade and stared at it, fascinated.

Lady C grinned. 'You'd be surprised at the things I hear and see and manage to get hold of.'

Denise, all ears now, smiled in a winning way at the girl and said, 'Sit yourself down and have a proper chat.'

But Lady C shook her head, her face clouding over as she snapped, 'I'm not stupid! You think you'll find out what I have and then you'll try and get it all from me.' Staring at Cathy for a moment, she said gently: 'Use it. Make him pay.'

As she walked away the girls all watched her in silence.

'What a nutter!' Denise said under her breath, because as small as Lady C might be, she was still a bona fide lunatic and as such you didn't upset her without just cause – and at least a claw hammer as a weapon.

Cathy looked at the blade once more and Denise took it from her hand.

'You won't need it anyway. Until they get you here properly, you're pretty safe. When the courts sign the papers, I mean. All he'll do today is play with you. Scare you. I know because he did the same with Sally when she first arrived. He daren't do anything more in case someone turns up to claim you or take you somewhere else. One last word of warning: he stinks. Keep as far away as possible.'

Cathy nodded, trying to take in everything and put it in some kind of order in her mind. It was difficult, and seeing the look on her face, Denise grasped her hand.

The bigger girl's face was full of understanding as she said gently, 'Don't let the old bugger get you down, he ain't worth it. None of them are. They act as if we're the shit on their shoes when in reality we're better than any of them. We are children, they are adults. They know we're their captives, that we can't go anywhere or tell anyone. But we fight back in our own way and you must learn to do it as well.

'Let him know you were the killer, not your mother, but don't admit it outright. Put the frighteners on the dirty old bastard and then keep your head. Use the bloody blade if it'll make you feel better, but bear in mind that if you mark him, he has something against you and can keep you here even longer.'

Cathy digested this information, nodded and took the blade back. In the last few days her life had been turned upside down, and she was sometimes hard put to sort herself out and try and survive what was happening. It was getting harder by the day.

'My boyfriend will come for me,' she said with pathetic bravado. 'Eamonn will come for me, I just know he will.'

Denise shrugged and smiled. ' 'Course he will, love, and fairies live at the bottom of our garden.'

Cathy frowned. Sighing heavily, Denise said: 'Get real, for Christ's sake. There is a way out, but it's disgusting. If you really want to go for it, I'll come with you. But that's in the future. For the moment, just be happy with surviving tonight and the next few weeks.'

Before Cathy could answer, Deirdre came into the room with the two female wardens. They were not in fact referred to as wardens but as care assistants, though as both were burly, heavy-set and assertive, Miss Brown and her companion Miss Jones obviously served that function. They were respected by all the girls for their superior strength and fairness. The women did their job and kept their own counsel. Not exactly friendly, they were impartial and never abused their power like Mr Hodges, Miss Henley or even Deirdre.

Now Miss Brown wagged a finger at Cathy and said, 'Follow me. Mr Hodges requests your presence.'

Cathy walked out of the now silent room and followed the woman fearfully. Miss Brown had huge feet encased in brown brogues. Her fat calves were visible through black stockings and Cathy watched them as they fought inside the nylon like a pair of melons, wobbling with each step.

When the woman stopped, Cathy nearly walked into her. Turning round, Miss Brown looked down at her and said gently: 'Frightened?'

Cathy nodded, all blue eyes and stretched skin. Her face had paled to a sickly grey. She looked into a raw-boned face, almost Russian in appearance. The woman's huge arms were barely concealed by her cardigan and blouse. She resembled a man in female clothes. Unexpectedly she smiled, revealing crooked teeth.

'Don't be. I'll look out for you, love.'

Tapping on Mr Hodges's door, she opened it and ushered Cathy into the room. 'Miss Connor for you, Mr Hodges.'

The man stared at them both for a second and then said, 'You may go, Brown.'

Miss Brown turned, saying as she left the room: 'I'll be outside, sir, ready to take her back to her room when you've finished.'

Cathy watched him close his eyes and then say through his teeth, 'I will ring when I need you, thank you very much.'

Miss Brown turned to face him and said heavily, 'It's in the statute book: "I must wait outside and return each girl to their designated room after any meeting with or unscheduled appearance before members of the staff". It is to protect you, sir, as well as the child.' She stressed the word 'child' and Cathy was made aware of the tension between the two adults in front of her.

'Miss Brown.' Mr Hodges's voice was hard now, low and menacing. 'I need to talk to the child, to assess her.'

Miss Brown smiled. 'She is not really supposed to be here, sir. Without the appropriate documentation, it is my job and Miss Jones's to see that everything is kept above board. After all, you wouldn't want to find yourself being investigated, would you, over something a child might say?'

She smiled at them both. 'I'll just be outside. Call if you need me.'

Cathy knew that the last words were as much for her as for Mr Hodges, and felt a lifting of her spirits. She had friends and allies in this hell-hole, and the knowledge was some consolation.

Shutting the door gently, the woman left.

Cathy clutched the blade in her hand as she looked at the man sitting behind the large ornate desk.

He smiled at her, a lascivious smile. Cathy had seen the

162

same smile on men's faces when her mother brought them home. It had always augured trouble for her and so she didn't smile back. Instead she looked at a spot just above the man's head and waited for him to speak.

Hodges kept silent, enjoying her fear. He looked her over from head to foot, and when he pushed himself up from his chair the action made Cathy jump.

He grinned. 'Don't be frightened. I won't hurt you, my dear. I just need to ask you a few questions.'

The blade was burning a hole in her hand. As he made his way slowly towards her, she felt her breathing quicken. Her mouth was dry and her heart was beating like a drum in her ears, the sound deafening.

She took a step back.

Frowning, Hodges stood before her, his sheer height intimidating to the girl before him. She could already smell the sourness of his breath and acrid body odour.

Unlike her encounters with her mother's friends, where she could walk away, run out of the flat or scream the place down, here there was no escape. She knew that without Miss Brown outside the door she would have been in real trouble. This man could have done whatever he liked, as often as he liked, with nothing to stop him.

'Keep still, girl. I have no intention of following you around my office.'

As his hand came down on her shoulder, she whimpered. The man liked this. Loved it. A child's fear was all part of the enjoyment for him and he smiled at her then, a nice friendly smile.

'Sit yourself down, girl.' He pointed to a chair and Cathy stumbled to it, glad to sit before her legs gave beneath her.

Reseating himself on the far side of his desk, he stared at her for long moments. 'Do you know why you're here?'

She shook her head. 'I shouldn't be here. I've done nothing. My mother took the blame.' Cathy was aware of what she had to do, and as she spoke her voice became stronger and clearer.

Mr Hodges frowned, unsure what she meant. 'Could you repeat that, please?'

Cathy spoke up loudly. 'I said, my mother took the blame.' She made herself smile as she saw the look of shock on his face.

'Do you realise what you just said?' His voice was almost jovial in his excitement.

Cathy took her courage in both hands and shook her head. 'I never said anything. Nothing at all, sir.'

Screwing up his eyes, indeed his whole face, he stared at the girl before him. He could have sworn on a stack of Bibles that she would not have the guts to come back at him, but there was more to her than met the eye.

He had big manly looking Brown outside the door and couldn't have any real fun, and on top of that, this slip of a thing was covertly threatening him. She actually dared threaten him! He would have to sort something out, here and now, or he would lose the advantage. Stepping away from the desk, he was on her in seconds and the blow which connected with her ear was sharp and painful, nearly knocking her from the chair.

Cathy felt the blade dig painfully into her palm as she squeezed her hands together and blood began to flow. Keeping both fists clenched, she knew she must not let him see the weapon unless she had to use it. It was evidence, it could be used against her.

As he raised his arm again she surprised not only herself but the man before her when she said: 'You dare, mister, and you just see what you get.'

He was so shocked by her vehement tone, he dropped

his hand to his side. 'I beg your pardon?' His voice was almost comical in its shock and confusion.

'My mum's bloke tried all that. I know what you're after, and I killed once to avoid that. I'd do it again too. No matter how long you keep me here, one day I have to be let out. And when I am, I'll make a point of coming back for you, mate. Mob-handed and all. Where I come from, people like you are despised. There's plenty I know would give me a hand to put you away.'

The street talk shocked him, even though he heard it all the time. It was the fact that the angelic-looking girl in front of him meant everything she said that frightened him the most. He could practically feel the hatred and animosity coming off her in waves.

'You dirty old bastard!' she hissed. The last few words were drawn out between her teeth, and the sheer force of them shocked both people in the room.

'All my life I've had to deal with people like you,' Cathy went on. 'Well, I've had enough of it. Now I want to go to me bed, and I want to go there alone.'

The inference of her words was not lost on Hodges who shook his head in utter disbelief. At that moment Brown poked her head around the door. Her face was expressionless but her demeanour showed them that she had listened to every word spoken in the room.

'Shall I take her now, sir? I have to lock her up with Wilden.'

Hodges nodded his head, his face grave as he watched them walk from the room. Brown slammed the door with a deafening retort that grated on his nerves.

No one, but no one, bested him. Especially not a chit of a girl.

Cathy Connor had made herself a bad enemy, and she knew it.

*

Miss Brown led the girl up the stairs to her room. 'I'll get you a bandage for your hand,' she promised.

Cathy looked down at the bloody fist in surprise. She had even forgotten that the blade was there. Miss Brown opened her palm and took the blade, placing it carefully in the top pocket of her blouse.

'We'll keep this between ourselves, OK?'

Cathy nodded.

'You did all right in there, love. Keep your pecker up. Hopefully you'll be out before you know it.'

Taking the back stairs, they made their way down to the kitchen. Deirdre and Miss Jones were drinking tea, and Deirdre's voice was high with annoyance as she said: 'What's *she* doing here? Henley will go mad.'

Miss Brown pushed the hapless woman back into her chair and said, 'She'll only know if you tell her. Now get the first aid box out, the girl's got a cut palm. You sort her out while we see to the lockup.'

Miss Jones followed her friend out of the kitchen, an inquisitive look on her face. Cathy knew that they would discuss everything and hoped they would not decide to punish her over the blade.

'How've you done this?' Deirdre's high voice was followed by a sniff as usual, and Cathy stifled a smile. The woman was really a fool, which at this moment was exactly what Cathy needed.

'Pour yourself a cup of tea and put plenty of sugar in it. It's good for shock,' Deirdre continued. Getting a tin bowl, she filled it with hot water and then poured some disinfectant into it. 'It'll sting, but it'll stop you getting any infection. Come on, sling your hand in and I'll tear up some rags and bandage it for you.'

Placing her hand gingerly in the hot water, Cathy sighed

as it soothed the pain then drew in her breath as the stinging began. Looking around the dingy kitchen, she wondered if she was really so bad that she deserved all this trouble. Ron's dead body was once more before her eyes, and her mother's words – '*What have you done now?*' – were ringing in her ears.

Did she cause all these things to happen to her? Was it something that she made happen? Even what had happened with Eamonn – did she somehow cause that?

Tears threatened and she took a deep breath, aware that in this environment tears were a sign of weakness and weakness meant more trouble.

'He don't mean it, old Hodges. He just can't help himself.' Deirdre's voice was low and unhappy.

Cathy stared at the woman in dismay, unable to believe her ears.

'It takes some men like that, you know.'

Cathy didn't answer, not sure that anyone could.

'Just you keep right out of his way and he'll leave you alone.'

Swirling her injured hand in the hot water, Cathy closed her eyes and prayed that soon she would figure a way out of this hell.

Denise was 'dormed', meaning she was trusted enough to be put in a small dormitory with other girls. This was a very shrewd step on the part of Hodges and Henley. She made sure there was no trouble between the girls there and kept them all in order. Unlike many of the others, who valued their private space and hankered after a small room of their own, Denise, although she would never admit it, preferred to be in company. Plenty of company. She was actually scared of the dark. Now she lay in bed wondering how Cathy was faring, knowing in her heart that they should all rebel in some way but unsure exactly how they could do that.

Although she was a hard nut, a heavy, she knew that it was futile even to attempt to get even with Hodges unless they could walk out of here directly afterwards. There *was* a way out, though it was a frightening and disgusting option. But maybe, just maybe, they could manage it, if the new girl was willing . . .

Hearing the locks being checked by the Two Misses, as they were known, she got off her bed and walked to the door.

'Is the new girl all right?' Her voice was loud and aggressive.

She heard answering laughter.

'Perfectly. She showed that old fucker a thing or two!'

The retreating footsteps were nearly drowned by the guffaws of the two women.

Leaning against the door, Denise breathed out a sigh of relief. She turned to the other girls who were all lying in bed waiting for her to speak and said, 'She'll do. The new girl will do.'

All of them were quiet then, for what Cathy had endured had been practised on most of them at some point. They were pleased that, whatever she had done, it had made the Two Misses laugh, which meant she had got one over on the old man. That was not easy, and unknown to her, Cathy's reputation in the Home was made that night.

Sally was still awake when Cathy finally came to bed.

'How'd it go?' Her voice was heavy with distress. 'You were gone so long I was getting worried about you. I saved some water in case you needed a wash.'

Cathy sat on her friend's bed and grinned. 'I'm fine. I—'

She was interrupted by a screech from Sally as she saw

the bandaged hand. 'What did the old git do? What's happened to your bleeding hand?'

'Nothing happened to me hand, you silly mare. I got one over on him and the worst thing is, he knows I did. He'll want to pay me back at some point but I'll be ready for him. I'm going to get me money's worth out of this place. One day I shall get meself out, but before I go I'll teach that old fucker a lesson he won't forget.'

The vehemence of her words and the steely resolution in every line of her body were a revelation to Sally. Cathy had seemed so quiet, ladylike even, that the change in her frightened the other girl.

'The world is full of people who want to use you, take advantage of you, make you do what *they* want even if it repels you. Well, Sal, I'm sick of the lot of it. First me mother – she used me – and then me mother's boyfriends, and now that old git. Well, I've made up me mind that I'm going to fight back, once and for all. No one will ever get the better of me again – and that includes Eamonn!'

Pulling off her clothes, Cathy got into bed with Sally. Cuddling up to try and get warm, she continued talking. This time her voice was lower, more reflective. 'Every man I've ever known has had an angle, some way of using women. With me mum's blokes it was the obvious – I mean, she was a brass. Most used her for her money or her body. Mostly her money. They lived off her, you know.

'The only bloke I ever had any time for was my Eamonn and even he's used me in more ways than one – though for all that I still have to have him. Can't be without him. I'm going to get meself out of here and back to the East End and my Eamonn. But this time I'll call the shots.'

Sally listened without saying a word.

As the shadows lengthened and the room became darker, the two girls' eyes grew heavier and heavier.

Soon they were asleep and dreaming of all the things they had been without for too long: food, warmth and especially love.

Chapter Eleven

Denise's smiling face at breakfast let Cathy know that her experience with Hodges had already been reported. Sitting at the table with a bowl of grey-skinned porridge and a slice of bread before her, she grinned happily. Her bandaged hand attracted the attention of all the girls around her.

'How'd it go then?'

Cathy, a natural storyteller, regaled them with her tale in as funny a fashion as she knew how, bringing tears of laughter to all the girls' eyes. They all knew, to different degrees, exactly what it was like to be up in front of Hodges, and admired the way this new girl had of making her ordeal humorous. It was a sign of strength, a strength that Cathy had been unaware she possessed until this moment.

As Lady C approached the table, Cathy smiled at her winningly. 'I lost your blade, I'm afraid.'

The girl shrugged. 'No worries, there's plenty more where that came from.' Her tone implied that she had a complete armoury at her disposal and the others started to worry about that fact.

'Can I have your bread?' She seemed to have lost her

violent train of thought and everyone breathed a sigh of relief.

'So what's the next step, Cathy?' Denise's voice was eager, interested.

Cathy sighed. 'The next step is getting out of here. From what Sally's already told me, even though I ain't really supposed to be here, that old trout Barton can get me sectioned. I ain't waiting around for that. Fuck her and Hodges. I'm going on the trot.'

Before they could talk any more, Deirdre clumped up to their table and told Cathy she was needed in her room.

Following the carer, Cathy walked innocently into her bedroom where the door was closed behind her. Hodges waited for her with his usual bland expression. Only his eyes shone with the evil inside him. He smiled slowly, making himself look frightening, and Cathy felt a sickness rise inside her as she realised what was going to happen to her.

On her bed lay an array of ropes and cords.

As Hodges stepped towards her, Cathy began to fight. Both he and Deirdre were amazed at the strength of her small body as she kicked and fought with all her might. Hodges laughed. This is what he wanted; the more she fought the more he would enjoy himself. It was the best part of his job – breaking the girls down, making them more amenable. He got a charge from seeing them helpless under his control.

Trussed up on the bed, Cathy watched as Deirdre was sent from the room.

Hodges smiled down at her, his face a mask of hatred. 'I'll leave you now,' he whispered, 'but I'll be back. And while I'm gone you can contemplate exactly what's going to happen to you. One thing is for sure, young lady. Nothing you dream up will match the reality.' He laughed once more, and left the room.

As he shut the door behind him, Cathy strained against her bonds and felt them tighten around her. All she could do now was play the waiting game, try to make herself relax. She couldn't let him beat her, she would not give him that satisfaction.

She knew now what it was like to be completely alone, and allowed herself the luxury of tears. Though whether they were tears of frustration or of rage, she wasn't sure herself.

Cathy's tie down was discussed by the girls. They had all been Hodges's victim at one time or another. The real shock to them was that Cathy Connor had not even been officially admitted to the institution before Hodges was up to his tricks again. This was unheard of. They speculated that the old bitch Barton might have formalised the arrangement quickly and therefore given him the push he needed to begin what he referred to as the breaking-in process.

Dinnertime came and went.

No sign of Cathy.

Suppertime came and went.

Still no sign of Cathy.

Sally Wilden was dormed in with Denise, and the two girls looked at one another fearfully. Both knew that Cathy's bonds would be tight; both knew she would receive nothing to eat or drink – both knew that the combination could be lethal.

Unlike the tie downs at other Homes, Hodges's tie downs were real acts of bondage. He had even been known to use handcuffs. The tightness of the bonds cut off all circulation and limbs went dead pretty quickly. One girl had had to be taken to an outside hospital after eighteen hours of this torment. Surely they wouldn't leave Cathy Connor all night as well?

Hodges wouldn't dare, they consoled themselves.

He wouldn't have the guts.

Betty Jones tracked Eamonn down to a small bedsit in Bethnal Green Road. It was owned by a young brass called Sylvia Darling. Eamonn used her place frequently, giving her a few pounds to leave the coast clear for him. Sylvia could ply her particular trade anywhere there was a wall and so the arrangement suited both of them.

A banging on the door brought Eamonn's head out from underneath the sour-smelling blankets, and a pithy retort from his lips.

Betty sighed and banged on the door once more. 'Open up, for Gawd's sake, Eamonn. I'm freezing me drawers off out here.'

Recognising the voice, he hauled himself from the bed and in nothing but his underpants opened the door. 'What time do you call this, woman? It's still the middle of the fucking night to me.'

Betty laughed. 'I thought you was supposed to have come up in the world?'

She looked around her with a dismissive eye, and on his dignity now, Eamonn pulled a cigarette from the pack on the bedside table and said quickly, 'Tell me what you want and piss off, Betty, I'm tired.'

As he lit the cigarette, it was snatched from his mouth by the irate little woman before him.

'Who you talking to, you little shit? I used to wipe your arse, and no matter how hard you think you are, or how big you've become, that will always give me the edge, get it? Now, put your kacks on and make me a cuppa and we can discuss why I'm here.'

Eamonn nearly smiled. He had always liked old Betty and suddenly remembered the times she had bunged him a few pennies as a child for a bar of chocolate. Deciding that he could offer her a bit of respect in the privacy of this room, he did as he was told while Betty smoked the cigarette for him.

Five minutes later, a cup of steaming tea in front of her, she began to speak.

'It's about young Cathy. I've been sniffing about like, making a real nuisance of meself to find out what the Social done with her.'

Eamonn's eyes kindled with interest for the first time since he'd let her into the room. 'And? Come on, Betty – where is she? Can I visit her, write her a letter?'

Betty looked into his handsome young face, alight with enthusiasm now, and could almost find it in her heart to pity him, despite the fearsome reputation she knew he was rapidly earning for himself as Danny Dixon's main man.

'It's not that easy, love, I'm afraid. You know what that lot up the offices are like – keep their mouths tighter than a duck's arse, they do. We're not related to Cathy, see, so they don't have to tell us nothing.

'But I got a bit pally with one of the clerks, said I'd do him a favour like if he'd do me one in return. He had a butcher's at Cathy's file and saw she was marked down for long-term fostering. He wouldn't tell me where exactly, but he said the family in question – the Hendersons – were a good-hearted bunch. Lah-di-dah and all from the sound of it.

'Cathy will be well treated by them, Eamonn. We don't have to worry about her even though we'll miss her. In fact, she'll probably be back here one day talking with a plum in her mouth. Imagine that – Madge Connor's daughter turned into a real little lady!'

Eamonn scowled darkly. 'I don't think I want to, ta very much. They've got no business yanking Cathy away from

Bethnal Green. She's my girl, she should be here with me.'

Betty smiled at him sadly. 'Talk sense, son. She's not fourteen yet. They're hardly going to hand her over to a known tearaway –' she put up one hand apologetically and swiftly added '– nor an old brass neither. I offered to have her, you know. Nothing I'd like better than to give that little girl a home. But they're having none of it. Better face it, Eamonn – Cathy's out of here for the duration. I don't think either you or me will see her again until she's sixteen and can tell 'em where to shove their foster care.'

She saw his fists clench and the tide of misery that darkened his blue eyes before he hastily averted them.

Betty rose to her feet tactfully. 'Well then, best be off, love. Look after yourself. Try and stay in one piece because sooner or later Cathy'll be back, you can count on that.'

She let herself out. Eamonn sat slumped at the table, head in his hands. If she hadn't known him for the bold-faced young villain he was, she could have sworn he was crying.

Cathy was delirious, her wrists and ankles so swollen and sore the pain was blurred now after twenty-four hours. Her heart was beating erratically and her hair was plastered to her head with sweat. Miss Henley was terrified and even Mr Hodges was beginning to worry, though a part of him enjoyed the scene before him.

But maybe he had gone too far this time . . .

Tie down was first introduced to mental institutions in the late 1800s. That is, officially. It had in fact been going on since time began. Lunatics could be treated in any way, as could prisoners. In homes and correctional institutions, it was often used as a last resort; at Benton School for Girls it was used before most other sanctions. Tie down was meant to be for epileptics primarily, so they didn't fall out of bed and damage themselves. It was a form of help for poor unfortunates who fitted during the night – that was the official line anyway. Other places used it for runners, people who might otherwise escape when left unwatched.

In Cathy's case it was for punishment.

She was tied in such a way as to render her motionless and also give the maximum of pain.

The looping of the cord around her neck, hands and finally feet guaranteed that if she struggled, she would strangle herself. With boys, Hodges tied them down on their stomach. Then they were much easier to get to if he felt that way inclined. He knew all the tie downs, had used them all over the years and rather fancied himself an expert on the subject. He would discuss it endlessly with like-minded fellows and usually felt a surge of heat in reliving his actions.

Now, as he looked down at the sufferer before him, her glazed terrified eyes and swollen limbs, he felt a prickle of fear. They didn't even have proper documentation for her yet. She wasn't supposed to be here.

As he cut the bonds that had dug deep into her flesh, he could hear the rapid, fearful breathing of his colleague.

'She needed this, you admitted as much yourself.'

Miss Henley didn't answer, not trusting herself to speak.

'She's a bitch of a child and this will keep her in order, mark my words.'

He was talking for effect and they both knew it.

As they massaged her wrists, both of them prayed she wouldn't die on them. Two deaths in eighteen months did not bear thinking of. In grim silence they ministered to the girl, both knowing that it had gone too far and neither having the guts to acknowledge that fact aloud.

Both nursed secrets, both knew the other's foibles, and

both were terrified of the possible consequences if these were unmasked. It was an unholy alliance. They would never betray one another.

The girls were quiet over their lessons and Mrs Daggers knew why. Hardly there five minutes and the little Connor piece had already caused havoc.

Mrs Daggers had worked in women's prisons and men's; she could read the signs, and realising that there could soon be a mutiny, she set the girls some work and took herself out of the room and harm's way.

She made for the top of the house and looked into the attic room that housed the cause of all this trouble: Cathy Connor.

'How is she?' asked Mrs Daggers in a low voice.

Miss Henley shrugged helplessly. 'OK, I think.'

Mr Hodges carried on rubbing Cathy's ankles, his breathing harsh in the confines of the room.

'How long was she unconscious?'

Miss Henley's voice was terse as she answered, 'I have no idea.'

Even Mrs Daggers was shocked. 'You mean, no one was watching her? She could have died, you stupid woman.'

Mr Hodges's head snapped round. 'Well, she hasn't. Now, if you have nothing constructive to add to this conversation, perhaps you'd care to fuck off out of it.' His language told the two women how badly worried he was, and they exchanged fearful glances.

'One of these days you'll go too far.'

The tall man's icy stare exhorted Mrs Daggers to silence but she was on the verge of hysteria and they all knew it. 'If this ever gets out . . .' Her voice was frightened.

Mr Hodges pulled himself up to his full height and said with unsullied dignity, '. . . then we'll all be up shit creek

without a paddle. Now, start massaging and pray we don't
have to bring in the outside doctor.'

'The girls are very quiet and I think there's a good
chance of trouble. My advice would be a good supper for
a change and some kind of activity tonight. If anything
happens to this child there's going to be murder done here
– and I don't mean this one.' Having said her piece, Mrs
Daggers began massaging Cathy's tortured limbs.

Although nothing was said in reply, she knew that the
warning had been taken on board and filed away for future
reference. She had done her bit. Now she could only wait
and see what fresh developments the day would bring.

Denise slipped from the classroom and waited in the
corridor for Miss Brown, whom she knew would be doing
her rounds.

'Please, miss, how's Cathy Connor?'

Miss Brown's normally rosy face was white and it looked
for a moment as if she did not recognise Denise's
distinctive figure.

'It's not good but she'll survive,' she finally divulged. 'I
could hammer that fucking Hodges myself! Stupid man.
I wish he'd get the shove or retire or something . . .' Her
voice trailed off.

After a few seconds she said sadly, 'I thought she was a
goner there, Denise, that I did. The thing is, even if I
reported what I saw there's so many of them involved in it,
including old Barton, no one would ever believe me.
Hodges is treated like bloody royalty by everyone in the
service. They all think he's the dog's bollocks. But I tell
you this: if that girl had died, I'd have gone to the papers.
I might never have worked again, but I'd have risked it.'

Denise nodded to let her know that she understood the
older woman's dilemma. This was her home as well as her

place of work. She was one of a growing army of women who, having worked in institutions for years, were now institutionalised themselves. Outside the walls of Benton School for Girls she was lost. This place was her life and she used what little bit of influence she had to make things easier for the girls in her charge. Denise knew that one Miss Brown or Miss Jones was worth a thousand Hodges, and yet they were rarer.

The kind ones were always the exception to the rule.

Having been in and out of Homes all her life, Denise was an expert on the staff.

'She's all right then?' Her deep voice was gruff with emotion.

Miss Brown nodded. Grabbing the girl by her shoulders, she said earnestly, 'Don't let them all go off over this. That would cause more trouble than it would solve. Give them the silent treatment. That scares the fuckers more.'

Denise smiled despite herself and nodded.

The twins, Doreen and Maureen, were amazed and delighted to discover they were to serve up what amounted to a feast in the eyes of the Benton girls: tomato soup and ham sandwiches, followed by Swiss roll and custard.

The news was not treated in quite the same way by the rest of the girls who, under orders from Denise, boycotted the canteen and sat stony-faced and hungry in the recreation room.

This news frightened Hodges and Henley more than a riot. It meant the girls were going to sit and await the outcome of their folly. Afraid to provoke them further, they eventually allowed the girls to stay in the rec room all night long. They chatted among themselves, waiting patiently for news of their friend.

*

Danny Dixon was pleased with his protégé and wanted to tell him so. Eamonn had been rounded up and now stood nervously in front of the man who paid his wages. The man who held the lives of everyone here in the palm of his hand.

Dixon wasn't scared of anyone at all. Even as a child he had not feared his violent bullying father or alcoholic mother. Joanie Dixon was legendary in the East End. She could knock a man out with a single punch. It was rumoured even her husband would cross the road rather than meet Joanie when she had the hump.

Growing up in such an environment, it was inevitable that young Dixon would eventually be a face of some description, but no one had guessed just how big he was to become. Hardened men who worked for him, who maimed for him, who terrified people for him, were wary in his presence.

Dixon knew that the fear he engendered in people was because no one knew how far he would go. His was a controlled violence. He didn't hurt people because they upset him, he would happily take an insult, yet he could attack the same person for no apparent reason whatsoever. His sheer unpredictability was his best asset in this business and he knew it, cultivated it, and enjoyed his notoriety.

He loved to listen to the old biddies talking all their trash about the East End hard men. It amused him no end to hear himself talked about in tones of awe. Dixon knew the score. Unlike his peers, he knew that bullshit was part and parcel of East End life. He prided himself on doing nothing more than playing the game. He had sussed out the life early and felt he knew a big secret that no one else shared.

In many respects he was right.

The boy before him reminded Danny very much of

himself. Eamonn Docherty Junior, as he was known, lived life with the express wish of accumulating money and spending it. He wanted the best and wanted it as quickly as possible. He would also do anything to further his own ends. Unlike most of Dixon's heavies this boy would never, ever draw a line. Had no boundaries.

Dixon admired this, even though he knew the lad would one day be dangerous because of these very qualities.

One day, Eamonn would want what he had. It was a simple fact of life. When that day came, he would deal with it. Until then he would use the boy, be his mentor.

Dixon believed in the old adage: It takes one to know one. In this case he was pretty sure he had met, if not his match then the nearest he would ever get to it.

Eamonn left ten minutes later two hundred pounds richer and unsure exactly what he had done to earn it other than beat a man nearly to death.

That beating had been bought and paid for already.

He wouldn't understand for a little while that the unexpected gift had been nothing more than a publicity exercise for himself and Dixon.

The beating would be talked of, naturally, but the two hundred pounds would be discussed everywhere. In every pub, club and drinking establishment.

Even his own men would discuss it.

It was sound economics.

Lessons would be learned.

For the moment, Dixon could sleep easier in his bed and Eamonn Docherty could bask in the kudos Dixon's largesse had afforded him.

Mary Barton was deeply concerned. Taking one look at the girl in the bed, she turned on Hodges ferociously.

'Get the doctor, you bloody fool of a man!'

As he lurched from the room she looked at her friend and colleague and raised her eyes heavenwards.

Miss Henley shook her head sorrowfully. 'No one was here with her. I thought he would have let it go after a couple of hours. I had no idea he had left her for the whole night.'

This was a lie and they both knew it. It was all part and parcel of the game they played. Everyone pretended that what they did was perfectly normal. No one actually admitted out loud that their treatment of the children in their care was abominable.

Nor would anyone ever admit that the money they skimmed from everything, from heating to food to clothing, was ever used for anything other than the most righteous and just of causes. It was a cruel and cynical game and they were all experts at it.

'What the hell will we say?' Miss Henley's voice was frightened.

Mrs Barton shrugged as if this were a normal day in a normal home. 'Why, the truth, of course. One of the other girls did this to her and we found her like it. What else can we say?'

Brown's voice came from the back of the room. 'Or we could say that the sadistic old bastard in charge of the place tied her up, nearly killed her, and came in during the night to have a look at his handiwork. Because you can guarantee that he did, ladies. And I bet he loved it! Especially when she was still lucid and knew what was happening to her. He could've done anything to her!

'Or we could say that she isn't actually supposed to be here, because she hasn't actually done anything wrong – unless we count the fact that you took one look at her and decided she should be locked up, Mrs Barton. I mean, that's why she's really here, isn't it?'

The two older women stared at June Brown in amazement.

'Have you gone off your head, woman?' Mrs Barton's voice was scandalised.

The heavy-set woman before them shrugged. 'Don't worry, I'll keep me trap shut, but I warn you all now: this place has got to sort itself out. Me and Jonesey are sick of it. Our job is to police the girls, not the bleedin' staff. Look at the pair of you! A dried-up old stick and a raving lesbian. And as for Hodges . . . he's a sick-minded fucking pervert! By Christ, how the hell you sleep at night, I don't know.'

Miss Henley's face was red and shiny with nervous perspiration. 'You can talk. What abo—'

June Brown interrupted her. 'Me and Jonesey have been together for years, lady. We ain't after little girls. Look at you and Denise . . . you think we don't know? She describes it all in graphic detail to give the other inmates a laugh and you think no one knows? You're really that fucking stupid? They talk about everything, and when they leave they take it with them, in their hearts and in their minds. One day it will all come out and I can't fucking wait to see the shit hit the fan then.'

She walked from the room, a fundamentally decent woman who, because of sexual preferences, was reduced to living a life of shame and humiliation in an institution where her so-called strangeness was more or less normal compared to the peccadiloes of the people in charge.

As she had remarked to her long-time friend, Gillian Jones: 'The price we have paid for our friendship is much too high. If we're unnatural, what the fuck does that make this lot?'

Life could be very unfair, as the Two Misses knew to their cost.

If they blew the whistle, it would be their word against

everyone else's and they both knew that they wouldn't stand a snowflake in hell's chance of ever being believed.

After a strong coffee laced with Scotch, Miss Brown let the doctor into the Home and played the game as she was supposed to. Ergo: she lied through her crooked teeth.

Chapter Twelve

The doctor was shocked and disgusted at the treatment meted out to the girl in the bed. He was on the verge of taking her to hospital when it was pointed out to him that she was a violent offender and had to be taken everywhere under guard.

The doctor, who only a few months previously had been brought in to help save a child who had mutilated herself and her dorm-mate, was not as shocked as he made himself out to be. Indeed, he dined out on his stories of this female institution, and in fact wished he were called there more often.

An actual tying up would be a very good story for his cronies and professional colleagues alike.

He had the girl lucid and sufficiently recovered to be spoken to and understood within one week – a feat he was proud of and which earned him the heartfelt gratitude of the authorities at Benton.

The doors, however, remained closed to him after that and he had to wonder at the fate of that particular girl as he did about others he had treated there. In his heart he knew he was part of a conspiracy of some sort, but wrongly believed it was to keep the good name of Deal as a holiday centre spotless. Mrs Barton knew human nature and sussed out the good doctor from the off, while he congratulated himself on the fact that the girl would have lost at least one limb, if not for him.

As it was she had a full complement of arms and legs and was making an excellent recovery.

Cathy was a silent and stoical patient.

He put the quietness down to the ordeal she had been through. He never dreamed it was Miss Henley's presence that kept the child so tight-lipped.

It would take twenty years and the admission of tie-down practices by the care authorities before he would piece together exactly what had gone on right under his nose.

Until that time he would congratulate himself on a job well done.

Denise was allowed to visit the sick girl on a regular basis. The fear everyone had experienced at Cathy's near demise had communicated itself to the residents of the Home and all were aware that, for once, they had the upper hand.

Food was plentiful, warmth was an everyday thing and the excessive punishments meted out were a thing of the past. Everyone knew it would not last and everyone was enjoying the respite while they could. No one more so than Denise.

As she looked down at the girl in the bed, she felt a tightening in her chest and realised it was a form of love.

Miss Henley and the others knew that Denise was the linchpin of the whole Home. That in her own way she worked with them to keep some kind of order; one word from her and there could be murder committed before their very eyes. Suddenly, the boot was on the other foot and, realising this, Denise milked it for all it was worth.

What Denise didn't know was that the guilty members of staff were already conspiring between them to remove both Cathy and herself from the Home as soon as was humanly possible.

Cathy opened her eyes and smiled gently. 'Me hands are still killing me.'

Denise winced. 'I bet they are, girl. They look painful even now.'

The tight bonds had cut off her circulation from the wrists. Eventually her hands had swollen badly and now, a week on, Cathy was losing her nails. The strange thing was, this was the most painful part of the whole ordeal.

'I hate having to be fed as well, I feel a right prat.' Cathy's voice was harder than before, her eyes more wary, but her small-boned body had an indomitable air that was obvious to any onlooker.

She had been through so much, in such a short space of time, that anything the world threw at her now would be as nothing. Unwittingly, Benton School for Girls had shaped the rest of her life.

Denise sensed this and was both elated and sorry. 'How long do you reckon then?' Denise's voice was low. Even though they were alone, neither was going to take any chance of being overheard.

'Another week and I'll be back on me pins. And then I want out.' Cathy's voice was wistful, the need to escape so strong she could almost taste it.

'Unlike me, see, you won't be pulled back in because you're not really supposed to be here anyway,' Denise whispered to her. 'I'll have to go right on the trot, me. South London is the last place I can go. I was thinking of Up West or even the North. Those twins, Maureen and Doreen, reckon I could make a good living up at a place called Lumb Lane in Bradford. Apparently it's really lucrative and all the women who work there look the business and have good pimps and everything.'

Her voice was strong and happy with the visions the twins' words had conjured up before her eyes. The thought of making plenty of money, and being in the company of real prostitutes again, was like a dream come true. Denise knew it was all she could expect from life. Even as a child she had accepted that for her, life would be a harsh struggle. It was how it had always been.

'You do realise what we have to do to get out, don't you?' she pressed.

Cathy nodded, her face clouding over for a moment, and then she smiled grimly. 'I'll do it and so will you. I'd do anything to escape this place.'

Both were quiet then, as if the enormity of what lay before them had rendered them both speechless.

Which was pretty much what had happened.

Mary Barton, for the first time in her life, was up against a brick wall.

A troublesome woman called Betty Jones had been asking all and sundry about the Connor child. She'd somehow found out about the initial scheme to foster her and kept asking why there had been no letters from or any news of the child. For the first time in her life, Mary was experiencing real fear.

Until Cathy Connor, she had done pretty much as she had pleased, both with the people she dealt with and the children she so cavalierly placed in homes, foster care or institutions. Now people wanted to know what was happening to her charges and she was having to justify herself. It was a sobering exercise.

Basically, like most bullies, Mary Barton was a coward.

She was happy when in complete control and lost once someone questioned her power.

Catherine Connor should never have been placed in Benton School for Girls and they all knew it. The little minx herself had actually had the effrontery to question her about the situation. Unheard of! No one ever questioned Mary Barton. It was like an eleventh Commandment, an unwritten law. But now everyone at work was querying her decisions and she was finding it difficult in the extreme.

How to explain why she'd placed the child here instead of with a private family? She had made out a report saying the child had attacked her and also Miss Henley. This was all it took normally. Now suddenly, the magistrate wanted to see the child for himself.

This Betty Jones was also causing untold trouble by offering the girl a home with her. As if Mrs Barton would allow a child to be put at risk in a house of ill repute, with a woman who sold her body to strangers for money! Miss Henley chose to forget the treatment meted out within Benton School for Girls by so-called respectable members of the establishment.

All in all, it was very worrying.

She found herself resenting the Connor girl more and more. She had never liked the child from the moment she had clapped eyes on her; now it seemed she might actually begin to hate her.

It was all the child's fault, of course. You did not bite the hand that fed and clothed you. It would be a hard lesson and the Connor child would learn it the hard way.

Of that Mary Barton was determined.

Once this little fiasco was sorted out, the girl was going into lock up in one of the more obscure mental establishments. That should take the leap out of her gallop.

*

Betty Jones's face was devoid of make-up and her hair was brushed into an unaccustomed bun. At first she had tried being herself, but as this seemed to get her nowhere she'd decided that the less like a whore she looked, the more chance she'd have of getting people to take her seriously. There was something up with Cathy; Social Services weren't being straight with her, she just knew it.

She'd decided to enlist the help of Richard Gates but all he could do was laugh at her changed appearance.

'I knew I recognised that face, but I couldn't place it. What on earth's the matter with you, woman? You look even worse than usual. You ain't joined the Salvation Army, have you?' He put back his head and roared with laughter once more.

Betty, forgetting what she was there for, snapped, 'Up yours, Gates. How dare you take the piss?' She stood up and made to walk out of the room. He stood up too and pulled her roughly back.

'Calm down, Betty. Be fair – you'd be shocked too if you saw me with a full head of hair and a Colgate smile, so it's the same difference, ain't it? Now, what can I do for you?'

Unlike his fellow policemen, Gates listened to anyone and everyone. You never knew where valuable information would come from next and he was a firm believer in taking all his sources seriously. Pillow talk had brought him more information than any amount of money. 'Even blaggers brag to brasses', was a favourite saying of his, and consequently he listened to them all.

Betty's face was still grim. Feeling magnanimous, he ordered them both tea and smiled at her. Betty allowed herself to be mollified.

'It's about Madge's girl – I heard through the grapevine that she's been fostered but now word is out that they've put her in some Home or other in Deal. Apparently it's a proper lock up. Well, she ain't done nothing so I can't understand why she's there. They won't let me see her, I've asked and asked.' She shrugged. 'You're me last resort.' She sipped her tea and warily watched the big man before her. If Gates gave her the heave-ho there was nothing left for her to try.

He stared at her for long moments. 'You don't half look rough, Betty. You wasn't all that great in your war paint, but now . . .'

Betty felt the sting of tears and Gates realised he'd gone too far.

'Come on, I was only joking. Lighten up, eh? Now, about little Cathy Connor . . . what's the full SP? She left the station with some hatchet-faced old bitch who was supposed to be taking her to a good foster home, apparently. How the hell did she come to be in a lock up?'

'Search me, Mr Gates. That's what I want to find out, see. I can't bear to think of her in one of them places – it ain't right after what she's been through, is it?' Betty could tell she had an interested audience in Gates. Finally she was going to get some help, even if it was just advice, and after the runaround of the last few weeks this in itself was a result.

Richard Gates's expression gave nothing away as he listened with growing concern to the plight of the girl he had already helped out of one very tight corner.

Cathy was amazed to see Denise by her bed at nine in the evening.

'How'd you get in here?'

Denise shook her head and pulled her up by her arms. 'Get dressed, we're out of here.'

Cathy's eyes widened in surprise. 'You what?'

'Miss Brown gave me the nod. I'm for the off tomorrow. If I get sectioned, I'm away for the duration. They're going to try and say we're not all the ticket. You'll be next, as soon as they think you can travel. We must go tonight!'

Cathy was frightened and it showed. She was still in pain from her fingers and had difficulty keeping her balance out of bed.

'Come on, Cathy, I'll help you. Let's just get a move on.'

The older girl helped her to dress, the urgency in her movements giving Cathy the impetus she needed to get herself moving.

'I've got keys to the front and back doors. All we have to deal with is the old fucker outside. We've already discussed that and I'm depending on you not to let any of it get you down. Just remember why we're doing it and you'll find the strength to tackle whatever has to be done. OK?'

Cathy nodded, and waited impatiently while her friend tied her shoelaces for her.

'Throw on your coat and get any personal things you want. We have about an hour to get shot.'

Cathy carefully dropped her few belongings into a paper bag then faced her friend resolutely. 'I'm frightened,' she admitted.

Denise's Oriental face looked grave, as if the wisdom of the ages was etched on it. 'I'm shitting meself too, if you want to know, but it's now or never as Ol' Elvis is always saying. Let's go. The Two Misses have both promised to be out of circulation until ten o'clock. That gives us an hour to be on our way. Down the back stairs and out the back will be easiest. You sure you can hack this?'

Cathy nodded. 'I ain't got much choice, have I?'

As they crept down the back stairs, darkness added to their mounting fright. But when they stepped into the brightness of the kitchen, the twins were waiting to urge them on.

'I've done you some sandwiches.' Maureen's voice was quivering with suppressed excitement. 'I only wish I had the guts to go with you both.'

Doreen was wide-eyed with excitement. 'We're going to start murders at ten o'clock in our dorm. We'll have the place jumping. You know what we're like when we have a fight. No one interferes.'

The twins grinned at one another in delight. Their fights were legendary, though they only ever fought one another.

'Thanks, girls. Look me up when you get out, OK? I'll see you both all right,' Denise promised.

This was said sincerely and the twins nodded.

'Take these, Cathy, they'll help your hands.' Doreen gave her a pair of woollen mittens. 'I nicked them off Henley.'

They all laughed.

'Now get yourselves through the back door and off. You'll get a lift, no trouble. Take care.'

The girls hugged each other, and suddenly Cathy was terrified of what waited for her outside the walls of Benton School for Girls. Like a man kept in prison for years and years, she found herself actually craving the comfort of the prison cell and fearing to leave it. After all, what was waiting outside could be even worse . . .

The cold air hit the two girls like a slap in the face. As they carefully locked the last door behind them, each took a deep breath. They were within the grounds now and that meant officially they were already runaways.

Both knew they had no chance of getting over the

fence. The only way out was to go through the front gate – which meant they had to deal with the Jailer. That was the nickname given to Barney Jennings. He was old by the girls' standards, being in his late-fifties. He was also the next worst thing to Hodges, being an incorrigible lecher. When he had to work inside the house itself, he had a nasty habit of trying to touch the girls, though most of his harassment of them was verbal. He would keep up a stream of filthy asides and innuendo.

The thing that really disgusted them about Barney was the fact that he had six fingers on each hand. Being gardener and odd job man, he often said that these were his green fingers, and made disgusting remarks to the girls about what those extra fingers could do. But getting past him was a doddle for older girls in the summer. When he knew they only had a few weeks left, for a small sexual favour he would let them out for the night.

The Two Misses also gave the girls who were about to leave more freedom than they would otherwise get, and if they were willing to service the old man in return for a few hours on the seafront, the warders turned a blind eye. It was the Two Misses' way of getting back at their employers and they turned a blind eye often enough to keep the Jailer a very happy man. Tonight, though, he would not be so amenable.

Denise was aware that Hodges and Barton would have explained the situation to him, and that he would be wary of losing the job he loved, even if they offered him sex.

The Jailer was inside the small lodge cottage as they knew he would be. As they came through his door he was drinking cocoa and reading the *Evening Standard*. The shocked look on his red-veined face told them all they needed to know.

Standing up, he began to bluster.

Denise pushed him back into his seat with a strength born of fear. 'Sit down, you old bastard, and shut your trap.'

Barney, a wiry man, strengthened by years of hard physical work, was wondering if he should retaliate when Denise pulled out a sharp knife.

Cathy's face was white with shock.

'I'll split you like a fucking pig, mate, from end to end. You just try and stop me and see what the fuck you get!' Denise's Oriental face was hard, eyes disappearing into their slanted sockets as she glared at the old man before her. 'They won't let me out anyway so I'll happily do more time for you, old son. Now give us the keys to the gate and we'll be on our way.'

She had not counted on his being the type who could not stand to be bested. No one put one over on Barney, he prided himself on that fact. Even in the war, Jerry had not got one over on Barney Jennings. The fact that he had bought and paid for his exemption certificate did not bother him one iota. While other men gave their lives for their country, he settled into a nice job out in Kent, without fear of raids, rationing or call-up papers.

If Denise had judged her man properly he would immediately have come to some kind of arrangement with them. But now he felt he had to do something. This chit of a girl was actually threatening him!

Smiling, he said pleasantly, 'Keep your hair on, girl. Let me see where I put me keys . . .' Standing, he played to perfection the part of an old man unsure where he'd put something. Placing his reading glasses on the arm of the overstuffed chair, he scratched his chin.

Denise and Cathy watched him warily.

'I know, girls, they're in my jacket pocket in the bedroom.' He began to walk towards Denise as if he was going to the bedroom. Instead he made a grab for her.

Without thinking, Cathy picked up a heavy ornament in one clumsy gloved hand and managed to hit Barney square on the skull with it. Denise saw the shocked look in the man's eyes before he crumpled on to the hearthrug. Shaking her head, she looked at the little figure before her and, laughing hysterically, said: 'You'll do.'

Cathy dropped the ornament, the pain in her hand excruciating. 'Is he all right?' Her voice was faint.

Denise nodded. 'Knocked out, that's all. I would have stabbed the fucker, I would. Just to get away from this fucking dump!'

Her hysteria had given way to choked-back tears. Finally collecting herself, Denise looked around the small cottage. It was comfortably furnished, and the rosy glow from the wood-burning fire made the place look jolly, cheerful even. It looked as if an old couple should live there, spending their twilight years chatting by the fire and eating home-made bread. It was a fairytale place.

The girls systematically turned it over without a second thought as they searched for money and valuables to keep them in food until they could start earning.

In an Ovaltine tin on a kitchen shelf Cathy found his hidden stash of money: ten five-pound notes secured with an elastic band. 'Here, look at this, Den.'

They split the money between them.

'This'll keep us going, my lovely.' Denise's face was alight with excitement.

Barney groaned.

Picking up the ornament, Denise thumped him once more.

'Denise, for fuck's sake!' The blow was very hard and as the man sank back on to the hearthrug, Cathy became scared.

'You could have killed him!'

Denise pushed him over on to his back with her toe. She stared at the Jailer for a few moments then, looking at her friend, said nastily, 'Fuck him. Fuck the lot of them. No one ever gave me nothing. I don't want nothing from them. I earned this every time I did Miss Henley her favours, every time I had Hodges bollocking me. I ain't learned much, but one thing I have learned is this: everyone wants to fuck you, girl, either physically or mentally. You have to put a limit on the shit you're willing to take and no turning back. I don't care if the old fucker does die. Why the hell should I? No one gives a toss about us, do they? Come on, let's get going. We've wasted enough time as it is.'

Five minutes later they were outside and running as if their lives depended on it.

The bright lights of Deal seafront looked welcoming. The rain began just as they hit the pier. A smell of fish and chips was tantalising and Cathy made to enter the chip shop, her hand automatically going to the money in her pocket.

Dragging her friend roughly away, Denise snapped: 'What are you, fucking stupid? If we go in there and crack a fiver it'll be all over Deal within half an hour. No, we make our way to the main road, we get in a lorry and then we concentrate on things like eating, sleeping and shitting, all right?'

Denise's sarcasm stung. Feeling small, Cathy followed her past the ruined castle and towards the road to London. She realised she was not as streetwise as she'd thought. Then again, she consoled herself, she had never been on the run before, so no wonder everything was new.

All she hoped was that she wouldn't make any more stupid mistakes like that. As they approached the road she thought of Eamonn and her heart gave a small lurch inside her chest. When he saw her, when she explained everything to him, she would be safe.

Cared for.

Loved.

Suddenly her hands were not so sore and the biting wind and rain weren't stinging her face as much. She felt a warm glow of anticipation, and, hurrying now, caught up with her friend.

Holding hands, they kept to the shelter of the roadside bushes, watching out for police cars and lorries. As they tramped through the mud, the two girls were quiet. Each was preoccupied with her own thoughts and each knew that until a lorry turned up and they were on board, they were still in grave danger.

Hodges, Henley and Barton would skin them alive and laugh while they did it if ever they set eyes on them again.

Derek Salmon was whistling along to Freddie and the Dreamers when he thought about his wife Abigail and the cheerful sound abruptly stopped. Suddenly 'How do you do what you do to me?' assumed a different significance. He switched off the radio and stared gloomily out into the dark night.

Abigail had left him six weeks previously for a sailor. She was a big accommodating woman of thirty-nine. Older than him by seven years, she had been the motherly type yet had loved sex. She would do anything sexual and enjoy every second of it.

Derek was small – wiry, he liked to call it – and afflicted with acne which had plagued him all his life. Abigail had not just been his wife, she had been everything to him: lover, friend, confidante. He had worked his arse off for her and now he was in digs and the sailor was snug in Derek's bed, with Derek's wife.

Life really was a bastard.

As he came off the docks and on to the main road he saw two girls hitching a lift. Normally he would have given them a wide berth. Plenty of drivers had been had over while giving a lift to young girls, threatened with the police and all sorts. But tonight the weather, his thoughts and the Freddie and the Dreamers song had made him feel lonely.

He stopped the lorry. Leaning out of the cab, he shouted, 'It stinks of fish, girls, but I'll take you as far as I can.'

Before he knew it the two girls were in his cab and he was smiling at them. 'You're drenched, loves.'

Denise instantly noted his kindly face and, wrinkling her nose against the smell in the lorry, asked sweetly: 'Got a fag, mate?'

Chapter Thirteen

Richard Gates was fuming.

It was ten-fifteen and he had just come off the phone to Social Services. The woman to whom he'd spoken, a Mrs Mary Barton, had not been at all forthcoming about Cathy Connor. After first wasting ten minutes establishing his bona fides as a policeman, she had then spent another ten telling him about the girl's supposedly aggressive behaviour. Eventually he had told her bluntly that if she did not tell him the real reason for Cathy's sojourn at Benton, he would come round to her house and personally shake it out of her, her husband, and any offspring such an unlikely union might have produced. This had reduced the woman to virtual apoplexy and the young WPC in the room with him and Betty to tears of laughter.

Finally he had been informed, in a decidedly offish manner, that if he would care to wait by the phone she would get someone at the school to ring him and explain the situation.

Slamming the phone down without even a 'Good evening,' he looked at the young WPC and then Betty and announced: 'This stinks. There's something not quite right going on here. According to that woman's superior, the girl was to have been taken to the Hendersons, whoever the fuck they are. According to Mary Barton, Cathy then attacked all and sundry and so was put into a secure unit.

'Now, I may be as thick as two short planks, but that little girl was incapable of fighting Muffin and the fucking Mule last time I saw her, and yet this bitch of a social worker reckons Cathy attacked her as they drove along.'

Betty looked flabbergasted.

The young WPC sighed heavily. 'I wish now I'd voiced me worries at the time, but to be fair, sir, we see this all the time, don't we? Kids being taken off willy-nilly. Barton looked a hard old cow but I thought she was taking the girl to a foster home. I never dreamed she would take her to a secure unit. I mean, even if the girl did attack her – and I have me doubts about that – Barton couldn't officially put her anywhere like that until the courts decided what to do with her. Cathy Connor would have had to be sentenced to be detained at Her Majesty's Pleasure, wouldn't she?'

Gates nodded. 'Yeah, she would. So how did she turn up at a secure unit that same night? There's something not right here and I'll find out what it is if I have to go to fucking Deal meself, tonight.'

Betty was scared and exhilarated all at the same time. She wanted to do the best for Cathy, who was a good kid, and now she had Gates behind her she felt much better. He was a man who managed to get things done – even if he did look like a reject from a Bela Lugosi film!

Denise was puffing away on a cigarette and chatting nineteen to the dozen with the lorry driver. Cathy kept quiet, smoking a Senior Service, quite happy for Denise to be the spokesperson. Lost in her own thoughts, trying to ignore the pain in her hands, she allowed Denise to monopolise the man and the conversation. The smell of fish was not so rife now they were used to it, and as the lorry travelled towards London Cathy felt her eyes growing heavy.

Denise was truly grateful to the man beside her, and even his acne and bad breath did not deter her. Being half Chinese and decidedly heavy, she knew she was never going to get the man of her dreams but this one, with his pleasant ways and kind heart, drew her in a way she had never experienced before.

She knew instinctively that they were safe with him. And coming from what they were used to, this in itself was a good feeling. He gave them cigarettes and kept up a stream of good-humoured banter as if they were long lost friends. Best of all, he didn't ask them any awkward questions.

Denise was well pleased with the way that things had turned out and as both girls warmed up and relaxed, she began to feel decidedly happy. They were on their way and they were safe.

Derek too was pleased. He liked the Chinese girl very much; she had a vulnerable look about her for all her size, and her chatter was interesting and funny. He saw the admiring glances she was throwing his way and smiled at her, knowing that this encounter was going to lead to much more and thanking his lucky stars he had had the foresight to stop and pick up the two girls.

Life was good again and big Abby was driven from his thoughts for good.

'Have another Senior Service, love,' he prompted Denise.

He was big-hearted and generous – just what the two runaways needed.

*

Mr Hodges was terrified to hear that not only had two of the girls escaped, but a Detective Constable from London was making enquiries by phone. Miss Henley had taken the call from a rattled-sounding Mary Barton and now she and Hodges himself were jumping out of their skin.

The Two Misses watched everything with quiet smiles and sat back to enjoy the show. Neither was in trouble, neither had done anything wrong; they were more interested in how the main actors in this squalid drama were going to extricate themselves from the mire.

All things considered it was turning into a good night all around.

Richard Gates took the call from Benton at just after eleven-thirty. Both the WPC and Betty listened avidly as he picked up the receiver.

'Detective Inspector Richard Gates here. Who's this I'm speaking to?' His voice was terse and aggressive. '. . . Mr Hodges, do you say? Could you spell that for me, please? I'd very much like to have everything accurately noted down for my report in the morning.'

He smiled at the two women and continued: 'What report? Why, my report to the court, of course. I realise that a mistake has been made and as the girl started off in my care, I intend to see that the mistake is rectified as soon as possible.'

He sighed theatrically and went on, 'Nice little thing, is Cathy. I've known her since she was a child. I understood she was to go to the Henderson family – can't understand what she's doing in a secure unit. Even you must find that strange, surely? Unless, of course, you can shed further light on the matter for me, such as court dates for assault charges, etc . . . No? Well, in that case I might just come down and pick the girl up myself. Save your Mrs Barton a job.'

As he listened to the shifty-sounding Hodges spluttering out excuses and trying to defend his actions, Gates lit himself a cigarette and sat back in his chair, totally relaxed.

Hodges was all over the place. Cathy could be removed as soon as Gates liked.

Betty, grinning from ear to ear, was wondering when they would be able to go and get the poor mite. She was looking forward to having her home again.

Cathy woke up as they made their way into North London. Denise was giggling and Cathy grinned back at her.

'Where are we?' she asked sleepily.

Denise's expression altered and Cathy realised the laughter had been shared with the lorry driver, not her.

'Look, Cath, I know this ain't part of the bargain, but I'm going to get you dropped off in Soho. All right?'

Cathy stared at her friend, puzzled. 'What do you mean?'

Denise closed her eyes and swallowed deeply before answering: 'Well, Derek here reckons he can get me set on in a proper job. So the best thing for you is to go to Soho. I've explained the whole thing to him and we both think you should keep away from the East End, at least for a few days. Let's face it, it'll be the first place they look, won't it? I mean to say, whether you should have been locked up or not, until we know what old Barton's done, we can't really relax, can we?

'Leave it a few days and then go round to where you used to live like. See how the land lies. They'll watch all your old haunts, the Old Bill. I can tell you, I know. I've been this route before.'

Cathy stared at her friend without really comprehending what she was saying. 'Where are you going then?' Her hands were aching again and she felt tired and cold.

'Like I said, I'm going with Derek here.'

Denise's face was sheepish, Derek Salmon's open and smiling. He couldn't really see what all the hag was about. As he drove he kept glancing over at the two girls, smiling at them until even Cathy found herself smiling back.

'But *where* are you going?' she persisted.

Denise sighed. 'Up North with him. He's dropping this lot off here then he's going for some more fish from a place called Grimsby, all right? What are you, the fucking police?'

It was said in a joking way but Cathy got the point all right. Denise had found herself a bloke and now it was every girl for herself.

'But what will I do in Soho?' Cathy's voice was desolate. 'I won't know anyone or anywhere.'

Denise laughed heartily. 'You've got twenty-five bleeding quid, you dozy-looking cow! You can go where the fuck you like.'

Denise was trying hard to jolly her along but could see Cathy's confusion and alarm. Her own eyes were sad as she said: 'I hate to drop you in it like this, mate, I really do but I've got meself a chance here, you know, a fresh start like. You're welcome to come too, if you want?'

Cathy shook her head. She knew that the offer was made out of residual friendship and loyalty which would be overstretched if she accepted. She closed her eyes and tried to smile.

'I forgot about the money.'

Denise grinned. 'How could you forget that? A small fortune.'

The two girls chatted more happily then but an hour later Cathy was standing alone in Oxford Street, with twenty-five pounds in her pocket and a heavy heart. As she waved off her friend she felt lonelier than she had ever done in her life. Walking along, she saw a sign for Dean Street and followed the road. It should take her into Soho; any road along here would, Denise had told her.

Carrying her few possessions, Cathy made her way in the dark and the cold towards the place where she hoped to find bright lights, food and drink, and a bed for the night.

Her hands were sore, her heart was too, but as cold and desolate as she felt, she knew she was on her way to a better life. Anything, *anything* in the world, would be better than Benton School for Girls.

Mr Hodges was terrified into silence and only a large brandy and Miss Henley's agitated twittering brought him round again.

'We're all finished, the lot of us. This policeman, this DI Gates, is coming here in the morning for Connor.'

Miss Henley shook her head in disbelief. 'But she's gone, didn't you explain to him? The police here have been notified, he'll find that out . . .'

Jumping up from his seat, Hodges roared: 'I'm fucking well aware of that, woman, but what the hell else could I do? The girl should never have been here in the first place, we all know that. Now it's up to Barton to sort this out and smooth things over. If she doesn't we're finished. All of us.'

Mary Barton's husband was usually an amiable man, cursed by a domineering wife but of the opinion that it was worth giving her free rein for a quiet life at home.

A High Court judge, Mr Justice Barton was nicknamed Unjust Barton – a nickname he was secretly proud of. He also prided himself on his handlebar moustache, his neatly brushed steel grey hair, and above all his firm hand with the criminal classes. He could intimidate a witness or counsel for the prosecution with equal ease and effectiveness.

His whole life was a game, a big happy game, and he saw everyone else as mere pawns. Even his flat-chested, bullet-nosed shrew of a wife.

Tonight, after partaking freely of a twelve-year-old malt at his club and enjoying the ministrations of a young friend, a lovely boy with blond good looks and a mouth like a vacuum cleaner, all he really wanted was to sleep. His wife, however, wouldn't let him.

The phone was ringing constantly and her high-pitched voice kept intruding on his slumber. Now, God damn her, she was telling him to get up in the no-nonsense voice she usually reserved for menials.

'Bugger off, woman, and leave me alone. I have a heavy day tomorrow. Leave a man be, can't you?' His voice became a roar and his wife flinched.

It was the look of sheer terror on her face which made him sit up and take notice. Mary was a lot of things, but timid and scared did not automatically spring to mind when thinking of her. Tonight, however, she looked dreadful.

'What's the matter? Is it one of the children?' he asked, alarmed. 'For Christ's sake, woman, what's wrong?'

Mary Barton started to cry and this alone was enough to bring her husband from his twin bed to hers. 'Oh, I've been a very naughty girl, but I was only trying to help those nice Hendersons . . .'

Mr Justice Barton looked at his wife as if he had never seen her before. Then, sighing, he took her into his arms. 'Come along, Mary. Tell me what you're wittering on about, woman, and I'll try and sort it out for you.'

He waited with baited breath for her to explain what all the bloody rumpus was about, his little blond friend in the forefront of his mind. Please God, she hadn't found out about that.

But as she started talking he began to relax. It was nothing to do with him, thank Christ. In fact, secretly, listening to his wife's dilemma, he felt a flicker of satisfaction. If he helped her out of this mess, she might just be a little bit more amenable in future.

Mary Barton, bitch of a woman, bugger of a wife and scourge of the Social Services, had dropped a prime bollock.

He could get a good bit of mileage out of this and intended to do just that.

Mary's tear-blotched face looked up at her husband's and both knew exactly what the other was thinking.

Nevertheless, they kept on playing the game. It was their idea of a civilised marriage.

Cathy walked through the door of a small Soho cafe. Finding a table as close to the heater as she could, she ordered herself a coffee and some toast and sat down to think.

Her hands were throbbing with pain and, taking the mittens off gingerly, she surveyed her fingers with horror. Most of her nails had fallen out and the open skin beneath was very sore.

When the Greek man behind the dingy counter noticed the state of them, he shook his head sadly.

'Stay there, sweetheart. I'll bring your order over to you. What you had – an accident of some kind? I'd say those need looking at by a doctor. Go on, sit back and get yourself warm.'

Gratefully she settled in her seat while the man brought over the coffee and toast.

'Let me have a little look, I won't hurt you.'

She was the only person in the coffee bar and was nervous because of it. He sensed this and laughed, his big round face alive with friendliness.

'Don't worry, I don't eat up little girls any more – I just nibble on their fingers.'

Cathy was startled into a smile by his banter and he smiled back at her, displaying large, uneven but very white teeth. He examined her hands and tutted. Holding her wrists gently, he said: 'You been tied up, girl?'

Tears stung her eyes and she shook her head. 'No, 'course not. I ain't been well, that's all.'

The man stared at her for a long while. Then: 'I don't think you should have them bandaged, they'll benefit more from the air, but you must keep them very clean, you understand me?'

Cathy nodded.

'You smell like an old fishmonger, girl. You need a bath and a change of clothes and a good rest by the look of it. Drink your coffee and eat up, I'll talk to you later.'

As he spoke, the door opened and two women came in. Cathy recognised them both at once as prostitutes. They had the same way about them as Madge had done. They gave her a cursory glance and sat themselves down, chatting and laughing happily.

Cathy ate her toast in peace and sipped at the hot coffee. She could feel her body gradually warming up but the pain in her hands had become almost unbearable.

The Greek man brought over two white pills and told her to take them, they would ease the pain. She took them without even asking what they were. Her hands were so sore she would have taken anything.

He also brought her over another coffee and she smiled at him gratefully. Pulling out her money she offered a five-pound note. He closed his eyes in distress, noticing the sidelong glances from the two prostitutes at the other table.

'What the hell are you doing, girl? Put that money away,

for Christ's sake. You're asking to get rolled. Those two would kill their own mothers for a few pounds.'

Seeing the frightened look on her face, he relented and, sitting beside her, said gently, 'Look – you're in Soho and you look like a runaway. I see them all the time. They come here thinking they'll have a good life, that things will be better for them here. Well, they very rarely are. You're just a little girl. All you can do to supplement your cash is sleep with men. You understand? Now, whatever you have run from, it can't be any worse than what you'll find here. So drink your coffee, it's on the house, then get yourself back to wherever it is you came from. Listen to me: I know what I'm talking about.'

Cathy heard him out then shrugged at the end of his speech. He obviously talked this way a lot; the words had a practised edge to them.

'I'm only staying a few days and then I'm going to some friends,' she said.

The cafe owner smiled sadly. 'I've heard that before. You sit there and get nice and warm. I'm open all night, I don't mind if you stay here. All I ask is that you think about what I said, eh?' He smiled and Cathy smiled back. 'I have a friend you might want to meet, a lady with a small boarding house. I can ring her if you like, my dear. She owes me a favour anyway.'

Cathy smiled widely. 'Thank you so very much, Mr . . .'

The big man nodded happily. 'Tony Gosa – they call me Tony Gosa.'

'Thank you, Mr Gosa. I appreciate your help.'

He stood up abruptly as the door opened once more, bringing in more prostitutes and a large African man dressed in a white suit and a leather stetson.

Cathy drank her coffee; the pain in her hands was receding and she finally relaxed, looking at the exotic people around her with interest. The women chatted and laughed, their perfume ripe and heavy as it wafted towards her. It reminded her of how *she* must smell, and indeed look, after the ride in the fish lorry. If she could get a bed for the night and a bath, a change of clothes and a rest, she would be fit and well enough to track down Eamonn. That was her main priority.

She knew she must keep away from the East End for a few days as Denise had warned her, but the money in her pocket would at least ensure her a place to stay.

Tony Gosa, the ever-genial host, brought her over a third cup of coffee and waved away any suggestion of payment. He looked sad-eyed and upset on her behalf and she felt relieved to have encountered such a sympathetic person.

Alone and frightened, a friend was just what she needed.

Duncan Goodings was fifty-seven years old, a rotund man with a ready smile and steely blue eyes. He was as fat as his sister, Mary Barton, was thin. He was also a much more resolute character than her, and even their own parents had conceded that that made him at once a strong and an irritating personality.

He had been summoned to his sister's house by her husband and had arrived formally dressed in his usual three-piece suit, making Mr Justice Barton wonder if there was any truth in the popular belief that the fellow never slept. He looked as awake and well groomed as any normal man did at nine in the morning on his way to the City.

Fortunately for Mary, her husband was perhaps the only person who could intimidate Duncan Goodings. Whether it was the judge's sheer size, his imposing appearance or his uncanny knack of grasping the underlying truth of any situation, Duncan wasn't sure. All he knew was, his brother-in-law was demanding he help out his sister, and help her out in record time, or he would want to know why.

Taking the large Scotch offered to him by his horse-faced bitch of a sister, Duncan tried unsuccessfully to smile. His face felt as if it would crack from the effort. Being summoned here in the middle of the night, leaving his young wife alone in bed, was not his idea of fun. Not that there had ever been many laughs to be had in this house. His sister's own children had abandoned the imposing residence as soon as they had finished university. Duncan sympathised with them. Anything would be better than living with these two.

'So what's all this about then?' The smug look on his brother-in-law's face spoke volumes and Duncan listened with growing uneasiness to his sister's rambling story. He'd known all along he should have stayed in bed with BiBi, his young, skinny, but very versatile Eurasian wife.

He had put heart and soul into rising to the top of the social work profession and now knew without a doubt that he was being asked to do something that was both illegal and immoral. For all his faults, and he knew they were legion, he had never in his life abused his position of trust. In fact, he prided himself on his integrity and fairness towards his subordinates.

Yet, as he listened to Mary's squalid little tale of power abused, he could see a way of turning it to his own advantage. This could be the very thing he needed to keep his sister out of his hair. Sometimes it was very hard to have to do what she asked, such as coming to dinner without his beloved BiBi, and pretending that she didn't even exist.

Yes, on reflection, this could all be turned to the good. Actually smiling now, aware that they needed him far more than he did them, he said, 'And this policeman, what's his name again?'

Both his sister and her husband knew when they were cornered and had the grace to look just the smallest bit ashamed.

Duncan Goodings had already made a mental note to get rid of the principal offenders in this drama quickly and without any publicity, especially Hodges, Henley and his own sister. All in all, this wasn't turning into such a bad night after all.

Smiling once more, he held out his glass for a refill of Scotch, and was gratified to see both his sister and her husband jump out of their seat in their eagerness to be hospitable.

Cathy was grateful to Tony Gosa, and so pleased to have made a friend in her first few hours in the West End that she followed him to the boarding house quite happily. As he led her through a maze of streets, she felt tired yet exhilarated. When he flagged down a cab she went with him without a second thought.

At three forty-five in the morning she walked through the door of a dilapidated building off Fulham Broadway. A large Greek woman welcomed her with open arms and relieved her of her bundle and her coat.

Mama Gosa was huge. Rolls of quivering fat undulated each time she moved and her chins wobbled happily as she exclaimed over and petted the small figure before her.

'Such a little thing, Tony. She needs food and warmth, yes?'

Cathy ate a large bowl of stew and afterwards was stripped and put into a steaming bath before she knew what was happening. Mama Gosa's hands were surprisingly gentle as she carefully washed Cathy's hands and helped her clean herself.

After another two white pills and a clean nightdress had

been given to her, she was settled in front of a roaring fire in the small front room. Mama Gosa left her there and told her to relax and maybe have a little sleep. She would be back later.

As Cathy lay on the rather dirty settee, she pondered on her good luck. Her hands were feeling much better and she was clean and fed. Thanks to Madge and her earlier life, Cathy knew that she had to watch out for herself, knew the pitfalls of being alone, yet she trusted these two foreign people.

Glancing around the room, she saw faded brown wallpaper and heavy oak furniture. On the walls hung icons and pictures of a dark-eyed scowling man in a big black hat. She sensed he was religious in some way, he had that heavily pious expression they all shared. In her short life, most people who looked like that had tried to tuck her up.

Satisfied that she had sussed out the situation, Cathy lay there and basked in the luxury of freedom and warmth.

The pills were making her light-headed and she felt her eyes closing. Her last thought before she fell asleep was of Eamonn and the joy on his face when he realised she was home at last. That she had come home for him.

Until she dared go in search of him, she would enjoy all that the Gosas had to offer. It didn't occur to her to wonder where her belongings were or, more importantly, her money.

Chapter Fourteen

Richard Gates was awake and contemplating whether to have a full cooked breakfast or black coffee and toast. As it did every morning, the full cooked breakfast won. Unconsciously rubbing the two large scars on his belly, he made his way naked to the kitchen.

The scars were a constant reminder to him of how close to death he had once come. Knifed when still a young PC, he had survived against heavy odds. The person who had knifed him had not come off so well, but Gates had stopped thinking about him years ago.

He had strong muscular arms and legs, and his stomach was heavy, full and surprisingly firm. The muscles having been slashed, he knew he would never look like Johnny Weissmuller again. But what the fuck? As he always thought – with his offbeat looks it didn't make one iota of difference.

Pulling a towel around him, he put the kettle on and picked up his mail, promptly throwing it all in a drawer. He looked at his letters only every few months or so. After all, why meet trouble head on? He rarely received anything of interest, only circulars and bills. He wasn't really close enough to anyone for personal mail.

As the bacon and tomatoes sizzled away, he walked through to his front room and turned on the radio. He liked noise around him in the mornings.

His flat was very tidy, and this fact always amazed people. It had a pristine cleanliness, almost like an operating theatre. The walls were painted white, he had a few good books, and his record collection was considered both weird and amazing by his few friends, containing everything from Burt Bacharach to the Stones. The carpet was deep brown, and there were two brown corduroy-covered two-seater sofas with brown Perspex arms. A large glass coffee table devoid of any clutter except for an ashtray finished off the room.

Not a photograph or personal memento to show who lived here. It looked like a room still waiting for its owner to stamp his personality upon it. Only his kitchen looked even remotely lived in. Gates loved to cook, had always loved to cook, and his pots and pans, recipe books and jars of spices, gave the flat its only touch of character.

He had a Belling electric stove with four large rings. It was the most expensive item in the flat and the most used. He also had an eight-track cassette which he played when one of his marathon cook-outs came over him.

Unlike his peers he didn't feel the need to enthuse about the Beatles or the other top groups. He liked what he liked, and his dealings every day with what he termed 'the scum of the earth' made him the highly individual man he was.

His small flat was his haven, his refuge from the maelstrom of work. He protected it accordingly.

The only other thing of note he possessed was his car, a large black Zephyr which he adored.

His sole concession to the fashions of his time were the wide kipper ties he wore, and even these were rapidly going out of style. Gates would stubbornly carry on wearing his. He had hundreds and he loved them.

A very private person, he knew he was considered strange by other people. But he could live with that and enjoyed his solitary life.

As he smoothed down his thin close-cropped hair and waited for the weather forecast, the phone rang. Swearing under his breath, he looked ruefully at his breakfast and went out into the hallway.

No one who knew him well would dare call him at home before ten o'clock. This had to be work, either a murder or a decent attempt at one. At the very least it had better be an armed robbery, nothing else would be allowed to spoil his breakfast.

In fact, the caller was Duncan Goodings and it was just as well he was unaware of the type of man he had to deal with. His nerves had never been Duncan's strongest point.

Cathy awoke and wondered where she was. A heavy smell of bacon was permeating the room and her stomach rumbled in sympathy. She was starving.

The fire was banked up and rain was hitting the windows with a steady rat-tat that was strangely reassuring. Stretching, she sat up and looked about her. In the cold light of day the room looked dilapidated, furniture and walls scuffed, carpet threadbare in places; but with the cheerful fire aglow it didn't look so bad. She had lived in worse, much worse, all her life.

As Cathy pushed her hair from her face with fingers that were feeling less painful, the door opened and Mama Gosa came in with a cup of tea.

'You look much better. Drink this up and I'll fetch your

few bits. I'm sure you want to get dressed and be on your way, yes?'

Cathy smiled and took the tea gratefully, her blue eyes open and trusting.

'You're looking quite bright this morning. A good sleep and a hot bath were just the things to get you on your feet, yes? Show me your poor hands and I'll see if we can do any more for you.'

Cathy put her cup on the floor and held out her hands. Though red and sore-looking, they really had improved and she and the Greek woman smiled at one another.

'Much better, yes? Now I have made you a nice big breakfast to see you on your way, so drink up and come and eat.'

Cathy was nonplussed for a moment. 'Must I leave today? I can pay – I have money.'

Mama Gosa grinned. 'We'll see, yes?'

She left the room and Cathy sipped at the tea and pondered her situation. This setup suited her. If she could camp out here for a few days, get her hands in better shape and have a much-needed rest, she would be able to face the world looking and feeling better than she had in a very long time.

She had an idea that her twenty-five pounds would come in very handy.

Suddenly it hit her that she was in effect on the run, and the unfairness of her situation stung. In just under four weeks she had been through more than most people endure in a lifetime. Yet, she consoled herself, she was still standing. She was still here, and she was coping. Admittedly, it was difficult to keep body and soul together at times, but she was making sure that she did.

Life with Madge had prepared her for the worst, and if you expected the worst anything other than that was a bonus – like this place. Denise and her knowhow had been a bonus too, and of course Eamonn was the very best bonus life could offer.

Following the smell of bacon and eggs, she made her way through the house to the kitchen. Her natural alertness was returning, together with her strength, and it occurred to her that there was really no reason why the two Greeks should give her their time and hospitality. Maybe she would be asked for something in return? No matter. She would cross that bridge when she came to it. She just hoped against hope that all they would want was money.

Smiling pleasantly, she went into the kitchen and began to eat her breakfast. The food was good and hot, the kitchen filthy. It didn't bother Cathy in the least. She knew she needed her strength and her wits about her. Hopefully she would recover both these things in this funny-looking refuge in Fulham.

Eamonn was still asleep and snoring when Patsy Fullerton crept from the bed. She was on the wrong side of thirty, with enormous breasts and backcombed bleached hair that made her look like a reject from a *Carry On* film.

As she struggled into her underwear and a very grubby Mary Quant mini-dress that did not really suit her short stubby legs, she watched the boy in the bed and shook her head in wonder. Three times, straight off, and not one word had he spoken to her. He was a funny little fucker.

Still, she reasoned, he was doing all right, had a few quid to fling about, and didn't spend half the night telling you all his troubles. She often joked that her job was more a line of therapy really. Most punters wanted a captive audience to listen to their woes more than they wanted an actual woman.

If they paid for oral sex they never kept their mouths shut, before, during or after the event. It pissed her off.

Still, she had her money safely tucked into her bag and had had a good night out with the young man asleep in the bed. That in itself was a touch as far as she was concerned. Normally she was lumbered with some old bastard with greasy hair, a greasier smile and even greasier money – usually not quite enough to pay for all the services she'd rendered.

Which didn't really bother her because at the end of the day, if you kept the fuckers happy then they'd come back, which was what her job was all about.

Her pimp was big, black and liked the good life. She provided it for him, along with a few other girls, and was quite happy to do so. Why, she didn't even know herself and had long ago stopped trying to puzzle it out.

She had no illusions that the boy in the bed would ever want her services regularly, although she had heard he was gradually going through every whore in London. And besides that she knew damn well he was being seen out and about with a regular bird called Caroline Harvey, daughter of a well-known 1950s face.

Funny then, that when he'd lost himself in the oblivion that Patsy provided and called out a girl's name, she had distinctly heard him say 'Cathy'. Girlfriend or no, Caroline Harvey was out of the running with Eamonn Docherty, did she but know it.

Caroline Harvey was small, plump and had the biggest violet-blue eyes anyone had ever seen in a woman. People were always saying her eyes reminded them of Elizabeth Taylor's. She mascaraed her lashes religiously, knowing they would enhance her best feature. Her breasts were small but full and her waist thick; she had long legs which she covered always in black stockings to hide the stretch-marks from a pregnancy when she was fourteen.

Her dark brown hair was cut in the latest style and she wore clothes that accentuated her figure. She knew what suited her, she knew what to say, and she knew exactly what was going on around her. She made a point of doing so.

All in all she was pleased with herself, very pleased with herself. More so since she had bagged Eamonn Docherty. He was an up-and-coming face and she loved the notoriety she earned by being seen with him.

At this moment, though, he was in her bad books. He had left her in a club the previous night and she had quickly arranged to stay at a friend's. She would never admit what she had in fact guessed: that Eamonn had simply forgotten her. Caroline couldn't actually bring herself to acknowledge that. Instead, she made her way home, encountering Patsy on the stairs of her lodging house.

The two women stared at one another. Patsy, knowing the score, grinned easily. 'He's a wanker, love.'

Caroline laughed good-naturedly. 'I know, but ain't they all?'

As she let herself into her flat she was smiling. Let Eamonn have his other birds. As long as the money kept coming her way, she didn't give a toss. All she wanted out of life was enough to spend, a hot cock and a bit of fun. She was also shrewd enough to put money by, something her mother had taught her years before.

'Never depend on no one but yourself' had been a constant theme, along with: 'If a man can't give you more than you can give yourself, then dump him.'

Both sayings had since been proven right, time and time again.

Plastering a big smile on her face Caroline said, 'What on earth happened to you last night?'

Eamonn, grinning sheepishly, replied, 'Sorry, babe, it was just one of those things, you know?' His voice begged forgiveness yet managed to convey impatience all at the same time.

Caroline shrugged. Pouting prettily she said, 'Well, don't let it happen again.'

When Eamonn had eaten his breakfast he told Caroline they were going flat hunting together. As far as Eamonn was concerned it was a purely temporary arrangement. But he didn't bother telling Caroline that and her happiness was complete.

Betty's flat was small and very clean, a fact that always surprised people when they first entered it. Unlike most of her contemporaries, she liked order and neatness. She reasoned there was enough shit to cope with in her everyday work; she didn't need it at home. Where most of the whores would go mad in their free time, buying up the markets and drinking themselves into a happier frame of mind, Betty was quite happy to scrub out her little flat, cook herself a nice meal and listen to the radio. Victor Sylvester was a favourite and she listened to *Housewife's Choice* every day. On a Sunday it was *Letter from America*, and of an evening she tried to be home for *Mystery Voice*.

Besides being clean and tidy, the flat was also relatively smart. The furniture, though second-hand, was good. Her two large wardrobes were her pride and joy. She had picked them up in Camden Market for a fiver. They were yew, had shined up a treat, and were fitted with everything from a full-length mirror to shoe racks. Her clothes looked lovely in them and Betty would often open the doors just to peek at her possessions.

This morning she opened her front door to Richard

Gates and smiled at the look on his face as he surveyed his surroundings.

'You've got it nice here, Betty.'

She grinned and preened herself with satisfaction. 'Thank you very much. Never was one for bringing me work home, know what I mean? Cup of tea, coffee?'

Ordinarily he would not have accepted anything in a brass's house, but today was the exception to the rule.

'Coffee would be lovely, thanks.'

He followed her through to the kitchen. Betty walked lightly in old carpet slippers, keeping her back very straight. It made him wonder what she had been like as a girl. She was delighted to have such an illustrious visitor and kept up a stream of chatter.

'I done this place all myself, you know. Over the years I looked about and found a few nice pieces. But my forte, if you like, is collecting thimbles.' She laughed at herself, and Gates didn't have it in his heart to laugh with her.

'You're a nice woman, Betty, do you know that? Probably have made some man a good wife.'

She shook her head in instant denial. 'I don't think so, Mr Gates. I've been tomming since I was twelve – takes the shine off all that, really. I'm happy enough with my life. I work to live these days, mate. I close me front door, and have my little bit of home and my radio and my thoughts. They're enough for me.' She sipped at her coffee in embarrassment for a moment after these revelations, then remembered the reason for his visit.

'So what's happening with Cathy? When are we off to get her?'

Gates walked through to her tiny front room. Perching himself precariously on one of her Queen Anne chairs, he said, 'Cathy went on the trot last night from that secure. I had some bigwig from Social Services on the phone. By his account she was aggressive and violent, something I don't believe, but no matter. The social worker who dumped her there – that old bag Barton – well, her old man's a judge. Like I give a flying fuck! Judges, street cleaners, they're all the same to me.

'But anyway, the bottom line is they're all well protected and we can't do fuck all. I even had a call from the Commissioner of Police, telling me politely to leave things alone. There's a big con going on and at some point in me life I'll find out what it is and have each and every one of them by the bollocks. But that's for later on, when I start me digging. For now I know they're all shitting bricks and that suits me.

'Officially Cathy went missing last night with another girl, Denise something or other, a half chat chink. Already on the bash, already on the ball. There's a Missing Persons out and that's it. I'm here both officially and unofficially because we're being asked nicely by the police in Deal to keep an eye out in the East End. They think Cathy'll make her way back here.

'It stinks like a pile of horseshit on your front-room carpet. I'll get to the bottom of it, lady, you can trust me for that much. And when I do, someone is going to wish that their mother had had access to the fucking pill on the night they were conceived!'

It was the longest she had ever heard him speak, and was the most emotional speech she had ever heard from anyone.

Looking round her little front room, with its displays of thimbles all neatly set out on shelves, and her few leather-bound books, Betty felt the sting of tears. Cathy would have loved it here, adored it.

They had always got on, Betty had always cared for the child. With Madge banged up she had seen herself inheriting a mother's status and had looked forward to it. Now the girl had gone missing and anything could have happened to her.

'I'll make sure that everyone keeps an eye out for her,' Gates continued. 'I reckon she'll make her way back here, don't you, Betty?'

She nodded sadly. 'If for no one else, she'll come back for Eamonn Docherty. She loves the bones of that boy.'

Gates frowned. 'Stupid little bitch! Can't she see that he's worse than his father? Christ, she must have more of her mother in her than I thought. By the way, any idea who the girl's father is?'

Betty laughed then, really laughed. 'Madge used to call her "Heinz Fifty-seven". Wicked, I know, but it was true enough. Madge had no idea whatsoever. She wasn't even sure what colour the baby would be. Madge is a big girl, and didn't realise she was carrying till she was nearly five and a half months. By then there was no chance of finding anyone who'd take responsibility, and no one the girl can run to now. Other than Eamonn, his dad or me.'

Gates nodded. 'Well, there's something not right anyway. I've had all the big guns down on me and that's a bit excessive for a thirteen-year-old runaway. A lot of people have had to go to a lot of trouble to sort this out, and I for one want to know why.'

'So do I, Mr Gates, sir,' Betty said sincerely, 'so do I.'

Mama Gosa watched the girl as she discreetly searched through her few belongings. The Greek woman's smile stayed fixed firmly in place. As the girl once more felt the lining of her coat, hoping against hope that the twenty-five pounds would miraculously reappear, the woman edged her nearer the door.

'What's wrong, eh?' Her smile was dangerous now and

Cathy saw this and sighed. She had been well and truly had over.

Looking at the woman face on she said heavily, 'Where's me money?'

Mama Gosa kept her lined face open and her eyes wide. 'What money? I don't know nothing about any money.'

Cathy stared the woman down. 'Me twenty-five quid. I had twenty-five quid and now it's gone and I want it, all right?'

For the first time the woman became uneasy. The little girl looked positively menacing for a moment.

Suddenly, everything caught up with Cathy. The last four weeks had taken a lot out of her. But she wasn't going to be robbed blind for nothing more than a hot meal and a few treacherous smiles. Standing up to the woman, she yelled: 'Where's me fucking money, you old cow? I want me fucking money! And if I don't get it soon, I'll wake the whole fucking neighbourhood. Now, where is it?'

Instinctively she picked up a breadknife from the table nearby. She looked down at it in her hand then into the frightened face of the woman before her and the rage left her body as abruptly as it had arrived.

Throwing the knife away from her, she sat down heavily, put her head into her hands and began to cry. The abject misery of her sobs made even the woman who had robbed her feel a slight twinge of regret for what she had done.

Cathy snatched up her things. She went back into the front room, took off the nightie and began to get dressed in her own clothes. Back in the kitchen, she looked at Mama Gosa and shook her head sadly.

'Lady, I hope you get what you deserve, I really do. One day you'll have over the wrong person and they'll really pay you back. When I tell me boyfriend what you've done he'll be very angry – and I'll tell him exactly where you live, hear me, and take him to your son's cafe. Either way, I'll see justice done.'

Picking up her bundle, she walked slowly from the room. She half expected something to hit her on the head or the back of the neck, but the woman let her go without a word.

At the front door Cathy turned and said, 'That was a very expensive bed and breakfast, and the funny thing is, I'd have given you the money anyway just to be able to stay. You stole it for nothing. All for nothing.'

Stepping outside into the coldness of the November day, she pulled her coat tighter around her and began to walk. People rushed past her, their days busy, lives ordered and purposeful. She wandered aimlessly along until she came to the North End Road market. She was cold and it was difficult to carry her things in a paper bag. She stole two jumpers and a small handbag.

Whatever happened, she had to get to the East End and she had to get there now. She couldn't afford to do any more hiding out – the Gosas had put paid to that.

As the rain began to fall heavily she felt the sting of tears and brushed them away. Crying was no good, it achieved nothing. She had done all the bloody crying she was going to do. Crying was for prats, and people with the time and the money and the comfort to indulge themselves. She had none of these things so she'd have to wait until she had. Then, she reasoned, she'd cry all day and all night in front of a nice fire, breaking off now and again for lovely hot drinks and the occasional delicacy. The thought made her smile gently.

She was learning, finally, what life was all about, and though it hurt it was also comforting. Because she'd learned now that facing the unknown was the scariest thing of all. She'd faced up to it at Benton and last night on the streets of Soho. Met it head on and won through. And now that the unknown no longer held such terrors for her, she was free to turn back, to the world she knew – the East End streets that she called home. Never mind if the police were looking out for her. She'd friends there, hadn't she, and a boyfriend who must be missing her madly.

Chapter Fifteen

Eamonn Senior sat in Betty's neat little flat and looked around him in amazement. A message telling him to come and see her as soon as he could had brought him here. For the first time in his life he'd stepped over the threshold of the woman he detested and Betty was pleased by the expression on his face.

'Jasus, Betty, you have the place gorgeous.' His voice was filled with reluctant admiration and the little woman smiled.

'Madge always liked it here. But I was never really one for other visitors, if you know what I mean.' He did and grinned to acknowledge what she was saying.

'What's happening with Cathy then?' he asked abruptly.

Betty lit a cigarette. Blowing out smoke, she said, 'She's gone on the trot and even Gates don't know where she is or why she went running. From what I can gather, some old bitch from the Social Services took her to a secure unit. Now they're all spouting a load of old fanny about the child being violent and dangerous or some such crap, but the bottom line is they screwed up and so now she's out there somewhere and we have to wait until she gets in touch.

'The Social Services want her back too and from what I gather, they'll lock her up and throw away the key if they get their hands on her, so if we do see her we have to help her and get her away as quick as we can.'

Eamonn listened in growing amazement. 'What the feck is all this shite about violent and dangerous? Are they sure they have the right person?'

Betty nodded her head in agreement. 'It's all mad, I know, but by all accounts they – her and this young girl she went on the trot with – attacked some old boy who was working at this Benton School for Girls. He had a couple of bad bangs on the bonce and he's said it was them. She's in trouble, Eamonn, even though Richard Gates is on her case and looking out for her. I know he means well, and he's come up trumps for an Old Bill, but the wall of silence is the best bet. I ain't telling him if I see Cathy, and neither should you. We have to try and help her get away. That's providing she turns up, of course. She could be anywhere. I just hope she's all right, you know?'

The two of them stared at each other for long, long moments. Both were thinking the same thing and neither wanted to put it into words.

Cathy had made her way back to Soho. She had walked all afternoon and decided she would return to the cafe and see if she could hustle back her money, or at least a part of it, from Tony Gosa.

It was now early evening and there were people everywhere. The shops were packed and the traffic was heavy. She looked around her with interest. Girls not much older than her were leaving their office jobs and making their way home. They wore smart, up-to-date clothes, Panda eyes and feathercuts. To Cathy they looked fantastic.

She was picturing Eamonn's face when she turned up

looking just like these girls – but the only way she would manage to do that was to get back her twenty-five quid. It was suddenly important to her to look good for him because she knew that looks played a big part in Eamonn's life. He spent a lot of his time combing his hair and looking in mirrors after all. She wanted to be his equal when she saw him again, someone to be looked at with pleasure and admiration. Not as a rag bag with scruffy clothes and a dirty face.

Tony Gosa did not look shocked to see her; in fact, he looked as if he'd been expecting her.

'What do you want?' His voice was loud and everyone in the small cafe looked at Cathy askance. It was filled with young people wearing fashionable clothes and fashionable sneers. Two girls of about sixteen sniggered at each other and pointed to her as if she were some kind of sideshow at a carnival.

'I want me fucking money!' Cathy's voice was equally loud and aggressive and everyone stopped what they were doing to stare at her openly. 'You had me over, mate, and I'm here to collect what's mine.'

Tony Gosa was amazed but showed no emotion whatsoever. As he walked from behind his counter, he grinned suavely at his customers. Then, taking her roughly by the arm, he propelled Cathy out of the door and on to the pavement in record time.

Bending over her, he said through his teeth: 'If I ever see you again, I'll cut your fucking throat, little girl. Now piss off and don't let me see you here again.'

The friendly face of the night before was gone. She heard him saying as he walked back into his cafe: 'You do people a favour and look how they repay you.'

Cathy was scarlet with rage and humiliation. Tears of frustration burned at the back of her eyes and she stood staring into the cafe while she wondered what to do. All that was left was jumping the trains and getting back to the East End that way; all her earlier dreams of turning up looking half decent were thrown out of the window. And on top of all that, her stomach thought her throat *had* been cut!

As she wandered up Old Compton Street she felt the wind biting into her face. She was hungry, cold and frightened. Frightened that there was nothing for her in the East End or the West End of London. She had no idea what the police were doing – whether they had her down as wanted, whether the blow to the Jailer's head would be enough to put her away good and proper this time.

She was so very confused.

Leaning against the wall by a strip club, hugging her few bits to her chest, her stolen clothes and pitiful belongings, she watched the world go by.

For the first time, she realised just how much trouble she was in. She might as well have taken the can for Ron's murder, because as things stood she was really not much better off.

Cold was settling all over London and fog beginning to come down when finally she pulled herself out of her reverie. It was late but people were still hurrying by her. There was loud music beating out of doors and windows, and the streets teemed with men and women all looking for excitement.

White with tiredness and pain, her fingers once more screaming with the cold, Cathy began to walk. Her predicament was becoming more and more serious as time wore on. She realised now what Denise had meant when she had said: 'There's no going back.'

The moment she had attacked that man at the school

she had put herself at the mercy of the system. If they caught her now they'd have every justification to send her back to Benton or somewhere even worse.

Why this thought had only just occurred to her, Cathy wasn't sure. All she knew was, she was in deep trouble and no one really cared enough to help her.

Caroline and Eamonn were in a small pub in Whitechapel; she was decked out in all her finery and Eamonn was watching her with pride. Caroline wasn't a bad-looking girl and her eyes were amazing.

Another reason she delighted him was her family connections. Caroline's father, Jack Harvey, had worked for a Maltese villain called Victor Messon.

Victor was a huge man who employed people like Jack Harvey to mind for him. Jack, it was rumoured, had also been a favoured friend. Everything had been hunky-dory between the two until they had both become enamoured of the same woman. She was a tiny Jewish girl called Rita Goldfinch, staggeringly beautiful with the biggest, softest brown eyes. At least, that was what Jack had always said. Like Caroline's, Rita's eyes attracted people, but unluckily for her she had attracted two violent men, each equally determined to get her.

They were both already married, though that wasn't a problem. They each wanted a mistress not another wife, though there were those who said that Victor would have left his old woman and set up home with the little Jewish girl.

He never got the chance.

Jack Harvey murdered the pair of them outside the Dean Swift pub. Now he was in Broadmoor, his criminal reputation only enhanced by this vicious act. He had beaten Victor to death with a wheelbrace and cut the throat of the long-suffering Rita, who had not really wanted either of them.

Jack's daughter had grown up accepting as her due the respect which the name 'Harvey' brought her. Her father was away, but he still had friends on the outside – that was how the story went. Caroline had never really bothered with him. It was her mother who still visited him and talked about him as if he were a mixture of the Pope and Charlton Heston, keeping his memory alive all over the East End.

Caroline cashed in on it, loving the notoriety. As for her father, she dropped him a Christmas card every year, plus a line every so often when her mother forced her to. Caroline wanted – in fact needed, the respect of people around her. And if she could win that respect from a face like Eamonn, her happiness would be complete.

As they sat in the Blind Beggar pub and listened to the juke box, a young man came in. He was fairly tall and dark, his hair cut in a college-boy style. He was wearing a mohair suit, Caroline noticed, her eyes going to him automatically. He smiled back at the girl with the big blue eyes in the corner of the little bar.

'Know him, do you?' Eamonn's voice was terse.

Caroline shrugged. 'No. Should I?' Her own voice dripped with sarcasm and something else. Something that Eamonn would not allow to pass unchallenged. It was full of smugness and daring.

Getting up, he walked to the stranger at the bar and said, 'You smiled at my bird.'

The young man turned towards him and grinned winningly. 'Free country. She's nice-looking. Take it as a compliment, mate. I only smiled.'

He had boyish good looks and he knew it. Eamonn sensed that this lad got himself along by his easy smile and his easy charm. He had car keys in his hand and the look of a boy who had been well brought up. Who had had everything a child should have.

All this went through Eamonn's mind in the split second it took him to smash a pint glass on the counter and slice open the boy's cheeks. He even wondered what the doting mum and dad would think about their son once he had scars all over that smiling face.

He wasn't a regular, or Eamonn would have known him. He was one of the new breed who used the East End pubs because they thought it gave them a bit of kudos, a bit of savvy. Well, he would have something to remind him of this night for the rest of his days.

'My name's Eamonn Docherty and I dare you to tell that to the Old Bill,' was his parting thrust.

Laughing, he walked from the pub, Caroline trailing behind him. No one stepped in to help the young man and no one phoned for an ambulance until they were sure that Eamonn was long gone. The boy held his torn face together with his fingers and looked around him in disbelief and shock.

Caroline followed Eamonn home in silence. They walked into the flat together. Still without speaking she took off her coat and faced the man she had decided to live with and love. His fist hit her in the face and she felt the bruising pain as his knuckles connected with her cheekbones.

He punched her to the ground and systematically rained blows on her head and body.

Still he didn't speak.

Curling herself into a ball, she relaxed her body and took what he offered.

Finally spent, he pulled open her legs and took her roughly and silently on the floor where she lay.

As she watched his eyes close and felt his seed spurt hotly inside her, she felt a moment's euphoria.

He was jealous. He had hurt her. Ergo he must love her.

No one had let Caroline Harvey into the big secret of what love really was and no one ever would.

Afterwards he cradled her to him like a child and whispered soft words into her ears. For those few minutes, she felt safer than she had ever felt in her life.

Cathy saw the man approach her and sidestepped to avoid him. They both did a little dance as each tried to pass the other. Finally she stood still and waited for him to walk around her.

He didn't.

Looking up, she saw a big man with a heavy beard. He looked foreign, maybe Russian. But, she conceded, that could just be because of his fur hat. He wore a heavy overcoat and a white scarf, looked smart but somehow menacing.

'Hello, young lady.'

His voice was deep and definitely a London one. Cathy tried to walk around him.

'Come on, young lady, what's the matter? Cat got your tongue?'

People were walking past them as if they didn't exist and Cathy stared up at the man with baleful eyes.

'You're in my way, mister.'

He looked down at her and laughed. 'Come on, come with me.'

He had hold of her arm and, gripping it tightly, pulled her down a small alleyway. Cathy tried to wrench her arm free. He just smiled at her. There were few lights down here and the stench of rubbish was overwhelming. He had pushed her against the wall. Taking off his gloves, he pulled two pound notes from his wallet.

Cathy stared at him in complete silence for a moment. As she tried to make a run for it, his hand caught her a blow across the face. It wasn't a heavy blow but it was enough to stun her.

'Don't be foolish, girl. Do what you're told and you'll get the two pounds, OK?' His voice was thick with excitement. He opened his overcoat and fumbled with his trousers. Cathy closed her eyes as she saw him remove his flaccid penis and start massaging it.

'Come on, little girl, put it in your mouth . . .' He spoke more softly now, cajoling her, and as she felt his hand go to the back of her head to force her down on to him, she lashed out with her arm. His second blow to her head hurt her badly.

The man was getting impatient and as Cathy stood trembling before him she felt the futility of trying to escape. He was massaging his member once more and pulling her head towards it, talking all the time.

'Come on, little girl, haven't I got two pounds for you? Just take it in your mouth and everything will be lovely. It will be fine. I only last a few seconds usually. There's a good little . . .'

Cathy felt the hot salty taste of his penis in her mouth and gagged as he thrust it into the very back of her throat. She couldn't move, couldn't do anything. He was enormous, and he was strong. Once more she was being coerced into doing something that she did not want to do.

As she tried to pull away he pushed harder at her, ramming his member further and further into her mouth. All the time he was talking and his hypnotic tone of voice only made her more frightened.

'There's a good girl. You see, it's nice, isn't it, really? Once you get the taste, you love it. All you little girlies love it, don't you?'

Another voice came unexpected out of the shadows. Hearing it, Cathy bit down as hard as she could on the man's erect and pumping penis.

'You fucking dirty old git! Leave the poor little mare alone. You should be fucking well ashamed of yourself.'

The man was trying to put away his exposed private parts and at the same time stop a tall and very vocal woman from hitting him with her large handbag.

'Go on, you dirty old bastard, before I call a policeman. I've never seen anything like it in all my life . . . and this little girl no more than twelve. It's a national disgrace.'

The woman's high-pitched protestations lent the man's feet wings and he disappeared out of the alley, taking his two pounds with him.

Cathy stood heaving against the wall. Nothing came up but bile. She hadn't eaten for a long time. The woman rubbed her back, feeling the girl's fragility and getting angry all over again.

'You poor little cow. You're only a sprite, ain't you? Come on, come with Desrae, I'll take care of you for a while. Christ knows, I came along at the right moment. Pushing your poor little head down like that . . . Wonder he didn't do you a damage, it is.'

Cathy felt the woman take her arm and allowed herself to be led along. She could still taste the man and was gagging even as they walked out of the alley and into the relative brightness of the road.

Cathy was worried that this woman, Desrae, would leave her alone again and kept her eyes peeled for the man in case he was nearby.

'I do believe there should be laws about dirty old gits like him – I really do, love. I mean, what a bloody palaver, eh? I bet he nearly choked you. I've had a few like that in my time, and believe me, love, it don't get no better.

Horrible feeling, ain't it? Queers are the worst fuckers for it, but a few of the older men go for it too these days. So I've been told anyway.'

Desrae, as she had called herself, kept up this conversation all the way to her flat in Greek Street. Opening a door, she pushed Cathy before her into a dingy hallway. 'Upstairs, first on the right, love. Mind the bleeding stairs – they're so steep it's like climbing Everest. Even Chris bleeding Bonnington would need crampons in this place!' She laughed at her own wit and was immediately attacked by a coughing fit.

As they walked up the dirty stairwell, littered with paper and old Durex, Cathy took in the smell of rubbish and cigarette smoke. Then Desrae opened another door and turned on a light.

Cathy was amazed to see a very nicely decorated hallway, all beige paintwork and green spider plants, and was then taken through into a lounge that housed a leather settee, two chairs and a big old dresser full of china and glassware.

'Put your bits down and I'll get you a stiff drink, love. I know you ain't old enough but a drop of the old gold watch is the best thing to get rid of the taste of cock.'

Desrae screeched with laughter again and set about turning on lamps and pouring them both a drink. As she placed a heavy cut-glass tumbler in Cathy's hand, the girl looked up at her in amazement. Desrae's hair was bleached and styled neatly in a French pleat. Her eyes were made up with heavy mascara and deep green shadow; lips a deep red slash. Her features were heavy yet strangely refined, and her smile was genuine and friendly.

Eyes twinkling with mischief, Desrae announced: 'Yes, my little love, you're right on your first guess. I am, in fact, a man.' And laughed again. 'But don't let that put you off, dear. I don't eat little girls up. And – what a bleeding touch – I very rarely want them to eat me!'

He screeched at his own wit once more and motioning with his glass, encouraged Cathy to down her whisky in one throw. 'Tastes like shit but it does the bleeding job, eh?'

Cathy tossed back the drink and erupted into a fit of coughing. A muscular arm was placed around her thin shoulders and Desrae kissed her on the forehead.

'You poor little mare. But don't worry, old Desrae will take good care of you now. You're as safe as the proverbial houses.' Seating the girl on the large sofa, he took her few things from her and then started to remove her shoes.

'I'll run you a bath, I think, and make you a bit of grub. Then me and you are going to have a natter. I ain't got nothing pressing on tonight. You're lucky it's me night off from the club or I wouldn't have found you, see.'

He carried on chatting about nothing all the time he ran the bath.

Cathy lay on the settee, listening yet not listening. The man-woman's voice had a soothing effect on her and she found she enjoyed the sound of it. Instinctively, she realised she was indeed safe and it no longer even seemed strange that her saviour should be a man in a dress and flesh-coloured tights. There was nothing in the world that could shock her now.

Five minutes later she was sitting in a bright pink bath, surrounded by bubbles and pink tiles, and sipping at a small hot toddy that Desrae assured her would cure all the ills of the world.

'Here, use this to tie your hair up.'

Cathy took the elastic band and proceeded to put her hair into a top knot.

'Beautiful hair you've got, love, and the most amazingly

delicate shoulders. Really shows breeding, that. I got shoulders like a fucking bricklayer – mind you, that's hardly surprising since I was one once.' The deep raucous laughter rang out once more and Cathy found herself laughing too.

'Thank you ever so much, I don't know what I'd have done . . .' Her voice trailed off and before she knew it, Cathy was crying. The kindnesses of her rescuer had undone her. The tears began to fall and then sobs, long held back, erupted harshly.

Desrae, upset himself, cuddled the girl in the bath tub and said loudly: 'Here, stop it. I'm filling up meself and I'll ruin me bleeding make-up.'

Half laughing and half crying, the strange pair hugged each other then chattered together in the bathroom for an hour. Cathy told him everything that had happened in the last month, enjoying the telling, getting it all off her chest and somehow straightening things out in her own mind. Finally she was spent.

Desrae, sitting back on his heels, looked at the little girl before him and shook his head sadly. 'Well, all I can say, Cathy Connor, is thank fuck you found me! There's some right strange ones out there, I can tell you. And coming from a man wearing women's clothes that probably sounds stranger still, eh?' Saying which, he picked up a large cerise towel and held it out for her to step into.

The towel was warm and enveloping; Cathy pulled it to her and swayed with tiredness. Desrae picked her up as easily as a kitten and carried her to the settee. 'Snuggle up there, love, and I'll get you some nice hot soup. Then we'll talk about what you're going to do next.'

Leaving her on the settee, in front of the gas fire, Desrae busied himself in his tiny kitchen, pouring out the tomato soup into a nice big bowl and cutting thin slices of bread and butter – minus the crusts, of course. All the time he worked, his mind was running over Cathy's predicament. The little girl in his lounge was underage, underfed and under cared for, in his opinion.

Desrae, himself a product of homes, was loath to get in touch with the police. Anyway, he reasoned, a lot of people couldn't distinguish between child molesters and homosexuals. Especially the Old Bill. He could be putting himself in the frame if he went to them. There was no way he was pushing her back out on the street, though, that was not even an option.

As for that Eamonn fella the girl was pinning her hopes on . . . about as much use as an ashtray on a speedboat him, was Desrae's opinion. Not only that, as soon as Cathy put a foot on her old stomping ground the Filth would be all over her like a rash.

No, the girl needed to keep away from there, and he'd have to point that out to her *toot sweet*.

Rubbing his large hands together and proudly surveying his handiwork, he carried in the tray and put it on a side table. He spoonfed Cathy her soup, all the while working out in his mind what he was going to do with her. Suddenly he had the most amazing idea.

'I've just had a thought, love.'

Cathy raised one eyebrow and smiled. 'What?'

'You can stay here and work for your keep.'

She frowned. 'What – do the tidying up and that?'

Desrae nodded and then said grandly: 'I'm going to learn you a bleeding trade, girl.'

Cathy was perplexed. 'What kind of trade?'

He grinned from ear to ear. 'I'm going to teach you how to maid, Cathy Connor. How to be a maid to a woman of a certain persuasion. That being the horizontal persuasion, admittedly.'

Cathy knew immediately what he meant and they both laughed.

'Me mum never had a maid, but I done her clearing up and that.'

Desrae dismissed Madge with a wave of one well-manicured hand. 'I'm talking about a real professional here, dear. I have all sorts of outfits and other things that I use in me job. I'll show you how to take care of them, and of me. And in the process I'll show you how to look after yourself. Deal?'

She grinned. 'Sounds good to me.'

She stared at the incongruously womanly figure before her and said gently: 'Thanks, Desrae. Thanks for helping me out.'

The words were inadequate, Cathy knew that, but they were heartfelt. Placing a long finger under Cathy's chin, Desrae turned her face up towards his own.

'You're welcome, darling. Now listen to Uncle Desrae: you have to keep away from the East End, at least for a while, all right? The Filth will be all over you if they catch sight, you understand? You hide out here for a while and we'll have a rethink in a few weeks, yes?'

Cathy nodded gratefully. 'I really can't thank you enough.'

Desrae chuckled merrily. 'Wait until you've maided for me a little while. You might change your bleeding tune, girl. Now, let's get you bedded down for the night and we'll talk some more in the morning, eh? You look bleeding knackered.'

Twenty minutes later Cathy was tucked up in a small single bed in Desrae's dressing room. Like the rest of the flat it was overdone and over-feminine and the smell of perfume was stifling. Cathy loved it. It was the nicest room she had ever slept in.

As Desrae removed his make-up and brushed out his hair, he wondered whatever had induced him to take on a young girl. Was it the reminder of what it had been like for him when he had first hit the West End as a teenager all those years ago? Or was it the need for company, a need that was becoming ever more pressing as the years wore on?

Whatever it was, the girl was here to stay for as long as she liked, and Desrae hoped that it would be a long, long time. There was something about Cathy, about her demeanour, her attitude, that met a need in himself.

She was vulnerable, and yet she had guts. She had been through the mill and yet she still had the ability to trust. He did not want to abuse that. He adored her already, from her big blue eyes to her tiny graceful little hands.

He only hoped that when she realised what the job entailed, it wouldn't put her off.

Sighing, he wiped cold cream all over his face and neck and, puckering his lips one last time, smiled into the mirror and said: 'You're not looking bad, girl, even at the grand old age of twenty-nine.' Desrae – Desmond Raymond – Smith was thirty-five, but would not admit that even to himself.

Finally, they were both in bed, each aware of the other's presence nearby and each glad of it.

Just as Desrae was dropping off, the bedroom door opened and Cathy came into his room in the overlarge nightie he had loaned her.

'What's the matter, love? You all right?'

She went to the bed and, slipping back the covers, climbed in beside her new friend. 'I was a bit frightened in there all on me own.' Her voice was small.

Desrae grinned. 'Go to sleep, love. You're as safe as

houses now. I told you that before and Desrae don't say anything unless it's true, all right?'

Cathy nodded. Five minutes later her soft breathing told the man that she was indeed asleep. As he listened to her, he marvelled at a God Who could answer the prayers of a homosexual transvestite. He had needed someone in his life and she had been sent to him in the shape of little Cathy Connor.

He lay there and felt that indeed his cup ranneth over. He smiled at the thought. He had known a few vicars in his time, in a professional capacity, and they had a funny old way of talking. They were a bit funny altogether, he reasoned, but he would not dwell on that tonight!

Instead he pulled the covers up over the girl's shoulders and closed his eyes. They slept like babies together, neither one of them moving till the morning.

Chapter Sixteen

Cathy awoke to the sounds of crockery being banged against glasses and the radio playing. It was all strange to her, and for a few seconds she wondered where she was. Then she opened her eyes and saw the dim winter sunshine coming through the heavy pink curtains and the events of the night before came to mind. She closed her eyes once more rather than think of that man, the alley, and the overwhelming stench around them.

Remembering the man-woman Desrae, though, she found herself smiling widely and a feeling of euphoria washed over her. Even after the terrible things that had befallen her during the last few weeks, she still felt she could trust the person who had saved her.

As she heard his dulcet tones singing along with the Monkees she smiled. 'Last Train to Clarksville' had never sounded quite like that before! Bursting into the room wearing a long blue peignoir and with his hair in rollers, he was still singing at the top of his considerable voice.

'Wake up, Cathy, and come and get something to eat,' he ordered. 'I've done us my favourite: smoked salmon and cream cheese on toast. Happy Harold will be upset when he sees it's all gone but what the fuck, eh, girl? Life's for the living, as a friend of mine always used to say.' He frowned and looked down at the girl in the bed then added sadly, 'That was before he died, of course. Took an overdose, deliberately and all. Silly man. I mean, life can be shit, I know, but any life's better than none at all, don't you think?'

Without waiting for an answer he put a large towelling dressing gown on the bed and flounced from the room. Wrapping herself in the sweet-smelling material, Cathy followed him. She had already realised that a lot of things he said did not really require an answer.

In the kitchen she looked at the plate before her with interest. There were indeed slices of pink smoked salmon and a mound of cream cheese. In addition there were scrambled eggs and slices of heavily buttered brown toast. Cathy tackled the hearty breakfast hungrily. Finally, feeling a large hand on her arm, she grinned as Desrae said: 'For Gawd's sake, girl, no one's going to snatch the bleeding food away from you. Slow down.'

Cathy ate more slowly, watching as Desrae nibbled his own tiny breakfast then wiped his mouth daintily on a napkin. It made her feel ashamed of how quickly she had bolted her own food.

'Drink your tea, love, I haven't sugared it yet. Sort yourself out. And there's plenty more where that came from so for fuck's sake eat a bit slower. You'll end up with indigestion.'

But Cathy had finished and was busy looking round the kitchen.

Like the rest of the flat it was clean and modern. Even the shelves were properly painted. In Cathy's short life shelves had always been of bare wood and encrusted with grime. She realised that if she was going to maid properly she had a lot to learn. Madge's slapdash ideas of cleanliness would not be welcome in this place. As if reading her mind, Desrae grinned.

'Looks lovely, don't it? I painted the walls meself. I like yellow – it's a sunny, friendly type of colour, though it washes me out. I mean, it doesn't suit my complexion at all. Still, sod that! I like to sit here and eat me grub, it puts me in a good mood, like. Colour's important, you know, in your surroundings. I try and choose happy colours if I can. Pinks, yellows, blues – well, light blues – and greens. Very relaxing colour, green is. Calming sort of colour. I'll learn you, dear. By the time I'm finished with you, love, you could maid for Danny la Rue.'

'You're still set on that then?' Cathy's voice was small, hesitant. The more she saw of this outlandish person, the more she wanted to be with him, though for the life of her she didn't know why. In reality she should have been terrified of him. A man, a grown man, dressed in women's clothes and acting more like a woman than any Cathy had ever seen.

Oh, she had heard about people like him: shirtlifters, shitstabbers and iron hoofs had been the nicknames used in the East End for homosexuals. They were called all sorts of things besides and treated with the utmost disrespect. There were not many who would dare walk the streets of Bethnal Green in full regalia, though a few worked the docks and took stick from the men and the women alike. Queers, men who looked like men, were barely tolerated, kept their sexual preferences to themselves and didn't advertise the fact.

No, Cathy had heard about queers, but this was the first queer transvestite she had ever encountered and she was amazed to find that they were such nice people. She could imagine, though, the reception that Desrae would get where he had come from, guessing correctly that he was from the East End himself originally and had moved away quick smart to somewhere more tolerant.

Obviously, his work was lucrative and he was doing very well; his flat was a palace in Cathy's eyes, filled with objects she had only ever seen in films before. There was even a TV in the corner of the living room, which in itself was amazing to the girl. Though Madge had earned enough over the years to give them what most people would have termed a good life, she had squandered all her money on booze, men and cheap clothes.

Cathy glanced up to find Desrae watching her. 'Am I still set on you maiding for me? Of course I am, love. The only thing is, I don't want to shock you, see. I mean, I know this is hard to believe,' he fluttered his eyelashes in an exaggerated way, 'but in case you haven't noticed, I am in fact a man.'

Cathy laughed delightedly. 'Seriously though, love – pour me out another cuppa, there's a sweet – I don't want to start you off on all this unless you're sure you can really handle it. If you're wary then we'll put our thinking caps back on and try to come up with something else, all right?'

Cathy filled up the man's cup and shook her head. 'I'll be all right, Desrae. Me mum was a brass. I mean, I take a lot of shocking.'

Desrae looked very serious for a second and said flatly, 'You were shocked last night, darlin', when I helped you out with that bloke.'

Cathy shrugged. 'That was different, wasn't it? I mean, I ain't got to do anything like that, have I?'

It was a question and a plea and Desrae's heart went out to the girl before him.

' 'Course you ain't, love. Fuck me, I only do that now and again these days, and then only with me regulars. I mean, you have to set yourself some standards, for goodness' sake.'

'So what have I got to do?' Cathy asked eagerly.

Desrae pulled his peignoir around him tightly and lit himself a Sobranie cigarette. It was the same shade as his wrap.

'Listen, love, I would not harm one hair on your head, let's get that straight now. You've had a bit of a time of it one way and another and I think you need somewhere to hide out, don't you? Well, I'm willing to let you do that here. Only for a week or two, mind, until the heat dies down. In that time I'll change your appearance a bit. Teach you a little about make-up and that. Style your hair.

'That aside, we're both agreed you'll keep away from the East End for a while. Myself, I think you'd be better off kissing the place goodbye once and for all, but that's your decision. As for your young fella, I'd say give him the Big E. But, like I say, that's up to you.' He sipped at his tea daintily then continued to speak.

'First things first, eh? I maided for years when I first came to the West End. Oh, I maided for a bitch of a man. A right bastard he was. Had lovely hair, though, real it was and all. Made a fortune he did. Mind you, he had his good points . . . but I digress. I ain't had a maid for years. Most of them are up and comings. You know, want to do your job really only they don't know how to go about it. You take them in, fall in love with the little fuckers and then they tuck you up. Pinch your customers, pinch your gold and pinch your self-respect too if you're not careful. No, I've looked out for meself for a few years. Now, however, I think I have found just the person for the job.

'I'll teach you how to care for my things – properly, mind. How to treat the customers, and a few little tricks to get by on. Nothing funny like, just the basics of Soho.

Where to shop . . . oh, lots of things. That's very much in the future though. First, I'll have to see about getting you some clothes and underwear. You can borrow my make-up until you can get your own. We need to give you some kind of image, don't we? You're a lovely-looking girl, and I reckon you'd scrub up a treat. Meantime, while all this is going on, I'll teach you how to maid. Most of my customers are regulars – always went for the regular trade meself. Built it up over the years. And then there's me boyfriend, of course.'

He laughed deeply at Cathy's shocked expression.

'Oh, I've got a boyfriend, love, and what he'll say about you I really don't know! Still, we'll worry about that later. First I'm going to get dressed and then I'm going to take some measurements and after that I'm going to get you some decent clothes. Can't have me maid looking like something the cat shat on, can I? What would all the other girls say, eh?'

Cathy shook her head in wonderment. Desrae made everything sound fun, easy and exciting. She only hoped that his happy-go-lucky ways rubbed off on her. If she needed anything at the moment it was some light relief. She wanted to hide away here in this nice flat, with this lovely man, lick her wounds and get herself sorted in both mind and body.

Here with Desrae she might have the chance to make a new life for herself. She couldn't face Eamonn yet, not until she was ready. Until she could meet him as an equal. Eamonn didn't like being burdened with other people's problems, he was too wrapped up in his own.

No, she would become a maid for this strange man, and hide herself away from the world until she was ready to make her triumphal return. She couldn't wait to see Eamonn's face when she did! Cathy hugged herself at the thought, and Desrae, seeing the stars in her eyes, pursed his lips thoughtfully.

Caroline awoke with a deep soreness between her legs and a dull heavy ache all over her body.

Eamonn's arms were around her and she instinctively snuggled into the warmth of his body. Wincing in pain, she realised that her eye was black and nearly closed. It felt too big for her face. Testing it once more, she opened it slowly and saw Eamonn looking down at her. There was a look of shame mingled with exhilaration on his handsome face.

He kissed her brow gently, small kisses interspersed with words of love and affection.

'I'm sorry, Caroline. I don't know what made me do it. You know I love you. I'll always love you. There's no one else for me.' He hugged her bruised body to him, causing her fresh pain – though not half so much as she would have felt had she known that all the time he soothed and comforted her his thoughts were on another girl entirely. Cathy . . . his Cathy . . . safely out of his rat's nest with the poncey Hendersons.

Part of Eamonn wanted to track them down and show them just what he thought of their cosy, do-gooding lifestyle. But another part – the part that had always envied the kids at school with clean clothes and hair and a well-fed look about them – knew that she was better off where she was. For the moment at least.

Come her sixteenth birthday, though, and he was going after her. Then she'd be free to lead her own life; free to love him as he knew he loved her. Loved her to death, in fact. Until then he'd have to content himself with this dopey slag who seemed to believe that the punishment he meted out was a sign of affection.

'I love you, Eamonn.'

She was telling the truth. Last night Caroline had fallen in love with danger, and all her life she would worship it. As she looked up at his darkly handsome face, his sparkling eyes and thick sensuous lips, she fell even deeper in love, believing this big handsome boy-man loved her too.

He had maimed another man for her. He would kill for her, so strong was his love and devotion. Smiling through her pain, Caroline ran her hand down his body and found his erect penis. Feeling the intense heat pervading her, she opened her legs in moist expectation.

She was not disappointed.

It was the best sex she had ever had in her life, and it was addictive. She could never have too much of Eamonn Docherty.

Cathy, dressed in a shirt deemed too small for Desrae and a pair of black tights, watched in amazement as he put on his 'face'. Even after watching her mother tart herself up for years, nothing had prepared her for the sight which met her eyes.

Covering his face thickly with panstick, Desrae blended it over his cheekbones expertly, subtly changing the contours and lines. Looking at her in delight, he waggled his eyebrows. 'Clever little git, ain't I?'

Then, making her laugh by pouting at himself in the mirror a few times and rolling his eyes, he pencilled a deep brown line around the outside of his lips.

'This makes them look fuller, see. Mine are a bit thin. Got a man's lips, me.'

He filled this all in with a bright pink lipstick, smoothing it by placing his lips together suggestively and pushing his tongue against the side of his face.

Cathy was roaring with laughter by then.

'Now for the old eyeballs, girl. This really is a feat of ex-fucking-traordinary danger. First time I saw someone do this, I was nearly as sick as a bleeding dog.'

Pulling down his lower lid, he drew inside it with a kohl pencil whose blackness immediately made his eyes look wider, more open. He fluttered his eyelashes, then began to apply thick blue greasy eyeshadow with a heavy brush. It took five minutes before he was satisfied. Then, blinking his eyes quickly, he looked at her again and grinned.

'Getting there, ain't I?'

The next step was the false eyelashes he applied with the same care and attention as a surgeon working in an operating theatre. He glued them to both top and bottom lids then, sitting back, proudly surveyed his handiwork.

Sucking in his cheeks, he looked at himself with a grave expression on his face. 'Now then, a brown blusher, I think – make the most of me cheekbones.' He picked up a large brush and stuck it in a pot of loose powder.

'Always act as if someone is watching you. I don't know who said that, but it's something I've lived by for years. They were dead right.' He applied the blusher with long sweeping upward strokes. 'All that's left now is the old Barnet Fair. I never wear wigs during the day unless I'm working.'

Taking out his rollers, he brushed his hair and backcombed it strenuously before styling it around his head in a wide halo and flicking it up at the ends.

'Eat your fucking heart out, Mandy Rice-Davis, that's what I say! I mean, who needs a woman with me about?'

Cathy was still laughing. 'You look great, not at all like a . . .' Her voice trailed off.

Placing one well-manicured hand over hers, Desrae said happily, 'Don't worry about what you nearly said, love, I take things like that as a compliment. I spend hours trying to look like a woman. Why should I be upset when you say I don't look like a bleeding bloke, eh?'

Cathy shook her head, unable to answer.

'You ever seen a bloke's tackle before?'

She nodded, unsure what was going to happen next. Desrae saw the look and laughed. 'Lovely you may be, but I think we've established that you're not my cup of tea, eh? No, love, don't worry. All I'm going to do is put on me body now. Nothing more. You'll see it for a split second, if that.'

Stripping off his nightwear, he stood naked before her for an instant. Then, picking up a pair of tiny shorts, he slid them up his legs. Taking his penis, he pushed it as far back between his thighs as he could. In the mirror Cathy saw it disappear completely as Desrae quickly pulled up the padded shorts. Arching his back, his long lean body posed like a ballet dancer's, he grinned.

'Clever, eh?'

Cathy giggled with delight.

'Now for the falsies and then we're cooking with gas!'

Ten minutes later he was dressed in a red jumper, thrusting false breasts pointing to the ceiling above it, and a black knee-length skirt. Black tights and high heels finished off the outfit.

'So what do you think, eh?'

Cathy sat back on the bed and shook her head in amazement. 'You look brilliant, Desrae. Blinding.'

He preened in mock admiration of himself. 'Not bad for an old sod even if I say it meself.' Then, smiling widely, he bellowed: 'Now let's get you some decent clothes.'

As they left the bedroom together it occurred to Cathy that this was the happiest she had ever been in her whole life. She felt safe, loved and secure.

It also occurred to her that it didn't really take much

to make people happy. Not as much as they thought, anyway.

Desrae walked into Tony Gosa's cafe with a wide smile and a very determined look in his eye. Tony, noticing him instantly, smiled warily back. 'Hello, what can I get you?'

Desrae said breathily, in his best girlie voice: 'Coffee, please. Sweet and warm, like you.'

Tony nodded and watched as he sat himself down. Desrae was known around Soho; he was a fixture there. Not because he was a transvestite, but because his long-time boyfriend was none other than Joey Pasquale.

Joey was a face, a real face.

He ran the West End through utter fear and terror. Joey was known to be hard; not hard but fair, like most successful villains, just hard. Joey's only known weaknesses were Desrae, whom he had been with for years, and his wife and son.

Tommy Pasquale was eighteen and had recently been introduced into his father's business. He was getting a big reputation fast. It was also rumoured that he had called Desrae 'Auntie' for years, though no one had ever had the guts to ask outright if this were true.

Desrae did not usually frequent places like Tony Gosa's; he used the nicer places in Piccadilly where they knew him and treated him with respect. No, he was sitting in Tony's cafe for a reason, and Tony had a feeling that whatever that reason was, it meant trouble for him.

As Tony placed the coffee in front of him, Desrae gave a wide smile. 'Put up any more poor little girls lately, have we?'

Tony's smile froze on his face.

'Does a blinding breakfast your mum, so my little niece was telling me anyway. Came looking for me, she did, and

I hear she spent a rather enlightening evening with you and your mother.'

Tony didn't say anything, he was incapable of speech.

'Name of Cathy. Remember her, do you? Only I think you charged her twenty-five quid. Yes, I think that was the amount. Or no, come to think of it, could have been fifty quid.' He pretended to concentrate, frowning deeply. 'Yeah, fifty quid I think it was. At least that's what she told me and my friend Joey. Very upset Joey was as well. Likes the kid a lot he does.'

Tony felt a cold sweat break out all over his body.

'Has he been in at all?' Desrae continued. 'I should imagine he's looking for me by now.'

Tony shook his head. Walking back to his till, he extracted the fifty pounds in record time and shoved it into Desrae's outstretched hands, apologising all the while. 'If she'd said she was your niece, I swear on my mother's eyes . . .'

Desrae interrupted him. 'Shut up, you Greek ponce. You'd sell your mother's eyesight for a few quid, and she'd sell yours. Cut the fanny and listen. As yet Joey knows nothing, but if I hear that any of my niece's business has been discussed anywhere, I'll bring you so much trouble you'll wish your mother had never bothered to open her legs the night you were conceived. Do you get my drift?'

'Yes . . . Listen, Desrae, if you say she's your niece, she's your niece. She can be your daughter for all I care, so long as I don't get no call from Mr Pasquale.'

Desrae laughed delightedly. 'Daughter would be a bit strong even for me, dearie. Niece will do nicely. Make a point of mentioning her around, would you? I'd appreciate it. Maybe I'll bring her in one day for a little chat.'

Tony swallowed hard. 'Your niece will always be welcome here, as you are.'

Desrae stood up and looked down at the smaller man before him.

'Frightened, aren't you? You're so frightened you'd suck my cock if I asked you nicely, wouldn't you?'

Tony was dismayed. Desrae was capable of anything, everyone knew that. His reputation was as fierce as his boyfriend's. No one had ever had Desrae over and lived to tell the tale. Unlike a lot of the queers around Soho, he was certainly not the victim type. For all his girlish voice and exaggerated mannerisms, Desrae could throw a punch like a docker and wasn't afraid to use a knife. Tony was trashed and he knew it. He also knew that if Desrae insisted on having his cock sucked, he would have to do it.

Desrae laughed once more. 'Don't worry, I'm fussy what I fuck. Always have been. You just watch yourself, mate. You ripped off the wrong person. You must be losing your touch, old chap.'

As he walked from the cafe in his black high heels, Tony Gosa breathed out a heavy sigh of relief. He should have guessed that little bitch would be trouble. Look at the way she'd come back in, looking for her money.

Well, if she had the protection of Desrae and Pasquale, she was one lucky little girl. Quite frankly, Tony hoped he never clapped eyes on her again.

Desrae walked around Soho, treated like visiting royalty wherever he went. As he swayed through the market he waved at whores and bouncers alike, greeting them all with his high voice and breathy, over-feminine laugh.

'I got me niece staying. Wait until you all meet her, she's a right little darling.'

Everyone feigned pleasure for him and waved happily as he passed by.

But Desrae knew exactly what he was doing, telling this

story. Once Cathy was accepted as his niece, however incongruous that might sound, she would actually *become* his relative in everyone's mind. Any questions about her would then be met with a blank wall of silence, which was exactly what he wanted.

He loved taking care of people, and now he had found a person he could care for who didn't already know his reputation and lifestyle. He wanted to make sure that when Cathy found out about them, she would already love him for himself.

As he made his way to Oxford Street with the fifty pounds in his bag and Cathy's measurements in his mind, he had an amusing thought. He would dress her like a little queen. She'd be a big queen's little princess!

He laughed out loud at his little joke.

What Joey would say when he saw her, Desrae didn't have a clue, but knowing Joey, he wouldn't say much. Which was a major part of his attraction. Joey trusted him implicitly. They trusted one another. There was more to their relationship than anyone had ever guessed and that suited them both right down to the ground.

Desrae's eyes misted over as he thought of his first meeting with Joey Pasquale. He always liked to think it had been fate that had brought them together.

Fifteen years before, one cold rainy night, he had been dressed in his finest and cruising the streets of Soho looking for a likely lad. A punter. Instead he had been dragged into a car and taken to waste ground over Notting Hill way. An old bombsite had been the place where he had learned what gang rape was.

When his kidnappers had realised he was not a woman they had gone mad, pulling at his penis, slashing at it with knives. Finally, after he had performed oral sex on them all, they had systematically raped him in the roughest of fashions, all laughing and enjoying themselves.

Desrae had been amazed at how young they were, only his own age. They were probably respectable types at heart who would forget the events of tonight and go on to lead perfectly normal lives. He knew already that many so-called he-men were some of the worst shitstabbers going. So many people lived a double life. The clubs he cruised had taught him all he needed to know about that.

Now he had been abused and humiliated by five young men who doubtless believed their actions were justified because Desrae wasn't one of the lads. He pulled himself to his knees and felt the sting of tears against the black eye he had received when they'd still thought he was a female.

One of the boys was doing up his flies. The flick knife still in his hand was making this very difficult.

Blood was dripping down Desrae's own thighs, and feeling the knife wound in his testes open up with his sudden movement, he made a dive for the knife. As he snatched it away, he brought his arm up with as much force as he could into the boy's neck.

The eight-inch blade sliced through the skin and severed the windpipe.

The others stood and watched in horror.

A hissing sound invaded the night, blanking out for them the rumble of trains passing by in the distance. The boy fell backwards, eyes staring up at the night sky.

One of the lads, the smallest, a puny type with thickly greased hair and a cheap leather jacket, kept saying over and over: 'Jesus fucking Christ! Jesus fucking Christ!'

Staring at the knife in his hand, Desrae looked at the others in amazement. A gurgling noise came from the boy on the ground and they all knew instinctively that he was dead.

Within seconds Desrae was alone.

The lads ran off, terrified and ashamed of what they had seen and done.

Tidying himself as best he could, Desrae tried to stand. His anus was raw, throbbing with pain and bleeding heavily. He knew he had to get to a doctor; had to get away from the dead boy before him. As he staggered off, the high heels he had slipped on so proudly hours before impeded his movements, and he stopped and took them off.

It was then that he saw a man coming towards him. His fear was so great he dropped to his knees and began to wail loudly. He was caught, found out. His life was over. Once they realised what he had done there would be hell to pay. No one would believe a word he said in his defence. He would be portrayed as a sexual deviant who had cold-bloodedly murdered an innocent young boy.

All this was going through his mind as he felt a heavy hand clamp down on his mouth. He wanted to scream in terror but could not. Then a voice whispered heavily in his ears, 'If you stop struggling for one bloody second I'll try and help you, love. Now, where's your wig and have you got a bag?'

Desrae looked up into the most handsome face he had ever seen. Swallowing down the tears, he answered the man's questions. 'I've lost them. Please help me! Please . . .'

The man was kind. He helped Desrae up and picked up his shoes for him.

'Listen, son, I've seen the body and I've guessed what happened. Now try and calm yourself down and I'll get your bits and bobs then take you home, OK?'

Desrae nodded. The man had said 'son'; he knew what he was and didn't care.

Ten minutes later he was sitting uncomfortably in a classy car, blood dripping all over the leather upholstery. The man was still talking, trying to calm him, and his deep voice was having the desired effect.

His rescuer took him to a doctor in Barnes. As he limped up the path Desrae wondered what the hell he was letting himself in for. The man must have guessed his feelings because he said gently, 'He's a proper doctor, stop worrying. An abortionist. I use him sometimes in my work, OK? There's not going to be any Old Bill called, so relax.'

Desrae didn't really have much choice.

He stayed with the doctor for three days, after being stitched up and sedated. His rescuer came every day and after introducing himself, made the boy a proposition.

He would take care of him, be friends with him, and every so often would want a favour in return. They both knew what the favour was, and both were quite happy with the arrangement. Desrae had been grateful to Joey Pasquale ever since.

Friendships like that were few and far between for men like him and he was wise enough to know it – because it was Joey's friendship he appreciated more than anything else. He had been provided with a flat and introduced into the best queer clubs London could offer. He had a blinding clientele and he had protection. His relationship with Joey guaranteed that. Their sex life was mutually satisfying and now a deep bond of affection and respect kept them together. Desrae knew how lucky he had been and thanked God for Joey every day of his life.

He adored his friend and protector. He only hoped that little Cathy would feel the same way.

When he finally let himself back into his flat he smiled to hear laughter coming from the kitchen. Cathy had met

Joey and they were obviously hitting it off. Desrae had had a feeling they would.

If anyone would understand his feelings for the girl, and his reason for taking her in, Joey would. He had after all, done practically the same thing.

Laden down with his purchases, Desrae walked into the kitchen and said heavily: 'What's this then, a bleeding mother's meeting?'

Cathy and Joey looked at one another and grinned.

Joey raised his deep brown eyes to the ceiling and said, equally as heavily, 'Not more fucking shopping, Des! What boutique you cleaned out now?' Looking at Cathy, he shook his head sorrowfully. 'You can't make a silk purse out of a bloke's ear.'

Still chuckling, she began to make another pot of tea and the atmosphere in the kitchen became almost festive.

After kissing Joey on the cheek, Desrae looked into his eyes and said: 'I couldn't leave her on the streets, could I?'

Joey shook his head. ' 'Course not. But I hope for both your sakes you got me some breakfast, girl, I'm starving.'

Desrae winked at him and smiled. Joey smiled back.

Cathy looked at the two of them and thanked God for leading her in the direction of Desrae and his boyfriend. If she had known their reputation she would still have thanked God, but it was to be a while before she really found out anything.

Chapter Seventeen

Eamonn was white-faced with shock, and he knew that he was in big trouble. All the time he had been working he had known that to upset his boss would be a very foolish thing to do. Now he had not only upset Dixon but had made the further mistake of boasting openly that he did not care.

Eamonn knew that this was the worst sin he could have committed and cursed Caroline and the drink, both of whom he held responsible for his own predicament. He'd been showing off in front of her, but without the drink would never have dreamed of saying what he'd said.

Namely that his boss was a silly old bastard who needed Eamonn a damn sight more than he needed Dixon. The words spoken in bravado, in a pub full of people, had instantly been reported back and more than likely exaggerated in the process.

Eamonn knew that in the last seven months he had made himself more than a few enemies, with his loud mouth and his ruthless ways. He acted the hard man all the time, from the moment he got up in the morning until he went to bed at night. He knew this, cultivated it. He wanted to be the most frightening face in the East End and was gradually achieving his wish. Other firms had tried to poach him. He was well known as a nutter, a head case – an up-and-coming man for the future.

Now he was terrified. As the two known hard men stood in the doorway of his flat, he felt a slackening of his sphincter muscle. Danny Dixon was a lot of things, but he was no fool. Now he would have to take Eamonn down a peg or two. If he didn't, he would lose his street credibility overnight.

Feeling the fear in his guts, Eamonn looked into Caroline's wide-eyed face and said heavily; 'I won't be long.'

The two heavies laughed gently. 'Don't wait up, love. We'll see he gets back safely.'

She watched as they took him from the house before giving way to helpless tears. Eamonn was everything to her, and she needed him now more than ever since she'd begun to suspect she was pregnant.

All she needed was for him to get wasted by Dixon; 'wasted' in the East End did not necessarily mean killed. Dixon could just as easily have him crippled; he had done that to people before. If anyone took money from him, he had their fingers chopped off with secateurs or had them tipped into baths of boiling water. He was not a man to upset, and even Caroline understood that what Eamonn had said was tantamount to mutiny.

She sat by the fire and waited.

There was nothing else she could do.

Danny Dixon was upset.

He had liked the boy Docherty and had enjoyed being his mentor. It was a funny thing that he had taken to Eamonn because normally he didn't take to anyone. Even his own kids, whom of course he loved, had never really endeared themselves to him. He had guessed that his feelings for the Irish boy were because he had seen in Eamonn himself as a young man. Seen himself reflected in the boy's hungry blue eyes and swaggering walk. He was full of bullshit and bravado, just seventeen after all. Yes, Eamonn reminded him so much of himself at that age that he'd allowed sentiment to cloud his judgement.

A few times in the past the boy had spoken carelessly and Dixon had let it slip. Now, though, Eamonn had pushed his luck too far.

Dixon knew that the boy had been giving Harvey's daughter a hammering. It was common knowledge that he battered the girl on a regular basis. This had disturbed Danny. He might not have a lot going for him in life but he had never, ever touched a female in anger, not even his wife who could try the patience of the Good Lord Himself when she had the hump.

Eamonn Docherty had to be taught a lesson and he had to be taught it soon.

People were talking about him, about what he'd said and how he'd said it. It annoyed Dixon to find some of his own hard men acting like fishwives, gossiping about the boy and his lifestyle. Telling Dixon other little things they felt he should know. He had realised long ago that Eamonn was not generally liked. Well, he wasn't too bothered by that; knew very well he wouldn't win a popularity contest himself. His role was not to be liked, it was to terrify. And so was the boy's.

Now Dixon had to terrify him, and frankly he wasn't feeling up to it at the moment.

He had broken his cardinal rule: he had begun to like an employee.

Cracking his heavy knuckles, he looked around the small

warehouse. It was full of stolen booty and smelled of tobacco and whisky. He opened a box and pulled out a bottle of Johnnie Walker. Opening it, he took a long swig.

His two minders exchanged glances. Surely Danny didn't need a drink before doing this little job? He noticed the looks and filed them away for future reference. These two men were like all the others: they were pretenders to the throne of Danny Dixon. Well, like the others, he would sort them out.

Maybe this session with Eamonn Junior would help with that. He would give the boy a good hiding, teach him a lesson and make sure it was well publicised.

A hiding would keep him in place, and all the others too. Satisfied with himself, he took another long swallow of the whisky. Wiping his mouth with the back of his hand, he shouted at his two minders: 'Had your fucking look, you two? Like a pair of fucking tarts, standing there watching me every move.'

The two men looked down at the floor and kept quiet. When Danny was in this mood the best thing to do was to keep your head down and your mouth shut.

Five minutes later they brought in Eamonn and watched smugly as he was beaten black and blue by Dixon. As a finale, he requested his baseball bat from his car and hammered the boy's legs until he was sure they were fractured at least. Leaving Eamonn bloody and unconscious on the warehouse floor, he walked out unsteadily.

'Take him to the quack and when he comes round, explain it was nothing personal, just sound business. If I hear what I want from him, his job's still there.'

A heavy nodded. Then, loading the boy into the back of a van, he drove him to the doctor's, all the time whistling along to the radio and wondering what his wife had got him in for tea.

*

The punter was small, so small he made even Cathy seem like a giant. Handing him a drink, gin with a splash of lime cordial, she smiled at him pleasantly and said she would see if Miss Desrae was ready to receive him. The man smiled at her, showing pristine white false teeth and a small pink tongue.

Walking through to the bedroom, Cathy said to Desrae in a stage whisper: 'It's Mr Middleton. I've given him a drink and taken his coat. He pays by cheque, doesn't he?'

Desrae, in the middle of putting on his stockings and suspenders, nodded. 'Yeah, give him a large drink, won't you? He can keep at it for bleeding ages and it's so boring. It's the clothes that do him, you see. Likes to see me tackle hanging by me stocking tops.'

At the moment, his tackle was concealed by a pair of black silk panties. Mr Middleton also liked to take these off with his very precarious teeth.

Desrae knew he sold fantasy and did his job every bit as well as any actor or actress. His customers really thought he was enjoying himself. Which, he believed, made him a performer in every sense of the word.

Cathy went back to the living room and topped up the man's drink, all the time smiling and chatting.

Mr Middleton was a banker, a very successful one. He was also married with four grown-up children, two daughters married in their turn and two sons doing very well in the City. His wife was a petite woman whose life revolved around her family, shopping and cooking. For her a regular sex life consisted of once every few months, whether they needed it or not. She had no idea that her husband preferred men. Grown men if possible, not girlie boys like many of the men who came to Soho. He had been

273

visiting Desrae for nigh on twelve years and they even exchanged Christmas gifts.

They were friends, confidants, and best of all they were both men who liked a laugh and some good company. The arrangement worked well.

Two minutes later Cathy led him through the flat and into Desrae's pink and gold bedroom. Shutting the door firmly behind her, she went to the lounge and picked up the used glass. Maiding was the easiest job in the world and in the six months she had been at Desrae's she had learned a lot. Like: never discuss anything personal with a customer. And never use their first name unless they request that you do. In fact, never presume anything, especially with the older men. And never, ever refer to what they were there for.

They were always treated as if they were valued guests rather than paying customers. Cathy collected the money, or remuneration as she had to call it. Desrae took the cheques, though only off good customers of long standing. Through his association with Joey Pasquale the cheques were made out to a shop he owned in Soho, and this way Desrae's name never appeared anywhere.

The punters could happily put their chequebooks into their accountants' hands without fear of anyone cottoning on to what they had really purchased.

Cathy heard the sound of deep laughter coming from the bedroom and grinned to herself. Desrae was a real professional. If only her own mother had had the sense to treat her job as a business.

She looked out of the window at the hustle and bustle of the street. The weak April sunshine was making the place look quite pleasant, but it was at night that Cathy loved Soho best. It was so bright, so alive, so full of music and laughter. She, of course, had only really seen it from this flat. Her first solo outing here had not been very successful, and she knew she still had a lot to learn.

Even doing Desrae's washing had been an eye-opener for her. Everything was hand-washed individually, without a thought for the cost or the time involved.

'You get what you pay for' was a favourite expression of Desrae's, and Cathy could see the truth of this statement every day. Her own clothes were beautiful. Desrae made sure she was dressed every bit as nicely as any well-heeled young lady. He enjoyed seeing her look so good, admired her all the time, which had given her back some much-needed confidence. Now she felt strong enough to venture further afield.

She needed to go back to the East End and find out what had happened to her mother and Eamonn.

Looking at herself in the mirror above the fireplace, she felt pleased with her appearance. She had filled out in all the right places, looked more like a woman of twenty now than a fourteen-year-old girl. Desrae had taught her how to apply cosmetics, how to make the best of herself, and it had certainly paid off. She was propositioned every time she left the flat, which was flattering, even though she would never have dreamed of taking up any of the offers.

The pimps all knew she was with Desrae and treated her with the utmost respect because of that fact. Cathy was sensible enough to know that she wouldn't last five minutes in Soho on her own, and that Desrae and Joey were her passport to the good life she led. In return Cathy loved Desrae fiercely, for his kindness to her and because she sensed in him the same need to be loved that she herself felt.

She knew that Desrae was frightened that once back in the East End, she would fall into the trap of returning there. The people she knew, the life she had once led, might call her back for good. Cathy knew that he was wrong, but could not convince Desrae of this fact.

On Saturday morning she was going to get dressed up and travel back to her old life. Prove to herself she had left it all behind, but for Eamonn. Three days to wait until she saw him again. She longed to see the admiration in his eyes that she saw in everyone else's.

She deserved that.

Picking up her bag, she gazed around the flat and sighed with satisfaction. It looked immaculate. Now she was going down the market to do a little bit of shopping for Desrae, then over to the Italian delicatessen on Old Compton Street for some nice pasta for their lunch.

As she let herself out of the flat she was a very happy girl. At long last life was being good to Cathy Connor.

Caroline was shocked when she finally saw Eamonn again. His face was swollen out of recognition, one eye heavily stitched and he was limping badly. At least his legs were not broken, and he'd been so grateful for that fact he had nearly cried.

As he lowered himself gently on to the bed, she exclaimed: 'Oh my God! Look at the state of your face.'

Eamonn shook his head painfully. 'Get me a stiff drink and shut your fucking trap.'

Caroline poured him a large Irish and handed it to him in silence.

He surveyed the flat disdainfully. 'Look at the state of this fucking place. Look at it, will you? It's like a shit-house. All the money I give you and I end up living in a pig sty.' Tossing back the drink, he bellowed, 'Clear this fucking place up now, girl.'

Caroline, her natural belligerence getting the better of her, said nastily, 'What fucking money, Eamonn? What you

give me goes on food and clothes. It's your job to take care
of the bills. If you had any sense you wouldn't have upset
Dixon. Where's the money going to come from now, eh?'
Even as she spoke she knew she was saying the wrong thing
but could not stop herself.

Eamonn's eyes narrowed and Caroline felt fear leap
inside her breast. He watched her out of the corner of his
eye. Rage was creeping up on him, sliding into his mind,
and he wanted to beat her, pummel her into the ground,
eliminate her. Because someone had hurt him and he could
not bear that affront to his pride.

Caroline's eyes softened and she said shyly, 'Please,
Eamonn, let me look after you.'

Trying to turn on the bed, he realised that in this
condition he would not be hurting anyone but himself. He
forced a smile and lowered his voice. 'Clean up a bit and
get me some grub. I need to rest.'

Caroline breathed a sigh of relief, yet felt a teeny bit
disappointed. She liked it when they fought. It was exciting
and made her feel more alive.

'I'll be back to normal in a couple of days, I just need to
rest up a bit, that's all,' he said.

They smiled at each other then, like conspirators.
Caroline opened a tin of soup and set about cleaning up
the tiny flat. All the time Eamonn watched her and thought
about what he was going to do next.

Tomorrow he would haul himself off to go and see
Dixon. He would apologise. He had a feeling he would
then get his job back. If not, it would at least stop any more
bad feeling. If Dixon gave him his cards, he could work out
where he was going to go from here.

He had had plenty of offers but would see how the land
lay before taking any of them up.

*

Danny Dixon sat in his office and smoked a cigar. He was hungover from the day before and his eyes were bloodshot and aching. His wife's strident voice upbraiding him all morning had not helped his mood. Sometimes he wondered why he didn't just kick her to the kerb and get himself a young bird with big tits and no mouth. He knew why, though. For all her faults his Jean was as sweet as a nut when it came to his businesses.

If he got a capture this second, Jean would swear black and blue that he was with her at the time, date and day he was supposed to have been out doing his skulduggery. She was a diamond in that respect. She was also good for PR. She visited around the East End, looked out for people and brought petty squabbles to his attention. She was an exemplary mother and a good cook. And when he did take a little bird from time to time, she turned a blind eye, knowing she would always be Queen while he wore the crown.

The office door opened and he quickly put out his cigar in the ashtray before him. Jean had told him that if she caught him smoking she would give him the mother of all hidings.

It was one of the heavies, Jake Jacobs.

'There's someone to see you, Mr Dixon.'

Danny blinked impatiently. 'Well, who is it then, man? Spit it out.'

Jacobs cleared his throat. 'It's young Docherty, sir. He wants a word like.'

Danny Dixon grinned. 'Then send him in.'

A minute later Eamonn hobbled into his office. Dixon made him stand.

'So what can I do for you then? As if I 'aven't done enough.'

Eamonn had rehearsed what he was going to say in his

mind all morning. Now, standing before this man who had badly injured him, he was having serious doubts about whether this was in fact a good idea.

Taking a deep breath, he began: 'I've come to apologise, Mr Dixon. It was the drink talking and not me. I don't know what possessed me to be so disrespectful to someone who has only ever shown me kindness and consideration. I know that I won't be working for you now and I accept that as my punishment, though it hurts me more than the hiding did. I felt I had to talk to you face to face so you would know how sincere I am, and also to prove to you how much your goodwill and friendship mean to me.'

Danny Dixon was impressed, and not just by the flowery words. He was more impressed by the fact that the boy had got himself here after a hiding that would have kept lesser men in bed for a week at least. He knew he had been accurate in his estimation of the young man and liked to be right about these things.

'Sit yourself down before you fall down.'

Eamonn lowered himself gingerly into a chair. Dixon stared at him for a few seconds.

'I've crippled people for less than what you did, son. You got off very lightly, I hope you realise that?'

Eamonn nodded his head vigorously. 'I do, Mr Dixon. I can only thank you for being so lenient with me.'

Dixon laughed then, a happy sound. 'Don't lay it on with a fucking trowel! Grovelling doesn't suit you, boy. Now, what do you want?'

Eamonn had trouble keeping the smile from his face. He knew that he was back in with a chance and was elated by that fact. He knew how to play the game and was playing it with as good a grace as he could muster.

'I would like the chance to prove to you that it was a

one-off aberration. If you could find it in your heart to give me a second chance, then no one would behave with more respect, more attention to detail, and more willingness to do any job you cared to give them. I want the chance to prove once and for all how much your goodwill means to me.'

He was gabbling now and knew it, but he had to try and give the man before him the right message and was doing the best he could under the circumstances.

Dixon watched him for a long while, making sure the boy felt the full weight of his scrutiny. If he were to take Eamonn back, he would have to do it without seeming too eager.

'Let me think it over. Your apology has been taken on board. I'll let you know my decision in a few days. Now, go home and rest. I admire you for coming out today and that will be considered along with everything you said. But I can't have anyone slagging me off, especially not an employee. You understand that much, surely?'

Eamonn nodded. He knew he had done well, knew that he had impressed the man both verbally and physically. He only hoped that he had done well enough to warrant a second chance.

As he limped from the building, Jake Jacobs watched him warily. Even he had to admire the young bugger, although he had never liked him. Eamonn had taken a hammering and had come and asked for his job back. That took bottle. But Jacobs still hoped his boss kicked the flash little bastard out on his arse, because Eamonn Docherty Junior was trouble and Dixon should have realised that by now.

Saturday was a bright April day with a promise of warmth. Cathy discarded her coat in favour of a light blue crêpe jacket from Biba. She looked beautiful.

As she alighted from the cab by Bethnal Green station, she breathed in the smells of the East End: hot bread mingled with the odour of the fish stalls. She saw little boys on their way to the synagogues and others carrying kindling and matches, going to light fires and turn on lights for the orthodox Jews in exchange for a penny. She saw the women's curlered heads wrapped in bright headscarves as they made their way to the Roman Road for their shopping, and street cleaners picking up papers and bottles from the Friday night fish suppers.

Her heart singing, she made her way towards Vallance Road where Madge had had her flat – and then stopped dead. She couldn't go to the old neighbours. Obviously they would have had a visit from the Old Bill and she was, after all, still on the run. Instead she turned and made her way towards Code Street in Shoreditch. Betty was her best bet; she would know all that was going on and would keep Cathy's visit a secret.

Cathy knew that people would notice her and that she would seem familiar to them, but she also knew she now looked very different from Madge's daughter, which was how most of them would remember her.

As she walked she looked around her, in search of familiar faces. She saw a few but bypassed them, knowing that to stop and chat would only lead to trouble. East Enders always wanted to know everything. She could tell them nothing, not because she didn't trust them but because what they didn't know couldn't hurt them.

If questioned about her they could speak the truth: they hadn't seen her.

As she walked up the stairs to Betty's flat her heart was in her mouth. But once she had knocked and her mother's friend had opened the door, a puzzled look on her face, she began to smile.

'It's me, Betty. Cathy Connor.'

Betty's face broke into a wide smile. Pulling the girl inside, she slammed the door shut and gave her a tight hug. She crushed Cathy to her chest as if she were Betty's own longlost child instead of someone else's.

'Oh, darling, I've been at me bleeding wit's end with worry about you.'

Cathy extricated herself from the woman's embrace and said happily, 'Don't I get a cuppa then?'

Betty grasped her hand and pulled her through to the kitchen, all the time exclaiming how beautiful she looked, how grown-up and prosperous. As she put the kettle on for tea, she said slyly: 'Sit yourself down, love, and tell me what you're doing for a living because you look marvellous.' The admiration in her voice pleased Cathy but she understood the implication behind the words.

'Well, I'm not doing the obvious if that's what you think.'

It was said in fun, but Betty heard the underlying note in her voice. Grinning, the old brass said, 'I should bleeding well hope not! But all the same, what *are* you doing, love? I mean, no one's heard a thing from you in six months. Sit yourself down properly and tell me all your news.'

Cathy took off her jacket and when she finally had her cup of tea, began to talk. She started to tell Betty about Benton School for Girls then said heavily: 'It's no good, Betty, I can't concentrate until you tell me what's happened to me mum. No one else can really help me with that. I feel terrible that she's away and I can't see her or anything. I mean, I can't even visit her, can I?'

Betty sipped at her tea and wondered how best to lie to the girl before her, because lie she would have to. If Madge Connor had had her way she would have had this little girl – well, Betty conceded, not so little these days but vulnerable all the same – banged up right beside her. She felt that Cathy had dragged her down and wanted to see the girl pay for that. It was only Gates's intervention via Susan P that had made Madge keep quiet for as long as she had.

If she saw Cathy she would talk this beautiful young girl into giving herself up, if she could, and taking the can. Not only for the murder of Ron but also for the assault that had occurred when Cathy had run away from that awful Home.

So keeping her face straight, Betty began a tale that both delighted the girl before her and assuaged her guilty feelings.

'Your mum is as happy as a sandboy, love. I mean, she ain't happy about being banged up, but she accepts it because it's kept you out of trouble. She doesn't want to see you locked up too. When she heard about you going on the trot, she wouldn't believe that you'd hit anyone, said it must have been whoever you was with who'd done the thumping like. You know your mum, love. I mean, for all her faults, she loves you in her own way.

'So now you know the score there, how about telling me what's been happening to you? You look so grown-up and if you don't mind me saying, you look as if you're doing all right.'

Cathy smiled and in a heavily edited account told Betty all about the lovely lady she was working for. Making out that Desrae was a real woman made her feel disloyal. Yet something inside her told her to be wary about exactly what she did say. As much as she loved Betty, brasses talked among themselves and if Cathy was still sought by the police, she didn't want to get caught out by Betty's chattering tongue.

Betty listened and smiled. She knew the score and admired the girl for keeping her business to herself.

Finally Cathy asked her what had happened to Eamonn, which was the question Betty had really been dreading. She had already explained about Eamonn Senior coming to the police station the night Cathy and Madge were arrested, and how helpful he had been, along with Gates. Now she had to lie once more to save the girl's feelings.

'Oh, he's fine, love. Worried about you, of course. Looked all over the place for you he did.' She saw the delight in Cathy's eyes and sighed inwardly. It would break the girl's heart to know what Eamonn had really been up to.

Then, as Betty looked at the beautiful young woman smiling joyfully at her, she felt she could not go on with the lie.

'Look, love,' she said, her own voice catching as she realised she must hurt Cathy, 'he has someone else now. Remember Caroline Harvey? Her dad was away for years. Still inside as a matter of fact.' She tried to make her voice light, tried to make it all sound quite normal. 'Well, Eamonn's been seeing her, or so I heard anyway.'

The devastation in Cathy's face was like a knife-blade thrust into her own heart.

Betty tried again. 'Listen to me, love, it's been seven months. That's a long time for a young feller like him.'

Cathy was quiet for a while. Finally she said: 'Where is he living then?'

Betty closed her eyes and said gently, 'He lives with Caroline. They're round by Vallance Road. One of old Moggs's places.'

Cathy nodded. Then, changing the subject, she said brightly: 'So how can we keep in touch like? I'll need to know how me mum is, won't I?'

'Aren't you on the phone?'

Cathy laughed, a genuine sound. 'Of course we are.'

Betty lit a cigarette. Taking a deep puff, she grinned at the girl before her. 'Give me the number and I'll keep in touch. You can always leave a message for me at the Two Puddings, I'm usually in there these days. They'll give it to me, no fears.'

They chatted for a while after that, about Madge and Betty's life without her friend and confidante. Eamonn was not mentioned again, but as Cathy left they both knew where her next stop would be.

Chapter Eighteen

Caroline's face was a picture as she answered the door to Cathy Connor. They knew each other slightly and each was more than aware of the other's involvement with Eamonn. Standing in the doorway, a cigarette between her lips and a smirk on her face, Caroline stared at the well-dressed young woman before her.

'Whatever you're selling, we ain't interested.'

Cathy smiled thinly. She was amazed at the change in the girl before her. Caroline Harvey had always been a bit of an icon to her. Her big violet eyes, fashionable clothes and large chest had all seemed to a younger Cathy to be the marks of a sophisticated woman. Now, she looked exactly what she was: a trollop. Which pleased Cathy no end.

'Out of me way, I've come to see Eamonn.'

Caroline stood where she was, all filter tip and cheap perfume. 'This is my drum, and you ain't coming in.'

Her voice said she was ready to fight and Cathy was slightly afraid, though not as terrified as she would have been a few months previously. Everyone knew that Caroline Harvey could handle herself but after all she'd been through, Cathy didn't scare easily these days. She pushed past her adversary and walked into the flat.

In the hallway she turned and said in a low voice: 'Don't even think about it, lady, or I'll wipe the fucking floor with you, see if I don't.'

Caroline was shocked at the girl's words. Cathy Connor was known to everyone as a nice girl, a bit mouthy but all right. Recently though the Old Bill had been all over the East End looking for her and now she had gained a reputation. You didn't go on the trot without a bit of bottle and it seemed that young Cathy Connor had acquired a serious amount of it in the last few months.

The two girls stared each other out.

Caroline was amazed at the transformation in her rival. Eamonn had mentioned Cathy now and again but Caroline hadn't really been too worried. Now she saw a young woman with style and aplomb, and that bothered her.

In the last six months with Eamonn she knew that she had gone downhill whereas Cathy Connor, God rot her, had turned into a regular pocket Venus.

Cathy marched into the bedsitting room and Caroline followed her silently. Eamonn lay asleep on the bed, his once handsome face barely recognisable. Cathy looked around the room in disbelief. Her eyes took in its squalor and she shook her head in disgust. The place stank. Caroline knew what she was thinking and it hurt. She didn't want to be judged by this girl, couldn't bear to be found lacking.

Opening his eyes painfully, Eamonn eased himself up in the crumpled bed and stared at Cathy as if he had never seen her before in his life.

'Hello, Eamonn. I see you're doing all right for yourself.'

Her voice was sarcastic and fraught with meaning. Eamonn had never felt so low in his life. To be caught like this when he'd always envisaged their eventual reunion as the full hearts and flowers number, a sixteen-year-old Cathy tremulous with pleasure just to see him again . . . Now it had all gone horribly wrong and he felt cheated.

'Hello, Cathy. How've you been?'

It sounded lame in his own ears. He realised too that he was unwashed, horribly battered, and that the whole place smelled sour. It was more than his pride could bear and he instantly turned surly and defensive.

Caroline stood silently by, aware of the shabby appearance she presented next to their smartly groomed young visitor. Caroline's hair needed washing, her make-up was last night's and her dressing-gown was stained. She felt twenty years older than her real eighteen and resented both Cathy and Eamonn for making her feel that way.

'I'll be in the kitchen,' she mumbled, and took herself off to avoid any further comparisons.

Cathy looked pointedly at Eamonn, making no move to come any closer to him.

'Didn't you wonder what had happened to me?'

Her voice sounded hurt yet resolute, as if she had already worked out how to deal with this situation. Eamonn was aware that for the first time he could remember, Cathy had the upper hand.

Never had she looked so good to him. Never had he seen her so well dressed, so sure of herself. At fourteen she was a woman. Desrae had seen to that.

Smoothing her skirt fastidiously, Cathy finally seated herself on the battered wicker chair next to the bed and looked closely at the boy she had loved all her life. His face was battered beyond recognition. His thick dark hair was plastered to his head with dried blood and sweat. His whole body looked limp as a beaten dog's.

'You look bleeding terrible!' she said, then tried

belatedly to make a joke of it. 'Who upset you this time?'

In his hurt pride and frustration at not being able to play the big man, Eamonn exploded furiously: 'What do you mean by that? You come round here, dressed like a high-class whore, and have the cheek to question me! Not a bloody word from you in fucking months and then you turn up for me like Lady bleeding Golightly and expect me to treat you like visiting royalty! Well, you had a wasted journey, love. I'm well settled here with Caroline.'

Cathy smiled but her eyes were sad as the unfairness of his words registered. 'I never came to get you, you're mistaken there, mate. I came to visit and see how you are, that's all. No more, no less. I've got someone else now, someone who cares about me deeply.'

She was thinking, of course, of her friend Desrae but Eamonn was not to know this. His face was a picture of hurt and surprise and Cathy felt an awful compulsion to laugh, even while the hateful things he'd said were tearing her up inside.

'Who is this bloke then? Got a white stick and a dog, has he?' said Eamonn nastily. He poured himself a whisky from the bottle on the bedside table and downed it in one.

'Like father, like son, eh?' Cathy swiped back. 'How is your dad, by the way? Still living off his little wife – or has he had her money away and gone off on the trot?'

The implication wasn't lost on Eamonn. She saw his face tighten.

'You're very mouthy all of a sudden.'

Cathy grinned. 'Oh, I can afford to be these days. I've got meself someone who takes very good care of me. He's lovely, you'd like him – or at least you'd respect him.' She looked pointedly at his recent injuries.

Eamonn stared dumbly back at her, humiliated beyond bearing and seeking only to hurt her with the worst insult he could find. Even in a rage, it would never have occurred to him to use violence against her. Not Cathy. Not ever.

'It must be your personality he likes then,' said Eamonn, slowly and deliberately. 'You're the worst shag I ever had.'

Cathy shut her eyes for a moment. Opening them, she picked up her bag and got to her feet, saying in a low voice: 'And you were the first shag I ever had. Remember that, Eamonn? I certainly do.'

He could not meet her eyes as shameful recollection flooded back.

'But I forgave you – God knows why,' she continued. 'All the time I was in that bloody awful school . . .' She could not go on. Dashing tears from her eyes, she walked towards the door.

'Cathy, don't go!' he called after her. 'I'm sorry, Cathy . . .'

Caroline, listening to it all from the kitchen, closed her eyes in distress at the feeling revealed in Eamonn's voice. She knew that if she waited a million years he would never, ever feel the same way about her.

Cathy looked back at him and shook her head.

'I won't stay, I've found out all I need to know, thanks. You haven't even asked me what happened to me in the last seven months. How I got on, how I got out of that fucking prison-like school they sent me to. You've asked me nothing about myself because from us being little kids it was always you. *You* who mattered, *you* who were the important one. Do me a favour, Eamonn, get yourself a job and a life. Look after Caroline in there,' she nodded towards the kitchen, 'because she's the only one who would put up with you. You're a big-headed, selfish bastard and I only wish to Christ I'd found that out years ago. You looked down on your dad, but let me tell you – he's more of a man than you'll ever be, mate.'

She walked towards the front door. He was mystified by her reference to a school when he knew she'd had a cushy foster home. He didn't stop to query her, though. His voice rang out harshly.

'Go on, piss off then, you little prat! Get out of here. Who needs you? You were the one who needed me, mate. You all need me.' He had pulled himself off the bed now and Caroline rushed into the room and tried to restrain him. He threw her from him roughly.

Cathy stared at them both and shook her head. 'Look at you, Eamonn. Take a bleeding good butcher's hook at yourself. You're scum. Only I never fully realised that until today.'

And opening the door, she walked away from him. As she went down the stairway she heard him mouthing obscenities at her and hunched her shoulders as if they could physically hurt her.

In the brightness of the street she took a deep breath and walked away, her head high, eyes burning with humiliation and suppressed tears. Hailing a cab, she made her way back to Soho, Desrae, and a life of peace if not happiness. She had done what she set out to do and now she had to go on from here.

Even though leaving Eamonn behind had been like tearing out her own heart.

Eamonn had been ranting and raving for nearly half an hour and Caroline was just about fed up with the lot of it. Seeing young Cathy with her sleek hair and nice clothes had made her realise exactly what she had allowed to happen to herself.

Eamonn had moulded her into what he wanted: a watered-down version of the Madges and other dock dollies he had grown up with. Like his father he needed a woman to keep him, not financially, not yet, but keep him on top. Keep him the master. As she sat in the chair vacated by Cathy and listened to him curse the female race, Caroline shuddered.

She placed a hand over her belly. If she was right, there was a baby inside her and she knew that because of the child to come she was trapped.

Until today, seeing Cathy Connor and listening to the girl give Eamonn as good as she got, Caroline had felt as if she had it all. She had Eamonn, the hard man, the worker. She had a home with him, and a baby on the way. Now she knew all she had was a troubled boy with a vicious streak and an almost psychotic jealousy.

Slumped in the chair, she wondered how the hell it had happened to her. She looked into the mirror on the dressing table, saw her reflection and shook her head. She looked awful. Morning sickness had drained her face of any colour and her hair needed a good wash. Yes, Eamonn had brought her down with him, and down he was. At rock bottom. He had even fouled the nest at work. Dixon had savagely beaten him, and now she was waiting for him to go back to being an enforcer, waiting for the money to come in again.

Caroline was turning into her mother.

That thought terrified her more than anything. Her mother stood by Jack because she dare not do anything else. He had murdered his mistress and his employer. After that his wife had had no choice but to wait for him. If she had taken up with another man, Jack would have seen her scarred for life. He still had connections who would do the job for him.

Standing up, Caroline began to gather her things together. She would go home to her mother and try and sort out everything from there. It took Eamonn a while to realise what she was doing. He thought at first she was finally cleaning up. But as she packed her bag, he started to shriek at her.

'You can fucking stop all that now! I ain't in the mood for hysterics, girl. Get me a drink and something to eat, and hurry up.'

Caroline ignored him and carried on getting her things together.

Eamonn pulled himself to the side of the bed.

'I mean it, Caroline. I'm telling you now, don't fucking wind me up today or I'll hammer you to within an inch of your bloody life. Now stop aggravating me, woman, and do what you're told. I mean it.'

She slipped off her dressing gown and pulled a jumper over her head. As she smoothed it down over her swollen breasts, she said, 'Bollocks, Eamonn. I'm out of here.'

Her voice was loud, firm. He looked at her in total amazement. 'What did you just say?' He narrowed his eyes as if this would enable him to hear her better.

'You heard.' Her voice was strong. It was as if she had turned into a different person. 'I've had enough, I'm going home to me mum's.'

Eamonn shook his head. 'No, you're not, lady. You're staying right here.'

Smiling smugly, Caroline said, 'You don't own me, Docherty. Never did. Go and chase your little mate, 'cos it sounded to me like you was more interested in her than in me. So, instead of wasting my time, I'm off. There's plenty of men out there, and I think I'll take a leaf out of Cathy Connor's book and go out and get meself one.'

She wanted to hurt him like he had hurt her. The blow as it connected with her face sent her reeling across the room. Lights exploded inside her head and she was nearly knocked out by the force of his punch.

Lying across the bed, she lifted her head. Still smiling, even through the blood that was pouring from her mouth, she said: 'You're not stopping me. I'm off, mate.'

Eamonn stared at the girl in total shock. Her lip was split and the inside looked like a piece of raw liver. There was blood everywhere: all over the bed, her face, her clothes. Yet still she was insisting she would go, leave him.

He punched her in the head, connecting with her ear. His heavy signet ring split the flesh. More blood. A lot of it.

Then he began to beat her, really beat her, putting all his strength into the blows, enjoying the yielding of her body beneath his fists. It was all her fault he'd lost the girl he really loved. If she hadn't been here, flaunting herself in front of Cathy, he could have talked her round, he knew he could. Cathy had to have guessed he'd get himself some female company while she was away, but guessing and seeing were very different. It was all Caroline's fault that Cathy had flown off the handle and said those terrible things. And now he'd lost her, lost his Cathy, because of this worthless bitch . . .

He was still punching Caroline when the door was kicked open and the two men from above came in and pulled him off her.

'Fucking hell, mate, you've killed her!'

His neighbour's voice was high with fear and distress. Eamonn stared down at the bloody mess on the bed then looked around him, bewildered.

His fists were covered in blood and bits of bone. Caroline Harvey was unrecognisable. Her hands were still across her stomach. She had died trying to protect her baby instead of herself.

The two men took in the scene and one of them began to retch, the dry sound the only noise in the room.

It was this that snapped Eamonn back to reality. Putting his head in his hands he whispered, 'What have I done? Oh God, what the fuck have I done?'

Jimmy Salter propelled Eamonn to the sink and washed his hands for him. Then, pulling him from the room, he made the other man lock the door. He put his own jacket around Eamonn's shoulders and said to his friend, Barry Callard, 'I'll take him to Dixon. Don't let on what's happened. People will think it's just one of their usual rows.'

Barry Callard was shocked to the core. Nodding, he went back up to the flat above. All he could see was Caroline Harvey's face, or rather the lack of it.

It would haunt him for the rest of his life.

Cathy went into a coffee bar in Brewer Street and ordered herself a large pot of coffee and a cake. Settling herself in the window, she stared out at the people passing by. Everyone seemed to be in a hurry, everyone seemed to have a place to go. It was a beautiful April day and the sun was still shining even though it was cold.

As she sipped her coffee she wondered how she was going to get on with her life now.

Eamonn had been in her mind so much, more so even than her mother; he had always been the most important thing to her. When she thought of poor Madge locked up in Holloway, and how she herself had been more worried about Eamonn, her heart felt sore. Yet he had been everything to her once.

Seeing him with Caroline in that awful flat, with his face battered, his clothes dirty, had opened her eyes. She had always felt that she needed him – without him would be only half alive. She had assumed he felt the same way about her. He had been her reason for living for so long, and now she was seeing him as her mother had seen him, as Betty had seen him, as his own father had seen him.

She thought of the lies she had told him and was glad that he thought she had found someone else. Had someone who cared for her, wanted her, needed her. The tragic part of it was she doubted it would ever be so. That part of her life, the ability to love and trust a man, had gone for ever. Eamonn was the only man she had ever lain with and at this moment she felt he would also be the last. She would never be a Caroline for anyone.

A shadow passed over her and she said desultorily, 'More coffee, please,' thinking it was the waitress.

'It's all right, love, I've ordered it already.'

Cathy looked up into Desrae's face. He was dressed in his straight gear, Sta-prest trousers and a black polo neck. His hair was tied back and he had on only a minimal amount of make-up. Dressed like this on a Saturday night? That told her how worried he was about her.

'I've cancelled all me customers,' he said now. 'Thought we'd have a nice girlie night in. What do you say?' As he spoke, a woman at a nearby table picked up her bag and coat. Looking at them both furiously, she moved to the other side of the coffee shop.

Desrae stared at the woman and smiled, saying loudly, 'Oh, thank fuck she moved away. The smell was simply horrendous!'

Wiping away the tears, Cathy gave him a smile she would have sworn she did not have in her. 'Oh Desrae, things can't be that bad if I've got you.'

'Joey's coming round later tonight, so we'll have a right laugh with him anyway,' he consoled her. 'Life's what you make it, girl, always bear that in mind. It's what you, me or that old bag at the other table with the face like a well-slapped arse, make it – dig? As those bleeding hippies say.'

Cathy laughed again, a small hurt sound. 'I loved him, Desrae. I loved him so very much.'

'You'll have a few more before you're ready to settle down, you mark my words, love,' he said gently. 'With your looks and nice ways, you'll have your pick of men.'

Cathy looked into his eyes and said seriously, 'Not for me, Desrae. Never again.'

Her voice was so sure, so serious, that for a moment he forgot that she was just a young girl. She sounded for all the world like an old, old woman.

Eamonn Senior was half drunk and could not take in what he was being told. Jimmy Salter was trying to tell him that his son had got himself into more trouble.

'Trouble? Fecking trouble? The boy's middle name is trouble,' he said airily, and belched. 'Now away from me door and leave me to meself.'

Jimmy Salter felt as if he would explode from annoyance. Danny Dixon had told him to bring the older man to him, and he had to do it. He didn't want to get involved and yet he was. Seriously.

Pushing his bullet head towards the large Irishman, he said through his teeth: 'Your boy has murdered Caroline Harvey. Now Danny Dixon wants to see you and you're going. He told me to bring you to him and that's exactly what I'm going to do.'

Somehow Eamonn grasped that this was trouble so grievous it would make the Lord Himself worried. Grabbing his coat, he followed the man down the path and climbed into his mini-van. Jimmy Salter was glad to see that shock had sobered up the big man beside him.

'He's killed that little girl Caroline, then?'

Jimmy nodded. 'Battered her to fuck, mate. Couldn't even recognise her.'

Eamonn shook his head, stunned by what he was hearing. 'Sure she was a sweet little thing, what would he want to be doing that to her for?'

Jimmy carried on driving. There was no answer to that kind of question.

'Jumping Jasus Christ and all the angels! Has the boy gone fecking mad? Are you sure that's what he's done, not just given her a dig like, a smack in the jaw?'

Jimmy pulled the car to the side of the road. He looked at the man beside him and said seriously, 'I dragged him off the poor little mare. He'd beaten her to a fucking pulp. Now will you just let me drive you to Dixon's then get meself home for me bleeding tea? Not that I'll have much appetite, knowing that poor little whore is underneath my kitchen, dead as a fucking doornail.'

Eamonn Senior was quiet for the rest of the journey. He was by now as sober as a judge.

Danny Dixon was in a quandary.

Eamonn had killed the daughter of a man known throughout the East End as a raving lunatic. Even from Broadmoor Harvey had a big rep. He kept in contact through visits and letters. He was a great letter writer, by all accounts, and still classed himself a man to be reckoned with.

If Danny helped the boy out then Harvey would hear of it, and a lot of other people too would turn against him over a thing like that. A man could murder other men, maim them, blow them up. But if the same man harmed a woman or a child, then public opinion would turn against him straight off.

For himself, Danny thought that Caroline had most probably asked for what she got. Most women like her did. She'd used her name and her father's notoriety to get things and to open doors. She was a slag, like a lot of the East End girls. He preferred the women of his own youth who'd been good girls, lived cleanly and didn't shack up with every Tom, Dick and Harry who had a big cock and a bit of wedge.

But this was a sign of the times. With loose morals came loose behaviour in other ways. If she had been Eamonn's wife he would have had respect for her. As it was, she'd been his fancy piece and so Danny felt nothing.

It was that clear-cut to him.

Now he was going to hand the boy over to his father. He'd see him all right with a few quid and tell him to get away, as far away as he could before Harvey made his presence felt. There was no way that nutter would let the murder of his daughter go unavenged.

No way in the world.

Father Seamus Jensen had heard Eamonn's confession and was now drinking a large Irish as he listened to the boy's father droning on about the old country and their associations with it. The priest did not really want to be reminded that he came from an extended family of villains and rebels. Didn't really want to be reminded that they were cousins on his mother's side, and certainly didn't want to be reminded of the times they had got drunk together as young men.

Seamus Jensen had entered the priesthood because he had been forced into it. His father was a well-known IRA man and before his execution by the British in Mountjoy Jail, had seen to it that his youngest son had been set on a different course. He had entered the Church, and after a few months had thanked God every day for the chance to serve Him. He also served himself, but didn't dwell on that fact too much.

Now, in his late-sixties, he enjoyed his life very much. He had his drink, his housekeeper – a fine woman who could cook white pudding like a native of Cork – and he had his parish house to live in. Most of all he had respect.

He didn't want Irish scum in his home. He liked to think of his fellow countrymen as poets and singers and hard done by, hard-working men. The Dochertys and their ilk were like a form of cancer in the body politic. Yet, he knew he had to help them.

Even though the boy had murdered a poor young lass, Father Seamus knew it was men like Docherty who put their money into his kitty again and again, while they sang songs about Irish colleens and the old wars against the British, thereby keeping the modern soldiers of Ireland in boots and guns. There was going to be a screaming shenanigan out there soon and it was eejits like Docherty who'd see it was all paid for.

'I've to make a few calls. Pour yourselves a drink and I'll see what I can do, OK?' Father Seamus told them.

Eamonn Junior nodded and said heavily, 'The lights of heaven to you, Father Jensen.'

Seamus Jensen rolled his eyes and said testily: 'No need to go that far, I'm not fecking well dead yet!'

Eamonn Senior sighed with relief as the man left the room. The priest would help his son, as Eamonn Senior would. Yet a part of him was crying out: Why?

Why had he to help him at all after what he had done?

He could only fall back on the old adage: blood really was thicker than water.

Chapter Nineteen

Seamus Jensen was not long making the arrangements. He came back to speak to the two men, his distaste evident to them both.

'You're away tonight. I've been in touch with a few friends and you're to leave on a boat at midnight.'

'Where are we going?'

'New York, the pair of you. It'll cost you your thousand from Mr Dixon but it'll be worth it. They'll get you papers, everything you need to live there and work. But you'll be expected to help them out at some point.'

Eamonn Senior nodded. He knew enough to have expected that.

'The boy's of interest to them, apparently. You can imagine why.'

Eamonn Senior nodded again. They had come out of the frying pan and into the fire. Hands shaking, he poured himself the last of the Jameson's from the bottle. 'Tell them we're willing to deal with them.'

The priest nodded.

People like Eamonn Junior only came along now and again. They were a strange aberration of human nature.

The people Seamus dealt with already knew Eamonn's name, knew of his reputation and wanted to persuade him to their way of thinking. He could be very useful to the Cause.

The priest saw the sadness in the boy's father's eyes and for the first time felt sympathy for him. 'They'll take good care of him, Eamonn, I promise you that.'

Eamonn Senior sniffed and wiped a hand across his face. 'Well,' he said, looking around the room with interest, 'they seem to have taken good care of you too. And you a man of the cloth.'

The unfortunate words were not lost on the man before him and no others were spoken until the car came to pick them both up. At the door Eamonn Senior looked at the priest and said brokenly: 'Will you go and see my wife for me, in a few weeks? Tell her you received a letter. That I'm dead or something.'

The priest nodded. 'I'll do what I can for her all right.'

There was nothing left to be said and so Eamonn got into the car with his boy and offered up a last silent goodbye to London. He knew he would never see it again.

His son sat beside him, quiet and shocked. His breathing seemed laboured, as did his movements. The two other men in the car were chatting between themselves, their voices a low drone in the background of Eamonn Senior's thoughts.

New York. Please God they'd find a bit of peace there. If his son would ever know peace again, of course.

He felt responsible for the boy's conduct, felt that if he had been a better father, more of a man, the lad would have stood a chance in life. Instead he was a nothing, a nobody, the vicious son of a notorious drunk.

He understood his son's need for respect – it was the driving force behind most men. Eamonn himself had taken his son's self-respect many years ago when he was a child. Now he could only try and give it back to him. If it wasn't already too late.

Cathy and Desrae made their way through Soho, giggling and laughing like schoolgirls. As they approached Old Compton Street, though, Desrae swore under his breath. 'Why don't they give them poor girls a break?'

They stood and watched as a hostess club was ransacked by the police. Women and girls of all ages stood out in the cold night air in flimsy dresses and open-toed high heels. The police were rounding them up and putting them into meat wagons. The men who frequented the club were allowed to go home. They had not technically done anything wrong.

As they went to pass by, Cathy grabbed at Desrae's arm and held him back. Then, to his utter astonishment, a well-known voice said: 'Hello, Desrae, who's your little friend?'

Richard Gates's voice was low as usual and Cathy looked up into his eyes, her own filled with terror.

Desrae smiled. 'This is me niece, Cathy Duke. Say hello to the nice man, dear.'

Cathy didn't say one word.

Gates looked down at her and smiled gently. 'You're looking well. Desrae looking after you, is he?'

Cathy nodded.

Desrae looked at the man and said loudly. 'Now listen here, you, there's nothing funny going on here. She just maids, that's all. I've never been into the female side of things and you of all people should know that.'

Gates chuckled gently. 'That's the thing I've always liked about you, Desrae. You're never afraid to open your big trap. Keep your voice down before we have half the Filth here listening to our conversation! I'm on another tack entirely, nothing to do with all this. I'm strictly East End, me. Now, I know this little girl and I happen to like her, all right? So you can stop looking so scared.'

He placed a hand on Cathy's shoulder and smiled. 'You all right, really?'

As Cathy was about to speak the sirens went off and the noise was deafening. They all waited until it was over before continuing with their walk.

'I'm up here looking round for an old friend of yours, really. Maybe you could help me? Eamonn Docherty Junior – seen him today?'

Cathy shook her head. Like most Londoners she thought it best never to admit anything to the police unless they had you bang to rights.

'He murdered his girlfriend today, battered her to death,' Gates said imperturbably.

She blurted out: 'What, Caroline? Caroline Harvey?' Her face was screwed up in disbelief.

'Yeah, Caroline Harvey. Did you see her at all today?'

Cathy shook her head. 'I ain't seen no one, Mr Gates. I rarely go anywhere without Desrae. He looks after me like.'

Gates stared at her for a while before saying, 'There's a lot worse than old Desrae in the world, love.'

Desrae said nastily, 'Not so much of the bleeding old, you!'

'Was you in the East End today, Cathy? Tell the truth.'

She shook her head once more. 'I've been with Dessie all day, haven't I?'

Desrae nodded, he knew what to say. 'We've been together since we got up this morning. Ask Joey if you don't believe me.'

'There won't be any need for that.' Gates patted Cathy's shoulder again and said, 'Look after yourself, all right? And if you need any help, anything at all, you call me, OK?'

As Cathy walked away with Desrae, she looked back over her shoulder at the man who had been so kind to her. He had let her go, knowing what she had done at that school.

Desrae marched them back to his flat. Closing the door behind them, he said heavily, 'If Gates is on your side, love, you're halfway home to anything you want in life. He ain't a bad one for an Old Bill. Bent as a nine-bob note, but a nice fella for all that. Now let's sit down and you can tell me what the fuck happened today. All of it, and in graphic detail.'

Cathy sat on the sofa and began to cry, thinking of poor Caroline. As Desrae cuddled her, she opened up her heart and mind. Holding her close, he whispered his love for her and told her that everything would be all right now, because he would make it so. Cathy Duke, as she now was, believed him. Desrae was the best thing that had ever happened to her, and she thanked God for leading her to him.

Tucked up in bed an hour later, she listened to the low drone of Desrae's conversation with Joey and allowed her thoughts to stray to Eamonn.

She remembered him when they were children, growing up together. Remembered how they had stuck together through everything, because all they had ever had was each other. She cried then, cried for the boy he was and for the boy he became. Cried because she had loved him, really loved him, and he had thrown away that love.

Of all the things that had happened to her, Eamonn's rejection of her had been the worst.

Father and son felt the movement of the tanker as it rolled out of Tilbury docks. The captain had taken them to their quarters and left them with some food and a bottle of whiskey. Eamonn Junior had not spoken a word all day and his father watched him warily, wondering if he knew what was going on around him.

This boy, his son, had murdered a defenceless girl, as once before he had robbed a young man of his life. Now the upshot of it all was they were sitting on a filthy cargo boat making their way to America. Maybe it was for the best. God had His pattern, and made you live by it.

Pouring his son a large drink, he placed it in the boy's trembling hands. Eamonn Junior drank it down and held out the glass for more. He needed total oblivion above all things. He needed to be drunk and out of his head. He needed to stop thinking.

Strangely, he wasn't thinking about poor Caroline, he was thinking about Cathy and what a fool he had been not to realise what he possessed in her. Having her in front of him again had shown him all he had given up. All he had abandoned. He had hated her in that moment, believing that she was to blame for all his troubles. Now he knew that he had no one to blame but himself.

Cathy was right: he was greedy, he was selfish and he used people. Now he had murdered for a second time, a girl who had loved him with all her heart. Poor Caroline. He had never really cared for her – she had been a possession, something he owned. Someone he had abused as he abused everyone.

As he had even abused Cathy Connor.

It was daybreak when he finally cried, but Eamonn being Eamonn, it was mostly for himself. The best part of his youth was gone, and with it any chance of seeing again the girl he loved.

Book Two

Truth is the most valuable thing we have. Let us economize with it.

– Mark Twain (Samuel Langhorne Clemens), 1835–1910

Chapter Twenty

1971

'Jasus, son, would you ever let a man fecking sleep?'

Eamonn Senior's voice was heavy with drink and tiredness. His son stared at him balefully while he tried to dress in the confined space of their bedroom.

'You'd better get up and let's get to work, Dad, for fuck's sake. You know what O'Halloran said yesterday and if you lose this job then you can fuck off out of it, I ain't keeping you.'

The older man looked at his handsome son and sighed heavily. The boy was working hard to try and get them some kind of life. They were robbing Peter to pay Paul, and after all this work and worry their home was a walk-up in the Bronx which housed only Irish, blacks and cockroaches.

The smell was worse than anything he had encountered in his life before and he was heartily sick of it. The heat of a New York summer here was bad enough, but the cold winter, with endless snow and ice, was doubly unbearable. If the boy would only listen to reason they'd be riding the pig's back. But he would not listen, wanted to do everything right this time. Wanted to have a regular job, a normal way of life. It was sickening.

Scratching his belly, the older man waited until he heard the pop of the gas under the coffee pot before pulling on his trousers. Dragging on his shirt, he began his daily complaint, shouting to be heard in the kitchen.

'If you'd only listen to sense, boy, we'd be living the life of Riley now and no mistake.'

Eamonn Junior rolled his eyes at the ceiling. Rinsing the cups under the tap, he tried to blot out his father's words. Every day it was the same thing and he was getting sick of it. The old man wanted him to become America's answer to Ned Kelly and get them a good living. In England, his father had told him that his way of life was bad. Now, though, in the States, he wanted the boy to capitalise on his reputation as a murderer and join what amounted to the Irish Mafia.

He stared out of the window and watched the street as he sipped his coffee. There were black faces everywhere; at first that had amazed him. England had a fair few, but America was positively overrun with them. It had been strange finding himself in a minority when they had first moved here, and time hadn't changed that. There was a very beautiful black girl living on his floor and Eamonn had chatted to her a few times before he realised she was a prostitute. He smiled now as he recalled asking her out, and her discussing the price! In England he had thought himself so knowledgeable about everything. Here he was a babe-in-arms.

The dock work had been easier to acquire than he had expected yet it was still physically arduous and his father was only taken on because of his Irish connections. They both knew and both used it in their own way. Strangely,

Eamonn did not miss his old job with Danny Dixon.

Eamonn loved New York. It was a seething mass of people, cultures and trouble. City Hall was the all-important centre of government for the province. People talked about it as if it were a mixture of the House of Lords and the worst military junta they could name. It was corrupt, it was splendid and it was there.

Yet as exciting as the city could be to him at times, he saw the ugliness of it keenly. Felt the tensions among the underclasses, and heard the way that people talked and talked and never really said anything. The bottom line was that New York was like any other big city: it was a good touch providing you had money. He needed money here more than he had ever needed it in London.

He realised his father was standing beside him, slurping black coffee and giving voice to his usual complaint. 'If you'd only listen to the Mahoneys, we'd be living like lords. Have the best of everything. The Irish run this fecking town though no one has realised it yet. The collections for Ireland are bringing in a fortune and anyone doing the job can cream off at least twenty-five per cent for their trouble. There's money to be made, good money, and you of all people should be seeing that. Christ, there was a time when you'd kill for a few quid . . .'

His voice trailed off. He knew when he had gone too far. 'Jasus, son, I could cut me tongue out, I could that.'

There was a deep silence. Finally it was broken by Eamonn Junior saying, 'Wrap up well, Dad, it's freezing out there.'

They left the apartment in silence. Eamonn Senior was still contrite over his words and as they walked down the stairs, squeezed his son's shoulder affectionately.

'This weather would cut the lungs from you. I don't ever remember being so cold.'

As they walked towards the bus depot a car stopped beside them and Petey Mahoney whistled them to stop. 'Jump in. I'll give you a lift. There's no work for you today anyways.' His heavy Cork accent was at odds with his smart clothes. He dressed like an upper-class WASP.

Eamonn Junior looked at the man expressionlessly. The smell of petrol from the car was heavy in his lungs, hot-smelling, hanging on the cold air. His father pushed him gently towards it and Petey, taking a roll of money from his pocket, slipped the older man a fifty. Smiling, he said: 'Get the hair of the dog that bit you. I'll take care of the little one.' He laughed at his own joke and Eamonn, knowing he had no choice, got into the car.

'Isn't this a lovely automobile?' Petey asked him as an opening gambit. Eamonn smiled. It was – a Pontiac Firebird, black and sleek, purring as they pulled away into the traffic.

'You could be driving one like this if you wasn't so pigheaded.' Petey held up his hand as if he were being challenged, yet Eamonn had said nothing. He never did. 'Don't start now! I'm just stating a fact. We need young men like you. You've already got a good reputation from home. Why do you always refuse to work for us?' The last was said with genuine interest. There were Paddies climbing over themselves to get in with the Mahoneys. Eamonn's complete indifference to them was what made him stand out.

They knew he had murdered twice. The girl was a sorry case, but such was life. The first murder, as a young boy, had been well executed and with just the right amount of ruthlessness to earn him the respect of his peers.

Eamonn could have found it in his heart to like him, if only Petey didn't keep on at him about joining the Mahoneys' firm. He shook his head and sighed. 'Can we just listen to the radio from now on?'

Petey, always affable, turned up the radio and said delightedly: 'At least you're talking, that's a new one with you. I call you the Silent Man. Tell me just this one thing and I'll shut me big gob – what made you change so much? I mean, why this stand after all you did in London, eh?'

They had stopped at traffic lights and Petey peered into the younger man's eyes, genuinely interested in what he was asking.

Turning down the radio, Eamonn said seriously, 'I killed a girl, a lovely young girl who should have had a long life ahead of her. I also killed a boy. He'd probably have done the same for me but still, I robbed two people of their lives in just a few years. I broke men's legs and arms for money, and I enjoyed it. I loved the power of it all, loved being in charge. After Caroline's death, I took stock. I wanted to be part of the real world again. I stopped wanting to control everything. I was a sick person, an evil person, and I could no longer live with that.'

Petey looked at him, and then as the lights finally changed, said gently: 'Is that all? I thought it was for some really good reason.'

The radio full on once more, they drove in silence to the headquarters of the Mahoneys, deep in the heart of Queens.

Jack Mahoney was big, six foot four inches, with the breadth to carry it off. His wife tried to keep him in shape but in the fast-food culture of America it was a losing battle. His belly was gigantic, a massive wobbling structure that she refused to have on top of her. This suited Jack because his tastes ran to tiny crop-haired black girls who he would swear gave the best blow jobs this side of the Atlantic. His seven daughters adored their big rumbustious father and he attended Mass every morning at six-thirty, rain or shine. Food and getting his cock sucked regularly were Jack's main hobbies. His work was a different kettle of fish altogether.

Jack controlled Mahoney enterprises through fear and through money. He believed that if you paid a man enough, you bought his loyalty. It had worked well for him till now. The Mahoneys had never had an informer or a turncoat.

But Jack also liked to keep the Irish around him happy. He knew that there was going to be a lot of trouble in the North back home, and even though he himself was a Southerner, Cork born and bred, he realised there was a lot of money to be made from helping out their Northern counterparts.

A large percentage of New York Irish lived on their memories, talking constantly of the Old Country and eating cabbage and corned beef, as a kind of sacred rite. It tasted nothing like the good food in Ireland but they didn't know that, because the majority of them were second- or third-generation Irish. While fuelling their nostalgia for the Auld Country, Jack was making a bundle from his Irish bars and was determined to keep it that way. His bars were alive with men and women singing rebel songs, eating Irish soda bread and drinking Jameson's. He had other businesses too, and to run these he needed muscle.

It seemed Eamonn Docherty was just the kind of employee they were looking for. It had never occurred to Jack that anyone might not want to work for him. If it had he would just have issued them with an ultimatum: work for me or I'll make sure you never work anywhere else. But for all that he knew he was a good employer. Once he had them, he looked after them in such a way that he was guaranteed their loyalty and gratitude for ever after.

Eamonn Docherty, according to the boy's father, was an

enforcer born and bred. Best of all, he had no convictions, political or otherwise. When asked about the state of Ireland, he had answered: 'Who gives a fuck?' Jack Mahoney's sentiments entirely, though he would never admit as much to anyone outside the family. So he had arranged for his younger brother Petey to pick up the errant youngster and bring him in.

Jack Mahoney's reputation was such that he was entertained in Little Italy and Chinatown – almost unheard of for an Irishman – but he was a staunch believer in organised crime and times were changing. The Italians and the Chinese were businessmen at heart and this was the time for them to befriend the Irish who were coming up fast in the various rackets.

He saw his brother parking the car and getting out of it with young Docherty. Jack watched the boy's arrogant stance closely and shook his head with a wry smile. The younger man was a fine specimen, but then his father had been a big handsome man in his day. Eamonn Senior could have been somebody but the easy life had always appealed to him too much. Men who lived off women were dirt to Jack, but the old man was Irish and you had to seem at least to be looking after your own.

Settling himself behind his large oak desk, Jack made himself look busy and important as the young man was shown into his office by Petey.

Eamonn Senior was sitting in a bar off Broadway. It was Irish-owned, the drink was not watered down and the company convivial. With a fifty-dollar bill, he was soon a welcome part of that company and was engrossed in conversation with a man called Willie McLaughlin on the pros and cons of a united Ireland. Three large Jameson's and he was well away, enjoying himself, when out of the corner of his eye he noted Jackie O'Malley, a bookmaker to whom he owed over two hundred dollars.

'In the money, are we?' Jackie's voice was sarcastic.

Eamonn Senior, with drink inside him and feeling good, was not too worried. 'Oh, it's a small touch I got from Petey Mahoney. He's out with my boy at the moment.'

Jackie knew this was a veiled threat and looking at the red-nosed man before him, suddenly became very angry. People like Docherty were users and O'Malley knew that if he let him off, others would expect the same consideration. He stared around the bar, at the shamrocks and the phoney Irish flags, the Waterford crystal behind the bar and the photos of Brendan Behan that adorned the walls. Overwhelmed with the futility of the struggle to keep his head above water, he said vehemently: 'I don't care who your son is gallivanting about with, I want the money you owe me, and I want it now!'

Eamonn Senior, full of whiskey and bravado, answered him lightly. 'Then you'll know what it's like to want, won't you?'

Jackie O'Malley had buried his wife three days before. He had been chasing money for weeks now; his wife's treatment had cost him a fortune, and in all honesty she hadn't even been worth it. His only son had come back for the funeral and returned to college with hardly a word. His daughter was having nothing to do with Jackie, and he himself was being chased by loan sharks because no one would pay him what they owed so he in turn could not make his repayments.

Now here was a piece of shite, a man devoid of anything that could be classed decency, more or less telling him to whistle for his money. People were watching the exchange. Jackie was being publicly belittled and was growing angrier by the second.

This had been the story of his life, used and abused by everyone. No respect, no one according him even common courtesy. He had been chasing his money for days, and no one was interested. He was a small operator, didn't have people like the Mahoneys or the Murphys to chase his debts for him, and it seemed that more and more people were turning to the bigger firms after they had in effect ripped Jackie off.

He snapped his fingers at the barman. 'Two large ones, here.'

The barman placed the two drinks on the bar and Jackie downed one at a gulp, then immediately followed it up with the other. Everyone watched in fascination as he then opened his coat and took out a long-barrelled gun. It was an old gun, one that had been used many years before by the old Moustache Petes. It was practically an antique.

He shot Eamonn Docherty Senior in the chest, the loudness of the retort making people in the bar run for cover and drowning out the game of baseball on the television set. Then, turning the gun on himself, Jackie placed it in his mouth and pulled the trigger.

The young barman looked at the brains spattered all over his T-shirt, saying, 'Jesus fucking Christ!' over and over again as he waited for the police to arrive.

The news hit the streets almost immediately and a policeman paid by the Mahoneys reported it to Petey while Eamonn was still closeted with Jack. Eamonn stared at the man before him.

Jack was huge, fat and undignified, a big, bumbling man with an aura of viciousness that was hard to ignore. Eamonn could see now why people were in awe of him. As big as he was, he moved in a surprisingly light fashion which belied his enormous body. It was a complete revelation to Eamonn to meet this soft-spoken man face to face. He had heard so much about him that to meet him was like gaining an audience with the Pope. Once you got there you were not sure what to say.

Jack gently explained to him what he wanted. He never used force unless he had to, was a great believer in the power of the spoken word.

'The thing is, I understand you are a very smooth operator. I've had great reports from London about you. I think that unfortunate incident with the girl was probably partly her own fault. Women can be the devil at times with their talking and their tantrums. I know, I have a wife and seven daughters, God help me. Now, I am after your expertise in the heavy department. I need young men, up and coming sorts, whom I can train and put in positions of prominence in business. I can offer you big rewards and the respect of the whole community. I can also make you rich beyond your dreams.'

His voice changed then. The camaraderie was gone as he finished: 'I do not offer my friendship lightly, nor do I like having it thrown back in my face. I only ever offer the hand of friendship personally once. If it's not accepted then I class that person as my enemy.'

Eamonn knew that he was being told that if he didn't take the job he would be a marked man. Mahoney could make sure he never worked again. Or he could make sure that he never breathed again. It was a Catch 22 situation. Forcing a smile on to his face, he asked gently, 'What about the pay?'

The big guy laughed. He had his man and could afford to be magnanimous. Even though they both knew he had got Eamonn by default, they forged a strange kind of friendship that day. It was based on mutual respect.

Eamonn had expected to dislike the man, yet found

himself admiring him, even wanting to be part of his enterprise. Jack Mahoney had taken the American Dream and turned it on its head. If for no other reason than that, Eamonn looked up to him. Deep inside, he also acknowledged that he was glad to be back doing what he did best. Doing what he enjoyed!

He felt the old adrenaline rush. Now he was back where he loved to be: in charge of himself, in charge of others. Deep inside, he'd known all along he had been kidding himself. He was born for this life, brought up for it. Why fight it any longer?

As he left the office he saw Petey waiting for him. The other man looked grave-faced, and as he broke the news to Eamonn, felt a great sorrow for him. The Mahoneys knew how great the pull of a patriarch could be. Their own father had been a lot worse than Eamonn Docherty Senior, and yet they had taken care of him.

It was family, blood, kin. It was what made the world go round and people strive to better themselves.

At the end of the day, family was all you had.

Eamonn Senior lay on the mortuary slab. His heavy face looked much older in repose.

His son looked down at the man he had both loved and hated, and felt a great grief inside him. He forgot all the times they had fought, forgot the times as a child when he had gone without food so the man on the slab could drink. Forgot the hidings he had endured during drunken rages.

He was seeing the man who had accompanied his son to a strange land because he knew how much trouble the boy was in. He was remembering how his father had tried, at least that once, to take care of him.

Swallowing down the tears, he tried to remember his mother. She had been a small woman with a ready smile who had adored her big husband and son. She had died a quick painful death from cancer at a very young age. Her face, so beautiful once, had been ravished by the pain of the tumour inside her breast.

He remembered the smell of the sick room, the heavy bitter scent of death. Until that moment he had forgotten it all. The pain had been too great to bear.

Now he could see the pale yellow of the bedspread, the whiteness of the sheets as she lay there, pale and so very thin, in her soft Irish brogue telling him to be a good boy and to do what his father said.

He had been too young to understand she was telling him goodbye.

The hospital staff had been kind to him afterwards. The nurses had given him tea and toast and he could remember his father crying. Those tears had frightened him. Eamonn couldn't remember him drinking before then.

He realised as he looked down at the dead man that his father had run away from this same memory for the rest of his life, had chased it away with whiskey.

He had done the best he could for his son, and inadvertently shaped him as an adult.

In some ways he supposed he should be grateful to his father – grateful for the fact that he had made Eamonn into the cold-hearted, violent killer he was today.

Chapter Twenty-One

Eamonn followed Petey into the warmth of the Lennox Bar on Lennox Avenue. It was a haunt for the waifs and strays of the bookie market – men who were either over-extended or couldn't get credit any more for various reasons.

In the Lennox Bar men who would otherwise be black-listed could gamble. All eyes turned to the doorway at their arrival, and a tall thin man with ginger hair and startlingly blue eyes slipped from his stool at the bar and made his way to the men's room. Without pausing in the bar area, Petey and Eamonn followed him.

They ambled through the men's room and out of the window. In the back alley the ginger-haired man was being held by Petey's two heavies, Paddy and Seamus O'Connor, who had been ordered to wait there in case of just such a manoeuvre.

Petey wiped a hand across his face and sighed heavily, a theatrical sound full of distress and hurt pride.

'Jasus, Jonjo, you're driving me up the fucking wall. I mean,' he looked around at Eamonn for confirmation of his words, 'we've been looking for you all day and me

fucking legs are playing me up and now I have to climb –
climb – through a fucking window in a fucking shit-house
bar and come and fucking get you! Are you on a fucking
death wish or what?'

Jonjo didn't answer.

Shaking his head, Petey nodded at Eamonn then leant
against the wall to light himself a cigarette. Eamonn walked
forward and punched the man to the ground. Jonjo put up
no resistance.

As he lay, curled in a foetal position on the filthy
ground, Eamonn proceeded to give him a kicking of epic
proportions. Blood was coming from Jonjo's face and
head. His eyes were closed, swollen shut, and his arms
hung in strange positions.

Hardly sweating, Eamonn started on the man's legs.
His face was impassive, the feeling of euphoria that bouts
of violence created in him taking over once more. The
O'Connor brothers watched in fascination, knowing they
were seeing the work of a master. It would make a good
story. Since Eamonn had joined the firm, he had become
the object of a great deal of interest. Though violence was
part of the job for all of them, this man had brought it to
the level of an art form.

As his parting shot, Eamonn took a box cutter. He bent
over the inert figure and removed its ears. Fortunately
Jonjo was already unconscious as blood ran in deep red
rivulets across the dusty ground. Straightening up,
Eamonn walked away, cleaning the knife on a piece of old
rag as he went.

'How about a beer before the next stop?' Petey was
aware that his own voice sounded high, almost girlish. In
fact, like this, the other man frightened him.

Eamonn just shook his head and got into the car.
Sighing heavily, Petey got in beside him and started the

engine. There was a very evident electricity in the air until Eamonn, forcing himself to relax, finally spoke.

'Who's next on the agenda?'

Petey grinned. 'You'll enjoy this one. It's a favour for a man called Carmine, an Italian brother. His daughter was married to a guy called Inglesias who beat the fuck out of her. She's divorced from him now but he still likes to intimidate her, you know? Anyway, the rub is he took the kids last week and didn't return them. I found out where he lives and we're going to pay him a little visit. He's scum.

'Carmine is not a made man but he's respected, which is why he's paying us big bucks to sort it out for him. He doesn't want to take a domestic to his Don, which is understandable in a way, but I also hate the motherfucker we're going to see. He's a pimp straight out of the old school. Beats his girls, puts them on drugs, and even has a specialist agency.'

Eamonn frowned. 'A specialist agency?'

Petey gave a twisted grin that made him look even uglier than he was. 'Listen to this one, Eamonn: this guy Inglesias brings in pregnant women for out-of-town businessmen who are into that type of kick. One of the women, a young Puerto Rican, only nineteen, is brought to an apartment and told that all she has to do is strip. She's told that there's a security guy gonna wait outside the apartment and once she's finished, he'll remove her from the building and she'll be five hundred dollars richer. The stupid bitch goes for it. After all, she's pregnant. She needs the money.'

He shrugged and then said huskily: 'They fucking raped her! A pregnant woman and they raped her. Seven men, one after the other, up her arse, you name it. Now I run women, you know that, everyone knows that. But I run fucking *women* – not kids, not pregnant women – but real honest-to-goodness whores who know what they're about.

She was dumped from a car by Central Park West, already in labour. Her kid died and she was left scarred for life. This low-life fucking scum needs to be sorted out once and for all.'

Eamonn shook his head. 'And this Carmine let his daughter marry this scum?'

'Until his daughter told him the score, he knew fucking nothing,' Petey explained. 'After the marriage, Inglesias thought he was safe. He had her terrified. Now, though, he thinks that with his money and connections he can get himself out of anything. We're going to let him know that that is bullshit. He's a dead man as far as I'm concerned. Or at least a living dead man, you know what I'm saying?'

Eamonn nodded. 'So where is he now, and what's the setup?'

'This is the good bit, see,' Petey sniggered. 'He thinks he's meeting me in connection with a business proposition. I've romanced him over the phone and talked sweet to him once or twice in a few bars. Carmine still don't know all the man's business, just thinks he's a regular pimp. So, I have Inglesias wetting his pants at the thought of the big bucks I'm gonna be bringing in for him. What we have today is a situation where he is meeting us in the privacy and comfort of his own home. We're gonna take the fucker in his natural habitat.'

Eamonn laughed now, relaxed and happy. 'Where are the children?'

Petey waved a hand dismissively. 'He gave them back yesterday. It was just another shitty thing to do, frightening his ex-wife by keeping the kids. He don't really want them. It's part of his make up. You know: I don't want you but I'm fucked if you'll ever forget me, little lady. Well, after this he's history.'

*

Crussofixio Inglesias looked at the girl beside him and smiled. She tried to smile back but it was difficult with a swollen mouth. He was so handsome, so good-looking, she still tried to believe that he was a nice guy, even though she knew now for definite that he wasn't.

'If you'd just done what I asked, none of this would have happened, eh?' He poked her in the chest with a long bony finger. It hurt.

She nodded. Even her short brown hair seemed to be trembling as she tried to be what he wanted her to be.

'Act like you're enjoying it. No man's gonna pay me good for a broad who looks like you do. I mean, you're looking ugly and you're looking like a frightened rabbit. Now there are times when that's what the man might want, a little rough stuff, want you to look frightened. Then it's good. It brings in the money. You're like an actress, you know. This is an art form.'

'But he hurt me, he made me hurt inside.'

Lighting a joint and breathing in deeply, Crussofixio scowled at the whore. He was that rare kind of man who gets aggressive on grass. Instead of mellowing him out, it made him more angry, and this was a man who was born angry. A man who honestly believed that women were there for men like him to exploit.

Crussofixio was sitting on a chair, legs splayed, watching the girl, a cruel smile on his face. Her tiny breasts were exposed but she hadn't realised that fact yet. The halter top had come undone and was hanging loose around her waist. Her breasts were barely buds, nothing there at all to interest a real man.

She looked what she was: a child. As Crussofixio stood up he seemed to loom over her, his six foot two inches heavy, running to fat.

'Look at yourself!' he ranted. 'You look like a slut, you

look like every other fucking whore on the streets of this town. I feed you, clothe you, take care of you, and *this* is what I get. You taking me for a fool, honeybunch? Because if you are, you better think twice, girl.'

She was terrified, starting to apologise to the man who had beaten her, but before he could raise his fist to her there was a knock on the door.

'Open it,' he snapped. 'I'm expecting some business associates.' He looked proudly at the girl's battered face. The men with whom he was going to work would see how tight he kept his ship. They would see just how good he was at his job from this demonstration of what it took to keep a girl in line.

As Eamonn and Petey walked into the apartment, Crussofixio smiled at them. The girl, convinced they were new punters, attempted to smile at them too, through her pain and tears.

Petey laughed loudly. 'What's going on? This your fucking daughter or something?' He stared at the girl. 'Put your tits away, love.'

He looked askance at Crussofixio who stared back, baffled. These men didn't look as if they were in his home to do business; in fact, they both looked totally wired. He recognised Eamonn as the mad Irishman everyone was talking about and felt a loosening of his bowels.

'One of my girls, she tried to fuck me with a john,' he explained nervously. 'I had to teach her a lesson, you know what it's like.'

Petey shook his head. 'No, I don't know what it's like. I never employed a little girl in my goddamn motherfucking life. How would I know what it's like?'

Crussofixio was in a quandary. Of all the things he had envisaged from this meeting, being criticised and intimidated had definitely not been on the agenda.

'Hey, man.' He tried to smile. 'I have to sort the bitches out myself, need to see that the work's done proper—'

Petey slapped his face. 'Fuck you, man. Fuck you and your shitty operation and your diseased fucking whores and your crappy little clubs. We don't want no part of you or anything to do with you. We're here over a fucking grudge, man, a fucking beef you got with your ex-wife's father, Carmine. I promised him I was going to cut off your fucking balls and bring them back to him in a handkerchief, and that's just what I'm going to do.

'Not only because I promised Carmine but because you stepped over the line, man, you stepped over all the lines of taste and fucking decency when you began supplying fucking pregnant women. Even the fucking niggers are disgusted with you.'

Crussofixio looked amazed and very frightened. He stared at the girl on the sofa. She sat watching everything with wide eyes and a chalk-white face. Her body was still trembling from the earlier beating. Petey took her gently by the arm and led her out of the room.

Crussofixio gaped at the two men before him with bulging eyes. He knew he was about to die, or even worse be left crippled, and remembered all the times he had hit on someone. Finally he knew what it was like to be on the receiving end of violence and he was terrified, because he knew how much he had enjoyed making people feel like this. He held up both arms as if to ward them off even though they had not made a move towards him as yet.

'Hey, guys, listen to me – Carmine is lying. I was married to his fucking tramp of a daughter, for fuck's sakes. This ain't business, it's a private family feud.'

Eamonn spoke for the first time. 'What about the pregnant women? I suppose they're a figment of our imagination as well, are they?' His London accent made the man before him jump, it was so harsh-sounding in the plush Manhattan apartment, so out of place.

'You're a big guy – big and running to fat. Letting yourself go now the money's coming your way,' Eamonn continued. 'You should never have let us in here today without covering firepower at least. You're a piece of scum in every way, Mr Inglesias, and this is your last day on earth. How does that feel, eh? Come on, tell me. I'm interested.'

Sitting down on the sofa so recently vacated by the young hooker, Inglesias cried into his long-fingered, perfectly manicured hands.

Eamonn shot him in the back of his head five times, leaving blood and bone and brains all over the white damask covers. Afterwards Petey removed his balls with the box cutter then, whistling, they made their way back down to their car.

As they pulled away, Eamonn said: 'You're really delivering his balls?'

'Too right I am,' Petey sniggered. 'These,' he held up the bloody handkerchief with pride, 'are worth over two hundred thousand dollars. We made a big fucking killing today, in more ways than one. We'll deliver these, have a late lunch, and then get out to do anything else that's on the agenda.'

Eamonn nodded his satisfaction with this suggestion. 'All in a day's work, eh?'

They were still laughing as they drove away.

Chapter Twenty-Two

Deirdra Mahoney was seventeen, pleasantly plump, with slanting green eyes and deep red hair, this being her crowning glory. Long and thick with a natural curl, it shone with gold lights and hung like a curtain down her back.

Deirdra knew that if her legs were short and chubby, and her breasts just a little too small, her glorious hair compensated for these deficiencies.

Unlike her six siblings, she knew her failings and worked on her good points. She was polite and quiet before her mother, deferential to her father, Jack, biding her time until Eamonn Docherty asked for her hand. He had been with her father for a year now, and had worked his way up to a very good position. She was certain he would. She had made it quite plain that it was what she was expecting; made it quite plain too that if he didn't toe the line in that respect, she would see her father and let him have the final word.

Once Deirdra had her man, she would finally have a life. A real life, one where she could be mistress of her own house, and have a car and some fun.

Jack Mahoney had his daughters watched like hawks, and this depressed her greatly. All the other girls at school had had some kind of sexual experience by now; all except her. She'd had to pretend – make something up. It didn't occur to her that maybe a lot of her schoolfriends had made up their stories as well.

She ran her hands lightly over her soft breasts and felt a tingling there. She wanted, needed, a man's hands on them. Sex was constantly on her mind; it was like a drug and she was obsessed by it.

'Deirdra, what on earth are you doing?'

She was brought back to reality by her mother's voice. Crossing her fingers, she answered lightly: 'Just looking out of the window, Ma. Watching the world go by.'

Maire Mahoney came into her eldest daughter's room. She straightened a pillow on the bed and smoothed the pink silk counterpane.

'Sure I wish you wouldn't sit on the bed, girl, you crease everything so.' It was a reprimand given daily and ignored daily. 'Would you not come down and play with the other girls?' Maire's voice was hesitant.

Deirdra laughed gently. 'I'm seventeen, Ma, I don't want to *play* any more. Did you ask Daddy about me going to the movies with Eamonn?'

Maire smiled then, making her prematurely aged face light up, showing an onlooker the beauty that had once been hers.

'Sure, you know you can go, girl, your father's over the moon about the two of yez. He's a good Irish Catholic. Jasus, there's enough of them in New York, I admit, but this one is more our kind.' She hesitated a few seconds before saying: 'Well, more your father's kind. He dotes on him. Talks about him all the time. Jasus, you'd think Jack was in love with him instead of you.'

Deirdra laughed with her mother. It was her father's liking for Eamonn that had made her determined to go for the handsome young man, rather than his obvious charms. She was in with a chance with Eamonn Docherty because her father knew and trusted him.

One thing she vowed: when she got him, there would not be one pink thing in her house. It would all be leather and glass, like the pictures in the magazines she studied.

'I just wanted to make sure it was OK with Dada before I went out, that was all,' she said humbly now.

Maire's face softened as she looked at her daughter. 'It's a good girl you are. I'm a lucky woman, even if I haven't a son to me name.'

Deirdra looked out of the window and Maire knew she was being in effect dismissed so left the room and her strange self-contained daughter. Only in her darker moments did she privately admit that getting the girl married and out of the house was in fact a pleasant prospect. Deirdra unnerved people, her sisters especially, and worst of all she unnerved her own mother.

Maria Castellano was listening to her husband's remarks with only half an ear. He bored her when he insisted on giving her the lowdown on everything he did. As she made herself a Spritzer she nodded her head, making her waist-length hair ripple. Her husband watched her fondly. She was exquisite. Perfect.

He loved her so very much.

John Castellano was a minor Capo in the New York Italian community. His father-in-law was a 'made man', meaning he was sworn into Cosa Nostra. It grieved John that he had not been put forward to be made, but he accepted the fact as he knew he had to. Maria's father was Paul Santorini. He ran a few teamsters, mainly in the construction business, made sure that the sites ran smoothly and that there was no need of a 'foreman' to oversee non-union workers. He took kickbacks and dealt in heroin. He loved only two things in his life: his wife and his daughter.

Maria knew her father had been amazed and a little upset over her choice of husband, but as she got everything she wanted, she got John. It had taken her just a week to tire of the muscle-bound mouse to whom she was shackled. But her father and mother would not hear of divorce, so she was stuck with him. For the time being at least. Her father had hinted that at a later date the marriage might be terminated, leaving her a grieving widow.

Maria had a natural Sicilian aptitude for the Mafia lifestyle. Death was nothing to her; she was a devout Catholic who believed that anything confessed was immediately forgiven and a place in Heaven assured. She used this as a sop to her conscience, and as a good way to do what she liked, when she liked.

She also used her father, her mother, and anyone else she happened to think could further her aims.

Maria's problem was she liked men too much, something her father had worried about when she was younger. She was currently embroiled in an affair with an Irishman – a big handsome gangster type from the Lower East Side. She knew her father would go ape shit if he found out, and that her husband John would kill the man without a second thought if he learned the truth.

It was a very exciting situation, and Maria milked it for all it was worth.

She had even invited her lover to the Ravenite Club in Little Italy. This was a known haunt of the Mafia and she'd wanted to be seen in there. The man reluctantly accompanied her and then fucked her rigid, all the while telling her she was a spoilt bitch.

Nevertheless Maria was falling in love with him and she was frightened and exhilarated by that fact. He was the first person ever to affect her. The first person to touch a chord inside her, deep inside, where her heart lay. He was the first man ever to tell her to shut her mouth. The first man to take her without asking her whether it was OK. The first man who had no fear of her father.

As she looked at her husband and waited for him to go to the club where he worked, she felt like laughing. He was a fool, a stupid ignorant Sicilian peasant. Dio! What on earth had she ever seen in him?

As John walked from the apartment, she kissed him on the lips. It was a wifely, lingering kiss which she knew would arouse him. She knew how much he wanted, needed and loved her, and that was the problem. Once she had her man, Maria didn't want him any more. It was the chase she craved, the need to conquer. But right now, she was expecting a visitor.

Eamonn Docherty found her naked and yielding as always. He let himself into the apartment with his own keys and went straight to the large bedroom where she lay sprawled awaiting him, sipping a glass of ice-cold champagne and stroking herself in anticipation.

Laughing, he took her there and then. Maria blew his mind. She also blew his cock – a pastime they both enjoyed.

Maria was snoring gently, her hair fanned out around her, making her look unusually vulnerable. Eamonn stared down at her in awe. She was gorgeous. He sighed and dressed quickly, his movements sure and deft after months of visiting this apartment. He could move around in the dark if he had to.

Maria opened one eye as he kissed her gently on the lips. 'I have to get going.'

Hazy with champagne and sex, she squinted at the bedside clock and said petulantly: 'It's only eleven, John won't be home for hours.'

'I have a bit of business to attend to.' His voice was firm, brooking no argument.

She knew by his tone of voice that it was useless to argue further with him. Instead she pouted sexily. 'Tomorrow?' Her voice was soft.

Eamonn knew how to play her games. He shrugged. 'Who knows?'

He strolled complacently from the apartment building, unaware of the two men watching from the car parked outside, too busy thinking about what he had to do. Maria was already forgotten.

The two men observed him hail a cab, and then followed him to Brannigan's Bar in Brooklyn. Stationing themselves across the street, they continued their surveillance.

As he walked inside, Eamonn was greeted by one and all before disappearing up a small flight of stairs. The men settled down for a long wait.

Paul Santorini listened to the two men before him with a mixture of interest and boredom. A small man, he dressed well, looked older than his years and had a razor-sharp mind.

His right-hand man, Ralph Borgatto, listened with more apparent interest. Ralph knew he would be expected to comment and that would take his considerable skills as a diplomat. He would have to agree that Maria was a whore, though one who looked like a madonna. He would be asked for his advice, and had to try and gauge his boss's own opinion from the few words he spoke now.

'He definitely has keys to the apartment, Mr Santorini. The janitor saw him let himself in. If John ever finds out . . .' the informant told him.

Paul Santorini held up his hand and said forcefully:

'When I want your opinion, I'll ask for it, OK? Just tell me where the lowlife went afterwards.'

The bigger man paled at his boss's words. 'He went to Brannigan's, up to the offices of the loan-sharking company he owns. From there he went to his fiancée's house. She's Deirdra Mahoney, one of Jack Mahoney's daughters. He got there pretty late, but she was up and opened the door to him herself. There was some kind of party going on, I think.'

Paul dismissed the men and turned to his friend and confidant, Ralph.

'What do you think, eh? I give her the best education that money can buy. I give her the husband she wants. I give the whore everything she wants. Now she's stupping an Irishman. If she wasn't my daughter, by the word of God Himself, I would break her face.'

Ralph sighed. His great head was covered in thick curly hair, and he had the olive skin and Roman nose of his forefathers. He looked as if he should be a shepherd on a mountainside, even in his thousand-dollar suit. His hands were huge, and he frequently joked he could strangle a man with just one of them. No one who knew him disputed this.

'Paul, can I be frank here?'

The older man nodded almost imperceptibly, which meant Ralph could be as honest as he liked as long as he told his boss exactly what he wanted to hear.

Taking a deep breath, he plunged in. 'I think we should let someone speak to her husband in private. That way, he'll sort it out. It's a matter of honour. You can bet your life that this Docherty knows who she is and exactly who he's dealing with. Word on the street about him is good. If he was one of us, he'd be a made man by now.'

Paul nodded. 'I know what you're saying. If only she

could have found herself the Italian equivalent, I'd be a happy man. I mean, if she had a child with this man it would be Irish, for Christ's sakes! If her mother knew it would break her heart.'

'Shall I get someone to speak to John or what?' Ralph urged gently.

Santorini lit himself a Havana cigar. Coughing, he said, 'Yeah, get the fucking ball rolling. It's a crying shame, though. From what I've heard, Docherty's a good guy.' He puffed on a cigar for a few moments before adding: 'For an Irish prick.'

Ralph agreed and poured them both a large Grappa. 'We'll get trouble from the Mahoneys over this, you realise that?' he commented. 'He's marrying one of Jack's daughters.'

Paul shrugged. 'So be it. I'll explain the circumstances if I have to. A man with as many daughters as Jack will be understanding, I know. If he isn't, I'll have his fucking brains blown out.'

'Whatever you say, Paul.'

Santorini knocked back his drink and said reflectively, 'You know the strange thing? I would have let her marry this Irishman if she had met him first. That's how much I love her. After this, though, I'll find her a husband who'll keep her occupied. I'll find her a man with the biggest *cajones* this side of the Hudson. I'll have her serviced morning, noon and night until she's pregnant and cowed. Look through the ranks and find me a real good-looking foot soldier. One who's known for womanising and charm as well as everything else. I'll give the bitch her match physically, then sit back and wait for grandchildren.'

The two men laughed at how easy everything was going to be, how clever they both were to have this thing sewn up.

Chapter Twenty-Three

Eamonn's eyes were bloodshot and red-rimmed. He glanced at himself in the mirror of the washroom and grimaced. His mouth tasted foul and he knew his breath was in danger of being condemned by the health officials. He pulled out some gum and chewed on it for a moment, relishing the taste of the spearmint and the feeling of having liquid in his mouth again. Sluicing his face under the cold water faucet, he tried to wake himself up, feeling a pounding headache begin.

Never again.

He smiled as he thought that. It was the same as usual. He got drunk, seriously drunk, every time he tied one on with Petey, and last night had been no exception.

After a few drinks and a meal in the Stakis restaurant on Broadway, they had adjourned to a topless bar a few blocks east. The girls were ugly, the drink plentiful and the hours negotiable. He had resisted the temptation of a redhead with breasts like lumps of concrete and finally slumped back in his seat unconscious.

He had woken up ten minutes ago as the cleaners

arrived. Petey was on the floor next to a blond-haired black woman with non-existent breasts and buck teeth. He always stayed true to type.

Tidying himself up as best he could, Eamonn walked back out into the club. It stank of cigarettes, testosterone and bad breath. Petey was still blissfully asleep, looking the Irish culchie he was with his face relaxed and smiling. Eamonn noticed with distaste that the woman had wet herself. Making sure his wallet was still in place, he left the bar and walked out into the morning light. It made his eyes hurt.

Making a right, he slipped into a Broadway diner in search of coffee and some breakfast before finding himself a cab. People were already about at five-thirty in the morning. He ordered a large coffee and a Danish, some eggs over easy and pancakes. He needed food, something to fill up the drink-soaked belly that was giving him cramps.

As he ate his mind was on Maria, his job and Deirdra. That was until a foxy little chick with a short skirt, smudged eye shadow and a colourful caftan came into the diner. Within five minutes he had bought her breakfast and was listening to her short life story.

The carefully edited version anyway.

He knew she was hooking; she had the look, even at eighteen. It took something away from the eyes, made them wary yet open. As if they knew something that no one else did. He also knew that once Petey saw her, he would find her a place and then they'd all earn. Himself included.

Eamonn had no qualms about what he was doing, he had long ago given up any hope of being a regular guy. There just wasn't any money in it.

*

John Castellano had been up all night, waiting outside the home of his rival on the Lower East Side with a gun, a set of handcuffs and a burning in his guts so acute he felt it would tear through his body and kill him stone dead.

Every time he thought of his wife with this man, he felt the urge to kill. Maria was blameless, her father had told him. She was bewitched by the Irishman, just a naive Catholic girl, brought up to trust and see good in other people. Now this man had taken their precious jewel and soiled her. She'd been too unworldly to see what was happening. Docherty had even talked her into giving him a door key.

His father-in-law had been surprised when his daughter's husband really seemed to swallow whole what he was saying, and a little part of John's mind had registered that fact. He knew deep inside who was at fault but he loved Maria and it was so much easier to blame that Irish bastard!

Now John gritted his teeth with annoyance. He had hoped to find his quarry straight off, but Docherty was proving elusive.

Well, John was a patient man, he would wait. He would track down his prey if it was the last thing he did. Lighting a cigarette, he settled himself once more in his car and watched the doorway to his enemy's apartment house. He would blow the Irishman away and laugh while he did it. This thought made him feel much better.

Cara Bowman was in fact seventeen, not eighteen, and had been hustling for nearly a year. Running away from a small town in Oklahoma, she had arrived in the Big Apple with thirty dollars and a suitcase of unsuitable clothes. She had turned her first trick within eight hours of getting off the bus.

Taken in by a black pimp called Alphonso, she had soon learned the harsh realities of life in New York with no money, no family and no friends to support her.

Meeting this man Eamonn was going to change all that. He had promised her a job – a proper one where she earned her money in comfort and could afford a decent place to live. She was still fresh-faced enough to make a go of her life in New York. She would save, go to classes, try and be somebody.

She certainly couldn't go home.

As she talked to the man beside her, Cara opened up like a little flower. Making him laugh. It felt more like a date than anything else and that pleased her. He spoke to her with respect, and listened to what she had to say. Better still, he didn't attempt to touch her once. Most men had to touch, even if it was only her face, her arm or her leg.

This man was different. Even in his crumpled suit, with a shadow on his strong chin and eyes rimmed with red, she could see he was a person to be reckoned with. His gold watch, his carefully cut hair and hand-made shoes told her all she needed to know.

She knew that what he was offering her was still hooking, but at least it was hooking with a bit of finesse. Nice clothes, a nice place to live, a nice enough kind of life. It sounded like heaven to her.

As they left the diner and got into a cab, she felt for the first time in months that life had something to offer her. She slipped her hand into his and felt him stiffen momentarily. As she looked at him, she saw a pained expression on his face, a tired, drawn look that made her feel sorry for him.

'Are you OK?' Her drawl was perfect; it sounded so smooth, so easy.

He smiled sadly at her. 'You're a very lovely girl.' Then

it hit him: she reminded him of Cathy, with her dainty build and blond hair. She had the same wary look in her eyes and the same fighting attitude. He closed his eyes and stroked her hair. She even felt the same as Cathy. His Cathy.

She rested her head on his shoulder and he could smell the street on her: fast food, cheap perfume and cigarette smoke. She smelt like a whore. The thought made him uneasy.

How was Cathy faring? Was she in the same position somewhere on the other side of the Atlantic? Were unknown men taking her body and using it in any way they wanted, all for a few seconds' gratification? He shuddered.

As they drew up outside his apartment building on Third Avenue, Eamonn felt sorry he had asked the girl home with him. She reminded him of what he had lost, what he had used and abused. She reminded him of his other life in London, and he'd started to resent her for this fact.

He paid off the cab, and then over the road saw the glint of sun on metal as a gun was pushed through the open window of the Buick convertible parked by the fire hydrant.

As the gun flashed, Eamonn pulled the girl to him.

It was all over in a split second. The car screeched away from the kerb, the cab disappeared round the corner, and Cara Bowman was lying in his arms, the back of her head blown away.

Maria watched her husband as he drank a cup of coffee and smoked another cigarette.

'What's the matter with you?' she said spitefully. 'You stay out all night, you come in this morning like a bear with a sore head and I can't get a civil word from you. Jesus H. Christ, you're depressing me.'

Her husky voice was higher than usual. Her face, devoid of make-up, showed its flaws. The harsh light revealed the broken veins on her cheeks and the sallowness of her Sicilian complexion. John was seeing his wife as she really was. Her foul mouth, her moods, her selfishness were all apparent for the first time as he looked at her.

'Shut the fuck up, Maria.'

Her face was a picture of shock as he spoke the words. 'What did you say?' she hissed.

Her husband closed his eyes and answered once more through his teeth. 'I said, shut the fuck up. I listen to you all the time. It's like a fucking long-playing record. Now shut up, Maria, before I give you something to whine about.'

John Castellano looked at her, his eyes hooded. Maria suddenly saw him as another woman might see him. If he'd married the right person he could have been a good husband. A good father.

'Fuck you, you bastard!' she couldn't stop herself from saying. 'If my father knew you spoke to me like th—'

His hand hit her on the jaw, a glancing blow that was powerful enough to knock her from her chair. As she sprawled on the floor he saw she was naked under her robe and for the first time it didn't make him want her.

She was abhorrent to him.

'Fuck you, bitch, and fuck your goddamn father as well. I know what you've been doing – he told me himself. Told me about the Irishman with the key to my fucking apartment. With a cock to stick up my darling so-called wife. So fuck you all – fuck your mother as well, for making you into the spoiled fucking whore you are!'

Pulling her robe around her, Maria scrambled to her feet. For the first time in her life she was frightened. She was in big trouble, and her father, whom she usually manipulated to get what she wanted, was a part of that trouble.

John watched her expression change and sneered. 'What the fuck are you anyway? There's plenty of hookers in the world with more respect for themselves than you have. I married you and you're mine now, no matter what you fucking want. You want to fuck the Irishman, eh? Well, I killed him this morning. I shot the bastard dead. Now you know what you caused. What you fucking asked for, you got at last. And you listen to me, Maria, and listen fucking good. There's going to be big changes around here. I'll take my belt to you in future if I even suspect you've looked at another man. I'm a fucking Italian, a real man, baby, and don't you ever forget that.'

Maria stared at the man she had married with such pomp and ceremony eight months previously and felt a wave of hatred so intense she could practically taste it.

'You've not killed Eamonn, no way!' she said passionately. 'You're not man enough to kill anyone. My father gave you to me – we live in his apartment, we eat with his money. We are owned by him. Once Eamonn and I go to him, he'll give me Eamonn as he's given me everything I've wanted, all my life.'

John walked over to where his wife stood by the oak cabinets of their kitchen. Bringing back his fist, he hit her again. This time he put all his weight behind it. Maria screamed as the punches rained down on her, afraid for her life. As he pushed her to the floor and proceeded to rape her, she wept in terror.

He pushed himself inside her, shouting: 'How's that, eh? Better than Irish cock, yeah? You like the one-eyed snake a little too much, I should have guessed that from the first. A hundred-dollar hooker couldn't move like you, baby.'

As he felt himself coming, he withdrew and spent himself all over her face and hair. 'I wouldn't waste a baby inside you, bitch. You're a fucking whore. A dirty, filthy whore.'

Spitting in her face, he stood up. He stared down at her, feeling a moment's euphoria at what he had done. At last he had her cowed. He had taken some of the fight from her.

He belted up his trousers and screamed, 'When I get home tonight, I want a meal on the table, I want you dressed decently and I want this place cleaned up. It's like a fucking pig sty.'

Maria lay on the floor, one hand covering her face. She did not move until she heard the door to the apartment close. Her face stung from the beating, and her eyes were already swelling. A trickle of blood mixed with snot seeped down her lip; she could taste it on her lips.

Staggering to her feet, she made her way to the phone. The large picture window graced a breathtaking view over Manhattan but the white furniture, grubby from neglect, looked grey in the morning light.

Slumping down on to the deep brown shag pile carpet, she lifted the receiver and dialled her father's number. Paul, woken from sleep by his daughter's hysterical voice, closed his eyes once more and sighed.

Petey was with Eamonn in his apartment, amazed by the way the man before him had crumpled and cried like a baby about an unknown hooker from fucking Oklahoma of all the Godforsaken places in the world. Eamonn had insisted on paying for the girl's funeral. The police, already well paid by the Mahoneys, had left the scene even richer and a deal less troubled about the death of the unknown girl. It was a drive-by-shooting, prelude to a mugging, was the official story. It would hit the inside pages of the *New*

York Times and be forgotten about by the next day.

Petey poured him another coffee and laced it liberally with whiskey. 'OK, so you were nearly hit,' he said. 'So we find out who is after you, and hit them first. It's no fucking big deal.'

Eamonn stared into Petey's large moon face and shook his head. 'She was just a kid, Petey. Don't you care that she died?'

The other man shrugged. 'In truth, I don't. Jasus, she was a hooker. Every time she plied her trade she took her life into her hands. You wasn't to blame.'

Eamonn looked at his friend and, wanting to believe what he was saying, nodded in agreement. Only he knew he had dragged the girl in front of him, let her take the bullet meant for him, and he wasn't going to admit that to anyone.

Petey's voice broke into his thoughts. 'We have to find out who the shooter was, OK? That's the priority now because you're still a target. Any ideas? Have you upset anyone? Have there been any threats or anything?'

Eamonn ran his hands through his thick dark hair and shook his head. 'It can only be one of two people: Maria's father, Paul Santorini, or her husband, John Castellano. They're the only people who might want to kill me.'

Petey whistled through his teeth. 'So it's the Italians, eh? I'd better tell this story to Jack, you know what he's like. But he'll try and sort it out for you. For all of us. You know what the Eyeties are like – they take everything so fucking personal.'

Eamonn had to agree, only just realising the trouble he was in.

Jack Mahoney would go mad.

*

Jack was already mad. At 6.45 he had taken a call from Paul Santorini's number two, telling him what was going down. Now he was about to lose one of his best men over a fucking woman. It was this that annoyed Jack more than anything. The fact that Eamonn was to marry his daughter at some point, didn't bother him; men were men and any woman who expected a man to stay faithful to her was a fool. But then, all his daughters were fools, he had seen to that himself. If Santorini had brought his girl up properly none of this would have happened.

He didn't say that, though. He knew better than to push the Italians. This could cause outright war.

Now he had his brother and the eejit Docherty on their way over to his home and had to try and make sense of all that had happened. This had come at the worst time; the FBI were sniffing round and the IRS were on their backs. Now he had to face the Italians *and* the fucking government, and on top of everything else his ulcer was playing him up.

John Castellano was getting into his car outside the club on Broadway when he saw his father-in-law coming towards him.

He knew instantly that he was in for trouble. His father-in-law's face was stern, eyes concealed behind dark glasses – always a bad sign. He didn't return John's greeting and that was when he got scared.

As Paul struck him hard in the face, John tried to fight him off. But the older man was stronger, and there was a point he had to make. He began to beat his son-in-law in front of all the people around them.

The bouncers from the club watched, their faces impassive. Passers-by paused, interested to see what was going down. A crowd formed as Paul Santorini beat his son-in-law to death.

Even when his victim was on the ground and begging for him to stop, still Paul beat him. Using fists encased in knuckle-dusters, he hammered the other man's face until it was unrecognisable. Finally, he took a length of lead piping from his driver and finished the job.

Then, breathing heavily, he straightened his hair, smoothed down his suit and walked with an unsteady gait back to his stretch limo by the kerb. Once he was inside, the car sped away.

The crowd was dispersing as the police arrived. As usual, no one had seen anything.

The bouncers shrugged and got on with their work. The man lying face down and drenched in blood was nothing to do with them any more. It didn't matter that until that moment John Castellano had paid their wages, joked with them, and asked after their families.

He was finished, the king was dead.

Long live the new king, whoever he might be.

Jack Mahoney's face was a picture as he took the call from his tout on the street. Putting down the phone, he sighed heavily.

'Castellano is dead, beaten to death by his father-in-law on Broadway an hour ago. I still can't believe you were fucking stupid enough to fuck a Mafia Capo's daughter! There's not enough fuckable women in New York already, but you have to choose a Mafia princess?'

Petey nearly laughed, the sound escaping as a soft snort, and it brought his brother's wrath down on him.

'You think this is funny, eh? You think this is amusing? You want to take on Paul Santorini, is that it? Only I'm willing to let you negotiate this one away if you think you can, little brother. Just say the fucking word. To keep our mutual friend here alive is going to take some doing, I can tell you. Santorini's lost face, you fucking pair of fools. He's also lost his temper which I understand is like the wrath of God. Do you two realise what's going down here, how serious this shit is?'

Feeling like a schoolboy caught out by his headmaster, Eamonn stood up. 'I'll go and see him, try to expl—'

Jack Mahoney put his head in his hands and laughed bitterly. 'Would you listen to this fucking eejit? Eamonn, if he so much as lays eyes on you, you're dead meat. I tell you something for nothing: I hope the piece of skirt was worth all this, I really do, because she'd need a cunt dripping diamonds before I'd lay my fucking life on the line.'

The three men stared at each other. Finally it was Petey who broke the silence.

'We wait until he contacts us, that's all we can do. Jack's right. If you go to see him, Eamonn, you'll antagonise him further. I've had men on the street all day finding out what's going down, and that isn't easy. The Italians keep themselves to themselves. Let's see what Santorini's next move is, then we'll take it from there.'

Five minutes later the phone rang and they were informed by an anonymous man that their club in Harlem had been fire bombed.

The ball had been set rolling.

Less than an hour later another call informed them that sixteen of their lorries were out of action at the Queens depot, and the drivers had all been sent home. At this, the three men left Jack's house and made their way to the riverside depot. If they were going to be killed, they all wanted it to be away from family and friends.

Jack was fuming, as much with the Italians as with Eamonn. 'All this for a fecking fuck!' was all they heard over and over again. Petey was beginning to take his brother's side; this was all a bit rich for the sake of a single woman – and her neither Irish nor black.

Paul Santorini was finally calming down. Inside the Ravenite Club he drank a few Grappas and waited to hear if his quarry had been located. He knew he was a laughing stock among his contemporaries, even though they would never dare show this inside the confines of the club. He also knew that he was looked on now as a weak man; his daughter's activities had been freely discussed all over Little Italy during the course of the day. She had got herself a reputation, had even brought her men to this very club, he understood now.

For that alone he could kill her.

He knew what the word was, and in his own way agreed with what was being said. But, God help her, Maria was a widow now and he would see to it that she repented of her whore's ways. Paul intended to put her under the jurisdiction of his cousin Carlos, a minor Mob figure and a family man. He would take her into his Las Vegas home – for a price. Paul refused ever to look on her face again. He would live this down if it was the last thing he did.

His Don had requested a meeting tonight at his home. Paul knew he was in for trouble and the knowledge made him even more uptight.

The Mafia was his extended family, his Don the head of it for Paul. He knew he had to swallow his cock and tell the man exactly what he wanted to hear if he were to keep his goodwill and, more importantly, his own life. He had broken the cardinal rule – settled a personal score on the street in front of witnesses.

His Don would not forgive that in a hurry.

Paul closed his eyes and saw his little Maria as she had

been, a child with beautiful eyes and hair. She had grown into a sensual woman, a whore of a woman, and now he had to pay the consequences of his devotion to her.

Paul Santorini's Don was called Pietro DeMarco. A small man, seventy years old, he kept himself fit by working out in a gym built into his office on Eighth Avenue. He dressed like a peasant, wearing a flat cap and a muffler. In the street, he acted like a fool, talking to everyone and making a big deal out of the smallest things.

He acted like this to take away any heat.

Unlike the younger men, he did not dress like an extra from *The Godfather*. He knew the importance of keeping a low profile. It was what had kept him alive for fifty years in America, and what had got him elected as Don twenty years previously. The FBI had tried to implicate him in racketeering many times and had always had to let the charges drop.

Now Don Pietro was annoyed.

One of his favourite Capos had committed an error of judgement so great it meant having to call him in for a talk. Straighten him out. This fact alone upset the Don.

He had always respected Paul Santorini, had liked him even. He knew all the talk concerning Santorini's daughter. A man with only sons himself, he understood how a father could love a daughter too much.

That was human nature.

But this daughter, if all the stories were true, was not a respectable woman.

Now there was trouble brewing with the Irish and the Don did not want this. The Irish were a force to be reckoned with, presently collecting money for a war in their homeland that beggared belief. Even the British Army were having trouble keeping them down; the Irish were a fighting nation and Don Pietro didn't want to have to face up to them over a mere woman.

The peace between the different nationalities had been good for everyone. Now they were in danger of outright war, and if that took off on the streets of New York then the Chinese and other immigrants might decide they wanted to muscle in.

Paul should have come to him, that was how it normally worked. Instead, they were waiting to see if the world as they knew it was about to be rocked on its foundations. Altogether a troublesome and annoying situation.

Don Pietro took his own pulse, a habit he had acquired a few years before. He had had a heart scare; it had turned out to be indigestion, but the scare had been enough for him. He took deep breaths and waited for Paul to come to him. Don Pietro knew he would arrive soon. It would be more than he dared to try and overlook a direct command.

He had looked on Paul as the next-in-line; now he would have to seek elsewhere. The men would hear of this and their respect for him would wane.

Unless he took steps to pre-empt that.

Chapter Twenty-Four

Jack Mahoney was resigned to his losses. He knew he could not claim on insurance for the vehicles at the Queens depot without involving the police. They would just have to be replaced from capital and the men paid while they couldn't work.

His legitimate businesses were a source of pride to Jack, and to have one of them practically ruined overnight broke his heart. As he had surveyed the damage done, he'd fought an urge to cry. The engines were all burnt out; the paintwork blistered from the force of the petrol bomb. He knew that if everything wasn't sorted out within the next few days, he would have to involve the other Irish families.

Something he really didn't want to do.

The O'Neills and the McBrides would be only too pleased to help out, but at a price. Currently the first family in the Irish community, the Mahoneys would be laying themselves open to all sorts of trouble if they asked for help.

Jack could end up forfeiting control of the IRA collections, a thing the other families wanted badly as hitherto they had been forced to hand the money over to the Mahoneys. Now there was a big bombing going down in Aldershot, England, and Jack was behind it one hundred per cent. He knew that the bigger the war in England, the more money to be made here.

He dealt directly with the IRA through his cousin in Cork. They trusted him, and if he went to them for help they would be only too glad to oblige.

Once more, though, at a price.

He didn't want to be beholden to them any further, he liked the situation just as it was. They needed him, trusted him, and this kept the other Irish families on their toes. It was a good arrangement in that respect.

But the IRA would take on the Mafia and laugh while they did it, if things became that bad. They were warriors fighting for freedom; the Mafia men were small fry to them. It could cause the biggest transatlantic incident since Pearl Harbor.

Bombing mainland England was one thing; bombing New York something else entirely. The families, Irish and Italian, were all wary of the FBI. They knew that their days were numbered and were all trying to become as legit as possible. Now there had been a murder, two bombings, and this was only the start. Jack Mahoney had to try and sort all this out once and for all. Then, if it all fell out of bed, he would have a rethink. See whom he could trust the most and who would want the least from him. He hadn't built up his businesses to have them taken from under his nose and jurisdiction by a few Irish navvies with an eye to the main chance.

Paul Santorini did not arrive at his Don's home until late evening. This gave Don Pietro another grudge against him. As Santorini was ushered into the Don's study he saw the steely glint in the old man's eyes.

'There was a time when you would have made your way to see me promptly. This, I think, is a sign of the times. No one has any respect any more. I'm an old man, I have little left in life except a good brain and a liking for punctuality.' He rose from his chair, his smallness belying his strength.

'I can only apologise, Don DeMarco,' Paul said lamely. 'This has been a wearing day. I have tried to uphold my family's honour . . .'

The Don interrupted him. 'Sit down, for Christ's sakes. What honour? Your daughter, may God forgive me for saying this, is the cause of all your problems. You know what my Don used to say to me: "Get rid of the cause and you solve your problem".'

Paul Santorini felt his heart sink down to his boots.

The old man walked around the study, his hands in the air. 'Honour, honour. That's all I hear about these days. But there's no honour among thieves. I have lived seventy years and that's all I have really learned.'

Paul listened respectfully; he could not do otherwise. He knew the old man would talk a while and then eventually get to the nub of what he wanted to say.

'I listen to everyone, I hear everything that goes on. I know that Maria has always liked the men.' He held up his hand as if Paul were going to disagree and carried on talking.

'This trouble with the Irish – she is behind it all. A man is dead by your hand. I understand that: he was violent to your child, it was all you could do. But a passer-by murdered in cold blood? The days of the family murdering in the street are long gone, I hope. Since Al Capone moved out of the Bronx and settled himself in Chicago, we have striven for respectability. The five families of New York are the most important families, you know this. We must set an example. Today I have had calls from all the other

Dons. They want to know what is happening. Why all this bloodshed. And, more importantly, they want to know where it leaves them. They want to meet and discuss this matter. I can understand their worries. I would feel exactly the same. Things like this can escalate.'

His voice changed imperceptibly and Paul was reminded forcibly of the threat this man could pose to him.

'I want this dealt with in the next twenty-four hours. If it isn't and I have to get involved on a personal level . . .' Don Pietro shrugged, leaving the rest unsaid.

'Now, a glass of Grappa, perhaps?' He poured the drinks slowly, giving Paul time to take in what he had said. As he placed the glass before him, Don Pietro smiled and said genially, 'I think Las Vegas is just the place for Maria.'

Paul jumped as he realised this man knew everything, had always known everything and always would.

'Despatch her soon, that's your main priority. That and settling things with the Irish. Mahoney is a force to be reckoned with in his own way.'

'Do you think I should meet them and try and build some bridges?'

Don Pietro smiled. 'I think that's exactly what you should do. This young man Docherty, I hear he is a good soldier, solid. Mahoney and his brothers all seem to think he is a man of substance and integrity. You've burned out their business in Queens, you've burned out their night-club. Now you have to try and make good that damage as best you can. I will not have a war, not with the Irish anyway. Let them fight among themselves, they like that. We have enough trouble keeping our own ranks in order. We don't need to fight the Irish – not because of a woman anyway. Even if she was *my* daughter.'

He laughed then, a rollicking sound, and Paul smiled along with him. He was being told to get everything back on an even keel or pay the price personally. He had to make reparation and swallow his pride while he did it.

Everyone who'd heard about Docherty seemed to take his side in the affair. The Italians liked men's men. Docherty seemed to be that and a bit more. He was what everyone wanted their sons to be: tough, strong and likeable.

Paul bowed to his mentor's command and set his mind to working out how to emerge from this situation with the least possible humiliation.

Eamonn walked through Little Italy with his hand inside his coat pocket. Cheek by jowl with Chinatown in Lower Manhattan, here the different cultures encroached upon one another and gave the area an almost carnival appearance. The commercial buildings and walk-ups were all brownstones with gaily painted fire escapes; many shady businesses hid behind respectable fronts here.

Eamonn's heart was in his mouth as he made his way to a restaurant on Canal Street – Angelo's, where the main people from the DeMarco family hung out.

He knew that to stop any more trouble from breaking out, he had to make himself known to the people involved and apologise. He owed that much to Jack and Petey Mahoney. If it meant sacrificing himself, then that's what he would have to do. He knew that his chances, whether running away or facing his antagonists head on, were not really very good.

Five minutes later, Eamonn was walking up the stairs to the private function room where Paul Santorini and his men sat discussing the current situation. All knew that the Don wanted it fixed as quickly as possible. All knew that Paul had already lost a substantial amount of face. As Eamonn entered the room they were all silent, watching him warily.

He was frisked by two men and again by a third before he was allowed to approach the table that held the ten hoodlums Paul Santorini held closest to him.

Maria was forgotten as the two men made eye contact.

Paul was impressed by the stranger before him. It took guts to walk into what could be termed a lion's den and he acknowledged that fact with good grace.

Eamonn stood before them respectfully, hands clasped in front of him, on show to all, his head hanging just low enough to show remorse without it looking as if he were frightened. His striking good looks and heavy physique were taken in and noted by the men around the table. However, they could say nothing until their Capo had had the first word.

Paul took his time. Then, sighing heavily, he said: 'To what do I owe this pleasure?'

Eamonn looked the man in the eye and said truthfully, 'I thought I would come and try to salvage the situation. I realise I have caused you and your family grave offence. For this I apologise, and ask respectfully that you take your revenge on me personally and leave my Irish family alone. They asked for none of this. I feel doubly responsible to have been the cause of their losing both money and prestige.'

He spoke in the flowery Italian way and the men warmed to this. His voice was strong; it did not in any way betray the fear they all knew he must be feeling.

'The friendship between our two peoples has been a source of pride to my Irish counterparts. We have all lived side by side for many years, each with our own interests. My selfishness in falling in love with your daughter was wrong and for that I offer to make reparation to you and your family. I ask you now, humbly, what I can do to make you forget what has happened and get us all back on our old footing?'

The Englishness of his accent surprised them. He had none of the Irish drawl they had expected. His strength of character was noted too, and approved of. He reminded them of themselves.

Paul was elated. Docherty coming and talking to him this way had saved him a lot of face – something that was dear to all Italians. After all, they were businessmen with a great deal to lose and it was up to him to make a gesture, an overture that suited everyone, especially Don Pietro.

Standing up, he walked around the table and advanced on the man who stood there. Eamonn held his breath as he saw Paul's approach, waiting to see what it signified.

Paul Santorini stood before him for about fifty seconds before embracing him, a gesture that was applauded by his men and which made Eamonn's heart race with relief.

He had done the right thing; he had come into the lion's den and with his flowery bullshit had made amends. The sweat under his armpits was drying even as he smiled at Paul Santorini. He had taken this man's married daughter and had fucked her rigid for months, and now the sap was letting it go. Eamonn had been the cause of two deaths and the man was letting it go. He could not believe his luck.

The thrust of the knife blade as it ripped through his clothing and then his belly didn't hurt at first. Eamonn was too shocked to realise what had happened.

As he dropped to his knees, he felt the blood seeping through his hands as he tried to press his insides back into his stomach where they belonged. When the blade was drawn across his cheek, he sank to the floor and into blessed unconsciousness.

His last thought was that the Italians were a race of slippery bastards and he should have realised that long before. He had come prepared to die, and it seemed that was exactly what he was going to do.

*

Jack and Petey sat in the waiting room at Lincoln Medical Center, waiting to hear the outcome of Eamonn's operation. Both were on tenterhooks; both realised that the situation with the Italians had now reached the point of no return. If they didn't retaliate, hard and fast, the other Irish families would see it as a sign of weakness.

Petey looked grey with worry and Jack felt a second's sorrow for his little brother. 'It's all right, Petey,' he said in a low voice. 'I've sorted it all out now.'

Petey shook his head in distress. 'Sure Eamonn was a good man, Jack. This has all got out of proportion, for Christ's sakes.'

Jack nodded and draped an arm sympathetically around his brother's shoulders. They looked alike despite their different shapes. Jack, big and cumbersome and heavy-jowled as he was had still some vestiges of his former good looks. Petey – small, bull-necked and round – looked what he was: a bruiser, a fighting man. But now his face was defeated at the thought of losing the one man he'd come to regard as a friend.

'I've asked Ireland for help. Someone's flying in the night.'

Petey was shocked at his brother's words, but knew better than to say so. Both men waited in silence to find out whether Eamonn Docherty would live or die.

Not many people knew where Don Pietro DeMarco lived on Long Island. Few of his Capos had ever visited his house. The Don believed that a man's home was his castle; he was with the English on that one.

He had brought up his children, and now tended the garden on his estate and liked to enjoy a glass of the wine he made there himself.

Once inside his compound he was no longer the Don, just a kindly husband, father and grandfather. He had three full-time bodyguards but these days he didn't really need them. After all, he was a respectable businessman now.

As he walked in his garden he admired the green shoots of the plants coming up after winter, plucking a dead leaf here and pulling up a weed there. He was at heart a peasant, knew this and relished the fact. It amused him to think that he had been responsible for many murders, and many illegal acts, yet inside he was interested only in the simplest things.

When the day came to meet his God, he would meet Him proudly and with a twinkle in his eye. If the God of his Church was as corrupt as His messengers on earth, the Don would be all right.

He walked into the house through the French doors, thinking at first that the man sitting in the chair was his eldest son Salvatore. But it couldn't be, he had been in Vegas for the last few years, looking after their holdings there. It was only when the Don walked into the light that he saw that the man in the chair was a stranger – and that he was also holding a small Sten gun.

'Mr DeMarco, my name's Daniel Connell and it's a pleasure to meet you.'

The thick Irish accent threw the elderly Don for a second and he faltered, all at once showing his age. His voice failed him as he tried to speak.

Daniel Connell laughed. 'Sure, don't worry, I haven't come to kill you, sir. I'm just here for a little chat. I understand that you're a man of sense. Well, I'm here to reason with you, having travelled all the way from Beirut. We're training an army out there, you see. But I understand there's been a small piece of trouble here that needs sorting out. So . . .' he opened his arms wide in an expansive gesture '. . . here I am.'

Don Pietro's eyes went to the door and the Irishman grinned. 'Locked. I know all your movements, sir. It's my job to find out these things, in whatever way I can. Now, if you'd be so kind as to sit down, I have a few things to say to you that I hope will clear up this mess once and for all.'

Don Pietro sat down in his old leather chair by the window. Daniel Connell got up from his seat. He locked the French doors, closed the heavy curtains. After pouring them both a large brandy, he settled himself comfortably once more in his chair and began to speak.

'The IRA are an organisation like your own, except we're political, we fight for a cause. Not that I'm saying anything against yourselves, just stating a fact. The Mahoneys gather money for us and we class them as good men. You know what I'm saying, don't you?

'Now you have what I understand is a loose cannon called Santorini. Forgive me for being blunt here, but he's dead already. I saw to that as soon as I got off the fecking plane. Docherty's a good man, and your lad had no business to be tearing him open and murdering the life out of him. What I want to tell you is this: we will keep you all in our hearts if this is left alone now. But if there's any retaliation, any single step out of line against the Irish, then you'll have a fecking war on your hands the likes of which you'd never believe. You're interfering with us, you see, and believe me, the fucking British Army are having trouble keeping us down so what chance would you have?

'We're linked with Baader Meinhof, the Libyans, every terrorist organisation in the world. Be sure to listen to me now because I do not want to be coming back here and having to explain it all again. Involved as we are in our own war, we don't really need another, but that's beside the point. If we came here to New York we'd finish you all off in a week. Now you get by because you have the politicians and the government agencies in your pocket, but they wouldn't be there for long if we waged a vendetta against you. I'm sure you can see the logic of what I'm saying?

'So I want your assurance that everything will go back to normal and will be left that way. No revenge attacks, nothing.

'If I have to come back here, I'll kill you slowly and with so much pain you'll wish you had never been born. This is no idle threat. Ask around about us with your European contacts – they'll tell you all you need to know. We have men training in Beirut, South America and Libya. We're everywhere, and like I said before, we're political, not out for money or any kind of gain. That's the difference between us.'

Don Pietro DeMarco was a sensible man. He knew he had been outfoxed and, if he were honest, outclassed. This man even knew what his movements at home were and exactly where to find him. He was apparently alone, yet with no one to help him he was in the Don's house, where his wife was resting and his grandchildren played.

Don Pietro knew when he was defeated and he knew it now. This man had vanquished him without even raising his voice. It was a sobering reversal for a man who had represented the full might of the Cosa Nostra for over twenty years.

'How did you dispose of Santorini?' he asked, struggling to keep his voice level.

Connell smiled. 'It was an IRA execution. I nailed him to the floor and after I'd crucified him, shot him in each knee and elbow. I stayed with him until he died – I like to see a job through. You'll find him at his house, in the games room.'

Don Pietro closed his eyes and nodded. 'I will do as you ask because I did not want this trouble myself. It was a domestic matter really. Men and their daughters, eh?'

Connell was impassive. 'In the IRA we leave family behind. We have to, we are soldiers. That's the difference between us, as I said before. We have women in the Cause who'd make your hit men look like pussy cats.'

The Don bowed his head silently and wondered when the other man was going to leave.

Connell tossed back his brandy and rose from his seat. He held out one large hairy hand and smiled benignly. 'No hard feelings, sir, it was just a matter of business.'

The Don shook his hand.

After Connell had left he sat down, drained his brandy and wondered what future there could be for a world where men like that roamed free.

Chapter Twenty-Five

Eamonn opened his eyes and looked around the room. It was full of flowers and cards. He tried to focus but found it difficult.

As he made a move he felt a tube coming from his side and realised he had to be in hospital. He remembered then what had happened to him and felt tears of relief that he was still alive sting his eyes. As they rolled down his face, a fresh-faced nurse came into the room and smiled at him.

'You're awake then?'

Eamonn tried once more to focus, and failed. The girl laughed. 'You've been awake on and off for the last week. Just relax, everything will be back to normal before you know it.'

Eamonn felt desperately weak, but his mind was alert. He struggled to keep his eyes open, sure that there was something he should be doing, a battle still to be won.

He drifted off to sleep. Petey and Jack were informed of the improvement in his condition by phone and breathed a collective sigh of relief.

*

The Mahoneys were trying to make sense of what had happened. Santorini's death was so bizarre it had made all the headlines. The men of the Mafia were talking about it everywhere. These men knew of death scenarios that would shock and repel, but the blasphemous attitude of the IRA in crucifying Santorini had amazed even them.

The Mahoneys were looked on with new respect and a certain reluctant admiration, and this augured well for the Irish.

The story of the home visit to Don Pietro was kept under wraps; that could have caused a major incident by a few loose cannon who would have found such disrespect too much to stomach.

Meanwhile Petey Mahoney was picking out the girls he wanted to work in his new enterprise. He was determined to prove himself to his brother and open another bar, similar to their one in Harlem but far more salubrious.

To Petey this meant the girls should be clean, have big tits and nice faces. He had the cash, he had the muscle and he had the knowhow. Jack would think it was a grand idea and the pats on the back would be great.

Petey and Jack had already realised that the Italians were with them now and the future was looking trouble-free. The new bar, to be called Petey's Place, would be up and running in less than a week. The liquor licence was already taken care of and the premises, an old gambling club, had been given a lick of gold paint and new brocade curtains. Even the bar had been newly varnished and the old tables and chairs scrubbed and polished for the first time in years. With low lighting from pink bulbs the place had a cosy, almost intimate feel and look to it.

Petey was proud of it.

He was auditioning in a friend's small topless bar called

Lautrec's. Word had hit the street that the new club was going to cater to men with real money. Consequently most of the girls from the lesser bars were there in all their painted splendour and with new outfits. Lipgloss and platform heels abounded and the smell of cheap perfume was overpowering.

Petey was in his element.

The girls, realising he was in charge, were all over him like a rash, and Petey, being Petey, was all over them. It was while he was watching a particularly bewitching young girl from Houston, with huge silicone boobs and a surgically enhanced face, that he was approached by one of the DeMarco Capos.

Petey knew the man by sight. He was one of the old-style Italians. He wore decent suits, his hair was still cut like a marine's and he always wore a tie with a matching handkerchief in his breast pocket.

Petey greeted him respectfully but warily. The man, Anthony Baggato, realising why, smiled easily. 'Mr Mahoney, I hope I haven't interrupted you at work? I just wanted to have a little chat with you. Is there anywhere we can go to talk privately?'

Petey nodded. Still wary, he made a big production out of taking the man through to his friend's office. If anything happened to him, he wanted plenty of witnesses.

Baggato was not very big, but he had presence. His easy smile and cold eyes made people uncomfortable. That one day he would be Don was not only his opinion but everyone else's since Santorini's death.

'Mr Mahoney – or may I call you Peter?'

Petey stood nervously by the door. 'Listen, Mr Baggato, say what you've got to say and then we'll talk names and other such shit. You come to me in the middle of the day, I am in a friend's club, I have work to do. We have all had a bit of a bother recently and what I want to know is: what the fuck do you want and is it trouble?'

Anthony Baggato smiled gently. The man's phraseology left a lot to be desired, but Anthony understood his feelings and tried his best to allay his fears.

'I am not here on family business – I am here on my own behalf. I need a supplier for something and have been told that you are the best man to deal with. That is as far as this visit goes. Supply and demand, it's what makes the world go round.'

Petey listened carefully. 'So what exactly would you like me to supply?'

Baggato grinned now, his face taking on a genial quality. 'I want you to supply me and mine with heroin.'

Petey's eyes widened.

'I understand your confusion, but you see, Mr Mahoney, this is to be a private transaction. I want to deal large amounts of the stuff. I want to be a big supplier, and to supply my own contacts in New York. This conversation is strictly off the record, by the way. This is a deal between me and you. No one else will ever be involved except for a few of my men. As you will know, the five Dons, the heads of our families, are anti-drugs, but what they don't know will not hurt them, *capisce*?

'Now, I need a good supplier, and I need one who will keep our business dealings quiet. I was impressed by your family over the Santorini affair. I feel that together we could make a good partnership.'

He wiped his mouth fastidiously with a snow-white handkerchief. 'I also know that you are a dealer, and that you have an in with the biggest supplier. I am talking South America here. I can guarantee you safe passage into Florida, Miami, and safe transfer of the drugs to any location in the United States. This is big, big business here, not nickels and dimes. I need your answer, and your word that our conversation will not be heard outside these four walls.'

Petey's eyes were nearly out on stalks. This was real money they were talking. Serious amounts of money, and he was already seeing an endless procession of dollar signs and noughts.

A million dollars' worth of heroin was easily passed on to the street. Ten million dollars' worth could be almost as easy. And why not be the man to do it? There was an endless demand, and the best thing with H was the fact that there were new customers for it every day. The biggest transaction Petey had ever done before was a six-ounce deal for thirty thousand dollars. He was on friendly terms with the Colombians through an ex-girlfriend's brother, Tito. If the profits were high enough, Jack Mahoney could probably be talked around.

Petey knew that Tito would have no trouble supplying the Italians through him, and indeed that it would be a match made in street heaven.

This was the deal of the century. Feeling like a dog with two tails and six lampposts, he held out his hand and said casually: 'Call me Petey, everyone does.'

This was the beginning of a friendly alliance that was to last for many years to come.

Eamonn had been out of hospital six weeks and was still getting back on his feet when he heard from Maria Santorini. He threw her letter away, feeling he wanted to draw a line under that part of his life and make amends to everyone concerned for the foolishness of his actions.

He made a point of seeing only Deirdra and trying to make himself love her, as much as Eamonn could love anyone. Only Cathy had ever touched that particular place in his heart, and in her absence he feared it had closed over.

Deirdra for her part listened with rapt attention to the blandishments of the handsome man she was going to marry and basked in his apparent delight in her and her conversation. She knew that she had got him by default but was determined to keep hold of him now.

The far-reaching effects of the events that took place after Eamonn's wounding had made things all the better for the Mahoneys businesswise. Not only were they collecting the Cause money, they were also involved in one of the biggest heroin operations in American history. Eamonn took to it all like a duck to water and Jack, after some initial reservations, found it in his heart to agree with Petey that an alliance with the Eyeties could only be a good thing.

It was this alliance that gave them even more credence and set them up as the foremost Irish family in New York state. They were catapulted into a world of real riches and real money. Eamonn and Petey ran the drug operation with the precision of a military exercise. They also laundered the money and made themselves almost legit.

Eamonn married Deirdra in the spring of 1974 in the church of St Anthony of Padua. The church on Sullivan Street in Manhattan had never housed such an illustrious wedding before. All the top families came and the Italian guests added extra panache to the Irish contingent in their wedding finery.

Deirdra, like a good Catholic girl, became pregnant on her wedding night, and Eamonn Docherty soon realised that he had taken on a woman with the sexual appetite of a man. Far from deterring him, he found it a turn on.

At first anyway.

Only time would tell what was to become of them all in

the future, but on that day they felt that life had dealt them some good cards.

The sun was shining, the bells rang out in exultation and the bride was happy.

What more could anyone want?

Book Three

Men are like children. They start on the breast and they very rarely leave it.

– Old Irish saying, Anon

Are you going to women? Don't forget the whip.

– Friedrich Nietzsche, 1844–1900

One murder made a villain,
Millions a hero.

– Beilby Porteus, 1731–1808

Book Three

Chapter Twenty-Six

London 1975

'Oh, piss off! You don't know what you're talking about!'

The man's voice was as much like a woman's as Geoff Capes's, but he was dressed in the full regalia: tight dress, high heels and bleached blond wig. His eyelashes defied every law of human nature and so did he.

Cathy sighed as she watched Desrae's temper rising. This man was a new recruit and his attitude had already caused problems, not only with Desrae but with all the other people working for them.

'Listen, Alfie,' Desrae told him, 'it's nothing personal but the other girls can't stand the fucking sight of you. And, quite honestly, at this moment in time I sympathise with them. You have a way about you that not only puts off your mates, it also pisses off the punters. Now you either sort yourself out, or me and you are going to have to part company.'

Alfie, otherwise known as Gabrielle, knew when he was beaten and decided to retire gracefully from the fray. Opening his heavily made-up eyes to their fullest extent, he feigned tears and shook his head sorrowfully. His purple-painted lips were trembling and Desrae closed his eyes in annoyance.

'It doesn't cut no ice with me, girl. All the tears in the world won't make me change my mind, OK? Either buck up or fuck off. I can't have all my girls up in arms over you and that's that. We ain't even open a week hardly and you're already making the place feel like a battlefield.'

Alfie walked from the little office with his dignity intact and his temper strictly under control. He knew he was beaten and accepted the fact gracefully – or as gracefully as a six-foot-two man in impossibly high heels can do.

When he had left, Cathy started to laugh. 'I'm sorry, Desrae, but his face! I mean, you nearly wet yourself when he said that due to circumstances beyond his control, he couldn't sleep with men under five foot three.'

Desrae roared then, rouged cheeks bunching up in amusement. 'It's his size – I don't know why the tall ones always wear the highest heels. It amazes me, it really does. A lot of the men, see, they like it up against the wall. Even with a bed in the room, they can get it in better like. So the truly big ones are out of bounds, really. But the littlest men always like the great big porkers. Life's strange, ain't it?'

Cathy nodded. Homosexual love did not bother her in the least, it was part and parcel of her everyday life. Thanks to Desrae's boyfriend and confidant, as he referred to Joey Pasquale, they had recently opened a small select drinking club in Wardour Street. The shop front was the usual tits and ass bookshop, as found all over Soho. This was legal and a money spinner, the more exotic magazines being kept under the proverbial counter. They owned two similar outlets in other Soho streets. But through the back of the Wardour Street shop were two large rooms, used now as a bar and meeting place for transvestites, transsexuals and drag queens.

There was a subtle difference between them all – Cathy had learned that much since being with Desrae.

Alfie was a drag queen; he wore the most outrageous clothes and acted so ultra-feminine that it was impossible to mistake him for anything other than what he was.

The transsexuals were often more like real women and so were harder to spot. Many of them lived their daily lives as women, and longed for the magic operation that would fulfil their dreams of biological femininity.

The transvestites were often just cross dressers or homosexuals who preferred dressing as women, for sexual or other reasons. Cathy found them all likeable and a majority loveable. Being square pegs in round holes, they were often more accepting of other people because of their own situation.

At twenty-two Cathy was beautiful, poised, and thanks to Desrae, happier than she had ever been.

Joey and Desrae were like the parents she'd never had; they both loved and looked out for her. Desrae fussed over her like a mother hen and everyone in Soho joked about his little girl.

The only thing that upset him was the fact that Cathy would have nothing to do with boys of her own age, preferring always to be with him and his cronies. She was too much of a loner for her own good.

Joey's businesses were doing well. He had bought the club primarily to keep Desrae happy, knowing that he would make a go of it. The kind of club he was running was needed in Soho, the only place homosexuals could really meet in peace. Soho was home to vice, prostitution, and all aspects of the sex industry – from books to films to trading in actual real live people. In fact, the concept of young men for sale was always big business. But Desrae, having been on the receiving end of rough trade in his life, didn't want anything to do with it. He looked down his nose at people who dealt in kiddy flesh.

As far as he was concerned, his club catered for grown men, and the people who worked there were grown men. 'Over twenty-one, legal and looking good', was his motto.

The small office they used above the sex shop was a riot of Desrae colours and Cathy, used to his Haut Bordello style by now, saw nothing unusual about the bright pink flock wallpaper. It looked OK to her. Joey had once walked into the office in sunglasses for a joke and Desrae had been mortally offended. Since then no one had made any jokes on the subject of his decorating tastes.

The club was all navy-blue velvet and grey, with pink accents throughout in the carpeting and seating. The navy-blue drapes had grey swags that made the place look almost respectable. All the people who worked at or used the club loved the feel and the look of the place, so Desrae felt he must have got something right.

The small bar area was his pride and joy – a single piece of oak carved with figures of men in all sorts of positions, sexual or otherwise. By the bar were high pink stools with chrome backs and legs. All in all, the place looked what it was: an expensive gay club. The clientele reflected this. They had everyone on their books and the membership fee of £150 per annum kept out what Desrae called the riff-raff.

One week into its opening they were already taking over £300 a night. Between £500 and £700 on Saturdays. It was small, select and lucrative. From politicians to businessmen, from actors to policemen, the place was full to the rafters every night. They all knew it wasn't just because the club was new; they were aware they had filled a gap in the market and as such were guaranteed to make their money back.

Cathy sipped her coffee and looked nervously at Desrae as he glanced over the idea she had written out and presented to him. It was the first time she had ever tried anything like this and she was anxious to know what he thought of her scheme.

'This is a terrific idea, love,' he said enthusiastically, 'but where are we going to stage these things?'

Cathy sat forward eagerly, her hair tumbling over her face. 'The strippers in the hostess clubs do their acts in much smaller spaces. Our acts can just move out into the centre of the room and perform. I know it'll be tight but I think it'll work, Des. After all, the music is piped from the back anyway and most of the girls will be miming, won't they?'

He nodded – Cathy could see his mind ticking over. She carried on selling her idea.

'A lot of the men we employ are natural-born artistes. I mean, look at Alfie when he dresses like Doris Day. Him singing along to 'Move Over, Darling' is hilarious. I've seen him do it in the dressing room before now and the other girls loved it. And Georgina's Diana Ross is fantastic, he looks so much like her—'

Desrae interrupted scathingly, 'Oh, yeah, if poor old Diana was fourteen stone!'

Cathy grinned. 'That's not the point here, is it? A resemblance to the person is enough. Your Marilyn Monroe is brilliant and you know it is.'

Desrae laughed now, pleased with the compliment. 'No way am I gonna sing in public.'

'You just need to dress up and tend the place. We can have the girls all dressed up as the women they want to be. I mean, it's a thought, isn't it? Having your drink served by

Carmen Miranda or Elizabeth Taylor has got to be better than by just any old drag queen, hasn't it? It'll give us the edge over the other clubs. The one in Greek Street is seedy and badly in need of a good clean and a decent clientele. We're going for the better end of the market and as such we need to offer something the other clubs haven't thought of.

'Did you see that politician the other night? Guess who was with him? Susan P, that's who. She wanted to have a look see. Told me that our place was the best she'd been in, and she'd recommend it to clients any day. Now what better accolade can we have than that? Susan's the biggest and best madam in London and she's branched out into using boys, as you know. Young men are big business and she said she would send people here and even supply us with men she thought would work better in a club atmosphere. She'd still take her cut from them, of course. But the point is, we can really make this place into a big business. Open other clubs, theme them . . .'

Desrae held up one perfectly manicured hand and said breathily: 'Hold on, love, we've only just opened this place and already you've got us having a chain.'

Cathy looked at her friend and said seriously, 'And why not – all over the country! There's a deep-seated need for them, and why shouldn't we be the ones to do it? Someone's going to sooner or later. The laws against homosexuality are being relaxed all the time. I want a club where gays and straights can come and enjoy themselves. We could even open a restaurant eventually . . .'

Desrae sat back in his Dayglo pink velour chair and shook his head in wonderment. 'You have given this a lot of thought, haven't you? A club where everyone can go and enjoy themselves? Now I've heard everything!'

Cathy had her argument ready. 'Look at the Valbonne,

Desrae. Many people go there to watch the TVs. You and I both know that. People-watching is a big thing these days, whether it's the punks at Tower Hill and Carnaby Street or the hippies in Camden Market. My generation want to experience everything. Gays are accepted now more than at any time previously. Now they're part and parcel of our everyday life. Let's cash in on it. This club we've got here is a contact club, which strictly speaking is illegal. But the next one we open doesn't have to be, does it?'

'All right, love. I'll talk to Joey, see what he thinks.'

Cathy smiled, knowing she was halfway there if Desrae was going to discuss it with his man. 'Where is Joey anyway?'

Desrae shrugged. 'He's got a load of hag at the moment with his bookies. He nearly bit my head off this morning when I rang to see if he fancied a bit of lunch.'

Cathy was surprised. 'That's not like him. Normally he's full of the joys of spring.'

Desrae smiled sadly. 'I think there's a lot more going on than he's saying, to be honest. Even his boy Tommy is out of sorts.'

'Tommy's always out of sorts these days.'

Desrae didn't answer. He knew that Tommy was obsessed with Cathy and found it hard to deal with the fact that she didn't want to know. He was more used to girls falling all over him.

'He's after a date, love. Why don't you put him out of his misery, eh, and go out with him?'

She shook her head. 'No way, Desrae. I don't want to go out with him, or anyone else for that matter. I'm happy as I am.'

Desrae didn't push the issue, but he wished he could make Cathy see that not all men were out for what they could get sexually. And anyway, sex could be a wonderful expression of love between two people. Even when they were of the same gender.

He looked over Cathy's carefully formulated plans once more and then the two of them were back on an even keel.

Joey sat in his house and stared at the walls, trying to find a way through his problems. Somewhere in the background his wife Martha, already drunk, was berating their housekeeper. He tried to put the ranting voice out of his mind and concentrate on the best course of action to take.

A small tight-knit crew of villains had recently come to the West End from Liverpool and they were trying to take the place over. Ordinarily Joey wouldn't have been too worried about that fact, but these were not the usual scallies. Far from it. They were a disciplined community with Irish connections and a love of unnecessary violence.

Joey was having trouble admitting that he was getting too old for it all. That was why he wanted the club with Desrae to work out. He wanted to retire and pass everything over to his young son Tommy who was a natural villain.

But that was easier said than done.

The head of the gang was a man called Derrick O'Hare – a huge Liverpool Irishman with a thick shock of sandy hair and deep-set blue eyes. He was built like a navvy and he spoke like one too. He had none of the finesse needed to be a boss in the West End. If he won power there would soon be anarchy. The West End had settled down happily over the last ten years and everyone involved was making money. Including the police.

Now it was all falling out of bed, and fast. Even Richard Gates was sniffing around and that in itself told Joey just how far this had all gone.

He should have nipped the Liverpool bunch in the bud but he hadn't bothered, believing as he always had that his reputation and presence in the West End would deter them from an outright bid to oust him.

It had deterred many before them, and he knew that he could still deter most people. But these Liverpool boys were a new breed. They dealt in everything and anything: weapons, drugs, sex. They sold women and boys, even children. Their sex shops were a big earner for them. They could supply the more hard-core magazines which they bragged openly came through the docks in Harwich from Germany, Holland and Sweden. They were already a force to be reckoned with up North and now they had come down South to take over the place.

They knew their market and they knew their clientele. They also knew they had to get rid of Joey Pasquale.

They had offered him money, tried to buy him out, and he had refused. Even found it amusing that they had the front to approach him. Now he realised just how dangerous they were. He knew his son would want to take them on and would even enjoy the challenge. But the more Joey heard about them, the more worried he became. Tommy would be taking on trouble the like of which he had never before encountered.

But take it on he would.

That was Tommy's way. He was his father's son. Twenty years earlier Joey would have stood his ground and fought. Now he just couldn't face it. This was a new breed of villain and in his more honest moments he admitted that they scared him.

It wasn't the violence – he had lived with that all his life – but he in common with most old-style criminals had always believed that violence had to be commensurate with the crime committed. These Liverpool lads, on the other hand, used violence all the time, even for the smaller jobs such as getting protection money. They broke limbs for just a few pounds. They were already gaining a reputation as men to fear, and Joey knew he was losing people to them every day.

Now his bookies were under threat.

He had just been approached in his own home, and warned for the final time that if he didn't accept their cash offer, they'd take what they wanted and ruin him. He closed his eyes and filled the empty room with his sigh. Tommy would fight them. But Tommy was young, full of bravado – and full of shit.

There was no saying who would win.

Tommy sat in the bar of the Mortimer Hotel in Piccadilly and sipped at his beer. As he waited for his contact he listened to a group of French tourists chatting together about the Queen and Buckingham Palace. One of the crowd was a tiny girl with huge blue eyes and blond hair; her resemblance to Cathy Duke was so striking he could not take his eyes from her. He knew he was making her feel uneasy and tried to concentrate on his *Daily Mirror*.

He was pleased when Dean Whiteside came into the bar and ordered himself a drink. As Dean sat down beside Tommy, he shook his head sadly. 'Still looking at all the blondes, I see. I'm a tit man meself. Don't give a toss what the boatrace is like as long as they have nice big knockers.'

Tommy laughed easily, knowing that Dean was joking. He had married his childhood sweetheart at eighteen, and ten years and four children later was still enamoured of her. Unlike many of his contemporaries, he didn't feel the need to prove himself a macho man by sleeping with anything that moved. His wife Stella was more than enough for him.

'You're a complete nut, Whiteside.'

Dean grinned. 'You're blonde mad, everyone knows that. By the way, you owe me a grand. That's what it cost to get you the info you was after.'

Tommy nodded. 'So what's the big news?'

Dean shook his head and sighed. 'All bad, mate. I tell you, Tommy, you'd better watch your back because these Scallies are here for the duration. They want it all. I spoke to an old lag this morning who had his face sliced up by them because he owed his bookie thirty-five quid. Can you believe it? Thirty-five fucking sobs. I mean, it's a joke. How the hell are they going to do business like that?'

'They're nutters, they don't reason like we do. All they're interested in is the bottom line. Who was striped up?'

Dean raised his blond eyebrows and said quietly: 'Old Dicky Drake, the bare-knuckle boxer. Most people swallowed him because he was once a face like. He's fucking punch drunk and barely making a living these days. No respect, Tommy. These people have no respect.'

Tommy was shocked. Dicky Drake was a legend in his own lifetime, *the* bare-knuckle boxer of his day, the most famous and the best loved. Dicky had thrown money to many people when he had been on top. Now in his sixties, and punchy, people tended to look after him. Which was only fair. Seeing him striped would cause many people in the East End and the South East to look to Joey to settle the score with the Liverpudlians.

'In a way that can only work for us. Everyone loves old Dicky and no one's going to swallow him getting hurt,' Tommy said tentatively.

Dean looked dubious. 'I dunno so much. I heard this morning that the same men have bought up nightclubs in Essex and Surrey. They've also been after a few of the old East End haunts. The thing is, Tommy, our generation don't give a fuck about the Dicky Drakes. What with the ICF, the Inner City Firm, and the National Front, the world's changing, mate. Nowadays people don't look at the old lags and say: "Give him respect, he was a face once." Now they say: "Kick the cunt's head in and get a bit of his rep." You know that in your heart. Even your dad's not frightening any more to a lot of the youngsters.'

It said something about the relationship between Dean and Tommy that he dared talk as he had about Joey Pasquale. Before Tommy could answer they were joined at their table by a large bald-headed man carrying a pint of Guinness.

'Hello, Tommy lad. Dean. Now what's two nice Catholic boys like yourselves doing in here, eh?'

Tommy looked into Richard Gates's face and laughed. 'Fuck off, Mr Gates. Get back to your nice little police station and leave the men and the boys to sort themselves out.'

Gates sipped his Guinness and said in a low voice that now held a menacing tone: 'How's your dad's new club then? Pulling in the right customers, is it? I saw a few famous faces go in there the other night. Be a right shame if I was to raid it now, wouldn't it? Especially with all this trouble coming from up Liverpool like.'

He leant towards the younger man and said slowly, 'Don't take me for a cunt, all right? I know what's going down and I want to try and avoid a complete gang war if I can. You villains can kill each other day and night for all I care. It's innocent bystanders getting hurt that bothers me, see. If the Liverpudlians decide to torch the club or one of the betting shops, then I have to try and sort it all out. I assume you're insured like, so you have to call me in to get your few quid. Now I know about this Liverpool firm and we could work together there. It's completely up to you. Either way, I'm up for it.'

Tommy ignored the policeman. Dean stood up and went to the toilet, leaving them alone.

'Up yours, Gates,' Tommy told him. 'I don't need the Filth, never have and never will. Now why don't you fuck off and go and put out some parking tickets, or whatever it is you do to earn your keep.'

Richard Gates was furious and they both knew it. In his own way he liked Tommy, and had always liked the boy's father. Gates believed that you were better off with the people you knew running things. He accepted that the Soho sex industry would always be run by someone, and that someone would never be the government.

He, like the old-time villains, believed that it was better off being run properly by one person than carved up and run piecemeal by too many people, all wanting a bite of the lucrative cherry. He didn't want O'Hare's lot getting a foothold in Soho. They were already in Blackpool, Nottingham, Leicester and their home town. They wanted it all, and that was not going to happen.

Anyway, like most Southerners he hated Scallies. They used intimidation and force, guns, fire, even dynamite to attain their ends.

He knew that this could turn into the biggest gang war Soho had ever seen, and he also knew that the blacks and the Chinese were keeping out of it.

The Scallies knew that Gerrard Street and the rest of Chinatown was out of bounds to them, and were sensible enough to accept that. The Chinks wouldn't roll over; they never had and certainly would not start doing it now. In fact, the Chinese were the best inhabitants of Soho in many ways. They sorted out their own differences and kept out of everyone else's.

The blacks were still in their own areas and only really came Up West to wine, dine or deal. That suited him as well. The blacks knew their limitations and accepted them. They were sometimes employed as heavies which fitted them down to the ground. The black community still hadn't bothered to unite. They fought each other as well as everyone else. Bob Marley's concept of all being brothers was great on a record but a non-starter if you lived in Brixton.

Gates's chief worry at this time was the Liverpool men, and he knew much more about what was going on there than he was going to tell Tommy Pasquale.

As he left the bar ten minutes later he felt more worried than he had in years.

Cathy looked lovely and she knew it. Dressed in a hand-kerchief skirt and gypsy top, she appeared much younger than her twenty-two years – the epitome of the fashionable young woman.

It was still early, only seven-thirty, and already there were people in the club's bar. This pleased her. The bar was Cathy's pride and joy, and as she smiled and waved at the customers she kept a sharp eye on the glasses and optics, seeing if anything needed replacing.

One of the customers, an MP who lived in London during the week and near his constituency at the weekends, grinned at her, showing expensive capped teeth. 'Hello, darling girl, and how are you?'

Cathy laughed. Fluttering her eyelashes, she said suggestively, 'You're looking very handsome tonight.'

He preened himself and Cathy inwardly laughed at the man who would one day be in Number 11 Downing Street. He was a complete arsehole and she was constantly amazed at the way he lived a double life. She had seen him in full drag and school uniform. She had also seen him on *Panorama*, shouting his mouth off about the Labour

Party's waste of resources and monetary instability. Still, she reasoned, whatever turned him on.

As she walked through to the front room, she saw Tommy come in at the shop and went over to him, smiling a greeting. 'Hello, Tommy, how are you?'

He stared at her, ranging his eyes over her from head to foot before answering. 'Kicking. And you?'

Blushing from his intense scrutiny, Cathy said stonily, 'I'm not too bad. Can I get you a drink? Your dad's up in the office with Desrae.'

'I'll have a large Scotch and then I'm going to take you outside and lick you all over until you scream.' He said this in a low voice and watched as her blush deepened painfully. He laughed cruelly and then was ashamed of himself for always trying to embarrass her. It was a self-defence mechanism.

Years before he had tried to kiss her, and when she had pushed him away he had continued, as men and boys do, to pull her against him and seek her lips. At the time she had kicked him so hard he had come away with tears in his eyes and since then had been obsessed with her. He knew some of her story from his father, but even though he understood why she felt as she did about sex, relationships and men, he still couldn't resist teasing her.

She was in his blood. He would do anything for her, even die for her, his feelings were so strong. Yet he knew she felt nothing for him, not even sisterly affection, and that hurt him more than he would ever admit.

Making his way up to the office, he caught his father embracing Desrae – something that always made him feel uneasy even though he had accepted their relationship years ago.

'All right, love's young dreams. Daddy's little soldier is

here now, so can we have less of the tonguing in public?' he said cheekily.

Desrae laughed. 'If this is public, love, I'd love to see somewhere private.' Then he discreetly left the office, knowing the two of them had things to talk about.

Tommy looked into his father's face and said simply, 'I'm going after them, Dad. I have to. This is personal now. They even striped up old Dicky Drake. I mean, these people have got to be stopped.'

Joey knew nothing he could say would change Tommy's feelings. 'I'll back you all I can, son, but I warn you: they won't be easy to get rid of.'

Tommy shrugged, that nonchalant gesture he had developed as a small boy with a villain for a father and a lush for a mother. It was another self-defence mechanism. 'You'll leave it all to me then?'

Joey laughed suddenly. 'Well, that's what you want, isn't it?'

Tommy nodded gravely. His father was handing everything over to him. This was a big day in his life and yet it felt wrong, as if his father was copping out somehow.

'Whether I want it or not, Dad, it looks like I'm getting it anyway, doesn't it?'

Joey didn't answer.

There was nothing more to say.

Chapter Twenty-Seven

Richard Gates sat in his unmarked police car and watched people going in and out of the small club in Wardour Street. The gay clubs didn't bother him. If it was all consenting adults, he didn't really give a toss. Unlike many of the men who worked for him, he wasn't a queer basher, racist or misogynist. He was after villains who committed real crimes, not just broke the law of the land. Everyone knew he turned a blind eye to many things. Since joining Vice, for instance, he had stopped a lot of the older women from getting busted for soliciting. He couldn't see the sense in fining them in Bow Street only to have them straight on the street again, earning money for the fine.

He wanted the youngsters off the streets, the ones who were not caught up properly in the life yet. He wanted them out of it once and for all. He knew how quickly people adapted to the life and the money. Especially younger women. The trouble was, though, they took drugs to make going on the game easier, then ended up permanently hooking to get their drugs. It was a vicious circle. At least if they worked for people like Susan P they had a bit of prestige and could save a few quid. Susan wouldn't touch addicts, and made sure that her girls were fully aware of that.

Gates watched the club for a couple of hours, taking down the names of anyone he recognised. He was impressed by the clientele and knew that Susan P would like half of them on her books. It showed Desrae had done his market research well. He had kept out the rougher elements; even rowdy nobs were not allowed inside. Laurence Olivier himself would have had trouble getting in with too many drinks inside him.

Gates got out of the car and went into the club; he followed on the heels of a High Court judge and his long-time male lover, a daytime television reporter. Walking through the sex shop, the two men in front averted their eyes from the magazines. *Brabusters* and *Big Jugs* weren't really their cup of tea. *Big Boys in Big Beds* was much more their line, and such titles were sold as art books for a high price in the very same establishment. Gates knew because he had had the shop raided a few months before. Now it had changed ownership, he was happy to let it be as long as he could gain access any time he wanted. Hard-core porn didn't bother him, unless it contained minors or animals.

Even Gates drew the line at that.

Desrae smiled at him prettily and signed to the doorman to let him through. As he walked into the smoky atmosphere he was accosted by a tall woman in a peach-coloured flowing dress and platform boots.

Desrae moved towards them both and said sotto voce: 'He's the Filth, love, and not one of the friendly ones, OK?'

The man sighed and walked away and Richard Gates chuckled as he said, 'How do you know I ain't changed what side I do me partin'?'

Desrae grinned, all lip gloss and pencilled-on eyebrows,

and answered him happily. 'If you ever do that, love, I'll be the first in line. Always loved a man with a belly. Something to grab hold of. Now drink first and then we'll chat. I do hope this isn't an official visit? I have more Masons in here than on the bench at the Old Bailey.'

'Or in the fucking dock for that matter, darlin'. I'll have a small Scotch, please. No, it's your man I want to see – Joey.'

As he spoke he saw Susan P come into the club dressed in a black leather catsuit. Her dark hair was blow-waved into a pageboy and her make-up was a work of art. She was half catwoman, half punk rocker, and it suited her. She was with two pop stars, both known pederasts.

Gates took his drink from Desrae and followed him up the stairs to the office. Cathy was in there with Joey, telling him about her plans for the next club, when they walked in. Her face broke into a wide smile as she saw DI Gates. 'Hello, Richard, what a surprise.'

He looked into that elfin face and felt the tightness in his guts he always experienced when he saw her. Her story had made him more aware of what was happening in the world, and now he followed up children's cases as much as he could. Seeing her in this club grieved him at times, because he knew she was in effect a fag hag now. At ease with the gay community because she knew they wanted only her and not her body.

And Cathy's body was made to be loved by a man, though he knew she would never believe that. Even a dirty joke upset her. That was how she had been left. That was what the so-called caring profession had done to her.

'I've come to see Joey about a few things, ladies,' Gates said briskly. 'Can I ask you two to leave us alone for a while?'

Pleased as punch at being referred to as a lady, Desrae

ushered Cathy out of the room. Sitting down, Gates looked around the office and said: 'Fuck me, it's like being caught in a queer's dream, this lot.'

Joey chuckled. 'You know what Desrae's like – over the top or what. Now what can I do for you?'

Gates said without any preamble: 'There's going to be a war unless I can stop it. You know and I know that the Scallies are out for the lot of it – everything you've got and more. I want to know what you know, and if you won't tell me, I'll drag your arse into the station.'

Joey laughed gently. 'Come on, Richard. You must know I can't talk freely about anything like that. You're a good Bill, a good filth, everyone knows that. But at the end of the day that is what you are and what you'll always be: a policeman. No one who grasses on the Scallies will live to tell the tale.'

Gates listened with his usual quiet demeanour. He knew that what this man was saying was true. If the Liverpool men were grassed, then that grass had better be ready for death.

'Whatever happens, I'm in on it, Joey,' he said heavily, 'and if that means I have to take you down, then I will.'

Joey shrugged; 'You'll do whatever you have to. And so will I.'

At the end of the day, his fear of the Liverpool gang was greater than his fear of the police.

Derrick O'Hare was laughing. He had a loud raucous bellow that generally made everyone else laugh with him. Today, though, his men were finding it hard to respond.

Deep inside they knew their boss was really a psychopath, and that he enjoyed inflicting pain. Enjoyed it a little too much for their liking. For instance, Derrick had personally taken out an eighteen-year-old burglar he had employed a few months before to do a few B&Es and collect information Derrick badly needed.

The boy had performed his job well, had kept his mouth shut and had looked forward to a long and happy association with the man who had employed him.

But when O'Hare had all the information he needed, on both criminals and straight people, he had shot the boy in the head and left him dead on a small country road in Essex. Now Chelmsford police were running around like blue-arsed flies trying to connect the boy with local villains, and failing dismally.

The boy had been a genius at his work; as young as he was, he could get into any house, anywhere, a skill taught to him by his father, an old-time safe breaker who had been shot to death in Marbella a few months previously. The boy was sound, trustworthy. There had been no need to kill him.

Derrick had kidded himself and his men that it was a security thing, when they all knew he just hadn't liked the boy. Had resented his youth and undoubted talent. Such was the mentality of Derrick O'Hare.

After the men had left his house in Manor Park he walked through to his conservatory and settled himself in a large cane chair to watch his two Dobermanns playing in the large ornately landscaped garden.

His girlfriend Lottie brought him out a drink. She was thirty-nine, still pretty and still well built. They had been together over nine years. Lottie was besotted with her big villain and Derrick was besotted with his blonde bimbo. Lottie played at being a fool, knew that was what he wanted, and she would do anything for this big man she loved with a vengeance. She had left her husband and child for him, and had never regretted it.

Now, kneeling between his legs, she performed fellatio

on him, knowing this always calmed him down after a business meeting. He was a man with a permanent hard on, and Lottie knew that to keep him by her side she had to keep him happy. She was pleased to do this.

Derrick, for his part, was still obsessed by her. He was convinced every man in the world wanted her, and consequently fucked her rigid to keep her mind on him. It was a strange relationship, and in its own way a good one. He owned Lottie, and she was quite happy to be owned.

Lee Bonham was sitting outside the sex shop in Wardour Street. He had been waiting for over an hour.

Lee was a small man with impatient green eyes and straggling black hair. He was always speeding, amphetamines were like food to him. Consequently he was as thin as a rake and in a constant state of agitation. Today he was dressed casually in a white T-shirt, black jeans and leather bomber jacket. For his job you had to look nondescript.

As a shooter for hire, he was one of the increasing number of nameless and faceless men who were making a good living in the London underworld. The police had trouble pointing the finger at them because they were so well protected.

It was all done in a civilised and friendly fashion. Lee was told the name and the location of his hit, and picked up his money once the job was done. This was a twenty-grand earner and he wanted it out of the way as quickly as possible.

He saw his mark leaving the shop and stepped out of the Ford Escort van in which he had been sitting. Crossing the busy road, he walked towards the man as he went to unlock his car, a rather nice Daimler Sovereign.

Lee tapped the man on the shoulder and pumped four bullets into his chest in a matter of seconds. He eased his dying victim to the pavement and ran back across the road, skilfully dodging the traffic. He was in his van and gone from the scene in double quick time. No one from the crowded street could pinpoint anything or anyone.

As usual one witness was sure he was black.

The police and the ambulance men were there in minutes, and all knew it was a complete waste of time.

Desrae needed more help than anyone. Sedated, they placed him in the ambulance and took him off as fast as possible. Joey was left with a coat covering his head as CID made their way to the scene.

A contract killing in Soho would make all the news broadcasts, and the police knew there would be a lot of pressure on them to find out who had done it. They also knew they had as much chance of finding the location of the proverbial snowball in hell.

Cathy had just got out of the bath at the flat when the doorbell rang. Pulling on a white silk negligee, she went to the door, a smile on her lovely face and a spring in her step. She was expecting Desrae; instead she found Tommy Pasquale.

'Hello, Tommy, I didn't expect you—' He pushed past and dragged her into the lounge. Cathy pulled herself away from him, alarmed at his strength.

'What's happened? Is Desrae OK?' she asked.

Tommy sank down on to the sofa and put his head in his hands. Cathy watched in horror and amazement as she saw the tears dripping through his fingers. Kneeling down beside him, she put one arm over his shoulders. 'Tommy, for God's sake, tell me what's happened.'

'Me dad . . . it's me dad. Someone murdered him today. Outside the shop in Wardour Street.'

Cathy was stunned. 'Are you sure?'

Tommy said aggressively through his tears: 'Of course I'm fucking sure! You don't make mistakes about that kind of thing, you silly bitch. They shot him, like a fucking dog. He was hit four times . . . four fucking times.' He broke down and sobbed.

Cathy put her hands to her mouth and Tommy felt an urge to take her in his arms. He needed her now, more than he had ever needed anyone in his life before. He had loved his father, loved and looked up to him.

'Desrae! My God, he'll go mad . . .' Cathy's voice was a whisper as she thought of the man who had loved Joey with all his heart.

'They've sedated him,' Tommy told her. 'He's all right for the moment. I've got to tell me mother yet . . . Oh Christ, Cathy, what am I gonna tell me mother and me sisters?' Gone was the hard man, the villain. Tommy was a lost and lonely boy, grieving for his loss and in agony over breaking the news to the living.

Taking him in her arms, Cathy cried with him. She had loved Joey as well. He had been so kind to her, and looked out for her and helped her fulfil her dreams.

As she felt Tommy's arms go around her waist she pressed herself against him, needing his comfort as much as he needed hers. When he began kissing her she responded, liking the feel of his lips on her face, liking the touch of his hands on her body as he slipped the silk negligee from her shoulders.

Sex to Cathy was all about her need for safety, not the basic urge it was to others. She badly wanted to feel loved now so she allowed Tommy to take her, aware that his need was as great as hers. As he pulled her gently on to the carpet before him, she opened her legs gracefully, tugging him down on top of her like an old pro. Instinctively she knew what he wanted and gave him it, moving her hips against his and rising to meet his every thrust as if they had coupled many times before. Their tears dried as both entered a twilight world of mutual gratification.

As he came inside her, Cathy caressed his face and whispered loving things in his ears.

Afterwards they lay together in the gathering darkness and talked as they had never done before. They talked about Joey, about Desrae, about their childhoods. They talked themselves into normal people again, both trying to make sense of the terrible thing that had befallen them.

Tommy realised that he loved Cathy Duke, had always loved her. He also realised that once this night was over she would be her old independent self again. He admitted privately that his father's death was almost worth the feeling of closeness he had achieved with this young girl with the big blue eyes and strange attitude towards sex and men. If nothing else came out of Joey Pasquale's death, he had tasted his Cathy, been caressed by her and loved by her. At least he had experienced that much.

As dawn broke over Soho and the first rays of the morning sun touched their naked bodies, Cathy got up and dressed herself.

Making a large pot of coffee, she took it into the lounge and woke the man to whom she felt so close now. As he sipped his coffee, Cathy saw that the frightened, shocked young boy was gone. He had been replaced by a bitter man who wanted to exact violent revenge for his father's murder.

'What are you going to do, Tommy?' she asked.

He smiled grimly. 'I'm going to hunt down that bastard O'Hare and kill him stone fucking dead.'

It was what she'd expected to hear, but it made her sad even so. Tommy had played at being the villain; now he had to live up to it. She had a feeling he would have no difficulty with that.

He was, after all, his father's son.

Desrae opened his eyes and looked about him, feeling ill. He knew at the back of his drug-clouded mind that something bad had happened, he just couldn't figure out what it was. As he tasted the bitterness in his mouth he remembered, and big fat tears rolled down his face. In the night one of the nurses had removed his make-up and false eyelashes and by the harsh light of day he knew he must look his age and, worse than that, just like a man.

He tried to rise. Glancing across the ward he saw a man in blue-striped pyjamas staring at him incredulously.

A small Scottish nurse came to the bedside and said gently: 'Can I get you a drink, dear?'

Desrae nodded, unable to speak for the silent tears that were pouring from his eyes. He felt he could scream with hurt and fear. Like a trapped animal he looked around the crowded ward at the other patients, all staring at the big transvestite who'd been brought in the night before.

It was the final humiliation.

'Had your fucking pennyworth, you ugly load of bastards?' he demanded. 'Seen the freak now, have you? Give you something to talk about at visiting time, I suppose. Wankers . . .'

As Desrae ranted and raved a doctor pressed a needle into his arm and he knew the blessed peace of oblivion once more, his last conscious thought being that Joey would have laughed to hear him because for once in his life he had talked like a man.

What would he do without his Joey?

When he woke in the evening he was in a small private

room and Cathy was sitting by the bed, holding his hand. Desrae smiled at her gratefully.

'I showed meself right up earlier, ducks.'

She smiled at him tenderly. 'So I heard. Here, I've brought you in all your make-up and a change of clothes.'

Desrae squeezed her hand and started to cry once more. 'They killed him – the Liverpool scum killed him. What will I do, Cathy? What on earth will I do without him?'

She kissed the man she loved so well and said in a strong voice: 'You'll get yourself dressed and then come home with me. Joey wouldn't want you upset like this, you know that. The Old Bill is waiting to talk to you and Gates is already outside. Keep your trap shut, Desrae, and tell them you saw nothing. Tommy's got everything in hand, OK?'

Desrae nodded, nonplussed at the businesslike tone of the girl's voice. 'You sound so different, love, I think I'm a bit scared of you.'

Cathy sighed and tried to grin. 'We're all in deep shit, Desrae. The Liverpool people are out to take everything Joey had. Tommy told me all about it last night. There's going to be a lot of trouble and we'll need our wits about us, OK?'

She kissed Desrae's stubbled cheeks. 'Once you get home, you can grieve in peace and we can find out what's happening. Now, do you feel strong enough to get up? I'll help you dress and everything, all right?'

He sat up in bed. 'Do I look really terrible?'

Cathy said sadly, 'Of course you do, you've just lost the most important person in your life.'

Desrae grabbed her hand and kissed it. 'You're important to me too, love – and don't you ever forget that.'

Before she could answer, Richard Gates came into the room.

'I'm sorry, Desrae. I liked Joey, you know that,' he said, and they believed him. 'Now what you must do is think back and tell me anything unusual that you saw. Anything at all.'

Desrae looked at him, all big-eyed innocence. 'But I didn't see anything, Mr Gates, I swear.'

Richard Gates knew he was lying and forced himself to make polite small talk, hoping for a change of heart. Cathy Duke, all in black, looked good enough to eat as usual. She knew more than she was saying. Gates too, understood that these people lived by a different law and that they would not be changing sides at this stage.

But he would get to the bottom of it all, he swore as much to himself.

He ended up giving a silent Desrae and Cathy a lift back to their flat. The irony of the situation was not lost on any of them.

Chapter Twenty-Eight

Richard Gates and Cathy sat and sipped their drinks. Desrae was having a nap in bed and they were making small talk. The subject of Joey came up and Cathy told Gates how good the dead man had been to her.

'I've been very lucky, what with you and Desrae and Joey looking out for me. He really was kind to me, you know.'

'I know that, love,' Richard said quietly. 'He thought the world of you, see. It's not hard even if I say it myself. I think the world of you too.'

It was the first time they had ever discussed their friendship, and Cathy was embarrassed. She gulped down her brandy and poured herself another.

Gates watched her. In his mind's eye he saw the kid in the police cell, her skinny arms and legs and huge blue eyes. That lost girl was still there if you looked for her hard enough. She was in Cathy's eyes.

He saw tears roll from those eyes on to her cheeks and pulled her into his arms. She let him, enjoying the feel of his large body and the comfort it offered. He stroked her hair and kissed her gently on the forehead, all the time telling her to relax, to let the tears flow and get it all out of her system.

He was thrilled to have a legitimate reason to cuddle her, hold her close. When she pulled away and blew her nose, he felt cheated. He also felt the first stirrings of an erection and cursed himself for it. But that was how Cathy affected him these days.

'I'm sorry, Richard. Can I get you another drink?'

He knew it was over, that it was time for him to go, and sighed heavily. 'I'll make me way home now, I need a few hours' sleep.'

They smiled at one another and a little later he left. Cathy watched him from the upstairs window and wondered what it was about the big bald-headed policeman that affected her so much. She could easily have stayed in his arms all night.

She heard Desrae moving about and went into the bedroom. He was sitting at his dressing table applying make-up.

'Where do you think you're going?' Cathy asked in surprise.

'Nowhere, but the girls will all be paying their respects soon and I want to look me best, if you don't mind.' He was busily pencilling in his eyebrows.

'I can always tell them to leave it till another time,' Cathy suggested. But Desrae shook his head.

'Best get it over with. Anyway, they'll cheer me up.' He applied more blusher and lipstick. 'A large G and T would go down a fucking treat.'

As Cathy made his drink the doorbell rang and the first of the 'girls' arrived – a small black man with a blond wig and tight hipster trousers. He was from the Valbonne and he and Desrae went back years. His name was Eugenie, and Cathy led him into the lounge.

Desrae looked like Queen Victoria in her black dress and mantilla and Cathy felt a sudden urge to laugh at the spectacle. With Desrae everything, even mourning, was so much larger than life.

At that moment the doorbell rang again and two more drag queens arrived, this time two men from the club, both in their daytime straight gear with only the bare minimum of make-up. Both burst into tears as they saw Desrae, and Cathy went to the kitchen and made a large pot of coffee. It was going to be a long day all right.

Bringing in the refreshments, and placing a bottle of Remy Martin on the table, she put on her coat and escaped into the daylight for a while.

She walked around to the club and let herself in. As she turned to shut the door she was pushed inside by two men. She opened her mouth to scream. A gloved hand was placed over her face and she was dragged through to the back of the shop.

'Keep your mouth shut and you'll be OK.'

The voice was unmistakably Liverpudlian and Cathy froze. The man dragged her up the stairs, copping a quick feel of her breasts as he did so. Inside the Dayglo pink office he pushed her away from him.

'What do you want?' she gasped.

The first man, blond and with arms like a Sumo wrestler's, laughed. 'We want all Pal Joey's books.'

Cathy shook her head firmly, recovering from her shock. 'Then you've come to the wrong place,' she said defiantly. 'He never kept anything here. This is *my* business, mine and Desrae's. Joey had nothing to do with it other than providing the capital.' She was amazed by the strength of her voice and the way she was standing up to them. Inside she was terrified but knew that these men must not see any weakness whatsoever.

The smaller of them began to tear the office apart and she stood and watched him. There was nothing they would want here, as far as she knew.

Five minutes later he shrugged and said to his companion: 'She's right.'

'Where's the safe?'

Cathy debated whether she should try and bluff her way out of it and decided against it. She went to the wall and removed the mirror Desrae spent all day looking in. Behind it was the safe. It contained money, about a thousand pounds, and a few documents pertaining to the club. Cathy unlocked it.

The larger man went through it all. Pocketing the money, he said nastily: 'Tell the queer we'll be back.'

Cathy answered coolly, 'And *you* tell O'Hare he won't get away with this.' Her voice and words stopped the men in their tracks. 'You can also tell him he doesn't frighten me. The people of Soho don't frighten easily.'

The bigger man laughed. 'If I had the time, I'd give you something to think about, lady.'

She snorted at him in derision. 'Don't kid yourself, sonny boy. It'd take a man to get a reaction from me and I don't see any in here, do you?' She saw his face go pale with rage and knew she'd gone too far but stood her ground.

The men must have had strict orders on what they could and could not do. They left, taking the money with them, and Cathy sank into Desrae's bright pink chair and tried to stem the wild beating of her heart. It was all going wrong. With Joey's death their security seemed to have disappeared. It was a sobering thought.

Pulling herself together, Cathy went down the stairs and locked herself into the club. Then she picked up the phone and called Susan P, to put her in the picture.

Within ten minutes Richard Gates was with her; Susan P must have contacted him.

'What did they take?' he demanded.

'Just the money from the safe – but I'm not pressing charges if that's what you want,' Cathy joked.

Richard laughed. 'I guessed as much. I just want to know what's going down, that's all.'

Cathy shrugged. 'So do I.'

He watched her as she made them both a coffee with shaking hands.

'Me and Desrae are really in danger, ain't we?' she said.

He nodded. 'Yes, darlin', you are in danger until we can get a handle on this Liverpool wanker.'

Cathy stared at him; his face was open to her. He got up and put some brandy in her coffee. 'Get that down your gregory, love, and we'll put our thinking caps on, eh?'

Cathy sipped the hot liquid and felt the warmth of it as it hit her stomach. Every time something bad happened to her, Richard Gates was there to pick up the pieces. She was grateful to him for that. He always made her feel safe – as if, while she was with him, no one and nothing could hurt her. It occurred to her then that he really cared for her, and she smiled to herself.

Another fatherly man like Joey – she had been blessed in that respect.

But Richard Gates's thoughts as he watched her were anything but fatherly.

Joscelyn Driscoll was listening to her husband's tirade against the police, the establishment and their Asian neighbours when Richard Gates walked in through the French doors. Both the Driscolls were shocked into silence.

Smiling, Gates pulled the man out of his chair by the shirt and proceeded to slap him around the room. Joscelyn, even though she hated the police, felt a moment's euphoria as she saw her old man getting a taste of what he'd doled out to her so often. Whatever had possessed her to marry a Liverpool wide boy, she still didn't know.

As her husband lay on the floor with Gates kicking him, she went to the kitchen to make one of her endless cups of tea. Let Lenny sort it out, she thought viciously. He was the one who had brought all the trouble to their door.

'Where's O'Hare?' Gates's voice was breathless, but as usual softly spoken.

Lenny Driscoll shook his head. 'I swear on me daughter's head, I have no idea what you're talking about, Mr Gates.'

Gates closed his eyes and said: 'You're not making this any easier for yourself, you Liverpool wanker. Now, for the last time, *where the fuck will I find O'Hare?*'

Lenny took the blows once more but still wouldn't answer. 'Please, Mr Gates,' he groaned, 'my life is worth more than that.'

'Your fucking life will be extinct if you don't tell me what I want to know, mate. Where's that bastard O'Hare?'

Lenny just lay on the floor curled up into a ball as he shook his head in denial. Picking up a small leather-covered stool, Gates began to beat the man with it mercilessly. Lenny took the punishment. It was all he could do.

The only interruption was when Joscelyn popped her head into the lounge and said gaily: 'Anyone for a cuppa?'

Dropping the stool, Gates nodded at her. 'Yeah, all right then.'

Sitting on the arm of a chair, he watched as Lenny Driscoll pulled himself up from the floor and tidied himself. It was the same everywhere Gates went: fear of Derrick O'Hare was far greater than fear of the police. It was beginning to annoy Gates.

Sipping his tea, he pondered on a man who could instil such terror, and obviously kill on a whim. O'Hare was an unknown quantity and that worried Gates. He liked to know exactly what he was dealing with.

Finishing his tea, he said to Lenny, 'Nothing personal, son.'

Lenny, battered and bruised, laughed painfully. 'No offence taken, Mr Gates.'

Gates left as he had arrived, by the back way, and grinned to himself. No offence had been taken, eh? Not unless Lenny could meet him down a dark alleyway one night. Then he had a feeling that offence would be taken – very seriously.

Cathy went back to the flat and was pleased to find Susan P with Desrae. The 'girls' were all gone.

'The doctor's been again and given him another shot. I think he'd be better off in bed, he lost it again earlier,' Susan told her.

They put a stoned and acquiescent Desrae to bed and then went into the lounge. Cathy told Susan P what had happened at the club. She hadn't wanted to tell her in front of Desrae.

'This O'Hare has to be sorted, and quick,' the other woman said grimly. 'If he gets what he wants, I'll have to deal with him anyway – unless I kill him, of course. I'm quite capable of that, you know.'

'It's like the world's gone mad, ain't it?' Cathy shuddered. 'But I tell you something – if anything happens to Tommy or anyone else, *I'll* kill him.'

Susan P felt an urge to laugh. The thought of little Cathy killing anyone was mad, yet inside she knew that the girl was capable of it, if the circumstances were right.

'Listen, darling, this man is dangerous with a capital D.

You just watch over Desrae and leave everything else to us. Tommy ain't going to take none of this lying down.'

'But what if he can't do anything?' Cathy fretted. 'After all, this man has already killed Joey, and whoever thought anyone would make a hit on him? If this man can kill Joey, then he really thinks he can do what he wants and that is what scares me. He has the North and now he wants the South – at least that's what Tommy says anyway.'

Susan P sighed. 'Listen to me. Tommy's not a mug, love. He'll sort it all out, you'll see. You just look after Desrae and leave all the planning to us. We know what we're dealing with and we're used to sorting these problems. It's par for the course in Soho.'

Cathy nodded and kept her own counsel. If this O'Hare wanted a war, then she for one was quite willing to give him one.

Flinty was a small man but strong, and a known grass. He knew everyone, and everything about everyone. No one knew his real name, he had been Flinty always. Even he wasn't sure any more about his given name. At sixty-five years old he was a gofer. In and out of prison for petty offences, he kept his eyes and his ears open and earned extra cash by telling tales, not only to the police but to other villains as well. If he heard a story, he took it to the person who would be most interested and picked up a few quid.

It was the way of the world. There were lots of Flintys about, except that in his own way he had brought grassing almost to a fine art.

Opening his front door he was all smiles. Twenty minutes earlier he had ordered himself a bottle of Scotch and a Chinese takeaway and was waiting for the cab driver to deliver it. Earlier in the day he had passed on a little bit of information to a policeman at Vine Street about a robbery due to go down in Essex. The man had paid him twenty-five quid for the info with a promise of the same again if anyone was nicked.

All in all, it was a neat day's work.

Seeing Gates on his doorstep, with his Chinese and Scotch, the smile dropped from Flinty's face.

Pushing his way into the small bedsit, Gates smiled. One of his rare real smiles. 'All right, Flinty? Long time no see, eh?' He placed the food and alcohol on the coffee table. Then, going to the kitchenette, he put on the kettle, filling it to the brim.

Flinty watched him with wary eyes. He didn't attempt to touch the food but eyed the drink with longing.

When the kettle had boiled, Gates turned down the Calor-gas stove and the kettle whistled softly in the silence of the room.

'Is it a cuppa you're after, Mr Gates?' Flinty already knew the answer, but he still asked the question.

Gates picked up the kettle with the help of a grubby tea towel and said menacingly, 'Take off your shoes and socks.'

Flinty paled and shook his head, saying, 'Oh, come on, Mr Gates, not that. You'd not do that to me, surely? I've always tried to help you out, you know I have . . .' His voice trailed off as the kettle was banged down once more on the small two-ring stove.

'Flinty, if you don't remove your socks, I'll fucking rip them off myself, OK? Now, you can make this hard or you can make it easy.'

The runty little man took off his shoes and socks, babbling: 'What do you want to know, Mr Gates? I'll tell you if I can, I always tell anything I learn. You must know that, surely?' He knew that Richard Gates would scald his feet without a second thought, and that all the screaming in the world would not do him any good. Screams in this houseful of bedsits were nothing unusual. It was that kind of place.

'Please, Mr Gates, tell me what you want and I swear on me mother's eyes I'll tell you what you want to know.' He had his feet exposed now and the smell was ripe in the cloying heat of the room.

'Jesus Christ, the hum of your feet is enough to make me scald the fuckers anyway! Don't you ever wash, Flinty?'

He shook his head. 'Where would I wash here? The bathroom's like a fucking war zone most of the time. The bath's filthy. I get by. Sometimes I bath at a friend's.'

'Sit yourself down and stick out your plates.' Flinty hesitated and Gates rolled his eyes to the ceiling. 'I'm getting annoyed now, Flinty. Just do as I ask and tell me what I want to know and you'll be OK.'

Flinty sat in the chair, his face a study of fear. Gates picked up the kettle once more and went to him, saying with a laugh: 'Sad little faces cut no ice with me, you cretin. I know what you are and you know that I know. You're a fucking nonce, mate. You prefer little boys to grown men. I know all about you so don't come the old soldier with me.'

Flinty dropped his gaze and stared instead at the steaming kettle of water hovering over his feet. Gates let a few drops escape and land on his legs. Even the thickness of his trousers, a tweed pair he had picked up from a second-hand stall in Camden, didn't prevent him from burning.

'Sorry, mate, bit of an accident there. I meant to hit your feet, see.'

Flinty closed his eyes. He was a coward. In his life he had been banged up many times and had endured humiliation after humiliation rather than have any pain inflicted on him. Now he resigned himself to his fate.

'What I want to know is, where can I get my hands on Derrick O'Hare?' Gates saw Flinty's face go even whiter and grinned. He had the little fucker; if anyone knew the whereabouts of the Liverpool lout, Flinty would.

The grass had tears in his eyes as he answered: 'Burn me now, Mr Gates. That's more than my life's worth.'

Gates let half the kettle of water land on the man's feet, and watched in fascination as blisters appeared like magic. Then, placing the kettle back on the gas ring, he proceeded to tie the weeping Flinty's hands behind his back with his own tie.

'Look, mate, I know this is painful and I'm sorry about that, but I *have* to know where the cunt is. If I have to, I shall pour all this water over your genitals. Now that *is* painful . . .'

Flinty went quiet and for a few seconds Gates thought he had died of fright. Looking into the man's face, he saw he was gritting his teeth, eyes tightly closed. He was willing to let Gates burn him rather than face O'Hare.

Putting the boiling kettle back on the hob and turning off the gas, he sighed heavily. Flinty's feet looked like two red pieces of meat, and Gates felt a moment's sorrow for what he had done. It was blanked out almost immediately by the knowledge that O'Hare could easily get away with anything while people were this frightened of him. Not since the Krays had Gates seen such a wall of silence.

It seemed no one wanted to fall foul of the Scouser and no one seemed able to persuade them otherwise.

Picking up the kettle once more, Gates tipped some over the man's genitalia. Flinty screamed, and Gates slammed the kettle on to the table. Knocking the Chinese to the floor, and opening the bottle of Scotch, he said quietly: 'You writhe in agony, you bastard, and remember

– this is nothing to what I'm going to do to you in a few minutes, all right? I'll fucking torture you all night if I have to but I'll find out what I want to know, OK?'

Flinty was traumatised, his face white, his lips blue. The hands trembling with shock behind his back made him look as if he were dancing in the chair. Spittle hung from his lips as he whispered: 'Please, Mr Gates, please stop hurting me.'

Gates took a deep drink from the bottle of Scotch and said reasonably: 'Tell me what I want to know, Flinty, and I'll see you get to a hospital, I can't be no fairer than that. I'll never let on where I got my information, you know that.'

Flinty shook his head and muttered, 'He's madder than you, he's madder than anyone. Untie me and I'll tell you his latest escapade.'

Richard untied the man's hands and Flinty lay back in the chair, panting. The pain must have been excruciating and Gates felt a sneaking admiration for the man's ability to keep quiet after all he had done to him. He gave Flinty the whisky and the man drank deeply.

'A few weeks ago, O'Hare tortured to death Billy Wright. You know old Billy, the tramp from Berwick Street?'

Gates nodded, not sure where this conversation was leading. Groaning now, Flinty began to talk once more.

'O'Hare bought him a drink and put him in his car. I was with them – I went along for the ride. O'Hare said we'd get a good drink and all he wanted was a bit of info. I do the same for faces as I do for the Filth, you know that. They skinned him alive, Mr Gates, old Billy Wright. In front of me eyes like. He honestly didn't know what they wanted from him, he'd have told them else. But that man O'Hare, he skinned him anyway. It was terrible, he's a fucking nutter. So, Mr Gates, I'd rather be tortured by you than him any day of the fucking week. Burn me, stab me – fuckin' shoot me, I don't give a toss. But keep me away from him.'

He took another long pull from the whisky bottle and Gates looked at him in silence for a while.

'I take it *you* had the information he wanted, Flinty. After all, you're still here to tell the tale, ain't you?'

'Too right I told him, Mr Gates, you'd have told him anything an' all but it didn't stop the cunt from starting in on poor old Billy Wright. I tried to save the poor old git, I swear on my daughter's he—'

'You ain't got a daughter, Flinty – she's dead, remember? Overdose, if I recall.'

Flinty ignored him. 'On her grave then, wherever that is, but I tell you now, Mr Gates, he's a fucking lunatic. I told him where that brown hatter Pasquale hung out because it's common knowledge. Joey was good to me over the years, but I'd have told O'Hare anything. Yes, even you, Mr Gates, would have shit it with him and his Bowie knife looming over your face. Now leave me alone.' He began to cry then in earnest.

Gates stared down at the man and spoke through gritted teeth. 'I'm not leaving till I get what I want, and believe me, Flinty, that ponce won't have nothing on me if I lose my temper. I think you should consider that, don't you?'

He refilled the kettle, saying as he did so: 'Next time I'll pour this in your mouth, and then, mate, you won't ever be telling anyone anything again, will you?'

Flinty put his head into his hands and said brokenly: 'He drinks in a spicler off Camden Market. It's the meeting place for his men. That's all I know, I swear.'

Gates smiled then, one of the lightning smiles that made

him look almost handsome. 'See how easy it was? All you had to do was tell me that, and me and you would never have fallen out, would we? I'll phone an ambulance for you now, OK?'

With that he left the flat, Flinty already gone from his mind. It was all in a day's work for Gates.

Half an hour later, he picked up two brothers from Tottenham – two black men called Lincoln and Roosevelt. The brothers were heavies for a price and every now and then Gates used them for 'persuasive' duties.

Both would kill their own grannies for a few quid – perfect credentials as far as Gates was concerned.

Tooled up with 'squirts' – ammonia in washing-up liquid bottles – knuckledusters and small telescopic coshes, they all wore Crombie overcoats with special poacher's pockets inside to house their baseball bats and pickaxe handles. Lincoln always used a baseball bat with eight-inch nails through the tip, for maximum damage.

As they arrived at the small spieler in Camden, they were all hyped up.

Lincoln turned to Gates and said cheerily: 'Five hundred, yeah?'

Gates nodded.

'Right then, who's the mark?'

The policeman had been dreading this and as he said, 'Derrick O'Hare,' waited for a refusal. He didn't get one.

'The Scouser, is it? What a touch! I hate fucking northerners.' Roosevelt's voice was jovial and Gates grinned.

'Let's go get them, shall we?'

The two men nodded.

As they walked inside the music hit them. It was Gilbert O'Sullivan singing *Clare* and the two black men mimed being sick, much to Gates's amusement. The doorman stared at them. Taking out a twenty-pound note, Gates tucked it into the man's breast pocket. He smiled and waved them through.

All dressed in Crombies, they looked just like any other lags on a night out. Gates had taken the precaution of wearing a black Homburg to hide his face and tell-tale bald head.

Inside the club it was dark. Girls in various stages of undress and drunkenness milled around looking for punters. They gave the blacks a wide berth which suited all three men. The gambling was subdued as it was early in the evening yet, only just past ten-thirty, and the main money spinner here was drink or the buying of drugs.

The air was thick with cannabis smoke. Amphetamines would go down later in the evening when men wanted to feel more alert as they gambled away their wages.

Going to the bar the men ordered shorts and looked around them. There was no sign of O'Hare. Pulling one of the girls towards him, Gates whispered: 'Where's Derrick's office? There's a tenner in it for you, love.'

The girl eyed him suspiciously then, taking the tenner, said slowly: 'Top of the stairs, turn right. But he ain't there.'

Gates knocked back his drink and ordered another. They people-watched for ten minutes before making their way to the stairs that led to the toilets and the upstairs offices. No one took any notice of them as they cut through the throng. Gates could not believe the lack of security. It was as if the man thought himself indestructible.

The office door stood open as they walked inside. Whatever ever O'Hare was up to, Gates decided, he didn't plan it from this little room. It was more of a book-keeping centre than anything else.

As they searched through the drawers, the door was

opened by a muscle-bound Scouser who said pointedly: 'Can I help you gentlemen at all?'

The three men behind him were all big too and all muscle-bound. But as Gates always said: Handsome is as handsome does. Some of the most muscle-bound men he had known were as weak as kittens.

Lincoln and Roosevelt felt the same way and the men began their tear-up in record time. The sudden appearance of the baseball bats and pickaxe handles took the smug looks off the faces of the Liverpudlians. They'd expected a fist fight. Instead they got a massacre.

But Gates, as he fought them, knew in his heart that tonight he would not get O'Hare. He enjoyed the fight all the same. Whatever happened, he was going to stop O'Hare before he harmed anyone else, especially Cathy.

If O'Hare wanted the West End and all it entailed, he would have to take it over Richard Gates's dead body.

Chapter Twenty-Nine

Derrick O'Hare sat in the bar of the Café Central and sipped a glass of ice-cold Chablis. He was dressed in a white linen suit and black shirt. His black loafers were hand-made and his socks bright green.

As a fashion statement he was a disaster; as a good tipper he was greeted with enthusiasm.

He sat at a small table, smiling and waving at passers-by who either waved back or dropped their eyes from this bloke who seemed to be drunk or mentally deranged.

It was his eyes that made people think he wasn't the ticket. They seemed to stare right through you. O'Hare knew this and used it to his own advantage. He enjoyed his notoriety, and also the money he garnered through intimidation. London to him was a criminal Mecca. He wanted it so badly he could taste it. He was even bringing down men from his other patches in Nottingham and Leicester to work with him here, putting them up in Bayswater and giving them large retainers until he needed them. He knew that muscle, and only muscle, would get him London. It was all the Southerners understood.

A tall man with a military bearing walked up to his table

and whispered something in his ear. Derrick rose from his seat and followed the man out of the bar and into a small ante-room. He grinned widely to see the man waiting there.

'Docherty, you bastard! Long time no see.'

Eamonn unfolded himself from his chair and shook hands with the man with whom he had been dealing for the last twelve months on IRA business.

'How was your flight?' asked O'Hare.

Eamonn shrugged and sat down again. 'The usual. This is my first time home for years though and it feels strange.' He didn't want to explain himself to O'Hare of all people.

'So tell me, what's been happening?' he asked. 'I hear there's skulduggery afoot.'

Derrick laughed harshly. 'I'm just putting a few old faces out to grass that's all. It's about time, eh? Come on, let's go out and eat and then we can talk. I hear you're staying in Park Lane. I can get you any kind of brass you desire. Just say the word: blonde, dark, black, white, big tits, little tits, long legs . . . Tell me your preference and I'll have it delivered to your door.'

Eamonn smiled, but it didn't reach his eyes. 'You don't have to pimp for me, Derrick, I'm quite capable of finding my own diversions. And I don't pay for it – never have and never will.'

O'Hare knew he had made a major faux pas. Shrugging, he said, 'I was paying, it was a gift. So no hard feelings, eh?'

Eamonn didn't leave his chair. Instead he poured himself another Scotch from the bottle in front of him.

'I'll skip dinner and get straight down to business, if you don't mind. The Cause contributions are drying up, and the Irish want to know why. So do I. You see, we need you and what you can offer us over here, but we don't need you that much. Your Liverpool contacts have been disappointing recently. We're running out of safe houses, and it's getting harder to position people we need in the smaller communities. Now you know what we need these things for.

'We are moving outwardly respectable Irish people into council estates. They will live as members of those communities until such time as we need them to do our work for us. These people are called sleepers, and your lot seem to be in a fucking coma these days because we haven't heard anything from or about them for months! Now we have paid you a lot of money for this venture and suddenly you're shafting us. We want to know the score.'

Derrick O'Hare was not scared of much, it wasn't in his nature, but the IRA scared even him.

Eamonn carried on talking, knowing he had the man on the hop and wanting to keep up the pressure.

'The reason I am here as opposed to one of the IRA big shots is because my London accent will go unnoticed, whereas an Irish accent in London is noted now and listened to. If one of the main men has to come over, you're a fucking dead man, O'Hare. Now where is the money and what's happening with the sleepers?'

Derrick had let the Cause go in recent months, mainly because he was bored with the whole situation. When he had first taken it all on it had been exciting and a lucrative money spinner. He had taken their money, set up the deal, and then gone on to bigger and better things – namely, financing the London takeover. Now he had to pay the piper and wasn't sure how he was supposed to do that. Nor was he sure exactly what the Irish and Americans wanted of him now.

'I've had a few problems meself,' he temporised. 'I'm in the middle of a big deal here and I have to oversee it personally. Once that's sorted out, I'll be back on top form with everyone.'

Brought up in an Anglo-Irish household, and having never been to Southern Ireland, let alone the North, he found the whole concept of an undercover army not only juvenile but mad. The British Army would soon rout them all out and that would be that, surely? Until then, he would appear to toe the line. The British Army had tanks, they had bombs, they had manpower. It was only a matter of time before this lot were banjaxed and either dead or locked up.

Eamonn picked up a newspaper and placed it on the table between them. 'How come you didn't know about this?'

Derrick saw a photograph of two people being led out of a small redbrick house. There were coats over their heads and a heavy caption above crying out: *IRA arms cache found in Liverpool council house.*

'That was yesterday's *Daily Mirror*. Even you must have heard of that. It's the biggest news story about at the moment.'

That O'Hare was stunned was evident; that he didn't really know what was going on in his own back yard was beyond Eamonn's comprehension.

'Like I say, I have other things on my mind at the moment,' he said, trying to shrug it off. 'Anyway, I couldn't have avoided that happening. Even you must see that much.'

Eamonn leant across the small rickety table and hissed: 'You should have known about that within minutes of its happening. We would have had lawyers and men from the Cause shouting about police corruption, framing, and anything else we could use to take the heat off. Instead we had to read about it like everyone else. Now you listen to me, O'Hare, and you listen fucking good. There's some big arses on the line and yours is the fucking biggest. The IRA even frighten the fucking Mafia. Take it from me because I know that from first-hand experience. A small-time Liverpool wanker means nothing to them. Fuck all.'

Derrick O'Hare was having trouble swallowing his pride. All he wanted to do was take Eamonn Docherty, his handsome face and thick well-cut hair, and throttle the life out of him. That was Derrick's answer to everything. But in the back of his mind was the memory of the £750,000 the IRA had paid him. He wanted to keep that money at all costs.

'These things happen,' he muttered lamely. 'I couldn't have stopped the police from raiding that house.'

Eamonn shook his head in disbelief. 'The money you were paid was so you could fund a few good informants in the local and national police! On a local level, you could have found out what was going down and we could have moved the people out overnight – before the neighbours knew anything, before the Filth knew anything. Instead they're awaiting a trip to prison for a seriously long time. Now I don't know about you, but that kind of thing aggravates the life out of me and mine. In New York you'd be hung, drawn and fucking quartered for that, and the same is usual in Belfast. Now it looks as if you might find it also happens in London. Because outside this room there are men waiting to escort you to your final fucking resting place.'

Knocking on the table top loudly, he summoned two large men into the room.

Derrick O'Hare was in a state of shock and it showed. His mouth was hanging open.

'From today, you're an ex-criminal and an ex-human being. All your assets are now ours and all your men are now ours.'

Derrick O'Hare, psychopath and gang boss, stared at Eamonn Docherty as if he had never seen him before. 'You're joking?'

Eamonn laughed contemptuously. 'What's to joke about? You fucked up big time. Now you have to pay the price.'

He walked out of the Café Central in broad daylight but Derrick O'Hare was not seen again for one week. Then only his head and his left hand came to light.

Lottie took her own life shortly after his few remains were found.

Lee Bonham was still speeding and still impatient. He knew the word on the street about Joey, also that the Irish had a few big wigs in town and had disposed of O'Hare. He also knew he was privy to information that even the British Government couldn't get hold of. It was a professional thing. He was tipped the wink by an old mate of his in the same line of work.

Lee had broken a cardinal rule and arranged a meet with the Irish connection, as he referred to Eamonn Docherty.

They met in a small pub called the Peterboat in Leigh-on-Sea, Essex, where they talked surrounded by day-trippers and locals, all enjoying a quiet Sunday drink. Both were dressed casually and looked for all the world just like every one else around them. But their conversation would have blown the mind of any eavesdropper.

'I had to kill Joey because it was a job,' Lee began. 'Nothing personal like, I hear he was a good man. But then again, they all are. This is my business. If ever you needed my services, I'd extend you the same courtesy I did O'Hare. Except I hear O'Hare upset a lot of people, including the Irish. Now I can't tell you how I came by this information, but the fact you're here shows me I'm right, don't it? See, I never did get paid for that job. You took O'Hare out a bit too sharpish for me. But I hear you're interested in anything to do with his business. I can fill you in on all you need to know, for a price – that price being the twenty grand I was to have been paid for taking out Joey. Now do we have a deal or not?'

Eamonn was impressed by the thin man before him. He knew Lee was speeding faster than an express train and yet a lot of hitters did the same thing. They said the speed gave them an added edge.

'I'll see what you have to say before I decide if it's worth twenty grand, OK? I can't be fairer than that.'

Lee shrugged and gulped at his lager shandy. The speed always made his mouth dryer than a buzzard's crotch, as he'd freely tell anyone who'd listen. Then he launched forth on his story.

'As you probably know, O'Hare was after the West End, that's why he wanted Joey's demise. Now Tommy Pasquale will want to shake your hand because he's been after O'Hare himself and had already set up a hit. What Tommy seems to have forgotten for the moment is that his father hid a lot of money for the bullion robbers – remember that robbery in the late sixties? Well, all the blokes involved are still banged up and keeping stumm. Joey was an old-style villain. He knew where the bullion was hidden but he kept it to himself and never once dipped into it. He knew that once the market was flooded with gold, there'd be a national inquiry. When the gang was released, then they could do what the fuck they liked and pay him for his silence. You see, when they were caught and convicted, they had to get word to someone to hide the stuff properly. Believe it or not, it was in a warehouse in fucking Norfolk for all that time.'

Lee laughed at the farcical situation.

'A little old lady had rented it to them for a fiver a fucking week. She didn't give a toss about what was in it, it was just a few quid to her on top of her pension. It was her old man's scrap yard, see. Anyway, the rub is word got to Joey and he had the stuff moved. Only he knew where it was. He didn't even trust a contact to take word to the men inside. "Careless talk costs lives", and all that old wartime crap, I suppose. Anyway, they all trusted him. They had to.

'Well, when one of them was banged up in Durham nick and under the influence of a bit of the old wacky baccy, he tells a face. The face tells O'Hare and O'Hare puts two and two together and decides he wants London and the bullion. What he didn't do, though, was find out off Joey where the bullion actually was. He killed Joey, then went out to the Essex marshes and looked for the stuff. It wasn't there. It's actually hidden near there, O'Hare was on the ball in some ways, but you see he listened to one of Joey's close companions, a bloke called Hemmings from Ilford. Hemmings, thinking he was on a touch, told O'Hare he thought the bullion was on the marshes. A lot of people thought that. Everyone knew Pasquale had hidden the bullion. For the record, my money's on Aveley Lakes of Tilbury. But either way, it don't matter, does it? Because no one is going to have the balls to touch it.

'The blokes who nicked it ain't cunts and they're getting out one day, you can bank on that. I wouldn't fancy them coming after me, no matter how much dosh I had. Let's face it, that's all they're going to think about, ain't it? Getting out, getting their stuff and getting on with lives that've been tragically foreshortened by the British judicial system. I bet even the fucking judge will shit himself the day that lot is released. But I digress.'

He took a large swallow of his drink and lit a Marlboro before continuing.

'The only person left who knows where the stuff is located is Tommy Pasquale, and that prat O'Hare should have allowed for that fact. I thought Tommy would be hit the same day, so father and son were out of the way. Apparently O'Hare decided otherwise. Maybe he thought Tommy was a wanker, I don't know. What I do know is Tommy Pasquale is a worthy successor to his father and will not be best pleased that you beat him to the job of killing the Scouser. Still, saying that, he'll still want to shake your hand, I suppose. I know I would.

'The only other person who might know the location is a face called Desrae. Joey Pasquale, married man and father, was also a shirtlifter in his spare time. Desrae is his boyfriend-cum-girlfriend. They recently opened a club in Wardour Street for rich men of a like persuasion. In other words, bigwigs who like men in big wigs.'

Lee laughed at his own joke and carried on.

'Tommy wasn't trashed at his dad's boyfriend. They get on well apparently. She, he or *it* also took in a little bird called Cathy Connor some years ago . . .'

As he felt his arm grabbed by Eamonn, Lee knocked his drink to the floor, the glass shattering and making everyone stare at them. It seemed to Eamonn to take an age for the barmaid to sweep up the glass, replenish their drinks and make her way back to the bar to start serving again.

'Cathy Connor? What's she look like? How old is she?'

Eamonn's voice was low and upset. Lee Bonham realised he had stumbled on a piece of information that the man was definitely interested in.

'She's a blonde, about twenty or so. Nice little bird, big blue eyes and great big tits. But she ain't on the game or nothing like that. She runs the bar with this Desrae and is quite respectable. Joey looked on her as a daughter, he really loved her. Like Desrae was the mum and he was the dad. What a weird fucking set-up, eh! But all that aside, they took good care of her. She lives with Desrae in a small flat in Soho – in Greek Street, I think. I hear she's a right little madam in her own way. Don't take no truck from anyone. But with Joey behind her, she wouldn't, would she? I mean, he was heavy muscle, eh?'

Eamonn shrugged, apparently recovered. 'Evidently O'Hare didn't think he was that heavy.'

Lee grinned. 'Whatever O'Hare thought is a bit fucking academic now, isn't it?'

'How do you know so much about everything?'

'My job is specialist, see. There's only a few of us and we tend to get told things in the course of our work. I mean, we have to be as trustworthy as the grave, don't we? So we find that people talk to us a bit more fluently than they'd talk to other people. It's funny, you know, but people try and justify the killing to me and to themselves. I don't have no allegiance to any particular gang of people. I kill anyone, anywhere, any time.'

Eamonn smiled. 'I'll bear that in mind. And I'll see you get your twenty grand.'

Lee nodded happily. 'Another beer?'

Eamonn shook his head and grinned. 'I'll have a large Scotch.'

'Have what you like, it's your round,' the other man joked. 'I'm just going for a piss.'

Laughing genuinely, Eamonn went to the bar and got the round in. He liked Lee Bonham – there was an honesty about him that was rather refreshing.

Cathy made Desrae another coffee and laced it liberally with brandy. In the weeks since Joey's death Desrae had gravitated between extreme melancholia and euphoric happiness as he tried to convince himself that Joey wasn't really dead. Cathy knew that it would take the funeral to put it all in perspective for him.

All she could do was listen and try to be a shoulder to cry on for her old mate.

She had cooked him meals, made him eat and forced him to put on make-up and wig. The police and press had finally left them alone and they were relying on Tommy to keep others away.

People meant well, but it was wearing listening to them all enthusing about Joey and it upset Desrae who had really loved him.

The doorbell rang and they both tensed.

'Ignore them and they'll go away. And don't let's put the phone back on the hook.' Cathy's voice was annoyed.

The bell rang persistently for over five minutes and the two of them sat there and listened to it. Finally, Cathy stood up. Storming from the room, she said: 'I'm going to tell them to fuck off and leave us alone!'

As she flung open the front door, she saw a face from the past, one she had never expected to see again.

'Hello, Cathy. Long time, no see.'

Hearing Eamonn's voice brought it all back to her so vividly, she felt as if she were once more back in Bethnal Green and Madge was shouting and hollering from the kitchen. It was the same old Eamonn, the man she had dreamed of, loved and trusted as a child.

And like Desrae, she realised, she would love only once and then with all her being.

'Well, aren't you going to ask me in? Offer me a cup of Rosie Lee?'

The tears came then. She threw herself into his arms. As he held her close and murmured words of comfort in her ear she felt that she had finally come home. Their last bitter parting was forgotten. He was the final part in the puzzle, the person who fitted in beside Desrae and Joey. Her first love, her only romantic love, her soulmate. Everything he had done was wiped out as soon as she heard his voice and they were back on their old footing.

Eamonn smiled, and Cathy was undone.

The first thing she noticed about him as she stood back and drank him in with her eyes was that he was all man. As soon as he touched her, she became all woman. It was an effect he was to have on her for years to come. Cathy saw Eamonn in a rosy glow; he had a sort of blinding brightness about him to which she responded. Nothing and no one would ever make her feel this way again.

As she pulled him into the flat and shut the door, she was smiling widely, her eyes tear-filled yet happier than they had been since Joey's death. She gestured him into the lounge and called excitedly to Desrae, so full of her own emotions that she didn't notice one crucial thing: Desrae and Eamonn took an instant dislike to one another. It was a quick, subtle thing but they were both aware of it from the second they clapped eyes on one another.

But Cathy, so pleased to have Eamonn near her once more, didn't notice anything amiss.

Like the old days, all she saw was him.

Chapter Thirty

Desrae was quiet and Cathy put it down to upset over Joey. Coming into the riotously pink bedroom, she placed a cup of coffee on the bedside table and grinned happily.

'I can't believe that Eamonn's back, I never thought I'd see him again.'

Pulling himself up in the bed, Desrae lit a cigarette and took a deep drag on it. 'I thought he was never going to go,' he said resentfully. 'Up half the night, talking and laughing . . .' His voice trailed off.

Cathy was sorry and her expressive blue eyes beseeched her friend as she said: 'Please, Desrae, he's a part of my life. I haven't laughed like that since . . . I don't know. Since Joey. We were just reminiscing, that's all, about being kids and our lives then.'

Desrae suddenly lost his rag. 'Tell him how you never ask after your mother any more, did you? Tell him that she's banged up for the fucking duration, and that if it wasn't for Susan P you'd know nothing about her? Tell him that they've put her on the psychiatric wing because she's as mad as a fucking March hare – tell him that, did you?

That she was attacked by another inmate and had her face slashed open . . .'

Cathy's face was white and stiff. Her eyes looked like twin pools of sea water, the salt tears making her shiny-lashed and vulnerable-looking.

'Is all of that true, Desrae? Is it really that bad for her in there?'

Desrae swallowed deeply, sorry now for his outburst. He'd been jealous of the girl's obvious feeling for Eamonn Docherty, whom he could tell was no good. He could smell people like Eamonn a mile away. Oh, they dressed nice and looked nice. Too nice, in fact. They collected people as they breezed through life, then used and discarded them like old rags.

Yes, he knew the Eamonn Dochertys of this world.

Desrae had wanted to protect Cathy from him, because he could see that the man was a predator. Now, in his chagrin, he had let the cat out of the bag about Madge and was instantly sorry.

All this time Cathy had thought her mother was well, as happy as she could be considering the circumstances, and that she was having an easy time of it in Holloway.

Desrae grabbed at the girl's hand but Cathy pulled away from him.

'How dare you, Desrae? How dare you decide what I should and shouldn't know? I'm a woman now and have the right to know what's happening to me and mine. I'm sorry that you don't like Eamonn, but that's too bad because I love him, and I always have. He's the brother, the lover and the husband I'll never have because I can't live like normal girls. You know that, Desrae, that's why I'm happy enough here in this excuse for a fucking flat, with its pink tassels and its chiffon fucking curtains and *you* – a raving queen who thinks he can dictate who I talk to, who

I associate with and who I care about. Well, Desrae, you've gone too far this time. My mother is *my* responsibility. I'll go and see Susan P now and see what the real score is.'

Desrae had never seen Cathy so upset. Never heard her raise her voice in such a manner. Unable to take back what he had said, he would have to take the consequences. Nothing would stop the girl from finding out about her mother now.

Oh, how he wished that Joey were here. He would have given Docherty his marching orders from the off. But Joey wasn't here any more and never would be again – and the sooner Desrae accepted that fact the better it would be for all of them.

Caitlin Moore was a small woman with long auburn hair that curled into spirals, and icy green eyes. Her porcelain white skin was untinged with even a hint of pinkness and was without blemish. In a strange way she was beautiful, in another way she was striking. In all ways she was evil.

Caitlin was the product of a Northern Irish father and a Southern Irish mother. Her mother had the rebel inside her – that was apparent to anyone. Her father, on the other hand, was an amicable little man with a penchant for hard work and a hatred of drink and the Mass. His only interest was getting the North back for the Irish Free State. A United Ireland. But such was his benign countenance people tended to listen to him, and smile, then agree or disagree according to their own beliefs. If anyone had said he was a leading light in the IRA, his work-mates and associates would have laughed themselves hoarse. But the fact was, he was a very big man in the Irish Army and his daughter was a zealous disciple.

Unlike her father, though, she didn't have the good nature to match her entrenched beliefs.

Caitlin was a hard woman, inside and out. She had planted two bombs already, though neither had gone off, the warnings being heeded now and strange Irish voices listened to. She looked forward to the day she could plant one and it would explode, taking English bastards with it. Raised from the cradle on rebel songs and the cause of a United Ireland, she was now as active as her father before her.

Living in her dingy flat and eking out an existence on a few pounds a week, like her neighbours, she waited and she listened. When the time was right again she would pick up the necessary paraphernalia and get her job done without a hitch as usual. Trained for three months in Beirut in the rudiments of bomb making and the art of self-defence, she was a seasoned and valued member of the Irish Republican Army.

She had no interest in men, in socialising or drinking. Her only vice was the cigarettes she smoked continuously one after another.

Her preferred reading matter was romantic novels and information on bombs. She read books on everything from the bouncing bomb in World War Two to the A Bomb in Hiroshima. Bombs and their devastating impact of carnage excited her. Even the big men of the Cause had expressed distaste for her gloating attitude.

But it was that attitude that had made her what she was; if she'd been more compassionate they would have tried to use her as a mouthpiece: the voice of modern Irish youth. As it was they kept her under wraps and used her as and when they needed her.

Abhorrent as she was to them, a woman could pass around London more easily than a man. But it didn't mean they had to like her, though they feigned liking when it suited them.

If it had been left to Caitlin, she would have blown up Parliament, the Queen, and fecking Buckingham Palace too. It wasn't just the Cause, though she believed in it passionately. It was also the heady feeling of playing God, having people's lives in your hands. Killing people was easy.

Killing English people was the summit of her dreams.

Hearing a knock on her door, she pushed the book she was reading under the mattress, and called out in her harsh Northern Irish accent: 'Who is it?' Her mind was racing because she wasn't due any visitors, and the cold sweat of fear trickled down her spine. She wasn't afraid of being caught; she was afraid that by being caught she would lose out on an opportunity to maim and kill.

'It's the man from the bank.'

She relaxed as she heard the passwords. Opening the door, she saw a large handsome man standing before her. He was dressed well, though casually, and had the most amazing teeth, white and straight, revealed as he smiled at her in a friendly way.

He pushed past her and walked into the room. 'Caitlin?' He held out his hand. 'Eamonn Docherty. I'm over from the States and have a message for you.'

Caitlin nodded solemnly. She knew of him, he was one of the Cause's best collectors in the USA and as such was spoken of in hushed tones of respect. Without him, none of them would be working at all.

'Pleased to meet you.' She shook his hand and then, sitting on the bed, pointed to the only chair in the room. 'Take a seat. I'll make you a coffee if you like?'

Eamonn sat down and shook his head. He began to speak immediately. 'You're to be used in two weeks. It's a car bomb, an English MP. You'll hear more nearer the time. There's a plant in the Houses of Parliament. She'll get in touch through the usual channels and then you'll know the name, the car and the location of your victim. I think he's to be hit outside his mistress's house – to add a bit of scandal as well as everything else. You OK with that?'

Caitlin nodded, her face expressionless as usual. 'Is it the Home Secretary, do you know?'

Eamonn didn't answer. Instead, he smiled easily. 'Nice room you've got here.'

Caitlin smiled back but it didn't quite reach her eyes, which unnerved the smooth handsome man before her. 'It's a shithole but it meets my needs.'

'*All* your needs? Who fulfils the personal ones?'

Caitlin stood up from the bed and signalled the interview was at an end. 'Have you anything else relevant to say to me?'

Eamonn shook his head, still smiling that maddening smile.

'Then I'll thank you to fuck off, Mr Docherty. It was nice meeting you at last. I've heard so much about you.'

'All of it true, of course.' His voice was mocking and she answered him in like manner.

'Of course. I heard you were a womanising piece of shite with a lust that makes Casanova himself look like a complete novice. But I'll give you a small piece of advice, shall I?'

She pointed a finger towards him as she spoke.

'I have respect in the Army because I do the job of a man; there's not a person in the Cause who would ever doubt me in that way. Now you may look on women as toys, Mr Docherty, as your playthings, but I don't understand those games and quite frankly you've greatly disappointed me. I had heard good things altogether about yourself, but now I see you're like all the men from this English culture. You're ignorant of women and how they think and feel. And that, Mr Docherty, will always be your downfall. Now take yourself and your supercilious smile out of here and we'll say no more about it.'

Eamonn was stunned at her reaction. He knew that normally he could charm the women with his smile and banter. Most of the ones he had met in the Cause were only interested in him as a man; they liked him and guessed, quite rightly, that he'd give them great sex, a few laughs then forget them the next day. They were often lonely, starved of affection, and enjoyed their time with him immensely.

He had heard of this Caitlin and convinced himself that he could crack her. All it would take was a few drinks and some flattering words. He had been wrong, however, and now the humiliation of being blanked by this woman was beginning to bite.

'You're a bit ahead of yourself here, lady. I wouldn't bed you even if you begged me for it.'

It was Caitlin's turn to smile now. She knew she had hit him where it hurt. She was enjoying the situation and decided to milk it for all it was worth.

'Now who'd beg you, I ask meself? Have you looked at yourself recently? You're a man who thinks women like him but, you see, only a certain type of woman goes for the likes of you. A whore or a fool. That's all. A real woman wouldn't look at you twice and deep down you know that.

'Deep down you know that if you could bed a real woman you'd stay with her, want her all the time, because she'd not be what you're used to at all. She'd be clean inside and out, she'd be decent and not giving herself to all and sundry with a pretty smile and a cock between his legs. Let's face it, if I slept with you now it'd be for loneliness and I have too much respect for myself to do anything like that. It's a shame that you've no respect – for yourself or for anyone else. You might find life a bit easier to swallow then. Now get out of here, and please God I never clap eyes on you again.'

Her thick accent was harsher than it had been, her words spoken with the degree of disdain that only a wronged woman can convey. Eamonn stalked out, his temper up and his colour even higher.

As he slammed out Caitlin mentally chalked up one to herself. Men were shite except for her father, and he was of a different stamp entirely from that eejit Docherty.

The scum of the earth, and an English accent to boot.

Susan P was just returning from the hairdresser's when she saw Cathy Duke walking towards her Knightsbridge flat. She stopped her black cab and called out to her.

'What's wrong, has anything else happened?' She could see that Cathy's face was white and strained.

'Can we go inside please, Susan? I need to talk to you.'

Five minutes later they were ensconced in Susan's flat with large Irish coffees and cigarettes. Cathy waited until they were both settled before she said with controlled fury: 'Why have you and Desrae kept me in the dark about my mother? What right did either of you have to do that to me?'

Susan listened to the girl in silence. She sipped her coffee and wondered what course of action to take. She could feign innocence but her days of even feigning it were long gone. She could take the easy way out and attack the girl, make her see that what she was saying was unfair. Or she could just tell her to piss off out of it.

Cathy stared into the eyes of the woman she had come to trust, even love, as a friend. It was seeing the girl's pained expression that made Susan P decide what she was going to do. For the first time in years she would speak from the heart.

'I was twenty when I came to Soho,' she began. 'That's old by today's standards, I know, but back in the early 1950s it was still the age of innocence for many women, myself included. I had had a baby a few weeks before, a boy. He had been adopted and I went a bit funny. The unmarried mothers' home kept me for three weeks and then gave me the arse kick. I was told I had sinned grievously and not to do it again. But, you see, my child was the product of rape.'

She stared at the girl opposite her and drew once more on her cigarette before continuing.

'The father of my child was also its grandfather. My father had been raping me since I was fifteen. My mother was dead and he was lonely, I suppose. Anyway, when she died he began to get closer to me and I accepted it, as you do. I was innocent about the world then, and when my father climbed into my bed I thought he wanted comfort, which of course he did. Only the comfort that he wanted was sexual. I knew, somewhere in the back of my mind, that it was wrong and told him so. I had no knowledge of sex, had never even talked to a boy let alone kissed one.' She laughed bitterly. 'I've made up for it since.

'Anyway, the bottom line is he forced me and after that it was a nightly thing. It went on for four years before I got pregnant. I was working in Woolworth's then in Bath where I was born. I was so fucking naive I didn't even realise I was pregnant until one of the women at work asked me if I was in trouble. When she saw my look of absolute wonderment she asked me if I had had my periods lately.

'Anyway, the long and the short of it was, I was in the club, five months gone, and with my own father to blame for it all. He feigned surprise and outrage when the woman took me home and voiced her suspicions, and I ended up in a home for unmarried mothers. He swore to me that if I told anyone the truth, he would dig up my mother and tell her I was a temptress. Oh, by the way, the pair of them were religious fanatics. I had had God rammed down my throat morning, noon and fucking night. That's how I learned what real sinners were. Not the criminals and the thieves but the lying bastards who hide behind a veneer of respectability – like the MPs and the do-gooders I cater for these days. But that's another story too.

'The boy was born and adopted, I saw him for one week only. He was beautiful but I had no feelings for him. I had learned by then about incest and everything else. Those places are a mine of information – but I expect you know that from your own experiences. Anyway, I came out of the Home and went to my father's house. He had a woman living there with her two daughters and I just knew, I knew in my heart, that he would harm them as well. He'd acquired a taste for it, you see. I saw the frightened look in their eyes, and I could tell. He had known the woman for a while and then just upped and married her. She was like my mother, a cold-hearted sort, all religion and swift kicks. It's funny, you know, but I've noticed that about the religious nuts – they love meting out punishment in the name of the Lord.

'Well, I left them all to it and came to London. I was on the game in a week and under the protection of a pimp called Johnny O within ten days. I got on with Johnny O and he liked me. Together we founded a house and made our dosh, and after we'd parted company I went on to do my thing and Johnny was murdered by a black man who decided he wanted what Johnny had, namely a seventeen-year-old girl who would do literally anything for money. Johnny O had a knack of finding that type, you know. A year later I had my father killed by a supposed hit-and-run driver. It was all I could do to avenge myself and protect the other young girls he might come into contact with.

'Now, if a Desrae had come along – and this is the reason I'm telling you my story, Cathy – I would have been a better person. All he wants is what's best for you. By his own lights he's trying to make you into a decent person, a kind person. In Soho girls aren't normally as lucky as you've been. They're used and abused by people. Someone else would have taken you off the street that night and put you back on it good and proper by the next morning. Now even you know that's true, don't you? As far as your mother is concerned, he was just trying to protect you. He knew it wasn't going to make things any easier for you if you knew of Madge's problems inside. You would have done the same for Desrae if the boot had been on the other foot, I know. To protect the people you love is crucial in a relationship of any kind, whether it's as a parent, a lover or a friend.'

Cathy listened and watched as Susan P bared her soul. In all the time she had known her, Susan had seemed the least vulnerable person she could imagine. But sitting there now, her big expressive eyes pained by the memories she had conjured up, Cathy sensed the depths of sorrow inside her.

'Desrae loves you like his own child. No other man will ever give you that – so remember it all your life. Love with no limits is very hard to find. He thought he was doing the right thing by keeping you in the dark. Don't hold that against him, just be grateful that he saved you from so many years of worry.'

Cathy finished her Irish coffee and sighed. Her face was so beautiful in the afternoon light that Susan P, without a second's thought, worked out just how much she could charge for Cathy with one of her clients. She put the thought out of her head as soon as it had arrived, but still she did it. It was a habit with her now.

'I loved me mum, you know,' Cathy said quietly. 'For all she was, Susan, I cared about her.'

Susan P laughed then, lightening the mood. 'Of course you loved her, she was your mother.'

Cathy stared around the pristine white room. It reminded her of a hospital, all glass, chrome and white brightness. Susan P in her deep red suit looked so at home in it. It was exactly like her: cold and clinical.

'Will you tell me the truth in future?'

Susan P nodded. 'I'll tell you it all now: she doesn't want anything to do with you. I'm sorry but it's the truth, she blames you for everything. She is a selfish, miserable old bitch, but I expect you already guessed as much. Still, I see she's OK because Desrae asked me to. Otherwise I wouldn't give Madge a second's thought. She's treated with a bit of respect because of me, and can do her time in peace. She was attacked by a woman prisoner called Barnes, Dilly Barnes, and I had her sorted out. Your mother is on the lock-up wing, the psychiatric wing, but she doesn't really need to be there any more. I paid through a friend who owes me a favour to keep her there. The regime is less strict and the food is much better. She can wear her own clothes and smoke as much as she likes, so stop worrying about her. Your mother is as right as rain, I promise you.'

Cathy stood up and walked to the window, her face closed. 'I used to hate her when I was small,' she confessed, 'but now I just pity her. I felt she should have helped me and she did in the end. I know she always had a fear of being banged up. But she did it for me, so I have to be grateful for that. I can't visit, though, in case people put two and two together.'

She turned and faced her friend. 'Could you get

something in there for me – a letter? I suppose I could write to her and use a different name or something. You could let her know it was really me . . .'

Her voice was hopeful suddenly as she tried to think of ways to make amends to the woman she felt she had abandoned. In her heart she acknowledged that it had been easier to listen to news from Desrae about her mother than to have to find out anything for herself. As an adult she realised that people like her mother drained you dry in the end. Madge would have had her dancing to a different tune every week if she'd been able to. She would also have made sure that her daughter had paid for each and every day Madge spent in prison because of her. It was this knowledge that was so difficult to take.

As a woman Cathy realised she didn't like her mother. Madge would never see that if she hadn't brought men home to earn money, then this whole sorry affair might have been avoided. She would take no blame on herself because Madge wasn't capable of taking blame. Not for anything.

But if Cathy didn't like her mother, she still loved her. In a strange way she knew that, as bad as Madge was, she had done the best for her child that she could. Self-destructive, amoral and selfish, Madge was someone who should never have had children.

Susan P watched the different expressions crossing the girl's lovely face and half guessed what they were for.

'Your mother is OK – stop worrying about her,' she said kindly. 'Now how about I get you a cab and you go home and make your peace with Desrae?'

'I was a bit hard on him, I suppose,' Cathy admitted, more cheerful now.

'You were feeling guilty, love – guilty because you don't really give a flying fuck about Madge. You've got a new life, a good one. And you've nothing to feel guilty about, believe me. People make their own lives in the end and if they fuck them up, and fuck other people's lives up in the process, then they don't deserve anything, especially from their children. I found my boy. You're the only person who knows this. He's a GP in Basingstoke of all places. I drove to his house and waited till I could see him. He looks just like my father. But I had no urge to touch him or talk to him. What good would it do to tell him his origins, eh? Let him have his life, and I hope it's a happy one. Take the same advice about your mother. Let her have her life now, she's had her chance. You have yours, and take the lessons you've learned here today to heart. In the end life is what you make it, love.'

Cathy embraced the other woman gently. 'Thank you, Susan. Thanks for everything.'

Susan P pushed her away with mock annoyance and said loudly, 'Well, keep the story of my son to yourself. Even Desrae doesn't know about that. Only you and Gates know. Richard and I go way back.'

Cathy nodded solemnly. 'I would never pass on anything you said, you know that.'

Susan stared thoughtfully at the girl before her. 'Do you know that Richard Gates is besotted with you, love?'

She saw the startled look in Cathy's eyes, and grinned. 'He's mad for you, I've seen it many times. Make him into a friend, love – you might find you need him one day. Richard is a fucker in many respects but he's a good friend. I know that from experience. Cultivate him. It'll be all to the good, you mark my words.'

Cathy smiled then.

'And when you open the next club, give me an option – I'll put money into it. I've already told Desrae. Once he starts to get over Joey, work will be the best thing for him,'

Susan advised. 'And like I said, cultivate Richard Gates. An Old Bill in the pocket is worth two in the station.'

'I'll take your word for that.' They both laughed.

Chapter Thirty-One

Eamonn and Tommy met in a small bar off the Roman Road. It was a spieler where they were both guaranteed protection from sightseers – pavement grasses – and the police. In a small back room, the two men faced each other warily.

'So, what can I do for you?' Tommy's voice betrayed no fear of the IRA's messenger and Eamonn respected him for that.

'It's more a case of what I can do for you, actually.'

Sitting at the table, Eamonn broke the seal on a bottle of Paddy and poured them both a good measure. They sipped their drinks, each weighing up the other, unsure exactly how to proceed.

Eventually Eamonn spoke.

'I despatched O'Hare. He tucked us up and had to be removed. I'm telling you this because as you are your father's successor, and the rightful heir to the West End, I want to work with you. Once you hear the terms I'm offering, I think you'll be amenable. However, you must understand that in passing on some information I am putting myself at risk. If you decide to throw my goodwill back into my boatrace, I may have to despatch you the same as I did O'Hare.'

Tommy laughed sardonically. 'Suddenly everyone's a fucking hard man.'

Eamonn grinned. 'I know what you're saying, but you haven't listened to me yet, have you?' He threw back his drink and explained the situation. He could see shock, horror, an almost feral reaction on Tommy's face as he listened to the story.

'I was already arranging talks with your father, though with respect I don't think he was really the man for the job. Italian-born, he saw the IRA as the British see them: terrorists and murderers. Whereas we see ourselves as an army, pretty much like Arafat saw himself and the PLO once. All we're asking is a fair crack of the whip in the North, no more and no less.'

'And O'Hare was under your protection, was one of your so-called army?'

Eamonn nodded. 'A mistake, I realise that now, but we have to deal with people who we know are not easily intimidated. O'Hare was a lot of things but a shitter he wasn't. Even when I gave him the capture, he was frightened, yeah, but not scared shitless – which he should have been. He was one mistake I won't be making again, I can tell you. And that's what brings me to you. Between us we could run the West End and Liverpool, the whole of fucking Britain if we wanted to. Once we win in the North, think of the opportunities you'd have to extend your operations there. Tommy Pasquale could become the main man – with our backing, of course. I can guarantee you an income of over one million a year, and believe me that's no exaggeration. If O'Hare had kept his side of the bargain he'd be alive and well, living the life of Riley, as my old dad used to say.'

Tommy nursed his drink for a while, letting everything Eamonn was saying sink in. Then: 'You want me to join the IRA?'

'Do I fuck! You'll be like an independent contractor – I think that's the best way to explain it – you'd work for us indirectly. I'll put people into key positions in Liverpool and other Northern cities. You'll watch the London end of the operation, though everyone else will report directly to you. Believe me, after O'Hare's death no one will take it on themselves to do anything more than grumble in private. We can, in effect, sew up the whole fucking country.'

Tommy shook his head in wonderment.

Eamonn laughed gently. 'Listen to me, I know this is a hell of a lot to take in . . .'

Tommy interrupted him sharply. 'I'm in, mate. No danger.'

The two men stared at one another then smiled.

'Tonight we make our way up to Scally land and we sort out a couple of faces. I want you seen and noticed by the community we're catering for. That way they'll have a working knowledge of what's in store should any of them decide to step out of line. Do you think you could handle that?' Eamonn enquired.

Tommy shrugged. 'Fair enough. What exactly does it entail?'

'Murder, that's what it entails,' Eamonn told him, 'and if you think you can't hack it, I need to know now.'

'I had a feeling you was going to say that,' Tommy said. 'What time do we leave?'

Eamonn grinned in appreciation. This time it reached his eyes, enhancing his handsome looks. 'Good man – I knew I could trust you. Cathy spoke highly of you and your father, which is why you're here now.'

Tommy smiled lazily, his brown eyes suddenly wary.

451

'She always spoke highly of you too, Mr Docherty! I understand you go back a long, long way?'

'We do that. But between you and me, Tommy, it'll be a purely business arrangement. We'll see about a friendship as we go along, yeah?'

Tommy clinked his glass against Eamonn's and nodded. 'Sounds good to me. Now, what are we getting up to in Liverpool . . . ?'

Terence Rankin was not a big man, not in terms of size anyway. In fact he was small by a hard man's standards. Barely five foot six, he was stocky, muscular, but short. Terence's place in the criminal underworld had been won because he was a psychopath, a mean, vicious and unrelenting lunatic. He was the man who always wanted to fight the biggest bloke in the pub, who baited them, took the piss out of them and humiliated them until they were honour bound to take a punch at the little man before them.

The little sober man before them, because Terence didn't drink, he didn't smoke and he didn't take drugs. He needed no artificial stimulants to make him aggressive. It was with him twenty-four hours of the day.

Now, as he sat in his four-bedroomed detached house in the Wirral, he was listening to his mother's voice as she berated him once more on the subject of his ex-wife.

Livvy Rankin was as big as her son was small, eighteen stone and nearly six foot tall. Her only child was her pride and joy and also the thorn in her side, as she would tell anyone who would listen to her.

'Why the hell you can't try and be nice to Tracey, I don't understand. I want the kids here weekends, and I want them here at Christmas and New Year and all the time you're roaring at the girl and scaring the life out of her, I don't get to see the children. Would you not give her a ring and say you're sorry? Apologise for hitting her father as well. Poor man, he must be sixty-five if he's a day and you had to thump him.' She shook her head in consternation.

Terence knew when he was beaten. He would do as his mother asked. He always did.

'I'll do it in the morning, go round and see her, then I'll bring the girls back to visit you. How's that, Ma?'

Livvy smiled. 'That would be grand. Now eat your fry. Are you going out at all?'

Terence nodded. 'I'm meeting a friend. You off to bingo?'

'Yeah, that's right.'

Livvy left for bingo with her cronies at 7.35. At 7.40, Terence was on his way to visit a prostitute called Mavis Henson. He was a regular, and saw her three times a week. He would reach her flat at eight o'clock precisely and stay for three hours. It was like a ritual to him. Mavis provided erotic sex, at a price. She was worth every penny.

Terence was whistling as he drove along, oblivious to the rest of the world. He had someone to see first, but would do that quickly. He hated to be late for a date with Mavis.

David Brewster was in the lounge of his small mid-terrace house in Knowsley watching the end of *Coronation Street*. Hilda Ogden and Elsie Tanner were having one of their periodic feuds and he was smiling as the end credits came up. His wife Louisa was sitting with their youngest child, Carrie, on her lap.

She said gaily, 'That Hilda Ogden is funny, eh, Davie? Playing the radio really loud to annoy Elsie. I thought I'd bust me sides.'

David grinned. He was a tall, heavy-set man with dark

wavy hair and a full beard. He was handsome enough, and knew it. His wife, however, was exquisite and David adored her. He loved *Coronation Street* too, though he pretended to watch it on sufferance because his wife liked it. He didn't fool her and they both knew it.

Carrie was nodding off. David picked her up and said: 'I'll put her to bed for you, love. Stick the kettle on and we'll have a cuppa. I have to slip out later.'

Louisa handed him the child and as he made his way upstairs, she went into the kitchen and put the kettle on. Just then, Terence Rankin walked through the back door of their house as if he owned it. Louisa opened her mouth to protest and he sideswiped her with the back of his hand, barely even pausing as he passed her. She was knocked against the sink. Popping his head into the lounge and finding it empty, he heard David's voice coming from upstairs.

'What was that noise, love?'

Terence Rankin's face was a mask of hatred, lips pulled back over his teeth. He took the stairs two at a time. David's older children, twin boys of twelve, watched as the man attacked their father on the landing.

He seemed to disappear under a rain of heavy blows and it took a while for them to realise that the intruder had something on his knuckles. The dusters Terence wore smashed through bone and gristle. Little Carrie walked out on to the landing and was knocked flying by the madman attacking her father.

Eventually it stopped.

Their father was lying in a pool of blood on the brand new orange and brown shagpile carpet, and their mother was standing at the top of the stairs, crying, her hands to her face. She looked at the man before her.

'But why? Why, Terry? What's he ever done to you?' She was shaking her head in bewilderment.

Terence Rankin looked at her long and hard before he said: 'He laughed at me, Louisa, I saw him. He laughed at me, and no one does that and gets away with it. Tell him he's out. No more work from me or anyone.'

With that he walked calmly from the house. He was fifteen minutes late for his date with Mavis and that annoyed him. She took one look at him and knew she was in for a night of it.

Sighing, she plastered a smile on her face and emptied her mind of everything but the man before her. With the Rankins of this world, you needed your wits about you. Your wits and your cunning.

He was a dangerous and slippery customer but he paid well, and that was the main thing.

Unlike Rankin, Michael Duffy *was* a big man.

Over six foot, he was built like the heavyweight boxer he once was with a handsome battered face from his days in the ring. Women adored him, which was a great shame because he much preferred the company of other men. Not that he was gay, far from it. But Michael Duffy had lost part of his penis many years before in a gang fight, and could not function physically with anyone. Not even himself.

No one knew about it, though, and it was because of this lack in himself that from time to time he gave vent to his frustration in outbursts of savage violence.

When he wasn't working for O'Hare, he kept himself pretty much to himself. It was the only way he could avoid becoming embroiled in pointless encounters with the women he craved but could not hope to satisfy.

He was in his flat when a call came for him to meet Eamonn Docherty. After feeding his Dobermann, he dressed carefully for the meeting. It was late in the evening and that suited Michael. He liked the night.

Like his counterpart, Terence Rankin, he knew nothing of his boss's demise. It wouldn't be common knowledge for a few days and by then it would be too late for him to do anything about it.

Mavis was lying on her stomach trying to rest. It had been a hectic couple of hours but even though Terence had been rough, she'd enjoyed herself. She liked rough sex sometimes, and Terence was a master of it.

However, tonight she was to receive money the like of which she had only ever dreamed of before, and now was the time to start really earning it. As Terence lay on the bed, trying to steady his breathing, she put her arm around him.

'That was great, Terry, really great.'

He turned to face her and nodded, agreeing with her. His orgasm had been intense and long. Now he felt relaxed and ready to sleep.

She stroked his face. 'Have a little nap if you like, Tel. Shall I make you another drink?'

He nodded. He felt heavy, his limbs and eyes like lead. As he tried to move once more, he found he couldn't for some reason and was afraid. He felt the movement of the bed as Mavis got up. He tried to focus and couldn't – everything was blurred. When she snapped the handcuffs on him, he couldn't resist. Mavis smiled down at him.

'Go to sleep, Terry, you'll soon feel better.'

He had no option; he did as she told him. Feeling much safer now he was contained, Mavis picked up the phone and began to dial. It was strange but she'd miss him in a funny sort of way, although she had a feeling she might be the only one.

*

By 11.45, both Michael Duffy and Terence Rankin were in a small warehouse by the Albert Dock. Michael had driven himself there, though Terence had been taken, very much against his will. Once the drug had worn off he was not the most happy of men, and his constant threats were beginning to get on Eamonn's and Tommy's nerves.

Finally, Eamonn had had enough. He cracked Terence over the head with a piece of wood he found lying on the floor. 'Now shut your fucking trap, will you!'

Terence stared up at him with deep hatred in his eyes and Eamonn knew that this man had to die, because if he did not Eamonn himself would never be safe again.

Michael Duffy had been easier than they'd thought; it hadn't taken as much to overpower him and now he lay on the dirty floor, quiet and watchful. He would try and talk his way out of this mess, Eamonn knew, and admired him for it. But there was no way Duffy was leaving the warehouse alive either. No fucking way.

These men were to act as examples for everyone who had worked for O'Hare. Their deaths would show exactly what happened to people who thought they could get out of their trees and tuck up the Irish.

It wasn't until Tommy and Eamonn had poured petrol on the two prisoners that the enormity of their situation hit home. The smell was heavy in the confined space and the two men were terrified. Tommy found it in his heart to feel pity for them, as bad as they were supposed to be. It was a terrible way to die. But they had asked for it, both of them, and he understood this much: when you ran a big organisation, you needed discipline. You needed the people who worked for you to know that they had to toe the line, had to listen to orders and obey them without dissent. Had to be one hundred per cent trustworthy.

If a few got it into their heads that they could overrule

you or take what was yours, then you had to set an example. This was a particularly gruesome example, but Tommy knew that it would do the job.

The two hardest men in Liverpool were to be burned alive for the common good. Once this news hit the streets, together with word of O'Hare's being found scattered all over the South East like a paperchase, only a raving lunatic would ever attempt to step out of line again.

It meant the Irish could rule from afar with their face installed to pass on orders. It meant peace of mind, not only for Eamonn and his IRA cronies, but also for the lower echelons of their empire. They needed to know that everything was under control; needed to know exactly how far they could go.

It was just good business, really.

'You cunts! You don't fucking scare me.'

Terence's voice was strong again, heavy with malice. Eamonn and Tommy ignored him. They sat at a table and broke open another bottle of Black Label.

Eamonn checked his watch. Five of their men were to witness the execution. It was the best way to keep order in the ranks and ensure that the murders became a talking point among them.

Terence began ranting and raving, spittle clinging to his lips as he writhed on the floor like a snake.

Eamonn laughed. 'Look at him! He's a fucking nutcase.'

Tommy laughed with him, the adrenaline beginning to surge through his veins. He knew he was in the company of a stronger will than his own and he relished it. With the Irish behind him, he was laughing all the way to the bank. After all, who would dare to challenge him now?

'How long now?' he asked.

Eamonn checked his watch. 'About another hour and a half. I want them all here to see this.'

Tommy watched the two men again. The petrol smell must have been awful for them. It was bad enough they knew they were going to die; it seemed cruel to leave them so long with petrol all over their clothes and skin.

Eamonn guessed his thoughts and said quietly: 'I know what you're thinking, but by the time the others arrive they'll both have accepted their fate. I know what I'm doing, believe me. I have a lot of experience in this type of work.' His voice was matter-of-fact. He betrayed no feelings for the men whatsoever.

Tommy nodded. 'Whatever you say, this is your show.'

Eamonn stared at him consideringly. 'You'll do,' he said finally.

Tommy grinned and held up his glass in a toast. 'Do you reckon we're safe to smoke?'

Eamonn laughed. 'Yeah, we're far enough away not to do them any damage. Yet.'

An hour and a half later the five witnesses were in place and whisky was poured for them all. Thirty minutes earlier Eamonn had injected both condemned men with a massive dose of Demerol. They were high as the proverbial kites. He dropped matches on to them without a second's thought.

Well fortified with Scotch, Eamonn and Tommy watched the spectacle impassively. The five witnesses, however, were not so lucky. They saw something they would never forget, and as far as Eamonn Docherty was concerned, that was exactly as it should be.

As the two men writhed on the floor, their hair and clothes being eaten by the flames, the witnesses stared in fascinated disgust. The smell of burning flesh was overpowering and the final twitching of the charred bodies obscene. Eamonn kept throwing on more petrol, making little explosions and flames erupt. He laughed while he did it and Tommy had to admit the man was an awesome sight.

When the spectacle was over, he turned to the others present, including Tommy, and said quietly: 'Let that be a lesson to you all. It is what happens when you fuck with me and mine. I will hunt you to the ends of the earth if necessary, and enjoy myself while I do it. In future, you report to me or my designated go-between. You keep your mouths shut and your ambition on hold. I'll give you all you want and more, but I will not tolerate anyone trying to branch out on their own. Do you all get the picture?'

Everyone nodded, even Tommy.

An hour later he and Eamonn were on their way to their hotel; they would drive back to London the next morning. In the car Tommy said quietly, 'I can't believe you did that so calmly.'

Eamonn shrugged. 'It had to be done. There's a lot at stake here. You have to understand that or you're no good to us.'

Tommy lit a cigarette, grateful to see that his hands were not shaking any more.

'Fancy a bit of supper before we retire to our virtuous couches?' Eamonn suggested.

Tommy agreed. He didn't want to be alone just yet. He wanted to be as drunk as a lord before he got into bed.

'No steak or pork for me tonight, I don't think. How about a Chinky?' Eamonn went on.

'Without the spare ribs?' Tommy joked queasily.

Eamonn grinned. 'But of course.'

Chapter Thirty-Two

Cathy and Desrae were soon back on their old footing. Both ashamed of themselves, they went out of their way to be kind to one another. Desrae even told himself that he would try to like Eamonn Docherty, if that's what it took to make his surrogate daughter happy. Since Eamonn's visit, Cathy had bloomed. She was up and dressed and in full make-up by seven-thirty every morning, but it was three days now since she had seen the Irishman and Desrae hoped he had not forgotten her.

As the days passed, Cathy ceased looking out of the window every ten seconds in the hope of seeing Eamonn come to her door. Now, with press attention focusing on other stories, they were talking about reopening the club for their regular customers. Cathy felt this would be the best thing for Desrae, and Desrae thought it would be the best thing for Cathy. Both of them needed to be busy for their own reasons.

Cathy was hurt inside, deeply wounded, that she had found Eamonn again only for him to abandon her once more. She went over and over their evening together and tried to see what she could have done to make him ignore her like this.

They had chatted, laughed and reminisced; they had talked of their childhood, their parents, and their lives since. He had kissed her as he'd left and she knew he had wanted her then. Should she have given in? After all, she had slept with Tommy when his father had died, and she didn't love Tommy. Eamonn clearly wanted her but she had held back, even though she'd known then that he was the only man she could ever love.

As she walked from the flat towards the club, Cathy was hailed by the Soho regulars. Her eyes were sad and her heart heavy, but she smiled and waved at everyone, stopping to talk to one of the hostesses from the Diamond Mine, a particularly rough club.

As she joked with the girl, her mind was still on Eamonn Docherty. His deep blue eyes and thick dark hair were all she could think of; his heavy body, muscular and strong, tormented her.

She walked into the shop fronting the club and smiled at Casper the manager. He was fifty-five with sparkling green eyes, a wrinkled face and the worst toupee anyone had ever seen. He had worn it for over twenty-five years and no one could remember what he looked like without it. Even when he paid one of his hostesses for twenty minutes of her time he didn't take it off and it was one of Soho's longest standing jokes.

But Casper, for all his ridiculous appearance and jokey manner, was a face in his own right, and one to be reckoned with in the West End. Everyone knew he could be very aggressive, dangerous if pushed, and consequently he was respected. If there was one person he really liked, though, it was Cathy Duke. He instantly noticed the sadness in her eyes.

'Are you all right, love? You look a bit under the weather. How's Desrae? He's coping, ain't he?'

'Yes. He's taking it hard but that's to be expected really. We're going to get the club going again. I thought it might be good for him, give him something to do instead of moping.'

Casper nodded solemnly. 'Good idea. I don't know how many people have rung about it like. You've lost a lot of business. There's a new one opening in Old Compton Street, above a shop. Small-time, I reckon, mainly for the working-class poofters, but whatever, it's all competition for you. If Joey had been alive he wouldn't have swallowed that, eh?'

Cathy listened in silence, her mind not really on business.

'Still, I reckon young Tommy won't swallow it either so you'd best be prepared for a bit of the old aggro soon. I hear the owner of the club is a Malteser, Victor Bagglioni. What a fucking gobful of a name that is, eh? I don't like foreigners. Nothing personal like, they just ain't right, are they?'

He always made Cathy smile. Putting a hand on his arm, she said, 'Don't change, Casper, you're a real tonic.'

He reddened. He liked to make his remarks as outrageous as possible, liked to shock people, and yet he knew that Cathy Duke was one of the few people who saw through him. Realised that deep down he was lonely, unhappy with his lot, but unable to change his way of life.

'There could be trouble here, Cathy,' he warned her gently.

She nodded and went through to the club to pour herself a brandy. It felt strange to be back, a different place now there was no prospect of seeing Joey stride in, shouting the odds and quelling any troublemakers with one glance of his hooded eyes.

'You'd better get in touch with Tommy,' Casper advised.

Cathy nodded, but no one had heard from him in days. Suddenly, after the tip off about the Maltese, she was frightened.

Eamonn was tired, but he knew he had to see Cathy. Now that everything was sorted out he had a few days to himself and she was the first thing on his agenda. As he made his way to the flat she lived in, he was whistling.

Then he saw her.

She was dressed simply in a cheesecloth blouse and long lemon-coloured skirt. She was braless and he could see the movement of her breasts through the thin fabric. Her long blond hair was pulled back by two combs and her narrow waist emphasised by a thick yellow belt. She looked like every other girl in 1970s London, except she was more beautiful than anyone he had ever seen in his life. The longing for her was still there and she brought back memories he had thought buried for ever.

As he watched her easy stride, he remembered their chaotic home in Bethnal Green, and the feeling of absolute calm she'd engendered in him then. As long as they'd had one another they were fine. He had used and abused her, and he knew that. But such was the bigness of Cathy's heart, she had forgiven him.

While still children they had been through more than most people would ever have to face in a whole lifetime. Yet they had found something in each other that had made them resilient, exceptionally close, fated to love because their lives were so similar and so blighted they could only ever find true happiness together. Only with one another could they really be whole.

As Cathy caught sight of him Eamonn saw a smile light

up her lovely face and his heart opened up to her. She ran to him, eyes bright and smile wide and trusting. How could he ever have hurt someone like Cathy? he wondered. Well, he was a different person now, with nothing to prove to anyone. He would treat her right this time, he swore to himself.

'Were you coming round to me?' Her voice was eager and hopeful.

'Where else would I be going? But listen, Cathy, come to my hotel. We can talk properly there. I don't think Desrae approves of me.'

It was said jokingly but Cathy understood him and nodded. She knew she should go home and tell Desrae about the trouble at the club and her worries over Tommy's disappearance. She knew exactly what she should do but, just like before, when Eamonn whistled she ran.

This time he would get anything he wanted from her.

Anything at all.

Cathy was impressed with Eamonn's hotel suite and it showed. The Ritz had been just a name to them as children; certainly neither of them had ever dreamed they would get to stay there one day. She was entranced by the decor, the ornamental mouldings, subtle colours and rich brocaded curtains.

The huge double bed was also fascinating, because Cathy knew she was going to end up in it and felt both frightened and exhilarated at the same time. For all her newfound confidence, being with Eamonn once more made her feel like a naive young girl again.

Opening a bottle of champagne, he grinned at her. 'Real Dom Perignon, not the watered-down shit you serve in your club.'

Cathy took the cut-glass flute from him and grinned.

'There's fuck all wrong with our champagne, mate. It's real enough, it's just no one's ever heard of the label.'

They both laughed.

Sitting beside her on the brocade love seat, he hugged her to him. 'I've missed you. I tried to ring but I was just so snowed under. I've been up to Liverpool, sorting out a few things.'

Cathy drank her glass of champagne in one long gulp and Eamonn laughed.

'I'm impressed. That's twenty quid a bottle. I can see this afternoon is going to cost me the national debt!'

Cathy was feeling light-headed with the unaccustomed champagne on top of the large brandy she had had earlier to calm her nerves.

'Why are you in England, Eamonn? The other night you talked and talked but didn't really tell me much.'

She was shrewd, he already knew that. Now he debated how much to tell her.

As he looked down into her eyes, she reached up and kissed him gently on the lips. 'I've missed you so much, Eamonn. All the feelings from before, they're still there inside me. You're the only man I have cared about, both as a friend and a lover.'

As he kissed her back, the old feelings stirred inside her. The feeling of being a part of someone, of being safe. As his fingers explored her breasts and face she felt the first promptings of desire, and rejoiced.

Taking her into the bedroom, Eamonn closed the heavy drapes and watched as she undressed. She was so shy, so obviously inexperienced, and this endeared her to him even more. Eamonn was used to predatory women by now. His wife, convent girl and devoted mother, was an aggressive lover. But Cathy, who worked in Soho and lived her daily life surrounded by sex, was timid.

Slipping naked into bed, she waited for him. The sheets were cold and her body was tingling with goosebumps, making her more aware of it than she had ever been before. As he undressed she watched him; the champagne was making her feel more relaxed, warm inside.

Practically leaping into bed, Eamonn ripped the covers from her and stared at her in the half-light. 'You're beautiful, Cathy.'

He touched one breast very gently. Kneeling beside her on the bed, he stared down at her in fascination. Cathy watched his face as he touched her then his mouth was closing around one nipple. She moaned. He was biting her now, very gently, making her want him more.

Opening her legs, he moved down her body and began to caress her with his tongue.

Eamonn was expert at oral sex, he knew that. Many women had squirmed beneath him and he loved it when he made them come, felt their orgasm. He used all his considerable skill on Cathy, rousing her to fever pitch until eventually he entered her. Riding her now, he watched her full breasts bouncing with each of his thrusts. Her tiny waist made them look bigger and he felt all the excitement of the visual aspect of sex, observing her as she moved beneath him.

Her eyes were closed, lips parted, long hair trailing over her face. He felt her orgasm build and encircle him, finally casting her adrift on the hard rhythmic thrusting that brought him swiftly to a shattering climax.

As he collapsed on top of her, she gathered him into her arms, hugging him to her. He kissed and nuzzled her. 'Oh Cathy, Cathy. That was wonderful . . . I've wanted you so much . . . you wouldn't believe.'

She lay beneath him, face buried in his neck, her body tingling still, revelling in the touch of his skin on hers.

Pulling himself up, he gazed down into her face and said gently, 'You enjoyed it, didn't you?'

Cathy smiled tremulously and nodded. He gathered her to him once more and they lay together in silence as he waited for his heart to stop its erratic beating and his breathing to return to normal. She wasn't lively, like his usual women, but then this was his Cathy, the girl he loved.

Hugging her a final time, he finally withdrew from her, and being Eamonn Docherty, his father's son, hoped he had given her a child. That would have been a real kick, made her his even when he wasn't here. As it was he had to go back to New York, and soon. Deirdra was making restless noises and threatening to arrive in London if he didn't hurry back.

After his wife's heavy body and sexual demands, Cathy was like a breath of fresh air. He loved the smell of her, the feel of her, everything about her, and intended to come to London often to see her.

He was holding her tight, trying to figure out how he was going to tell her about his wife and family yet keep her sweet enough to wait until the next time he was over.

She had told him about the threat from Maltese Victor, and he suddenly realised how he could walk away and still keep Cathy's good opinion. He had a little plan and would act on it as soon as possible. That way he could come out of this with her undying love and affection.

He told himself he would do anything to keep that.

Chapter Thirty-Three

Cathy was on cloud nine and it showed. It was as if the girl had been lit up from inside and in a way Desrae envied her.

He remembered how it felt to be young, in love, and also in lust. For him it had been Joey, who had been worthy of that regard. He wasn't so sure about this Docherty who was too smooth by half. He was convinced Eamonn was going to leave Cathy's life as suddenly as he'd entered it and could do nothing to prevent that hurt. All he could do was stand by the girl as best he could.

For now, though, he had the worry of the predatory Maltese, the fact that Tommy was apparently on the missing list, and threats to the club hanging over his head.

'Do you think anything can have happened to Tommy, Desrae?' Cathy asked him in a small voice.

'I really don't know, love. I even rang his mum's, pretending I was a business associate looking for him. She hasn't seen him either, only she didn't sound too bothered about it. She was pissed as usual.'

Cathy looked worried. 'I'll get the boys out on the street, shall I? See if they can come up with anything.'

Desrae shook his head. 'No, love, not yet. We don't

know for sure that anything's happened and if we go looking for him then word will get round. Leave it for another twenty-four hours and see what develops, OK? I'll have a word with Gates, see what he can come up with.'

'Fair enough. Eamonn will know what to do anyway. He'll be round soon.'

Desrae forced a smile on to his face. 'That'll be nice for you.'

Cathy knew how much it had taken for him to say that. She hugged her friend. 'Oh, leave it out, Desrae, I've known him all my life.'

He shook his head sadly and grabbed her hands. 'All I'm saying, love, is be careful, that's all. But I'm here for you when you need me, you know that.'

His voice said he thought that would be sooner than either of them knew.

Maltese Victor was pleased with himself. No one had seen hide nor hair of Tommy Pasquale for days and the Soho community was agog, waiting to see who the new baron was going to be.

Never had there been such excitement and speculation in the West End. Joey's death and Tommy's sudden disappearance, coupled with the death of O'Hare, had made even the laziest whore interested in what was going on around her.

As Victor stepped out of his club on to Old Compton Street, he hailed a couple of touts who worked for him. When he crossed over to walk into Dean Street he was smiling after the respect they had shown him.

It was early evening, the place was coming alive and all the garish lights were being turned on ready for the night's business. Victor loved Soho, loved every part of it. He had liked old Joey, but now he was gone the place was open to anyone with a bit of nous. And Victor had that in abundance.

When the car pulled up beside him and he was hailed, he turned happily, knowing the voice and feeling safe. His old associate Demetrious Scalpie smiled at him, and Victor smiled back. Scalpie was a small-time villain, a Greek with a Maltese wife and a Maltese mentality. Victor was waiting for the man to give him his due respect. He could hear the strains of Blue Mink's 'Banner Man' coming from a nearby bar, smell the onions and offal sold by a street vendor.

Life was good, and Victor was happy.

When the shot hit him in the chest, at first he thought he was imagining it. There was no pain at all, just a heaviness as he was forced backwards. The second shot hit him in the shoulder, nearly taking off his arm. As the blood flowed he stared at it, amazed. Then he looked up at Scalpie. The man's face was creased into a smile as he aimed the gun at his friend's head.

Then Victor knew no more.

Scalpie was back inside his car and off down Dean Street before the screaming hostess who had witnessed it all was back inside her club to tell the tale.

Victor lay on the dirty pavement, his eyes still registering shock as they stared blindly up at the night sky.

By the time the police arrived, two clubs in the vicinity were closed and in the others no one had seen anything.

No one had heard anything.

And no one gave a shit anyway.

Desrae smiled at Eamonn and he smiled back at him. Neither smiles quite reached their eyes but it was the best they could do. Cathy, pleased that there was no real animosity, was happy enough. As she poured them all drinks, she felt a warm glow inside her. Eamonn looked so handsome this evening. She drank him in with her eyes as he made small talk with Desrae.

The phone rang and Desrae answered it, eyes widening with surprise as he took in what had just been said. Putting down the receiver, he looked at Cathy and shook his head in amazement. 'Maltese Victor is dead, can you believe it?'

Eamonn, the big man, happy with his role in everything, grinned. 'Gunned down in Dean Street, about one hour ago, yeah?'

Desrae stared at him, eyes now registering a grudging respect. 'How do you know?'

'Because I made it happen. Now I've asked around about you, Desrae, and I know that you're sound, so anything I say is not to leave this room, OK?'

Cathy and Desrae nodded.

'I wiped him out as a favour to Cathy. I know Joey's death was a blow and that you will need a bit of muscle. I've arranged that muscle for you. I also had a hand in the murder of O'Hare, but that was personal, nothing to do with Joey. I just did you all a favour without knowing it.' He was smug, enjoying their attention.

Desrae was intrigued. 'But you're living in New York. What the fuck was O'Hare to you? Where did he fit into the picture?'

'I'm involved in a lot of organised crime in the States, and that business extends to England. I obviously have other interests in New York, but my main enterprise is here, in dear old Blighty.' He smiled to take the edge from his next words. 'I'm involved with the IRA.'

Cathy's mouth dropped open. 'But they're terrorists! They're just a load of fanatics . . . What the fuck are you doing with them? You hated being half Irish. You would never admit to it. When your dad used to spout off about them, you used to do your nut. What's changed?'

Eamonn looked down at the carpet as he answered. 'Over here they're terrorists. In New York, in the Irish community, they're fucking heroes, a real army. I collect for them, Cath, it's big business and only the strongest are good enough to work for them.' He was having to defend himself and it was annoying.

Cathy's face drained of blood; even her lips were pale. 'They're murderers, that's all. Innocent people died in the last bombing . . .'

Eamonn laughed gently. 'Oh, and Joey and people like him aren't murderers too? I never took you for a hypocrite, Cathy.'

She stood up and paced the room.

'I don't care what you say. Joey and his sort stick with killing their own; I'm not saying that's right, not at all, but Joey Pasquale would never have planted a bomb where women and children could be maimed and harmed. He would never have done anything like that. He lived as a criminal and, God love him, died as one but I was proud to know him. I wish he'd been my father for all they say about him.

'But this . . . no way can I accept this, Eamonn. They're not an army, they're terrorists, and you can tell all your new friends in New York that I think they fucking stink! You should have seen the papers here a while ago when they bombed an army barracks. It was carnage. That's not war, not real war. That's just killing for killing's sake, and in the name of God as well – as if He had anything to do with it!'

Eamonn was stunned. Where was the adulation, the thanks for a job well done? In America he was treated like visiting royalty – even the Mafia gave him respect. Yet here in London his Cathy was talking to him like they were still little kids.

'My God, Cathy, you've got a fucking nerve!' he

exploded. 'I took out a man for you today, one who was a danger to you, and what thanks do I get, eh? I get a lecture off a young girl with the brains of a fucking amoeba and the nous of a dead cat. I had a man killed for you, to keep you safe, and you turn on me like this? I can't fucking believe it!'

Cathy saw the bewildered look in his eyes and felt the first stirrings of sorrow. He really could not see what he had done. It had always been the same with him. Eamonn never could see that he was wrong. It was like the night he'd killed for the first time. All he'd been interested in was getting an alibi. All he had ever really been interested in was himself.

'Do you remember that Christmas, Eamonn, when your dad dumped me mum for the little widow and we went round there, me and me mum . . .'

Desrae interrupted her. 'What the hell has that got to do with anything?'

Cathy turned on him and roared: 'If you listen, you might learn something. Now, do you remember that, Eamonn?'

He nodded. 'Of course I remember. What about it?'

'Well, when we got back that day, you'd eaten all the chicken. Every bit of it, picked the fucking bird clean.'

Eamonn shrugged. 'So what?'

Cathy looked into his face, her eyes pained and flat. 'That's you all over. You took what you wanted and didn't give a toss about me, me mum, no one. And that's how you've always been. You'll never change all the time you've got a hole in your arse. Don't talk to me about causes and armies, I'm not interested. If you're involved it's for personal gain and nothing else.'

Desrae watched the two antagonists wide-eyed.

'Well, you got that much right anyway. I ain't a

screamer for the Cause, but I earn a good fucking wedge from it and that's how I'll stay. I don't tell you what to do, how to earn your living, so don't you ever try and tell me, lady. My wife doesn't tell me what to do, no woman ever will, and a few of them have tried . . .' And then he realised just what he had said.

The three people in the room fell silent, the atmosphere charged like an electrical storm.

Standing up, Desrae smoothed down his herringbone skirt and said heavily, 'I'll make a pot of tea, Cathy. Call me when you need me.'

'So you've got a wife then?' Cathy's voice was low now. 'Is she in the IRA as well? Is that how you got involved?'

Eamonn shook his head. 'Listen, Cathy love, I know it's a shock, all of it, but at least I'm telling you the truth . . .'

She laughed then, a bitter, harsh sound. 'Oh, fuck off, Eamonn. You wasn't going to tell me about Mrs fucking Docherty. Are there any little Dochertys yet?'

He wiped a hand across his face and sighed. 'Three. All boys. Jack and the twins, Declan and Michael. I didn't tell you because I didn't want to spoil everything. I couldn't get in touch with you after I had to leave on the quick . . .'

Cathy's eyes were slits now as she said, 'Oh, yes, when you murdered poor old Caroline. Let's not forget her, shall we?'

'How can I ever forget her? I'll have to live with what I did all me life. I see her every day . . .'

Cathy pushed him hard in the chest. 'Well, it hasn't stopped you shagging around, has it? Three kids, a wife, and silly little mares like me on the side. Killing her hasn't cramped your style at all, has it, you two-faced fucking bastard! I'll give you IRA . . .' She shook her head in loathing. 'Go on, get out of here and leave me alone.'

'So you don't want to know about Tommy then? Me and Tommy?'

She looked at him hard. 'What about Tommy, what do you mean? He wouldn't have anything to do with the likes of you. He's decent and kind like his father. A villain, I admit that, but not a murderer. Not a fanatical Irish loony. He's half Italian, for Christ's sakes . . .'

Eamonn grinned once more and Cathy felt an urge to slam her fist into his perfect teeth and break them all. 'Well, he was very interested in what we had to say.'

'What do you want him to do then?'

'That is none of your business. Let's just say he's been with us for the last few days and he's due back home this afternoon.'

'You're bad, Eamonn. Everything you touch is tainted by you, and I let you touch me.'

She shuddered, unable to bear the memory.

'I let you touch me and you are scum. That's all you are, you and all your fucking cronies – Irish scum. Go back to New York and your wife and your kids, though I feel sorry for them, having you as a father. You'd sell them off if it got you what you wanted, wouldn't you? Just go, and I hope to Christ I never clap eyes on you again.'

Eamonn saw the disgust in her eyes and tried once more to reason with her. 'Cathy, please. Let's not part like this.'

Walking past him, she left the room. She picked up her coat and called through to Desrae in the kitchen: 'I'm out of here, I'll be back later.'

Without another word she left the flat.

As Eamonn went to follow her, Desrae stood before him. In his high heels he was as tall as their visitor and his grim expression made Eamonn think twice about pushing past.

'You've fucked yourself, mate. Leave her alone, let her

go. You have no bloody idea of the suffering your lot have caused. One of the women who works near here lost her son in Ireland. This ain't America, mate, this is London and it's us lot you want to blow to pieces in the name of the Cause. For someone supposedly so shrewd, I can't believe that didn't occur to you.'

Eamonn dropped his eyes but kept on arguing. 'You're the hypocrites. You know of people who kill, who harm others, you know what I'm talking about. Yet you condemn me.'

Desrae nodded sagely. 'I know what you're saying, but it's all relative, ain't it? Joey might have taken out O'Hare if he'd thought of it first, but that's all he would have done. To Joey and O'Hare and even Maltese Victor, it was an occupational hazard, if you like. None of them would ever have planted a bomb on a train or in a pub to kill a stranger. Can't you see the logic of what I'm saying? Are you so fucking hardened to what you do that you can't see it from our point of view?

'You aren't living in a country where there's signs all over the Underground saying: *If you see a suspicious package, leave it and inform the police.* You're not living in a country where every Irish accent is suspect – where people are trying to drum out their neighbours just because they're Irish. You haven't got your young men fighting a guerrilla war in Belfast and Armagh, patrolling the streets and having hand grenades and snipers' bullets aimed at them. All you're doing is supplying the money for maniacs to do just that, to blow up innocents and maim children. If you loved your own kids, you'd understand what I am talking about. You'd understand what poor Cathy is trying to say to you.'

'The English are ignorant,' Eamonn growled. 'You're the dinosaurs of the world. The Raj is gone, you don't own an empire any more . . .'

Desrae laughed. 'Northern Ireland is a part of Britain, my love. The people in it are British. You're bombing your own, you fool! Killing people you don't even know: women, children, innocent men providing for their families.

'We had five bombs go off in London in January and the one in Manchester killed nineteen people. You are murdering scum, you and all your so-called compatriots. I admit I didn't like you from the moment I clapped eyes on you, I knew there was something wrong, something I didn't trust, and now I realise what it was. You and people like you – you talk about causes and fucking crap like that, but it's just plain and simple greed. You're safe in America, where they know fuck all about this. They ain't frightened of jumping on a train or a bus, knowing that a bomb could blow them sky high. Oh, no, they're nice and safe, rattling their fucking collecting tins for the glorious Cause!

'Now I think the best thing you can do is get out of here and leave that girl alone. She has enough to contend with, without you and your warped outlook on life.'

Eamonn was so annoyed he felt a tightening in his chest, heard the blood thundering in his ears. He wanted to take back his arm and fell the man before him.

Really hurt him, as Eamonn was hurting inside.

'How dare you talk to me about warped?' he blustered. 'A man dressed as a woman, with a wig, false eyelashes and latex tits. You've got the cheek of the devil to call *me* fucking warped . . .'

Desrae laughed scornfully as he interrupted. 'I might dress as a woman, mate, and live my life as one, but I can sleep easy in my bed at night. Can you? Think about that on your way home to New fucking York. I ain't got nothing on my conscience, nothing at all.'

Eamonn, half strangled by his anger, walked from the

flat without another word. He felt the stagnant city air on his face and he breathed it in deeply. They were all ignorant fools. He was glad he had got out of London. They thought they knew it all, thought they were so sophisticated, but they didn't have a clue.

He couldn't find a black cab so walked to the Underground. It was only then that he realised there was a bomb scare. As he marched into the nearest pub, he felt his anger leave him. White faces and the talk of the IRA all around him were all that he needed.

Sitting in a corner, he got quietly drunk until the all clear was given. The TV coverage on the set in the corner mocked him. He would go back to New York and forget about Cathy, he promised himself.

But he knew in his heart that it would be easier said than done.

Cathy saw Tommy that same night. It was 10.30 in the evening and he had tracked her down to the club. She was sitting alone at one of the tables, drinking brandy and Coke. He could see she was half drunk.

Casper had warned him already that she had a face like a well-slapped arse, and in his opinion was better left alone. Tommy had merely smiled and walked through to find her. Desrae had filled him in on the events of the day, leaving out the fact that he thought Cathy had slept with Docherty. Now all Tommy wanted was to be near her, to talk to her and try to cheer her up.

As Cathy looked up at him, it occurred to her for the first time that he was a good-looking man. With his thick dark hair and hazel eyes he was actually very handsome. She smiled at him, a lop-sided drunken grin.

Tommy smiled back. 'I thought I might find you here, Cathy.'

'Help yourself to a drink, Tom. I'm already a bit drunk.'

'I think that's the understatement of the year, ain't it?'

Cathy laughed, but it was a lost, lonely sound. 'So you're in the IRA and all now, are you?' she slurred, looking at him with a pained expression on her face. 'It seems everyone I know is a closet terrorist these days.' She straightened up in her chair, trying to look dignified and sober. 'I've got to go to Acton next week, see one of the TVs who works a club there. Could you use your influence to make sure there are no bombs along the way, please? I'd ask Eamonn, but I think he might make sure there was one at the moment.'

Tommy closed his eyes and shook his head. 'Did you really, honestly, think I'd have anything to do with all that, eh? Come off it. Docherty spoke too soon, love. I'd never agree to anything like that. I wouldn't.'

Cathy looked at him through narrowed eyes. 'Honest? Honest to God, you're not bullshitting me?'

Tommy covered her hand with his. 'Would I bullshit you about something this important? Please, Cathy, it's me you're talking to now, not bloody Docherty. I would not have anything to do with any of it. It's taken me all this time to convince them I wouldn't open me trap about what they wanted to discuss. Believe me, there were a few moments when I thought me number was up. They're heavy duty, love.'

Cathy was so relieved she felt her whole body sag. 'Oh, Tommy, if I thought you was involved in all that, I'd hate you till the day I died. I know we might not be pillars of the community, but all that is too much, mate. Too much for anyone. All that death, all that killing.'

She was on the verge of tears. 'How can Eamonn be associated with it? How can he feel that he's doing something worthwhile, something decent? He's making money off other people's grief, other people's heart-break . . .'

Taking her gently in his arms, Tommy hugged her tight. 'That's not me, Cath, you know that. I'm your common or garden villain, me. Nothing more and nothing less. Fuck me, I couldn't be a part of all that. Stop thinking about it now, eh? Docherty's gone from your life now. Good riddance to bad rubbish, I reckon.'

Cathy giggled at the childish saying. 'I love you, Tommy Pasquale. You're a good man.'

Her words, drunk as she was, were music to his ears. He loved her, and the night he'd spent with her when his father was killed had been the best of his life, even though it had been tinged with sadness.

'Things can only get better now, Cathy. We have each other, we have our youth and the chance to make a good life together. Let's put everything behind us, eh?'

She pulled away from him and sniffed loudly. 'I want another brandy, a great big fuck-off brandy. Then I want to have a laugh. Let's go round to one of the hostess clubs and get stonked out of our brains. Or better still, let's go to the Roxy or the Vortex, see all the punks in their finery . . .'

Tommy laughed delightedly. 'Let's get you home, eh?'

Cathy pouted. 'I ain't ready to go home yet. I want to be free of the flat, Desrae, and everything for a little while.'

Suddenly, her face became serious. 'Do you think I ought to phone up Gates, tell him about Eamonn?'

'No, that's the last thing you should think of doing!' Tommy looked alarmed. 'Just put the lot of it out of your head, love, all right?'

Cathy, aggressive now, answered him in a tight voice: 'What are you saying? He's in it up to his neck. I think this is one instance where grassing is well in order. Think of all the people Eamonn has helped to hurt, kill or maim.' She tried to stand up, and gripped the side of the table to steady herself. 'I'm going to ring Gates now, tell him where the fucker is. I'll give him the Ritz! Murdering bastard.'

Tommy pulled her on to his lap and held her to him tightly. 'Cathy . . . Cathy, love, don't be stupid. They'd kill you before you could turn around. These people are ruthless. You'd only be hurting yourself. For every Eamonn Docherty who gets a capture, there's twenty more to take his place. Let it go, girl. Just let it go. Now let's have a couple of drinks, love, and then we'll go and do whatever you want, OK?'

He was frightened now, and trying desperately to placate her, because he had in fact become an active worker for the very people she wanted to grass up to the police. They were his passport to controlling the West End, and this little girl, as much as he loved her, was not going to fuck that up for him. He would get her drunk, get her home, and then talk some sense into her in the morning.

She was a loose cannon at the moment and he would have to watch her very, very carefully.

'I loved him, you know, Tommy.' Her voice was faint now. She looked ready to drop.

'I know you did, and he loved you. But try and forget about him, you've got me.'

Her eyes lit up. 'Yes, I have, haven't I? Let's to go bed.'

Tommy smiled then, a real smile. How long had he dreamed of her saying that to him?

'We'll go to bed later, love, all right?'

She leant against him happily, Eamonn forgotten for the moment. The drink was taking over. 'I think you're lovely, Tommy. Can I have another brandy, please?' She seemed calmer now, and her eyelids were beginning to droop.

'Shall I take you home, love?'

As he led her from the small back-room club, she kissed Casper on the cheek.

'She's out of her brain, Tommy,' he said with a worried look at her.

Tommy picked her up and carried her out on to the pavement. 'Tell me something I don't know! Lock up, Casper, there's a mate.'

As the doorman watched him carry Cathy up the road he felt sad. She had taken Joey's death badly; they all had in one way or another.

London was becoming a different place nowadays, the skinheads, the punks and other such weirdos everywhere. No one was safe, what with violence on the streets and IRA bombs everywhere.

What was the world coming to? he wondered. It hadn't been like this in his day.

Chapter Thirty-Four

Cathy woke up in her single bed with a mouth that was so dry she thought her tongue was going to stick to it. Her eyes felt as if someone was poking red hot needles into them.

She was awake only a minute before she realised she was naked, and so was Tommy Pasquale. He lay beside her, snoring. The events of the day before gradually filtered back into her pounding head. She could remember everything about her fight with Eamonn and afterwards going to the club. She could only vaguely remember Tommy coming in. After that everything was a blur.

Pulling up the covers, she could smell the musky scent of sex. They had slept together in every sense, that much was evident. She had obviously consented, Tommy wasn't the type to take advantage. What the hell had she been thinking of?

Tommy had loved her for a long, long time. If he knew she had also slept with Eamonn, he would be broken-hearted. He was decent and kind, a man to look up to in her world. Many women wanted him because of his good looks and outgoing personality. He was articulate, intelligent and kind, a real catch in Soho terms.

But in her heart of hearts she understood that the only person she really wanted was Eamonn Docherty, even knowing what she did now. Though she would send him away from her if she saw him again, he would always be in her heart.

Eamonn was the only person in the world she would ever truly love. Now, because of all the upset he had caused, she was lying beside a man who was worth ten of Eamonn Docherty, twenty of him. A man who would give her anything she wanted in the world; a man who would love her and honour her and keep her. How many women had heard those words and known they would never be fulfilled? It was just a bit of mumbo-jumbo in the wedding service. Yet Tommy would take those words and make them true for her.

Life was wrong, bad, upside down. Nothing was ever what you thought it would be. No one was ever what you thought they were. All her life she had had to look out for herself, and she would carry on doing just that.

She would pledge herself to Tommy Pasquale, give herself to him. It was all that was left for her. Looking on his handsome face she felt that the love she bore this man, this friend, was a decent, clean love and through it she might redeem herself. Waking him gently by kissing his brow, she smiled down at him.

He awoke immediately, pleased as punch to find himself in her bed, although he'd known when he'd slept with her that he was doing wrong; she was so drunk she would have got into bed with the Hunchback of Notre Dame. Now he consoled himself with the thought that he seemed to have done the right thing after all. She was pleased to be here with him.

'I love you, Cathy.'

'I know you do.'

She didn't say she loved him back and they were both aware of that fact.

'So where do we go from here?'

'I'll buy a flat and we'll get married, Cathy. Be a real couple,' he suggested.

'If that's what you want, Tommy.'

He felt a small flicker of annoyance at her answer, but swallowed it down. He wanted her to be as enthusiastic as he was, feel as happy as he felt, even when he knew it was out of the question. But he would make her feel like that in time, he promised himself that much at least.

'That's what I want, Cathy,' he said lovingly.

She kissed him tenderly on the lips, as a sister or a mother might. 'Then that's what you shall have.'

Richard Gates was beside himself, so angry he could kill.

Cathy Duke, little Cathy, was marrying Tommy Pasquale and everyone was acting as if it was the greatest event since the fucking Coronation!

On top of all that he knew through a series of grasses that Docherty had been back in town though no one was holding up their hand to seeing him. If he'd seen anyone in Soho it would have been Cathy bloody two-faced Duke.

As Gates bellowed at his co-workers, bellowed at his contacts and bellowed at strangers in shops and pubs, he realised that he had a serious problem. Susan P found his behaviour highly amusing and that was more annoying than anything.

'Very dog-in-the-manger, Richard,' she chided him.

'It's not that, Susan, and you know it. She's throwing herself away on that bloody fool and someone should tell her.'

Susan P lit a cigarette and blew out smoke noisily. 'Someone like you, you mean? The girl is happy, the boy is happy, and Desrae is positively delirious, looking forward to grandchildren, if you don't mind. I think it's the best thing for Cathy and so does everyone else. It's only you who seems to be against it, and I know the reason as well as you.'

Richard Gates felt himself blushing and that made him angrier than ever. 'I should nick you, Susan, and you know *that* as well as I do, but I like to feel I look out for my friends, such as they are. And now, if you want to *stay* my friend, I would advise you to shut your fucking trap.'

Susan screamed with laughter. 'You know what you need, don't you, Mr Gates? A good fuck, get it all out of your system. Here, I'll make you laugh, shall I, give you a good crack? I've recently acquired a house in Westminster that was owned by an ex-minister. Now my MPs can canoodle to their hearts' content because it's got one of those silly bells that tell them when they have to go and vote. If that doesn't make you laugh, nothing will. How's that for giving the establishment one up the arse, eh?'

Richard smiled despite himself. 'You're as a mad as a hatter, Sue.'

'Seriously though, Richard,' she told him, 'you really should face up to what you feel, then you can deal with it. Admit the truth, man, get it off your chest. God knows it's going no further than these four walls.'

He took a deep breath, forcing himself to put his thoughts into words for the first time. 'I've never been a common or garden Old Bill, as you know. I keep my job and rise in it because I make a point of finding out people's foibles, their little secrets. That way I can play my games in peace. But where that girl's concerned, I don't know whether I'm on my arse or my elbow . . .

'Yes, I admit, I would make love to her if I could. I would make love to her morning, noon and night. And I'll tell you something else – she'd love it, I know she would. Cathy needs someone like me . . .'

He broke off in mid-sentence and they were both quiet for a while. Then Susan P went over to him and embraced him, a sisterly hug.

'My God, man, you have got it bad.'

He shook his head in despair. 'I know that, girl. Don't I fucking know it?'

'If you really cared you'd be pleased for her, because she's happy now.'

Richard laughed, a humourless sound. 'But that's just it, Susan. *Is* she happy?'

Cathy tried on the white suit once more and modelled it for Desrae. It was a lacy Ossie Clarke number which made her look taller, slimmer, and much more sophisticated. Desrae himself was like a cat with a whole pint of cream, absolutely over the moon to have this chance of dressing himself up in some expensive new finery. He had chosen a dark purple creation for the wedding, with a purple and orange hat and handbag as matching accessories.

In the six weeks since Joey's death and the subsequent events, Cathy felt she had gained a modicum of peace. She would soon be Mrs Tommy Pasquale and would have a lovely flat of her own in Soho. Tommy had wanted to move out to Hampstead or even Knightsbridge, but Cathy was adamant that she wanted to stay there.

He knew she needed to be near Desrae and eventually agreed that it would be the best thing for a while. Cathy knew that Tommy wasn't too pleased about it, but he would do whatever she wanted and she loved him for that. As time had gone by she had found herself caring more for him than she'd expected to. He was kind, considerate, and loved her so much it was painful to see at times.

Suddenly, Desrae stopped his chatter about the wedding and put a blunt question to Cathy.

'Have you seen the doctor, love?'

She blushed. 'What for?'

'Because you're pregnant, of course.' Cathy was annoyed and it showed. Desrae was unrepentant. 'I know your cycle better than you do, love. You're pregnant all right, so why don't you just admit it?' One of his foibles was the fact that he loved to buy Cathy's sanitary wear. He obviously hoped that the people in the shop would think it was for him, though he would never admit that to anyone.

'I think I'm just late, that's all, Desrae. Joey's death and everything else, I think it's just delayed things.'

'You and I both know that's a load of old cods, love.' He put an arm around her shoulders. 'Do you know who the father is?'

Cathy didn't answer for a moment.

She had resented Madge because she didn't know who had fathered her child, and now Cathy herself was in exactly the same predicament.

'Of course I do. It's Tommy.'

Desrae sighed. 'All right then, if that's what you say, then it's Tommy. I hope it's his, meself, but I'm not too sure about you, love. What do you really think, or should I say want?'

'I know that Tommy is the father, I just know. Women do.' This was said in such a way as to leave Desrae in no doubt that it was something he could never experience.

'Well, obviously you're being a bit of a crosspatch. I'll just put it down to you being in the club. What does Tommy think about it all?'

'I haven't told him yet, not until I'm really sure.'

Desrae looked out of the window and said airily, 'Oh look, there's a dirty great pig flying over Greek Street. So, let's talk about this properly, shall we? When are you going to tell him? He'll be over the moon, you know that.'

'With respect, Desrae, I'll tell him when I'm ready and not before. It's my baby, my life and my decision.'

'I'm well aware of that but I hope you haven't forgotten the fact you are marrying that boy in two weeks' time. I hope you've plucked up the courage to tell him something this important by then or what chance does your marriage have?'

Cathy collapsed on to the sofa and started to cry gently. 'I think it's Tommy's but I can't be sure.'

Desrae hugged her consolingly. 'You'll know when it's born. If it looks Italian it's your man's, and if it looks Irish then it's Mr Charisma's. That's easy enough, eh?' he joked. 'Anyway, they're both dark so it won't make one iota of difference to young Tommy. He'll love it, believe it's his and take good care of it. Now stop worrying, will you? Just enjoy yourself. Christ knows we need something to cheer us up, all of us.'

'I feel so guilty. I'm doing what me mum did. I'm having a child and I have no idea who fathere—'

Desrae interrupted her. 'Listen, love, at least you can narrow it down to two. With people like your mum it could have been one of hundreds! So stop berating yourself and enjoy it all. I'm really looking forward to being a grandmother.'

'You're right,' Cathy said, and brightened up. 'So long as it's got me and you, it's going to be OK.'

Desrae smiled, but it bothered him that poor old Tommy wasn't even brought into the equation.

A fortnight later, Desrae sat in his kitchen and thought about the day ahead. It was to be a quiet wedding, just himself, Casper as best man, Susan P, and the bride and groom. Tommy's mother had shown no inclination to attend and neither had his sisters.

Desrae felt sad and lonely this morning. Even though Cathy would only be moving around the corner, he would miss her presence in the flat. Miss having someone to talk to, to be with, to look after. But, as he lectured himself, if he had been a real mother, this day would have come eventually. And there was the baby to look forward to.

He and Cathy would make sure that her child had all the things they'd never had: security, love and money. Plenty of money. Children needed to be cushioned from the harsh realities of life, needed people and money behind them to become somebody. In his mind he wove dreams of private schools, with himself decked out in all his finery watching the child collect a degree or whatever it was people got in private schools.

He had a goal in life once more. He would be Cathy's right arm, her mother and father rolled into one. With her child he would redeem himself from a life of promiscuity and sexual gratification. There would never be another Joey. Fortunately, Joey had left Desrae with enough money that he need only keep his punters if he wanted them. But he did not want them any more.

He would retire, and take on the club full-time. Be there for Cathy and the baby and make sure that they all lived happily ever after, Tommy included.

He stared at the purple creation hanging on the back of the kitchen door and beamed with pleasure.

The photos would be wonderful with his Zandra Rhodes outfit and Cathy's lace suit. It was a bit austere as far as he was concerned, but he knew Cathy didn't like bright colours as much as he did. You only had to listen to her go on about the flat. Wanted it all like Susan P's, all white walls and glass and minimalist, whatever the fuck that meant.

Once a baby was crawling all over the place, those white walls would be a no no all right, Desrae thought smugly.

As the 8.30 news was announced he put some toast on and plugged in the kettle. A cup of Rosie Lee and a bit of Holy Ghost, that's what his little girl wanted this morning.

Humming, he prepared a tray with a rosebud in a vase to set it off and went to wake Cathy. He knocked on the door and went in, looking down at the girl who had become like his own flesh and blood and feeling tears well up in his eyes. She looked so childlike, so beautiful in sleep, that it made Desrae feel as if he were looking on a great painting or sculpture. Leaving the tray by the bed, he shook her awake gently.

'Come on, sleepyhead. It's the big day today.'

Cathy, who was dreaming of Eamonn, a nice home and a lovely baby, opened her eyes and burst into tears.

Desrae hugged her tightly. 'It's just wedding day nerves, love. Come on, eat up your breakfast and I'll run you a bath. Then you'll be as right as rain.'

But she wasn't and they both knew why.

The deed was finally done nevertheless and Casper was making a speech at the reception in the club. All the girls had turned up there as a surprise and Cathy was glad to see them. They had all tried to outdo each other with their outfits and Susan P had admired each and every one of them.

One particularly tall transsexual was dressed as Cilla Black and really did look like her. After requests from everyone he had sung 'Step Inside, Love' with great conviction. Cathy told him that when they opened the new club, he would be better off miming.

Now Casper was making his speech and his words brought a lump to the throat of everyone there.

'I know you all care about Cathy, as I do. We wish her all the best of health and happiness, as we do Tommy – a man's man and his father's son.'

Everyone clapped here and Casper knew he was on to a winner.

'Desrae looks every bit the mother of the bride, and the father as well . . .'

Everyone laughed except Desrae so he hurried on, 'All that is left for me to say is: may you have many happy years together and many lovely children. All named after us, of course.'

Everyone clapped some more and kissed the bride and congratulated the groom. Tommy wasn't the type to be kissed by TVs and they all knew that. For most of the girls the closest they had come to male behaviour in years was shaking his hand.

The reception soon gathered momentum as hostesses, bouncers and assorted visitors turned up, laden down with presents and champagne by the bucketful. Cathy could not help but feel happy, seeing the celebrations all around her. Tommy was so delighted his eyes shone with joy and she knew she had done the right thing. He would be a good father, a good husband. As Desrae said, she could have done a lot worse.

After two glasses of champagne she decided to go outside and get some air. She walked into the darkness of the shop, amazed to find that it was evening already. She opened the shop door and was about to step out on to the pavement when a hand grabbed her. Before she could scream a voice said, 'Don't worry, it's only me.'

Richard Gates's voice was the last one she'd expected to hear. Turning towards him, she smiled happily.

'Susan said you might be along. How are you?' She hadn't seen him for a long time, she realised. Too long.

'Oh, I'm all right. So how does it feel to be an old married woman then? Any different?'

She smiled ruefully. 'Not really, I still feel like Cathy Connor inside. I expect I always will. It'll take a bit of getting used to: Pasquale. By the way, I understand I have you to thank for getting me a birth certificate and everything. I appreciate it.'

Richard looked embarrassed. 'Think of it as a small wedding present.'

She put her hand against his cheek for a moment. 'You've always been so kind to me, haven't you? Even when I had all that trouble as a kid, you helped me out. You know I did it, don't you? Susan P told me never to tell you for definite. Well, I'm ignoring her advice because I want you to know that I count myself very lucky to have you as my friend. Even if you are an Old Bill.' She laughed to take the emotion out of her words, and make him understand more than she was saying.

'Can I kiss the bride, do you think, or do I have to ask your husband's permission?'

Cathy laughed. 'Of course you can kiss the bride. I can't think of anyone else I would rather kiss.'

She was teasing him and it broke his heart. As she stepped into his embrace, expecting a peck on the cheek, his arms enveloped her and then he was pressing his mouth hungrily to hers and her lips were parting in answer to his.

It was a deep kiss, a sensual kiss, and inside she felt herself responding to him, which made her frightened. He held her to him like a vice; she could feel the hardness of his belly and the strength of his arms. Then the fear left her and she relaxed and kissed him back.

So much passion going into one kiss with a man old

enough to be her father, and whom she had always looked on in that light.

Sexual attraction was still hard for her to comprehend. Cathy had felt it with Eamonn, never with Tommy. Now she realised she was in its grip again, with the last man on earth she'd have dreamed of. They kissed for what seemed an age before Cathy gently freed herself from his grasp. Her breathing was erratic and her heart beating a tattoo inside her chest.

In the half-light Richard looked younger, and his deep-set eyes were fathomless as she stared into them.

'I love you, Cathy,' he said hoarsely. 'God help me, I always have. And if you were honest, you'd admit you feel the same way. You don't kiss strangers like that, love.'

He pulled her to him tightly, and once again she felt safe inside his arms, warm and protected. They stayed like that until the shrill ringing of the telephone forced them apart. Cathy walked to the counter and answered it automatically, before it brought out Casper or someone else. She didn't want to be caught with Richard in the darkened shop.

'Hello?'

The voice on the other end of the line made her go pale. It was Eamonn calling from New York.

'Happy wedding day, Cathy. I hope you'll both be very happy.'

She was stunned. 'How did you know? Who told you?' Her mind was whirling.

'Tommy did, love – I speak to him all the time. I just want you to know that there's no hard feelings, eh? Let's still be friends. We'll have to see one another in the future when I come over to liaise with your husband and I'd like to think there was no animosity between us. After all . . .'

Without speaking, she put the phone back on its rest then took it off the hook.

He had lied to her. Tommy had lied to her. All his talk of shunning the men of violence had been a sham. Money was everything to him as it was to Eamonn. Now she had tied herself to a man who had lied to her, deceived her. He'd known that lying over something so serious would break her heart if she found out. She placed her hands protectively over her belly and felt tears fill her eyes.

Richard watched the changing emotions on her face and pulled her into his arms once more.

'Tell me what's wrong,' he urged. 'Who was that on the phone, love? Come on, you can tell me anything, you know that.'

And as she looked up into his loving eyes, his kind concerned face, she knew she could never tell him a word of this. The consequences would be too far-reaching, might even endanger him. Tommy would break her neck as soon as look at her if she ever spoke of what she knew, but he still believed she didn't know what he was up to and that was for the best.

As Richard held her to him the door to the club opened and Desrae and Casper walked into the shop.

'What's going on here then?' Desrae's voice was loud.

'A little too much to drink, and a bit emotional, eh, Cathy?' Gates's voice was carefully calm. Cathy looked gratefully into his eyes. Casper placed the phone back in its cradle and she stared at it as though it might jump off the counter and bite her.

'Leave her with me a second, Desrae, then I'll bring her back inside, OK?' Gates's voice was a quiet command and Casper, sensing something was afoot, took Desrae's arm and guided him back inside the club.

Surrounded by pornographic books and films, posters of undressed women and men with other men in provocative poses, Richard took Cathy into his arms once

497

more. Holding her to him tightly, he said, 'Listen to me: no matter what happens, no matter what you do, I'll always be there for you. Remember that, won't you? I am here for you, darling.'

Cathy allowed herself to be held and caressed by him, knowing there were some things she could never tell anyone, even Desrae.

She had a secret from Tommy and he had a secret from her. What a way to start a marriage! What a way to face the rest of your life, because she knew that now she had married him, he would see her dead before he'd see her with another man.

It was this knowledge that frightened her most of all.

Book Four

Frisch weht der Wind der Heimat zu;
– mein Irisch Kind, wo weilest du?
Freshly blows the wind homewards;
– my Irish child, where you are dwelling?

> – *Tristan und Isolde,*
> Wagner, 1813–83

Be all my sins remembered.

> – *Hamlet,*
> William Shakespeare, 1564–1616

I love thee with the breath, smiles, tears, of all my life!
And if God choose I shall but love thee better after death.

> – *Sonnets from the Portuguese,*
> Elizabeth Barrett Browning, 1806–61

Chapter Thirty-Five

New York 1987

'For fuck's sakes, Deirdra, will you get the kids out of my fucking study and into the garden? Everywhere I look there's brats. Now do what I ask you. Immediately.'

Deirdra, her long red hair dyed now, doe eyes a startling green still but her figure heavy from constant childbirth, walked into Eamonn's study and said pointedly: 'It's your only daughter's birthday party. Of course there are children all over the place. What did you expect me to do – not invite her friends, their parents, what? You tell me, Mr Big Man, you seem to know everything.'

'Don't be funny, Deirdra. All I ask is that you keep them out of my study, that's all.'

She shook her head, making her full red cheeks wobble like jellies. 'We have nine children. This house is *always* full of children, you fool of a man. What's another twenty or so, I ask you? Anyway, if Norah goes in there you never say a word. It's only the boys you're ever cross with.'

Eamonn frowned. 'Because they're little bastards, that's

why. Anyway, where the fuck is Jack Jr? He was supposed to be here by now – I told him three-thirty.'

Deirdra shrugged. Her eldest son, named for his grandfather, held no interest for her. In fact, none of the children did.

'How do I know where he is? Out whoring like his father does, I expect.'

Eamonn closed his eyes and took a deep breath. His wife goaded him constantly and it was wearing. He looked at her as she stood before him. There was no trace left of the seventeen-year-old girl he had married. Deirdra was old before her time.

He knew her weakness and used it shamelessly. His wife was sex mad, at least with him anyway. The heavier she grew, the more sex she wanted. She did nothing for him, her big fat body did nothing for him, and they both knew that. But still he gave her what she called her due, or had until recently.

Now he gained a perverse satisfaction from seeing her ask for it, beg for it. He liked to refuse.

He loved his children and she professed to love them too, but in reality she had no interest in them once they hit three. Deirdra liked babies but he was fucked if she was getting any more from him. Nine children were enough for any man. The college fees alone would keep a small country going for a year, but Eamonn had the money, it wasn't that. It was the fact that he didn't really want her as the mother of his children.

Already Norah, the only girl, was getting too like her mother. Emulating her, with her pseudo-intellectual friends and her pathetic pretence that she understood exactly what they were saying. Deirdra was in fact a sandwich short of a picnic, seriously challenged in the brain department, and he really should point that out to her.

But today wasn't the time.

There was a party for the kids, and the parents would all be here soon, and Eamonn would have to play the convivial host no matter how much he was dreading it. Today he did not need a party of any kind. Especially one that Deirdra had arranged. She would have squandered a fortune on the arrangements, and would make sure that everyone knew just how expensive it had all been. For someone who had always had money, she had an uncanny knack of acting like a parvenu.

As she stared at him from her green eyes – once her best feature, now covered in too much shadow and false eyelashes – he felt the usual tightening in the base of his neck. She really was a pain. Her tiny tits were encased in a padded bra, but her hips still looked as if they could easily carry a wide load. Her waist was thick, her arms and legs over-plump. Even her neck had a small roll of fat around it, as did the rims of her eyes. She looked like a little red-headed pig, he thought, smiling.

'What's the joke? Me, I suppose.' Her voice sounded hurt.

'Don't be so stupid, I was just thinking of our Norah being a whole eight years old today.'

Deirdra laughed then, a happy little sound. 'Christ, eight! The time goes so fast.'

Not fast enough, was Eamonn's opinion, but he wisely kept it to himself. His wife walked towards him on her impossibly high heels and tried to put an arm around his neck. He moved expertly away from her.

'Come off it, Deirdra, the kids will be on top of us in a minute.'

'Come upstairs, the au pair can watch them. Come on, Eamonn, it's been ages.'

He pushed her away roughly. 'Leave it out, love, I have

a mountain of work to get through before I can have a bit of fun at the party. Are your mum and dad definitely coming?'

She nodded, pouting in disappointment. 'You're getting it somewhere, Eamonn, because you're not asking me for it.'

He sighed heavily. 'Leave it, Deirdra. Not now, eh?'

Before she could answer the twins burst into the room, faces bright and green eyes full of tears.

'Daddy, Daddy, Dennis is driving us all mad! He's got a slug gun.'

Eamonn put his head in his hands and sighed heavily.

Eight sons and they were all limbs of Satan.

The Dochertys' house on Long Island was beautiful, ablaze with chandeliers, the rooms all high-ceilinged and embellished with ornamental plasterwork. The decor was subtle because Eamonn had warned the gay decorator that if he saw any hot pinks or Dayglo oranges he would personally take the man outside and shoot him through the back of the head. Something in his voice had penetrated the man's Valium trance and he had heeded the warning. The result was a very lovely, spare and understated house.

Deirdra hated it.

Eamonn loved it.

As usual he had won.

As far as he was concerned, the house was his finest achievement. Worth over two million dollars, it was also a shrewd investment. With fifteen bedrooms, eight receptions, a ballroom and two kitchens, it was ideal for the Dochertys and their nine children.

The gardens were massive, over five acres, and all securely walled. The only access was through security gates. Eamonn wanted it to be the American equivalent of a country estate and acted the Lord of the Manor in his own home. He also had a flat in Upper Manhattan where he met his girlfriends, and kept a long-term mistress off Bleccker Street. She was called Jasmine, a tiny blonde actress who spent most of her time resting. But she gave great head, and her tits were not only stunning but bought and paid for by him, so that Eamonn felt he'd made another good investment.

All in all life was good.

Now, dressed in a dinner suit, he looked every bit the successful man as he greeted his guests – though in the back of his mind he felt a black tie dinner for a child's eighth birthday was going a bit too far. He would have preferred the kids to have had jelly and ice cream and a few games. Fuck knows, the two Norland nannies cost him the national debt and the au pair wasn't cheap either. Why couldn't they have arranged something?

But he smiled as everyone arrived, and made small talk, and kept his eye on Deirdra who liked to drink a bit too much and was liable to cause a scene if she overindulged.

It was just on nine-thirty when he thought his eyes were playing him up. Standing at the top of his sweeping staircase, he could have sworn for a moment he saw Cathy Connor. He had just glimpsed her out of the corner of his eye.

He had come upstairs to belt the living daylights out of the twins who had found a tube of icing and drawn a large pink penis on Norah's birthday cake. He personally had found it hilarious; the caterers, another load of tight-assed fags his wife had hired, had found it disgusting. The twins had just been found out. Liam, aged ten, had grassed them up without a second's thought.

It didn't matter how hard Eamonn tried to instil his East End values into the boys, they just ignored him.

Eamonn had told them time and time again: You never tell on family or friends. He doubted they would ever learn that lesson.

Making his way hurriedly downstairs again, he walked into the ballroom and scanned the throng of people.

Everything was decorated in lemon and silver: lemon yellow balloons proclaimed 'Eight Today' on them, and silver balloons announced 'Birthday Girl'. The birthday girl herself was dressed in lemon and silver also and being on the plump side like her mother, looked like a fat girl always does in lace and bows: stupid.

In his heart of hearts Eamonn felt sorry for the child, knowing that she was desperately trying to please her mother. She was talking to all the grown-ups about the Metropolitan Museum of Arts, and finding it difficult. Deirdra tried to coach the girl but it was really a case of the blind leading the blind where culture was concerned.

He was idly scanning the room when he saw that blond head again. His heart lifted, and he felt a pulse ticking inside his temple. Then she turned around and his hopes died.

It wasn't Cathy.

It was a stranger, though that wasn't so surprising. Deirdra was a bitch for inviting unknown people she classed as 'interesting'. Well, fuck interesting, this particular stranger was layable, that would do for him. Eamonn homed in on her.

'How do you do? I'm the man of the house. And you might be . . . ?'

Usually his accent alone was enough to seduce the American women, they couldn't resist it. This lady, however, was a different kettle of fish. On closer inspection she was not all he had hoped. She had the blue eyes, the cheekbones and the chin, but that was as far as the similarity to Cathy went.

In the nasal tones of Brooklyn she told him: 'I'm Carol Van Dutty, and I'm a sculptress. Your wife is interested in one of my works. It's a particularly fine piece, actually, Deirdra has quite an eye . . .'

He interrupted her before she hit him full swing with the sales pitch.

'My wife, honey, wouldn't know a sculpture from a hole in her arse. Now if you'll excuse me, I'll leave you and forget about you until I'm forced at gunpoint to write you a cheque.'

Carol Van Dutty, real name Rebekka Splint, watched wide-eyed as the handsome hunk walked away from her.

Eamonn was upset and it showed. He really had thought he had seen Cathy. He had felt her near to him, sensed her presence. All an illusion, of course.

He saw his daughter and sighed once more. Norah looked at him with the bewildered eyes of an eight year old totally out of her depth. He walked towards her, greeting people as he went.

'Hi, baby, what's cooking?'

Norah laughed, a happy carefree sound, and he was disarmed. She was only a kid, for Christ's sakes, and here she was, made up like a fucking carnival dancer.

'Come on, sweetcakes. What say me and you retire to my study and smoke a cigar and enjoy a brandy? Christ, you're eight, it's time you started drinking and smoking at least.' Norah giggled into her gloved hands. He felt a surge of real affection for her; if his wife would leave her alone she'd be a terrific kid.

Eamonn took her hand. As they moved through the crowd and made their way to the door, they were stopped by a business associate of his, an Italian named Johnny Galdi.

'Terrific party, Eamonn, and is this the little birthday

girl?' He chucked her under the chin with his heavy hand. Norah moved her head away and the man laughed. 'Not interested in boys yet, huh?'

'She's shy, Johnny, she's her daddy's girl.'

Johnny squeezed the eighteen-year-old bimbette on his arm and laughed gustily. 'Ain't they all?'

Johnny was sixty if he was a day and suddenly he made Eamonn feel depressed. Would that be him eventually, still chasing tail at sixty? Still looking for that elusive female, the one he'd want to fuck until they were too old and too decrepit but they could still reminisce?

He led Norah to his study, spying Deirdra on the way. She was surrounded by a group of young men, all hanging on her every word. This depressed him as well, because he knew they were all out to put the touch on her for something. She paraded struggling actors, painters, sculptors, and every other fucking wacko she could find, around his home, forever listening to their crap with wide eyes and an open chequebook. How had his life come to this?

Inside the study he poured himself a large Johnnie Walker Blue Label, and a Coke for Norah. They sat side by side on the Victorian loveseat his wife insisted was 'just the thing' for his study and he tried to make conversation with his only daughter.

'How's school?'

'It's OK.'

'How's your friends?'

'They're OK.'

'How's everything going?'

'OK.'

'Jesus Christ, Norah, is that all you can say? That school costs over three thousand dollars a term and all you can say is OK?'

She looked at him with puzzled eyes. 'Are you OK, Daddy?'

Shaking his head he laughed, but it was an exasperated sound.

'I'm a child, Daddy, I'm not supposed to talk to you. Don't you watch *Oprah*?'

She was making one of her mother's adult jokes and it saddened Eamonn. Made him feel like crying, in fact. Suddenly he was terribly upset. He put an arm around her shoulders.

'Listen to me, pumpkin, all that crap Mommy tells you to say . . . well, next time she coaches you, tell her I said you're not to listen. Be a child, Norah, while you've got the chance. My father used to say to me: "Don't try and be so old, son. One day you'll be old for the rest of your life." Do you understand what I'm saying here?'

Norah nodded. 'Of course I understand, Daddy, and I know I'm a child. But you try and tell Mommy that! I haven't got one real friend here tonight. I wanted to go to McDonald's like my friends, but Mommy said that was low-class.'

She sighed like an old woman. Her little face was a picture of world weariness as she said sadly, 'I wish I had more sisters – to take Mommy's mind off of me a bit, you know?'

He hugged her to him tightly, his eyes filled with unaccustomed tears at the loneliness in his child's voice. 'I'll talk to Mommy, OK? Tell her to lay off you, how's that?'

'She won't listen, Daddy. She thinks I'm going to be the next great woman of America. She wants me to be famous for something. The trouble is, I'm not very good at anything much.' Her voice was small, broken. It angered him. She was eight years old and already her mother had made her feel like a failure.

'Daddy, can I go now, please? I mean, to bed, not back to the party. Could you square it with Mommy? She wants me to sing later and, Daddy, I really don't want to.'

'OK, Norah, I'll tell her me and you got drunk and I had to put you to bed because you were singing dirty Irish songs your grandfather taught you. How's that?'

She smiled tremulously. 'Goodnight, Daddy. I love you.'

He pulled her to him once more. 'And I love you, princess. Sweet dreams.'

At the door she turned and smiled again, and his heart went out to her. He drained his brandy when she had gone then picked up the phone. As he dialled, he thought of his daughter's worries and determined to talk to his wife tonight and sort this out once and for all.

He heard the voice he was longing to hear on the answer-phone at the other end of the line, and listened to it sadly.

'There's nobody here to take your call. Please leave a message and we'll get back to you as soon as we can.'

Cathy's voice.

Sometimes when he rang she answered the phone and they exchanged idle chit-chat. Just hearing her voice gave him an erection.

He didn't leave a message but replaced the receiver and stared for long moments at the phone.

In twelve years he had made over thirty trips to Britain, and never once had he seen her. Tommy always had an excuse as to why she could not attend so much as a small dinner with him. Eamonn knew she held a grudge and it broke his heart. She was still the only woman he had ever really wanted.

He poured himself another large brandy and walked to the French windows to look out on to his garden. By his study was a replica of the rose garden at Hampton Court, and there he could just make out his son Jack with his arm around the waist of a tiny dark-haired girl. But he could also see the twins and young Paul, who was only seven but with the devilment of a serial killer, about to launch a bucket of water over their eldest brother and his girl.

Before Eamonn could open the window to protest, the dirty deed was done. He could hear the girl's screams even over the lousy jazz band his wife had booked for the evening's entertainment. He went back to his desk, and turned off the light. He had decided to go on the missing list tonight. Let Deirdra sort out the little buggers, he didn't have the heart for it. Personally, he thought their escapades quite funny and liked to see their high spirits, especially when his wife had all her so-called friends in the house.

He knew it was petty, but at these times he rather enjoyed her humiliation.

She'd wanted the Von Trapp family; she'd got a crowd of hooligans called the Dochertys.

Life had its compensations.

Deirdra finally located her husband towards midnight, half drunk and still laughing over the incident with the boys. She was fuming.

'How could you, Eamonn, in front of all our friends! How could you humiliate me like this? Everyone's been asking where you are. My father is worried about you and so is Uncle Petey. He's gone off to search for you. How could you do this to me, Eamonn?'

Her voice was a high-pitched whine that grated on his ears.

'On top of everything else, you sent Norah to bed! I've

told the au pair to get her dressed again so she can sing her solo . . .'

Eamonn stood up and banged his fist on the desk. 'Oh no, you don't! That child is not making an exhibition of herself tonight. If you get her out of bed and bring her down for this toffee-nosed bunch to snigger at, I'll give you such a slap across the chops you'll have bells ringing in your head for days!'

Deirdra was nonplussed. 'I beg your pardon?'

'You heard. Now get back there and I'll be in soon. You tell them that Norah has fallen asleep, and then tell the fucking band to stop playing Miles Davis and give us something everyone can dance to, OK? That noise is going right through my head. This is supposed to be a party, for fuck's sake. Who could dance to that dirge going on at the moment, I ask you?'

Deirdra rushed from the room. Eamonn followed her sedately. As he hit the ballroom he was once again a genial host, from his smile to his effortless small talk. Even his wife couldn't fault him.

The band struck up 'Summertime', and people danced to it slowly. A black singer called Marcella who had come with Petey started to sing along and suddenly it was a real party. Ten minutes later the band was playing 'You Are The Sunshine of My Life' and everyone was singing along.

It was now a party party and even Deirdra realised as much. All her sophisticated dreams had gone out of the window but she finally relaxed and began to enjoy herself.

Jack made his way over to his son-in-law.

As Marcella started to sing 'Danny Boy', the older man's eyes misted up. He always got emotional over that song, most Irishmen did.

'I see you're getting choked.' Eamonn's voice was scornful.

'Sure you're a dreadful man, you know, you have no soul.' Jack grinned, wiping his eyes. 'How's that eejit of a daughter of mine these days? Christ, but she's piling on the pounds. It must be like mounting a fecking elephant.'

Eamonn was saved from answering by the arrival of Petey and Anthony Baggato, both well on in drink and cocaine.

'We're all meeting tomorrow at the Ravenite, be there,' Anthony told him.

Eamonn nodded. 'What's the talk on the wire taps and everything else?'

Anthony shrugged. 'They're out for the big fish, they don't know about us. Unlike others I could name, we keep a low profile.'

'If only they knew, eh?' Petey said jovially.

'Great party,' Anthony told Eamonn.

'Yeah, thanks to me. If it was left to Deirdra we'd all be standing around talking about Russian authors and minimalist painters. Oh, and politics, mustn't forget that.'

'Fuck politics, and fuck the Russians. They're all bastard Communists anyway,' growled Jack.

Eamonn laughed. 'Not the writers, or the ones she professes to read anyway. They're all dissidents, whatever the fuck that is.'

Petey shrugged and said seriously, 'Probably the Russian word for queers. Most of these authors are strange, you know. I've seen that on the *Johnny Carson Show*. All those words in their head and when they get interviewed they talk about fuck all. I notice things like that.' He felt he had said something very profound and was very pleased with himself.

An hour later the party started to break up, and an hour after that Eamonn was ready for his bed.

The trouble was, so was Deirdra.

*

As they undressed she kept up a running stream of conversation. How well her party had gone, how everyone had told her how great it had been. How everyone had complimented her on the food and the decor.

In short, how clever she was.

As he climbed into bed Eamonn said softly, 'It was the kid's birthday. Tomorrow I'm taking Norah to McDonald's and giving her a real treat for once. Get a few of her friends together.'

Deirdra didn't answer. He turned over and pulled the quilt up to his neck. Switching on the lights, she went to the bathroom and was gone some time, getting herself ready. He lay gritting his teeth in bed. It was going to be one of those nights. Lying there, he faced the inevitable.

Fondling himself, he pictured Cathy in his mind. Her hair, her eyes, her breasts. He pictured her legs opening to him, her eyes inviting him. By the time Deirdra came back and turned off the lights, he was ready for her.

As she caressed him she felt the stiffness of his manhood and chuckled with delight. 'We *are* a big boy tonight.'

With his usual mockery he said, 'And it's all for you, baby.'

All the time he was kneading Cathy's breasts, lifting Cathy's body up to his, eating her with a fervour that Deirdra found amazing, and finally pumping into Cathy as if their lives depended on it. As he felt his wife's orgasm, he started to experience his own. In his mind Cathy was panting beneath him, her breasts heaving with her need for him, her wetness for him only, her moans for him only.

As he collapsed on top of his wife, she placed her arms around his neck and sighed. 'That was good, baby, the best.'

She really believed she had made him feel like that. He

felt bad for her suddenly, wanted to tell her the truth: that it would take Arnold Schwarzenegger to lift it for him where she was concerned.

Instead, he kissed her on the lips and rolled off her. He felt lonely, lonelier than he had ever been in his entire life. He had everything most people could want: a fine home, a nice family and enough money to buy his own island if he wanted to. Yet at this moment he would exchange it all for one kiss, one night with Cathy.

As his wife snored softly beside him, Eamonn lay awake and remembered his childhood with Cathy and his father.

If only he'd known then what he knew now. Oscar Wilde said that youth was wasted on the young, and he was right. When you were young you wasted not only your own life, but usually someone else's as well.

Sleep, that night, was a hell of a long time coming.

Chapter Thirty-Six

Eamonn listened as Petey and Jack argued about one of their collectors. The man's name was Michael Flynn and his brother in Ireland had been denounced by the IRA as an informant. Word had come from Belfast to give him the bad news. In other words, make him disappear.

Petey was not so sure they should get involved; Jack's attitude was that they had been given their orders and should carry them out with the minimum of fuss. Eamonn was indifferent.

The Mahoney name was still enough to strike fear into the hearts of many people in New York State, as far afield as Florida, Miami and Boston. They were the main collectors for the IRA now, and through this had gone on to bigger and better things, from drug dealing to smuggling. Anything that anyone wanted, anywhere, at any time.

Eamonn would in fact be just as happy if they left the Cause, stopped collecting for it, because he'd made a fortune from it and was still making a fortune in other ways.

His nightclubs alone brought him in enough to live on comfortably for the rest of his natural life. They were all real businessmen these days, with office space in Manhattan and invites to City Hall. He himself paid over a million dollars a year in rent for his own offices off Wall Street and knew that his legitimate businesses would more than meet his needs these days.

Which was probably what was causing this dissatisfaction with his life. He had the houses, the cars, the holidays . . . He had a wife, a fine family. In reality he had everything he had ever wanted.

And it still wasn't enough. He wanted someone he could respect, someone he could love. He wanted a woman he could possess, and be possessed by. Someone who would always love him, no matter what.

He sighed and Jack said snidely, 'Are we running on too much for you, Eamonn? Only I know business bores you these days.'

He didn't rise to the bait. 'Look, either kill him or leave him be,' he said. 'There's two choices here. I can't see what the problem is. I'll arrange it, if you like,' he offered. 'That way it's down to me and you don't have to square it with your conscience or anyone else's.'

Petey slammed his fist on to the desk, the noise deafening in the small room.

'I'm fucking sick of all this! They talk and we jump. It's like we have no lives or minds of our own any more. This is getting beyond a fucking joke. Michael has done nothing wrong. He's mortified at what his brother did . . .'

Eamonn stood up and said gently: 'Give it a rest, Petey. It's done. Let's forget about it.'

The three men stared at each other balefully, each with their own thoughts, each knowing they had arrived at an impasse.

It had been coming on them for a while.

Familiarity breeds contempt. They were all aware of that

fact but had never thought it would apply to them. Now they found it did. Each wanted different things from life, and at times like this their individual wants and needs seemed more important than the future of the collecting business.

Petey wanted out; had wanted it for a long time.

Jack wanted out, but knew that as the elder brother he could do nothing without bringing trouble on to everyone else's head.

Eamonn didn't really care either way. He swung between wanting more and more, and wanting none of it.

Petey's voice was bitter. 'Life's shite. Even with all we've got, life's still shite.'

'Well, you know what they say, little brother: "Life's better shite in a good suit, than shite on your uppers." Remember that next time you decide you want to cross the Cause, because they'd kill you and not give a fuck.'

'I'll get it sorted,' Eamonn said again. 'Now I'm off. I've got Tommy Pasquale over this week and I need to get things set up for him.'

The other men nodded, understanding that what he was really saying was: Life goes on.

Eamonn snorted derisively. 'What a load of tossers we are. We have everything and yet we have nothing. Frightening thought, isn't it?'

He left a deafening silence behind him.

Eamonn arrived home at 7.30 and sat down to his meal with Deirdra and the children. He was smiling and laughing with them, and his wife joined in. She was on top form until they'd finished dessert and the coffee was brought in. Then the children, as if given a secret message, all asked to leave the table.

Deirdra poured Eamonn his coffee and added sugar and cream. 'I've some news for you, Eamonn.'

He sipped his coffee, half an ear on his wife and the other half on the baseball game he could hear coming from the children's den. He smiled absentmindedly at her. 'What's that then?'

Deirdra pushed her hair from her face and grinned. 'Guess. Come on, try and guess.'

She was like a big kid and he decided to humour her. Christ knows he didn't spend much time with her, the least he could do was be civil. It made life easier in the end.

'What's the big news, chicken? You know I'm useless at guessing games.'

She beamed at his use of the name 'chicken'. It was what he used to call her when they were first married. When he still liked her.

Because she knew better than anyone that it wasn't keeping his love that was the difficulty in her marriage; she would be happy if he could just *like* her again.

Placing her hands on her cheeks, as she had once seen Demi Moore do in a film, she said gaily: 'I'm pregnant again.'

She still smiled even as she saw him blanch. She still forced a smile as she saw his lips set into a grim line, and she was smiling as he threw his napkin on to the table and put his head in his hands.

'You're joking. Tell me you're joking!' His voice was low, angry.

She shook her head, her smile gone now, her face as white and strained as his.

They were both silent for a while, each staring at the other like antagonists before a fight. Deirdra was having trouble holding his gaze. She was distraught. For all these years she had tried to keep this man interested in her. When she had married him, she had seen him as her escape route, a chance to have a really good life of her own. But instead she had fallen deeply in love with him, and it had never left her. No matter what he did, how he used her, how he spoke to her or neglected her – and he neglected her shamefully at times – she still carried on loving him.

She had tried to be a sophisticated woman for him, tried to make a home he would want to come back to. Had given him child after child to tie him to her. And now, finally, she had to admit: she had failed. The look on his face would have broken the strongest of spirits. It was certainly breaking hers.

'I don't fucking believe you, Deirdra,' he began harshly. 'Ain't we got enough kids? Bearing in mind the fact you lose all interest in the poor little fuckers when they start walking and talking. We agreed after Paul that nine was more than enough. But no, you think that by having another child, and probably another after that, you'll make me want you.

'Well, lady, you can't make people love you. You just can't. I've tried. You're the mother of my children, and God help me I've got enough of them. But that is it, that's as far as it goes. You hold no attraction for me, you never really did. You're a shallow, boring, spoiled little mare, like one of those Jewish princesses you knock about with, only Irish.

'Money cushions you, has always cushioned you. But you can't buy my love with money or with babies, darlin'. The sooner you realise that the better. I pay the bills, I make sure we all have everything we need, but that's as far as it goes. Have the baby, go for it, but I'll never come to your bed again after this. You'll not catch me out again. No fucking way. It's a chore, Deirdra, a fucking chore, mounting you and heaving away on top. I think about everyone and anyone while I'm doing it, because you hold no interest for me. So, you have this baby and make the most of it, because it's the last one you'll ever get from me.'

Deirdra sat and took all he had to say without batting an eyelid. What was it about Eamonn Docherty that made her want him so much she couldn't bear the thought of living without him, even though she knew that then her life could only be better? Without him she would grow, become someone, the person she really was. Instead she'd tried everything and anything to be what she thought he wanted her to be.

She suddenly saw him with stunning clarity for the first time ever. Saw him for what he really was. Shaking, she lit a cigarette. Her hands were trembling, her heart beating too fast. Utter humiliation was burning inside her.

'Do you know something, Eamonn?'

He didn't even look at her as he answered. 'What?'

'I've given fifteen years of my life to you.' Her voice was low, but surprisingly clear. No trace of the usual tears or temper. 'I have spent nearly seven of those years pregnant . . .'

'Well, whose fault was that?' he interrupted.

She placed both hands flat on the table and yelled, 'Listen to me, *I* am talking now!'

He was so shocked, he did as she asked.

'God help me, I've loved you through all those years. When you stayed out all night. When you came home with the smell of another woman on your body. When you didn't even remember that it was Easter, or Christmas, or one of the kids' birthday. How many times did you fly off to Las Vegas on Christmas Eve? How many times did you visit England or somewhere else and not even ask me if I minded you going, let alone did I want to come? Oh, I admit I've been difficult over the years, but it was because

I loved you so very much. Now I have been given the final humiliation. So, in future, I won't ask you for anything.

'I'll have my child. I'll have this baby. *My* baby. And as God is my witness I'll never trouble you again, though how a wife asking for a bit of her husband's time or affection is wrong, I really don't see. You could have pretended you cared, Eamonn. Christ knows you could at least have pretended. You have been cruel, so cruel, over the years. But I never stopped caring and hoping.'

She stood up then and her dignity amazed him.

'If you want to leave, then go, I'll understand. If you stay we will play our game of pretend as usual. God knows I'm used to it, I've played the game for fifteen long years. But even I can see it's a pointless exercise now.'

As she walked from the room he was stunned.

That Deirdra could talk to him like that!

She closed the door softly behind her and he suddenly felt as if he had lost something precious; a great void welled up inside him, one he knew would never be filled.

Because he had deliberately destroyed someone. A small person, an insignificant person.

And that person was his wife.

Eamonn made his way to the apartment in Manhattan that he always rented for Tommy's visits. It was off Fifth Avenue, central for everywhere and upmarket enough to walk out of at night without too much fear of being mugged. As he got into the lift he was whistling, because from Tommy he got his news of Cathy.

Over the years he had thought of her so much it was unbelievable. Sometimes he thought about her for days on end, going into a minor depression over her. Knowing that Tommy had her whenever he wanted was like a knife thrusting under his ribs. Listening to the other man constantly singing her praises made him jealous inside. He wanted what Tommy had.

And he could have had it so easily!

He played at being mates with his English counterpart. He acted the big man, taking Tommy out and around New York, hoping all the time that his friend was going to go home and tell his wife how well Eamonn Docherty was doing.

He knew it was childish, stupid, but it was what he had been doing for years.

Through Tommy, he felt he had access to Cathy, even though he had not laid eyes on her in all that time.

Tommy answered the door with a wide smile. Eamonn walked inside and heard the shower running. He raised his eyebrows meaningfully.

'You were quick. Not an hour off the plane and already you've got a bit of company, eh?'

Tommy looked sheepish. 'It's Carla, I always ring her. We've got an understanding.'

Eamonn walked through and sat down on the white leather sofa. The view of the Manhattan skyline was breathtaking, but he was used to all that now. It didn't interest him. In fact, at times he yearned for a look at the good old Thames. As full of shit and polluted as it was, he missed it. Like he missed a proper cup of tea, a full English breakfast and Saturday night up the Palais.

He grinned at his own thoughts. 'So how's everything back home?' he enquired.

Tommy shrugged. 'Same as ever.'

'How's the wife and kid?'

Tommy sat down and said happily, 'They're both fine. Kitty gets more like her mother every day. Although she's dark like me, she has the blue eyes and the temper of her mum. 'Course, if Cathy knew about Carla, my life wouldn't be worth living! But it's like anything else, you know, Eamonn. I need things – things she doesn't give me.'

Eamonn nodded, but for the life of him could think of nothing better than having Cathy there day and night to make love to, talk to, be with. But, unlike Tommy, he wasn't married to her.

'What doesn't the delectable Cathy give you, eh?' he asked curiously.

Tommy sat back in his chair and Eamonn was startled to realise that his visitor was already high.

'For a start, she doesn't ever give herself – Cathy. She has never given herself to me. From the day we married there's been something standing between us, I don't know what it is . . .' He was quiet for a moment before he said in a slurred voice: 'Yes, I do know. I'm lying. She hates me working for the IRA, no matter how far from the violence I am. That's why she won't ever have anything to do with you.' His voice trailed off.

Eamonn had never expected to hear such frankness from Tommy, even though he suspected the reason for it had more to do with drugs than true confession.

'Have you had a bit of coke?'

Tommy laughed then, a high-pitched, stoned laugh. 'Just a bit, plus some grass and a few ludes. I mean, might as well make a party of it, eh?'

Eamonn nodded.

There was no work being discussed here, that much was evident. Carla, six foot two and twelve stone of Puerto Rican womanhood, came out of the shower and smiled at him. She would happily take the two of them to bed but even Eamonn balked at that.

Getting up, he peeled five hundred-dollar bills from the

roll in his pocket and told Carla to make herself scarce for a few hours. Tommy, stoned out of his brain, was unaware she had left for a while. He just wanted to talk about himself.

'The thing with Cathy is, I love her but she has such high expectations, you know? She holds herself up like some kind of icon, and everyone has to live up to her. Every time there's something on the news about Ireland, I get the silent treatment. She drives me mad. If she said something, something concrete, I'd have a handle, you know, something to come back at her with. But I don't. She doesn't even use my money because thanks to the clubs she has more than enough of her own. I don't know why she stays married to me, and that's the truth. But then, in fairness, she has never once done the dirty on me with another man, that much I do know. Sometimes I wish she would, I really do. But then I look at her and I'm undone. I could never be without her. I'd kill first, kill her even, before I let anyone else possess her. It's crazy, isn't it? I would see her dead rather than see her with someone she could love, who could get a reaction from her. Because I sure as hell can't.'

Eamonn was shocked to the core. Never, in the twelve years they had worked together, had Tommy ever voiced anything but praise for his wife. Never had he given an inkling that things were as bad between them as this. His words now were a revelation, the shocking testimony of a man's wasted life.

As Eamonn had wasted his.

Tommy needed the devotion of a Deirdra, while Eamonn needed a woman like Cathy because only she was strong enough for him. He knew Tommy was drinking, had noticed that over the years. He should have realised why. Part of him was sorry for the man before him, and part of him was glad because he knew at last that Cathy wasn't happy, wasn't in love with another man. Which meant there was still hope for him.

As he listened to Tommy rambling on, Eamonn realised just how sad a man he himself really was. For all he had, as much as he had achieved, deep inside he was still the same spiteful boy who had clawed his way out of Bethnal Green, East London.

He wasn't proud of that fact. But Eamonn, being Eamonn, he wasn't ashamed of it either.

Later that night he took Tommy to a private club in Brooklyn Heights. Eamonn had bought the club five years previously with Petey and they used it sometimes when they wanted to entertain particular clients. It was a hostess club, except the women in it were high-class and were also specialists in their chosen profession. It looked like a dungeon inside and a tall woman in her forties, wearing a long red wig and high leather boots, was the resident dominatrix.

Barbarella catered for everyone and anyone, charging them astronomical prices to live out their most lurid and degrading fantasies. She had movie stars and even an ex-president or two on her books, and joked she could whip for America if it was an Olympic sport.

Barbarella dealt in humiliation and pain, and she knew her clientele well. In the dimness of her small dungeon rooms she beat everyone's secret out of them.

She also catered for people who liked inflicting pain, and the recipients were paid well in good old-fashioned dollar bills. She had women on her books who took a beating twice-nightly and loved it, their only stipulation being they didn't get hit on the face or arms, where it might show.

Even Barbarella had been amazed at the number of men

who wanted to inflict pain, who enjoyed hearing women beg and plead for mercy. Over the years she had got to know Tommy well; he preferred to be dominant, she knew, but was no serious threat to her slaves. Tonight she gave him a woman called Fenella. She was a fellatio expert who boasted she had sucked over a thousand cocks and loved them all. While she performed, she liked the men to pull her hair and attempt to choke her. It gave her performance an added edge.

As Tommy, coked up and full of drink, made his way into one of the smaller rooms with Fenella, Eamonn went through to the bar and ordered himself a drink. This had never really been his scene but he had perceived a gap in the market for such an establishment – an upmarket gap. There were plenty of these places that were like doss houses, but he had given this one sophistication and social acceptability.

He was proud of it in a way. When he saw the famous names and faces there it gave him a feeling of acute glee, because he knew every time he looked at these people that he was better than them. He provided them with their sick entertainment, took serious amounts of money from them, and could still look down his nose at them.

He had had two drinks and sorted out a few minor problems with Barbarella when a young man with long hair and a leather vest came over to them.

'You'd better see to your friend, Mr Docherty, I think it's time he went home,' he said in urgent tones.

Raising his eyebrows at Barbarella, Eamonn made his way to Tommy's room. He walked through the door, the young man close on his heels. What he saw then made him think he was caught in a bad dream.

He had never seen so much blood. It was everywhere: all over the bed, the walls, the floor, even the ceiling.

Tommy was covered in it, and for a split second Eamonn thought that he had been the victim of a hit. It was only when he saw the girl with her throat gaping open that he realised it was her blood everywhere.

She was soaked with it, all over her hair, her clothes, her body. Big fat red clots lay beside her on the floor, like pieces of liver.

Eamonn felt the bile rise inside his chest, and heard himself gagging. He shook his head in denial of what his eyes were witnessing.

He heard a voice coming through the haze of redness.

'We'll have to move her, Mr Docherty. We can't have the police in here, it'd be the end of us. I warned her time and again about winding up the puntcrs.'

The boy's voice was oddly calm and reasonable. Eamonn turned to look at him, feeling as though he was caught up in some surreal nightmare.

Tommy was crying brokenly. Tears and snot vied for possession of his face. He wiped at his eyes like a small child. He was naked from the waist down, and standing in a pool of the girl's blood. It was oozing up between his toes like a luxuriant carpet.

'Thankfully, like most of the girls who work here, she has no family – not close anyway. She was from Kansas, a runaway. She can just disappear. Her type often do.'

The boy's matter-of-fact voice was more chilling than the scene before Eamonn because in fact he was no longer seeing it. Instead it was Caroline's battered body that had returned to haunt him. He was back in the East End, a scared boy again. In Tommy's distraught face he could see and hear himself.

'What happened?' he forced himself to ask.

'From what I can gather off your friend here, she kept on taunting him. Fenella was like that. She was a submissive, but at times she liked to liven the games up, you know? She liked to make them really hurt her, because some of them just play-act. I heard her scream – I mean, you get used to screams in an establishment such as this, but I'm personally trained by Barbarella and I know the difference between a cry of delight and a scream of fear. I hold the pass keys, it's my job to monitor everyone. I came in and saw he'd slashed her with his glass. It's down on the floor there.'

The young man paused and said sympathetically, 'But she was a troublesome girl, so I wouldn't be too hard on your friend. Someone was going to do it to her sooner or later. Fenella had a death wish, you see.'

Eamonn nodded mutely.

'I'll call Barbarella in and we'll get this fixed,' continued the boy. 'There's a shower through that door. Get your friend under it and I'll find him some clothes, OK?'

Tommy was still crying and shivering from shock. Eamonn tried to move him but the other man was totally rigid and refused to go with him to the shower. A few minutes passed then Barbarella came in, minus her wig and boots, together with two large women. All carried black refuse bags and cleaning materials.

Eamonn stood and watched as Tommy cried and cried. Big bubbles of snot blew from his nose, and endless tears rained down his cheeks. Eamonn just watched him, fascinated.

'God, I'd have laid money on your friend. Who'd have thought he was wacko? Seemed a regular guy to me,' said Barbarella, shaken for once. Then: 'I'll have her taken to Mario's – they'll dispose of her body in the next cremation. Trust me, tomorrow she'll be blowing in the wind.'

Eamonn listened with a feeling of acute sickness inside him. When had everybody stopped caring? When had the world come to this? On top of everything else, he felt responsible. He had brought Tommy here, told him the score.

Cathy had been right years ago, but it had taken Eamonn this long to see himself clearly: he was scum.

Chapter Thirty-Seven

It was forty-eight hours since the girl's death and Tommy still had not spoken one word. He just sat in a chair in the Manhattan apartment and stared into space. Eamonn had tried talking to him, getting him to drink a cup of tea, to eat. All to no avail.

He knew that Tommy was in shock but he didn't know what to do about it. Jack and Petey had both told him to get in touch with one of the more amenable doctors. In other words, pay someone to treat him and keep it quiet. Eamonn had quickly found the right place. The discreet ambulance and three specially trained paramedics were coming for Tommy soon. There was just one thing more Eamonn had to do.

He dialled Cathy's number and recited the first prayer he could remember saying for years. He wasn't sure if it was a prayer for forgiveness or a plea to God to bring his Cathy back to him at last.

When Cathy walked through Customs at JFK, Eamonn was waiting. He wanted to kiss her but one glance at her set pale face told him it would not be a good idea. He had to content himself with squeezing her hand then keeping an arm casually around her shoulders as he guided her to the waiting stretch limo.

As they travelled on the expressway, she stared silently out of the window.

And Eamonn stared at her. Twelve years on she still looked like the girl he had left in England. She didn't look like a grown woman, the mother of an adolescent daughter. He had half expected to meet a screaming harridan, demanding to know what had happened to her husband. He should have known better. This was Cathy at her iciest.

She had come in on the night plane after he'd called to say that Tommy was in trouble, ill, and had been taken to a private sanatorium. She should look tired, red-eyed. Instead she looked crisp and fresh, but her utter coldness put Eamonn off his stroke. How could he tell this severe, unforgiving stranger the truth about her husband?

As if reading his mind she snapped at him, 'For Christ's sake, Eamonn, you've dragged me all the way across the Atlantic. I hope it wasn't on a fucking whim! Is Tommy OK or what? Will you please explain!'

She saw the confusion in his eyes and watched as he nervously adjusted his cuffs with hands that shook. Her swearing, her calmness, her utter contempt, had thrown him.

She laughed mockingly. 'Have the IRA put the word out on him, is that it? Oh, I know he's dipped into the Cause money because he told me. My dear husband is a gambler, a serious one. He owes money all over the Smoke. Spends his nights with hostesses after he's taken them to the casinos. Oh yes, my Tommy who really loves me and his daughter has got the gambling bug. He's always had it, only he could control it once upon a time. Not any more, though. So what's the score? I haven't much time – I need to get back to England and pick up the pieces of my life.'

The bitterness in her voice spurred him into action. Her life was laid bare to him with those few words. He felt he wanted to protect her, take care of her . . . even though she would probably rather be bitten by a poisonous snake.

Briefly, he told her what had happened.

Cathy's face tightened imperceptibly but she didn't show any other emotion and even that was gone in the blink of an eye. She stared out of the car window once more. He lit her cigarette.

It was another glorious New York day. The sun was high, the traffic thick, and the pollution could knock you to the ground. Inside the air-conditioned car he watched as she smoked her cigarette, hands steady, breathing shallow.

'What is it with men and death, eh?' She shook her head sadly. 'I killed, and you know why. Now I live with it all the time; it's blighted my life. I stayed with Tommy because of what happened to me as a child. I married him to escape you, and then I found out he was in as deep as you were with death. Everyone I have ever loved has been involved in death.

'I fall asleep,' she whispered, 'and I dream and then I see Ron and the blood everywhere. And do you know what's the worst thing? For all he was, he didn't deserve to die like that. Poor old Madge was on a losing streak all her life. It was inevitable that something like that would happen one day. Only as a child I didn't know that, did I? I loved my mum despite the squalor and the neglect. I loved her, I really did. Now I love my child, and she knows I do. I tell her so every day of her life.'

He heard the bitterness and loneliness in her voice and his heart went out to her.

'I have to look out for her, you see. I can't risk her

ending up like we have, you, me and Tommy . . . poor Tommy who just wants to be happy. Kitty can't bear him, she sees through him, knows that he's weak. I never loved Tommy but I stayed with him. It was easier to be Mrs Pasquale with the perks of the position than it was to go and make a proper life for myself. Besides, I'm incapable of ever loving a man. The closest I ever came to it was with you.'

Eamonn felt poleaxed. Of all the things he'd thought she'd say, this was the most unexpected. Yet it was music to his ears.

'Where is Kitty?' he asked. 'Who's taking care of her?'

Cathy put out her cigarette and immediately lit another. 'She's at boarding school, and Desrae will have her if I need to stay on out of term-time. So, Tommy . . . the sanatorium, are they taking good care of him?'

Eamonn nodded, happier now he could tell her something concrete. 'It's the best, a privately owned establishment in the suburbs. The doctors are sound—'

She interrupted him. 'You mean, they can be bought off, paid to forget what their patient has done?' Then she stared at him through slitted eyes. 'Are they going to let him come home?'

Eamonn shook his head. 'He needs specialist care. They say he's had a breakdown of some sort. According to the doctor it had been coming on for a long time. The incident in the club, brought it all to a head.'

Cathy gave a chilly little smile. 'Every time a bomb goes off, I reproach him with my eyes, can't bear him near me. And he can't stand it either. But he can't get out. He explained that to me years ago.' She leant forward and he could see the swell of her breasts through the thin material of her blouse.

'You're all owned and you can't see it. For all this wealth, you're not your own men any more and you never will be. I asked you once, many years ago, if you could sleep. Well, maybe you can but Tommy couldn't, and neither could I. Do you know, I almost envy him. At least this way he'll be out of it now. Even the IRA won't want to deal with a fucking madman, surely?'

They didn't talk any more after that. She was right about one thing – Eamonn was no longer his own man. But as far as Tommy went she was wrong. He wasn't out of it. Not yet.

Tommy sat in the luxurious room, dressed in silk pyjamas, staring vacantly at nothing. Cathy sat beside him and looked into his eyes. She knew that wherever he was now, he was a world away from this hospital and the life he had led in the past.

She sighed. 'How much is all this costing?'

Eamonn was quick to reassure her. 'I'm paying, don't worry about it.'

She looked at him, her blue eyes flat and hard as she answered. 'I had no intention of paying. I just wondered how much it cost to turn your back on murder in a discreet private bin. No, carry on, you be the Good Samaritan, it suits you. There's a twisted morality here. You caused this, and now you can rectify it.'

She stood up. 'I'd like to go and book into a hotel, if you don't mind.' She was so cold, so distant, he felt she was a stranger. That he had never really known her.

'I have an apartment you can use while you're here,' he suggested. 'A hotel is no place on your own.'

She nodded. 'Whatever. So long as you don't think you can come and go as you please.'

He bit his lip to prevent a retort. 'I'll take you now.

537

Would you like to speak to the doctor before you go?'

'What for? You've told me all I need to know.'

Cathy sat in Eamonn's apartment and stared at the city of Manhattan, lit up with coloured lights and stars. It was a beautiful, breathtaking sight and she enjoyed looking at it. Somehow it brought her peace.

Eamonn had filled the fridge with food, and there was a full bar with anything a person could desire. She had poured herself a generous measure of Napoleon brandy which she sipped as she sat in the dark and looked out over the city.

One entire wall of the apartment was made of glass and it was so stunning she forgot her worries for a while as she looked at the view. It was a huge apartment and despite herself she'd been impressed. This annoyed her, because she knew it was what Eamonn had intended.

He wanted her to know how well he was doing, how much money he had. She settled back in her seat, still staring out at the view but seeing only Eamonn now.

Every time she looked at her daughter she saw him. He was Kitty's father though Tommy had never once cottoned on. All those years and Cathy had not conceived again. At times she had wanted another child so much it had made her ache inside. It would have been something to offer her husband. They had come together as man and wife many times but Tommy had always known that she didn't really want sex with him. Didn't want the contact.

Afterwards, they would lie together in silence, both feeling that something dreadfully wrong had happened, which of course it had. They had taken something beautiful, something wonderful, and destroyed each other with it. He had given her his love, and she had thrown it back in his face.

Cathy swallowed down tears and poured herself more brandy. She needed to anaesthetise herself tonight, because if she didn't she would ring Eamonn and ask him to come to her in her loneliness. For all her fighting talk, she would still go to bed with him because she wanted him, God help her, she had always wanted him. He was like a part of her, like her second self.

She had loved him all her life and couldn't stop herself now. But she must never let him know that because then he would take advantage of her. He wouldn't be able to help himself: it was how he was made.

Eamonn was in a sports bar off Madison Square Gardens, eating a rib-eye steak and deep in conversation with a large man called Igor Travenovich. Igor was a Chechen who had fled to America five years before and was now the head of a Russian family similar to the Mahoneys.

The two men got on well. They were both hard-nosed and business-minded before anything else. Their similarities made them good friends. Both egoists, they couldn't help but like what they saw in each other.

'You understand the stuff must reach London before seven days? I hear the carrier is ill. Has had many troubles,' Igor told Eamonn.

'It's sorted, everything will run to schedule, I promise.'

Igor nodded. 'You understand I must make sure that everything is fine, yes?'

Eamonn laughed through a mouthful of steak. 'I would do the same, mate. So don't worry. No offence meant and definitely none taken.'

Igor nodded. He had the bearing of a military man, the squared shoulders and steady-eyed look.

Eamonn knew that the Russians and the Chechens and all the other breakaway states were going to mean trouble at some point. In New York there was such a variety of criminals it made you dizzy to contemplate their number. Eamonn had dealt with many different nationalities over the years, from Cubans to Jamaicans, South Americans to Chinese.

Each had their own speciality, and each their own way of doing things. Eamonn, never averse to learning new tricks or taking on new business, had enjoyed his forays into their worlds. The Mafia and the Irish were now dealing with people who resembled themselves fifty years before – new races who came to the US with the express intention of making money.

Eamonn could identify with that, because he had felt the same way. America was a cultural melting pot and he knew that England these days was not far behind. With England, though, the size of the country curtailed much of the criminal activity. America was so vast, there was more than enough room for everyone. Now that the Irish and the Italians were practically legal, the new rich – the Russians and all the Eastern Europeans – were coming in and making New York their own with their violence and black market money.

'I hear the London man has had a very bad time of it,' Igor commented.

Eamonn smiled, showing his expensive teeth. He always vowed that one of his sons would become a dentist. It was one of his jokes that in America it was a sure road to riches without ever needing to use a gun.

He wasn't joking now. 'Look, Igor, as long as I deliver my end of the bargain, I don't see why you should stoop so low as to listen to gossip. The man has problems. We all have problems at some time. It's in hand, it's sorted. Your merchandise will arrive on time. Let me worry about Tommy and drop this conversation – now.'

Igor fell silent, eating his ribs and shrimp. Eamonn clicked his fingers for the bill, even though they had not finished their meal, and ten minutes later they left the restaurant.

Igor shook hands before getting into a yellow cab. Eamonn walked past the Gardens, watching the comings and goings of the people for the game.

He felt deflated. Igor had dared to query the way he was handling Tommy. It showed the consensus was the Irish were losing ground. He had noticed some alarming new developments over the last few years. The Russians were now banking everywhere; they were the new Mafia. They were jumping into bed with everyone, and then jumping out again after administering a right royal fucking.

Tommy's mistake was known to them now and that wasn't good at all. Tommy Pasquale had become a liability. It was Eamonn's job to take him out. But in his heart he knew there was another reason why Tommy had to die.

Eamonn wanted for himself what Tommy had been given but had never really possessed: Cathy.

Chapter Thirty-Eight

Cathy had fallen asleep on the sofa. Even though she was in a strange city, and on a strange mission, her sleep was untroubled. She lay there, her face at peace, her breathing regular and shallow. Her sleep was deep enough for her to avoid dreams.

Eamonn stared down at her: at her soft skin, her long eyelashes, visible in the breaking dawn, and her breasts, spilling from her robe. He felt himself hardening. Never had he wanted a woman more. Never had he gazed upon anyone with such longing.

Her arms were above her head, the pose childlike. It was how she had slept as a little girl, with him beside her in the bed, his cold feet always on her back.

The thought made him smile.

He knew that he should not have let himself in, even if he did own the apartment. She was entitled to her privacy, entitled to be alone and to use the place as her home. But he had sneaked in just to look at her, just to see her in repose.

He stared at her body hungrily. He could just see her pubic hair through the thin material of her negligee. It was still thick, blond and luxuriant.

He put his hand up to his face, covering his mouth. He suddenly felt a great urge to cry. To weep over their wasted lives.

'Make the most of it, Eamonn, this is the nearest you'll ever get to me.'

Her voice was low, husky, and it made him start. Looking at his face, Cathy smiled lazily. Then, sitting up, she read-justed her clothing. As she covered her breasts he felt a great sadness, a sense of loss inside him. For him she represented safety and love; had done since they were children. It was this that attracted him to her still.

He sat beside her and said brokenly, 'I just wanted to look at you, that's all. Just look at you like I used to when we were children.'

She heard the plea in his voice and knew that it was answered inside her; she wanted what he wanted. She wanted to pull him on to her, wanted to take his hand and place it on her breasts. She wanted him to ride her hard, to use her roughly. She had dreamed of it often enough over the years.

Instead she sighed gently.

'We're not children any more, you know, we're all grown up and we've both made complete shite of our lives. I have my club – it's one of the best known places in London now, the *La Cage* of Soho. It's a tourist place, a good night out. And I have Kitty. If I didn't have her, I don't know what I would have done over the years.'

She was silent then, filled with thoughts of her daughter. Eamonn watched her profile. She had not changed since a girl. She was the one person he had ever really loved, he knew that now, unequivocally.

'I love you, Cathy. Always did, always will.'

She turned to face him, her eyes pained. 'That's not fair, Eamonn, and you know it.' Her eyes were shiny with unshed tears. He knew then that she still loved him; deep inside she had never stopped loving him.

People like Cathy loved one hundred per cent. They were loyal to their lovers, wanting only them. She would forgive her lover anything. The bond forged as children was still strong and he sensed that she would let him take her now with no more protests.

He pulled her to him then, opening her mouth with his own, forcing her lips apart with his tongue. He tasted of cigarettes and Grappa, smelt of smoke and Paco Rabanne, always his aftershave.

She felt the touch of him as if it was burning through her clothes, felt the heat spread over her body, into her breasts and between her legs.

She was pulling his clothes from him, ripping at his shirt, the buttons flying everywhere, dragging at his body. Forcing him down between her legs, making him eat her, taste her. Arching her back to meet him as he gently kneaded her breasts and feasted on her.

As she felt the beginnings of her orgasm, she held his face to her body, wanting to drown him in her juices. He was hard, ready for her, and as he rose above her she watched him enter her, his thickness making her want him more. Never had she felt like this before, never in her life had she wanted anyone more.

It was a revelation to her, that these feelings had been inside her for so long, suppressed, unused.

She met him thrust for thrust, and as she felt him tighten, felt his whole body stiffen, she climaxed again, a longer, more intense orgasm than before.

It was over in minutes but neither of them had ever experienced anything like it.

He held her to him, feeling all-powerful, as if he could squeeze her until he broke her bones. Their breathing was still erratic, he could feel the quick beating of her heart. Finally he knew the meaning of real love-making and it was a revelation. He knew that he would never again feel like this with anyone.

They didn't speak, there was nothing to say. Eventually he rose and picked her up like a doll, taking her into the bedroom. As they lay on the bed together, they both felt as if they had come home. Tommy was forgotten, Deirdra was forgotten, their children were forgotten as they enjoyed each other.

It was a honeymoon period, a time for them alone, and they both knew they had to savour it while it lasted. Whatever happened now, they were once more an item, once more together, and neither wanted to think further than that.

Harvey O'Connor, a third-generation Irishman, was dressed in a white coat and loafers. His good suit was covered up, around his neck he had a stethoscope and in his top pocket a collection of scissors and medical implements.

He looked at himself in the mirror of the washroom and winked approvingly. He was nondescript, his sandy hair and brows making him blend into any crowd. As he left the washroom he smiled at two young nurses and they smiled back absentmindedly.

In the pocket of his white coat he had a syringe already prepared and as he entered Tommy's room he was smiling reassuringly. Tommy was still in a state of shock, still staring ahead. His breakfast was beside him, uneaten. The smell of eggs was rife in the room, and made Harvey screw up his nose in distaste.

He took the syringe from his pocket. It contained a mixture of insulin and cyanide. No one was too concerned what he did; the death certificate had already been written out hours ago. It was just a case of taking the appropriate steps. In other words, administering the injection and leaving the hospital with the minimum of fuss.

A nurse, a middle-aged Mexican called Juanita, would discover the body and alert the right people. As Harvey pushed the needle into Tommy's arm, he noticed the man's healthy muscular physique and sighed. It was a shame, but it had to be done.

This was worth twenty thousand dollars to him, and unlike most jobs he was to talk about it to certain people.

It was to become known that a murder had been committed.

Whether it was the prick of the needle or the inherent urge to live which is strong in everyone, Tommy turned to face him, pulling his arm away in the process. Harvey dragged Tommy closer, forcing the needle in deeper. He plunged the poison into his system and watched in satisfaction as Tommy's eyes glazed over and his life was quickly extinguished.

Harvey let out a deep sigh of relief. The last thing he wanted was to have to beat the man to death, or try and suffocate him.

Positioning the body on the bed in a sleep position, he closed Tommy's eyes and pulled the sheet up around his neck. Then, smiling gently, he picked up a piece of Tommy's breakfast toast, scooped some scrambled egg on to it, and ate it. It was cold, but he was ravenous. He even sipped at the coffee, grimacing with contempt at its cheap taste. Hospitals were the pits where food was concerned.

On cue, Juanita entered the room at nine-fifteen. He left then, and let the woman do her stuff. It was a job well done, and a profitable hour's work. What the hell? He had even had breakfast thrown in.

*

The call came at 10.35, as Eamonn and Cathy emerged from the shower. Eamonn took it and afterwards showed the practised sadness of a funeral director as he told Cathy the news.

'Tommy had a massive coronary this morning. There was nothing that anyone could do. It was due to the drugs he had taken, and his lifestyle.'

Cathy sat stunned, numb with shock, as she listened to him talking. While she had been making love, her husband, poor Tommy, had been dying.

Eamonn guessed her thoughts and said gently, 'Come on, Cathy, we weren't to know, were we?'

She shook her head, her distress evident. He went to her and pulled her into his arms. She tried to break away but he held her tighter.

'Don't do this, Cathy, don't beat yourself up. You weren't to know what was going on, none of us was.'

She understood the logic of his words, but could not accept them yet. But she allowed him to hold her. Suddenly, she was cold, so cold. Her body felt as if it had been locked into a freezer, so chilled had she become.

Eamonn dressed himself then, knowing he would have to take her to identify her husband's body. As he slipped on his shoes he heard the buzzer sound. Coming out of the bathroom, he saw his wife and two youngest children standing in the hallway.

Cathy was white-faced, grim-looking.

Deirdra smiled at them both and said cheerily, 'Good morning.' She held out her hand to Cathy. 'I don't believe we've met?'

Eamonn closed his eyes and felt a sinking in his heart. Cathy stared at Norah as if she had seen a ghost. He ushered his wife and children through to the lounge and said sadly, 'This is Tommy Pasquale's wife, Cathy. Cathy, this is my wife, Deirdra.'

His wife stood there, all dignity and viciousness.

'Tommy died this morning,' he told her. 'I'm just taking Cathy to the hospital to sort things out.' He saw with satisfaction the shock on Deirdra's face. She even put her hand to her mouth, a gesture which on any other woman he would have enjoyed. As it was her pudgy hand annoyed the life out of him.

'My God, I'm so sorry.' Deirdra knew she was in the wrong, knew she was 'out of order', as her husband would have said. Knew that she had been barking up the wrong tree.

'So what brings you here anyway?' He pressed home his advantage. 'I thought I mentioned I was letting the place to some friends?'

He knew he was being unfair but to catch her like this, to have the chance to put her on the spot, was too much to resist. Cathy stared at the two antagonists and felt her heart sink. So this was Eamonn's wife, this was the woman she had envied over the years. This plump, unhappy woman, with the beautiful hair and the clothes that did nothing for her.

Deirdra didn't answer her husband; Norah did. 'Mummy said we'd come and get you, and make you come home with us.' Her little voice was matter-of-fact, her eyes dancing.

Eamonn knew that Cathy was aware of the situation and thanked God she wasn't a woman to panic, to let others unnerve her.

Cathy stared once more at the little girl and then said softly, 'I'd better get dressed.' She turned to Eamonn and said, 'Thank you so much for all your help. I'll be fine now, really. I know Tommy would have appreciated what you've done, he always had a high regard for you.'

Deirdra was mortified. This woman had just lost her husband and she, Deirdra, had arrived like the avenging angel.

'Please, my husband will take you to do whatever you have to,' she said hastily. 'I met Tommy many times at our house. He was a good man. He spoke of you and your daughter many times.'

In her ignorance, Deirdra had hit on the one thing to make Cathy crumple. At the other woman's words, she felt the tears come then her whole body began to shake with an ague-like shuddering. She collapsed on to the settee, her legs weak, eyes pouring tears.

Norah, a sensitive child, put her hand on Cathy's arm. 'Mommy, shall I get the lady a glass of water?'

Paul, only seven and frightened by all the emotion in the room, began to cry. Eamonn picked him up and cradled him in his arms. His eyes bored into his wife's. He conveyed his utter contempt for her in a matter of milliseconds. Even Deirdra's sadness and pain didn't make him any easier on her. He wanted to hurt her, wanted to make her pay for her intrusion, and he was doing just that.

Five minutes later she and the children were gone, her halting condolences still ringing in Cathy's ears as Eamonn poured her a stiff drink and forced her to sip it.

Finally, Cathy spoke to him. 'She wasn't what I expected.'

Eamonn sighed heavily. 'She wasn't what I expected either, but there you go. We were both disappointed in our own way.'

Cathy nodded sadly. 'Tommy tried, but I never really gave him a chance, you know? I was very hard on him, and yet I'm a hypocrite. A twenty-four-carat hypocrite. I made his life hell because of his involvement in the Cause. Yet you were the instigator of it all, and I don't care any more. Or not at this moment anyway. How I'll feel once I'm back in London, I don't know. I am as selfish as you, and I must admit that to myself.'

He took her hands in his. 'You're not selfish, you gave him a good life. He spoke highly of you and your daughter.'

'She's not his daughter, Eamonn, she's *your* daughter. I always knew deep down, but seeing your little girl today . . . they look like sisters. They're so alike it's unbelievable. That was Kitty as a younger child. That was her, from her hair to her voice. Tommy knew, I think, deep inside. All those years and we never had another, never once did I fall pregnant. She has his name, but nothing else.'

'He was her father, he brought her up, he loved her.'

Cathy shook her head. 'Kitty never liked him. I know that's weird, but it's true. She never really took to him, prefers Desrae, loves him, but pretty much blanked out her so-called daddy. In the end he gave her a wide berth. They were antagonists as she grew older. She won't be heartbroken over the news and neither am I, really. Isn't that a terrible thing to admit? In some ways I feel relieved about it all. Desrae will mourn him properly, but he'll be the only one. Tommy's mother died a couple of years ago, he had no one really close.'

They were silent for a while, each with their own thoughts.

'I'd like to see Kitty, I really would,' Eamonn said at last.

Cathy smiled at him through her tears. 'When you visit London, come to me. Promise me that you'll always come to me, Eamonn?' Her voice was heavy with distress. 'Don't abandon me now, after all this.'

She sounded so desolate. Then, as if she were playing a

part, she pulled herself together. Standing up, she said seriously, 'I'll have to make arrangements to take him home.'

Eamonn shook his head. 'We'll bury him here, that's the best thing. I can arrange it in no time.'

Cathy looked at the man she loved more than anything in the world and with those few words, in her heart, recognised that Tommy Pasquale had not had a massive heart attack. Somehow, this man was responsible for his death.

Yet, even knowing that, she couldn't hate him, because now that Tommy was gone, the drunken, drugged up Tommy, the gambling Tommy, the man with debts all over London, she could finally be free. Really free. Because she had known since the day of her marriage that Tommy would never have allowed her to leave him, he would have seen her dead first.

Her only thought was: *We are all tainted, the three of us. We're all tainted somehow and we will pay for it in the end.*

Jack Mahoney was in his Queens office. The area was once called Blissville and normally, as he looked over the industrial wasteland it had become, that made him smile. Not today. He shook his head sadly as he listened to Petey and Eamonn arguing.

'He had to go. Igor was nervous; Anthony Baggato even mentioned it, for fuck's sake. Tommy *had to go*. Now will you all leave it, please? I sorted it as I sorted Flynn. As I sort fucking everything out for this firm.' Eamonn's voice was loud, hard. 'I liked Tommy well enough, we all did, but he made a fatal mistake and we can't afford too many of those.'

Petey was not impressed. 'You did this all off your own back, Eamonn. We should have been consulted.'

'I did consult you, for fuck's sake!'

Petey bellowed at his friend: 'Only after the fucking deed was done! Harve told me, for Christ's sakes. I should have known before him. I should have been involved, but you just did what you wanted as usual, Eamonn. Fuck me, and fuck Jack.'

'I wasted him to keep us in the frame. If we'd swallowed him and his antics, we would all have been dead men pretty damn quick. Can't you see what's going down here? Igor isn't a fool, he isn't fucking stupid. He's involved with the Armenians, the Russians, and anyone else you'd care to mention. I can't afford to have him worried about anything, anything at all.'

Jack spoke finally. 'So who's going to mule now? Who's going to take the stuff over to England?'

Eamonn shrugged. 'I am. I'll take it over this time and set up something else while I'm there.'

Petey looked disgusted. 'I suppose you'll be holding the hand of Tommy's bereaved widow, eh? The fucking whore! You've been stupping her since she arrived, you think I don't know about it? That's why you wanted him out of the frame. This ain't nothing to do with business, this is pure fucking, nothing more nor less.'

Eamonn's fist made contact with Petey's chin a split second after he'd finished speaking. Petey was launched into the air and over the desk at a speed that belied his size.

Jack rushed to his unconscious brother and, looking up, said sadly, 'The truth always hurts, Eamonn. Remember that in the future. If you were Mafia, touching a dead man's wife would mean death.'

Eamonn laughed then – a nasty vicious sound. 'Well, we ain't the fucking Mafia and Petey ain't no fucking Lucky Luciano! When he wakes up, you tell him to think long and hard before he ever strikes up a conversation like that again. If he does, I'll fucking kill him.'

With that he left the office, his rage so acute he could almost taste it. Sitting in his car in the small parking lot, Eamonn let his temper subside.

Petey had in fact hit the nail right on the proverbial head, which was what had made him so annoyed. He tried to justify himself then. Tommy knew that as a prime mover in the overseas network he had no right to make himself vulnerable. What they were involved in could put them all away for so long, the word 'parole' would have left the dictionary by the time they were released.

Tommy knew the score, he must have been on a death wish. No one in their right mind would fuck with the Irish, or the American Irish, or for that matter the Armenians or the Russians. It was laughable that Petey, the man Eamonn had come to look on as a brother, who would steal the lead from a church roof and confess in that same church days later, should be the one to point out to him the immorality of his relationship with Cathy Pasquale. Even Jack, whose daughter he was married to, had not done that. Jack was a man's man, he knew the score.

He also knew his daughter's failings.

Eamonn's mind drifted back to long ago and a Mafia Don's daughter, then to Caroline whom he had killed without mercy in a moment of rage.

Women were his downfall.

Somehow he brought out the worst in them, and they brought out the worst in him.

But not Cathy. Never Cathy. She had been a constant throughout his life.

He saw Petey walking unsteadily to his car and felt the first flush of shame. He knew that they were probably as close as any two men were ever going to be. Getting out of the car, he walked over to Petey. It was a blinding day, the sun high, the air thick with the smells of gas and industrial smoke.

'I'm sorry, Petey.' Eamonn's voice was quick. Out of the corner of his eye he could see Jack observing them from his window.

Petey looked at him; his big moon face was hurt-looking and open. That was part of Petey's attraction. He shook his head sadly. 'You've changed, Eamonn. I never thought I'd see the day you'd raise your hand to me – *me* of all people. If you were anyone else I'd kill you for that. Rip your heart out.'

Eamonn sighed heavily. 'These are strange times, eh?'

Petey nodded. 'Very strange. We're killing all and sundry. What's the difference if we start killing one another?'

He shrugged nonchalantly. 'Years ago this was all I wanted from life, you know. I thought I wanted things: money, prestige. Now I look at any ordinary family in Central Park and I fucking envy them. Even though I know they're probably struggling to survive, I envy them because, unlike me, they sleep easily at night. They're not having to decide who lives and who dies. They don't have to listen to men always talking death and destruction. They don't have to be on constant guard in case someone is waiting to put them out of the fucking frame. Suddenly, I see myself as others would see me if they knew my life. What it consists of.

'I'm getting out, Eamonn, I have to,' he said vehemently. 'I'm telling the Irish they can do what they like, I'm taking early retirement and concentrating on my clubs and investments. Now I expect you'll be asked to put *me* away. It'll be interesting to see if you can do it. You know where I am – I won't hide or try to run. I'll leave it all to your conscience.'

With that he got into his car and drove away.

Walking back to his own car, Eamonn got in and sat

behind the wheel. But he didn't go anywhere; he didn't know where he wanted to go. Even Cathy was pushed from his mind by the enormity of Petey's words.

He watched the activity around him with new eyes. Listened to the sounds of industrial machines, heard the lone voice of a man singing.

Life went on.

No matter what happened to you personally, life went on for everyone else.

Two days later they cremated Tommy. Fine Lawn, the small company the Mahoneys used for occasions such as this, was a beautiful place just inside Staten Island. The service was attended by Cathy, Eamonn, Petey and Jack. No one spoke, and the short eulogy was uninformative. The priest had not known the deceased and it showed.

Cathy stood dry-eyed as her husband's coffin was carried along the small conveyor belt and disappeared behind the black curtains, ready for his fiery committal. Eamonn gripped her hand and she felt a measure of pity for the man in the coffin. If she had given him even a small amount of herself, he would have been happy.

But the revelation on her wedding day had killed any chance of that.

Yet the man beside her, who was the instigator of all their problems, she had forgiven. Or at least had accepted him for what he was. Why had she found it so difficult to do the same for poor old Tommy?

She knew the answer to that question; it was because she could not help loving Eamonn Docherty. Deep inside she knew he wasn't worth it. But that didn't stop her wanting the man beside her so much it was like an obsession. He was on her mind all the time, his touch was all she craved. Eamonn was once more her all, as he had been throughout her life, if she had only admitted it to herself sooner.

She took his hand as they left, the birdsong and the greenness of this place suddenly making her depressed. Cathy longed for the noise and traffic of Soho, for Desrae, for Kitty. And if she could have her Eamonn one weekend a month as he had promised, then life for her would be complete.

She didn't need anything else.

Chapter Thirty-Nine

As they walked through Heathrow, Cathy noticed that Eamonn was very subdued. Small wonder that he was wary of coming to England after his past associations. Caroline's murder enquiry was still open and no one could ever feel completely safe with something like that hanging over them.

It seemed that death always hung over them like a spectre, constantly hanging over their heads, when she wanted only to be happy with the man she loved.

Eamonn watched closely as his two large suitcases were put through the X-ray machine. He picked them up and put them on a trolley with Cathy's luggage then walked through customs with her, his natural grace and her natural beauty making heads turn in their direction.

A black cab took them back to Soho. Both were relieved to be on the home stretch of their journey – Cathy because she missed her home, Eamonn because the contents of those cases would have guaranteed him a hefty prison sentence if they had been discovered.

He sighed heavily as the journey finally got under way. Cathy put her hand into his and he held it tightly. The touch of her skin was like an electric shock coursing through his body. He finally had what he wanted, finally had Cathy in his grasp.

As he gazed at her, his eyes felt as if they had been given the opportunity to look into heaven. Such was the power of his feelings for the woman beside him, at that moment he wanted nothing more from life than this: just to hold her hand.

Desrae was dressed in his finest: a pale pink Oscar de la Renta suit with pearl buttons. He smoothed it over his thighs, and admired himself in the mirror in Cathy's bedroom. He checked the room once more and was satisfied. The whole place was immaculate, and full of flowers, the bouquets filling the flat with their fragrance. In the small hallway he had placed a large bowl of sunflowers, and everywhere else were roses and gypsophila.

It looked lovely.

As he thought of poor Tommy, his eyes misted over with tears. Tommy was the son of the man he had adored for so long. It really was like losing his own boy. He was upset that Cathy had let the funeral happen in the States without his knowledge, but guessed, wrongly, that she'd been trying to save him from sadness and stress.

He walked from the bedroom and went to Kitty's room. She was lying on the bed, all long legs and coltish prettiness.

'All right, darling? Can I get you anything? Tea, perhaps?'

Kitty looked at him with huge blue eyes and shook her head. 'Not for me, thanks, Auntie Des. I've just had a glass of milk. What time is Mummy due?'

'Anytime. I thought she might ring from the airport, but I thought wrong as usual. She's probably up to her eyes, poor lamb.'

Kitty sat up, and put down the book she was reading. 'Do you think she'll be sorry that Daddy's died?' Her voice was low, genuinely curious, and for a split second Desrae felt a terrific urge to slap the girl's face. It was unnatural, the way she had shrugged off her father's death as if nothing had happened.

'Your father was a good ma—'

Kitty interrupted him. 'I know that – he was my father after all.' Her voice had the haughty quality she adopted from time to time. 'All I'm saying is, do you think that Mummy will be so devastated she might be ill or something? One of the girls at school, Sarah Palmer, her daddy died and her mummy tried to kill herself. Cut her wrists. It was awful.'

Desrae softened then. 'Mummy loved your daddy very much. We all did, love. But Mummy's a strong lady, a real East Ender. She'll rally round – for you if for no other reason.'

Kitty smiled then, transforming her whole face. 'That's a relief.' Her voice was a child's once more and Desrae was sad for the girl. Losing her father so young was not easy for her. He made his way to the kitchen and put on the kettle. The girl was his pride and joy, his grandchild. Even if she did call him Auntie. Not many girls would have welcomed a transvestite to their school open days but Kitty did. As she said: Auntie Dessie was Auntie Dessie and she didn't care what anyone else thought.

Desrae loved taking the girl around the West End with him, showing her off to people, going shopping. He could deny her nothing – which often caused friction between him and Cathy, who felt the girl was spoiled enough as it was.

As he prepared a tray, he heard the door of the flat open. Cathy was home, thank God! And God love her, she'd need him now more than she ever had before. He heard Kitty's screech of delight and smiled. Those two would always have each other – at least that would never change.

Walking out into the hall, straightening his wig, he stood frozen to the spot when he saw who Cathy had in tow: Eamonn Docherty, as large as life and twice as good-looking, his smile fixed and his hand on Cathy's arm in a protective gesture. Desrae knew immediately that he had administered a bit more than tea and sympathy.

It was there, in their eyes, their faces. The shock of it was overwhelming. Tommy wasn't even cold and they were already at it!

Picking up his jacket, he smiled tensely and said in a high-pitched voice: 'Well, I'd better be on me way. Pop round later, love, and let me know how it all went, eh?'

Cathy's face was anxious as she looked at her oldest friend. 'Aren't you staying?'

Eamonn said heavily, 'I was just leaving, Desrae, I have my bags in the cab. There's no need for you to go.' He smiled once more at Kitty, his eyes boring into her. Then, after kissing Cathy chastely on the cheek, he was gone.

The girl, unaware of the atmosphere, said loudly after the door had closed, 'Who was that, Mum? He's a real hunk.'

Cathy smiled. 'That's your Uncle Eamonn.' Her eyes met Desrae's, begging him not to say anything in front of the child.

'Mum, he's gorgeous! Why haven't I ever met him before if he's my uncle?'

Cathy laughed. 'Can I get me coat off and have a cup of tea before the twenty questions start?'

Kitty, at eleven already taller than her mother, made a mock grimace. 'I'll go and finish my book, let you and

Auntie Dessie talk, and make the tea, and then I want a chat with you on my own, OK?' Cathy nodded.

Desrae put down his jacket and Cathy followed him into the kitchen. 'Thanks for taking care of Kitty, Desrae, I really appreciated it.'

He didn't answer. He stood staring at his friend, his own face hard. 'What was *he* doing with you then? Mr Wonderful . . .'

Cathy sat at the table and put her head in her hands. 'Mr Wonderful helped me enormously actually, Desrae. He took care of the funeral arrangements, everything. I don't know what I would have done without him. Now, can I have a cup of tea? I'm parched. It's a long old flight from New York and the journey back into London was a traffic nightmare. I really don't need you and your bad attitude at the moment.'

Desrae was wrongfooted now and he knew it. 'I'm sorry, it was just a shock, seeing him here. You looked so very cosy together . . .' Placing a cup of tea before her, Desrae said unhappily, 'Tommy was special to me, you know that. He was my last link with Joey. My Joey was still alive inside his eldest son.'

Cathy was remorseful now for her own reaction. 'I know, and I'm sorry too, Desrae. It's been hard all round.'

'I had his sisters on the phone. I don't think they were very happy about the funeral being over there. I must be honest, I can't understand it myself.'

Cathy wiped a hand across her face. 'It just seemed like the best thing at the time.' She sipped her tea and lit a cigarette.

'It was quick, painless. He wouldn't have known much about it, at least we can be thankful for that. Now, if you don't mind, I really don't want to talk about it. As for Eamonn, he's a married man with nine children – yes,

Desrae, I said *nine* children, and another on the way. And if you think that makes me and him an item, then you're right. But all we're guilty of is picking up our old friendship. If Tommy's death showed me anything it was that life's too short to waste. Now, I think I'll drink me tea and see my daughter. I've missed her.'

She looked into her friend's face. 'And I've missed you too. A hell of a lot.'

Then, seeing the grief in Desrae's eyes, she cried. She cried because at last she had seen someone who was really sorry that Tommy was dead.

Wang Cheng was a small man, impossibly small even for a Chinese. He was only four foot ten inches, and his skinny body looked like a child's. As he bowed to Eamonn, he was smiling.

'Meester Docherty. How pleasant to see you.'

Eamonn gave a small bow back and then, laughing, the big man embraced the tiny one. Up in a small flat in Gerrard Street he unpacked his cases and transferred his clothes into two identical receptacles. This was achieved in minutes.

'No trouble at the airport?'

Eamonn shook his head. 'None at all. They're exceptional, I was impressed.'

Weng grinned agreeably. 'Such a big worry for such small items, yes?'

'Well, I'll have to find another mule,' Eamonn told him. 'Tommy passed away unexpectedly in New York.'

Cheng looked suitably sombre. 'I heard – my cousin in Chinatown told me. Very sad, such a nice man as well.'

Eamonn knew that Cheng was well aware of the circumstances; not much got past the old rinky dinks. But he carried on the pretence nevertheless.

'Yes, very sad. In his prime.'

'You make him sound like a piece of beef,' Cheng joked politely. 'Now I will bid you good day, I have to deliver these as soon as possible. I look forward to seeing you again before you leave.'

'Always a man of few words, eh, Mr Cheng?' Eamonn laughed.

'Western people talk for hours, Mr Docherty, but they rarely say anything of importance. I wish you a safe journey to your hotel.'

Eamonn picked up his suitcases and left, chuckling. Mr Cheng was a card, but he was also a very important part of their operation. The Chinese knew this and acted accordingly. Eamonn wished he could introduce him to Igor, the two of them would get on famously.

Instead of making his way as usual to the Ritz, he jumped in a black cab and went to Knightsbridge. He was using a contact's flat there. It would make it much easier for him and Cathy to meet.

He was humming a tune to himself as he made his way to his destination. He was back in his beloved London, and life was finally looking up. As he gazed greedily out at the busy streets his mind was on Cathy and her daughter Kitty, the beautiful child of his body.

Life had its compensations. It was just a shame it took so long to find them.

Kitty was curled up on the bed, her head in her mother's lap. Cathy looked down on her child and felt the tightening in her gut that seeing her daughter's lovely face always produced inside her. She had the best features of both her parents: her mother's sapphire eyes, her father's thick brown hair. Her skin was a porcelain white. Even her teeth were perfect.

'I'll miss Daddy, I suppose.' Kitty's voice was low, heavy with sadness.

Cathy sighed, heartbroken for her child. 'Sometimes when people die it's a relief for their families. I feel a little like that, though I wouldn't say it to Desrae.'

'Auntie Desrae loved Daddy too much. I loved him, Mummy, but I feel awful because I didn't really *like* him. Does that sound terrible?'

Cathy shook her head.

'You're very pretty, Mummy, I expect you'll marry again.'

'I beg your pardon?'

Cathy was shocked.

'Well, a lot of the girls in school, their mummies marry all the time and none of them is as pretty as you. Everyone says that at school. You're like a celebrity there.'

Kitty said this with pride and Cathy laughed. 'Well, I'm not a celebrity, not really.'

'You have the best club in London, everyone knows that at school because I tell them all about it. They think it's marvellous having men dressed as women all over the place. Auntie Desrae is the mascot of the whole school. Everyone is interested in him and how he looks without his clothes on. But I never tell them things like that, it's too private.'

'I'm glad to hear it.' Cathy loved Desrae, and to think of him being discussed by a bunch of kids as some kind of weirdo really upset her.

'I've told you before,' she said, 'Desrae is as much a woman as I am. He is a transsexual. But he feels he's too old to have the operation. Some men have it and afterwards live their lives as women. Desrae lives his life as a woman anyway, and he's a fine woman, a good person through and through.'

Kitty stared at her mother solemnly. 'I know, Mummy, but the girls ask stupid questions, like does he have periods, and things like that.'

Cathy suppressed a smile. 'And what do you say to them?'

Kitty tried her hardest to look all mysterious and superior as she answered. 'I just give them a cold look, and don't answer them.'

'Good girl. Now would you like to ask me anything about Daddy? I'll answer your questions as best I can, love.'

Kitty looked up at her mother with wide eyes and said honestly: 'What's to ask? He died, and really, Mummy, that's that.'

Cathy smiled down at her daughter but the girl's answer bothered her. She should feel something, surely? But maybe Eamonn's child was incapable of feeling the normal human reactions . . .

Cathy arrived at the Knightsbridge flat at 10.15. She was dressed casually in jeans and a white silk shirt, her make-up light, lipstick pale coral. She looked understated and stunning. Eamonn opened the door to her in a towelling robe.

'I have champagne on ice, and a few delicacies lined up for when we've built up an appetite.'

She followed him through to the lounge and as he handed her a glass of ice-cold Dom Perignon, said casually, 'I haven't got long. I'm supposed to be at the club. Kitty's with Desrae, and the girls – I use that term loosely – are all dying for a glimpse of me.'

As she sipped champagne, he undid the buttons of her blouse, freeing her naked breasts. He stared down at her and whispered, 'I love you, Cathy, I adore you.'

She smiled at him then, a long, slow, languorous smile. 'Same here.'

He kissed her, and within minutes they were in bed.

As they lay entwined later, both limp, skin shining with a fine film of sweat, she spoke what was on her mind.

'This is it now, for us. You'll come to me often as you promised you would. I can't be without you, Eamonn.'

He hugged her to him. 'I'll be here every month for a long weekend. There are a lot of things I have to take care of in America, you know that. But believe me when I say, I'd walk out on Deirdra and the kids in the morning, if that's what you wanted. You only have to say the word.'

She kissed his shoulder. 'I wouldn't be responsible for that. I want to have a relationship with you more than anything, but you have commitments and so do I. We can keep up a transatlantic romance. I can come out to you and you can come out to me. A weekend shopping in New York every few weeks would suit me down to the ground. That way we both make the effort and see more of each other than we thought.'

He was pleased, happy that she wanted to do this for him. He squeezed her to him tightly. 'That would be fantastic, darling. Whatever you want, I'll do.'

She grinned then, mischievously. 'Well, I can think of some unfinished business . . .'

He laughed loudly at her words. 'You're sex mad!'

'Only with you, Eamonn, only with you.'

He looked into her eyes then and said seriously, 'Remember that, because if another man touched you, I'd kill him.'

Cathy tried to joke though his words, and the meaning behind them, frightened her a bit. He sounded so intense.

'Thank God for that! I thought for a second you'd have killed *me*.'

Eamonn still wasn't laughing as he answered. 'I wouldn't rule that out entirely either.'

Cathy was stunned. He meant what he said.

She was saved from answering by the trilling of the phone. Eamonn picked it up and grunted into the mouthpiece. She watched while his erection subsided as if someone had burst it with a sharp pin.

He listened for a few minutes and then put down the phone.

'What's wrong, Eamonn? What's happened?' Her earlier thoughts were pushed from her mind at the sight of his white face.

'I have to travel home tomorrow, but I'll be back soon, I promise.'

She stared at his drawn expression and said forcefully, 'For Christ's sake, man, what's happened?'

He lay back against the pillows, eyes dead in his face, mouth turned down at the corners like a child.

'Just work, that's all. Just work.'

As Cathy comforted Eamonn in London, Jack Mahoney was mourning his brother in New York.

Earlier that day, as Petey and his latest girlfriend lay in their bed, tired after an afternoon's love-making, two masked men had burst in on them. They had opened fire with two Berettas, silencers only making the sound more harsh and deadly.

Between them the lovers took 200 bullets, the girl's lovely face being one of the first things to be destroyed. Lying entwined, they took the full force of the men's rage. It was all over in seconds, leaving only parodies of two people in love.

In the silence afterwards the only sound to be heard was the slow dripping of blood on to the expensive carpeting.

When Cathy walked into her home at 2.30 the next afternoon, Desrae was waiting for her, like a big wronged husband. His face was a tight angry red, eyes heavy-lidded with malevolence.

'Well, well, well, you took your fucking time!'

Cathy closed her eyes and said through her teeth, 'Not now, Desrae, OK? I've had more than enough to keep me going without you on my case as well.'

Kitty was listening from her bedroom, ears practically uncurling in her effort to overhear the conversation between her mother and Desrae.

'How's Eamonn? All right, is he? I assume that's where you've been. My God, girl, but you've got a nerve! Tommy, God love him, not cold in his grave, and your only trumping the man he worked for! What happened to all your high falutin' talk of yesteryear, eh? I seem to remember you referring to him as scum, amongst other things. What happened to change all that, eh? The old pork sword prove too enticing, did it?'

Cathy bellowed at him then, her own fury making her want to hurt her friend. 'Yes, that's it precisely. I couldn't wait to jump in the kip with him. I wish I'd followed my heart and done it years ago. So now you know, don't you? Happy, are you, Desrae? Happy now that you've made me admit I'm a no-good slut?

'I put up with more than enough from Saint Tommy. Believe me, I took my fair share over the years with him. I never loved him, not even when I married him. He was a weak and sad man, a drug addict and a drunk, you know that in your heart. He worked with Eamonn, and knew what he was getting into, and lied to me about it, lied to me for years, even though I knew what was going on, what he was really doing. I spurned Eamonn over it, but at least he was honest about it.

'Where do you think all Tommy's money came from over the years, eh? What did you think he was doing in New York all those times? Shopping? He was no better than Eamonn, so you have no right to judge him – or me for that matter.'

Desrae was white with shock and anger. 'You and Docherty . . . My God, you've held a torch for him all your life, haven't you?'

'Yes, I have held a torch for him. I love him, Desrae, and if you can't handle that fact, then there's nothing more for us to say, is there?'

Picking up his coat, Desrae stormed from the flat, slamming the door behind him.

Cathy stood alone and forlorn in the lounge.

Kitty crept out into the hall and said in a frightened voice: 'Mummy, why were you shouting like that?'

Cathy went to her child and embraced her tightly. 'Because friends argue sometimes, darling. They argue over the silliest things.'

One of Desrae's protégés, a young man called Colin Masters, stage name Roberta, was singing his rendition of Cilla Black's 'Surprise, Surprise'. At the end of the song, he always pulled off his wig and dress and stood, a young man, waiting for the audience to clap and cheer, which they always did, rapturously.

But Desrae took no joy in his performance tonight.

Though the club was packed as usual to the rafters, he took no joy from that either. Walking through the dressing rooms he smelt the familiar odours of marijuana and perfume. There were ten men in there, all in various stages of undress. Normally he was the life and soul, chatting and talking, joking and praising.

Instead he watched them silently, a sad smile on his face. Camilla, a huge black man who did a haunting rendition of Dionne Warwick's 'Walk On By', greeted him happily. 'Did you hear, girl?'

He stood, all thirteen stone of him, with his hands on his hips and his surgically enhanced breasts standing to attention like a sixteen year old's. With full stage make-up and no wig, he looked strange and somehow vulnerable.

'No. What, love?' Desrae's voice was dull.

Camilla grinned. 'I have had the offer of a lifetime.' He flapped his hands with a girlish glee that belied his huge frame. 'Six months in Las Vegas, what do you think of that, eh?'

Desrae smiled happily for his friend. 'Good luck to you, you'll enjoy it.'

Camilla screeched with laughter. 'The man who asked me – a really nice guy by the way, not averse to a bit of the old shirt-lifting – wants me to stay at his place and maybe see what evolves.'

Desrae smiled then, sadly. All the TVs were looking for the same thing: a man to love. Someone to treat them with respect, someone to love them back. Desrae knew from experience that the chances of finding it were very small. But he didn't have the heart to say so.

'Good on you, Camilla. I wish you the best of luck. But don't forget you're still into me and the club for fifteen hundred quid what you owe on the tits.'

'Don't worry, that's all been taken care of,' Camilla said coyly. 'Hank – that's his name by the way – is going to clear all my debts here before I leave.'

The girls all jibed at him for this and Desrae poured himself a glass of vodka from a bottle on the courtesy table, then sitting in a vacant seat, sipped it and checked over his own make-up. Little Joanie, a small white man who bore a staggering likeness to Judy Garland, said softly: 'You all right, Desrae?'

He nodded. ' 'Course I am, just tired, that's all.'

'Well, girl, I hate to say it but you look rough, you know what I'm saying?' Joanie's voice was low, heavily feminine and sexy.

Desrae nodded.

'How's Cathy? I haven't seen her for a while, the girls thought she'd have been in by now. Terrible about her husband, wasn't it? So young and fit for a heart attack.' He flapped his hands. 'Still she's a good-looking girl, and a real one at that. Won't be too long before she has a few men around her door, eh? She's so young to be a widow, and so pretty. Beautiful in fact.'

Desrae pursed his lips and didn't answer. Instead he finished his drink in one gulp and left the dressing room.

All the girls stared after him as he left.

'What's wrong with her then? Looks like she got her cock caught in her Spandex.'

Everyone laughed, but Joanie said forcefully, 'Tommy was like his son, all he had left of Joey Pasquale. It must be a bitter blow, losing him like that. I wouldn't have minded a love affair like they had.'

All the girls were quiet then, each thinking the same thing.

Desrae had been one of the lucky ones. At least he had experienced it. The most the majority of them would ever experience was raw sex and a quick goodbye. Joey had loved Desrae, everyone knew that. They were a legend in Soho, even all these years after his death, and the fact that his only son had loved Desrae as a surrogate mother had made him the envy of every TV. Even Tommy's daughter was a big part of Desrae's life. The girl called him Auntie Desrae.

A picture of a young Desrae and Joey Pasquale, both laughing gaily at the camera, hung above the bar. All the girls looked at it constantly and prayed that one day it would happen to them.

After all, if it could happen to Desrae there was hope for them all.

Joanie was singing 'Over the Rainbow' as Cathy spied Desrae at the bar. It was just after twelve and Kitty was ensconced with the girls in the dressing room, having a fuss made over her and getting tips on make-up and clothes.

Cathy knew that her daughter's forays into the club gave her enough kudos at school to keep her name in lights there till the year 2000. She didn't think it was a bad thing for Kitty to get to know the girls who worked for her. They might be men dressed as women, but they were all nice people, all the type you would want around your children if you knew them as well as she did.

They adored Kitty, and she adored them.

As Cathy approached the bar she smiled at the young men behind it. All dressed in silver sequinned bikinis, all with blond wigs and deep pink lipstick, they looked like girls, beautiful young girls. One of them winked at her and made a sad face at Desrae, trying to let Cathy know that he was down in the dumps.

She put her hand on Desrae's shoulder. He could see her in the mirror behind the bar. Cathy whispered in his ear, 'I'm so sorry, Desrae, I had no right to go off like that.'

It was enough. Turning, he said breathily: 'Hark at him hit the high notes!' As the audience broke into rapturous applause, the sound deafening, they smiled at one another, all their anger forgotten.

They stood together, surveying their club. It was a success story. No one would have dreamed, all those years ago, just how much of a success it was to become. It was a huge place now with a restaurant, three bars and an illustrious list of guest artistes. They even had a resident drag act who was rapidly making a name for himself on TV.

It was their baby, their goal together, and they had achieved all they had set out to do.

As Desrae embraced Cathy, there was a collective sigh from the bar staff.

'Had a row, have we?'

Desrae snapped back, ' 'Course we have. All women row, love, it's what sets us apart from the men.'

Cathy accepted a mineral water and sipped at it.

'If he's what you want, love, then that's fine by me. After all, who am I to tell you what to do, eh?' But Desrae's voice was sad, troubled.

Cathy kissed him full on the lips. 'You're my mother, father and best friend, all rolled into one. That's what you are, lady.'

Desrae preened with pleasure at the words but said sarkily, 'Not so much of the father bit, love, if you don't mind.'

Cathy giggled, but then said seriously, 'What would I do without you, Desrae? You're my rock, my shelter in a storm, my only real family.'

He cupped her chin in one large hand and said gently, 'Other than Kitty, of course – we must never forget young Kitty.'

As Desrae looked into Cathy's fine blue eyes he felt an urge to cry. All his instincts told him that, one day, Eamonn Docherty would hurt his beloved Cathy. Hurt her very badly. But she could see no wrong in him.

All he could do was wait, listen, and eventually be there

to pick up the pieces. After all, that's what friends were for, wasn't it?

Outside the club a woman watched the doorway. She was heavy-set and wrapped up well even though the weather was quite mild. She lit a cigarette with stubby fingers and drew on it deeply. As Cathy left with Kitty, the woman followed them back to their flat and then after they had gone inside, kept up her vigil once more: smoking and staring up at the lighted windows until the place was in darkness.

Only then did she walk away.

Book Five

Farewell, love, and all thy laws forever,
Thy baited hooks shall tangle me no more.

– Sir Thomas Wyatt, c.1503–42

Chapter Forty

London 1990

Cathy was packing for one of her weekends in New York. Desrae watched her, both of them carefully not mentioning the fact that they were once more at loggerheads.

'So, I'll go and visit Kitty, shall I?'

Cathy nodded. 'If you don't mind, Desrae. Look, I know you don't like me going, but surely you don't begrudge me a few days a month away from everything? I need the break as much as anything else.'

Desrae snorted. 'You mean, you need a bleeding good rogering!'

Slowly Cathy began to smile.

Desrae smiled too.

'You should listen to yourself,' she said tartly. 'Rogering indeed! I hope you don't tell my daughter that!'

Cathy placed an arm lovingly around her friend's shoulders. 'Please, Desrae, I need him. It's hard to explain but me and Eamonn, we go back years. It's like when I'm with Eamonn, I'm a whole person again. As if he's a part of me and without him I can't function. I know how you feel about him, and I understand that, but I can't give him up – not for you, Kitty, anyone.'

The finality in her voice hit Desrae like a slap across the face and, sighing, he bowed to the inevitable. Over the last three years Cathy had emerged from her shell and even Desrae had to admit that the woman before him was strong, able, and very, very determined. Nothing could keep her from her New York jaunts. A few times she had taken Kitty, and her daughter had loved it there. But most of the time Cathy went alone, so that she could be with Eamonn.

'Shall I make us a cuppa?' Desrae offered.

Cathy nodded, sorting through her underwear. 'That would be lovely. Splash a drop of Scotch in mine, I could do with a livener.'

Desrae left the room and went to make the tea, as happy in Cathy's home as he was in his own. When the doorbell rang he walked through to answer it, as always admiring his friend's taste in furnishings. Unlike his place, Cathy's was all subdued colours and antique furniture. It looked classy, or at least that's how Desrae always thought of it, though he felt if he lived in the place, it would be a bit too much like living in a museum.

As he opened the door, his face broke into a wide smile. 'Hello, Mickey! Long time, no see.'

Mickey, otherwise known as Michaela, stepped into Cathy's flat but there was no answering smile on his face. In full drag he looked stunning. Today, without make-up and dressed in slacks and jumper, he looked what he really was – a thirty-year-old man who dressed effeminately. He also looked worried.

'What's wrong?' Desrae asked him.

Mickey sighed heavily. 'Is Cathy about? I'll tell you together, OK?'

Desrae nodded, taking him through to the lounge and calling for Cathy. Five minutes later, armed with cups of tea, Cathy and Desrae listened in amazement to Mickey's announcement.

'Casper's topped himself.'

'*What!*'

Mickey sipped at his tea and daintily wiped his mouth. 'I said, ladies, Casper's topped himself. He was found this afternoon in his car. He'd put a hose through and died of carbon monoxide poisoning. He'd been dead since last night, I reckon. He left the club about two and even old Daniella said he looked really rough. But then, he's looked rough for weeks.'

'Who found him?'

'His neighbour. Apparently she'd asked for a loan of his lawnmower, of all things, and found him in his garage. She phoned the Old Bill and then the club. Shrewd old bird, by all accounts. Used to flog her arse on Park Lane years ago.'

'But why would Casper do that? He was fit as a fiddle and the shops were doing really well.'

Mickey sighed. 'I spoke to one of the boys in the shop in Old Compton Street. He said Casper was in trouble with Terry Campbell. By all accounts Terry had been in a few times looking for him, and Casper had told them all to say they didn't know where he was.'

'Terry Campbell? But what could Casper have in common with him? He's a pimp, the lowest kind and all. He deals in spring chickens – little boys.'

Desrae tut-tutted. 'If Terry Campbell was after him then he was doing something he shouldn't have been or he would have come to one of us, that stands to reason. I think we should have a good look at the stock in the shops. If he was selling anything under the counter, then we'd best know about it. See, Terry makes films, does the more lucrative books. Kids was always his forte.

'I remember him from years ago – used to cruise Soho looking for the young girls, offering them a place to stay and a hot meal, then he'd set up a deal and the girls would get a fucking shock. Terry only used them once or twice. They couldn't take more than that. He catered for men who liked a gang bang, five or six at a time, and videoed it all. The men paid a big price and got a nice souvenir video to remind them of their handiwork. The bloke isn't welcome around these parts and he knows it, but for all that he still has a good business. He just makes sure he keeps out of everyone's way.'

Desrae looked at Cathy and said sadly, 'He must have hooked Casper in.'

Cathy was horrified. If any of those videos were on sale in her shops . . .

She stood up. 'I'll cancel me flight. If Casper's been using our premises to peddle that crap, then I think we'd best sort it all out before we have Vice on our arses.' She looked at the two people before her and sighed. 'I'd never have believed it, though, not of Casper.'

Desrae wiped a hand across his mouth, as if to stem a feeling of sickness, and then replied: 'There's more to this than meets the eye. I'll talk to Gates, see what he can come up with.'

Cathy brightened. 'Good idea. After that we'd best have a chat with Susan P. She'll know the score with Campbell anyway.'

Desrae squeezed Mickey's hand. 'Thanks for letting us know so soon.'

Mickey shrugged. 'Someone had to get it sorted. Might as well be me as anyone else.' But for some reason he couldn't look Desrae in the eyes.

*

Cathy was tense and subdued as she turned the shops over looking for videos or books that should not be there. If Casper had been selling anything too risky, she was liable to lose her shops and a hell of a lot more besides: the respect of the Soho community, for a start, as well as the goodwill of the police. If Casper hadn't topped himself, she might well have done it for him, the mood she was in.

Richard came into the Wardour Street shops and she looked at him anxiously. He smiled. 'Relax, Cathy, I ain't going to nick anyone.'

She said sadly, 'I can't believe it, can you?'

'There must be something fishy going down because Casper was a diamond,' the policeman said. 'If he was peddling for Campbell, then Campbell had something over him, I'd lay money on that. What we need to do is find out what the rub was. Once we know that we're halfway home.'

Cathy gestured at the shelves. 'There's nothing here as far as I can see.'

'There's nothing at his house either – I had it searched as soon as I knew what was going down. We need to find that fucker Campbell and have a word with him. Maybe he can shed some light on it all.'

Cathy lit a cigarette. Taking a long pull, she sighed, blowing out smoke.

'Have you had the floorboards up?'

She shook her head.

'Well, I think that's where I'll start then. I mean, he's hardly going to have stuff that iffy under the counter, is he?'

'I suppose not.'

'Definitely not. What we need to do is find his contacts, anyone who might have an inkling what's going down.

Campbell is a nonce and caters for nonces, but he's branched out over the last few years into brothels. He keeps one in Paddington but the place changes addresses more often than you change your drawers. He uses empty houses to hold his parties. Afterwards they clear up and fuck off. It's hard to tie the ponce down. But someone, somewhere, knows all his moves, it stands to reason. If we can't find Campbell himself, we find one of his oppos then move in for the kill.'

'But where does Casper fit in? He hated nonces, you know that as well as I do.'

Richard shrugged. 'As my old mum used to say: It'll all come out in the wash. Now I'll start taking up the boards and you can put the kettle on. We'll worry about anything else when we have to. Meet trouble head on, so to speak.'

He smiled at her to take the edge off his words and Cathy did as he asked, but all the time her mind was whirling. Casper had been her friend, a good friend. She would never have believed it if someone had told her he was a nonsense. There was something wrong here and she was determined to find out exactly what it was.

Mickey went to the club after he had visited Cathy's flat and finished brushing out his wigs and pressing his dresses for the evening show. His close friend Leyla, a large-boned Mancunian with a deep throaty voice and impossibly large breasts, sighed heavily as he consoled Mickey.

'Poor old Casper, eh? What do you reckon the score was there? Do you think he was up to something?'

Mickey shrugged.

Leyla, always letting his mouth go, said loudly, 'Well, you spent a lot of time with him. Didn't you suss anything? I mean, you and him was mates . . .'

Mickey grabbed him by the chin and, pressing his face

close, said nastily, 'Why don't you just shut up, Leyla, give your brain a breather?'

Leyla's heavily made-up eyes were wide with shock – which was what Desrae noticed when he walked in.

'What the fuck's going on here?'

Leyla said quietly, 'Just a girlish tiff, that's all.'

Mickey stood up and said, in a high breathy voice, 'Sorry, Leyla. I think I'm overwrought, what with Casper and everything.' His eyes filled with tears and his bosom heaved and both Leyla and Desrae were all over him, petting him and telling him to sit down and relax. He'd had a big shock, as Desrae pointed out over and over again.

Mickey allowed them to fuss him, but when Desrae left the room to get them all a large brandy, he stared at Leyla malevolently and whispered: 'You keep your thoughts to yourself, OK? Otherwise you might just find yourself in big trouble.'

Leyla, real name Ronald MacVey, felt the first stirrings of fear. Michaela had always been a bit different from the other girls, had always kept his distance. After work, the others often made their way to a club in Tavistock Street where they loved to party in full drag and make-up, and put on a show for the straight men and women who enjoyed drag watching. Michaela had never done that. Now he thought about it, Michaela rarely mixed with his co-workers outside the club. A few of the other girls thought he had a secret lover, a real name. It happened like that sometimes. They got a politician or a TV star and afterwards kept a low profile.

Now, though, Leyla wondered what the hell Mickey was involved in that would make him utter such violent threats? Surely Casper had just topped himself? It happened a lot in the sex game. It got to you in the end. Maybe he couldn't hack it with the toms no more. Maybe he had had a thing with Michaela. Whatever it was, it was frightening Michaela, and he was bloody terrifying Leyla.

Cathy and Richard were in her flat drinking more tea and trying to think where Casper could have hidden anything he knew to be dangerous. The floorboards had been pulled up and all the shops turned inside out but there wasn't a thing to go on.

'I've had my boys pull his house apart, same again. Not a fucking sausage. Maybe we're barking up the wrong tree,' Richard said gloomily.

'So there was no note, to say why he topped himself?'

'Maybe the post mortem will show up something. Assisted suicide isn't unheard of, you know.'

Cathy's eyes widened. 'You mean, he was murdered?'

Richard scratched his chin. 'It wouldn't be the first time, would it? And if Terry Campbell is involved then I wouldn't rule out nothing. What time is Peter from the shop supposed to be here? He could give us a lead maybe.'

Cathy glanced at the clock on the mantelpiece. 'About an hour ago. Peter's only young, and I think he's frightened of the Old Bill so go easy on him. He only came out about a year ago and he's nineteen top whack. He's very effeminate, too, so don't intimidate him, OK?'

Richard grinned. His deep-set blue eyes looked positively evil as he answered: 'Why would I intimidate him?'

'You look frightening at the best of times. When you smile you can look terrifying, and you know it. You play on it. Only people like me and Susan P know that deep down you're like a teddy bear.'

He rolled his eyes and groaned. 'Well, don't let that get around my men, will you? I'd lose all me street cred overnight.'

Before Cathy could answer the doorbell rang. She came back accompanied by Peter's boyfriend, a small rotund man in his fifties called Brian Hacker. Brian was a business-man dealing in overseas investments – namely time shares. He had a permanent smile that displayed many gold teeth and was so black-skinned he shone like a well-oiled piece of ebony.

'Where's Peter?' Richard demanded bluntly.

'He's gone, taken his clothes, everything. He's also taken my jewellery and petty cash.' Brian looked very upset. 'I always keep about a grand in the flat. For expenses, you know. That's gone. He's gone.'

'Do you think he's fucked off, or do you think someone has removed him from the premises?'

Brian thought for a few seconds, then: 'I think he's fucked off, meself. He looked frightened this morning. I can't explain it, but he wasn't right, you know? I think something or someone has scared him away. We were happy enough, no big love affair but we got on well and had a rapport of sorts. I took care of him, and he took care of me. I like a bit of the exotic now and again; Peter provided it.'

He looked at Cathy as he said the last part and she nodded.

'Have you any idea where he could have gone?'

Brian thought hard. 'Originally he's from a place in Essex called Little Dunmow or something like that. His sister still lives out that way, but they weren't close. You know what the gay community is like: most of us leave our families behind with our old lives. It's difficult for some people to accept the real us, especially family. I know his parents have nothing to do with him. In fact, his father threatened him with a shotgun last time he visited his mother. Peter was a sensitive boy, really felt things. He was very cut up about it.'

Richard lit a cigarette. Blowing the smoke towards the ceiling, he asked, 'Did he have any other friends he might have gone to?'

Brian shook his head. 'Not that I know of, and that's the truth. The boy was small-boned, very feminine-looking, you know what I'm saying? One look at him and you knew he was a pillow pusher. Even his voice sounded like a bad recording of Judy Garland. He took a lot of flak because of that, kept himself to himself. He'd already had a few beatings, see. Other than working in the shop and being with me, he didn't really have another life. I took care of him, made sure he was OK.' His voice broke and he coughed to hide his distress.

Richard rolled his eyes at the ceiling. 'So there was no one else?' he persisted insensitively. 'A lot of the boys had their daddies, men like yourself, but they also have a lover on the quiet. You're sure there was no one else?'

Brian thought for a few seconds before answering.

'That boy was a loner, man, and in all honesty I don't have no truck with boys who have secret lives. That's how you get AIDS, man, you hear what I'm saying? He wasn't promiscuous, I know that, I'd lay my last penny on it. He had me and I was enough for what he wanted.'

'Did he leave anything behind at all?'

Brian shook his head. 'It's like he never existed. Not even a pair of pants in the laundry basket. I checked.'

Richard stubbed out his cigarette. Then: 'Do you know of a man called Terry Campbell?'

Brian nodded. 'Heard of him certainly, but I don't know him. I like the exotic, man, I admit that, but what Campbell offers ain't my cup of tea.' He paused for a second and then said seriously, 'You telling me that Peter was involved with *him*?'

Richard saw fear and repugnance in the man's eyes and

shook his head. 'Not directly, no, but the man he worked with might have been. Casper, his co-worker, topped himself.'

Brian's eyes widened, showing yellowing whites. 'Is that a fact? Nice old man too. Always polite when I went into the shop. He put the hit on Peter, you know. Peter told him no. Casper wanted him to do a bit of video work, but the boy was shy, man, really shy. That wasn't his trip at all. He was effeminate but not a performer, you know what I'm saying?'

'Well, thanks for your help, we appreciate it,' Gates said. 'If Peter gets in touch, you make sure you let us know, OK?'

Brian nodded. 'Gonna miss that boy, he was good company in his own way. Never argued, never caused no upset. Just a nice boy, you know what I'm saying?'

Cathy touched the man's arm and said gently, 'You're right there, he was a very nice young man.'

Brian stood up to leave, then turning towards Gates said seriously: 'He ain't gonna get himself hurt, is he? I mean, if that Campbell is involved then something dirty is going down. I have a few faces in Brixton and Tulse Hill if you need a bit of extra muscle, know what I'm saying?'

'I know what you're saying and I'll bear it in mind,' Gates told him.

'That boy wouldn't leave me without a word unless he was in big trouble, and he wouldn't rob me, man, because he knew he didn't have to. I would have given him the money if he'd asked. And I certainly never kept anyone in my home longer than they wanted to be there, you understand me?'

'We'll find him, don't worry,' Richard promised.

Brian nodded. 'I sure hope so. I hate to think of him running scared, and if Campbell is involved then he really has something to be scared of, doesn't he?' As he walked to the door he added an afterthought: 'I don't know if this will help, but I heard through the grapevine that Campbell has a flat in Norwood. I remember someone saying something about it a while ago. He bought it for his sister. You know she's black, not light-skinned like him?'

Cathy shook her head.

'Yeah, black as night, man. I heard another rumour too: that his sis has two children, and some people say they're Campbell's.' He grimaced. 'And they call me and mine weird, man! But I never wanted no one I was related to, you know what I'm saying?'

Cathy showed the man to the door. When she walked back into the lounge, Richard commented: 'If he'd said "you know what I'm saying" once more, I think I would have done him a permanent damage.'

'It's just his way. I liked him. He's obviously worried about Peter and so am I. Do you think the boy knows anything?'

'He either knows something or suspects something. Until we locate him, we can't speculate. I'm interested in this stuff about Campbell's sister. I heard the rumours years ago. Campbell is light-skinned, looks Mediterranean, but his father was black. The sister is stunning, apparently, and he's always been that bit too close to her. The parents were divorced. His father was an old-time bouncer: big, black and mean. His mother's only a little woman, but a real hard bitch. I remember having dealings with her years ago when Terry was first spreading his wings. Started out pimping for his cousin and gradually progressed to the big time. His real name is Trevale, he prefers Terry, for business purposes anyway. He's a Jamaican white man and thrives on it. Straddles two cultures and uses them both to his advantage. I think his mum needs a visit, as does Peter's sister. I'll get on to it now. Want to come with me?'

Cathy nodded. 'This is all really weird, isn't it? I mean, we don't actually know if anything's wrong, do we? It's all supposition.'

Richard gave one of his rare unforced smiles, and Cathy was reminded of how good-looking he could be when he wasn't acting his usual hard-faced self.

'Look, Cathy, where Campbell is concerned nothing is ever cut and dried. He's everyone's worst nightmare. He's scum, but he's clever scum. The lives he's ruined can't even be counted. I remember the first time I came across his handiwork. It was a young boy working the Cross. We'd brought him in for soliciting. The poor little fucker had tried to pull an off-duty Vice copper. Anyway, the long and the short of it was he was scarred up like you've never seen. I mean, this kid had been tortured in the name of fun. With cigarettes and knives and all sorts. If I told you it all you'd throw up, Cathy. I know I nearly did. I felt sorry for him, he was completely destroyed.

'Well, it was all Campbell's doing, and a while later we raided a bloke's house in Cheam, of all fucking places, and saw the boy being mutilated on a video. I have never wanted to harm anyone as much as I did that day! We've been after Campbell a few times but he always slides off the hook. Now, though, I intend to get the fucker, get him once and for all.'

Richard looked so upset Cathy had an urge to go to him and comfort him. The thought nearly made her smile because he was a big strong man who looked after everyone else. Instead she said softly, 'You're a nice man, Richard Gates, you know that, don't you?'

He looked up at her. 'Well, let's keep that between ourselves, shall we?'

'I'll get my coat.'

'You do that, it looks like it might rain.'

He helped her on with it, enjoying the feel of her close to him. Enjoying having a legitimate reason to touch her.

Together they left her flat and made their way to the Railton Road and Trevale's mother's house.

Chapter Forty-One

Terry Campbell looked at the boy beside him and smiled. The boy didn't smile back. He was staring at Terry's mobile phone, and trying to figure out a way to get his hands on it. He had no idea where he was, or what was going to happen to him. All he could remember was having a drink with this man, and then waking up here.

Johnny Cartwright was nearly eighteen, though he looked much younger than that. He wore his hair long and flowing, his eyes were a deep green and his teeth were white and even.

He knew he was good-looking. He had been making a living on the streets of London for over two years and in that time had heard a lot about Terry Campbell. When Campbell had approached him the night before, Johnny had decided to take the proffered drink and then scoot at the first opportunity. He'd heard whispers about what happened to the boys Campbell took up with.

But at the same time, he was not a man you insulted. You just avoided him as best you could.

Now Terry walked to the corner of the room and opened a small fridge. Inside there was beer and wine and also bottled milk shakes. He took out a strawberry one and handed it to the boy. Then he went to the window and stared out of it.

The boy stayed where he was on the bed. His head was thumping, and he knew it must be due to some kind of drugs. He had the heavy lethargy only they left you with. He took a guess at Mogadon but could have been wrong.

Terry turned to him briefly and said, 'There's glue in the cupboard if that's your poison. Otherwise I have a few sweeties you might want. You're the entertainment for a few of my friends tonight, and if you do a good job and don't panic, there's a two-hundred quid bonus for you, right? But if you start a load of upset then you get nothing but a good hiding, understand me?'

Johnny sipped at the cold milk shake, its sweetness soothing to his dry throat. He saw the camera equipment around the room, and the large-screen TV, and his heart sank. On a table by the bed were handcuffs and other sexual paraphernalia.

Finishing his milk shake, he felt the bile rise inside him and feared he was going to vomit. It was partly the milk on his empty stomach but mainly fear. He knew he was in for a nightmare experience. He had heard about these parties and knew that boys who had attended them had sometimes never been seen again.

Then he smiled grimly to himself. He was HIV. Well, maybe he'd pay back a few debts later this evening – though one of the older boys had said that many of the men who hired them and their like were HIV themselves. Johnny lay back on the bed, his head whirling.

What did it matter anyway? Who gave a toss about him? He'd take what drugs were on offer and try to get the night over with.

'How many men are coming?'

The boy's voice was low and Terry didn't look at him as he said nonchalantly, 'About eight, maybe more.' Johnny felt his heart racing once again and closed his eyes in distress. He heard Campbell laugh. 'Don't worry, there's a girl being delivered here later. Between you, you should be all right. She's fifteen but a virgin by all accounts. She'll take most of the flak, I should imagine. Relax and enjoy it. Think of the money and what you can do with it.'

The boy nodded. His face was a sickly green colour and his mouth was slack. 'What sweeties have you got?'

'That's the spirit, son,' he said approvingly. 'Think of this as a little business venture and you'll be as right as ninepence. It's only ever trouble if you make it trouble, do you get my drift?'

The boy knew he was being threatened and kept silent. All he had to do was get tonight over with.

Myra Campbell was small, only four foot nine, and slim, with tiny childlike breasts and a handspan waist. Her bleached blond hair was cut very short, and her eyes were still made up in the panda style she had adopted in the late-sixties. For her age she was an attractive woman.

But her childlike demeanour hid a devious personality that was at times frightening in its singlemindedness.

She lived for her son Trevale, her eldest child. No one could ever say anything bad about him; no one could ever convince her he was evil. To Myra he was her life. She adored him, and he adored her. That was how it had always been.

When she placed a cup of coffee in front of Cathy, the two women eyed each other up. They instantly disliked one another. Cathy saw through the dainty little woman like a pane of glass, and that alone would make Myra her enemy. She had spent her whole life deluding people and the few who saw through her she hated with an intensity that was frightening. In fact, Myra Campbell made Cathy's skin crawl.

The feeling was mutual. Myra hated Cathy's holier-than-thou expression, but most of all she hated her for the way she looked.

Richard Gates watched the exchange in fascination. Myra went to the kitchen to fetch her own drink, and Cathy met his eyes and made a face.

The house was beautiful though over-clean. You could sense that this room was rarely used; only on high days and holidays. The carpet was expensive; everything in the room was expensive. From the Edwardian loveseat to the antique vases on the mantel it was a lovely, tasteful place. One to be savoured and enjoyed. A room to read in, to relax in.

But it felt drained of life, of enjoyment, of hope. The atmosphere was stifling and Cathy could not wait to leave.

Myra came back into the room and sat on the edge of her chair. She eyed her two visitors warily. 'So what's all this in aid of then? My boy, I suppose.' She pursed her lips, and both Cathy and Richard knew she was not expecting an answer. 'I don't know why you lot keep picking on him. He does some bloody good things for people but you don't shout abo—'

Richard interrupted her. 'Up for the Nobel peace prize, is he? Him and Mother Teresa, for taking in all the waifs and strays from the Cross and giving them a living? Is that what you're referring to?'

Myra snorted, and her voice was low and bitter as she said, 'Fuck you, Richard Gates, and all your sort. My baby is a good boy, a kind boy, and nothing you make up will ever convince me otherwise.'

He laughed. 'You've changed your tune! Years ago he was just a high-spirited lad and everyone was making him do things he didn't want to do. You've developed plenty of trap since then and all!'

Myra stood up, thin body bristling with indignation as she paced the room, drawing deeply on a cigarette. 'He's my baby and I ain't going to let anyone bad mouth him to me. Do you dig what I'm saying, Mr Gates?'

Cathy put her coffee cup on a low table and said, 'No one's accusing your son of anything yet. We just need to talk to him, that's all, ask him a few questions. Is he at his sister's? What's his address?'

Myra stared at the younger woman before her and smiled, a cold smile that didn't touch her heavily made-up eyes. 'Do I look that fucking stupid, love? I ain't got no address for my boy, and if I did have I wouldn't give it to you under torture. As for my daughter, I have nothing to do with her at all. She's a whore.'

She spat out the words like bullets and Richard jeered: 'Is that because she's doing what you've always wanted to do, eh? Fucking your son?' He was deliberately goading her.

Myra's face paled. Talking between her teeth, she said heavily, 'Get out of my home. Get out now, both of you. I invited you in, and now I want you to leave.'

Cathy stood up. The two women were both small-boned, both delicate, both very angry.

'Your son is responsible for the ruin of many young lives, Mrs Campbell, doesn't that bother you at all?'

Richard watched them, his face impassive.

'He ain't never ruined no one, lady, you got it all wrong as usual. Like everyone always gets it wrong where my boy's concerned. It's all hearsay and talkology. His solicitor will explain that to you, as he's explained it to the police many times. No one has ever said a bad word against my boy except the Filth, and let's face it, they ain't exactly whiter than white these days, are they?'

Cathy was getting even angrier. 'Your son is scum, and after meeting you I can understand why. Look at you, in your ivory tower, knowing your adored little baby is taking children from the streets and using them, ruining their chance in life and disposing of them afterwards like rubbish. All this stuff in here,' she swept an arm around the room, 'was paid for by other people's degradation and shame. He caters for the lowest of the low and he's in good company because he was taught everything he knows by you, wasn't he?'

Myra raised her hand to slap Cathy's face. Cathy's hand with its long pale pink nails grabbed at the woman's wrist and, twisting it, she put Myra on her knees. As she heard the woman cry out in pain, Cathy laughed.

'Don't even think about striking me, lady, because I'd rip your hair out by the roots and ram it down your throat! Remember that, won't you? I won't rest until your boy's banged up or off the streets permanently. You tell him that from me, Cathy Pasquale.'

Richard was staring at her as if she had just grown horns and a beard in front of his eyes.

Cathy shoved Myra away from her and walked from the room. Richard followed her. Neither of them spoke until they were sitting in his Cosworth outside Myra's three-storey house. Cathy was still shaking with fury, her face white and mouth set in a grim line.

Richard lit a cigarette and passed it to her. Taking it, she swallowed back tears.

'I could have come across someone like him, couldn't I, when I was a girl? Instead I met you and Desrae and Joey. I've just realised all over again how lucky I was.'

She faced him, eyes filled with pain and confusion. 'What makes these people like they are, Richard? I hear all this shit about abusers being abused themselves, but I've never wanted to abuse anyone, ever. And I was abused all my life, throughout my childhood. My real life began when I killed Ron. I still remember that night, remember what I did to him, and yet, if I hadn't I would never have had the good life I enjoy now. The material things I have now, I should say. Maybe that's my punishment eh? Instead of prison I got money, wealth even, but I was never, ever able to get peace of mind.'

Richard put a strong arm around her and pulled her to him, holding her tightly. As she breathed in the scent of him she felt safe and secure once more. She always had done with him, right from the night he had sat beside her in the police cell and wrapped her in an old blanket.

Richard hugged her to him as if his life depended on it. He kissed her gently, smelling the peach shampoo and hint of musky perfume she always wore. He wished she'd cry, because he knew that if anyone needed to cry it was the woman in his arms.

Instead she pulled away from him and, smiling sadly, said: 'Campbell's sister, I think, don't you?'

'Oh, so we're seeing Terry's sister first, are we, and not young Peter's?'

Cathy nodded. 'I think somehow she'll have more to tell us than his mummy.'

Richard started the car up and sighed heavily. 'I wouldn't bank on it, love, but we can but try.'

Shaquila Campbell was stunning.

Tall and slim, she carried herself like an African princess. She was small-breasted with a tiny waist and long, long legs that were shapely and slim. In her high heels she was nearly six foot tall. There was nothing of her mother in her, and Cathy surmised that her father must have been a handsome man.

Shaquila's eyes were black as coal and almond-shaped, her nose a small bud in the centre of her face, her wide mouth sensuous and sexy. Her high cheekbones accentuated her African features. Her teeth were a pristine white and she looked as if she was always on the verge of smiling.

Not now, though. She stood on the doorstep of an attractive house off Kensington High Street, a small boy in her arms, back ramrod straight. Both Cathy and Richard were impressed by the calm and proud picture she made.

'Shaquila Campbell?' Richard's voice was his usual soft drawl.

The woman nodded. Resting the child higher on her hip, she looked them both over before asking, 'What can I do for you?'

'I'm a police officer. I need to ask you a few questions about your brother, Trevale.'

The girl's calm deserted her and she tried unsuccessfully to shut the door in their faces. Richard pushed against it and gently forced it back open.

'I really think you should let us in. If I come back with a warrant it isn't going to make things any easier for you, is it? At the moment I just want a few words, that's all.'

Shaquila bit on her bottom lip. 'There ain't anything I can tell you about my brother.'

Her voice was now pure Jamaican – quite different from the way she had spoken previously.

Cathy stepped towards her, saying, 'Please let us in, it's important we talk to you.' The little boy smiled at her, then shyly hid his face in his mother's breast. Cathy smiled back at him and her heart went out to the tall girl in front of her. She could practically smell her fear.

'Come inside, but I'm sure I ain't got nothing to tell you.'

They followed the woman into a large high-ceilinged room and sat down at her invitation on a white leather sofa. The room was bare: no pictures on the wall, no ornaments, nothing. Just a plain brown carpet and white leather suite. A chrome and glass coffee table dominated the room, and a large wide-screen TV was stuck in one corner.

The only touch of frivolity came from curtains. Of rich gold brocade, they stretched across the large picture window and added colour and warmth to the pale magnolia walls.

As they settled themselves the girl placed the small boy on the floor where he promptly lay down and began to suck his thumb. The sound was loud in the room.

'He's beautiful.'

Cathy's voice was sincere and Shaquila smiled her thanks before asking Richard: 'What do you want? What is my brother supposed to have done now?' Her voice was resigned, as if people coming and questioning her about her brother was an everyday occurrence.

Richard spoke first. 'Do you have any idea of Terry's whereabouts at this time?'

Shaquila shrugged. 'No, why should I?' Her tone told them she was not going to be an easy nut to crack.

'I understand you and he are very close?'

The words were spoken with Richard's usual quietness, but the underlying message was clear and Shaquila's eyes were hooded as she replied, 'Of course we're close. He's my brother.'

'He's also the father of your children and if I know anything about it there's a law in this country about that. It's called incest.'

Shaquila smiled icily. 'Actually, it's perfectly legal. We're both over the age of consent and can do what the hell we like in the privacy of our own home. I know that for a fact.

Now, if you and this lady here have finished your questioning, I'd like my flat back, please. I know nothing about Terry: where he is, where he lives or who he's with. So you're just wasting your time.' The West Indian inflection was gone now. She sounded like Trevor Macdonald with a poker up his jumper.

Cathy was embarrassed, but Shaquila and Richard were not. He smiled grimly at her.

'You do know what he's involved in, don't you? You know about him taking kids off the streets and using them for his porno films and his parties – his private parties where young boys and girls are raped repeatedly by brutes of men? Your lad's a handsome boy. I understand he has a sister. What about in years to come? Do you think Terry'll balk at his daughter when he never thought twice about pumping up his own sister? Think about what I'm saying, Shaquila, because while you and your mother protect him, he has a licence to do exactly what he wants.'

Shaquila's beautiful eyes were filled with tears. As she opened her mouth to answer him, Richard's pager began to bleep. He stood up and took it from his pocket. 'There's a phone in the hall, may I use it?'

Shaquila shrugged nonchalantly. She knew he was going to use it, with or without her permission. He was that kind of man, she had already sussed that much out for herself.

Alone with the girl, Cathy stared at her in morbid fascination. 'Richard's right, you know, we really do need your help with this.'

Shaquila wiped a hand across her face wearily. 'I don't speak to the police. Surely you understand that?'

Cathy grinned. 'I'm not the police, love, I'm a Soho club owner trying to find out why an employee of mine committed suicide. It seems your brother was very much involved. I also have a stake in a couple of sex shops –

nothing exotic, all legal and above board – but I have to know if my employee was selling your brother's contraband stuff through my outlets.

'It's not just the nicking I care about, it's the content of your brother's home movies that bothers me,' she went on. 'I was on the streets meself, a long time ago. I know what's waiting for a lot of the kids out there. Your brother, whatever he may be to you, is the cause of a lot of heartache and degradation. He's the cause of young girls and boys dying, do you know that? He cruises the streets looking for vulnerable kids, offers them the earth and then abuses them. All for money.'

Cathy's next words were spoken softly, with much emotion.

'I have a child myself, a teenage daughter, all budding breasts and long legs. Her name's Kitty. I wasn't well cared for when I was young. My mother was a dock dolly, an old pro. The worst kind. I wanted better for my child, and I'm sure you do for yours.'

Shaquila stared into her face and burst out passionately: 'Sometimes I look at my kids and I hate them – I hate them because they were forced on me! I stick up for Terry, but I can tell you have never met him. He is one bad motherfucker. Always was. I can't leave this house – I even have to have food delivered. I have to sit here, day in and day out, and wait on his calls. And then I have to act as if I'm the happiest woman alive. I have to suck my brother's cock because if I didn't he'd slit my throat without a second thought.

'I know my brother, I know him better than anyone. I've been at his mercy all my life. My mother hates me because he's forcing on me what she wants really. I was used by my father and then by my brother. We came from a weird household and I know I can never be rid of him until he's dead. Putting him in prison wouldn't answer my prayers because all the time he breathes I'm in danger. So, as much as I'd like to help you, I can't.'

The words were spoken with a sincerity that made Cathy want to cry with despair. Because this beautiful, articulate woman was trapped in a situation where she could not help herself or her children.

'I'm truly sorry,' Cathy told her.

Shaquila laughed tearfully. 'Not half so sorry as I am. But, you see, for me there's no escape. None whatsoever.'

Cathy took a card out of her handbag and placed it on the arm of the chair next to Shaquila's hand. 'That's my number. Ring me, please, and I'll help you. I promise you, I'll help you.'

Shaquila looked into her eyes and said, 'You really mean that, don't you?'

'Of course I mean it, Shaquila. I've been there, I know what other people are capable of. Really capable of. Not many people find that out in this life. But I'll get you away. I promise I'll get you away from him.'

'If only life was that easy.'

Shaquila's voice was once more weary and dead-sounding. Cathy put her hand on the woman's cheek and smiled at her. 'Life's never easy, Shaquila. People like us know that only too well, but every now and then it throws us a lifeline and we have to take it.'

She picked up her handbag and walked to the front door. 'Ring me, OK? And I'll make sure you're taken somewhere even Richard Gates won't find you.'

With that she hurried him from the flat. Shaquila needed to think, and Cathy had accepted that fact. She herself was silent all the way home.

Chapter Forty-Two

Once back at her flat, Cathy relaxed. She made a pot of tea and as she poured it, gave Richard a shaky smile.

'That was one of the worst experiences of my life. I have never felt such empathy, such a feeling of - total understanding, with another human being.'

Richard didn't speak; he knew she had to talk and get whatever was troubling her off her chest.

She sat down wearily.

'Why are women always at someone's beck and call, eh? What is it with us? We spend our whole lives waiting for a man either to love us or fuck us. Or else we end up with someone we don't want but can't get rid of. Men these days have no respect for women at all. None whatsoever. Terry Campbell wants his sister and he gets her because she's too frightened not to do as he says. And there's millions of women in that position, maybe not with their brothers – which just makes Shaquila's situation even worse – but with husbands, boyfriends, lovers. You read about it all the time in the papers. A man killed his wife and kids because she wanted a divorce. A man killed his girlfriend because she met someone else. It's as if women have become as throwaway as the society we live in.

'I've had men try and take advantage of me all my life. Even as a little kid I had "uncles" who wanted me to sit on their laps, wanted me to touch them. One bloke me mother had used to pretend he was tickling me just to cop a quick feel off a four year old. By the time I started school I knew more about the male psyche and sexual needs than most women do on their wedding day. And the worst thing of all is, because child sex is so horrible to think about, people tend to avert their eyes from it. They ignored the fact that I was at risk and they ignore it now just when it's becoming the biggest business in the world.'

Richard placed his large hand over her small one.

'I know that, love, you don't need to tell me – I see it every day. I've dealt with little boys of ten or eleven who are HIV positive. I've seen them asleep on the Embankment, wide open to whoever wants to prey on them. If it were down to me I'd have the kerb crawlers' and the nonces' names put in all the papers with their photos, I'd have their wives and families contacted. I'd fuck them good and proper. I'd have a convicted paedophile's name put in a local paper together with his picture so his new neighbours would be able to keep a tight rein on their kids. Instead, these bastards are let out and move districts, get council priority because they are so "vulnerable" – I mean, for some unknown reason everyone wants to kick their head in! – and so they settle in a new community where they start watching the kids swimming or fishing or up the park, and begin their games all over again. So, believe me, darling, you're preaching to the fucking converted.'

Cathy looked at him closely. His deep-set eyes were hurting; he saw too much, knew too much. Richard Gates was a kind man who cared, really cared, about people, but his intimidating physical presence sent out a completely different message. He looked like a thug, he knew it and used it. The reality was something much more complex.

'Let's get over to Dunmow or whatever the place is called. See Peter's sister, find out what she can tell us, eh? Maybe she'll be able to shed some light on his whereabouts,' Cathy suggested.

Richard agreed. As he stood up he placed a heavy hand on her shoulder and once more she was reminded of his physical strength.

'We'll sort this out, I promise. Just keep telling yourself that at least Kitty is safe. You have done a blinding job with that girl and should be proud of her. Next time we read all that old pony and trap about abused people being abusers, you and I can laugh, because we know it's not true. People abuse because they want to, because there's a fucking weird kink in their make-up that makes them want to own and control other people. That's all it is: control. Kitty has you and Des and me and Susan – all classed as strange by most people. But you see, Cathy, unlike us lot, most people haven't been let in on the secret yet.'

'And what's the secret then?'

He stared down into her eyes, his heart breaking with the want of her as he answered: 'We know that deep down some people are evil because they want to be. No matter how they dress it up, how the social workers and the goodie two shoes word it, *we* know the truth. The abusers are getting more and more prevalent and no one is helping the victims. All the energy is directed to the perpetrators, the nonces, the rapists, the fucking scum. But you and me, Cathy, we know it's a waste of time. The best we can do is help the little people, the abused kids and the runaways, to fight back.

'So come on, girl, Little Dunmow is calling. Let's get our arses in gear and see what else we can find out.'

*

Trevale 'Terry' Campbell was upset.

He had just had a call to tell him about a visit from a Vice officer called Richard Gates. He had arrived at Trevale's mother's home – her *home*, for Christ's sake! – with a tiny blonde, and that bitch had actually threatened Trevale's mother with physical violence. Within fifteen minutes of the call he knew who the little blonde was, and that she was involved because that stupid cunt Casper had topped himself.

Although his handsome face was impassive, his mind was working like a computer. How dare they go to his family? How dare they visit his mother's home? Now the spy he paid to watch his sister, a small Asian called Gunil, had told him that she also had received a visit from the same people who had been to his mother's house. They were going to pay for that but first he had to speak to Shaquila.

He stormed up the pathway to his sister's flat. Shaquila had the door open before he reached it, her face stretched into the parody of a smile.

'Terry darling, what's wrong? What's happened?'

He pushed her into the hallway and slammed the door shut behind him. 'Have a nice little visit, did they, the Old Bill? Thanks for letting me know they were here, Shaquila. Thanks a fucking bunch for that, girl.' His high cheekbones looked as if the skin had been pulled tight over them. He was talking through his teeth, a sure sign of trouble to come.

Shaquila licked her lips, brain racing to find an excuse for her errant behaviour. 'I tried to ring you, but I just kept getting the Orange answerphone. I assumed you'd turned your phone off for business. I was going to try you again in a minute, I swear, Terry. Why would I lie to you? Where would that get me?'

Her voice was full of panic and he watched her, savouring her fear and confusion for a few seconds before he relaxed. Shaquila wouldn't dare cross him. She didn't have the guts.

'There's fuck all wrong with my phone, love. Everyone else has got through OK.'

She could feel the hysteria building inside her. Her brother was vicious if crossed; he would make her hurt, make her hurt badly, and feel he had been just and honourable in teaching her a lesson.

'I swear on the kids' lives, Terry, I would never let you down. Why would I want to spoil what we've got? How would I ever cope without you, baby?'

He was relaxing, she could feel it. He loved it when she begged him, it was part of his make up. He needed to be sweet-talked, to be cosseted, to be in control.

He could see her hands shaking, hear the tremor in her voice. He could afford to play the big man.

'All right, Shaquila. Relax, girl. I have to make sure you're in line, you know that. Now what did they want?'

He followed her through to the kitchen, and as she put the kettle on he sat at the scrubbed pine table and looked out at the long, perfectly tended garden. His daughter was playing on the swing. Her hair was neatly braided in pigtails; her almond-shaped eyes dull and devoid of life. She gave him a dutiful little wave and carried on her aimless swinging.

'They were asking me if I knew where you were, and I told them no. I asked them what they wanted you for and they wouldn't tell me. I just sat it out until they went. I didn't know what else to do.'

Getting up, he went to her and slid his arms around her from behind. He caressed her breasts as he talked. 'That's my girl. Me and you against the world, eh? Fuck them, they can't prove nothing. I tell you – that fucking Pasquale bird has pushed her nose into something she shouldn't have! But I have an idea that'll sort her out. I'll teach that white bitch to try and put the hit on me.'

Shaquila turned to face him. 'What are you going to do?' She tried to sound excited at the prospect of something bad happening.

'Never you mind. Make me that tea then I think me and you will retire for a quick half hour of fun. What do you say?'

Shaquila felt her heart sink down into her boots, but she plastered a wide smile on her face as she said gaily, 'All right then, Terry, if you've got the time.'

He stared into her black eyes and said hoarsely, 'I've always got the time for you, darling.'

Cathy knocked on the door of the cottage in Little Dunmow. They had both admired the scenery on the way down, having forgotten how beautiful the Essex countryside could be. The cottage was down a lane, and looked like something out of a magazine. It even had roses round the green-painted front door.

There was no answer and Cathy knocked again, this time louder. Richard looked through the window at the front and then beckoned her to follow him round the back of the cottage. It was so small, like a doll's house. Roughcast, it was painted a dull white, and the windows were leaded lights, painted black. It stood on half an acre of land and as they walked round the side of the cottage, they both admired the beautifully tended garden.

The sun had sneaked out from behind a cloud and now lit the scene before them as if it were a painting. Cathy half expected Peter Rabbit to scamper across the grass towards her.

'Ain't it gorgeous, Cathy?'

She followed Richard down the winding back garden to two cement-built outhouses. He surveyed everything around him. There was a small conservatory on the back of the cottage, full of wicker furniture and houseplants.

'Isn't that a picture, girl? Relaxed and tranquil. Just the place for a young shirtlifter who needs a rest, eh?'

Cathy stared at him in surprise. What the hell was he on about now?

Opening the door of the nearer building, he shouted inside: 'Get your arse out here, son. I saw you poodling down the garden from the front of the house. Maybe your sister should invest in some net curtains, eh?'

Cathy watched as Peter emerged from the building looking shamefaced. He couldn't look her in the eyes.

'I'm sorry, I just panicked,' he said in a high breathy voice.

'Now your sister seems to me to be a woman of taste,' Richard said genially. 'So I reckon there must be a nice cold beer in the fridge, and if there is I'd love one. Shall we make our way inside, son?'

Peter nodded and they followed him down the garden path and through the conservatory to an antique pine kitchen.

'This is a beautiful property, bigger than it looks as well,' Richard commented.

'This is an extension. Me sister's husband's a builder, see. They can't have kids so they sink everything into this place. I love it here – it's so restful. It was once a farm labourer's cottage, a small one-bedroomed affair. It was the thatched roof that cost them really, and now they have a couple of bedrooms up there. Done a wonderful job, they have.'

All the time he talked Peter was pouring out beer. He

led them back into the conservatory and waited until they were seated before he started to cry.

'I'm so sorry for the trouble I've caused, Mrs Pasquale, but I was so scared. That Campbell threatened me! I didn't know what to do, and then when Casper killed himself, well, I just freaked. I really didn't want to get involved, you know?'

Cathy nodded sympathetically. 'I believe that, Peter, but we need to learn what Casper was up to – what he was dealing in. Until we find that out we can't really do anything to sort it. I'm sure you can see that?' He nodded and wiped his eyes.

Richard watched him, exasperated. 'What was the score, son? Don't keep us in suspense.'

Peter rapidly began to talk. 'Campbell was into the bestial books at first. You know, the Thai ones – women with horses and donkeys, that sort of thing. They were a real seller and he shifted quite a few. He split the proceeds with Casper, sixty-forty. Well, I told Casper to be careful. I mean, we all know you're not stupid, Mrs Pasquale, don't we? Not only that but you'd been very good to me. I pointed that out to Casper, but he said to keep me beak out of it and just keep stumm.

'Well, the next thing was we had videos and that, with kids, only Casper said they weren't really kids but older boys and girls dressed up to look younger. I never swallowed that one! I put a few of them on when he weren't there, and let me tell you, those were real kids.'

'Where are the videos then? We tore the shops apart and didn't find anything.'

'Casper took them all and destroyed them the night before he topped himself. You see, Terry Campbell was on to him . . .'

Richard raised his eyes to the ceiling and bellowed:

'About what, you stupid little fucker? You're talking away but you ain't telling us nothing.'

Peter's tear-filled eyes closed for a few seconds before he continued. 'He was on to him about the films, of course. Casper was making his own copies and selling them on. That's what riled Campbell so much: Casper was selling them to Michaela's boyfriend.'

Cathy was wide-eyed as she said: 'Who's Michaela's boyfriend then?'

Peter looked at Richard as he answered. 'It's Edward Durrant. Mickey's been seeing him on and off for years.'

Cathy saw Richard's reaction to that. 'Will one of you let me in on all this, please?' she insisted.

He looked at her and said, 'Eddie Durrant is an alias – that's fucking Trevale's half-brother's name! He uses Durrant because Campbell is such a fucker of a name in town. He doesn't want to be associated with Trevale, they hate one another. Eddie's a bad man, but I've never known him involved in anything like this.'

Peter shook his head. 'He ain't involved, he just wanted something on Terry, see. Now he's threatening him with all sorts, there's going to be big trouble, and Michaela's behind it all. If he'd kept out of it this would never have happened. You see, when Terry found out about it, he was going to kill Casper over Eddie's involvement. Eddie was trying to blackmail Terry using the films. He has a few faces in the Home Office, as you probably know, Mr Gates. This was his way of paying back his brother, see. It's personal, it's family, and that's the worst type of feuding if you ask me.'

'Eddie Durrant,' Richard said in amazement. 'I thought he was still out in South America?'

'He was, but he's back for a big deal,' the young man said importantly. 'Don't ask me what the deal is, I don't know and I wouldn't tell you if I did. All I know is, he wants Terry and this is his way of getting to him. Eddie's mum died recently in East London, and he's cut up about it. Casper told me Terry sent a wreath and the card said something about: "One down, one to go". When Casper realised who he was dealing with, he cleared the stuff and topped himself.'

'Surely, though, he couldn't have known he was dealing with Eddie? I mean, Casper would have known the connection between him and Terry,' Richard queried.

Peter nodded. 'Yes, but he done the deal through Michaela, see. That's what he told me anyway. He didn't know the connection between Michaela and Eddie, there's not many who do. Michaela's a real transsexual, not so much a drag queen. Eddie's bisexual. And, let's face it, Michaela would sink to his knees for anyone. That's what he's always been like. The funny thing is, he's worked for Terry in the past in some of his movies. There's one called *One Woman, One Man and His Dog*. It's a spoof on the television programme. That stars Michaela, a German Shepherd and some old boy done up to look like Seth off *Emmerdale Farm*. Make you sick if you watched it. Sick as a fucking dog.'

Cathy was amazed and disgusted. 'And how did Casper get involved with it all?'

'He owed money – gambling debts. It was his only real vice. He approached a lender, Dizzy McAlpine, the Rastaman from Tulse Hill. He always tips Terry the wink about his big lends, then Terry approaches the person if they can be used in some way and pays off the lion's share of the debt. The person then works for him. He did that with Casper and the films. But then Casper, seeing the money they were making, got a bit greedy. When Michaela approached him about making copies and selling them on the European market, he jumped at the chance. He really thought Terry would never be none the wiser. The silly old bastard!' Peter started to cry again.

'So where's this Eddie now then?' Richard pressed.

'I don't know. I never had any dealings with him, see. If anyone knows it will be Michaela. That's who you want to see.'

'So Michaela's running between two camps?'

Peter gave a sickly smile and said, 'I couldn't have put it better meself. And let's face it, it wouldn't be the first time, would it? That bitch would do anything for money. Anything.'

Richard stood up. 'We'd better get back to the Smoke. We need to talk to Michaela, find out what the score is. All this trouble over a family fucking feud. It's a joke, really.'

Cathy was still confused. 'It's crazy, really crazy.'

Peter looked at her sadly. 'Casper was a fool. I warned him what would happen and he wouldn't listen. That Michaela is a cow, a real bitch. He knew exactly what he was doing – set Casper up like a fucking lemon.'

'Well, don't you worry, we'll have it all sorted before you know it, Peter, and then you can come back to work. I think you ought to get back in touch with Brian, too, he's worried about you.'

Peter looked wistful. 'I miss him, but I'll wait and see what the score is. I don't want anything to do with either of them brothers, Eddie or Terry. They're dangerous. The whole family's weird.'

Richard laughed then, a deep rollicking sound. 'You can say that again! The mother's a few paving slabs short of a patio and the sister ain't much better.'

As they drove back towards London, they discussed this strange turn of events.

'If it's a family feud, we really needn't concern ourselves now Casper's out of the way,' Cathy began.

Richard nodded. 'I'll have to keep digging, but as far as I can see, you're in the clear. If Casper's moved the stuff and destroyed it, you're no longer in the frame.'

Well, that was a relief. But Cathy hoped Shaquila got in touch; she would very much like to help her out. Yes, she would help her and her children in any way she could. What goes around comes around. She had found Desrae and Richard. She would repay the debt by helping the black woman and her kids. It was the least she could do.

Desrae was waiting in Cathy's flat when they got back. His make-up was smudged, face rigid with fear. As soon as they walked through the door he burst into great racking sobs.

Flinging himself into Cathy's arms, he cried: 'He was here! That Terry Campbell . . . he was here. They've taken Kitty from school, Cathy. They've taken her!'

On closer inspection Cathy and Richard saw he had the beginnings of a black eye, and bruising around his cheekbone.

'Calm down, woman, and tell me what happened,' Richard ordered.

Cathy was beginning to feel the first stirrings of panic. 'What do you mean, they've got Kitty? How could they have got her, for Christ's sake?'

'A woman picked her up from the school, apparently. I rang for our usual Wednesday night chat and I was told Kitty wasn't there. I asked to speak to the Head and she said a woman showed up with some story that you were bad and Kitty was needed at home. Kitty knew the woman so they assumed it was OK. Kitty was desperate to get back to you, see.'

Cathy sank on to the sofa and groaned.

'Then he turned up at my place,' Desrae continued. 'He hit me, started shouting at me, telling me no one went to his house, no one fucked with his family and you would pay the price. I didn't know what the fuck he was talking about at first, I thought it was about Casper, see. Then he said I was to tell you he had your kid and you would never see her again until you paid him up. Those were his exact words. Paid him up.'

'You mean, he's ransoming her?' Cathy said in a frightened voice.

Richard shook his head. 'It means, love, he's going to teach her a lesson and *then* you'll get her back. He don't want money, he wants face. Respect. He's going to teach you a lesson.'

Cathy stared at him in utter confusion. Then the meaning of his words dawned on her and she shook her head. Her face contorted into a white, hatred-filled grimace, she bellowed, 'He'd better not touch my baby! I'll kill him if he touches my baby . . .'

Then she lost it.

The other two tried to hold her down in the chair as she fought them to get out of the flat and go looking for her child, single-handed.

Kitty was everything to her. The only good, untouched part of her life was her love for her daughter. She had always prided herself on what a fine job she had done, how well Kitty was protected. The whole idea of boarding school had been to keep the girl out of harm's way. Now someone had walked in and calmly taken her, and that person was a sicko, a psychopath. A man who had given his own sister two children against her will. A man whose name instilled fear into the whole of London because he was unpredictable, amoral and a byword for viciousness.

This was the man who had taken Cathy's child, her baby.

As a red mist gathered before her eyes she heard a loud wailing. It took an age for her to realise the sound was coming from her.

Chapter Forty-Three

Cathy was calmer. Desrae had given her three Valium and now she sat in the lounge, staring at the wall.

Richard was terrified. He had never seen a woman so changed. It was as if someone had taken away the real Cathy and replaced her with a shadow of the person she once was. Her face was a sickly, green-tinged white, and her eyes were wide and staring. They seemed to have taken over her face. Even her hair looked defeated, hanging limply over her shoulders.

'I'll kill him. Before God, I'll kill him if he touches my baby.' Her voice was a dead, flat monotone.

Richard held her tightly to him for a moment. 'We'll find her, don't worry. Now, I have to go – see what I can dig up, OK? I'll find Durrant, ask him for help. Stop worrying. Campbell won't really do anything to Kitty, that's just posturing. His way of scaring you. He would never dare touch her. Believe me, Cathy, I know what I'm talking about.'

He was lying in his teeth but couldn't see what else to do.

Even as they spoke Kitty could be the victim of a gang rape or worse.

He was relieved when Susan P walked into the room accompanied by her minder, Tulson. The latter was big, black and quiet – the perfect man as far as Susan P was concerned. He watched over her, kept his own counsel and took his wages with no more than a word or two.

Cathy rushed into her friend's arms and cried once more. Fear for her child was sending her off her head. 'We must find her, Susan! Before he defiles her, before he does something bad to her. She's only a kid, only fourteen. If anything happens to her, I'll go fucking mad.'

Susan patted her, whispering words of endearment, telling her everything would be OK. When Richard finally left, she sat Cathy down, looked her in the eye and said firmly: 'Pull yourself together, Cathy. This ain't helping matters. You need to be strong now. We need you to be stronger than you've ever been before. Kitty needs you. We're going to find her, OK?'

Cathy nodded, the sense of this making inroads into her brain. Susan P's calm voice was having an effect.

'If you lose it, we're one down on our posse. Do you understand me?' Opening her bag, Susan P took out a small vial of powder and quickly cut a few lines on the coffee table. 'Snort that, it's Charlie. I know you don't normally touch it but it'll give you an edge, and you need that tonight.'

Cathy did as she was told, taking the small straw from her friend and snorting up the cocaine quickly.

'Now I have been in touch with every contact I have, and I can guarantee you we will have a lead before the night's over. What we need is a small clue as to where he would take her. Once we have that, we're on our way.'

Susan was talking for effect and she knew it. Unless someone told them where she was they had no chance of finding the girl, no chance whatsoever.

Given the fact that Campbell had been using and abusing for years without suffering so much as a fine for living off immoral earnings, it seemed foolish to hope he would make a mistake this time. But where there was life there was hope, as the saying went, and Susan P knew she had to keep up Cathy's spirits.

Michaela was sitting in Campbell's car. Terry was giving him a fixed-rate reward: in criminal parlance that meant the sum paid over had already been negotiated and earned.

Michaela didn't count it, he knew it would all be there. Slipping the two thousand into his handbag, he said, 'You won't hurt her, will you, Terry? She's a good kid, you know, and I only did this as a favour to you.'

Terry laughed coarsely. 'What I do with her is my business, OK? I kept my end of the bargain, and you kept yours. The girl's my property now, nothing to do with you at all. Keep your nose and your mouth out of my business and we'll be fine. Interfere and I'll take your fucking head off your shoulders, wig and all. Dig?'

But Michaela wasn't satisfied. 'I delivered her on the proviso you did not hurt her. Listen to me, Terry. That little girl is a sweetie, she's a good kid, and her mother will move heaven and earth to find her, as will Richard Gates and Susan P. Now you promised me you was just going to use her as a bit of leverage, no more and no less.'

Terry Campbell smiled, displaying even white teeth, and then he said roughly: 'I lied.'

Michaela paled underneath his Mary Quant panstick. 'You bastard! You know I'd never have done anything if I'd thought you'd hurt her. What's brought about this change then?'

'Her mother actually went into my home – my fucking home! – where my children live. She also went to my mother's house and threatened her. Threatened *my mother.*' Campbell took a deep breath. 'No one fucks with my family and gets away with it. This is personal. That fucking bitch needs a lesson and I'm going to see that she gets one.'

Then Terry opened the car door and pushed him out roughly. 'Fuck off, bitch! I've got what I wanted and you supplied it to me. Now leave me alone and keep your mouth shut.'

Michaela knew when to retreat and did so. As he watched the car pull away he thought that two grand wasn't enough for what he'd just done. He should have asked for five. Flagging down a black cab, he made his way to Eddie Durrant's flat in Bayswater.

He had really burned his boats now. He couldn't go back to his house, the club – anywhere. Cathy would know who had taken her daughter from school, would know Michaela had tucked her up. If anything happened to Kitty, he was a dead man.

But Michaela had always been a selfish, two-faced liar; it was in his nature. Two grand was two grand after all. He needed money to go to South America and get The Op, the surgical procedure that would change his life.

A girl had to look out for number one – especially when that girl was in fact a man.

Louis Bardell was twenty-eight. His smooth olive skin, deep green eyes and thick black hair made him strikingly attractive. He knew people looked at him and he enjoyed it. He was also a homosexual with a taste for the exotic: young boys.

As he and a pair of soulmates came out of his Kensington flat, Louis saw a large thuggish-looking bald man leaning against his dark blue Mercedes. Glancing at his friends, he pulled himself up to his full height and said loudly: 'Get off my car, there's a good chap, before I call the police.'

The man stood upright and Louis saw just how large he was. His two friends took a step back.

'I *am* the police. Shall we go inside? I need to talk to you about something.'

'I'm sorry but I'm on my way out for the evening . . .' His voice trailed off as Richard Gates smiled threateningly down at him. 'Inside, please, all of you.'

Back in the house Richard watched as Louis and his friends all seated themselves in the high-ceilinged drawing room.

'Nice place.'

Louis snorted. 'Take a good look, dearic, it's the nearest you'll ever get to real money.'

Richard said pleasantly, 'If you don't shut your fucking mouth, I'll see to it that you're banged up in Brixton for the next few days, helping me with enquiries – and that's the nearest *you'll* ever get to having your arse torn out!'

Louis and his friends all shuddered.

'Pain is a horrible thing, isn't it, lads?' Gates went on. 'I know I don't like it, not personally, though I enjoy inflicting it on people. Funny that, isn't it? I could take out a knife and cut off your ears and laugh me head off, but if you accidentally scratched me, I'd do me crust. You see, I hate pain, personal pain.'

Richard smiled at Louis.

'And that's something we have in common, isn't it? Because you like hurting people, don't you? You like hurting little boys and girls. I know that's true because I have a video of you doing just that. You see, Trevale sold those videos he made of you in action. It wasn't such a private party. You're number one in the paedophile electric blue charts all over Europe. You're famous, mate.'

Louis was now a sickly white. His whole demeanour had changed in a few seconds. Licking his lips, he shook his head in confusion. 'I don't know what you're talking about.'

'Your big green eyes are striking, hard to mistake. I understand you also have a rather unusual tattoo on your right buttock: a snake chasing itself. Want to take down your trousers and prove me wrong? No, thought not. You're looking at a long stretch, Sonny Jim,' he concluded. 'There ain't enough money in the world to stop this prosecution taking place.'

'You'd better be very careful what you say, Mr . . .'

Richard smiled. 'Gates. Detective Inspector Richard Gates. Would you like me to tattoo the name on your other cheek, by any chance? In case you forget it?' He turned to the other two men and smiled once more. It was one of his better smiles, a cross between a grimace and a death's head. 'You two gentlemen are quiet. What's wrong, cat got your tongues?'

The two men, one a computer analyst and the other a professional footballer, stared at him in distress and fear.

'What exactly are you after?' This from the analyst.

'I'm after the location of Terry Campbell's little soiree, the one he's having tonight. I heard through the grapevine he was having one of his private parties. Well, they would have to be private, wouldn't they? I mean, it's hardly the type of occasion you'd invite your mother or sister to, is it?'

The footballer, a twenty-five-year-old Frenchman, had the grace to look ashamed and instinctively Richard knew he had his man.

He looked at Richard and spoke softly. 'No one knows the location until an hour before. That's how it's always worked in the past.'

'OK,' Richard decided, 'we're all going to sit here together and have a lovely little chat, a few Scotches, and when we know the location, I can get along there and fuck up the night's entertainment.' He rubbed his hands together in a parody of Uriah Heep and squealed in a girlish voice: 'Boy, am I looking forward to that!'

Kitty was terrified. When she had seen Michaela at the school she had at first been concerned, fearing that her mother was ill. But Michaela had been quick to reassure her that her mother was in fact OK; Desrae was holding a private party and he wanted Kitty to be there. The story about Cathy's being unwell was just for the school's benefit.

It wasn't until they had hit London and she had been taken to a strange house that she'd realised something was not right. Her first sight of Trevale Campbell had been terrifying. He just stared at her, then made her put her arms above her head and turn around slowly. All the time she did it he watched her critically.

Michaela was nowhere to be seen. When Kitty attempted to walk to the front door, the man took her roughly by the arm and slammed her into a chair so hard it jarred her spine. The girl realised she was in danger, but had no idea why this was happening. What could the man want with her?

Then he put on a video and told her to watch it, and learn.

It was only after she had seen the video that she understood just how much trouble she was in.

Trevale Campbell was loving every second of her distress.

This was pay back in a big way.

If that bitch's mother thought she'd get away with desecrating his home then she had another think coming.

And when he had sorted out the daughter, he was going to sort out the mother as well.

He was going to force her to watch the video of her daughter's coming of age.

Eddie Durrant was very big, and handsome with the dark, almond-shaped eyes of his father and perfect coffee-coloured skin. A violent criminal, he hated his half-brother Trevale with a vengeance. Eddie's mother had been a young white East End girl called Renee. She had given birth at sixteen, and his father had abandoned her though he always kept an eye on his son.

Like Trevale, Eddie was his father's son.

He'd urged his boys to be hard, to be tough, to be the best. He'd forced them into violent confrontations as children, made them fight when they were together, making the victor his best boy for the day.

Eddie had always resented the fact that his father had lived with Trevale's mother after discarding his own.

As he grew into adulthood he had the same kink in his nature as his half-brother. Both took kindness for weakness, and both respected strength, and strength alone. Both used and abused everyone and anyone. Both saw money as the only commodity, and violent sexual activity as something that was their right. It would never have occurred to them that feelings were involved. At least, the feelings of other people.

When Eddie had found out that his brother was making a small fortune with his sex films business, he had made it his own business to hop in and take a slice of the action. Not because he needed the money or because he wanted a new venture, but because it pleased him to put one over on Trevale. Michaela had come up trumps as Eddie had known he would.

Now, as he heard the latest development in the story, Eddie felt annoyed and elated all at the same time.

'You're telling me that my brother has taken the daughter of Cathy Pasquale and is going to use her at one of his parties tonight?'

Michaela nodded, worried about what he had done. Seeing Eddie had made him realise he had a foot in both camps and that could be a dangerous thing. A very dangerous thing. But he wanted to score a little more money before he made his departure for Rio.

Michaela put on his little-girl-lost face and said breathily: 'I had to do what he asked, Eddie. I mean, if I'd refused to go and get her, he'd have hurt me bad, wouldn't he?'

Eddie looked at the man-woman before him and felt disgust rise inside him. 'That Pasquale woman has been good to you. Don't you have any loyalty to anyone, Mickey?'

Michaela shrugged. 'Of course I do, but I can't fight Terry, you know that. Once you go back to South America, I'll be left to fend for myself again. I can't afford to have your brother as an enemy.'

Eddie laughed humourlessly. 'But you can afford to have Cathy Pasquale as your enemy, is that it?'

Michaela was not at all pleased with the way the conversation was progressing. 'Look, Eddie, I just did what I had to do, OK? I'm sorry, I liked the girl, I like Cathy . . . fuck me, I like them all but I have to watch my own arse. This could be an earner you know, for us both. If we tell Cathy we can get her daughter back she'll pay well, I know she will.'

Eddie sat opposite him, resting his chin in one large cupped hand. 'You don't say?'

Warming to his theme, Michaela nodded furiously. 'At least ten grand, maybe more.'

Eddie waved his hand dismissively. 'You are willing to sell the life of a young girl, the daughter of a woman who was very good to you. Who loaned you money for your breast op, who gave you a job when you needed one, who has taken you into her club and by the sound of it, her family. I just want to get this straight in my own mind, see. I want to know for sure that you really are that fucking low! Christ, I thought Trevale was a piece of dirt, but you, Michaela – you take the biscuit.'

Mickey pouted. 'Well, when you put it like that, of course it sounds bad. But you're not looking at it from my point of view, are you? I've worked my butt off in that club for Cathy, night after night. She ain't given it to me for nothing, has she? I mean, it's in her interest to treat us well, isn't it? She is a nice woman, granted, but at the end of the day she's still my employer – it's not like it's family, is it? She's rolling in it, fucking stinking rich. Why shouldn't I have a bit of what she's got, eh?'

'You really think you can justify what you've done, don't you?' Eddie's voice was high with disbelief. 'Look – I asked you to help me set up my brother. *That* was personal. Then you go behind my back and work out a completely new deal with him. Then –' he laughed – 'this is the bit I really like, you think you can come here and make even more money by using me to blackmail the woman who has been good to you, and who incidentally has never done a fucking thing to me. Is that right? Am I reading all this correctly?'

Eddie stood up. 'Get your coat back on. Me and you are going to pay this woman a little visit.'

Michaela nearly fainted. 'I beg your pardon?'

'You heard me. You are going to see this bitch and tell her what's happened to her daughter – and if she decides to kick your ass, I ain't going to stop her, honey pie. In fact, I might just give her a hand. In all the years I've known you, Mickey, I knew you was a user, but this lot takes the fucking red rosette. But then, you see, there's another side to all this. Now I can get my brother wasted without even raising my hand. *That*, to me, sounds like good business.'

Michaela was stunned. 'Come on, Eddie, you wouldn't sell me down the river? You wouldn't do this to me?'

He smoothed his hand across his shaven head and said gaily: 'Oh, but I would. You just watch me.'

Eddie finally tracked Cathy down to the club where she was waiting with Susan P and Desrae to learn the location of the party. When he walked into the office with Michaela, Susan and Desrae both stared as if they had seen a ghost.

'Eddie Durrant and the Lovely Michaela – to what do we owe this pleasure?' Susan P's voice was heavy with malice.

'Long time no see, Susan. You're looking good, baby. But then, you always did,' Eddie said smoothly. He smiled at Cathy, holding out one perfectly manicured hand. 'Mrs Pasquale? A pleasure I'm sure.'

Cathy stared at him with relief. If this was Trevale's brother, the one who hated him, then they were in with a chance. The coke had kicked in by now and her mind was razor sharp though her hands were trembling. Then it registered properly that this was Michaela standing with him: Michaela who had taken Cathy's baby from school and delivered her to the man who would destroy her innocence.

As Cathy flew across the room and grabbed at him, no one else moved a muscle.

Ripping his wig off his head, Cathy proceeded to punch, kick and pummel the slim-hipped young man lying abjectly on the floor before her. Grabbing his face in her hand, she looked down into his eyes.

'I'll see you dead, you bastard, over this night's work. I'll see you screaming in fucking pain and I'll laugh, mate. And if you think you've got a handful with me, you wait until the girls get their hands on you!'

As Michaela, crying and wailing, tried to explain himself, Eddie Durrant said: 'Can it, Mickey.' Then he told Cathy and the others exactly what Michaela had done. As he spoke Mickey saw his chances of survival slipping further away with every word.

In the club the night was just picking up. Red, a large-boned Irishman with a Danny la Rue laugh and the clothes of Carmen Miranda, was just going into his opening number. They could hear him singing 'I, I, I, I, I, I love you *very* much,' in a strangely mixed Irish-Mexican accent.

It always went down a bomb, and tonight was no different.

Susan P listened then said: 'So where's the girl, do you know?'

Eddie nodded sagely. 'But I want something in return.'

Desrae snorted. 'Well, spit it out, nigger, we ain't got all fucking night!'

Eddie faced him and smiled, his eyes hard. 'I ain't no one's nigger, and if you think I'm after money, I'm not. I am after the cessation of my brother's power of breathing – if you understand me?'

Cathy nodded. 'Don't you worry, if I get my hands on him he will never draw fucking breath again.'

Eddie appeared satisfied with this. 'The house your daughter is in is just off Kensington High Street,' he told the assembled gathering. 'It's my half-sister's house, but she ain't there. He packed her off today with the kids. I assume he'll move your girl there just before the party begins.'

He looked at his watch. 'It's just after nine-thirty, and the parties usually don't start until around eleven, eleven-thirty. All the heroes like to get well tanked up beforehand, prepare themselves for their night's entertainment. We should catch her then.'

'And we should catch Trevale there, too, shouldn't we?' Cathy asked, her voice a whisper.

'Of course.'

Everyone moved at once. Michaela was still lying on the floor, scared and bloodied. Cathy looked down at him. 'I'll deal with you later, Mickey.'

'I'll watch him,' Eddie promised. 'You get yourselves off and when you come back you can tell me all about it.'

Cathy nodded, her eyes dead. 'You can bank on that, Mr Durrant.'

The big black man grinned and spread his arms in a gesture of friendliness. 'Please, call me Eddie. All my friends do.'

No one answered. They left the office in double-quick time. Eddie smiled down at Michaela. 'Now then, they have a well-stocked bar, can I get you a drink after all?'

Michaela stared up at the man he had slept with on numerous occasions and said thickly, 'You bastard.'

'But of course! Everyone knows my daddy never married my mummy,' Eddie said pleasantly. 'It's the root of *all* my problems.'

Helping himself to a large Remy Martin he savoured the taste, anticipating the moment when he would be told his half-brother was dead.

Chapter Forty-Four

Johnny Cartwright watched as Terry Campbell forced the girl into the room. She was terrified. Her hands were tied behind her back, and he felt sorry for her, really sorry, because he knew that she was to join him as tonight's entertainment. With her long dark hair and her huge blue eyes she was stunning, and he knew she would take a lot of the heat off him.

As she lay on the floor he could see her whole body trembling. She was already in a state from either drugs or shock, maybe a mixture of both. One thing was for certain: she had no real idea what was going on around her. Her eyes were wild, like a trapped animal's, a long streamer of spittle was hanging from her mouth and her lips were pulled back over her teeth in a grimace of terror.

He found it in his heart to feel sorry for her.

He had been in this room for hours, and as the day wore on had become resigned to what was going to happen to him. He had been selling himself for a long while so the thought was frightening but not exactly new to him.

This girl, however, was different. You could tell she wasn't in the life by her abject fear, her neat clothes and her cleanliness. He guessed, rightly, that she was a stolen child. His deep green eyes were sad as he saw Trevale pulling her on to the large bed. Her skinny kid's legs were on show, and her underwear, school issue navy blue drawers, were baggy on her. Johnny knew that this would be a major selling point for the people who were to come to this so-called party.

She was tall for a young one, but had the fresh-faced look they craved, neither girl nor woman. Flat breasts and sparse pubic hair were the order of the day for these people, he knew that himself. After all, he sold himself on a daily basis, knew more about it than all the so-called psychologists and social workers. They merely observed, had never participated.

Kitty had decided to fight back and tried to claw the man as he dragged her on to the bed. He punched her as hard as he could in the thigh, careful not to mark her face. The dead leg penetrated even the Demerol with which she had been injected and she screamed in agony. Two minutes later she had her mouth taped and her arms tied to the headboard, pulled above her head.

Terry was just lighting a joint when the first visitors arrived. Johnny sat quietly, watching the man and the woman as they came through the door. They were in their fifties and well dressed in matching leather jackets. Terry greeted them like a maître d' in a fashionable restaurant. The woman was heavy-set with exaggerated eye make-up and backcombed hair. Johnny took her to be an ageing prostitute; the man beside her was obviously her partner.

It was strange the way these people seemed to find each other without the aid of clubs or anything normal people used to socialise.

The woman was staring at Kitty as if she had just been given the winning lottery numbers before the draw.

The man watched Johnny, who stared back at him impassively. He could hear Terry telling them how the two kids were going to do a scene, and how they were going to video it, and if they wanted an individual show it would cost extra, and that if they wanted the tape edited professionally that would also cost more, but it was worth it because the quality was exceptional.

The woman was already haggling for a private hour with the girl and Johnny watched and listened, amazed at the level to which people could sink. He thought he had seen it all in his young life but this cold-blooded trade in flesh was overwhelming even for him.

He smiled at the man gently, knowing what was expected of him and delivering it. He wanted to walk out of this room at some point and, with Terry Campbell that meant toeing the line. He hoped he could get close enough to the girl to tell her that. But the state she was in, she probably wouldn't be able to take onboard what he was saying anyway.

But he'd try.

The man ruffled Johnny's hair, running his fingers through its thickness. He looked up with his deep green eyes and the man was immediately enamoured. If Johnny could make a good impression, the man might insist on a one-to-one and if he had the money then Terry would agree to it, bringing in someone else for the other customers. His luck was out, though. The man was soon happily greeting two friends who had just shown up.

He was a crowd man. Johnny felt his heart sink down into his boots. Still, it had been worth a try. The two men were dressed in bondage and Johnny's heart sank even lower. The bondage gays could be vicious bastards; he knew, he'd already had a few in his time. They associated pleasure with pain. Funny how they seemed to enjoy inflicting it more than receiving it, though.

He smiled again, because he knew that the odds of his passing on the HIV virus were growing shorter and shorter. If they made him bleed, and he had a feeling that's exactly what they were going to do, he would give them an extra little present tonight, other than his body and his self-respect.

Terry was pleased by the boy's professional behaviour. Terry knew that a lot of the paedophiles felt better if the child seemed willing because then they could kid themselves that he had acquiesced and was happy with what they were doing. It reinforced their belief that children loved it all really, whatever the experts might say.

Everyone had a drink, even Johnny. He gulped down the vodka thirstily, hoping to get drunk as well as drugged out of his head. He saw Terry forcing vodka down the girl's throat, too. He could hear her choking. Everyone laughed, it was comical to them. Terry carried on pouring the neat spirit into her, and the girl drank quite a lot before passing out.

Johnny was pleased for her; hoped she didn't wake up until it was all over.

The woman, who turned out to be an estate agent – Johnny knew this because she was discussing the sale of a property in Willesden that could be used the next week – then asked Terry again how much for some time on her own with the girl.

He looked at her and considered the matter. 'I'll give you an hour, you give me the loan of the Willesden house next week for nix. I can't be fairer than that, can I?'

The woman laughed. Her teeth were stained yellow from smoking and her make-up was so thick it cracked and flaked off in little pieces. Terry then proceeded to usher the men and the boy through to the adjoining room.

Johnny had expected something like this. The other

room was equipped with a bed and a stock of drinks. As they moved through, Terry's minder delivered two more party-goers to him.

These were City gent types, suited and booted and carrying briefcases. Unlike the others, they were quiet. Accepting a drink, they stood together and Johnny guessed they were lovers who indulged in the exotic every now and then, when they could afford it. He kept his gaze on the door, hoping the girl was OK. He certainly wouldn't have fancied being left alone with the big dyke.

The two leather-clad men approached him. One caressed his hair while the other stroked his genitals through his trousers.

'Take your clothes off, son, we want to see what we're getting.'

Terry nodded at him and Johnny started to undress slowly. The men all watched in anticipation. Johnny closed his eyes and went on to auto pilot. He heard a groan from the other room and glanced towards the doorway, hoping the girl was all right.

He prayed they would both be all right.

Kitty could see the woman through her drunkenness. It was very hard to focus for more than a few seconds, though. Somewhere in the back of her mind she knew that something bad had happened, but could not remember for the life of her what it was.

Opening her eyes once more, she saw a woman leaning over her. Her face wore a garish mixture of bright make-up and she stank of perfume.

When Kitty realised the woman was kissing her breasts, she felt such distress that she vomited, vodka flying all over the woman's hair and shoulders. Kitty felt an urge to laugh and scream all at the same time. She couldn't do either, however, because she was finding it difficult to breathe. The vomit had come through her throat and nose, and tied as she was on her back, she was fighting for breath.

The woman was now sitting upright, face contorted with rage. She slapped Kitty hard across the face.

The girl could feel herself passing out and her last thought was of her mother. As she sank into the welcoming blackness, she wondered if Cathy was looking for her; if she knew that she had been taken from school.

The woman tried to clean herself up. She heard a commotion in the other room and opened the door a crack. There was pandemonium out there. People were all over the place: uniform, plainclothes, and in her terror she was amazed to see at least two transvestites. She assumed they had come for the party.

Shutting the door, she surveyed the room. She opened the curtains and tried to force open the window. It was nailed shut. But then it would be, wouldn't it? There had been instances where the kids had jumped out, and the party had had to be abandoned.

Her eyes darted around the room in terror. If she was found in here alone with the girl who was making weird wheezing sounds now, she was well and truly fucked. Not only her job, but her standing in the community, in her local church and with her neighbours, would be put in jeopardy.

Picking up a piece of wood from the large fireplace, she decided she'd try and smash the window open. As she picked up the weapon the door was opened and she was confronted by the boy Johnny. He was shouting at the top of his voice: 'There's a girl in here! Come and help her, she's choking.'

He was kneeling on the bed now, trying to untie the girl's hands. As the woman stood there, a tiny blonde came into the room and she knew immediately that this was the girl's mother. Only a mother could have that ferocious look in her eyes, only a mother could have hatred all over her face as she looked at her.

The boy was pulling the girl to a sitting position, and then the tiny blonde was wiping the girl's face, cleaning out her mouth and nose. Suddenly the girl coughed and took a few deep breaths. It occurred to the woman then that the girl had nearly died, had nearly suffocated in her own vomit.

As she watched, fascinated, the tiny woman handed the girl over to the boy then she got off the bed and walked across the room. She was so tiny, like a little doll.

The lesbian was tall, five ten, big-boned, wide-cheeked. She looked every bit like one of her Slav ancestors. She had the heavy hips and brick thighs of a working woman.

She was strong.

But not strong enough for this tiny woman in the throes of a violent rage. As the girl's mother attacked her, she was forced practically head first through the window from which she had been trying to escape.

Then it was all over. A large man with a bald head and a rounded belly was pulling her off, laughing as he did so. 'Come on, Cathy, let the police take over now. We've got Kitty, she's fine. Come on, love, let go.' He was trying to pry Cathy's fingers from the woman's hair.

'I'll fucking kill you, you hear me? If you go to prison I'll get you there, I'll get you wherever you go, lady. You're mine, your arse is mine!' Cathy's voice was a chilling whisper that was loud in the empty room. 'You touched my baby – you touched my little girl. I'll rip your heart out and sing like Julie Andrews while I do it. Remember that, lady.'

Estelle Parkinson was just finding out what it felt like to be on the receiving end of pure aggression.

Richard looked at the little tableau then stared hard at Estelle. 'You'll have a shiner there girl, and your hair's falling out in clumps. But that's fuck all to what you'll get in prison. I hope it was worth it all, love, I really do, because life as you knew it is over for you now.'

Estelle Parkinson stared at the man before her; she could feel his hatred of her as she knew he wanted her to. She dropped her eyes first. As she was escorted from the room, a large transvestite punched her in the back of the head, sending her and her captor reeling across the floor.

Everyone laughed. It was partly relief and partly embarrassment. For many of the officers there it was a first encounter with this side of the sex trade, and they all hoped it would be their last.

Desrae walked into the bedroom, dreading what he might find, but one look at Cathy and he knew that whatever happened, Kitty was safe now. He looked at the young boy, Johnny, at his lovely hair and gorgeous eyes, and saw himself all those years ago. Only he had been lucky enough to find Joey. Who did this boy have? Putting his arm around the boy, Desrae cuddled him close.

'There, there, son. You're safe now. The cavalry arrived just in time and the nice policemen are going to take all the nasty people away. What a bleeding touch, eh?' He smiled at the boy who finally began to cry.

Desrae comforted him, knowing that after tonight, this boy would become a fixture in his life. Not for any sexual motive, but because he had been in the right place at the right time.

Desrae loved taking care of people and now he had another lame duck to look after. Life had its compensations – but God found a strange way of delivering them sometimes.

*

Kitty's stomach had been pumped out and she had been examined by the best doctors available.

She was intact, untouched.

Cathy thanked God and sat beside her daughter's bed, holding her hand as she slept off the drugs and the shock. With a bit of luck she wouldn't remember much of what had gone on. If she did, then they'd make sure she got the best counselling that money could buy.

Richard sat beside her, one heavy hand on Cathy's knee. They sat there in silence together, like the parents of a much loved child, united in their adoration of the girl before them.

'She'll be all right, Cathy, I promise you.'

Cathy glanced at him and smiled wanly. 'I can't believe people could actually do that. Yet I should know they do, I should know better than anyone.'

Richard sighed and pulled her into his arms, gently stroking her back. 'Go on, have a good cry, let it all out. You've had a big shock, Cathy. Your child was taken and nearly raped, you're entitled to have a good weep.'

She tried to smile through her tears. 'What would I do without you, Richard?' Her voice was low, tired-sounding. 'You've always been there for me from day one. From the first moment I met you, I knew I could trust you – even though you were the scariest individual I'd ever laid eyes on. I sensed something in you: the kindness, the caring. I said that to Desrae once and he roared.'

Richard shrugged. 'Well, he would, wouldn't he? Unlike you he doesn't see the real me. I rarely let anyone see it.'

Cathy looked into his eyes. 'I know that better than anyone. Everyone thinks you're a vicious thug who masquerades as a policeman, and really you're a lovely man.'

He grinned. His teeth had always been one of his best points and he knew that. 'I'm a lovely man, am I? Well, don't let on about it. I don't want me street cred ballsed up at this late stage.'

Desrae came into the room then so Cathy couldn't answer. He took in the scene before him and sighed heavily.

'You two look like love's young bleeding dream sitting there, wrapped around each other. Makes me feel quite jealous.' He looked at Kitty and shook his head in distress. 'The poor lamb! Look, Cathy, no disrespect, love, but you look bleeding terrible. Get your arse off home. They've said she'll sleep till the morning, and I think you need a stiff drink and a hot bath . . .'

Cathy was shaking her head when Richard pulled her from her seat.

'He's right. Come on, love. I'll take you home. Get a couple hours' sleep and then I'll run you back here before I go into work, OK? I've left everything in the capable hands of my assistant. He's about as much use as an ashtray on a motorboat, but he knows the score. He'll book them then I'll deliver them to the CPS. So I've got a bit of time.'

Desrae pushed them towards the door. 'Tomorrow they'll be questioning Kitty. She'll need you with her, and you'll need your wits about you. Get a few hours' sleep and freshen up, for Gawd's sakes.'

Cathy saw the logic of this and did what her old friend had suggested.

With one last glance at her daughter she walked from the room. They were back at her flat in twenty minutes, and Richard ran her a hot bath while she made them both coffee. As she sank into the steaming fragrant water, he walked in bringing her a brandy and a cigarette.

She smiled her thanks. 'You spoil me, Richard.'

'You're worth spoiling, though I regret putting in the bubble bath. I've done meself out of a quick look at your womanly tackle.'

Cathy laughed, a heavy tired sound. 'I'm so relieved she's OK, Richard. I was so frightened . . . terrified of what might have happened to her.'

He stopped that line of thought. 'Well, she's fine. We got there in time and she'll get over it, darling, we'll all see to that.'

She took a gulp of brandy, enjoying the burning sensation.

'You were like a bleeding wild cat! That Parkinson woman's face . . . I hope I'm never on the receiving end of your anger, girl.'

Cathy blushed. 'I wanted to kill her. Honestly, Richard, I could quite easily have shot her if I'd had a gun.'

'Now you know why they don't want guns sold over the counter here. In the States firearms are easily available and no one really knows what they're capable of in anger. The sad thing is, once you're calmer you regret it. Even though that woman was a nutter, if you'd topped her you'd have had it on your conscience.'

Cathy thought about what he'd said then answered him. 'I don't know so much. What she was going to do with my child was obscene, disgusting. Maybe I would have been sorry, I don't know. All I do know for sure is, if I'd had a gun then, I'd have blown her away.'

Richard stared down at her. She looked so beautiful, her hair pinned up in a French pleat and her face devoid of make-up. She was all blue eyes and pink lips.

He loved her.

He loved her so much that at times it was like a physical pain. Sometimes he fantasised about being married to her, imagined that she loved him as much as he loved her. That they had a child together, that they lived together as man and wife, and loved together as man and wife. The bubbles were obscuring her, but he sneaked a look at one pale pink nipple and felt the beginnings of an erection. Standing up abruptly, he went from the bathroom and sat in the lounge drinking his brandy.

She came in a while later, wrapped in a large white towel, her skin rosy from the hot water, smelling of sandalwood and toothpaste. 'That does feel better.' She curled up beside him on the sofa, and as he saw her settling herself comfortably he felt an urge to take her, whether she wanted him or not.

But he didn't. It was like everything as far as she was concerned: he kept it in his mind, never allowing it to spill over into his meetings with her.

He knew she loved him as a friend and contented himself with that.

She slipped a hand into his. 'Thank you again, Richard. I seem to spend my life thanking you for one thing or another, don't I?'

Her touch acted on him like an electric shock. 'You're welcome. Let me get you another drink.'

He poured another large brandy and she downed it practically in one gulp.

'I feel squiffy, but very relaxed.' She stifled a yawn. Moving round in the seat she lay against him, allowing him to put an arm around her. She snuggled against him and murmured, 'You make me feel so safe. I've never felt like that before, not with anyone.'

'It's because I'm a policeman, and you know what they say about us, don't you? Defenders of the populace, and all that crap.'

Cathy giggled. 'You know what I mean. After the night we've had, I should never feel safe again. I nearly lost my child, the only thing in this life I really care about. But now, snuggled up here with you, I can finally relax. I can always be myself with you, don't have to pretend to be anything I'm not. You know the real me, the real Cathy Connor. I'll always be Cathy Connor inside, always. Little Cathy Connor who you helped, who you looked out for.'

She took another sip of brandy. 'Don't you wish you were married, had a family?'

He squeezed her to him and said jokingly: 'I have Kitty, I have you and Susan P. I've even got fucking Desrae, so help me! What would I want with a wife, eh? I'd be bored out of me brains.'

'I'm so glad I had Kitty,' Cathy said thoughtfully. 'I wish I had another child, I wish I'd had loads of them. I wish I could have been a normal person. You know what I mean: met a boy, got married, had kids, had a mortgage, gone to a little part-time job for me pin money. I'd have loved all that. Cooking dinners, washing and ironing, scrubbing floors . . .'

'I'll marry you and you can do all that for me. But I warn you, I make a lot of washing.'

She laughed at his words. 'Me and you married! Can you imagine that?' Her laughter died as she realised that he could imagine that. Instinctively she placed a hand on his cheek. 'Any woman would be glad to be taken care of by you, Richard. As I've always said, you're . . .'

He finished the sentence for her. 'I know, I'm a lovely man. I'll have that put on me grave. "Here lies Richard Gates, he was a *lovely* man". '

'A very, very lovely man actually.' She was kneeling on the sofa now. Leaning against him, she kissed him gently on the lips. She knew what he wanted from her, and such was her gratitude she was willing to grant him anything.

'Love me, Richard. Love me however you want.'

He looked into her eyes. She was half drunk, but not drunk enough not to know what she was about.

As she dropped the towel from her body he saw her for the first time without clothes. He saw the pink tones of her skin, the softness of her rounded stomach, the fine line of her ribcage. His breathing was becoming heavier. He felt a film of sweat break out on his brow. He saw the pink slit between her legs as she lay back on the sofa and held out her arms to him.

He could smell her, and she smelt beautiful as he had always known she would.

The downy hair between her legs was honey-coloured, and he felt an urge to press his face against it, taste her, take her, as he had imagined himself doing so many times in his life. Instead he covered her with the towel and, gathering her to him, held her tightly, feeling the sting of tears as she held on to him just as tightly.

Her voice was small. 'Don't you want me?'

He closed his eyes. Oh, how he wanted her, how he had dreamed of her saying those very words to him. But he wanted her only when she wanted him also, and not from gratitude or because she wanted to confer a favour. As much as he was tempted to take her now, he knew he couldn't. Knew that he would hate himself afterwards; that it would change their relationship.

He picked her up and carried her through to her bedroom. He plonked her down on the bed without ceremony and said: 'Come on, girl, get a few zeds in. I'll crash on the couch and wake you with a nice cuppa in the morning.'

She lay on the bed watching him, sorry now for what she had done. She looked so forlorn he felt a moment's pity for her.

'Look, Cathy, it's not a case of not wanting you, darlin',

but if we got together I'd like it to be because we care for one another like adults, as man and woman. Not because you feel you owe me one, OK?'

She nodded sadly and he kissed her lightly on the cheek before leaving the room.

As she lay there she felt a strange urge to cry, because it suddenly dawned on her that she *did* want him as a woman; wanted him desperately. Not because she was grateful, but because he was a man whom she respected and cared about. Loved even.

Why had she never realised that before?

Now she had offended him, after all he had done for her. A big tear squeezed its way out of her eye and she wiped it away furiously. She had taken his love for granted all her life, and now she realised why she enjoyed being with him so much, why they were such good friends. Because, deep down, she wanted Richard Gates as much as he seemed to want her, and now she had ruined it.

She didn't sleep that night even though she was tired out, emotionally and physically. Neither did Richard.

Both lay awake until dawn, aware that only a door separated them.

Chapter Forty-Five

Kitty was much better the next day, and the hospital said they were only going to keep her in a few days more for observation. She seemed to have no recollection of her ordeal and everyone agreed that until she remembered it, it might be wisest to leave her alone, not try and force the memories.

This suited Cathy down to the ground. The less said about the ordeal the better, as far as she was concerned.

Richard made sure that the police were kept informed, and that Kitty was left in peace. It seemed all the girl wanted to do was sleep. The doctors said to let her. She would find her own way to deal with what had happened.

Cathy held her daughter's hand, a silent loving presence, which was all that Kitty really required. As long as her mother, Desrae or Richard was with her, she was happy. And for Cathy just to see her daughter fit and well was enough. Just to know that she was there, safe and secure.

After a long sleep Kitty awoke and smiled at her. 'I'm a bit hungry now, Mum. Can I have something to eat?'

Cathy grinned. 'Of course you can. All the girls are

coming in later to say hello. That should give them all something to talk about in here, eh?'

Kitty's eyes twinkled at the thought of the nurses' and doctors' faces when the 'girls' arrived. Knowing them, they'd all be in full drag, trying to outdo one another as usual. Then she thought of Michaela and her eyes clouded over.

'Why did Michaela come and get me, Mum?'

Cathy was nonplussed for a few seconds. 'No one knows yet, darling.'

Kitty looked at the bedcover. She was picking at it nervously with her fingers. 'I don't want to see him, Mum.'

With those words, Cathy realised that her daughter remembered more than she was letting on. But she would play the game. Kitty was like her mother.

'Don't worry, baby,' Cathy reassured her. 'Everything is fine now, and nothing bad will ever happen to you again. That's a promise, OK?'

Kitty tried to smile. 'I love you, Mum. I really love you.'

Cathy gathered her into her arms and they cried together. They were still sitting like this when Desrae turned up with all the girls from the club. They swept into the room like a gaggle of exotic birds, all lip-liner and false eyelashes. Baskets of flowers and fruit were placed on the bed, magazines and chocolates were put into the small locker and a rather gaudy lime-green bedjacket ceremoniously placed around Kitty's shoulders.

As they all fussed over her, kissed her and remarked on how beautiful she was, Desrae whispered to Cathy: 'Susan P's outside. Get yourself home for a few hours.'

Cathy nodded. After taking her leave of everyone, she left the hospital and climbed gratefully into Susan's car.

When they were stuck in traffic, Susan P finally spoke. 'How is she?'

'She remembers more than she's letting on, Sue, but she seems to be coping OK.'

Susan P rolled down the window of her Lotus and shouted out to a passing jay walker: 'You on a fucking death wish or what?' Without waiting for an answer she went on to Cathy: 'Eddie Durrant wants to know when we're going to keep our side of the bargain?'

Cathy leant back against the leather seat and took a deep breath, letting it out slowly. 'It'll have to be done soon, won't it? What's the score with Michaela?'

Susan shrugged. 'Disposed of this morning. His body will be washed up in a few years off the Essex Marshes. He's history.'

Cathy lit a cigarette and stared out at the passing traffic. 'I was good to him, you know. Helped him out many times.'

'Look, there's plenty of Michaelas around,' her friend said. 'Think of the girls I employ. They have the best clients, the best of everything, and still they try and turn tricks behind me back. It's human nature. They don't think of what we've had to do to get where we are. It's a case of: "Well, you're all right. You've got plenty of spondulicks. What's the matter with me creaming a little extra off the top?" Cunts, the lot of them.'

Susan honked her horn as they pulled into Dean Street; a cab was blocking the road. Two men emerged, the worse for wear, and made their way into the Groucho Club. One was a big TV producer and Susan P smiled and waved at him.

'One of me best customers, him. Likes women to walk up and down his back in needle-sharp high heels. A right nut. Still, he ain't no trouble and that's always a touch, eh?'

Cathy couldn't help but laugh. Then: 'You've been

marvellous through all this. I can't thank you enough, Susan.'

The older woman slapped her on the leg. 'Oh, leave it out. Don't come over all mushy, I can't take that. We're mates, and mates help each other out.'

'Thanks all the same, I really did appreciate it. And as for Michaela – thanks for that and all.'

Susan glanced at her. 'Don't thank me. It was Fate who got rid of her, love, the same as Fate's getting rid of Campbell. It's arranged. All we have to do is wait. He's going to cut his wrists in jail. At least, that's what I *think* is going to happen. It's more a case of when, and only Richard can tell us that. Hopefully then we'll see the back of Eddie Durrant.'

'What's happening with all the other people at the party?' Cathy's voice was bitter.

Susan P grinned. 'Quite a catch! The lesbo estate agent has made a full statement. There was also a High Court judge, a plasterer from Bow, and a couple of people from the Foreign Office. What a lovely thought, eh? How these fuckers find each other, I don't know. Still, birds of a feather and all that.'

They pulled up outside Cathy's flat. 'Durrant's in there. I'll dump the car and be with you in about fifteen minutes, OK? Richard's up there as well. He'll know more by now, I hope.'

Eddie Durrant was installed in Cathy's lounge with a large Scotch and a Cuban cigar. Cathy was amazed once more by how good-looking and presentable he was. Gates was quiet as usual. Waiting until he had something to say before he spoke.

Cathy was glad of Eddie Durrant's presence because she was still embarrassed about the events of the night before. She smiled at her visitors.

'How's your daughter?' asked Eddie.

Cathy went over to Durrant and held out her hand to him. As he shook it she answered him. 'Fine, thank you.'

'Good. That's good to hear. Children are precious.'

'They certainly are. Can I get you a refill?'

'A coffee would be great, but first I think you should hear what Mr Gates has to say.'

Richard spoke very quietly, but his words struck a chill.

'Campbell won't make a statement. He's convinced the other people will be too scared to give evidence against him. We have decided that he is to be taken out in custody. That's difficult, but not impossible. He dies tomorrow. The others will be scapegoats. They'll all be done. The boy, Johnny, is willing to testify, and we're hoping Kitty will be deemed too traumatised to appear in court. We'll have her statement read out.

'We've got enough to keep us all very busy and in fact Campbell's "suicide" will only compound his guilt in the eyes of the jury. Plus we can dress it all up pretty much how we like once he's out of the way. So, Mr Durrant, that's that.'

The big black man nodded, pleased as punch with the new developments. 'You're my kind of policeman, Mr Gates. Justice is very rarely served in these cases, as you know. I suppose the High Court judge will get off lightly?' His voice was mocking and Richard ignored him.

The phone rang. Cathy walked through to the kitchen to answer it. It was Eamonn, and as she heard his voice she realised she had not thought of him once in the previous twenty-four hours. She didn't answer immediately, and Eamonn, thinking they had a bad connection, said loudly: 'Is everything all right? I've tried to ring a few times but there was no answer.'

She saw the flashing light on the answerphone; it was

true. She gave him a quick summary of all that had happened. When she'd finished, he said, 'Is she OK?'

Cathy nodded, forgetting he couldn't see her.

'Will you be all right for next weekend then? I've missed you, Cathy, really missed you, darlin'.'

She felt a faint irritation as he spoke. 'Did you hear what I just said, Eamonn? My daughter, my only child, was taken by a paedophile and nearly raped – gang raped – and you honestly think I'll be OK to dump her and come to New York this weekend? Are you really that stupid?'

Eamonn went quiet at the end of the phone. 'I'll ring you at the weekend, Cathy,' he said finally. 'I can tell you're not yourself. You know I don't mean to be selfi—'

She interrupted him loudly, forgetting she had company in the next room.

'Oh, bollocks, Eamonn! You've always been a selfish bastard, always will be and all. If the boot was on the other foot then I'd have been on the first plane to New York in case you needed me. But that's not your style, is it? You don't like people to be complicated, do you? Everything has to be nice and trouble-free, doesn't it? Well, you'll see me when you see me and not before! My daughter, *our* daughter, needs me, and I'll see she's taken care of.'

'I think you're being a bit hard here, Cathy. I'm not the enemy . . .'

'No, you're not, I am dealing with my enemies but thanks for the offer to help – it's much appreciated. Even if you haven't actually made it yet!'

'Cathy, please darlin', listen to me.' His voice was all solicitude and calculated charm. 'If you need me, I'm here. I just thought you might like a break. I'm sorry, I didn't mean to make you cross. I'll get the next plane, charter a jet, anything to fucking well make you happy. OK?'

'That won't be necessary, I still have a few loose ends to tie up here. I'll be in touch soon.'

Eamonn knew he was being dismissed and it annoyed him. Swallowing down his anger he said sweetly: 'I love you, baby, remember that.'

'I love you too, Eamonn.' Putting down the phone, she realised it was true, she *did* still love him – but not as much as she had once thought.

As she turned to the door, she saw Richard standing there and realised he had heard only the last part of the conversation. She knew that instinctively and it hurt her because he was worth fifty Eamonns.

His eyes accused her, and for a split second she felt an urge to scream out all her frustration. Instead, she smiled warmly at him.

'I'm just making the coffee.'

He smiled back. 'Take your time, there's no hurry. How's Eamonn these days?'

Suddenly Cathy felt annoyed with them both. All she had on her plate, all she had to cope with, and the two men in her life were both giving her grief.

'He's great, thanks,' she said sarcastically. 'Coming over at the weekend to hold my hand and fuck the arse off me. You know Eamonn – always there when you need him. I don't bleedin' think.'

'There's no need to take that tone with me, Cathy. I ain't the enemy, love.'

She sighed, all the fight leaving her. He had used the same word as Eamonn. Maybe all men were secretly enemies of women? It was a thought anyway.

'Oh, fuck off and all, you. I ain't in the mood.'

Richard walked away from her, and she heard the front door slam a few seconds later. Tearing through the flat, she followed him out on to the street. It was busy with the evening traffic and the influx of nightly visitors.

'Richard, please wait!' Her voice was high. She caught up with him on the corner of Greek Street. 'Please, Richard, forgive me. Please, I'm sorry. I was upset, just upset. I didn't mean it, I swear I didn't mean it.'

He looked down at her. He knew she was telling him the truth but it had hurt. After everything that had passed between them, it had really hurt.

She clung to him, and the passers-by watched them with interest, the little blonde and the big bald-headed man.

Slipping his arms around her, he held her to him tightly. 'All right, Cathy. Relax, girl, calm down. You're forgiven, OK? Now please stop crying, darlin', come on. All friends have a few tear ups, it's only natural.'

He walked her back to the flat, all the time comforting her. When they got inside Eddie Durrant had tactfully disappeared. He held her again as she cried, repeating over and over again: 'I'm sorry. Please believe me, I'm sorry.'

Eventually he looked into her face and said gently, 'Look, Cathy, you've had a rough time of it. I understand that. Now let's have a coffee, eh? I want to visit Kitty and I want something to eat. So let's get back to normal.'

She nodded. Even with red eyes and a running nose she was still incredibly beautiful to him. No matter what she looked like, he would always see his Cathy. That was how he would always think of her.

Why he would always love her.

Trevale Campbell was pleased with himself. He had not made a statement and had refused even to talk when they had questioned him. He was confident he would soon be released because the other people involved would cut their own throats before they tied him in with all that had happened. He had made sure that his reputation as a hard man, a maniac, would serve him in good stead in just such circumstances as these.

As he lay on his bunk, planning his revenge against everyone, the cell door opened. He sat up, a wide smile on his face as he saw two burly policemen enter.

'Can I go? Have you finally realised you're holding an innocent man, you fucking cretins?' He was all arrogance and bravado.

They shut the cell door behind them. When he was knocked to the ground by the bigger of the two men, he assumed they were going to try for a forced confession. Well, he hoped they marked him good. It would all be in his favour – he might even sue the fuckers. He smiled at the thought and chuckled loudly.

'Kick the fuck out of me, boys, I want you to. I'm inviting you to.' The smile left his face when he saw the Stanley knife blade. He tried to get up, but was held down in a vice-like grip.

'Good night, Mr Campbell.'

The razor-sharp blade was swiped across each wrist and then across his throat for good measure. Then the men let go of him and walked quickly from the cell. He lay there, blood pumping out of him, hearing their laughter from beyond the door.

Pulling himself to his feet, he staggered to the metal grille. It was closed. He looked around the cell. It was dirty, covered in graffiti. The smell from the toilet was overpowering. Suddenly Trevale Campbell realised he was going to die here. In this squalid little cell. Alone.

Twenty minutes later they came back, bringing a cup of tea and a sandwich for the detained man. It all looked very thoughtful. A new prisoner was being put in with him, really to serve as witness to his 'suicide'. This young man, pulled in for dangerous driving, nearly passed out at the sight before him.

There was blood everywhere, all over the place, but it was the dead man's staring face that did it for him. His eyes were bulging and he looked more angry than anyone the boy had ever seen in his life.

On the floor of the cell was a single word, written in letters of blood. *BASTARDS.*

Back at her flat, Cathy, alone now, picked up the dirty cups and glasses and took them out to the kitchen. She pressed the button on her answerphone, and as she loaded the dishwasher she played back her messages.

The first one was from Eamonn, and she listened to it with only half an ear. Normally his voice made her go peculiar. Today it was just another message on the tape. The second was from Michaela, and Cathy listened to it with disbelief on her face and hatred in her heart.

'Hi, Cathy, just trying to track you down . . . I'll call again later.' Mickey must have been making sure that neither Cathy nor Desrae was going to the school for any reason. That made sense, when he was intending to go there himself. She hoped he rotted in Hell.

The third message made her jump. She recognised the voice. It was unmistakably Shaquila Campbell.

'Mrs Pasquale? It's Shaquila here, can you ring me? I have some information I think you might be interested in.' She gave her mobile number and rang off.

Cathy didn't bother listening to the other messages. Instead she picked up her coat and left the flat. An hour later she was at Shaquila's flat.

The other woman let her in nervously. 'Listen, you should have rung me. If Terry knew . . . I mean, yesterday he got so upset . . .'

Cathy placed a hand on the woman's arm. 'Calm down, Shaquila. You have nothing to fear from him ever again.'

Shaquila's eyes widened. 'What are you telling me?'

'He's dead,' Cathy whispered. 'Or at least he will be soon, if he's not already.'

Shaquila looked at her as if she were mad.

'He's dead, believe me, the man's gone from your life,' Cathy insisted. 'He's had what's known on the streets as an assisted suicide. He's cut his wrists and throat. Or he's going to at some point tonight.'

Shaquila's voice was flat. 'Is this for real?'

Cathy nodded. 'It's for real. You can relax, Shaquila, he ain't never coming back.'

The other woman closed her eyes and her body seemed to sway with emotion. 'Oh, how I have dreamed of this day! You don't know what it's like.'

Cathy laughed gently. 'I do, Shaquila, believe me.'

'Was it your daughter he had yesterday?'

Cathy nodded again. 'I got to her just in time, but thank you for warning me even if I didn't get the message. I know what it took for you to defy him like that.'

'I was terrified. I didn't see the girl, I just heard him talking about it. I remembered your daughter's name was Kitty and I put two and two together. I hope she's OK?'

'Shaken, subdued, but OK. Thanks again.'

Shaquila suddenly laughed out loud. 'He's really dead?'

Cathy said gaily, 'As a bleeding doornail.'

They toasted Terry's death in red wine, and like two old friends laughed and chatted together. Shaquila was a woman given a reprieve from a living death.

'What are you going to do now?' Cathy asked her.

She shook her head. 'I don't know. It will be so good just to be able to move about freely, you know? Not to have to wait in for him to come and take me, when and as often as he wants. I can finally be free.'

'Do you think you'll ever settle? You know, with another man?'

Shaquila laughed bitterly. 'I don't want no man, thank you very much, and before you ask I don't want no woman either. I just want to be happy. I want to bring up my babies and just be happy.'

'I know what you mean, but you're beautiful, Shaquila, men will want you. With your looks, you won't be alone for long.'

She shrugged. 'We'll see. How about you? You married, divorced, what?'

'Widowed. But I have a man. He's in the States so I see him every month. It suits us. I also have a man I think I love more, but he's older than me, a different person altogether from the man I have already.'

'How much older?'

Cathy thought. 'About sixteen years or so. I'm not sure exactly. He looks older than he actually is.'

'There's an old African saying: The older the buck, the harder the horn.'

They laughed once more.

'Thanks again, Shaquila, I really appreciate the way you tried to help me,' Cathy told her.

Shaquila took the small blonde woman in her arms and they embraced as only women can.

'Thank you, Cathy. You have taken away a nightmare that has lasted nearly all my life.'

'Well, the nightmare's over now.' She glanced at her watch. 'I'd better be going, Shaquila. I have to get back to the hospital.'

They embraced once more.

'Don't be a stranger now, you hear?'

Cathy smiled. 'I won't. Take care.'

Shaquila nodded. 'You too, and thanks again.'

She shut her door and heaved a sigh of relief. Her life, her real life, was just about to start. Squeezing her hands into fists, she did a little jump for joy.

That night in the club Cathy celebrated with everyone, but inside she was sad. Richard was with one of Susan P's girls and it was obvious they knew each other very well. As she saw him chatting to the tall brunette Cathy felt a stab of pain go through her heart. She realised she was jealous.

Susan P watched and went over to her. The worse for wear after more cocaine than usual, she opened her mouth before she realised what she was saying.

'She's one of his regulars. Yvonne's a real professional and knows just what Richard likes.'

Cathy smiled. 'I wouldn't have thought he paid for it?'

'Oh, he pays all right. Likes a bit of exotic now and then does our Richard. Knows what he wants and takes it. With a tom there's no tie, is there? That's what makes them so attractive to some men. They fuck them, have a laugh and then leave them.'

'I suppose so.'

Susan P looked at her friend and said gently: 'Have I just put me big foot in it?'

Cathy shrugged. ' 'Course not.'

'He really cares about you. You realise that, don't you?'

'I care about him too, as a friend. A good friend.' And as she watched him with the tall statuesque prostitute she knew that that was all they could ever be to one another. Just friends.

Now that the danger was over, she wasn't sure she wanted anything more. Maybe last night's feelings for Richard had just been because of all that had happened.

And besides, she had Eamonn. Eamonn, her Irish boy, the man who had taken her virginity, the man she loved with all her heart and soul.

Could you love two men? Cathy thought she did, in two very different ways. Suddenly it occurred to her that she might well *love* two men, but she didn't *need* either of them.

One was a lover, one a good friend – the best friend anyone could have.

And that was exactly how she would leave it.

Terry Campbell's death in custody hit all the papers. The apparent suicide was one of many that had taken place over the last few years.

As the word hit the street many people breathed a sigh of relief. The only person to cry for Trevale was his mother. The news broke Myra's heart.

She had loved her son with a passion that was as fierce as it had been perverse. She followed him within the year and was buried with him, Shaquila saw to that, but there was no headstone, nothing. Not a thing to say that either of them ever existed.

Shaquila saw to that as well.

Chapter Forty-Six

Kitty opened the door to the flat. When she saw who the visitor was she squealed with delight. 'Mum, it's Richard!'

He walked into the flat with his usual fierce expression carefully concealed. Kitty adored him and on the occasions when they met he always managed to look like a benevolent uncle.

'Hello, Kitty Cat, and how are you?'

She hugged him. There was something about him that made her feel safe and at home in his presence.

'I'm OK. Auntie Susan's coming round later. Are you staying for a while?'

He smiled down at her and said in his low husky voice, 'Only for a few minutes.'

Cathy was busy making a pot of coffee when he came into the kitchen. She smiled at him tremulously. 'Hello, Richard. Sit down, I'll make us a drink and then we can chat.'

As he played with Kitty, Cathy watched them. There was something about Richard that made you either love him or loathe him, and she and her daughter loved him. Richard was like a mainstay to Kitty, a big kind uncle who'd bought

her sweets when she was a little girl, and then fan magazines as she became a young woman. He wasn't empty-
handed now; he was never empty-handed where Kitty was
concerned.

Opening his overcoat, he removed two movie
magazines and slipped them under the kitchen table to the
girl. Kitty left the room with them and Cathy laughed.

'You always bring her that crap, every time. I ban
them and you bring them. How am I supposed to
discipline her?'

He shrugged. 'She's a kid, for Christ's sake, so let her
be one. Anyway, all the girls love anything to do with Tom
Cruise or River Phoenix.'

'She'll become an airhead.'

'All women are airheads. They don't mature until their
thirties.' He said this with a rueful smile and Cathy, placing
the coffee on the table, slapped him on his bald head.

'You've got some front . . .'

He interrupted her then. 'Yeah – more front than
Brighton. Do you know, she reminds me of you when you
was a kid. That same leggy look, the same freshness.
Though in fairness you've weathered well, girl, considering
all that's happened to you.'

Cathy felt tears prickling her eyes. What she would have
done without this man's friendship over the years, she
didn't know. He was the rock she had clung to as the tides
washed over her. No matter what had happened he was
there beside her, helping her.

'So, Richard, what brings you here then?'

He took a deep breath; he hated to be the bearer of bad
news and had a feeling that this woman had had all the bad
news she could take in the last few weeks.

'Your mother was released a few days ago. I was only
told this morning. I thought I ought to warn you.'

Cathy went white with shock. 'Are we in any kind of danger?' she asked him finally.

'I really have no idea,' Richard admitted. 'As far as I can make out she was released into the community. You know she was being treated on a psychiatric basis towards the end? It seems they moved her out of Cookham Wood and into a small hospital in Essex called Rampton. She did so well there that they released her. Now no one seems to know where the fuck she's gone. They had arranged accommodation, social workers had fixed back-up for her, and she was to be a day patient at Basildon Hospital, but Madge pissed off more or less immediately after they left her. No one has seen or heard from her since.'

Cathy bit her lip.

'She is classed as a manic depressive,' he went on. 'As long as she takes her medication, she's fine. Dolmatil evens her out, like. Now, though, it seems she has decided to look after herself, and quite frankly I'd say be wary for a while. She'll turn up, her sort always does.'

Cathy interrupted him. 'Normally on the street. Half the bag ladies are out of the mental hospitals, aren't they? Is she dangerous, Richard? Tell me, please. Not for me, but for Kitty. I need to know.'

He shrugged. 'The doctor's report says she's no danger to society, otherwise they'd never have let her out, but whether she's a danger to you, I have no real idea.'

Cathy lit a cigarette and pulled on it deeply. 'If it's not one thing, it's another,' she said wearily.

'Just keep a weather eye out, that's all you have to do. Once she turns up we can all breathe easily again. I mean, she might be sweet as a nut. We really don't know.'

Cathy laid her hand on top of his. 'You're so very good to me. What would I do without you?'

'You'd have survived. You're a survivor like me.'

'I nearly didn't the day I first met up with old Desrae, but that's a story for the dark winter nights. But all that aside, I'm worried. Not for me, for Kitty. I've never told her about her granny. There didn't seem any point.'

'Well, there is now, and she'll cope with it. I mean, think about it. At fourteen she's seen more of life than most adults. More than you wanted her to see, I know but you've brought her up smashing, she's a credit to you, darlin', and you should appreciate that fact. You done a blinding job with her. She'll cope.'

Cathy finished her coffee before answering him.

'I'll see what happens first. If I hear from my mother then I'll have to sort something out, won't I?'

Richard nodded. 'I suppose so. Like you say, worry when there's something to worry about, eh? Now I'd better go. I have to work for a living – which is more than I can say for you lot.'

After he'd left Cathy sat at the table and pondered this new situation. She wanted to see her mother, and she didn't want to see her mother. It had been a long time. Far too long really for either of them to know the other. Remembering her childhood, she tried to concentrate only on the good bits, the fun bits, but it was hard. Ron's face swam before her eyes and she shut them tight, trying to blot out the image.

So much that was bad had happened in her life, and all because of Madge and her job. In reality Cathy should hate her, but she couldn't. Madge was her flesh and blood, her only relative after Kitty. Her only family.

Desrae opened his front door with a wide smile on his face. He had been expecting Kitty. Instead he found a shabby woman with dyed red hair standing on his doorstep.

'Can I help you, love?' Desrae took a quick look down

Greek Street in case someone saw him talking to this old bag lady.

'Are you Desrae?'

He nodded. 'What can I do for you, my love? Collecting for something, are you?'

The woman shook her head. 'I am here about Cathy Duke, or Connor as she was known.'

Desrae narrowed thickly mascaraed eyes and said in a deep voice: 'What about her? And it's Pasquale these days.'

The woman sighed. 'I ain't here for trouble. I just need to see her for five minutes, that's all. I have some information for her.'

'And what kind of information would you have, dear, if you don't mind me asking?'

She sucked on her teeth a moment before answering. 'Important information, that's what.'

Desrae rolled his eyes heavenwards. 'You trying to wind me up, love? Now who are you? When I know that I'll decide if I'm going to tell her anything. I can't be no fairer than that, can I?'

'My name is Betty Jones, I've known Cathy since she was born. I was a friend of her mother's. Maybe she's mentioned me? I see her now and again. She visits me like.'

'Well, why didn't you ring her?'

Growing impatient, Betty said sarcastically: 'Because what I have to say is best said to her face. I have never known her address. I was never invited to her home. But I still care for her, as I always have, and I need to see her urgently. I was told you could get me to her.'

Desrae was in a quandary. He wanted to know what was going on, but he didn't want it to seem as if he was interfering. He had heard of this Betty Jones all right, but wasn't sure what to do now that she was actually on his doorstep.

'What's this all about then?' he pressed.

'It's about Madge, her mother. That's what it's all about.'

Desrae stepped back. 'You'd better come inside.'

As they walked up the stairs, his mind was working overtime. If Madge were back, then that could only mean trouble for Cathy. And what about Kitty? The girl had no idea that her grandmother had been in prison for murder. She was not going to know either, if it was up to Desrae. That youngster had been through more than enough.

Betty stared around her at the gaudy colours in the sitting room and finally perched on the edge of the two-seater settee. Desrae sprawled in a chair and for a few moments the two weighed each other up.

'Madge turned up at my house two days ago,' Betty began. 'I've been trying to decide what to do with her ever since. I know she's been up here, watching out for her daughter. I'm worried about her. Madge isn't all the ticket these days. Not that she ever really was.' Betty sighed heavily. 'I wouldn't put it past her to do Cathy a damage if she could. Not that she's said anything, it's more a feeling, you know?'

'Do you think Cathy should be told, is that it?' Desrae asked, feeling dismayed at the news.

Betty shrugged. 'Look, here's my number. I have to get back, I want to keep me eye on Madge. She thinks I've gone out shopping. I'll have to cab it back as it is. Do what you think is best, and then let me know. Here, give me your number and I can tell you what's going on from my end. Whatever happens, we have to protect Cathy and her daughter. Madge is as mad as a hatter. Years ago, she was a laugh: not any more. She scares me, mate.' Betty shuddered. 'I don't really want her at my place but there's not a lot I can do, is there? I can't ding her out, can I?'

Desrae shook his head understandingly. 'Look, take this.' He thrust a twenty-pound note into the woman's hand. 'Get a cab. And write me down your address as well. I'll pop on me thinking wig and try to come up with something, OK? I don't like to rush you off like this but Kitty, Cathy's girl, is due here and I think it's best if she doesn't see you,' Desrae said tactfully.

Betty nodded. 'I bet she's a beauty. Cathy was stunning as a child – really stunning. I envied Madge that little girl, I really did. Maybe I should have taken her over . . . Madge probably would have let me. But the past's the past, isn't it? Not a lot you can do about it once it's gone.'

Desrae shook his head sadly. 'No, you're right there. Leave the past in the past, as my old Joey used to say, Gawd love him. We'll all look out for Cathy and then she'll be fine, eh?'

Betty smiled, happier now she felt someone else was involved. 'You're a very nice woman, Miss Desrae, Cathy was lucky to have found you.' The words were sincere and Desrae smiled sadly.

'No, I was the lucky one. But thank you all the same.'

He showed her to the door then picked up the phone. There was only one person to deal with this effectively, and that was Susan P. If anyone could sort out this mess, then she was the woman to do it.

Madge looked terrible. As she walked along the Roman Road, people stared at her. Years before she would have known everyone, and indeed she recognised a good few faces now but she knew no one would recognise her. Her face, striped up in prison, had puckered scars along each cheek. Her hair was grey, straggly and unkempt. Her eyes had disappeared into the bags beneath them.

She looked what she was, and she knew it.

As she hit the second-hand stall she sorted through the clothes, looking for a dress or a suit, a good coat and maybe a pair of shoes. Her clothes from prison were well past their sell-by date and she knew she needed to tidy herself up.

Especially if she was going to see her girl. Madge smiled at the thought.

A woman looking for a new top jostled her and Madge, used to prison life, knocked her flying with one meaty forearm.

The stallholder stared in amazement at the old lady with the face like the back end of a bus. 'Calm yourself down, love . . .' Her words were cut off by the expression on the old woman's face. Madge looked ferocious, and her scars, a sure sign to any East Ender of a prison sentence served, stilled the stallholder's tongue.

Madge carried on looking, undisturbed. After twenty minutes she had what she wanted, and when she bartered the stallholder down the woman didn't say a word. As Madge moved away with her purchases, the woman looked after her and breathed a sigh of relief. The youngsters were aggressive enough, without old-age pensioners jumping on the bleeding bandwagon!

Madge stayed down the Roman all afternoon, enjoying the familiar sights and smells. She treated herself to a few eels and ate them standing by the stall, eyes taking in everything around her.

She was really out, she was home. But she still had old scores to settle and settle them she would.

Betty made them a pot of tea. She had arrived home before Madge which had pleased her. Her friend need not know she had been anywhere.

'Had a nice time, duck? The clothes look a treat on you.

She does a good deal that young Marion, doesn't she? Got meself a lovely lambswool coat off her last year.'

Madge nodded and sipped at her tea.

'Come on, cheer up,' Betty urged. 'You're out now. Soon you'll have your own little place, and can pick up your life again.'

Madge stared at her friend for a while and then she began to laugh. It was a chilling sound that made Betty uneasy all over again.

'Give over, Madge, that wasn't meant as a joke.'

She stopped laughing. Her voice hard, she said: 'But it is a joke, isn't it?' Her face took on a mock-puzzled expression then. 'I mean, I do the time for my daughter – my daughter the whorcmaster – and she gets a good life, a nice husband, money, respectability, the whole fucking enchilada. And what the fuck do I get, eh? Fuck all, that's what. And you can't see the joke, Betty? You must be losing your sense of humour in your old age. I find it fucking hilarious, personally.

'But I'll sort her out, don't you worry about that,' she said ferociously. 'I'll sort her out once and for all. The spawn of the fucking devil her! Never knew a real day's peace from the moment I birthed her. Should have put her down the toilet like I did the others.'

Betty was shocked and this made Madge laugh again.

'All those fucking years and not a word from her. You don't know what it's like inside, Betty. It destroys you a little bit more every day. I had a long time to think about what that little mare did to me, and I'll repay her, don't you worry about that.'

Betty felt the sting of tears. Where was the old Madge? Where was the slapdash, haphazard friend she'd had for so long?

'Coming up the pub?' Madge's voice was normal again.

Betty nodded. There was a phone there and she knew she had to get some help. She could no longer cope with Madge Connor on her own.

Madge and Betty sat in The Two Puddings in Stratford, sipping port and lemon. Madge had wanted to see it again after all the years inside. They had cabbed it there and now sat quietly watching the world go by.

'It's all changed, Betty,' Madge was saying. 'I mean, when they gave me the twenty quid as I left I thought I had a fucking fortune, but it's fuck all these days, isn't it? The price of everything is astronomical. How young girls manage with a couple of kids, I don't know.'

Betty nodded in agreement. 'I know, the prices are a joke. It's that Margaret Thatcher I blame. Whoever voted her in needs treatment, if you ask me.'

Madge finished her drink. 'Bit posh in here and all if you ask me – full of them yuppies by the looks of it. Read about them in the papers I did. The money they earn!'

Betty smiled. This was more like it, Madge was talking normally again. 'You seem a bit better, love,' she said.

Madge smiled, and there was a glimmer of a resemblance to the girl she had once been. 'I am better now I have a plan. Yes, I feel much more relaxed.'

Just then, a young man walked past their table on the way to the toilets and eyed them with derision.

'Had your fucking look, you ugly little cunt?' Madge's voice was loud and hard. The people in the bar turned to stare at her. The boy was shocked which suited Madge. Her face was screwed up into a mask of hatred.

'Go on, piss off,' she bawled. 'Go and pull yourself, bleeding plonker. And on your way back, don't you dare look in my direction again.'

Betty was red with embarrassment and shock. 'Leave it

out, Madge, it ain't the old days now. You can get nicked for threatening behaviour these days.'

'Up yours, Betty,' Madge said scornfully, 'and up his and all. Who did he think he was, looking at me like I was a piece of dirt? Who's he, for fuck's sake, that makes him better than me? Answer me that one if you can.'

Betty was distressed. 'Come on, I'll get us another drink.' She walked up to the bar, keeping her eye on the door.

The barmaid said softly, 'You'll have to keep that old dear in line or you're both out, love. I can't have me customers spoken to like that.'

Betty mumbled an apology and ordered the drinks, all the time thinking that Carlos the Jackal would be hard put to keep Madge in line.

When the door opened and Richard Gates walked through it, Betty felt as though she had been given the keys to the Bank of England. Never in her life had she been so pleased to see anyone, especially an Old Bill.

Madge saw him too. She glared across at Betty and shook her fist threateningly.

Richard said quietly: 'Long time no see, Madge.'

She stared up at him, and he saw the ravages that time had inflicted on her face.

'Not long enough for me, mate.' Animosity was coming off her in waves.

As he escorted her from the premises, Betty followed them, leaving the drinks on the bar. Outside, Susan P was waiting in her Lotus. Richard put Madge into the back seat and climbed in beside her. Betty watched as her friend was driven away, feeling she had done something bad, very bad. But she knew that if Madge had hurt Cathy, she would never have forgiven herself.

Going back into the pub, she drank both her drink and

Madge's, giving her friend a final toast as she did so. She had a feeling she wouldn't be seeing old Madge again.

'Well, well, well, if it isn't Mr Gates, the villain's friend. I might have guessed I'd see you at some point.'

Richard ran one hand over his bald head. 'You're a complete prat, Madge. You'll never change, will you?'

She snorted and then said nastily, 'And how are you, Miss P? All right, are you? You both look like you're doing very well. Nice cars, nice clothes. The scene has definitely changed since I've been away, eh? Even me daughter seems to be somebody now. Well, let me tell you this: you're all nothings, nobodies. Outside the Smoke no one's heard your names, or even knows you exist. You're big fishes in a little pond.'

Susan P watched the old woman in her mirror, wondering what the hell they were going to do with her now they had her.

'You're to leave Cathy alone. If we thought you wanted to see her because you're her mother and she's your child, we'd take you to her. But you don't, do you, Madge? You want to hurt her. As if you didn't do enough to hurt her in the past.' Richard's voice was low, barely audible. The quieter his voice became, the more deadly he was. Madge knew this and kept her peace. Then suddenly she exploded.

'Fuck you, Gates, and fuck you an' all, you lesbian bitch. I have nothing to lose any more. Nothing at all. You don't scare me, any of you. She owes me, the little whore, and now I'm going to collect. Her clubs and her kid and her nice husband . . . when did she ever give a shit about me, I ask you? I grafted for that little mare, I flogged my arse to keep her clothed and fed.'

Madge actually believed what she was saying, Richard and Susan P realised in shock.

'I gave up the best years of my life for her, and now she wants to blank me out like I never even existed. Well, she can't. I done a lot of bird for that little madam and the thought of her doing well gets right up my fireman's.'

Richard sighed. 'You have already broken your parole agreement. I can get you banged up again tonight. You were supposed to go and stay in the accommodation allocated to you by Social Services. Instead you did a runner. Now I'm going to take you back to the nick with me and let that be an end to it. If I recommend you have another assessment in, say, one year and go back inside *pro tem*, they'll listen to me, Madge. I'll say you're a danger to your daughter and granddaughter. I'll tell them you threatened me, say I think you're a danger to the public. Then, when you're banged up once more . . .'

Susan P interrupted him then. 'I'll see to it that you get your just deserts in prison.'

Madge grinned. 'Fuck you, lady.'

Susan P screeched the car to a halt by the kerb. Turning in her seat, she grabbed Madge by the hair and, dragging her face towards her own, said viciously: 'No, Madge, it's fuck *you*, because if I choose to, you'll fucking die, lady. And you know I can make that happen. I looked after you in that nick. I saw to it you was left alone. Because Cathy asked me to, wanted me to. You know she couldn't visit, she was on the run. And later, though I could have arranged it, I knew you were too vicious an old crone to let her see you. So just watch yourself, lady, because if Cathy gets so much as a fucking cold, I'll blame you.'

Madge was shocked. 'I'm getting all the blame as usual, am I?' she whined. 'You don't know her. You'll all learn as I did what she's really like . . .'

Susan P pushed her back into her seat and sighed. 'Tell her the score, Richard, I want to go home.'

'OK. You're going on a little journey, Madge. Fancy that, do you? Or would you rather go straight back in the clink?'

He smiled at her expression. Let her sweat, it'd do her good. All he wanted was her well out of the way, somewhere he could keep an eye on her. Prison was not the place for her now. She needed help and he was going to see she got it.

Cathy was wary for a while but after a few months, thoughts of her mother faded from her mind. She believed that Madge had decided to leave her alone and get on with her own life. In a way, she was sad. She had wanted to see her, talk to her. But it obviously was not to be. Gradually her life hit an even keel and she began to live once more. Richard and Susan never told her anything, and nor did Desrae.

They had all decided that in this matter ignorance was bliss so far as Cathy was concerned.

Book Six

Come, let us take our fill of love until the morning; let us solace ourselves with loves. For the goodman is not at home, he is gone a long journey.

– Proverbs, 7:18–19

Liberavi animam meam.
I have freed my soul.

– St Bernard, 1090–1153

Chapter Forty-Seven

New York 1995

Cathy walked out of Saks on Fifth Avenue laden down with bags. She felt full of beans. Springtime always made her feel good as if life were beginning again and everyone had a new chance.

That morning she had walked through Central Park alone, watching the rollerbladers, enjoying a cigarette and coffee from a street vendor, and watching the world go by. Everywhere was budding, becoming beautiful. The grass was greener than ever, the trees being slowly dressed for the summer with leaves, and the sun was strong, making even the Atlantic wind bearable.

She had come to love New York, to love America. In the eight years she had visited regularly she had become a New Yorker in as far as she knew the city well. It was now a second home to her. So much so that a year before she had bought herself a loft apartment off Bleccker Street. It reminded her of London's Soho, and the artists and trendy young men and women who thronged the streets made her feel at home.

She ate in Chinatown, a light lunch of Chow Mein and prawns washed down with herbal tea, then walked with her purchases toward Little Italy where she was to meet Eamonn at 2.30. As she strolled through the crowded streets she smiled at people and the usually abrupt New Yorkers smiled back. Maybe it was her sunny countenance, or maybe the coming of spring had affected them too.

As Cathy walked into The Baker's Bar she spotted Anthony Baggato. 'No Eamonn then?'

Anthony loved her. He loved her face, her hair and her British accent. 'He'll be here soon, princess, let me get you a drink.'

He snapped his fingers and a waitress came over to them. She was dressed in a brief black dress and impossibly high heels. Cathy smiled at her.

'I'll have a glass of white wine, please.'

The girl took the order and both Cathy and Anthony watched as she sashayed back to the counter.

Cathy laughed out loud. 'You're terrible, Anthony.'

He held up his arms in a gesture of resignation. 'I look, I wish, I enjoy. At my age it's the only excitement I get, for Christ's sake.'

He was now huge. In his early sixties, he weighed over eighteen stone. As he spoke he still watched the girl. She was all of twenty with a hard, petulant expression about her lovely face.

'I don't know, Cathy, how much shopping can a woman do? Every time I see you, you're laden down with packages. I hope you make that Irish putz pay for it all?'

'I'm an independent woman. I earn my own money and spend my own money.'

Anthony played the Sicilian then. Jokingly he raised his shoulders and said loudly: 'Why couldn't I have found someone like you? My wife shops constantly and all she buys is crap. My home, a million-dollar apartment, is full of crap. That's why I never go there.' Anthony had traded in the last but one wife five years before. His new wife was twenty-eight, a chorus-girl type with full red lips, collagen enhanced, and a pair of breasts that defied the laws of gravity.

Eamonn came into the bar, and as he saw Cathy his spirits soared. She looked, as usual, good enough to eat. Dressed in a tight white suit, showing off her legs and well-turned ankles, she was as gorgeous as any movie star.

He was still entranced by her eight years on in their relationship. Today, despite all his worries – and they were legion – she still gave him a boost.

'So, I catch you together again. What is it with you two, eh? You seeing Anthony behind my back or what?'

They all laughed as Cathy replied, 'Well, I'm just glad we've been found out. It's been such a strain keeping a secret.' She sipped her wine as the men talked business.

Anthony said, 'What's the rub with Igor?'

Eamonn shrugged. 'He's the same as usual. Same shit as usual.'

Anthony laughed. 'So what you're telling me is, the red shit has not yet hit the fan?'

'The emphasis being on *yet*,' Eamonn said gloomily.

Both men looked worried for a moment and then Eamonn brightened. 'We've still got plenty of time, and if push comes to shove I'll sort it out myself. It's not as if I haven't done it before.'

'What's all this then?' Cathy enquired. 'You always seem to talk in riddles.'

The two men looked at her, and Cathy saw the tension around their eyes as they smiled at her.

'Never mind about it, honey, it's all crap.' Anthony

stood up with difficulty. 'I'd better be off, I have to meet Jack soon.'

He kissed Cathy's hand in a gentlemanly gesture. 'Until we meet again. And don't forget, baby, when you're sick of this schmuck, give me a call. What time's your flight tomorrow?'

'Eight-fifteen – in the morning that is.' She grimaced. 'I really don't want to go, Anthony, but duty and business call. As you know yourself.'

'That's one hell of a club you have there. I enjoyed it when I came over. Eight-fifteen, you say?' He looked at Eamonn, a hard penetrating stare. 'So you're off to London tomorrow? Well, then, goodbye. Until the next time.'

As he left the bar Cathy and Eamonn watched him go. He lumbered these days, but still had his old commanding presence.

'What was all that about? The meaningful stare and everything else?' Cathy wondered.

Eamonn shrugged. 'I have no idea. Now then, what do you want to do?'

She smiled flirtatiously. 'What do you think I want to do? I leave tomorrow. I got in some steaks, some wine and some salad. Dinner, bath, bed. In that order.'

Eamonn grinned. 'Sounds good to me.' But even as he spoke, Cathy could see he was worried about something.

Eamonn kissed her on the nose. 'Listen, I'll put you in a cab. I have to go home, sort out a few things. I'll get to you about six, is that OK?'

Cathy nodded, secretly upset that he was leaving her again so soon. 'That's fine by me,' she said brightly.

Deirdra smiled unpleasantly at her husband as he walked into the Long Island house. 'And to what do we owe this pleasure?'

He ignored her sarcasm. 'Was anything delivered today?'

'Some suitcases – I put them in the garage. They're very heavy. What's in them, for Christ's sake?'

Eamonn turned and walked from the room, leaving his wife fuming. Since the birth of Hattie, their youngest daughter, seven years before, he had not touched her. They lived as man and wife, attended functions together, even made chit-chat at the breakfast table – that was when he stayed home, of course – but other than that there was little contact between them.

One thing she knew: he wasn't out chasing skirt. Most of the time he was in the house with her and the children. Only a couple of times a month was he on the missing list. For Deirdra, that was enough. This was how her life was going to be and she accepted it.

Eamonn went out to the garage and looked at the two cases. They were the same as usual, nondescript, but carried more inside their lining than ever before. It was this fact that was so scary.

His usual mule had been taken out by a young black mugger on East 110th Street and Lexington. Eamonn was now left with the merchandise, and no way of getting it to London short of taking it himself. But he was due in Washington tomorrow afternoon. It was a Mafia connection meet and he had to be there.

As he stared at the cases he thought of Anthony's idea and tried to push it from his mind. He couldn't do this to Cathy, not her. But he knew in his heart that he didn't really have a choice. Also, she would never know what he had done. The merchandise was undetectable. In all the years they had been muling for the Russians, they had never once had a capture, either this end or in London.

It was foolproof.

The merchandise was worth millions, and was always paid for up front. In the 1990s, the need for it had grown and they were dealing with contacts all over the world now.

He closed his eyes and wondered what Cathy's reaction would be if she knew what he was involved in this time. It didn't bear thinking about.

Cathy was dressed in a little white number, purchased that morning from Saks. It showed off her tan perfectly and the cut was such that it enhanced her breasts and made her waist look even smaller. As she opened the door she was surprised to see Eamonn standing there with two suitcases.

'Surely you haven't left home?'

Her voice was so shocked that he forced a laugh. 'They're a present. A gift for my transatlantic lover.'

Cathy looked at the two huge Samsonite cases. 'You're joking?'

'No, these are for you. I know my gifts usually run to Cartier, and in fact I have a bauble in my breast pocket from that very establishment. But I saw these and I thought: Just the thing for my Cathy. Strong, lockable and safe.'

He put them down in the bedroom. She was still bemused.

'Suitcases? Now I've seen everything. You never cease to amaze me, Eamonn Docherty.'

He smiled at her. She had accepted his 'gift' as he'd known she would. As he poured himself a drink she began to cook the steaks. She cooked them the English way, with plenty of salt and pepper and Eamonn's favourite Worcestershire sauce.

They sat and ate, chatting as lovers do about their lives and dreams. As they finished the wine and smoked cigarettes, Cathy said: 'You know, Eamonn, it's funny.

When I saw you with the cases, for a second I really thought you had left home. I know I've always said that I didn't want us to live together, but that's because you are now a New Yorker and London is my town. But I really hoped in that split second you were going to tell me we'd always be together.

'I know it's silly, we both have commitments, we both have other lives, other people, other businesses. There's so much to keep us apart. But I really felt overjoyed for a moment, believing you were coming to me. I realised that if we'd both taken different paths, we could have been together today. Truly together. Not just for our long weekends every few weeks.'

She sipped her wine. 'I guess what I'm trying to say is: I love you more than I realised. I love you enough to try and overcome everything that keeps us apart.' She looked into his eyes. Usually they were a soft limpid blue like sea water. But today they held a hint of sadness which in turn hurt her. She felt a yearning to put the happiness back in his eyes and his heart.

He took her hand in his. 'I love you, Cathy, and we will be together one day, I promise you that much. Maybe sooner than either of us thinks.'

Now she had spoken the words aloud he could talk to her. Up until this moment she had always said there were too many things against their being together, not the least his ten children. Even he could understand her, as a woman, being loath to take a man from that many kids. Though it was most definitely a woman thing. He could walk out of the door in the morning if he had to. He would still see his children. No one would, or could, stop him from doing that.

But it had had to come from her. The final word had to come from Cathy.

'Remember when we were kids and used to snuggle up together, trying to keep warm? Whoever would have dreamed that our lives would have taken this path? That we'd both be so successful in our chosen careers?' he mused.

Cathy nodded and then said sadly, 'That we'd both murder . . .'

Eamonn shushed her, gripping her wrist painfully. 'I hate it when you talk that crap, Cathy. What's past is past. We can't change it. We both made mistakes. Yours was pretty much unavoidable. Mine . . . well, mine was like everything else I touch. A complete fuck-up, a waste of a life. Caroline would probably be married to someone now, have a family . . .' He broke off, his eyes desolate.

'I have been responsible for so many bad things, Cathy, things that I could never talk about, even to you. But once we get together properly, I am going to make sure you are the happiest woman in the world, I promise you that.'

She smiled happily. 'One day, eh? One day we'll really be together?' He nodded. Taking his hand, she led him to the bedroom.

The view from the loft was stunning and they lay together in the half light and watched as the stars came out one by one. As they clung together entwined, their love-making over, his eyes were drawn to the cases by the bed. They seemed to be mocking him.

All his grand talk, and he was using the woman he professed to love so much because he was once more in a tight corner. He *had* to go to Washington. Since Petey's death, Jack had left all the negotiating to him, had left pretty much everything to him. It was the price Eamonn had paid for the demise of his friend. Though Jack never said anything Eamonn knew his father-in-law felt he should have fought Petey's corner, told the IRA that Petey had a right to his freedom. Jack, a first-generation Irishman, should have known better than that. Once you were in the Cause only death took you out of it.

As Cathy breathed softly beside him, Eamonn felt a chill travel over him. If she got so much as an inkling of what the cases contained, or any idea what it was to be used for, she'd hate him till the day she died.

He lit a cigarette and lay in the darkness, his love asleep beside him and his own mind in turmoil. It was comparatively easy getting the stuff to England. The bugbear would be getting it out of Cathy's flat without her realising what she had been carrying.

Which was where Mr Cheng came into the equation.

Which was where it got really difficult.

Eamonn was angry with himself, and felt the unaccustomed fear that accompanied that anger. He was in trouble, deep trouble, with the Italians as well as the Irish. His dealings with the Eastern Europeans had caused friction in the world he was living in. Even though Anthony Baggato was party to everything, Eamonn still didn't have the protection he needed.

The Irish would abandon him if they knew what he was involved in. He was in way over his head. After all his dubious dealings over the years, he had taken on the Russians with confidence, never dreaming it would all get so out of hand.

As he lay beside the only woman he had ever loved, Eamonn felt the deep loneliness that accompanies the betrayal of a friend or a lover. Because he *was* betraying her. Even after it was all over, he would know what he had done to her and that was going to be hard.

He knew he should stop it all, take Cathy out of the equation, himself suffer the consequences, but he knew he wouldn't. There was a lot of money involved, but apart from that he had made a promise to deliver and he would. He *had* to.

He lay awake, his mind whirling. Dawn was breaking, and still sleep eluded him.

Cathy, however, slept safe and happy in the arms of the man she loved.

Cathy was eating breakfast: a couple of eggs over easy and some Bisquick pancakes with maple syrup, four strips of streaky bacon, and a huge cup of filter coffee.

Eamonn watched her, jealous of her appetite. He himself could eat nothing, would eat nothing, until he had word that the merchandise was out of her possession and safely stashed.

'You look awful, Eamonn, are you OK?' Her voice was concerned and he shrugged.

'A spring cold, I think. I felt shivery in the night. I'll be fine.'

She ate her breakfast ravenously; their love-making always gave her an appetite.

Eamonn was on his fifth cigarette.

'Are you sure you're not worrying about anything? Maybe I can help?'

He shook his head and snapped testily, his anger tinged with shame, 'For fuck's sake, Cathy, give it a rest, will you? I said, I'm fine.'

She stopped eating and stared at him with wide eyes. 'Jesus, Eamonn, I was only asking. There's no need to bite my bleedin' head off.'

She pushed her plate away. 'I have to get packed, I must leave for the airport soon. I won't need both the cases. I mean, I've got plenty of clothes here now I have this place. One will do.'

Eamonn felt panic welling up inside him. 'I thought you

were taking all that stuff home?' he said casually. 'You know, you were saying you should take some of it back to England. The winter stuff. I thought you were going to give it to Desrae's friend, the one who loves American clothes.' He was gabbling and he knew it.

Cathy laughed. 'Oh, fancy you remembering that! I'd forgotten all about poor Joanie. You're right – I did promise him some of my old stuff. He's about the same build. When he's wearing his falsies anyway.'

'Might as well make use of the suitcases now I've bought them for you. Seems a shame to leave one here doing nothing. Anyway, every time you pack your things in them, I want you to think of me.'

He was jocular and Cathy laughed with him, pleased that he seemed more cheerful.

'I'd best make a start, then get a shower. I'll have to leave soon.'

As Cathy packed both cases she was singing. The sound broke his heart in the quiet of the morning.

Eamonn watched Cathy's plane take off. He had felt it was never going to go. Step one was underway. As he had kissed her one last time, he had felt like Judas in the Garden of Gethsemane.

He made his way to the car park to pick up his BMW and roar back into town. He was nearly crying. No matter how often he told himself that nothing could or would go wrong, he was still terrified.

Back in his office, the telephone rang. It was Anthony Baggato. 'I take it you understood my message yesterday?'

'She's got the stuff,' Eamonn told him, 'but she has no idea about it.'

'That's as it should be,' Baggato boomed. 'The fewer people who know about it the better. I certainly wouldn't want it getting around town that I was involved. Are you ready for the trip to Washington?'

Eamonn said wearily, 'Yeah. What do you think they want from me?'

'I really have no idea,' the other man said. 'They do this now and again, it keeps people on their toes. As long as you ain't been creaming off them you have nothing to worry about.' He paused. 'Tell me you haven't been that stupid?'

Eamonn was annoyed. 'What would be the fucking point? All that's nickels and dimes compared to what we're involved in.'

Anthony chuckled. 'Very true. You're right, I apologise. But even I get nervous at times like this. It's all askew, all going wrong. I'm a superstitious man, all Italians are. I even went to Mass this morning, first time in years. But like the Bible says: God loves a sinner. And I'm definitely one of those.' He paused, then said casually, 'If, by some chance, they find out about Igor and everything, can I count on you to keep me out of it?'

Eamonn's darkly handsome face was marred by the look of contempt he bestowed unseen on his fat friend. 'What you mean is, let them kill me and Jack and a few others, so long as you live to see a ripe old age, eh?'

Anthony laughed disarmingly. 'If you put it like that, yes, that's exactly what I mean.'

'Have you heard a whisper or something?' Eamonn's voice was terse.

'I swear on my children's heads, I've heard nothing,' the Italian told him. 'You know Fancini died last night?'

Eamonn blanched. 'You're putting me on?'

'He was shot twice, once in the back of his head, once under the chin. A real Mob killing. Even the police have sussed that one. The body was left in his driveway, in his car. Whoever ordered the hit wanted him found. Did you have any dealings with him?'

Eamonn didn't answer. Fancini was a minor man, who had been Eamonn's outside contact with Igor's associates in Atlantic City. Even Anthony was unaware of his involvement as far as Eamonn knew, though he had seen them together on a few occasions.

'Are you telling me that the Mob's hit on Fancini because of us?' he said finally.

'No, all I'm telling you is the facts. Fancini got the bullet last night. Whoever whacked him did it as an example.'

When there was no response, Baggato sighed and said: 'Well, gotta go. I wish you peace. Remember, these are the big men you're seeing. They make my outfit look like toy soldiers. Be careful, just be very careful, and don't incriminate yourself or anyone else.'

'What if they know already?' Eamonn asked slowly.

'If they know, you offer them a slice of the pie, a fucking big piece of pie. If necessary, you offer them the *whole* pie. You'll know what to do. You're not a fool, even they know that, and your Irish connection gives you a measure of safety. Name drop. Use what you've got. If they're on to you, you're a fucking dead man unless you can cut some kind of deal.'

'How the fuck did we ever get involved in all this?'

Anthony did laugh then, a harsh humourless sound. 'That's the easy one. Through greed. You know, this is a lesson really. Everything has a lesson in it. We had more money than the fucking Catholic Church but we wanted more, and we didn't want to share our good fortune – what the old Dons call "wetting their beaks". No, we wanted it all, and so it follows that when it goes wrong, only we take the shit. We didn't delegate, you know what I'm saying?'

Eamonn was quiet. After Anthony had hung up he sat gnawing on his thumbnail, a nervous habit from childhood. He was in a tight corner, in trouble with too many people this time, and they were all experts in their own field.

For the first time in his life Eamonn Docherty was out of his depth.

Chapter Forty-Eight

Cathy's arrival home coincided with Kitty's school holiday and Desrae's birthday. No one knew how old he was exactly, but that didn't matter. Desrae liked to enjoy his birthdays and no one had ever had the guts to ask just how many he'd enjoyed.

The girls at the club had arranged a theme night. Everyone was to be dressed in Roman attire – which to most of the drag queens meant dressing as Cleopatra, while they hoped against hope to meet their very own Mark Antony.

Cathy had gone straight from the airport to the club, and now was there, waiting to see what the girls were going to look like this evening. Bertie, one of the bar staff, had taken her cases through to the dressing room.

Sitting on a bar stool, a cigarette in one hand and a mineral water in the other, she looked immaculate, not at all as if she had just travelled from the States. Her make-up was perfect, and other than the fine lines around her eyes denoting tiredness, she looked stunning. Her little Versace suit was uncrumpled, and her tanned legs ended in a pair of periwinkle blue sandals the exact colour of her suit and eyes.

The girls in the club all looked at her with awe, and a tinge of jealousy. It didn't matter what they spent on themselves, they were still men dressed as women, and even though a lot of them, especially the transsexuals, looked better than the majority of women, they still felt second best next to Cathy Pasquale. Mainly because she had that quiet dignity, that certain aura, that only a few lucky people have.

She smiled a greeting as Richard came into the club. 'Bit early even for you, isn't it?' she joked.

'Give us a break, Cath. I'm here on business as well as pleasure. The pleasure part is being able to chat with you. The business part might not be so welcome.'

Cathy heard the inflection in his voice. She frowned. 'What do you mean?'

He didn't answer because the lights on the club's stage had just been turned on and eighteen Cleopatras walked out simultaneously, all make-up, perfume and good-natured bitchiness.

Gates closed his eyes and said in a pained voice: 'Now I've seen everything. Even Susan P is coming as Cleopatra. I hope you're not?'

'Of course I am,' Cathy said indignantly, 'and so is Kitty. It's weird but instead of a real Roman night, we've ended up with a Cleo night. All the men, including you, must come as Caesar or Mark Antony. Though looking at you, I'd say Nero would be nearer the mark.'

'I can just see me in a toga, with my knobbly knees!' As the girls on the stage went through their paces, he motioned Cathy through into her office. She followed him, intrigued. She wasn't too worried. Richard often consulted her about things, and depending what it was – say a young girl missing or a young man being pursued by a predatory male, she might then have heard or seen something. He knew better than to question her about real villainy. He had his own grasses who sorted all that out.

Inside the office, she shut the door but the strains of the girls all singing 'Happy Birthday' still penetrated through.

'That sounds fucking horrendous!'

Cathy rolled her eyes at the ceiling. 'Desrae will love it. One of the bigger girls, Black Matilda, all of eighteen stone, wanted to dress as Marilyn Monroe. In fact, I didn't see him on the stage so I wouldn't be surprised if he came like it anyway. The poor woman would turn in her grave if she could see him.'

Cathy roared, enjoying the thought and looking forward to the night's revelry.

'Do you know a Mr Cheng?' Gates asked suddenly.

Surprised, she nodded. 'Everyone knows Mr Cheng – Little Cheng, as we call him. Why, what's he supposed to have done?'

Gates sighed. 'It's not what *he's* supposed to have done. Don't come all East End innocence with me, Cathy. Have you ever had any dealings with him via Docherty? Has he ever asked you to deliver anything or take a message to Cheng?'

Cathy felt the hairs on the back of her neck prickle with fear. She averted her eyes from Richard's fierce gaze.

'Never. Eamonn has never asked me to do anything like that. Why would he? And what's more, why would he be involved with the Chinese?' She had regained her equilibrium.

Richard said thoughtfully: 'Susan P knows about it, but I can't get a word out of her, and she's frightened, very frightened. I've never seen her like it before. Surely that should tell you something? I have it on good authority that something big is going down, and many people are in on it. I'm frightened, Cathy. For you, for Susan, and for the others involved even though I don't know them. Have you seen anything suspicious recently, either here or in the States? Think, woman, think and tell me. I hear it's so big even the main men are terrified of it.

'All I know is, Docherty's been mentioned and so has Cheng. Now I need to put those two together and find something they have in common. The only thing I can think of is drugs, but even a large cache wouldn't cause the terror I've seen in my narks. It's as if they all want to escape, but can't get out. Now I'm asking you one last time, Cathy, can you help me? I'm stumped. If it's not drugs, what the fuck can it be?'

She looked at him, mystified and wary.

'Is it to do with the IRA?' he questioned her. 'I've heard a few whispers that Docherty's involved with them. Is that what this is all about? Only if it is, tell me. I've taken a good kick back over the years not to pull him in; Susan P arranged it a long time ago. I swallow that bastard because he has some high-placed friends, not just in the Met but in Special Branch as well. Both you and I know the Irish wouldn't have gained such a hold without friends in high places. That stands to reason, doesn't it? But this is different and I need to know what's behind it.'

Cathy shook her head. 'I'm sorry, Richard, but I really don't know anything,' she said sadly. 'I'd tell you if I did.'

Gates was looking older and more tired than she had ever seen him.

'There's a conspiracy going on right under our noses, Cathy, and we are powerless to stop it. The Russians are over here, the new Mafia of the Western world, with money, guns and power. Money in great amounts can buy power, you see. People like me, supposedly enforcing the law, are powerless to stop them.

'They come over, put our girls on the game – and it's

not like the old days. These people tie the women to their flats, won't let them move. They take all their money and use them till they're well and truly worn out. This is what we have here now – an underclass of women and boys and little girls being used to make money for the bigger fish. Long live capitalism – the Russians have experienced it and they love it. You can buy justice in this country, buy your way out of a prison sentence, buy whatever it is you fucking want. I should know, I've sold plenty of so-called justice over the years. It's taken me all this time to see how wrong I was.'

The bitterness in his voice, and his defeated expression, made Cathy sad. She realised she had been his last resort – his only chance of finding out what was going on. Walking over to him, she slid her hands around his neck. He pulled her to him tightly.

'Oh, Cathy, what happened to the good old days, eh? When we all had a little tickle and no one got hurt. The real baddies were banged up and the nice baddies were roaming free. Now it's a different world.'

'I think the truth is we're out of our league now. As you say, the New Mafia, the Russians and all the rest of the Eastern bloc, well, they've got the same hunger as we had once. Now we're all rich, we want a nice quiet life, don't we? We're safe and secure and they're threatening us. It's the law of nature, the survival of the fittest.'

Her usual cheerful tone of voice had deserted her. She sounded hollow, not her normal chirpy self at all.

'Well, I for one want out of it all. I'm past ducking and diving. Even the club gives me the pip at times. So I do understand what you're saying.'

Richard wanted to take her and hold her, she sounded so lonely. He wanted to tell her he loved her. But he knew he wouldn't.

She had offered herself to him once, and he, like a fool, had refused her. Thinking it was just because she was sorry for him, wanted to love him from gratitude. Over the years he had wished time and again that he had taken her up on that offer. Because he knew he could love her, physically and mentally, better than any man, better than Eamonn Docherty ever could. She was with Eamonn for the same reason Richard had thought she wanted to be with him: because she felt she owed it to him. All they had been through as children had made her see the Irishman through rose-tinted spectacles. To her Eamonn was a product of his environment, the same as she was.

But the truth was her loyalty was totally misplaced. Eamonn was a user and would use even her without a second's thought.

Richard knew that as well as he knew his own name and address. But Cathy would never see it, not until Docherty finally tucked her up good and proper. And knowing her lover, that would happen one day. He just hoped it wasn't going to be now with all the rumours of something seriously big going down, something so huge even Richard Gates couldn't protect Cathy if she stood in the wrong people's way.

Eamonn had taken the Washington shuttle from Newark airport and by late afternoon was ensconced in the Hilton International bar, a drink beside him and a nervous feeling in his belly. He was taken up to a suite soon afterwards and felt like the condemned man on his last walk.

He tried to pull himself together.

Smiling amiably at the man sent to escort him, he was answered with a stony stare. That in itself didn't augur well, but he figured this man was probably like that even with his mother. Muscle had to look mean; it was part of the job description.

Inside the suite he saw four men, all known to him, all the last people he had expected to meet here.

There was Patrick O'Rourke, his IRA contact from Ireland, as large as life and twice as ugly, red hair tied back in a straggly ponytail and ice-blue eyes cold with disdain.

There was Sammy Colderi, the Las Vegas Don, short, portly, and looking as if he didn't know what the hell he was doing here.

Beside him was Manny Steinschloss, a Jewish entrepreneur who ran his own personal bank strictly outside the law.

But the main worry for Eamonn was that the fourth man was a New York Don, the head of the five families: Gesu Molineri. He was a huge man in his late-sixties, quietly spoken and notoriously reclusive. He kept a low profile at all times and to see him here frightened Eamonn more than seeing O'Rourke, deadly as the Irishman could be.

Molineri smiled grimly. 'Please, Mr Docherty, be seated.'

Eamonn sat down, willing himself to be calm. He had been frisked in the limo from the airport so they were all aware he wasn't armed. A glass of whisky was placed before him but he didn't touch it. Instead he lit a cigarette, pleased to see that his hands were not shaking, and trying to look relaxed.

Molineri spoke again.

'I have had a little disagreement with the Chechen – Igor. You know him, yes? We had a small dispute for a while over territory. He seemed to think he could just move into the East Side; I told him he couldn't. Yesterday he died. But, you see, before he died, we had a long chat. About you.'

He paused to let his words sink in.

'And about a few other things, principally events that occur in London. Nothing I need really concern myself with, you understand, but interesting all the same.'

Eamonn could hear the steady thud of his heart beating in his ears, the roaring sound that only acute fear produces.

'I got in touch with Mr O'Rourke. We have a few dealings in Libya together – I am sure you can guess our business there. Yes, unknown to you, I have been in touch with your friends for many years. Even the FBI knew this. You, however, did not.' He smiled to take the edge off his words.

'Mr O'Rourke has always held a high opinion of you, especially after you disposed of your great friend, Petey Mahoney. As an Italian I understand it was purely business, and that business must be your god; friendship was secondary. I admired this in you. I have heard many good things about you over the years, and your dealings with Igor and the Russians . . . I admired those as well. Admired the way you carried your trade right under our fucking noses!'

His voice was hard now and Eamonn realised they were coming to the crunch.

'Now, though, it is time for us to reconsider. Plutonium is the new gold, more expensive than diamonds even. Easy to get hold of if you know the right people – which you did. You have made a lot of money from this enterprise and now we are willing to take the burden from you. I already have customers lined up as far afield as India and Pakistan. In short, I want what you've got, and I intend to get it.'

'What's it got to do with all of you? I mean, why are the four of you here?'

Molineri laughed heavily. 'Mr O'Rourke is here to show

solidarity, though he will wet his beak. Steinschloss is to be our banker, the Russians trust him, and will also wet his beak. Sammy is here because we want to use Las Vegas as the front for our operation.'

Sammy looked as shocked as Eamonn felt. He was strictly gambling and prostitution, even the Feds knew that and left him pretty much to his own devices. All the more reason for the family to use him then, Eamonn realised. No one would ever suspect him of international arms dealing.

'So where do I fit in?' He knew he had lost the contract and now was only interested in letting himself out of it as easily as possible.

'You, I am afraid, have to explain to the Chinese that we want the stuff you just transported to England. It's a heavy load, and we have customers waiting. If you explain everything properly, that they are dealing with powerful people, you will be let off with your life and the lives of your family. I already have a buyer for it, though I suppose the Chinese had one as well. They can come to me, I'll be happy to supply them in the future. I have made a deal with the Russians. Good men that they are, they took Igor's death well. Like us, they understand it wasn't anything personal. Just business. His brother is to be my main agent in Moscow.'

Eamonn felt the constriction in his throat. They had it all cut and dried.

'The Chinese won't just give it up,' he told them, dismayed. 'Can we not wait until the next delivery? Try and keep the peace?'

Molineri laughed then. 'Fuck the Chinese, Mr Docherty. Get it, remove it, and make sure it is in my possession within four days.'

With that Eamonn drained his Scotch. He needed it.

*

Desrae was dressed as Cleopatra. His black wig suited him and his eyelashes could have broken a pane of glass, the mascara caked on them enough to make the *Guinness Book of Records*.

It was coming up for midnight. Inside the club all was noise and bright lights. Regulars were allowed in, but it was pretty much a private party. A constant floor show was going on, over two hundred people were eating and drinking – the noise was deafening and giving Cathy a headache. She saw Gates and Susan P whispering together in a corner and her heart sank.

Since his earlier visit she had been worried, very worried. Her eyes stayed on her daughter at all times. She felt that Kitty was in danger – though from whom she didn't know. Joanie, the worse for wear, was singing now, a dirty rugby song, being egged on by the punters and the other girls. Kitty, also dressed as Cleopatra, was laughing uproariously, but everyone knew she didn't understand the words of the song. Which was just as well.

Cathy went over to Susan and Richard. 'Watch Kitty for me, will you? I have to slip back to my flat. I won't be long.' She was going to put on her own costume and see if she could get in touch with Eamonn.

She hurried through the streets, conscious of a deep feeling of foreboding. She hoped Eamonn was back from Washington; she needed to talk to him. She let herself into her flat, shutting the door behind her and walking through to the lounge.

Little Cheng turned to face her as she came into the room. Shock at seeing him in her home registered on her face.

'What the hell are you doing here?'

A large man came from behind and pinned her arms to her sides.

She shook her head in disbelief. 'What's going on? What are you doing here?' She could hear the panic welling up inside her, making her voice high and quavery. Cheng was feared in Soho, many of the Chinese were. But they normally kept to their own. What could he want with her? Her mind was whirling.

'Where is it, Mrs Pasquale?' His voice was tight.

'Where's what, Mr Cheng? I don't know what you're talking about.'

He walked up to her, his little body stiff with threat. Taking out a long slim-bladed knife, he held it to her face. 'I do not have time for this, Mrs Pasquale. I need to know as soon as possible where my merchandise is. Now tell me what I want to know.'

Trying to pull herself free, Cathy finally surrendered to the panic inside her. She became hysterical. The knife had a strange smell – the smell of cold steel. It was cool against her skin and as she realised what he was going to do, she opened her mouth to scream. Using all her strength, she kicked out at the little man and pulled free from the bigger Chinese behind her. She ran for the door but he caught her by the hair and dragged her back into the room.

Lying prone on the floor, she began to take a beating the like of which she had never thought to experience in her life. Ten minutes later she was half-conscious, talking rubbish but somehow holding the attention of the man above her.

'The cases, Mrs Pasquale. Where are the cases?'

She was in such pain his words seemed to drift towards her on a warm red tide. She told him where she'd left her cases. As she lost consciousness, her final thought was that this was all Eamonn's fault.

She had been set up by the man she loved.

Cheng looked down at her gravely. He had what he

needed. Glancing at the bigger man, he nodded. 'She can't be left alive.'

He stood up, his suit stiff with blood, and sighed. He had always liked Cathy Pasquale, everybody did.

But Docherty had phoned an hour ago, had tried to tell him that he needed the merchandise back, that he was to deal with the others from now on. Cheng knew a double cross when he heard one. He didn't trust Docherty. There was something afoot and Cheng had a buyer all lined up. He was not going to let them down. Not for anyone.

As the bigger man went to work with the knife, Cheng visited the bathroom and tidied himself up as best he could. Then, thinking quickly, he went into the lounge and said heavily: 'Rape her – it'll look more like a domestic robbery.'

The other man nodded, pleased with this turn of events.

Mr Cheng left the flat then. There were some things he did not choose to witness. He had his standards.

Desrae was well drunk. It was a great party. Even Kitty had been allowed a few glasses of champagne and looked all starry-eyed and grown-up. The cabaret consisted now of young men in leather dancing to soul numbers.

Susan P, coked up and hot to trot, suddenly said to Richard, 'Where the fuck has Cathy got to?'

He glanced at his watch. Cathy had been gone over two hours. Fear drenched him like a cold shower. He looked at Susan P. 'Come with me. I think she might be in trouble.' They handed Kitty over to Desrae and made their way out of the club, apprehension plain on their faces.

As they walked through the streets of Soho they made an incongruous pair. Richard was dressed in one of his out-of-date suits, his heavy body making him lumber along. Susan P was costumed as Cleopatra, her gait unsteady, eyes dark with worry. More than a few people turned to stare at them. Even in a wacko place like Soho they looked strange.

They found Cathy five minutes later.

As Richard phoned the ambulance and police, Susan P. threw up repeatedly in the toilet. It was the worst sight she had ever seen. One she would never, ever forget.

Cradling Cathy's ruined head in his lap, Richard Gates cried bitter tears. It looked very much as if he had lost her.

This wasn't the lively, lovely woman he had seen only a few hours ago. This was a battered, mutilated stranger, her closed eyes so swollen the eyelashes had disappeared. She lay in his lap like a broken doll. But the worst of it for him was knowing that she had been raped. Brutally raped. He could see the bloodstains on her legs and clothes.

His Cathy, whom he loved more than anything in the world, was dying in his arms. He felt as if he would go mad with grief. Tears streaming, he whispered over and over: 'Hang on, Cathy, please hang on.'

He was still saying that when the paramedics and police arrived.

He went in the ambulance with her. If she died, if his Cathy died, then so would the people responsible. If it took him the rest of his days, he'd track them down and kill them, one by one.

Eamonn had been trying Cathy's number all morning but all he got was her voice on the answerphone. Slamming down the phone, he stared out at the view from his offices in Plaza Tower.

The phone rang and he picked it up.

It was Desrae, her breathy voice coming down the line from England.

'Oh my God, Eamonn, she's dying! Cathy's dying. Oh,

please come. *Please*. I don't know what to do . . . They've cut her to ribbons. You can barely see her face for the stitches! Oh God, oh dear God, help her someone . . .' Then, after the broken words, the gut-wrenching, heartfelt sobs.

'I'll be there, Desrae. Don't worry.' But for a moment after he'd hung up he could not move. He thought back over the years, remembering Cathy, lovely and loving. *Cut to ribbons* . . . And it was all his fault.

Ten minutes later he was collecting his car from the underground car park when two Chinese men walked towards him. The car parking valet suddenly turned away and walked out of the small booth he used, towards the daylight at the exit.

Eamonn knew, before he turned and saw the men, what was going to happen to him. He was surprised the Chinese had got to him first. He had expected the Italians to be the assassins. He knew it was stupid trying to run, but despite everything the life force was still strong in him.

They caught him easily and cut his throat as he struggled on the ground. Afterwards his heart was stabbed through to the backbone twice in rapid succession.

It was a quick professional job.

He lay on the dirty, oil-stained floor, the blue eyes Cathy had loved so much staring up into the darkness.

His last thought was a hope that soon he would be joining her.

Cathy's attack was not treated as a rape and robbery as Mr Cheng had hoped. Richard Gates saw to that.

He sat by her bed, holding her hand, until he was told that she was stable and her vital signs were good. He stared down at this travesty of the beautiful woman he loved and felt hot tears sting his eyes. He had loved her, he still loved her, and he was willing her to survive.

A distraught Desrae was being looked after by Susan P, who was also taking care of Kitty. Cathy's daughter was so upset that they had had to have her sedated. No one had allowed her to see her mother. It was decided she was too young to take that.

Richard resigned from the job five days after Cathy was found. He left without a backward glance and stayed at the hospital from then on. If she died, he would go with her. There'd be nothing to keep him on this rotten earth if Cathy left him.

The nurses were afraid of him, even while they marvelled at his tenderness as he washed her, tidied her hair, and sat endlessly holding her hand. They gave up trying to make him go home. He was there for the duration, they accepted that.

But Cathy lay, mute and unmoving, and no one knew what she could hear, feel or understand.

There was no mention of turning off the ventilator. Richard Gates would kill anyone who tried.

Chapter Forty-Nine

Betty walked into Broadmoor and underwent the usual searches until finally she was taken through to see Madge. Her friend loved her room there and kept it spotless; she had finally been diagnosed as a paranoid schizophrenic and with her new medication was much better.

In Holloway, where Gates had had her taken for parole violation, she had bitten off another woman's nose in a fit of anger over a match-thin roll up. On the recommendation of two prison psychiatrists, she was finally put away properly.

She would never be coming home.

Betty hugged her friend and they chatted for a while. Madge made them both a cup of tea, and as they sipped it Betty showed her the photos of Kitty and Cathy which she had brought with her.

Madge admired them all happily.

'That Kitty is the image of me mother, you know. Got the Irish look to her. The widow's peak and the black hair. Good-looking girl. Can I keep these?'

Betty nodded and Madge put them on her small bedside table. Later she would pin them to the wall with all the others.

'I wish she'd visit me, though. I'd love to see her. Cathy was always so full of life, wasn't she, Betty? Remember how she used to make us laugh when she was small? Those big blue eyes staring up at us.'

Betty nodded and grinned. This was Madge on a good day. On others, despite her medication, she raged against her only child and grandchild, threatening to kill them, Betty, and everyone else who had ever betrayed or even slighted her in any way.

Betty was sad, but knew that in her own way Madge was happy. Or at least as happy as she would ever be.

As she looked at the photos of Cathy, she felt the sting of tears. It was terrible to think of her slowly dying in hospital, in a coma. She hadn't told Madge – it didn't seem right somehow. Let her live in a world where everything had been great, where Cathy's childhood had been ideal and Madge herself a woman of renown, a loving mother, capable housewife and good provider. In Madge's mind that was how it had been for her and the daughter she had loved so much.

Mr Cheng was walking along Brewer Street. It was very late and the Soho streets were quiet but the little man's gait was cocky. He had no fears, knew his reputation would stand him in good stead. No one would ever challenge him; he would be safe in his own world.

A smile played around his lips as he went into an inconspicuous doorway. He walked up a flight of stairs and into a tiny flat. A petite Eurasian girl with short cropped hair and non-existent breasts was waiting for him.

She bowed and smiled, displaying small white teeth. Her almond-shaped eyes were welcoming. She said in broken English: 'I have been expecting you, sir. I have everything ready.'

Cheng was already undoing his shirt as he followed her through the flat, the smile on his face now bright as daylight. As he sat on the leather sofa and accepted a cup of herbal tea, he was shocked to hear a familiar voice say: 'Hello, Mr Cheng, long time no see.'

Richard Gates was standing behind him. Such was the man's shock he dropped his tea on to the white carpet.

The girl didn't move a muscle. Her face was closed now; she was detached from what was happening around her. Richard nodded at her. She picked up her coat and left the flat.

The little man looked at Richard warily. 'What can I do for you, Mr Gates?'

Richard laughed heartily. 'You, you old cunt, can tell me what you were taking from Cathy Pasquale's drum the night you had her attacked and raped. By the way, before you try and bullshit me, I know you were there. I had a meeting with the man you hired to do your dirty work. He is at this moment on a mortuary slab in Deptford, so none of your funny business. All he knew was, you took suitcases from the club. That was all. So what was in them – drugs?'

Cheng narrowed his eyes and kept silent.

Richard said politely, 'Have you ever heard the expression: You can do more with a soft voice than a big stick? Only everyone knows how quietly spoken I am, and how I will batter people without a second's thought. You see, I love Cathy, and you hurt her, and I just want to know why before I kill you. You can handle that? Understand what I'm saying?'

Cheng nodded.

'Now you can make this easy on yourself, or you can make it hard. It's entirely up to you. I can beat the truth out of you, I can remove certain parts of your anatomy, or

I can gouge out your eyes. All things that will hurt but not kill you. So what's it to be?'

Still Cheng said nothing.

Taking a length of rope from his pocket, Richard tied Cheng's hands behind his back. The man didn't attempt to struggle, he knew it was useless. Richard admired him for that, even as he hated him.

'One more time: *what was in the cases?*'

Still Cheng didn't answer. The man's face was a study in obstinacy. His narrow-lipped mouth was set in a stubborn line and his eyes were distant. He jumped, though, when he saw Richard turn on a hairdryer. Gates turned the setting to very hot and held it close to the man's face.

Cheng tried to move his head away.

'You'd be surprised the damage you can do with one of these,' Gates said nonchalantly. 'It's why they stopped letting them into certain nicks. Good torture weapons. They burn the skin lovely, blister it up a treat.'

As he spoke Susan P let herself into the flat. When Cheng saw her he felt a wave of nausea wash over him. She was smiling at him. In her hand she held a small hammer and a bag of nails. Susan P's trademark when upset was to have people nailed to the furniture. For the first time Cheng was afraid.

Richard Gates turned off the hairdryer and laughed loudly. 'Hello, darlin', come to join in the fun?'

Susan grinned. She was wearing a short leather mini-skirt and a see-through blouse. Her nipples were erect from the cold and her skin was flushed a pretty pink colour.

'Has he told you yet?'

Richard pulled a mock-tragic expression. 'Afraid not, my love.'

Susan tutted loudly. 'I enjoy my work, Mr Cheng. This is a little trick I learned off an old lag I knew once. Nice bloke he was, a torturer for the old-time gangs. Died as he lived, violently, but then that's par for the course in our game, ain't it? Nothing personal usually. But this *is* personal.'

She bent down and said through gritted teeth: 'This is very fucking personal. You only had to rob that girl, not fucking rape and leave her for dead, you Chinese cunt. Now my advice to you is start talking, mate, because I'm looking forward to this. In fact, I can't wait to get fucking started. I'll nail your cock to the fucking floor, and laugh while I'm doing it. In my bag I have a whole host of goodies – all designed to make you scream in pain. And you can scream in here, as you know. It's soundproofed. Your little punchbag got a hefty wedge to deliver you to us, and we intend to get our money's worth.'

Cheng looked from one to the other and sighed. 'If I tell you what you want to know, do you give me your word I will be killed quickly, cleanly?'

Richard nodded. 'You'll be hanged. I can't be no fairer than that, can I?'

Cheng closed his eyes and thanked them.

'It was plutonium, not drugs,' he said. 'Everyone thinks of drugs but they're old hat. The real money now is coming from Russia. There is a big market for the plutonium they make. The Indians want it, the Iraqis, the Libyans . . . Some people think India will be the next superpower. And superpowers all want one thing, don't they? Nuclear weapons. Cathy Pasquale didn't know she was carrying the stuff. But she wasn't stupid. When she came back unexpectedly and found me there, I had to dispose of her and make it look like a robbery.

'It was nothing personal, just business. Eamonn Docherty was the instigator. He had her mule for him after he lost his contact in New York. Then he tried to double cross me. The Mafia and the Russians have become allies over in the States – I learned this through a contact our there. Docherty was killed on my orders. The Irish or the Italians would have got to him eventually. Believe me, Mr Gates, this is international. You can kill me, yes, but if you go after all the other players in this drama, you'll be killing for the next ten years.'

Richard let the information sink in. Only one part of it interested him.

So Docherty had tucked Cathy up, as he had always tucked her up, one way or another, ever since they were children. He marvelled at a man who could put a woman in danger like that, a woman he had professed to love.

He sighed and rubbed his hand over his face, suddenly deflated.

But he would kill Cheng, even though he knew that hanging was too good for him. He would stand and watch as the man took his last breath. It was all he could do to assuage his hurt over Cathy's condition.

'Why the rape, though? Why put her through that?' Susan P's voice was loud in the small room.

Cheng shrugged. 'I thought it would look better on the police report. She came in while the burglary was on – a good-looking woman. The robber raped her then panicked. It happens.'

Susan P was fit to be tied. 'So that was it then? You just thought it would look better on a police report? Cathy was violated because *you* thought it would look better on a police report, eh?'

He closed his eyes and nodded. 'I am being truthful. Telling you what you want to know. If it's any consolation, the man you killed was never used by me again. As you know yourselves, we all have to give orders we don't necessarily like. Well, I hated to give that one but it was necessary. Cathy Pasquale could not have been left alive with any knowledge of this operation. Her close relationship with you, Mr Gates, made that essential. I could never have what we were doing made common knowledge. Surely even you can understand that?'

Susan P was so angry she felt that she could quite happily have a heart attack and not even notice it. This man was sitting in front of her, calmly telling her how he had had her friend raped and murdered, and actually trying to justify it!

Taking back her arm, she let him have the full force of the hammer across the face. The crunch of bone was audible in the room as Cheng's cheekbone was demolished.

'You Chinese bastard, I'll fucking kill you with my bare hands! That girl was decent, fucking decent. She'd made it. Against all the odds, she'd made it and made a go of her life. For what, eh? For you to come and waste her as part of a business transaction?'

Her voice was thick with tears and rage.

'So some sand niggers, some fucking Arabs, could take the Russians' nuclear shite and probably blow us all up in years to come? You took her life for *that*? She's lying in a hospital bed in a fucking coma and you sit there and tell me that it's *just fucking business*? Well, this is business and all, mate. My friend Richard might have given you some fairy story about being hanged, but I promised you fuck all, mate. So I'm going to beat you to death, like Cathy was beaten to death. Like a mad dog would be beaten.

'And shall I tell you something else, eh? I'm going to enjoy it, every fucking minute of it. Because that girl was worth fifty of you or Eamonn bloody Docherty. She is one of the few truly decent people I have ever known. All her life she was shat on in one way or another and I watched her fight back and become someone. From a little kid she had what it takes to survive in this shit hole of a world, and then you come along and think you can just fucking take her out of the ball game.

'Well, you picked on the wrong people this time, Mr Cheng. You had the audacity to fuck with me and mine and I will make you pay dearly for that.'

Cheng looked pleadingly into Richard Gates's eyes. His face was already half destroyed from the hammer blow.

Richard turned his back. 'As the lady said, she didn't make you no promises. And I sure as hell have no intention of arguing with her.'

He laughed then, and afterwards watched in cold silence as Susan P put Mr Cheng to bed for the last time.

Killing Cheng would not make Cathy any better, but at least it made them feel as if they had done something to right a terrible wrong.

In the best tradition of Soho they had had their pay back.

The two nurses on the ward stared down at the woman in the bed. She looked terrifying. They shook their heads in wonderment.

'In a way, I think it would be better if she *did* die. I mean, if she comes out of it, it'll be a long slow road to recovery. She'd be looking at years of plastic surgery, let alone everything else. It's a real shame, isn't it?' said one of them.

The other nurse nodded. 'Weird bunch, though, aren't they? Especially her so-called aunt, the bloke in the dress. I nearly died when I first saw him! But he seems to really care for her.'

Her colleague chuckled. 'You should have seen the consultant's face when he first clapped eyes on Auntie.

Nearly died he did! She shook hands and his disappeared into hers. What a laugh! I almost wet meself, and Staff laughed out loud.'

She monitored the drip then said, 'And what about the big bald-headed bloke, the policeman? He was crying again today, I saw him myself.'

Her friend nodded sagely. 'Her daughter's lovely, though. If this Cathy Pasquale looked anything like her, then she was a good-looking woman. Especially those eyes. What a shame, eh? She was raped as well. Who would do that to another human being?'

The first nurse didn't answer.

In their job they daily saw pain and suffering and none of it was ever truly understandable, though many people who survived major traumas like this said they had learned from the experience. It remained to be seen what priceless insight Cathy Pasquale had gained – or if indeed she would even be capable of rational thought again.

While the night nurses were chattering, Cheng's body was discovered by a tramp underneath the arches in Shoreditch. He robbed the body before making an anonymous call to the police. He got a few credit cards, a hundred pounds in cash, and a beautiful silver and diamond dragon charm.

It was a lucky dragon, said to bring the wearer wealth, health and happiness. Shame it hadn't worked for Little Cheng.

Epilogue

Che gelida manina.
Your tiny hand is frozen.

– Giacosa and Illica, *La Bohème*

Chapter Fifty

Richard made himself a cup of coffee and brought it back to Cathy's room. It was seven months since the attack and though she was off the ventilator now, she was still not conscious.

As he sipped his drink he looked out over the grounds of the nursing home in Sussex. She had been transferred here two months previously. They had agreed that he would be more or less resident in the room with her.

Richard had a small Z-bed that he slept on at night and in the day he did pretty much everything for Cathy. He washed her and changed her clothes. He brushed her hair, massaged her limbs and sat holding her tiny hand in his large meaty one.

Cathy looked awful. The scars on her face and body were horrific, still a vivid red, raised up and sore-looking. No one who saw her there would ever have believed that this woman had once been beautiful.

There were no photos to remind them; no photos in case she woke and saw herself and remembered. There was no mirror in the room either. Richard had seen to that.

As the nurses went about their business they heard the

low drone of his voice, constantly talking to her. He talked all the time: telling her that he loved her, relating how well her daughter was doing, promising that they would have great times once she was on the mend.

It broke their hearts.

The big bald man, with his heavy belly and sad blue eyes, had become like a mascot to them. They had all got to know him, and all liked him. Even the more grudging members of staff sometimes secretly wondered what it must be like to have someone who loved you so much. They had all seen coma patients left for months without visits once the initial shock wore off for family and friends. But not Cathy Pasquale.

She was very thin now, just skin and bone. The doctors had administered a glucose drip to try and fatten her up. She was in a state of semi-coma, neither dead nor fully alive.

She could stay like that for ever. The doctors had diagnosed her as being in a vegetative state. But it was a lottery with brain injuries. As Richard Gates tirelessly pointed out, people had been known to wake up after years had passed. They knew there was no way this patient was being left to die: 'in her own best interests'. There would be no court consulted for permission to starve Cathy to death.

Richard sipped his coffee and talked to her. 'Kitty will be here later with Desrae. They're been away to Lanzarote. Desrae has a few friends out there. Remember Joanie? Well, he's bought a great bar there apparently. We'll all go when you're better.'

Her tiny birdlike hand was cold in his and he held it tighter. He gazed out of the window as he chatted to her, trying to ignore the tears that blurred his vision.

'I thought we'd have something nice for dinner. I got in

some pasta. They let me use the kitchens here, as I've told you before, and I'm doing us all a meal, me and the nurses. Hope they live to tell the tale.' He laughed gently.

'All the girls at the club send their love, and Susan P is dropping by this afternoon to see you. She's bringing you in some clean nightclothes. The laundry here leaves a lot to be desired, and somehow I hate seeing your lovely things taken away in a trolley, your name taped inside like a school kid's.'

His voice was louder now and he thought of the indignities she daily suffered. 'She's going to wax your legs as well. You know what she's like – if her legs ain't waxed, she won't leave the house.' He chuckled though his face was shadowed with sadness still and his shoulders were stooped. Worry and the full force of his desperate, impotent love for her had aged him.

He put his cup on the beside locker and picked up her hairbrush. When he looked down at her he was stunned into silence.

Cathy's eyes were open and she was looking at him.

Those deep blue eyes he had dreamed of for so many years were actually looking into his. Her scarred, destroyed face had been brought back to life. It was as if he had witnessed a miracle.

He held his breath. There wasn't a sound in the room. He could hear the whirring of the overhead fan in the hallway, and the clatter of cups as the tea lady made her rounds. Outside he could hear a car pulling up, the sound of people chatting underneath the window, their voices so normal, so everyday, they made him want to cry.

Cathy's eyes were open. She was looking at him still. She blinked just once before closing them again, as if the effort had been too much for her.

Sitting in his chair once more, legs weak from shock, a

cold sweat covering his body, Richard took her hand in his again. It felt cold still, like a baby's hand, lost in his huge paw.

'I know you can hear me, I've always known. Please come back, Cathy, I'm begging you now. Come back to us all. Kitty needs you, I need you, Desrae needs you. You've left such a gaping void in all our lives. Please, Cathy, if you can hear me, let me know. Squeeze my hand, blink, anything.'

He stared at her drawn face, the scars livid against it though he didn't see them. To him she would always be his lovely Cathy. She was still his Cathy, her eyes had shown him that. Opening his own eyes wide, he tried to hold back the tears. Looking out at the summer sky he felt the sadness of a man who had wished devoutly for something and believed he had been given it.

They had said this could happen.

He had been warned about it.

As he held back the tears he swallowed deeply. It was like summer outside. October and the weather was glorious. An Indian summer they were calling it. He didn't much care what time of year it was if only Cathy were here to enjoy it with him.

He gave way to the tears. Thick and salty, he let them roll freely down his face. There was no one to see them, after all.

'Stop crying, Richard, please.'

He looked at her hard, unsure if she had really spoken or if he had imagined it.

Her eyes were still closed.

'Cathy? Talk to me, Cathy, please.'

He stared down at her then like a man demented, the tears still rolling down his cheeks, his eyes blurred and stinging.

'I'm thirsty. What time will I get a drink?' Her eyes were open again and he could see she was fully conscious. She knew what she was saying. She was back with him once more.

He gathered her into his arms and held her to him. 'I love you, girl. God help me, I love you so much.'

She smiled gently, her skin feeling oddly tight, not like her own face at all. 'I know you do, Richard, but all I want is a drink.'

He kissed her on the forehead then, a big wet smacking kiss. 'I'll get you a drink, darling, I'll get you whatever you want. All you have to do is ask.'

'I know, Richard. I know.'

He knew then that she had heard him, heard every word of love he had spoken over the last months, and his heart soared with the knowledge.

Cathy had a long road ahead of her, but with his help, and Kitty's, and Desrae's and Susan's, she would come through it all.

She'd had a life that most people would have given up on long ago. Her start had been rough, she'd made some wrong choices along the way, but she had always done what she had felt to be right.

She had loved too well and almost been destroyed.

Now, though, he would see to it that she led a life of complete happiness. He would take care of her as a man should take care of a woman: protect her, love her, cherish her.

Most of all he would cherish her.

They smiled at one another then, as if Cathy had heard his thoughts and was silently answering them.

He hoped in his heart that that was the case. It was what he wanted more than anything in the world.

Hard Girls

Martina Cole

HARD LIVES. HARD LESSONS. IT'S MURDER ON
THE STREETS.

*Danielle Crosby had a body to die for. A body she sold to the
highest bidder. But she ended up paying for it with her life.*

When a prostitute's body is found lifeless, mutilated and
brutally raped, DCI Annie Carr has never seen anything
like it and never wants to again. Kate Burrows, retired
DCI and now consultant, has plenty of experience when
it comes to murder – after all she caught the Grantley
Ripper and broke the biggest paedophile ring in the
South East. She is determined to help put the killer
behind bars. But whoever it is won't be easily caught.
And when another girl's body is found, even more
horrifically disfigured than the last, it's clear the killer is
just warming up . . .

In a ruthless world where everyone's out for themselves,
Annie and Kate must dig deep if they hope to catch a
callous serial killer who knows no limits and makes no
mistakes. For some, prostitution is seriously big
business. But how many people will pay the ultimate
price?

Utterly riveting, HARD GIRLS is a gripping and disturb-
ing thriller that will have you hooked until the very last
page.

'Cole is brilliant at portraying the good among the bad,
and vice versa, so until the very end we never quite
know who to trust. This is the very stuff that makes her
so compelling' *Daily Mirror*

978 0 7553 2870 3

headline

The Take

Martina Cole

IF YOU WANT IT BADLY ENOUGH, TAKE IT . . .

Freddie Jackson is just out of prison. He's done his time, made the right connections, and now he's ready to use them. His wife Jackie dreams of having her husband home, but she's forgotten the rows, the violence and the girls Freddie can't leave alone.

Bitter, resentful and increasingly unstable, Jackie sees her life crumble while her little sister Maggie's star rises. In love with Freddie's cousin Jimmy, Maggie is determined not to end up like her sister.

Families should stick together, but behind closed doors, jealousy and betrayal fester until everyone's life is infected. For the Jacksons, loyalty cannot win out. In their world you can trust no one. In their world everyone is on the take.

**THE TAKE is now a major four-part
television drama on Sky One.**

978 0 7553 5777 2

headline

Now you can buy any of these bestselling books
by **Martina Cole** from your bookshop
or *direct from her publisher*.

FREE P&P AND UK DELIVERY
(Overseas and Ireland £3.50 per book)

Dangerous Lady	£7.99
The Ladykiller	£7.99
Goodnight Lady	£7.99
The Jump	£7.99
The Runaway	£7.99
Two Women	£7.99
Broken	£7.99
Faceless	£7.99
Maura's Game	£7.99
The Know	£7.99
The Graft	£7.99
The Take	£7.99
Close	£7.99
Faces	£7.99
The Business	£7.99
Hard Girls	£7.99

TO ORDER SIMPLY CALL THIS NUMBER

01235 400 414

or visit our website: www.headline.co.uk

Prices and availability subject to change without notice.